Wise Fools

◆

March 2022

Gail,

Thank you for reading my novel.

Enjoy!

Wise Fools

———— ◆ ————

Tim McGhee *Tim A. McG*

Writers Club Press
San Jose New York Lincoln Shanghai

Wise Fools

Writers Club Press
an imprint of iUniverse.com, Inc.

For information address:
iUniverse.com, Inc.
5220 S 16th, Ste. 200
Lincoln, NE 68512
www.iuniverse.com

ISBN: 0-595-18327-1

Printed in the United States of America

Dedicated To:

The oppressed.

Those who went before us to fight oppression.

Those who keep the fight for justice alive today.

Those who have given up, that they may find the will to have another go at it.

Those who never give up, that they may inspire us all.

The young fans of any game whom admire those who play the game for keeps.

and,

The romantic.

Foreword

◆

An Understanding: It is important you read this.

The University of West Virginia is a fictitious state-supported institution of higher learning located in the fictitious town of Montani. The bigoted philosophies of the administration, athletic department, and coaching staff of the fictitious University of West Virginia do not in any way reflect those of West Virginia University. In fact, the West Virginia University administration, athletic department, coaching staffs and the individuals within have long been noted for and are highly respected for their commitment to fairness and equality. I am proud of them.

Any resemblance of the characters to any person living or dead is purely coincidental, with exception of those politicians, television, music, and movie personalities, writers, athletes, and any others who at that time in history had been accepted into the public domain. Since I tend to think in musical lyrics and selections from literature, I wrote my protagonist to do the same. The artists credited with those lyrics and selections are duly noted. They do not necessarily endorse this novel.

Although *Wise Fools* is set in a definite period and derived from the history of that period, the book is more accurately described as fiction and less accurately as historical fiction.

Most importantly, I believe as many others do that people as a whole are benevolent. Unfortunately, there have been and still are a few among us who have spread corruption and iniquity. This element is woven throughout *Wise Fools*. Some of these characters are depicted as West

Virginians. These portrayals are by no means a blanket incrimination of the citizens of my state I've always called home. West Virginians are good folks, as good as those from anywhere else. I've been here long enough to know that is true.

If the story of *Wise Fools* is an indictment, it is one of the thoughts and beliefs that prevailed in the period. Despite the enlightenment of the decade of the sixties, intolerance remained in the year 1975. If my novel gives readers a reason to reconsider those trying times with regard to making it better for today, that would make my years of writing more meaningful.

Tim McGhee

Acknowledgement

◆

Many folks stood with me as I wrote this book. I must first thank those most important to me: my wife Cindy, and my daughters Megan and Annie. I have surrounded myself with pretty, bright, kind, independently-thinking women, and I'm much better because of them. With regard to my novel, Cindy introduced me to the concepts of Internet publishing and shorter, clearer sentences. Megan and Annie kept me honest by reminding me I'm fighting the creeping aspects of age and desperately want to be my protagonist Mason. The ladies at times thought I had a rather unusual hobby. While not particularly wanting me to hunt deer and after having a chance to watch me play golf, they decided it was better for all to keep me at the keyboard.

I also thank my mother-in-law Deanie Samosky. We really haven't talked about my book and that doesn't matter. She's the most outstanding person I know and has had a profound effect on my life.

My good friends, Anna Parkman and Ross Parkman, read the book early. They said they truly liked the story and the characters, but made me aware of the fact that I'm grammatically challenged. In spite of my flaws, they provided much encouragement. Joyce Babineau also read and had good, constructive comments for me. Near its completion, Joyce read the final draft, provided web site support, and started selling books. I can't ask for much more than that. Barbie Dallmann, through her business service Happy Fingers, formatted the book for iUniverse, sparing me, The Lost Child of the Internet, the pain of doing so and saving my family from watching a grown man cry.

There are those friends who helped me indirectly. I appreciate them and I want them to know it. My "day job mates": my boss Rick Sample thought it was interesting I did this, said he didn't care what time I got up to write just as long as I was in front of a customer at eight AM, and told me to make my e-mails shorter. Other business associates, friends John Pistella, Jon Hill, Gerry Henwood, and Mark Colman concurred with Rick about the e-mails. They also kept me in line by "busting my chops" for being a writer, regularly saying things like, "No, Tim…I seriously doubt Winona Ryder will get anywhere near your book." Others who kept me going sometimes without even knowing it: my men at the Y; Sid and Libby; my in-law sibs Pete Samosky, who will give you cause to think, Paul Samosky, who will give you cause to laugh, and Sara Samosky, who will step away from her practice as a pediatrician and give you cause to bake cookies; Susan Poindexter, Glenn English, Dirk Cline, Ken McBride, Mary Frances McBride, Sallie Dalton, fellow writers Lisa Lynn and Dan Kehde, and especially my daughters' numerous friends. You all gave me support. I can't do anything without you.

I hope everyone enjoys reading *Wise Fools* as much as I enjoyed making it up, channeling it to the amusement of others, and writing it.

Sunday November 2, 1975
Mid-afternoon

Re-examination

Fame in athletics is fleeting, as are victories and a really good relationship with a woman. But, as it is common to say, I digress. Just eight days, eight goddamn days ago we were on a big time roll. We were seven and oh and ranked number eleven in the nation as we landed in the dinky airport in State College, Pennsylvania. Christ, you'd think the number three team in the nation would have the ability to land jets without making you feel as if you had to have a tether and a tailhook. But I got off the plane unscathed, made the sign of the cross, and boarded one of the buses taking us to the edifice of scholarly football, Beaver Stadium. Beaver Stadium, the home of The Pennsylvania State University, a school we had not defeated on the gridiron since 1952 and had never beaten on the SAT college boards. So what we were smaller and slower and stupider? Our team was determined to take this one away from the Nittany Lions on their turf in front of their fans. What the hell is a Nittany anyway?

I, Mason Bricker, lifelong West Virginian, believe! I believe in my Ridge Runners, the pride of the University of West Virginia, albeit much maligned in the press, defined as the guys who ran around in no shoes, are missing most of their teeth, and have vertical family trees. How wrong they are, because West Virginia's players come from the same high schools and prep schools as those of the Big Schools: Penn State, Pittsburgh, Ohio State, Michigan, and Notre Dame. That's right, only three of our players are from the state. We are: yours truly, a smallish village idiot walk-on, Vinny the quarterback, and Cap'n Teddy, the biggest redneck in height, girth, and image you'll ever meet. The out-of-state papers can't bust on our boys because our boys are their boys, only ours are to be honest a little lower on the food chain. The aforementioned Big Schools got their choices due to past regard and reputations of the quality beef out of that eastern and midwestern area. They got the Blue Chips. Blue Chips are players who rate a 'can't miss.' They are the biggest, strongest, fastest, meanest mothers you'll ever see, and damnit are they cocky. They've had this aura about them since they played Pop Warner, and because of that they got more respect than normal teenagers ever get. Blue Chips bring pride to a community. 'My Blue Chip can beat your Blue Chip,' they say, town leaders and factory workers alike. And after watching their Blue Chip run/tackle/catch/pass/block/hit, feeling proud as if they fathered/birthed the boy himself/herself, the pride swells to even greater proportions as the college recruiters come. First the front men, the assistant coaches, arrive to sell the mamas and the papas on how they are going to take care of their boy. Then as signing day approaches, if the boy is Really Blue, the heavy artillery, the head coaches from the Big Schools pay their visits. These Coaching Legends pull on the prize recruit to continue his matriculation at their respective schools, bringing their Big School fame and Big School expense accounts to the locals, eating at local restaurants and staying at local inns, to the unabashed delight of the locals themselves.

But let's go back to the boy. Imagine being seventeen years old, having just screwed the cap back on your Clearasil, and a Legendary Coach knocks on your door. Think you'll be impressed—with yourself? A heady time this recruiting period is. I wouldn't know, having only experienced the whole thing vicariously through my good buddy Vinny Vacca, but that's another story for another time. Thing is, the Big Schools get the Blue Chips, and the leftovers, those who are head cases, a half step slower, a few pounds too light, or an oomph or two weaker, these Wallflowers of the Big Recruiting Dance go to places like The University of West Virginia.

Now, this isn't all settled early. The status of a Blue Chip can come and go during those prep years. Talk about a stark dose of teen reality:

what does the kid who at age sixteen was damned certain he was headed for State College do a year later when he finds himself in Montani, West Virginia? Sometimes, he folds his tent, playing out his career, partying a lot, simply going through the motions, which is possible at a Wallflower school. Not Michael Burton, linebacker extraordinaire, a Pennsylvania boy who saw six of his high school opponents, six whose football skills he matched at least go to Penn State, leaving him behind at the last moment, stuck as the metaphorical bus rolled away. Michael came here with the Wallflowers but didn't give up. He worked and worked hard, becoming stronger and quicker and more and more a student of the game. Michael put all he had into it, so much so that he this summer was named to the *Playboy* pre-season All-America list complete with photos just thirty pages over from Miss August. Vinny, the star running back Arthur O'Neill, and I worked out with Michael over summer break, two hours a day with the weights, noon runs up the climbing grade of Lewis Hill, wind sprints in the heat of the afternoon, endless streams of pushups on the searing turf with Michael's back muscles glistening in the July sun like cut black onyx. I matched this man rep for rep and I'm a stronger, faster, beefier, better ballplayer for it. But Michael always had the edge. On the wall positioned at eye level just so he could see them before he laid down to bench press, he had printed in large letters with an ink marker the names of those six opponents, a constant reminder. Michael takes every game seriously. Hell, Michael takes breakfast seriously. But, October twenty-fifth in State College, PA was his anointed Game of the Year and everything led up to that focused moment.

Michael had put a tremendous amount of pressure on himself to perform well in this what is certain to be his consensus All-America year, but he doubled his efforts for that fourth Saturday in October. To no surprise, he exceeded those expectations. After Penn State got a cheap early touchdown on a punt return during which they clipped, blocking me in the back right when I had the return man dead nuts, Michael and his defense dropped the hammer. First they prevented disaster after a Lion d-back picked a Ridge Runner QB Bobby Kay floater deep near their goal line. Michael stopped them cold and allowed them only a chip shot field goal for three. Then Kay, positively sucking as he was, fumbled the snap from center, again putting our backs against the wall. The D didn't give a yard, forcing Penn State to kick another short one when they should have had a sure seven. It was thirteen nothing, but if not for Michael and the Immovable Objects it could have just as easily been lights out in the first quarter.

The respective offenses effectively did nothing else for the remainder of the game. Kay's play, despite the airhead not being able to get us anywhere, was upgraded to Not A Detriment as he stopped giving them away. But Michael…damn…he was fuckin' crazy all over the field, hitting, making plays, and hitting still more, inspiring his fellow defenders to raise their games. As a result, the West Virginia defense did not allow the Lions a single first down.

There were no scores moving through the fourth quarter. The Legend of Happy Valley, coaching his team to a thirteen zip lead but impatient probably because he knew his offense was getting its ass kicked, called for a pass over the middle in a running situation to get something going. How was he to know that the boy he left at the train station four years ago was the man playing the game of his life, patrolling the middle? In short, he couldn't have and the pass was thrown and Michael caught it and took it the other way toward and down the sidelines, making every NFL scout in attendance, already very impressed with my man's play that day, stand in awe of his footspeed. We converted and at six thirty remaining it was thirteen seven, officially a ball game.

The offenses still could go nowhere and traded punts. After we punted yet again, with our Swedish Bomber Anders Borgstrom beautifully pinning Penn State deep on its ten yard line, all the Lions had to do was get two first downs and run the clock down. No way. Michael with the fury of a grizzly bear attacked the Lion runner, popping the ball out of his hands into those of Tim Seiler, a Ridge Runner d-lineman. Even Kay couldn't keep Mr. Arthur Touchdown from running the ball across the goal line on the second play. Our priceless kicker Raj Retnitraj knocked it through and we had the lead. The lead, fourteen thirteen, against the number three team in the land, on the road, with thirty-six seconds left, prepared to end the misery by which Penn State held sway over a couple of generations of Runner fans all over the nation.

The West Virginia bench, from coach to starter to reserve to assistant trainer, was cranked. Thirty-six short ticks off the clock and we had the upset. It was absolutely a beautiful moment to be a Ridge Runner. I was caught between savoring every facet of it all and doing my job on the kickoff team: run fast, stay in your lane, hit somebody. Simple enough.

Raj teed the ball up to the snorts and hoots and foul language from both sides, then backed away, raised his hand, dropped it, and approached the ball. To prevent a long return, he expertly dribbled a squib kick just over the Penn State line halfway down the field much like a golfer who knew what the hell he or she was doing would choke up on his seven-iron and dink the ball out of the rough to the nearby pin. A Lion reserve guard who didn't know what the hell he was doing fielded the squib, ran about at random, and froze in his tracks in my lane, allowing me to pound him to the turf with an unexpected devastating blow, theretofore the proudest moment of my life. The way our D had been playing, this game was ours. Ours, baby!

The history of the University of West Virginia football, however, can be summarized by the next four plays. Play number one: our safety Chandler Childress batted down a long ball. Nineteen seconds remaining. Play number two: The Legend tried to slip one under us, but his worst nightmare Michael was there to break it up. Thirteen seconds left. Then, play number three, the PSU QB after hysterically scrambling went for a first down pass on the sidelines where Ridge Runner Joe Osbourne, in real life a gun nut, just about ripped the receiver's head off, making him drop the ball. Three seconds to live for Penn State, and there's a flag on the play. The little yellow hanky of the official was laying near the head of the Lion QB. Our Mr. Andy Baum, although swearing to God Almighty he didn't do it, was charged by the judge, jury, and executioner with a personal foul for having laid out the quarterback after he threw the football, not very legal. That was fifteen yards against us, placing the ball at the midfield stripe with time for one more Penn State play.

The Legend isn't legendary for nothing. He obviously had a feeling. A cold front that had swooped through Pittsburgh late that morning was traveling east and approaching Happy Valley. In the last series of plays, the winds had picked up strength. In the estimation of an assistant coach, probably a goddamned weather coach for all we in Montani can know and observe in awe, they were blowing for the most part behind the Nittany Lions. The Coach sent his field goal team onto the field.

At the fifty plus ten through the end zone and another seven for the snap and hold, the Lions' Ernie Ernst, a kicker with a lively leg to his credit, would have to boom one sixty-seven yards, an NCAA record. Penn State's undefeated season and national championship hopes rested on the toes of Mr. Ernst.

We on the U sidelines were barely content to hold our celebration until the kick fell short. For, Ridge Runner fans, we hadn't a clue of the significance of the changes of the atmospheric conditions and knew, no, were damned sure this kick was in desperation.

Just as Ernie mightily swung his leg and met the ball, the breath of God, I'm certain it was His breath, blew a gust and got under that ball. This blast of wind carried it so high and so fast that the ball miraculously got to the goalposts and, in compensation for Ernie's natural hook, bounced off the inside of the left upright and articulated through for three points. No flags, no time left for us. Seasons change and so did we. The Guess Who. Yeah. Guess who lost. In a matter of a few seconds, we went from one-point winners to two point losers. No more undefeated season for the Runners. No more climb up the polls. And the streak remained alive at twenty-four games.

At the nucleus of a hundred screaming and jumping guys in white hats and black shoes, with three dozen or so civilian accompaniment and seventy thousand fans extolling mostly in relief of not having to live with the reality of dropping a football game to their less fortunate brethren from the south, within this disorganized collegiate post-victory mayhem we stood. We were fifty in number, mostly still, incredulously looking at the goalpost the football only a few moments before had split after being kicked from the most unlikely distance of sixty-seven yards, two fuckin' thirds the length of a football field, probably requiring FAA approval if you'd look into it. And then the winds brought the rains, that horizontal variety that soaks every square inch of your body if you for some odd reason choose to stand out in it, which about twenty of us did, still staring at that infernal goalpost. We were there, unable to fathom what we possibly did in another life to deserve such punishment. Bad karma. It's not my fault. Now you have it, now you don't.

Pleading with myself to take my eyes away from the crash site, I found Vinny to my left, mesmerized by the uprights and the crowd rushing out of the rain, also steeped in the overwhelming waves. Vinny and I met at Ridge Field in September 1963, a couple of second graders about to watch the U get pounded by Navy and Roger Staubach. Becoming friends instantly, we haven't missed a home game and had then even managed to get our parents to traverse the two hundred fifty miles between Weirton and Mullens twice a month and get us together. Early on, Vinny was the quarterback and I was the receiver. We exchanged countless numbers of passes over those twelve years. We always said, "We're going to Montani and we're getting out there together, mark my words!"

Then Vinny became a Blue Chip as a result of his natural leadership and football abilities and the Big Schools wooed him in a Big way. He was six-two and a hundred eighty pounds, could throw a ball seventy-five yards, fifty while standing on his knees. I, on the other hand, was a not-so-big five-eleven and one sixty-five, fast and loved to hit, but played in a league of not-so-big southern West Virginia schools comprised of guys whose football careers would end after their final high school game. Vinny played with and against a lot of boys who would be suiting up on Saturdays the next year. Largely for those reasons the Fighting Irish of Notre Dame and the Buckeyes of Ohio State battled for Vinny's services, while Princeton and Brown had a gentleman's competition for me, probably because I was peaking in a biorhythm sense and had some neurochemical release on the day I took my SAT college boards. Anyway, on the weekend before we were to sign with our respective colleges, we individually and collectively said 'fuck it.' Vinny called Coach Dennis Lawson of the Ridge Runners and proposed a deal: he would sign with West Virginia if he was allowed to bring me along. Lawson didn't know me, but my friend was a Very Blue Chip, possibly Indigo. The coach presented a counteroffer, "You, Vinny, sign and your buddy is an invited walk-on." Vinny covered the telephone transmitter with his hand as we spent a couple of seconds deciding. "You've got us!" The dream was on! Then Vinny went to tell his dad, which trust me, was a very difficult thing to do.

We stood there soaked to the gills as the rains lessened from torrential to heavy. Vinny is the third team QB, holder for Raj the kicker, and keeper of the offensive clipboard chart. Really, not bad for a sophomore, but you do it and you'll find out you want a promotion. I'm the only walk-on on the traveling squad, a kick coverage team resident headhunter, and a third-team receiver, happy to have that chance but also wanting more. We looked to each other, water flowing from our respective headgear, saying without speaking, "This bites." Then I saw to the right of Vinny's shoulder a man, a big man in the West Virginia whites, number fifty-five, double nickel, prostrate in the mud, occasionally heaving and twitching. Michael. He was the living example of being…so close. Vinny and I approached him and helped him to his feet. We walked with Michael toward the dressing room, rain splattering us, facing the woe.

The locker room, the buses to the airport, and the plane were somber, reflecting the feeling we shared, a void inside each of us from which there was no recovery in sight. An occasional murmur heard over the noises a passenger airliner makes while in flight were the only clues that The University of West Virginia hadn't placed a cadaver in each seat. Not a bad metaphor. Victories are shared, but defeat is personal. A part of each of us died that day and the renewal of our souls would take time. Jetting away through the dark to home was the beginning of putting it all into perspective and growing from it.

That is, if we landed safely. Montani also has an aircraft carrier for an airport. For a fact, ex-Navy pilots are preferred to negotiate their craft to our airfield on top of a shaved hill. But, that night the length of the runway wasn't the challenge. No one knew what the hell was going on as the stewardesses scrambled about, opening and closing the door to the cockpit, trying but not succeeding to hide the anxious looks on their pretty faces. Joe sat across the aisle from Vinny and me. He turned to me and whispered, "I haven't heard the landing gear drop." I looked into his face and he put his finger to his lips in the international sign for 'secret.' Then he stared ahead like a good soldier. I began to pray.

A stew, the green-eyed one, announced, "We are about to land and I ask you all as a precautionary measure to assume the crash landing position. Wrap your arms around your legs and place your head between your knees." We had all been football players since we were very young and therefore took orders without asking why. I turned to Vinny, who had become as white as a descendent from the Mediterranean can get. I gave him a thumbs-up.

Someone said softly, "Place your head between your knees and kiss your ass goodbye!" Macabre, definitely. Only five years ago, the football team of our sister university, Marshall, was on a plane that slammed into the hillside at their home airport in Huntington, West Virginia. No survivors. Jesus, I prayed, please get me out of this one.

Suddenly there was a thud, a high-pitched motor noise, and another thud. "They're down!" shouted the normally reserved Joe. Then there was the distinct thump of a plane landing. One stewardess had to be helped from her seat. A couple of Runners got sick. I turned to Vinny again. The color was coming back to his face. "Think we could help the bishop out and get a few converts right now?" I asked. He was unable to talk.

I overheard the captain telling Coach Lawson the landing gear was somehow stuck and wouldn't come down. After trying desperately to engage it, he dumped his remaining fuel and prepared for a belly landing. About a hundred feet up, the wheels dropped.

I'd rather be lucky than good.

Every emergency vehicle in a seven county area was parked on the tarmac. We disembarked the plane and silently boarded the two buses to transport us to The Ridge. Halfway down the road, someone on my bus said in singsong, "Hi, honey, I'm home!" "How was your day, sweetheart?" was the response. "Oh, just the usual." We all roared with laughter. A level of acceptance had been found…but other issues, demons much more damaging to the heart of our team, were yet to surface.

Sunday November 2, 1975
Re-examination continued

We as a team watched, or rather endured, the film of the game the next day. It wasn't that bad, or half of it at least. Our defense was remarkable, really dominating Penn State. I never thought I'd use those last three words together, but it was true, man! We stuffed them! But, our offense reeked of a malodorous flounder lying eyes up on a Carolina ocean pier in the middle of an August afternoon. No sustained drives; just run the ball, run the ball, pass, punt. Strangely, however, Lawson was a man of few words. Very little critique. No yelling. No sarcasm. Even the assistants and coordinators followed The Coach's lead, sometimes with odd looks on their faces, but they nevertheless went along. "Good game. Tough breaks. If you play like that against NC State Saturday, you'll kill 'em," said Lawson. Lawson: the older, taller, thinner one-time athlete. The head man. Grey, more wrinkled, but the head man. Dominating. Therefore, I think we were too confused to speak. I mean, there's a guy who would normally rip you a new one for so much as a missed count, and that day he seemed almost distracted.

"Practice tomorrow, same time," said Lawson in a tone of dismissal. This is major college football. Of course there was going to be practice tomorrow. I don't know why he said that. His brain was scrambled and I couldn't figure out why. Another oddity.

We all sat motionless, looking askance, waiting for someone from the old TV show *Candid Camera* to appear. Then the brave Monty Cash got up and so did everyone else. Meeting adjourned.

Vinny and I were in his 1975 red Chevy Caprice convertible with white leather interior, sitting at the intersection onto Braust just below the stadium, looking like a couple of pimps as we always do when we ride the Big Red. The Gunner was wearing one of those ridiculous-looking silk print shirts and hip-ass tight slacks combos with square-toed shoes and a full-length leather coat, the same kind of crap he wears to the games, the same kind of crap all my teammates wear to the games. Granted, Vinny and the black guys make any cloth-ing ensemble look great, but I've told him he could stand some improvement in that department. He ignores me. That day, he was just one step away from a "leisure suit." All he needed was that shirt-like coat with the lapels of his shirt-like shirt draped over them, both wide enough to make an entire extra leisure suit. The whole thing was usually (okay, always) made from some fabric originating from an oil well and processed through a DuPont reactor. The "suit" spanned the color spectrum, solid, sometimes textured, but thankfully covering the shirt with its print ranging from floral to scenes depicting American Indian buffalo hunting to the indescribable. Vinny's was solid navy that day, right below acceptable.

This summer I visited my late father's friend, stockbroker Stan Mumphord, Stan the Money Man, in Manhattan. I was wearing one of those "leisure suits" when I stepped off the plane at LaGuardia. I thought I was dressed-up. Stan thought otherwise. "You look like cattle fornicating," he said. We rearranged our schedule quickly so Stan could take me to his tailor and get me some real clothes: cotton button-down shirts, white and oxford blue, summer-weight tan slacks, worsted wool gray slacks, Bass Weejuns, a navy blazer, rep ties, sleeveless tees and boxers.

I didn't influence Vinny in any way. Frankly, all my black teammates weren't swayed either. They all lovingly refer to me, among other things, as "Ivy," despite my day-to-day preference for Levis, natural-fabric shirts, tan workboots, and a cord or wool blazer. That's what I wore to the meeting. Needless to say, I looked out-of-place.

Back to Vinny's car. I decided to speak first.

"Was that weird or what?" I asked.

Vinny responded succinctly, "Yes."

I continued, "That was so strange I think he's come up with some sort of punishment that we won't know about until, say, we're thirty years old."

Vinny likes my mind. "Like what?"

"Like an annuity that pays off in twelve years by delivering cattle to our houses."

"What would be wrong with that?" The Gunner asked wryly. "Besides, if Joan were riding one wearing nothing but a g-string…"

Joan. He knows what changes my subject. He wanted to steer the conversation away from his offense being in the tank, despite being third team and it not really being his offense. If Vinny Vacca is only one thing, it is loyal.

But Joan. "Let's see. Ten years she'd be late thirties; yeah, most definitely I'd take her," I said, "I hadn't thought about Joan for nigh on fifteen minutes. Why did you get me started again?"

"That has to be a record for the semester," he announced.

"The old mark was twelve minutes set by me and seven others."

Vinny puts up with these…rather odd feelings I have for Joan. Odd in that she's eight years and three degrees ahead of me in life. I have placed a very acceptable sorority woman on hold for Joan Kissinger. Margaret Joan Kissinger, PhD, Northwestern, 1975, instructor, English Department, The University of West Virginia, specializing in American Literature, no relation to Secretary of State Henry despite both of their families being the "Who's Who" variety. I'm the tutor designated to help her with (or through) her three ALit sections. Why me? All the grad students were otherwise assigned. There was a hole to fill in ALit, so I the English major was asked to fill it. I'm not one to argue. Besides, I may be a sophomore football-wise, but I'm a junior with regard to academics. My ionospheric SAT verbals got me out of freshman comp, so I had ALit last year. It's a good fit. I aced, and the English brass likes me. Obviously. They gave me to Joan.

Joan: five-six or so, average height, and that's where she stops being average. She has the eyes of Ali McGraw, the smile of Natalie Wood, the bosom of Raquel Welch, and the lower below-the-waist section of Susan St. James. She could easily be slipped into Miss St. James Forty-Niners jersey, or be inserted into any Mary Tyler Moore role and no one would flinch, just as long as cup sizes are not a prerogative.

When I first saw her I would have done what I always do and ignore my constantly flashing hormones, but that PhD…a chance to be literary in the tub by candlelight, that kept me coming back. An intellectual honey. Wow.

Then she really plucked my heartstrings. More about that later.

My eyes and Joan's first met at a gathering of department folks in August at her new house on the big hill. Montani is a small town of older buildings and houses scattered on the hills extending up the banks of the Pine River, a navigable waterway on which the crew teams dodge barges every morning. Pittsburgh's only an hour away by interstate. The Steel City has a big influence on Montani. My College Town is a scaled-down version of the Foundry charm I've come to appreciate while hanging around The Gunner in Weirton for so long. And, scaled-down is the key word here. Small town Montani would be a helluva lot smaller if it weren't for the invasion of the twenty thousand students every August. As I said, I've stayed here in the summer. What a great place! Other times…what a wild place! But the hills; the fact remains that if you attend The University of West Virginia, you'll have to drive or walk up and down the hills for your four years of undergrad, more if you go to a professional school. Bad for your transmission, but good for your quads and your ass.

Joan's new house…I get off track a lot…deal with it. She overlooks the Pine and the downtown on just about as beautiful of a lot as you can find here. Huh, beautiful…Her home is tastefully decorated—no expense spared, though—she's gotta have a rich old man. I've a little nuevo net worth, which we'll get to later, but Joan was and remains out, way out, of my financial realm. Like the South Atlantic League to the Majors. Which, of course, adds to the mystique. To move on, I was there with Michael who has as his special lady Ellen Herron, a lovely English grad assistant with red locks cut long and mid-seventies flowing, hazel eyes, and tanned legs with a capital L. Ellen was dressed in green shorts and a white Izod. Was she wearing shoes? Probably. I didn't make it down to her feet. But, and not because of Ellen, I like going places with Michael. He's smart. I look smart. He's a badass. I look like a badass. He's a black man. I'm descended from Irish Catholics, so I feel cool with Michael. He's a nice guy with his shit together. The fact that he on the football field pounds his opponents into submission is just part of his personality. Michael in his black jumpsuit showed exactly why he can do that. He's my male mentor, despite sharing his wardrobe with Vinny.

I have a female mentor. It's not Joan, she's my love object. My female mentor is Michele Taranucci, PhD, Duquesne, 1975, instructor, specializing in creative writing, which is where my interests lie. Our first conversation at Joan's party went something like this:

Michele: Hi, I'm Michele Taranucci, your creative writing instructor.

Mason: Hi, Mason Bricker, your student.

Michele: I know. Lemme ask ya, what the hell are you doing here?

Mason: Well, the same thing you're doing here, just meeting everybody.

Michele: Not here, Mr. Intelligence. College, here, West Virginia.

Mason: Uh…I don't follow you.

Michele: I saw your verbals. I read a few pieces of yours from last year. What the hell are you doing here? You should be at Chicago or Princeton or something.

Mason: Well, Michele, if I may call you Michele—

Michele: Go ahead, just don't call me at home.

Mason: Okay…to answer your question, it's kind of complicated, but I'm here to play football.

Michele: Well, you'd better be a starter.

Michele was and is good looking. Putting it mildly, she ranks right up there with some of the fine Italian women. That day she wore her shorts and her sport shirt, looking like a more muscular version of Ellen, with her hair in a bob, and her crocodile stuck out farther. Although she stands about ten pounds from Joan's perfection, the crackers acid test (meaning I wouldn't kick her out of bed for eating crackers) certainly applied with Dr.

Taranucci. The problem for Michele that day was one that is similar to that of a very gifted violinist. Everyone wants to have something that makes him or her unique, especially in a social gathering. Michele is that musician, but Joan is Isaac Stern. Dr. Taranucci is a wonderfully talented violinist, to continue my efforts at a good cheesy metaphor, but in the shadows of the maestro. Apparently, from observing her for the remainder of the evening, Michele had figured out this thing with Joan is going to happen as long as she remains as her colleague, so she has decided to lead with her scintillating personality to give her the edge she thinks she needs. Just the kind of woman one would think one would fall for. The good news is Michele has become a good friend. The bad news is Joan…well, I wasn't then objective enough to call it either way.

I'll never forget what Joan was wearing the day…instant…I saw her. She had a madras blouse over a summer-light white camisole, inviting my eyes to her tastefully covered breasts. The blouse was unbuttoned to her waist and tied…Holy Mary. Progressively straight-leg denims and blue flats…Joan was elegant in her simplicity. Brown hair in a bangs and a flip framed her pretty face lighted with glistening brown eyes. She was so beautiful it hurt. But, it's not just me. I have discovered from our several walks we have had across campus that Joan turns heads at the rate only a chiropractor would appreciate. Almost every guy in her classes does not cut, an amazing statistic nationwide for men and English. A couple of my high school buddies are in her nine o'clock. She is all they can talk about. They think I'm some sort of demigod just for my association with her. They always ask me if I've bonked her yet (they really say 'bonked'). I try to tell them it's not like that with her. That's the same thing I try to tell myself, but once daily I then raised and still raise my head for a quick glance at Joan and, for those couple of moments, before I shake it off and shove me back to reality, I think maybe it's possible.

Joan is genuinely upbeat and positive, as one might think a beautiful, wealthy, bright woman would be. It's simply astounding how many things she has going right in her life. I've pondered the subject and, not knowing if her mother's a lush or if her father beats them all, I can think of only one minor flaw, so minor you don't notice it unless you've taken this subject to almost obsession. It is: she has short legs. Shapely, but short. Okay, shorter legs. Shorter than Judy Lambert, my friend and housemate, who has legs up to her boobs. But I had to find something, and there it is. She compensates with spike heels and the imperfection is barely noticeable and rather sexy.

I've talked to Joan a lot about a lot of things other than school and American Literature this semester. We've discussed a) Politics. She's a rich liberal. I'm a fiscal conservative. You can imagine the discussions that have arisen from that. Think John Maynard Keynes in lingerie vs. a muscle-bound Milton Friedman; b) Religion. We're both Catholic, but we have both admitted neither of us strictly follows the Church. I try not to tell myself that could come in handy at a later date; c) Money. Believe it or not, I, to my utter surprise, own stock in her family's bank, Batavia Bank, near her hometown Chicago. Small world. Jeez, really small world. The subject came up and I waited two weeks and mentioned it to her. It's not a big holding, just that one and a couple of others Stan the Money Man thought it would be good to come out of the bear market with. We bought ten months from meeting her. The more I think about it, the weirder it gets. Stranger still, she reacted to the news as if I told her I had a Christmas Club there. My attempt to impress her and join her socioeconomic group failed. That pissed me off a little bit. Anyway, on to d) Sports. She's asked many questions about football. She said she had never followed it before but is, because of me, fascinated by it. After hearing that, I conjured the image of my little honey in a tiny parochial school plaid skirt, knee socks, and shoulder pads and had a difficult time keeping my composure. e) Men. They would be much better off and would get many more women if they did not think with their dicks, she once said. I immediately started thinking with mine. Luckily, the phone rang. And f) Women. She is not malicious in her conversation about or descriptions of other women. Regardless, she is aware that because of her striking beauty all the coeds despise her. And I think she is hurt by it, and would like to change it. She wants them to like her. I bet she's had this trouble before.

After all the time I have spent with her, I realize I craved being around her. And because of her being the subject of ridicule by the coeds, I feel sorry for her in a way no one possibly understands. I want to be her hero, the man, and as men try to do to fix it for her, to make it better for her. I want to let her know that despite the malice of the covetous female and the abject lust of the lecherous male, she is to me just perfect just the way she is, and most importantly for whom she is. Joan, the woman. Joan, the academic. Joan, the professional. Joan, the woman. Perfect. Everything about her. Perfect.

Therefore, I have spent the past several weeks knowing I was but one embrace away from falling in love with her.

Back to the post-Penn State depression my fellow West Virginians and I suffer annually. After disembarking from my bus at the stadium the evening after Penn State, I drove home in my red '70 Datsun 510, dubbed the Tazmanian Devil because of its boxy construction and open mouth feature due to the missing grill. Stan has put me in a position to buy a much cooler ride, but my feelings about spending my early teen years poor then becoming a benefactor of one of my dad's buddies impels me to be among the inconspicuously rich. Rich. Rich, my ass. It's just a hundred fifty fuckin' thousand dollars. In comparison to Arab princes, it's an hour's worth of production on a small oil well. So, I don the cloak of driving a 'bomb.' Vinny had gone to see Jean, a gorgeous but sometimes manipulative woman who thinks I'm evil. Judy and our other housemate Alice Calire, a woman possessing a little body that would stop a train, were out of town. I was alone. Just as I placed my key in the lock, a car screamed up Donnelly Avenue beside the cemetery, horn blowing.

Turning left onto my Wagner Road without a signal, I saw it was Michele's bronze Toyota Corolla with her driving and…God, almighty…Joan in the passenger seat. They had never been here, I exclaimed to myself. Was the house clean? Was all the paraphernalia still sitting on the dining room table? I didn't know. It didn't matter. They parked. Two doors alternately slammed. I heard the tap-tap on the sidewalk, then up the stairs, then Joan, marvelous in her Pendleton, straight legs, and pumps, was on the porch. She launched herself into my arms and squeezed tightly, saying, "You're safe! You're safe!" I was bewildered but refused to ask questions, pulling her against me, feeling for the first time those wonderfully rounded breasts I had always wondered about.

Joan wept, still buried in my chest. Michele appeared on the porch, also dressed casual, no details, as my mind was buried in Joan. Dr. Taranucci smiled at us like we were getting ready to leave the house for our senior prom. I looked at her, most likely quizzically.

"Uh, we heard your plane was in trouble." Michele said.

"Wha—Wha—," it was as if Joan should have been there all along.

After thinking about just how safe and sound I was, Michele anticipated a miscommunication. "We were at Dr. Cost's party. Sirens were everywhere. First estimates came back at a dozen killed, ten more injured."

Then, I got it. Joan felt so good I hesitated to tell them the truth. When I did, she released her grasp on me and slowly, as the conversation continued, backed away. She grew conspicuous and suggested they get back to Dr. Cost's dinner.

I stood, stranded on my porch as they drove off.

*   *   *   *   *

I awoke at nine thirty the following Sunday morning feeling the effects of my last hits of the day: the guard on the kickoff and the third one on my bong. I'm relatively small, but I play like I'm fifty pounds bigger. I know no other way. My body constantly feels the punishment.

So I suck in a lot of marijuana smoke. They cancel each other out. I managed to navigate my way downstairs, hungover from potential unrealized: significant victory, certain death, and incredible love. Orange juice cooled the blaze in my throat. I went back upstairs, showered, dressed, and walked to mass, there praying for understanding.

Vinny and I met at church and headed over to the weird football meeting. After we drove home, I told him the story of the occurrence on the porch, a happening outside my reckoning.

"Let's get a beer," my friend said.

He was quiet through the first couple of swigs. After he took himself deep in thought, much deeper than I have seen Vinny go, so deep I could see it on his face, he retrieved himself and spoke.

"I don't know what you are going to say about what I am going to say, but here goes: you have two weeks. I don't like it and I am not going to co-sign for it, but it's your life and your heart and your pecker, so go for it, but give it two weeks." Vinny drew a long swig, satisfied with his contribution.

Stunned, thinking he would try to talk me out of her, I probed. "Two weeks. Isn't that kinda arbitrary?"

"No, I just picked it out of the air," Vinny answered, then took a short tug on the bottle. I just sat there. "I know what the fuck arbitrary means. Listen, Mason," he continued, "You two, both of you, have only just begun. I stress, both of you. She wants you, but she just doesn't know how yet. Work on it for two weeks. If nothing happens, call Jennifer Pierce. Something will happen there, I guarantee it."

I ignored the Jennifer remark, the reference to the 'very acceptable sorority woman.' "Two weeks," I said. "That's the day after Pittsburgh."

"Again, just out of the air."

We went upstairs and each loaded the bong to celebrate the plan.

If Vinny is correct about Joan and her true feelings for me, she surely had a strange way of showing it. Professional but perky describes Dr.

Kissinger's mood toward me the day after, Monday, and actually that entire week. You'd think she'd at least be happy to see me. Others were. Everyone else in the department as well as students of Joan's I know all, without exception, considering the flight difficulties and the ever-so-close loss to a top-ranked rival, gave me extra-special attention that week. I'm not saying I demand it. Normally I'm the opposite. I just want to blend. But in this case I wanted Joan to be consistent, not only with the crowd, but with herself. What else should I expect from a woman who drove all over town looking for me, then upon finding me, ran up my porch steps crying, throwing herself in my arms, damned glad I was there? What did that mean? I was at best perplexed, but more precisely, I was hurt.

It was painful to be treated like a business associate, and then to, here's the killer, be within earshot of her description of some guy she had just met and the way he makes her feel. I allowed myself to think I knew what was going on, and so did Michele, who looked like she was kinda embarrassed for her. But that game is for doubles, and even though I couldn't right away think of a girl who did those things for me, except maybe Judy when she goes on one of her jogs about town, wearing her extremely skimpy, possibly illegal Dolfin silky running shorts, calling attention to her already accentuated legs, length of which are measured in meters, or Alice, who fills up a pair of denim anything, any length, with her butt, best when she on "Calire Cut-off Days," in April and August and September, is drifting through her Engineering building and making pocket protectors pop out. I would have talked about them, but they are our housemates and deserve a bit more respect than being on display in the meatcase. Huh…I guess I just did that.

Before I had a chance to make full use of my jock-playing-the-field image, Michele caught me swaggering down the hallway. She called me into her office, a room crowded with knickknacks, photos, prints, and academic slop. How she accumulated so much shit in a couple of months I'll never know. I sauntered in. Maybe she wants me, I thought. Michele closed the door and walked behind her desk.

"Don't do it."

"Do what?" I queried, smirking.

"Don't lower yourself to the use of her tactics."

"Her. Who's her?" I asked, a smart-ass.

"You know who."

"She's nothing."

"Oh, yeah? Well, you'd have a difficult time playing seven card stud right now, stud, because I'm calling your bluff."

We stared at each other, motionless, for a fifteen count. Then, the breaking of my heart overwhelmed me. The tears flowed, not individually, like a snowy wind blew in my face, but a hard tissue-drencher with pounding twitches, my second in less than forty-eight hours. The emotions blew out so hard, I felt I was an observer watching me in Michele's arms, letting it all out.

After a couple of minutes and a couple of requests for messages by Michele, I sat up under my own will and strength. Breathing deeply, I finally spoke.

"Well, I guess the secret's out."

"I knew a few weeks ago," she said.

"Now, how in the hell did you know that?"

"I don't know. It was just a day of looks. First, you'd look at her. Then, she'd look at you. Back and forth. Back and forth. Like clay court tennis. It was driving me mad. I wanted to scream, 'Just do each other, already! I'll watch the door!'"

Still, I didn't believe it. I searched for other reasons for the outburst. "You know, I don't know, Michele. A lot of things have happened. Or almost happened. The game. I mean, to play your guts out, then lose on a weather pattern. Then, that landing. I really haven't allowed myself to think about that yet."

"Then, Joan showing you she cares a great deal for you, then not showing you."

"Yeah, not showing me," my voice trailing.

Michele arched her back to stretch. She, too, has…no, no. I'm in enough trouble already.

"I wish I knew what to tell you," Michele said, "This interoffice stuff is difficult, but then there is the fact…that age difference, and not how I feel about it. I think if you two can find a way, go for it. However, she's so…so, like a banker in some regards, like her father, and his father, and his father…and, you know, it's worked so well for a hundred fifty years, why should she change? Loving you would be a completely different way of looking at romance. It'd be like a bank actually dropping loan rates. Why should they do it? Am I making any sense? I often don't."

I interrupted, thinking it was an appropriate time to tell her this. No, I changed my mind.

"Okay, what is it?" she said.

"No."

"Look, nothing you say right now can surprise me. Let it out."

Knowing that this could take a long explanation of some rather odd events, I against my own wishes told her, "Do you know I own stock in her family's bank?"

Michele rocked back, then responded, "Holy shit! How did that happen? Does she know?" Michele asked, loving every minute of it. I dig the way she trusts me.

"Yeah, one day when I wanted to impress her, and the subject came up, I said, 'There's something you should know…'"

Michele laughed, "How did she take it?"

"Like you would think. As if I were a pimple on a gnat's ass."

"Yeah, but Christ! How many shares do you own?" Michele didn't mind asking the inquiring questions. I didn't answer. She gave me that room, then slapped her lap. "Okay, I have to ask. How did you get the money?"

"My dad," was the very short version of a long story.

She paused with regard to my lack of candor. "Damn good story," said Michele, accepting just that, "Damn good. Is your broker married?"

"Divorced." I smiled.

"A catch. Don't tell my mother. Jeez Louise, Mason, I have learned so much today. Thank you for having a nervous breakdown in my office."

"Thank you. Only you, baby." I stood and extended my hand. She took it and stood, then hugged me. Michele is the best woman friend a man could ever have. She is so perceptive and so caring. If I wasn't already in love with one English instructor, I'd surely have a difficult time resisting the urge to fall for her. What the hell am I saying? Screw up a perfectly good relationship? Man, sometimes I think I have to be under twenty-four-hour watch.

Sunday, November 2, 1975
Mid-afternoon

Re-examination continued

Okay, so that last statement sounded like Jock-Stud Man. I just have these feelings I sometimes have a difficult time expressing. Michele's my friend and I am cognizant of the fact that it's better for both of us to stay that way. I guess I am beyond friendship with Joan, but that makes a romantic relationship sound as if it is on a higher order. I'd do anything for Joan, but I'd also do anything for Michele and Vinny and Michael and Arthur and Judy and Alice. Friends and lovers are juxtaposed, and that could be a reason they sometimes find it hard to co-exist. That explains Jean. God, I can't believe it! I just figured her out! That's scary.

The week carried on as it had started. Joan acted toward me as if she were the good older sister. Michele had the subtle essence of a sage, always checking in with me with words of encouragement or wisdom.

Vinny gave me the countdown everyday. "Twelve days. How's it going?" I would reply, "She's friendly, but that guy Alan Karbin keeps calling and she keeps laughing at the things he says." Alan, the scourge of the jealous man, desirable Alan, real estate broker, Mercedes two-seater, intelligent, rich, handsome, trustworthy, loyal, helpful, friendly, courteous, kind, obedient, cheerful, thrifty, brave, clean, and reverent fuckin' Alan. What Alan did to her over that weekend is beyond me because as of eight thirty Monday morning Joan couldn't and wouldn't stop talking about that son-of-a-bitch Alan.

Then I met him. Thursday. He came by to pick up Joan for lunch, the pencilneck. About six foot, one fifty five, with the looks of a tennis player; country club handsome. Joan introduced us. I saw it coming. I took my blazer off in my office for the first time that semester and walked into the hallway, standing before him in a ribbed tee and Levis, tan boots and no belt. Dr. Kissinger stumbled a bit over the introduction. The message was clear: I've got thirty pounds of beef and a few hundred SAT points on you, club boy. Will it be a battle of wits or shall I just kick your sorry ass right here?

The conversation was pleasant and rather pointless, then they took off. I stood victorious. The department assistant Kathleen strolled by. She told me I had a nice frame. That's all I needed. I smiled, thanked her, told her she was pretty attractive herself, and walked back into my office to the solace of my desk and my sportcoat.

The lofty effects of my mastery over the loser Joan had chosen for a boyfriend wore off much more quickly than I could have imagined. I had been relegated by the happy young adult couple to what was chronologically my station in life. At the same time, my state of melancholy yearning for The Woman overwhelmed me. These two enduring emotions did battle in my brain as I sat, remaining as intelligent and as physically overpowering as I had presented to that fucker Alan, but losing footing to the landslide of reality facing me. In contest with that, a third feeling much like the second crept into my mind: I couldn't let her go. Call it what you will; undying love, a pride so strong I risk being extirpated by it, or just the ignorance of nineteen year old obstinance. I had invested time in this woman. Think time, dream time. Recognizing the feeling coming on, I reflected back to those times only I knew about. The off-white ceiling of my room provided the blank-page backdrop as I would lie in my bed and allow my imagination to stir and ultimately overthrow any rational thought I had in rumination of Joan. Combinations and permutations of Joan. Thinking of dreaming about Joan, a derivative fantasy. Seldom if ever sexual in nature, I would merely see us together, walking hand-in-hand through the autumn colors of rustling leaves at our feet, talking. I would make her laugh that Laugh of hers that sends me orbiting, a Laugh which belies the professorial persona she carries. It is a Laugh that tells me I and only I know better, that there is a woman of ardor beneath the bred culture she shows everyone else. And she would Laugh again, and place her arm around my athletic waist, and gaze at me as if impressed and safe. Safe, trusting in my strength and my love in the way that I could be her protector, warding off all men superficial and superfluous, the kind of men who selfishly chase around after beautiful women as prizes. I would be in the windows to her soul her true man, settling with her before a fire, holding her head to my shoulders as she silently stroked my chest, absorbing the heat, the glow of the flames reflecting from her absolutely gorgeous brown eyes, symbolic of the burning desire she has for me. Me. I, the one man who adores her as she deserves, the miracle she is.

Deciding I wasn't worth a damn to anybody there in that state of mind, I took a walk. I was alone, at that time no color at my feet, only the death of the deciduous leaves sopping on the concrete of the sidewalk from the recent drizzle of that part of fall signifying 'it's over, see you in March.' I paced with a random brain, never before being this lost in Joan. The old brick buildings of The U's downtown campus were in the forefront of gray clouds, buildings which usually added character and flavor to the common business district of Montani, but that day seemed deformed. I was depressed, With regard to my presence here at The U, my attempt to run with the football studs and how meaningful I truly could be to Joan; I felt as if it were all a big mistake. But my instincts of the athlete I am made claws to pull me out of this funk. This is the same drive that jerks me off the turf after someone has jacked a forearm into my jaw. With these instincts my hope flickered like a pilot light. I refused to let go.

I found myself downtown, not searching for Joan, but there anyway because when had pain ever stopped me from doing anything? The old facades and storefronts on streets whose existences were being seriously challenged by malls reminded me of myself; the guy on the football field who could hurt people, but being replaced by the sleeker models, and the romantic watching the front of possessions and disposable income approach the horizon. Compelled to a jewelry store, which is most odd since I never had any interest in precious metals or stones, for investment purposes or otherwise, I went on automatic. And before I knew it, I exited the store, placed my American Express card back into my blazer pocket, with a small box in hand. It contained a sparkling one-carat diamond ring with a three-stud mount and an eighteen-carat gold band; small enough for everyday, big enough to attract attention, size six, wouldn't you know it, the same size as Joan's left ring finger, the size of which I know from the recesses of my memory in recall of an obscure conversation I had with her some weeks back.

The short walk from the downtown to my home took me through ranks and files of company houses built by a long-since closed steel mill, now housing the unlikely neighbors of the retired mill workers who knew at one time how to drink and get into fights and U students who know how to party but are too high to get into fights. Climbing the stairs to the porch where I held Joan, the thought of which has always since clamped my heart, I went to my room and placed the ring in my small

wall safe I for which I really can't remember why I had installed. I looked
up. Like the dreams on my ceiling, this thousand dollar purchase, one of
which thanks to Stan the Money Man I can afford, was dangerously close
to obsession. But my awareness of all details Joan and the strange twist I
had put on the events of the day, and the fortuity of it all, rendered me
steadfast and renewed my spirit in the zealous pursuit of my Dream
Woman. I try so hard to be beyond my years on earth, but sometimes it's
good I'm nineteen, because I think I'm so goddamned invincible. That
keeps me in the fight. For at times the fight is all I have.

The fight is all I have. I knew I was going to have a great day in practice.

Practice. The West Virginia football team was on Monday of last
week at the outset of a schism as a result of Lawson's inattention to the
problems that had beset the offense during the Penn State game. The
defense had played great enough to beat a couple of NFL teams, much
less any college team, but the offense suffered so, not being able to cross
the goal line or get in field goal range or even string together a few first
downs. Lawson's handling of this matter riled the defensive players. A
few of the lesser committed ones started in on the offensive guys. Bobby
Kay, quarterback, was the initial target. He is just a sophomore, a big
kid, six-four, two hundred, a thrower of 'frozen ropes,' passes that whip
from the end of his arm on line, high velocity, only the slightest of a
parabola existent, thirty yards sometimes. A cannon for an arm this boy
has, but something is lacking. Actually two things are missing. First,
Bobby is not the brightest light bulb on the team. He has a difficult time
in school, still unable to get anywhere near declaring a major course of
study. He has problems in quarterback meetings, during which he
attempts to decipher that week's opposition's defense. The coaches
know of his limitation and downgraded The U offense to compensate
for it, because they want that 'rope' out there. Strange, because we ran
the ball a lot, not affording the Big Kid, The Kid, or just Kid many
chances to use his ropes. They want, supposedly, to give him experience
now, and he will grow and throw many ropes for the Runners, and then

for the National Football League. Supposedly. But Bobby is so Bobby sometimes, it seemed almost as if there's some other incentive for Coach Lawson to put Kid out there.

Second is an intangible: The Kid's lack of leadership ability. Problem is, you have to really look to uncover this one. We are seven and one, having dropped down to thirteenth in the most recent polls after Penn State. Not bad. Great for a bunch of Wallflowers. If someone would have told me back in August we'd be here in late October, I'da taken it. But we beat Maryland, Kentucky, Indiana, Boston College, and Virginia Tech in the first five games. As of this weekend, those five teams have combined for fifteen victories out of forty-five games. They're not the kind of teams to make you quake in your boots. Our sixth game against undefeated Miami, on the road in the Orange Bowl stadium, was our first big test. To put it mildly, The Kid lost it. Passes went awry, huddle commands were garbled, and his voice was shaking. It was obvious to those around that he was barely treading water. Fortunately, the defense forced turnovers and Raj kicked five three-pointers outside the forty. We escaped south Florida with our record intact. The coaches, in anticipation of questions that arose, issued a statement, "It was tough. We won. If it ain't broke, don't fix it."

Temple was a cupcake and Bobby did great. Then we played the Penn State game I talked about. Oh, my God, it was awful. He was visibly rattled. I was embarrassed for him. The Kid was definitely overly challenged and it happened on national television. And then the meeting the next day, or the 'non-meeting' as it could be called. It was obvious that, despite our loss of confidence in Bobby Kay, the Sunshine Soldier, he was handpicked by the higher-ups as our quarterback, our leader. It was difficult to figure out. More accurately, it was sad.

Sadder still is the fact that we have not only one, but two QBs with ability and skills and who also are held in high esteem by us individually and as a team. Number two man is Lendel Ward, a junior, six-one, one ninety, big arm, not quite like The Kid, but powerful enough to get the job done, and a running ability like few others. When Lendel gets flushed out of the pocket by the opposition, he has the knack to make our impending disaster a disaster for the other team. He is bright, a political science major, a three four five average GPA, and is a community leader, volunteering time at the Med Center. Everyone respects Lendel. Being a black player, he without trying bridges the black-white gap that is there but is not talked about. With Lendel and with our belief in him, all of us, we would have beaten Penn State by a touchdown.

The third quarterback, the man I work with in the running of the 'scout team,' the group that plays against the first team defense on Wednesdays to prepare them for Saturday's game, is my best friend Vinny. He's a sophomore, a Blue Chip recruit, six-two, now one eighty-five, bright, powerful arm, footspeed, and, most importantly, a fourth quarter guy. You talk about poise. He faces Michael and Joe every week and he makes them work. Michael has told me that Vinny is a big part of the reason the defense is so tough. But the fans only see him as the clipboard boy or the holder for kicks. Vinny, with his abilities and his pride and his desire and competitive spirit, is most certainly there. However, with Lendel being so good and Bobby being the favored one, The Gunner may not see playing time. But he's a Runner to the core and we're going to stay here until they tell us to leave. Until then, our Saturdays are on Wednesdays.

There are options, definitely; Lendel and Vinny. But the Kid is the man. And in my estimation, as long as Kid is our quarterback, the rift between offense and defense will grow.

Bobby does have some things in his favor. Fortunately for him and for West Virginia football, the team is comprised of players whose talents either weren't widely known to the big-time recruiters four or five years ago, or possibly didn't even exist, but who each individually grew to the stature of the outstanding players they are today. In our ability to take the Nittany Lions down to a lucky field goal, we have shown that we are an anomaly among Wallflowers, right up there with the Big Schools. This year in 1975 the Ridge Runners are for real.

So, in an effort to explain what each football player does and his contribution to the team, let's talk about the guys who carry The Kid.

It starts with every team on the lines. They are the big boys, standing six-one to six-six and tipping the scales at two forty-five to two seventy. The average fan doesn't notice them because they don't play out in the open field and don't handle the ball. They're in the obscurity of the Trenches. On occasion, you'll see a defensive tackle get a quarterback, and you might spot an offensive guard rock a linebacker back on his heels, but that's the extent of their public exposure. However, every coach to a man will tell you that a football team doesn't go anywhere without a good line on both sides of the ball. This year, West Virginia has those players. We have Ted Gerlach, John Pettibone, Montgomery Cash, Reginald Smith, and Marty Louisinsky when we have the ball, as well as Andy Baum, Francis Lionel, Andy Bruzinsky, and Tim Seiler on defense. This year, West Virginia has those players. Our big boys rule the Trenches. Our big boys rock and roll.

The big boys have their own ways of doing things. A lineman, for instance, because they are basically buried within humanity and humbleness draw their identity from the team, and are therefore inwardly hurt most by defeats or poor team play. But, differences extend further. An offensive lineman relies on blocking assignments, patterns, and technique to get his job done. The defensive guys must fight through this organization and because of that are often more intuitive. I've read that a psychologist has studied these differences. He said he could look at the locker areas of linemen and tell which side of the ball he lines up on. Offense: neat. Defense: disarray. These may be generalizations, but sometimes it helps to have an idea how that other guy thinks. Otherwise, why would you even want to look in a lineman's locker? And if you did, are you going to tell him to clean it up?

Now consider the men the linemen either block for or try to stop: the offensive backs, running backs in particular. Showboats they are. He acts as if the crowd is watching the game through a camera lens spotted on him. Confident of their abilities, they know they are the stars. They get the ball and dip, cut, and dodge in a dance-like fashion. If the game were on stage, they'd have a lead. My friend Arthur is in civilian life one of the nicest guys you could meet, and at the same time, he is one of the cockiest and one of the most talented football players on the team. But he backs it up with his splendid play. He's strong and fast. We know we can count on Arthur when we need something done. He delivers, and he doesn't let us forget about it.

Contrast him with the fullbacks. Lining up beside the running back, their primary assignment is to block for him. They're like a lineman who can get the ball, which they do whenever it is necessary for a big man to grind it out for a few crucial yards. Like all football players, they're tough, and mean. But our fullback, Frank Adams, prides himself on the ability to play regardless of anything, like deep bruises or even broken bones. In a way, he internalizes the running back's confidence without the showmanship.

On the outside of the offense and around the defensive perimeter are a rather odd bunch, a group of loners in a team sport played before tens of thousands. The wide receivers, the men who catch passes, and the defensive backs, the men assigned to stop them, are guys who are physically detached from the area of most of the play, but within themselves know how critical they are. Receivers on a good day touch the ball maybe five times, and an outstanding d-back may intercept only eight passes all season, but they ply their skills in a charged zone which requires the best athletes on the team. Everyone knows that one great play by one of them either way could turn the game. Our wideouts, Dhali Sellers and Clark Nestor, as well as Tom Smith and Dave Beck, never fail to catch The Kid's passes and make him look good. The Runner d-backs, Shane Evans, Dougie Roland, Bill Turpin, and Chandler Childress, are rock solid, having only given up one touchdown all year, a cheap one against Miami. The West Virginia recruiters in the winter and spring of 1972 and 1973 hit the prep school mother lode with regard to these highly adroit football players. I'm the number five receiver, third team. Having played with and against these guys all year, I know what it takes to do the job. That doesn't mean I have it. If I did, I'd be on scholarship. But, our receivers and d-backs certainly have it. They can match up against anybody in the nation.

These players with different contributions and varying motivations must be held together as a unit by some cohesive force. On offense, that's the quarterback. The QB directs the huddle and handles the ball every play. He is viewed as a religious leader by some, a politician by others, and a clown by still more, depending upon the team record. The defense, on the other hand, consists of a group of folks working for a common purpose but individually are renegades and in some psychological profiles have been shown to have suicidal tendencies. It takes a special guy to show them the way. They are led by the linebackers. These players physically resemble fullbacks with the leadership qualities of a quarterback, and have a distasteful but very necessary homicidal edge. They thrive in the havoc that defines defensive football, but, as the leader they must keep their thoughts organized, almost professional and detached, as possibly an assassin would.

My two buddies from defense are the linebackers. Michael Burton is the middle linebacker, a position of structured mayhem made famous by the Chicago Bears' Dick Butkus. Michael fits the job like he sent in a resume for it. Like Arthur, a nice guy off the field, a great friend, but holy hell on the gridiron. I find that fascinating. Equally so is Joe Osbourne, a special linebacker in our defense called the musket back (hillbilly musket...get it?), a combination linebacker/defensive back. Joe is the consummate solitary man: a future CIA agent, dedicated to

the Second Amendment of The Constitution, and a sometimes reluctant proponent of the Fourth Amendment. He is rumored to have done
some dirty work in Angola for the spies last summer. I can believe it. Joe
for some reason known only to a Higher Order has befriended me. We
don't hang out together; Joe wouldn't do that. But he has had me over to
his apartment to show me his extensive gun collection, including Israeli
automatic weapons and a grenade launcher. Strange. Stranger still is
that, despite exuding his Neanderthal-McCarthy era beliefs about
females, Oz has this unusual quality about him that attracts women by
the flocks; something beyond his obviously handsome six-two two
hundred pounds, a basal charm of the classic strong, silent type. They
know he's not going to open up, but he is a good scratching post for
their animal urges. What kills them is Joe doesn't seem to pay attention.
What kills me is they keep coming back. Regardless, if the Cold War
heats up in Montani, I know where I'm going.

This team I have described, a bunch raised mostly in Pennsylvania
and Ohio, a squad playing great ball in the final moments of the Penn
State game, was then yesterday when two and seven North Carolina
State rode into town teetering on the edge of a chasm. It was offense vs.
defense, two units needing to remain together, but finding it very difficult to do that. This has been a natural tendency among football teams
since coaches implemented the, as the Korean War generation calls it,
the 'two platoon system.' One 'platoon,' as they say, to move the ball and
another 'platoon' to stop the other guys. These differing purposes mesh
when things are going well. However, when it's tough, i.e. when we're
losing, the natural contentions surface and the sneering gathers
momentum. The captains of the team, Ted Gerlach and Michael, tried
to get everyone to chill out, but on the opposite sides of the ball themselves had a difficult time taking their own advice. Among all there were
rampant references to questions about ability, toughness, willingness to

hit, manhood, and sexual preferences. And as we took the field for the opening kickoff, everyone among the forty-four in the first two teams had been referred to as a wimp and a pussy.

Amid this state of disarray, I had my finest moment as a Ridge Runner when the Wolfpack return man couldn't get the handle on the ball. After a few seconds of fumbling around he looked up just in time to see the top of my helmet which, resembling a warhead, drilled him into the turf. The ball flew out of his hands and into the endzone where Michael recovered it for a touchdown. We celebrated wildly as Raj lined up for the extra point. He hit it, and that was the end of that and the beginning of a slide that lasted the whole game. To put it mildly, everybody sucked and NC State stole one on the road, twenty-one seven, an upset of major proportions nominally, but in reality, after the rains came at State College we didn't have a prayer.

The dressing room was a quiet as a library as we all shuffled around, averting direct gazes, just wanting to shower and dress and avoid the press and get the hell out of there. We all parted, never in more of a state of confusion. With our game against numero uno Pittsburgh in just seven days, we looked like a team doomed.

I walked home with Vinny. We vented. Our feelings were interlocked and valid: a) we were tired of being scout team heroes on Wednesdays and standing around on Saturdays, b) we can play as well or possibly even better than those losers, c) maybe we should talk to the coaches about some way to show our worth, and d) hell, yes, talk to the coaches; what the hell can we lose, and e) if all that doesn't work, let's take this Gunner to Cheetah aerial circus somewhere where we would be appreciated.

Arriving at our house to the Hallowe'en party Judy and Alice were having, we really didn't feel any better, despite the fact that there were sorority sisters and other coeds prancing around in suggestive costumes. Most everybody stopped their individual reveling to offer us sympathy, which we humbly accepted. Vinny then found Jean and approached her for commiseration. Her friend Jennifer, my preferred-by-my-friends woman, found me and told me it will be all right. Jennifer Pierce, tall, slender, dressed very well like Catwoman of Batman fame, mask removed to display her almond-shaped brown eyes I could look at for…a while, then I had to excuse myself to rest, which meant retiring to the smoking room and doing a solitary bong hit while obsessing about Joan.

I stopped by my room to change clothes, asking myself why, when there was a real woman down there donning a tight black outfit, I just wanted to think about an unavailable college instructor. I placed in my bureau drawer the black-and-white framed photo of Joan and me in her office I kept on my desk, the one I for a few extra football tickets conned from the newspaper reporter doing a story on the instructor and her tutor. Feeling guilty for doing so, I rationalized I am in college and had to be prepared for any eventuality.

While getting clothes from my closet, I found a box on my bed. I examined the exterior as Alice came upstairs to tell me a man had dropped it off after the game. That's all she knew. She turned and I looked at her caboose. She turned back and told me she caught me, then laughed and walked away. I was just happy most all of my facilities were still there.

After slipping on a light blue long sleeve polo shirt, Levis, and my trusty work boots, I picked up the package and headed upstairs for the smoker. Arriving, I sat the box on the bed and proceeded to my first order of business. Recently I had been paranoid, not of the cops or the FBI, but of turning into that naked guy in the classic movie, *Reefer Madness*. Sure, it would be fun to have two equally naked chicks dancing around me, but at what price? Loss of brain function? I therefore eschewed the powerful Maui Wowie for the home grown stash from nearby Preston County Vinny called Weed Lite. I loaded our bong, Atlas, with the lite variety and took a big hit. Tingling, not from anticipation of what was in the box, I opened the box.

There, I found two large black and white glossies of two men with a briefcase in a wooded setting, bank account transcripts, and a handwritten letter to me, Mason Bricker, from a PD Doughtery, a total stranger. PD wrote, 'These photos and the photostats from the bank will undoubtedly raise some questions. I'd like to come by and answer them tomorrow at, say, around five PM? Hope to see you then. Call me at the Hotel Montani to confirm. PD.' I grabbed the box and went down to my room to check this out. Telephoning the hotel and asking for PD Doughtery, I was greeted on the line by a very pleasant fellow with a slight black accent. He asked if five was okay. I said yes. He said he had to go. I rested the transmitter of my phone in its cradle and wondered what the hell was going on. Turning to the box, I again pulled the pictures out. Readily I saw to my surprise that one of the men was Coach Lawson. The other was some fat, bald guy. An examination of the photostats showed that they were of Lawson's bank account and were of a series of cash deposits apparently, for $9,500 each everyday between September 25 and September 26 and between September 29 and October 3. Possessing a moderate buzz, I needed a second opinion. I moved downstairs to find Vinny.

The party was in full swing, or as swinging as a bunch of Pi Gamma Pi sisters can make it. They were all pretty, but were not prone to drink green goddamn and gator or anything like that. I spotted The Gunner talking to Jean and Judy. My blue eyes turn slightly red with a modicum of marijuana, which is the reason why I don't smoke before sunset, lending some rigidity to my drug habit. No, that's bullshit. Anyway, I must have looked high, because the women immediately suspected I wanted Vinny to keep me company in the smoker. I told them I was finished for the day and this was concerning another matter. Sure, they retorted. Then come with me, I said. Judy stayed to be a hostess, but Jean came along, which was okay with me because it was either see it here or find out about it in the sack.

Vinny looked over the contents of the box. He picked out Lawson pretty fast and also didn't recognize the other fellow. Finding the

account photostats interesting, he surmised it was a payoff for something. But what? What could be important enough to pay off a coach?

Jean sensed I was distraught over something. In a fit of kindness, she
suggested I dress for the occasion and join the party. I replied I couldn't
think of anything, which was code for I'll just stay up here. She then told
me I was very creative and I could come up with something if I tried.
She and Vinny left for Vinny's room. A little sweet love for the clipboard
jockey, I guessed.

I sat on my bed and dreamed of Joan. Wondering where she and Alan
were or what they were doing or wearing or not wearing…I reached for
the telephone, picked up the receiver and dialed 5-5-5-4-8-7-…and
slammed it back down in the cradle. Any idiot man would have called
her by now. Not doing the things common to the masses was the reason
why she was still talking to me in a civil tone. Then, it hit me…

It was time for some good college fun. I had a beige cowboy hat on
the upper shelf of my closet. I retrieved it, along with my blue bathrobe.
After fetching a pair of cutoff sweatpants shorts and a gray T-shirt out
of my drawer, I stripped and put it all on, then laced my boots over long
gray woolen socks. I went to the party as Hawkeye Pierce of TV's
*M*A*S*H*, a show I used to like until they tried to make a message out
of each and every scene. Just killed it. My costume went over well until
Vinny came down dressed in Levis, an Oxford cloth button-down, a tan
cord blazer, and brown workboots and announced he was me. Everyone
thought that was funny. I thought Judy and Alice were going to lose vital
organs they laughed so hard. I was flattered, but I also quickly realized I
was a bit repetitive in my wardrobe. Fuck 'em. Vinny looked good as me.

I mingled and talked with a lot of females. Probably because they
were tipped off by Judy and Alice, no women mentioned football. But,
the guys couldn't resist. Here the distant hero stood before them, and
they could hitch on to me to live out some of their frustrated glory fantasies of the days of yore. Whatever. I let 'em have a piece of me.

After a half-hour or so, I ended up with Jennifer, my 'secret' admirer. I structured the conversation toward her, asking questions about her and her past and her family and anything to keep it going. She's from Charleston, her dad's a doctor, she went to the Catholic schools there, she's studying marketing, she never liked Richard Nixon, and on and on and on…While I was listening, I couldn't help but realize that only a week ago I held, actually held Joan on my front porch. I wanted to do it again, but I managed to keep my interest in Jennifer while thinking about Joan. I stood there with Jen and all the students, but hoping my Dr. Kissinger would walk through my front door, my mood oscillating from optimism to hopelessness and all points in between.

Later that evening, yesterday evening, Jennifer and I ended up in my room making out like college sophomores should, that is, with each other. I had Jefferson Starship's latest on the cassette deck for her, then Led Zeppelin's *Physical Graffiti* for me. It was interesting. The way Jennifer stretched out on my bed I thought I was with Julie Newmar herself. But, probably because my mind was with someone else and I didn't probe for sex, she sensed I was far and away. She finally mentioned her perceptions to me and blamed it for me on the outcome of the game. I agreed with her and apologized.

"Mason," she said lying on her side, "You're a troubled spirit."

I thought this was her exit speech. Gone before she was gotten.

"I can help you," she continued, "Just open up to me. Give me a chance to help you."

I paused to reflect, then smiled and replied before I knew it, before I had really considered if that's what I really wanted, "That would be nice."

Jennifer positively beamed, "Trust in me, Mason. I work wonders."

I guess she had done this before, but, what the hell, I'm her project. And don't forget about Stephen Stills. If you can't be with the one you love, love the one you're with.

Sunday, November 2, 1975
Mid-afternoon

Looking back to earlier this morning

The party started breaking up about midnight. Sorority chicks must get their rest, I guess. I drove Jennifer to her house.

"Call me tomorrow afternoon. I want to see how you are," she said, "You know, make sure you're okay."

I agreed to Jen's twelve-step recovery program for whatever ailed me, the accidental boyfriend.

With all my housemates romantically occupied and with my new girlfriend safely nestled in her greek house, I drove. The University of West Virginia is separated into two distinct campuses by a hill, the final geographical arbiter in Almost Heaven. Over the hill is the Overhill campus, a spacious setting of academics, rolling ridges of classroom buildings and dormitories. Overhill is where the medical, law, and engineering schools are located. A big farm was offered to The U in the Land Grant Act of the eighteen somethings, affording us the opportunity to sink money into the sprawling structures needed to allow us a shot at having quality professional schools such as medical, law, and engineering (Alice's domain). The alums who shadowed the hallways and labs and libraries of these buildings are the ones who make the jack and foot the bills of today. Despite the fact it has been said that The U's medical and law and engineering schools rank nationally in the same position West Virginia holds when alphabetized, the grads match up well enough with everyone else to keep us all alive. Don't give me that Ivy or Big Ten or Seven Sisters or TJ-UVa bullshit. I'll put our doctors, lawyers, and engineers head-to-head with those from Harvard and Yale and Virginia and Michigan and Purdue any day. And don't wait for me to do that. It's already happening, and I've heard no complaints. So, fuck them.

The downtown campus is a completely different story, all shoe-horned together on a hillside with no preconceived plan. Starting with the frats on the top, one descends, with regard to mean datum only, through ancient dorms and old classroom buildings of real brick and actual ivy, the newest and most modern of which being the student center. If you're arts (like me) or sciences or education or business (like Vinny, Judy, Michael, and Arthur), you spend your time downtown, so called because it is jammed into the smallest space possible beside Montani's business district. The reference to this place as a "downtown" is evident of the propensity of West Virginians to pump up the mediocre. And, mediocre can be used to describe the piece of paper you're issued when you complete your one hundred twenty-eight hours of prescribed course work here. I have to be honest: no one in California is going to sound the horns when you walk in with your degree from The University of West Virginia. But, it's like being a Wallflower. You can make it what wish. I just don't see Judy or Alice or Vinny or Michael or Arthur or me even doing anything ever that can be described as mediocre.

I found myself driving around Ridge Field for the fifth time. The Ridge was dropped onto the downtown and makes that campus the focal point every football Saturday. There's little extra room anyway, but when you cram forty thousand onto this hillside, I have found the safest place to be is on the field. When ABC Sports comes calling, usually annually when either Penn State or Pittsburgh is in town, the backdrop is the panorama above and around The Ridge, the downtown campus. However, the viewer in Minnesota doesn't see the rather distinguished campus to the right or the stately homes of old Montani on the hills. The guy in front of his TV in Illinois doesn't even see the frats, for Chissake. Positioned over the West stands of The Ridge and directly in view of the camera is our unique off-campus housing. Old, dirty white company houses extend up and down the hillside, built so closely together neighbors can through open windows exchange loaded hash pipes or pies and cakes after they unload their hash pipes. It looks like college football being telecast from atop a coal camp, feeding The Image. The U doesn't recruit on these Saturdays. It's ugly.

I, however, am charmed.

Motoring away from The Ridge and circumscribing Montani on all the roads, digging for album rock on FM, I evaluated my life, November 1975 edition. Football officially blew and I had photographic record of my head coach putting himself in a compromising position of some sort, although for what or why I would not understand until that afternoon. I was completely free to do anything. My dad's dead, my mother just died, my brother's in Pittsburgh with his own life he does not wish to share, and my older sister and my younger sister are in Virginia trying to be as normal as possible. I am a walk-on, meaning I can step away from football and no one would care, being in line to be a reserve until my Senior Day. Michael and Arthur are headed for stardom. Jennifer would miss me until she would snare another lost soul. Joan is and always will be taken care of. Michele's on the academia fast track. Vinny, Alice, and Judy all have their own lives and families. Me? I am all alone, isolated. I could stay in the smoker and do hourly bongs and no one would guess something was wrong until the rent was due.

Jennifer. Frankly, my evening with her left me empty. After just an hour, I was looking for a way out. This is bad, since Jennifer is the good friend of my best friend's girlfriend, and the sorority sister of my two housemates, also my good friends. Any such quick action could mean pain for everyone. Looks like I'm destined to grow old with her. What if I married Jennifer and, say, ten years and three children later, I run into, say, Joan at, say, O'Hare Airport? What if we then, during that chance meeting in 1988, decided that embrace on my porch was real and we were Meant To Be? What a mess that would be. I knew then I had to talk to Joan as soon as possible. Problem was, I knew if I would make a profession of love to her, after witnessing how fast she withdrew from me on my porch, and after her and Alan, the wimp Alan; after all this, she would think I was a jerk. It would be, 'That's nice' or 'Mason, I'm already in a relationship.' The other problem is, I knew it was There for us. I just knew it. So, I drove around listening to Uriah Heep and Deep Purple and Pink Floyd feeling the highs and lows, the tears and the laughter. Men are not equipped to handle this. It was becoming apparent to me that I had the genetic makeup to bust the wedge as a member of the kickoff team. Deny pain. Internalize feelings. But I knew I loved her, whatever love is for me. Hell, I didn't know. I did know that life without my woman would positively be the worst. I had to do something.

I drove up to my house at two in the morning, exhausted. Beside the door, I discovered Judy's marker on IN and the others OUT. I moved mine and walked upstairs to my room. Almost by reflex, I pulled the wooden box out of my bookshelf and opened it to display the Congressional Medal of Honor my father won in the war, along with a hand-inked thin-papered copy of William Wordworth, *Character of a Happy Warrior*. My favorite passage reads, "…Who, doomed to go in company with pain, / And fear, and bloodshed, miserable train! / Turns his necessity to glorious gain; / In face of these doth exercise a power / Which is our human nature's highest dower." I knew what my father would have said to me then. "Fight the gallant fight, my son."

Holding the medallion of the Medal of Honor in the palm of my hand, I longed for my father to be beside me once again telling the story. It is a story of fear and duty, of going for broke and feeling very lucky, and of lying on the edge of the beach awaiting rescue with his men whose lives he had saved, praying to God to spare him from that solitary sniper's bullet which would end it all right then and there before it all would be over.

It is a story told many times, always at the request of me, the proud son, and confirmed by Frank Bricker's buddies from Company Able. In early November 1942, Sergeant Bricker and a unit of United States Marines under his command were stuck behind enemy lines in the South Pacific. The Battle of Guadalcanal had been brutally fought by both sides for a few months, but that November the Japanese sensed they were losing it badly. They therefore threw everything they had at that very crucial point of the line, an atoll which would be remembered by the Marine Corps there and afar, then and now, as 'that fucking island.'

There was, however, no sense of history in Sgt. Bricker's outfit. They were simply trying to save their respective asses. Outnumbered twenty men to one, it certainly didn't look good. And worse still, the Sergeant had been separated from his unit, a group of ten men under cover but low on ammo and who were being absolutely hammered by a nest of Japanese.

Frank could see his men and see the nest. He decided at that time that life as he knew it was over. Thinking correctly he was undetected by the enemy, he figured he had no choice but to go after the nest and try to spring his men. Fortunately for him, as a result of a scavenger hunt on dead enemy solders, he had six grenades, a bazooka, and two machine guns. Unfortunately for him, he would upon his first shot blow his cover early. Fortunately for his men, Frank had a soul that was strung together with manhood and grandiosity and he just didn't give a damn about his personal safety.

Knowing that first shot better be accurate and decisive, Frank placed his bazooka on his shoulder, aiming it through the dense jungle foliage. He squeezed the St. Jude's medal his girl Colleen had given him at the train station back in West Virginia two short years earlier, thanked Mary, Mother of God he was Catholic, then fired the bazooka rocket into the enemy nest to their total surprise. Frank thought only half of them had died immediately, because the other half started peppering him with automatic rifle rounds and machine gun fire, a reaction very similar to hornets after being swatted by a stick, which my dad used to do for sport as a kid.

To his amazement, Dad uncovered another nest behind the one he had bombed out. They took over attacking his buddies while the original nest focused on Frank. And by the mercy of Jesus Christ Himself, he discovered a hole carved out of the base of a big tree beside him. He sought cover there while he collected his thoughts. Not wanting to remain in that tree for the rest of his life, Frank stepped out just enough to lob a couple of grenades in the direction of the nests. On line, one pineapple hit the first nest as the other went beyond and struck the second one. He thought the double concussion stunned at least or killed at best every enemy soldier.

At that time, my dad was really pissed off. In an image the men he saved have said would be permanently chiseled into their memories, Sergeant Frank Bricker exited the tree with the bazooka strapped to his back and a machine gun in each arm. Rockets and grenades dangling from his belt, he was a US Marine armed and in battle, straddling that fine line between bravery and abject ignorance, machine guns blaring, walking toward and into the nests behind the bullets, creating Asian carnage and ripping it to shreds.

It is said Frank held his fire and stood amid the Japanese death that only minutes before was filled with life and had his buddies pinned, owning their butts. The quiet was almost deafening as Sarge kicked around in what were gunnery stations of five to seven soldiers each. Finding nothing apparently alive, my dad said he took no chances and grotesquely planted a round or two in each head he uncovered. Then he walked away and toward the men whose lives he had spared for another day and another battle, lives he had changed. He had changed his own and had set the scales by which those yet born would be measured. But all they knew then was that they could pick up what armaments they possessed and get the hell out of there.

Maybe it was not obvious to them standing with their feet planted firmly on that fucking island, but Frank's buddies, being the good Marines they were, knew a badass when they saw one. They eventually reported their Sergeant's act of heroism they considered to be above and beyond the call of duty. The story made it up the ranks until it reached mythical proportions, ending up with the proper authorities who presented Frank Bricker with the medal I held. We as a species really don't know why anything comes to pass, but fourteen years later Frank would sire a son who would grow to develop a great appreciation for what he had done, for his buddies and for his country. This, of course coming after a son who held in total disdain about anything concerning his father. One out of two is not bad from long range, which is where my father lived his life.

After the war victorious, Frank the hero came home to parades and speeches, then a wedding mass in full dress blues with the Medal around his neck and his sabre to his side. He and his bride, the graceful Colleen O'Hare, drove to Beckley in a borrowed automobile to honeymoon and then, as it is said, the party was over. The war hero took a very common man's job with the railroad and life continued even after the excitement of living was gone.

Within, Frank Bricker suffered a great deal from this tremendous change, a change that took him from Marine Corps showpiece traveling Hawaii and California and Washington DC to a fireman stoking coal on a locomotive in Mullens, West Virginia, breathing soot through a wet cold bandana, eye brows and eyelashes singed as he opened the door to the firebox, shoveling black diamond, its radiant embers all he could see through the ash laden air in the tunnels, day by day, month by month, first a son, then a daughter, shovel for a shift, head of the household, home on the mountain, crying babies, shovel coal, ash, tunnel…

Not being one to lay back and complain, Frank had to figure out some way to get himself out of the emotional foxhole in which he was pinned. Woodworking, carpentry, painting with oils all brought somewhat of a sense of fulfillment, a roadside café on his highway 'from tedium to apathy and back again,' as Robert Higgins wrote in my dad's favorite novel, *Mister Roberts*. Frank was that Lieutenant Douglas Roberts with his tin-can assignment, mired in the backwaters, an appetite for action unfulfilled. He was a warrior and there was no war, but the adrenaline rushes kept coming....

As Mom told me once, Frank arrived home from one of his day turns on a spring afternoon captivating in its clear, cool air. Ron was crying incessantly and my mom was pregnant and worried about money. The hero paused briefly, then proceeded straight to his bedroom and changed into his USMC-issue sweat suit and sneakers. He threw an, 'I'll be back soon,' over his shoulder and took off for the other side of town.

Twenty-four minutes and four flat miles later, after a run both exhilarating and therapeutic, tiny Ron was still wailing and Colleen was still with child and the bills hadn't gone away, but Frank was a changed man. He was changed so much so that he made that run daily, despite rain, broiling heat, knee-deep snow, reports of Communists poised to overtake Europe and Asia, layoffs and markoffs. Frank cut a nice figure jaunting through the Guyandotte valley, although the citizenry of Mullens silently thought their hero had gone into one too many battles without his helmet, as most folks in the mid-1940s considered of anybody doing anything differently.

Possessing both an ability much greater than the general populace to deal with pain and discomfort as well as a natural aptitude for speed, Frank was becoming quite fast. His talents were enough that upon being visited by one of his Guadalcanal buddies, this man after witnessing his hero pass children on bicycles and adults in automobiles, and knowing a speedy badass when he saw one, reported his findings to the proper authorities. The story moved up the ranks until it reached mythical proportions, so much so US Marine coaches with stopwatches made the trek to Mullens to put the clock on their boy. Their boy, my dad, cleaned the clock.

The war hero that day received a second call to duty to train at Parris Island for the 1948 Olympic Games to be held in war-ravaged-but-quickly-being-rebuilt London, England. Dad packed his bags and took to the railroad again, but this time as a passenger. Standing with Colleen and toddling Ron and infant Junie, they exchanged kisses and he made promises of more medals.

For the next year, Frank thrived in the good things of a top athlete's life: good clothes, good shoes, good food, and good coaching. His status both as a Guadalcanal hero and a Marine Corps sprinter put him back in the forefront he so much preferred. And the extra training paid off immensely, as Dad quickly became the military's number one man in the quarter mile, winning or placing in the big meets of that year, seemingly peaking for the Olympics in '48.

The top American track and field athletes gathered at the Los Angeles Coliseum that June. My dad was among them, man, with thousands of servicemen and my mom in the stands, watching their Sergeant Bricker, 'Bazooka Frank,' a fluid, powerful running machine. He made it through the early heats and finished fourth in the semis, earning place in the finals. Wow. Finals in the US Olympic Trials. That has to be the coolest thing anybody in my family has done, aside from Dad taking out those two machine gun nests. But it was in the top two.

The finals. Dad told me he drew lane three, pretty good, he thought. He said he stood there, the calmest of the eight, he figured. He told me if he could single-handedly pick a fight with a dozen Japanese soldiers, any race has to be a piece of cake. I to this day have to agree with him.

I've seen pictures of the runners being called to their marks. Dad's high-waisted musculature contrasted with the long leanness of the other runners. I've seen film of the runners getting set. I saw the smoke of the gunfire, and I saw the man in lane three hit the deck hard as the others rounded the first turn. A photo of my dad's starting attempt shows that his starting blocks fell apart when he shoved off on them. It is said Dad pulled himself up from the cinders screaming 'Semper Fi!!' He gave chase, but he was so far behind even two machine guns in his hands and a bazooka strapped to his back wouldn't have done any good.

The Corps protested, but all Olympic Trials are final. Dad, very respectful of Rudyard Kipling and himself a man who has met triumph and disaster and treated those two impostors the same, graciously thanked the President of the U. S. Olympic Committee and accepted his fate. Boarding with his wife on the next train back to the Mountain State, Frank took up again as a fireman on the railroad, again normal. Almost.

After a stint as a USMC drill instructor revisiting Parris Island, just about as big of a badass one can get, The Governor of West Virginia and his wife invited Frank and Colleen for dinner at the Governor's Mansion in Charleston. There, the four of them enjoyed hobnobbing with each other, the Chief Executive and the Hero, and the First Lady and the Wife of the Hero. After much viewing of china and crystal and much sipping of fine whiskey and amid clouds of the smoke of Cuban cigars, the Governor, relishing the company of the rawboned, strapping, testosterone-laden ex-Marine, offered my dad as thanks for what he has done for the state anything West Virginia could provide him. After a minute of due consideration, Dad requested four years of all-expense-paid college educations at any of the fine state institutions for his two children. Surprisingly, according to my dad, the Governor agreed and for added measure threw in two season tickets on the fifty at Ridge Field…for life. At that point, my dad told me he should have gone for lifetime employment with one of the state agencies, but that's the thing about bargaining, you just don't know. Anyway, the two men shook hands. Not bad, as my dad said, for coming in butt-kissing eighth.

With their children's futures taken care of, my mom and dad would leave Ron and Junie with Momma Bricker on the days of home games and pack the car for the long drive up US Route 19 for Montani. Five weeks in the fall, they were in their respective heavens. Colleen thoroughly enjoyed being among the wealthy of the state and was just thrilled when the First Lady greeted her by her first name in front of everybody. And Frank, not really concerned with them or with anybody for that matter, simply loved to watch the game, a spectator of speed in action. He was certain that if it were not for Hitler and Hirohito he too could have donned the navy and silver and would have been 'flyin' down the sidelines.' But, as he told me, if he hadn't picked up that extra grenade a half-hour before the skirmish on Guadalcanal, none of that would have been possible. You just don't know, he said.

After several years of the fall outings, motherhood around the Appalachian mines had worn on Colleen. She looked forward to giving the children to Momma and reading a few books. Frank didn't care. He simply turned to his number one son, the nine-year-old Ron, his boy on the ballfields, a youngster whose heart was in it but was not excelling up to Dad's expectations. The hero thought spending a weekend with his son in the company of a real football team could give Ron the edge Frank knew he needed. It worked for a few years. My dad exposed my brother to the rewards of being a top athlete while introducing him to the intricacies of the art of football and the use of the speed which by genetics the boy was bound to possess. They talked of the day when the ex-Marine would watch his offspring fly down the sidelines, fulfilling a dream of the hero and making up for the mechanical failure at the Olympic trials.

In a cruel twist of fate, Ron carried to high school an extra thirty pounds of fat that rendered him as slow as a summer breeze. My brother's spirit was broken as he was the prime subject of sophomore hazing due largely to his girth, his lack of heart, and his lack of natural ability, a combination no amount of exposure and coaching and influence could overcome. Finally, and still more cruelly to my dad, Ron in a gross act of defiance over the him one day couple of years later proclaimed his freedom from football and his desire to pursue the theatre.

I was there for this. Through my seven year old eyes, I could see Frank was trapped in what later I would understand to be in that jungle foxhole again, for he himself a rebel had raised a boy who had just committed a rebellious act. With wisdom he lobbed no grenades at his son. He simply let go. And go Ron did.

Frank was presented a problem. The West Virginia home opener was only a few days away and he had no one to accompany him to the game. He spent a majority of that time trying to talk the fifteen-year-old daughter Junie into it, but after seeing what happened to her mother and her brother, she wanted no part of it. So, just a couple of days before the trip remained, we discovered each other. I, the bookish second son, somewhat introverted and ignored, took the hero up on his offer, showing up early that Saturday morning with a blanket and the 1962 World Almanac in hand.

We talked about everything in that six-hour trip. I read statistics and sports results from the book. I asked him questions, lots of questions, about the war and running. Then we got to the game. It was the first time I walked into Ridge Field, appearing from the gate tunnel and watching the whole thing open up before me. I was literally enchanted. From our vantage point on the fifty, I could see the teams go through their warm up drills surrounded by people filing in from the campus above. Two things were etched in my mind: The dark red brick of the old building climbing above the score box, which I would later find to be Woodside Hall, and the smothering of people in the place I would find out later to be the end zone in what was called The Bowl. I showed my dad my discoveries and proclaimed in my boyhood innocence that I wanted to be in both places. Dad told me Woodside was a classroom building for quiet study and the end zone was a place of noise and roughness. One place you read, I responded, and one place you play football. And then I met Vinny. And as it turned out his father was also an ex-Marine, so the men got along and became friends.

We boys were brought into an electrified state by the crowd noise that built and held until the final gun sounded. That excitement has never left us. In that game and in every game as I grew to be a young man, from the same seats, with Woodside and The Bowl, I looked forward to the day that I, too, could come to school here and read and play football.

As it turned out, I had the Bricker speed, the motorin' lineage that can be traced from Frank to his father Charles, a man who used to race against horses at county fairs all around southwestern Virginia, along with his father Daniel. I loved the game of tag as a child. No one could catch me. No one. This so pleased my father, for his experience with Ron had been a struggle. And when I turned eight and it was time for Pop Warner football, he was there along side me at the tryouts.

One problem arose. It seems that I didn't particularly like contact. In the open field, I ran away from them all. But in the mix of things, I cringed. The thing that came natural to a lot of boys, the ability, the desire to stick their helmets in there, I avoided. Therefore, despite my speed I was of little use on defense. I felt the displeasure around me from my coaches, my fellow players, my father. Both he and I had heard the small-town talk: there's another Bricker not worth a damn on the field. When's he gonna start auditioning for plays? I'm sure it hit my father in the gut, but I'm also pretty certain that he within himself had taken the blame for Ron's sudden aversion for the sport and everything else Frank. He didn't want the same fate to fall on me. He didn't want me to leave the game but most importantly he didn't want me to leave him.

Dad started working with me. He had me tackle him, not an easy prospect at his two hundred pounds. That helped some, but there was still a lot missing. For all that, he handled me in a Socratic fashion. Dad spoke with me often about courage and fortitude. He told me of many instances he came upon in the war where American soldiers he fought with screwed up the will necessary to get the job done. He evoked duty, that if I were to wear the uniform and the pads I had a duty to my team-mates to play the game as it should be played. Then he told me again what he had done on Guadalcanal and at the age of nine again showed me the Medal. For the first time, I got it. I was always impressed by the feel, the weight, by the colorful ribbon, but mostly by the story behind it. I had heard it all before, but it then finally hit me: my dad's a war hero and here's the Medal of Honor to prove it. He possessed the bravery. I could, too, I thought. My game improved immediately.

I wasn't hard-nosed, but I stopped avoiding contact. I took my shots and gave out a few. And Dad's philosophical approach to coaching me his son gathered momentum. He told me more stories of the war and his pursuit of Olympic gold. As I grew, we had the courage ourselves to delve into those most difficult of topics, like religion and girls. He was a man I could trust with everything.

I played junior high ball as an eighth grader with a bunch of ninth grade guys who were absolutely the toughest sons-of-bucks alive. Yet, I surprised myself and those around me by turning into a ball-seeking missile, a headhunter. I loved to hit. I sought not only contact, but colli-sions. In fact, I did it so well that I earned a starting assignment in the defensive backfield for the opener. And I played my heart out. I poured it all onto the field, just like my teammates. We had a great time.

One Monday morning toward the end of the season I met my father at breakfast. We discussed the usual over eggs and toast and sausage: President Nixon, Ridge Runner football, and my upcoming game with Beckley Junior High. During a pause in the conversation, he removed a box from a paper sack and handed it to me. I opened the box to find his medal, along with the inked copy of the Wordsworth poem. He asked me if I knew what the word 'epitome' meant. I said with confidence the dictionary definition: a brief summary. My dad then told me it meant to him, 'stands for.' He said I was the epitome of courage, that I had responded to duty as any man should, and that I am now the hero of the family. Taking his Medal of Honor out of the box, he placed it around my neck much in the same way it had been done on him almost twenty-seven years before. He then stood and grasped my hand.

We talked more about honor and bravery until he had to go to the railroad for work. I stood at the top of the hill and watched him wave as he rounded the corner at the bottom.

That day, Frank Bricker, United States Marine Corps drill sergeant, sprinter, and hero, and my dad, died in a locomotive accident.

I wore the Medal to his funeral. Mustering all the courage my father said I had, I gave him a solitary salute as the seventeen guns sounded overhead.

Sunday, November 2, 1975
2:30 PM

The resolve for ultimate romance

I saw my father in full dress blues, looking young and slim and tanned as he might have after the South Pacific campaign. He put his white-gloved right hand on my shoulder.

"Stick it out with West Virginia football, son, and get Vinny to do the same. And, never, I repeat never is a woman too good for the romancing from a Bricker."

"Is that the problem, Dad?" I asked. "Do I think I can't stack up to any man she would want?"

"If you think you deserve her, she deserves you."

I felt excited and scared. I mean, this is my Dad. "I'm hip, Dad. Have you seen her?"

"You'd be amazed what we can see from Up Here."

"You made it Up There. There was no doubt, Dad," *I said, even after having this conversation with him before.*

"Yeah," my dad said, *fading away. After a few seconds, he reappeared as clearly as before.* "Guess who I met the other day?" *he asked.*

Who?" *I replied, thrilled to hear about other folks from heaven.* "Martin Luther King, Jr.? Bobby Kennedy?" *It had to be somebody famous for him to bring it up, as he always does.*

"No. The Japanese soldiers from Guadalcanal."

I didn't allow myself to be fully aware of how odd that was. This is heaven. Anything could happen, I guess. "That's interesting, Dad."

"Yeah, in an earthly sense. But we're beyond that political and geographical crap Up Here. Now, about this Joan. You'd better stop wasting your time and get to it, boy, before we send somebody down there to steal her away from you."

I thought of someone being sent here at birth. He'd be even younger than me. "How could you do that, Dad?"

"Transference of souls. Everyday procedure." He made it sound like he was building a birdhouse or something.

"You do those things?"

"Sometimes."

"Damn," *I said, swearing to Dad. In heaven. He's right. I'd better get a move-on.* "What's this Alan guy really like, anyway?"

"If you're worried about him, you're wasting your time. There are others who should concern you; others you don't even know. Others she doesn't even know. I've told you too much already. Son, you'd be happy with her. Tell her how you feel. Tell her...."

There is a knock at the door, or something

"Open," I said in a groggy voice.

"A little nippy-nap?" Vinny asked, already in.

I shook my head. "I had another one of those Dad dreams," I said, moving with a little stiffness from the acid-rocker hit on the NC State return man.

"How was he dressed this time?" Vinny asked.

"Dress blues."

"That's okay. Nothing like the leprechaun, though."

"That's true, Bill."

"Who did ol' Bazooka meet this time?" The Gunner asked. My subconscious has sent us through this drill before.

"The Japanese guys he blew away on Guadalcanal," I replied.

"That's weird. Almost as strange as meeting Millard Fillmore."

"But, not like when he met Pappy Boyington." Obscure to most all, Pappy more often than not invaded my conscious thought. Right behind my dad, Pappy is my hero. I read his book *Baa Baa Black Sheep*, written by the flamboyant, irreverent drunk of a Marine World War II flying ace who lived it. The way he took a bunch of loser pilots and turned them into a top-drawer fighter squadron…I wish he were coach of the Wallflower Runners.

"Yeah," Vinny responded, "especially when you consider Boyington may not be dead yet. Now, what was it your old man told you to do this time?" The pattern re-emerges.

"It's what he told us to do: stick it out."

"You heard it here first, Ridge Runners fans."

I continued, "He also told me to tell Joan what I'm thinking."

"You can't do that! She'd call the police!"

Purposefully ignoring his remark, I said, "You know, I've decided since we've been sitting here I'm going to write her a letter."

"Good move. You write real good," Vinny emphasized the poor grammar with a hillbilly accent, funny coming from an Italian-American.

"It's non-threatening."

"Especially if you don't deliver it naked."

"You're a riot, Vacca. Really, if it's crafted right, I can convey my true feelings."

"If you don't say fuck or anything like that."

"Only if it's appropriate," I added.

Vinny changed the subject, "The mystery man still going to show up at five?"

"Yes. You gonna be here?"

"No. Jean needs me."

"Sounds like no foreplay today," I said smiling.

"Whatever it takes," Vinny replied, wagging his eyebrows then switching to something else, "That was another strange meeting we had today, wasn't it?"

I considered that. "After yesterday, you'd think they'd shackle us all to the walls and take cattle prods to our bare butts."

"You'd like that, wouldn't you, Longhorn?"

"Kiss my ass, Vinny," is all I could think to say, trying to shake this cattle thing I'm developing.

"You know, he's obviously favoring The Kid," said Vinny, declining my request, "I mean, he's not saying anything to him in public. But, the defense; they bit the big one, too."

"And, they had their own meeting. No coaches," I added.

"Have you talked to Michael about that?"

"Uh…I think I'll leave Michael alone for a while."

"Goddamn," Vinny swore, "If we played Pitt this afternoon, they'd score a hundred."

"And we'd probably go negative," I finished.

Vinny drew his face into a look of pensiveness. He spoke, "You know, a lot has to change before Saturday."

"No shit, Sherlock."

Unfazed by my last remark, my friend continued, "Maybe we'll be part of that change."

The possibilities hit me. "Maybe. Just maybe," I replied.

The Gunner looked right at me, "Hah!" I laughed aloud. Prison humor.

"I'm going to leave you alone to write your woman," he announced, "Can I read it?"

"Okay, but there will be no references to sex."

"Still, can I read it?"

"Okay," I conceded.

"Can I read it before she reads it?"

"No! Go away." Vinny obeyed me with a smile.

Sunday, November 2, 1975
2:40 PM

Precursor to The Letter

This is a good situation. I will be able to present myself in the best light, give her time to think, and also give her a chance to respond on her terms. No shock factor, as in 'I love you. Ta-Da!!' No pressure, like, 'You're adorable; what do you think of me?' I know, I just know that a woman as beautiful as she has been approached romantically in many, many ways. I therefore feel I will have some, maybe a lot of uniqueness in my delivery. And with Joan, unique is the key.

Goddamn, I can't do this. Who the hell am I trying to fool? If I were one to describe the situation with trite phrases, I would go with 'out of her league.' See how banal I am? I'm starting to repeat myself. But that summarizes it. The differences are remarkable. Okay, let's try it. We,

Joan and I, are common in our: a) intellect; obviously, through our conversations, and b) chassis; I know we'd look good lying bare together on silk sheets, and c) fuck, that's about it. Is that any way to launch a relationship? Brains and body? Well, maybe. Anyway, there is so much to overcome. So much. Possibly too much. Upbringing. Lifestyle. Net worth. Age. Education. Christ! This isn't going to work.

But it has to. It must, to fulfill the meaning of the embrace. It's up to me. She's not going to do anything about it. Why should she? There is a world of Alans out there, ready to feed her the truffles to which she has become accustomed. And considering the Alans, they're interchangeable, like integrated chips. There is no reason for her to overcome it all. This truly is my call.

I'd better get up for this letter. Gotta get in the right frame of mind. This is the biggest letter I have written to date. The implications are large, baby. I'm pumped! Cranked! It's mine, baby! Mine!

That sounds like I'm writing the National Football League! Don't be foolish. She's a woman. Just tell her how you feel.

Feel. There's a big word. Why. There's another one. Why? I don't know, I just feel it. I feel love. God, I hope the guys on the team never find out about this. But, that's stupid. Vinny's mentioned that. They will find out. Okay, I'm cool with that. This would be a lot easier if this were Jennifer. Normal. Then, let's compare Jennifer and Joan. Let's compare on categories associated with this boyfriend/girlfriend stuff: a) Social acceptance. Jennifer in a rout. No talk from the 'streets.' Not that that would bother me, but Joan may have a hard time with it. b) Ease of relationship. Also Jennifer. No family strife. No school administration on our backs. c) Upbringing. Lifestyle. A tie, so Jennifer is still up. d) Rack. Joan, popping out all over. e) Fanny. Another dead heat. f) Legs. Jennifer, all the way up 'til tomorrow. g) Overall beauty. Joan in a close one. No, really, farther away than I'm willing to admit. Joan. In a big way. h) Intellect. Joan, easily. Jennifer, sometimes you just want to say, 'Uh-huh.' And i) Desire for me. Jennifer. She is willing to accept my foibles without pulling a Jean and wanting to change them. That's sweet. All right. It's The Catwoman.

Sunday November 2, 1975
4:00 PM

November 2, 1975

My dearest Joan,

I have a matter I need to discuss with you. It's such a sensitive matter that we can't talk in your office. A restaurant is not good, not in this small town. The telephone can be an instrument of torture. And semaphore and Morse code are not practical since it is next to impossible to convey emotion with flags and dashes and dots. And there is little hope for me telling you this in your home or in my home. So, I write you this letter. It's a good medium because it gives you a chance to think before you respond. I do indeed want you to think and think hard as you read. I ask you to think about how good this is for both of us.

Seventy-one days ago, my life was nice but rather uneventful. I worked out. I read. I wrote. It was good despite the fact that I had virtually no contact with females. As it happens sometimes, it became easier and less painful to neglect them. So, that I did.

Then you burst forth onto the scene with your brown eyes and your PhD and your perpetual optimism and everything else wonderful about you, just about wrecking my plans for stoicism toward women. In just seventy-one days you have changed my life very much for the better. I am surrounded by you as I work so diligently for you, as I listen so intently to you, as I take joy in explaining things to you (remember: football is not life), as I walk around campus hoping you're around the next corner, as I answer every ringing telephone hoping you are calling, as I run faster and jump higher, feeling more and more like the man I want to be. All this, my dear Joan, because you are in my soul.

And why not? You are beautiful. You are bright. You are funny. You are kind. You are a sweetheart. No wonder I have fallen in love with you.

Please, Joan, don't make the mistake of disregarding my love for you as just another schoolboy crush. It is much more that that; much, much more

First, I am not just another schoolboy. You're good, but so am I. I have a lot to back it up, this profession of love for you. True, I could soar with a great woman like you. But, I too have much to offer. Let's talk about it sometime.

Next, Joan, look at us. Watch our interaction. Notice the way we stand and talk. Listen to our laughter. Observe our eyes. There is something to us, Joan. We are a man and a woman waiting for romance to happen.

That's the key. Look at us, together. Forget Mason Bricker, academic junior, and Joan Kissinger, English instructor. Remove the labels. We are Joan and Mason, lovers. Follow our eyes and you will find the way to my arms.

It's there, Joan.

We're there.

With all my love,
Mason

*   *   *   *   *

I read the letter a couple of times. A feeling of relief overcame me as I saw in print that which I had felt for so long, that which I had held within with due regard to position, station, and fear of laying it all out to a gorgeous woman. Knowing this read great, but considering the circumstances surrounding writing anything to any member of English faculty, I appraised the letter in terms of lucidity and sentence structure. I'm satisfied I have gotten the point across concisely and I have said it clearly and well. That, however, brought up another point. Maybe had I said it too 'concisely,' too 'well?' I mean, it was only a couple of pages of handwritten stationary. I had boxed up my entire love for Joan into that neat little package. Will she get to the end and say, 'Is this it? Is this all?' I'm sure she has received rambling, flowery epistles taken right out of Horace's works, if he ever wrote any on the wooing of older, more educated women who had most likely seen and heard it all. Then I reconsidered Horace, who as a first century BC Roman poet stressed moderation in life and, despite probably not even pursuing a woman such as Dr. Kissinger, wouldn't have been rambling or flowery anyway.

After reading my creation a half-dozen more times with all this in mind, I decided to my satisfaction the letter is me. It's direct, a quality of which in terms of romance I have not displayed to Joan, much to my frustration. It held within this directness passion. In just a few words I've poured my feelings out, without compromising or optimizing them. Michele would be proud. And, most importantly, the letter revealed and verified the control I have over these boundless passions. I'm pushing the edge of the envelope here with regard to both life in the seventies and faculty/student propriety. Anything that would make her apprehensive about my ability and willingness to be appropriate with my love for her would nip this letter in the bud. However, I'm pleased with the letter, with what it does for me, and what I bet it will do for her.

I laid back on my bed and looked up to the ceiling. I could see Joan opening the envelope, reading the letter, clutching it to her bosom, and laying back on her own bed and looking up at her ceiling and imagining us together. Writing this letter is one of the wisest things I have ever done. I just know it.

Sunday November 2, 1975
4:30 PM

November 2, 1975

Dear Junie and Camy,

How are my favorite sisters? Enough with the bullshit. I have a lot to tell you so I'd better get to it. However, to do this, I will have to write two letters: How It Is and How I'd Like It To Be.

How It Is

Football, how do they say, in a word, sucks. We've dropped two straight games, our offense hasn't scored since the Industrial Revolution, and everybody is in everybody's face. Fingers are pointing, the coach could turn into a real joke (more on that later), and picket lines are just around the corner with anarchy not far behind. And, worse still, Vinny and I aren't getting any offense playing time. I paid my dues; you'd think they'd put me in every now and then without having to sacrifice my body against the opponent's four man kickoff return wedge. As for Vinny, he's spending entirely too much time of the bench for a QB of his calibre. Plus, he's got writer's cramp from using that clipboard every week. It's awful. Film at eleven.

School's pretty good. My classes are for the most part still enjoyable. I really like my job as a tutor. Joan Kissinger is such a great professor to work for. She gives me free rein on taking care of the students. Plus, she is just about as lovely as any one woman can be. Plus, her classes are superb. Sometimes she gets me involved. I think I'd like to teach college someday.

Judy and Alice and Vinny say hello.

Have I told you how wonderful Joan is?

How I'd Like It To Be

I was in my office one day last week when Joan walked in wearing a black strapless gown complete with a thigh-high slit and pearls. She sauntered to me. I stood, in many ways. Draping her arms around my neck, she gazed into my eyes and said, "My darling Mason, how I do love you." I responded, "Well, golly, Joan, I love you, too." She whispered, "What are you waiting for?" Remembering this was my signal, our lips met, writhed, and then parted with a juicy smack. "Oh, Mason," she said, "you are such a forgetful darling. You left your novel, the one which you will complete and will bring you fame, by my bed." "Oh," I said, "I'm sorry. Thank you for bringing it." "Sweetmeat," she replied, "I didn't bring it. It remains at my house, by my bed." "Oh," I said. "Come get it tonight," Joan suggested, very suggestively, "And if you leave it there again, we'll just have to do this over and over until you get it right!"

By the way, I'm the #1 receiver, Vinny's starting, and we beat the hell out of Pitt.

Love, Your bro, Mason.

Beat Pitt my ass. Looked damned likely eight days ago. Now, tension, turmoil; we make the ninety-fourth Congress look like Sunday School. The combative Congress, impotent against the shockingly popular President Gerald Ford, Watergate survivor, All America center from the University of Michigan; in thirty-five years as a congressman did not sponsor one piece of major legislation; probably wore a leather helmet…where was I? Oh and, and that's a big *and,* the worst could possibly sit in that box and is heretofore very unknown.

I sealed and addressed the letter to my sisters and applied the required ten-cent stamp. Then I sealed the letter to Joan after reading it a couple dozen times more to make sure I got it right. I looked up a delivery service which makes Sunday deliveries. All-Week Delivery, 555-7777. I called them. They said they'd be by in fifteen minutes. I guess today's a light day for obsessive customers. I took the letter downstairs, put on some coffee, spun some Paul Rogers and Free ('She said 'love?' / Lord above!'; *All Right Now*) and laid down on the sofa. I awaited All-Week's arrival.

I am alone. Too bad for Mr. Doughtery that Judy and Alice aren't here so he can see that the state of the American coed is very much alive and wonderfully well.

The doorbell startled me from a shallow slumber. I stood, stretched, and walked to open the door. Two men are there. One is a short, chubby man in a forest green jacket and forest green slacks and black leather institutional shoes. The other is a light skinned black man, slender, just over six feet, with closely cropped African hair and a thin mustache. He looked to be in his thirties, despite being dressed young in a leather jacket, a cream silk shirt, designer jeans, and European shoes. I guessed correctly that the guy in the green uniform is from the delivery service. I excused myself to the other guy and handed the delivery man the letter to Joan, addressed, didn't bitch about the five dollars, tipped him a couple, and sent him on his way. Then, I turned my attention to the other fellow.

"I'm sorry. Yes?"

"Hello, I'm PD Doughtery."

"Hi, I'm Mason Bricker. I've been expecting you," I said, extending my hand. Mr. Doughtery clasped it confidently, consistent with his manner. I guess he is someone who possibly played some kind of college ball somewhere at sometime and is now successful in another endeavor, the life I would like to lead.

"Please, Mr. Doughtery, come in."

"Thank you. And call me PD," he said as he entered.

"Certainly. Call me Mason. Thanks for coming here today."

"Thanks for having me."

"Can I get you a drink? A beer? Miller Lite or Iron City?"

"Crossing the state line, are you?"

"You're not taking pictures, are you?"

We both laughed. "I'll have an IC," he said.

I fetched the beers. "Can I take your coat?"

"No thanks. I won't be in your hair that long."

I led PD up to my room.

"This looks to be a well-worn pathway. Get beers. Go to your room."

I feigned laughter, "Ah, ha,ha,ha. You'd be surprised how little that happens."

"No, I wouldn't," PD said as he slapped my back. It's nice to see aging guys have a sense of humor, even if I'm the subject.

We walked in. The walls are blue with mahogany baseboards and trim. Decoration is the visages of Jim Morrison, Crosby, Stills, Nash, and Young, a rare color photo of *Cuckoo's Nest* author and pharmacist Ken Kesey, and the abusive Jack Tatum of the Oakland Raiders. The queen size bed is to the left with the head against one of the windows. The door to the bath leads off to the left of the bed. The right is crowded with a big bookcase under the other window filled with books and sound equipment and cassettes. My desk is against the wall at the right when you enter. Somehow, I have found room for a lounge chair in the only corner you can see. A couple of throw rugs over the hardwood floor and three lamps, by the bed, by the chair, and on the desk, and you've got my room. Quintessential funky collegiate.

"Nice digs," PD said. I think he meant it.

"Thanks. I brought you up here because even though I don't know what the hell is going on, it probably should be kept in confidence. As of now, only Vinny Vacca and I know of the box and its contents." I lied a little bit....

"Ah," he sighed, taking a seat in the lounge chair. "Vinny Vacca. Turned down Notre Dame and Ohio State to stay at home. One helluva quarterback. What a guy. Seriously, what a guy. What brings you here?"

"Vinny. Otherwise, I'm lucky to have a helmet," I said as I sat on my bed. "Vinny and I met at The Ridge. We haven't missed a home game since we were in the second grade. We're not about to stop now, even though West Virginia football has apparently entered the Sleaze Zone. Am I right about that?" I probed.

PD guzzled on his IC and gazed at me in that way which makes you want to say, 'What?' Then he started, evasively "Why you, you may ask? Well, I've known of you for a long time. I knew Leonard Myers. He spoke highly of you and your father. Leonard's as well as your father's passings were tragic. But, I've kept my eyes on you."

Leonard Myers was one of the men from Company Able, a good businessman. I was under his tutelage in money management when, just a year after my dad's death and five minutes before I was to go to his house, a neighbor discovered that Mr. Myers had put a bullet through his head. Then he left my mother, my brother, my sisters, and me some cash. That pissed off his distant relatives. Regardless, it took a long time for me not to feel as if I had some kind of a curse on old Marines.

"That's scary," I replied to PD.

"Don't be frightened or shocked. I'm a banker, in Trust for fifteen years. I know Stan Mumphord."

The Money Man. Another one who crawled off of Guadalcanal with my dad. For a second, I was concerned my confidence with Stan had been violated. It must have shown.

"Stan and I don't discuss your account. He only talks of what a pleasure it is to work with you."

"It's a pleasure to deal with Stan. But, I know he has much bigger customers. Or I hope he does."

PD sipped again. "Stan has told me nothing about anybody, but it seems as if everyone of Stan's clients in 1973 and 1974 and this year is smiling. And that is in part why I came to you."

"Uh," I uttered, a bit confused, "Be more specific."

"First," PD began, "if you were with Stan during those times, you understand risk and you understand reward. I happen to know Stan shorted the last half of '73 and most of '74, then bought late '74. Made money while everyone else was sucking wind on the way down, then turned it on a dime and made money on the way up. Played it like a Stradivarius. And that bank idea." PD smacked his lips as he kissed the tips of his fingers like a French chef. "The maestro. So, I think you will understand very well the contents of the box. I think you won't be frightened away by it. And, since you are your father's son, I think you will do the right thing with it." PD rocked back in my chair and looked satisfied.

Enough is enough. "What's going on here, PD?"

"Myron McNabb, the Beckley resident multi-millionaire and holdover Aryan, has paid your head coach Denny Lawson a cool sixty-five K to perform the very difficult task of benching the better QB, Lendel Ward, who just so happens to be black, in favor of his worst choice for QB, Bobby Kay, who happens to be white."

I sat, stunned. I couldn't believe what I just heard. PD gave me time. I took a big belt of Iron City, then uttered my first words, long in coming, but definite, "That makes me want to vomit."

"Tell *me*," PD replied.

We are still, contemplating in our own universes. Finally, I motioned to the box on the bed. "I guess there's some weighty evidence sitting there."

"Yep," he said, "Photographs of the two men, and I use the term loosely, exchanging the briefcases supposedly full of money. Photostats of account records showing the exchange of money from both parties, documents to which I have sworn a blood oath never to reveal the source. Affidavits detailing the knowledge of the transfer of the cash. Weighty evidence, indeed. Two copies of everything."

"What do expect me to do with it?" I asked immediately.

"What do you think you should do with it?"

I'm stumped, "Well, I don't know. I haven't thought about it, you know, the best place. I…uh…kinda think Lendel should see it. I…I would like to run that by Michael Burton. They're the two black leaders on the team. And Arthur O'Neill, that's three. Help me out here, PD. Are these the correct answers?"

"I've chosen well. They are the correct answers. Now, what do you think you four should do with it?"

I am in a fog. I still couldn't believe…but I went on, "The newspapers would love to have this. Nothing sells better than a scandal. And this is a *scandal*."

"Right. Everyone's trying to be the next Woodward and Bernstein," PD mused.

"I guess that makes you Deep Throat."

"No, no!" PD said emphatically with laughter. "I'm nobody. If you don't take it, I burn it."

"Say *what*?"

"I've got a family, a good career, senior vice-president of a bank."

I examined PD's face and paused, "So, I'm your last resort—where did you say you worked?"

"First National Huntington—"

"Oh-ho-ho-ho!" I roared. "Huntington! The Marshall connection. Taking the U down! Boy, you guys are ruthless!"

"The University of West Virginia, 1960. BA in psychology. Played football up here, end."

Now I'm really confused. The answers to all my natural dissentions are 'take the box and run with it.' But, I'm just not ready for that. "Why this, PD? You know what this revelation is going to do to the football program up here, our football program. Yours and mine."

PD drained his beer. "I know," he said, "It would make it much more difficult to recruit blacks, to say the least. But, Mason, my man, let me ask you a question…you ever sell out?"

Further perplexed, I threw my hands in the air, "Fuck, I don't know, PD," I sputtered, "I mean, yes, but I don't…no. No, I don't know."

PD leaned in to me, deep brown eyes firm. "When you're a black man," he said, "selling out is a way of life."

I felt it. I got it. I hadn't understood fully why he's here, but now it is much clearer to me. I have a chance to not sell out. And, with regard to my friends Michael and Arthur and all my black teammates, I think I'd better take it.

"Okay, PD, I'm in." I said with confidence.

"Congratulations, Mason." He shook my hand. "Let me ask you: You ever read Kipling? His works, his poem, *If*?"

"Only about every week. My dad read it to me. I read it to him the night before he died. It was one of his favorite selections of literature."

"Well, son, it worked. You are a man."

Tears jumped into my eyes. PD reached over and placed his right hand on my shoulder. This man, hombre, dude, this fellow I didn't even know fifteen minutes ago, a man who knew my dad and some of his buddies, evoked my dad and brought the emotions out in me. They're there on the surface, I guess, and it doesn't take much. Shit, I hate to cry in front of other guys, unless you have just lost on a sixty-seven yard desperation field goal or are watching *Brian's Song*. Trying to pull myself back together, I searched for answers to other questions.

"Why would a football coach do that, PD?" I choked out.

PD sat back, assuming the position of wisdom. "First, Myron made it available. Temptation. Second, Coach Lawson's ethics aren't exactly his strong suit. I've met the man. You get the impression that you shouldn't turn your back to him. Third, Lendel's that much better than Bobby. It would take sixty-five thousand to bench my man Lendel Ward. Fourth, look at today. The front-runner among Democrats for President in '76? George Wallace."

"Oh, fuck, you're right, PD," I sighed. "Goddamn, it's not better, it's worse."

"Yep," PD confirmed, "His trip overseas got 'em all fooled. Like he's seen Jesus or something."

"I guess you can fool enough of the people all the time," I said, misquoting Lincoln purposefully.

"But the big reason looming over it all," PD continued, "is that Myron saw Dennis coming and he knew he could enlist the coach, as a mercenary at least, in his war. And his war, if he gets by with this, could escalate."

PD's right. Exclusivity in football is not news. But, we're supposed to be making reforms in this country. Something like this, buying a coach to sideline a black who otherwise would be a star, sends us, all of us, back in the wrong direction. To the back of the bus. But, this time with · Rosa Parks on the curb and Governor Wallace driving.

"I hope I can do you well, PD," I said, tying it all together in a tone of unsure faithfulness.

"Don't worry. You're perfect," PD said, "The logistics are good: third team receiver, walk-on, conscientious student toiling away in the English department. And, most importantly, I believe you will consider all the possibilities and act wisely. And when you act, I believe, as you did in '73 and '74, you will act decisively." He surely knows a helluva lot about me.

"Those were Stan's ideas," I said humbly.

"Yes, but even though you were only seventeen, you were the head of the household and it was your money and your butt, as Stan verifies by his receiving a phone call a day from you. You always do what you have to do. That's what I've heard about you, Mason Bricker."

Stan had obviously revealed a lot about our business relationship to PD, but it had all been complimentary. I'm always up for compliments.

PD looked at his watch. "I've gotta four hour drive ahead of me," he announced. "And I've taken up enough of your time. There's your evidence," he said, nodding toward the box on the bed. Strangely, we hadn't gone through it during the time he was here. "Do what we talked about. Call if you have questions." He handed me a business card, 'PD Doughtery, Senior Vice President, First National Huntington Bank.' "It's a pleasure to finally meet you, Mason."

"Certainly, the pleasure is mine," I returned.

PD stood and shook my hand again. I led him downstairs. Still no one else is here. I walked onto the porch with him.

"I won't ask you about the game this weekend," he said, finally mentioning the subject we had both unconsciously omitted.

"Things don't look good anyway. Now this."

"You do it your way. But, it is yours to do." PD extended his hand a third time. "Good luck, my friend."

"Thank you. I'm going to need it."

Dusk is falling quickly, as it always seems to do during these months when the days are getting shorter at an accelerating pace. PD walked down the stairs and toward his gold Trans-Am.

"Not your typical banker's ride," I threw at him.

"I'm not your typical banker," he tossed back with a smile.

I have to concur.

Sunday November 2, 1975
6:50 PM

The presentation of the evidence

I sat parked near our house in my Tazmanian Devil listening on FM radio to the alternative progressive rock I so loved but couldn't tell you from where it progressed. Before I could examine the subject of the progression of my life within the regression of societal attitudes to the status quo of the South in the mid-sixties, headlights shined from behind me and in my rearview mirror. The lights flashed bright a couple of times then turned off before I heard the thud common to the closing of the door of all American-made automobiles, a thud on which I am sure Detroit spends millions and millions. It's a sound that makes all owners of those well-built union-made frames feel warm and secure subconsciously at least, reminiscent perhaps of a noise from the womb. Vinny disturbed my contemplation of that thud by opening my passenger door, getting in, and closing it, creating an Oriental clank of two pieces of sheet metal slapping together. That's a sound that makes us Americans feel warm and secure subconsciously at least in our xenophobia. A Miller Lite was in The Gunner's hand as he was dressed much more reasonably in a bomber's jacket, tan cotton sweater, black denim slacks, Weejuns, and no socks. We stared at each other.

Vinny deadpanned, "This had better be good," implying he had to throw his clothes on in a hurry.

"It's good," I said, "It's so wicked, it's good." I started my Taz, dropped it into first, and pulled out into Wagner Road. I drove down that brick street silently, flicked my turn signal left, and turned.

"Goddamnit, tell me!" exclaimed Vinny.

Just because I knew I could I waited, driving that short block and turning right onto South Hale Street. Then I started. "You ever wonder why The Kid is the quarterback?"

"All the time."

"Wonder no more."

Vinny turned to me, "When you're smug, you're a jerk."

Boy, Jean must have really been upset about her pony leaving early. "There are bigger jerks in the world."

"Oh, yeah?" Vinny is testy.

"Yeah, like Dennis Lawson," I said, driving past The Flame and turning right.

"Agreed, especially over the past several days."

"And," I added, "Myron McNabb."

Vinny was quick to ask, "Who the hell is he?"

I rolled to a stop at the red light. "The millionaire from Beckley keeping you and Lendel on the pine." On the signal of green, I drove straight, past the public library, past the municipal building, in silence. I stopped at the next red awaiting for a turn left on White Street.

"What the hell are you talking about?" Vinny asked, finally, deliberately.

"Just what I said," I responded. The light turned green and I turned left. "We're going to Bill's to meet Michael and Arthur." I drove on, twisting my torso to get the file from the back seat. "Here. Look this over."

Vinny examined the photos and copies. "This is the stuff from the box. I've seen this already. Did you meet who's behind this? Who's behind this?"

"I'll tell only you, and if you tell anybody else, we'll have to kill each other."

"Quit fuckin' with me. Who?"

"A banker from Huntington. Ex-Runner end. Black guy." We're stopped by the light at Hale and White heading for University Avenue and the downtown campus.

"How does he know?"

"One of McNabb's Nazi cronies has seen the error of his ways and confessed"

"Okay. McHitler pays off Lawson. Lendel and I are destined to life on the sidelines. McKlink spies on McHitler, tells your banker end, then the banker end tells you. Why you?"

"I'm a sucker for you ethnic types."

"Mason! Goddamnit!"

"Look, Vinny, you've just gotta believe! Look at the photos. Look at the paper. C'mon! What do you need, a fuckin' Senate resolution?"

"Why you? Simple question. Or, didn't you ask it?"

"He knows buddies of my father, like Stan the Money Man."

"Then why are you getting Michael and Arthur involved?" asked Vinny.

"I couldn't in good conscience not tell them."

Driving up through and beyond Hillside, we sat in silence for a minute. Vinny broke. "You gonna tell Lendel?"

"Yes, but Michael first."

"Why Michael?"

"He'll know the best way to do it."

"Why can't you tell Lendel just like you told me?"

"Because you're Vinny and he's Lendel. I know you and Michael knows Lendel."

"You gonna tell anybody else?"

"For maximum effect, *The Montani Mail* would be good. *The Pittsburgh Advocate* would love to have it, especially this week, but I first think we four should talk about this."

"Oh, no. You three. I'm not in on this. I could lose my scholarship. My father would cut me off. I'm in the streets. I'm not independently wealthy like you."

I yelled as we drove past Michele's house on University, "When the hell is a hundred-and-a-half grand independently wealthy? Jesus, Vinny! Your part of the dealership is more than that, rich boy!"

"My point exactly."

We're silent again as we drive past McDonald's, now in Overhill. Vinny and I haven't had that independently-bullshit argument for a long time. That makes me think: Joan by now has to have my letter. Funny how I forgot about that. I guess this football mess has monopolized my thoughts. Good. I need something to keep me from worrying about it until I see her tomorrow. Actually, it is such a good letter, if Joan's not sprawled on my bed wearing nothing but one of my button-downs when I get home I'll presume she had a problem with it.

"Look," Vinny stated, "I'm just inquisitive. I want to know, but I don't want to blow. As in my ride and my piece of the pie.

"Fair enough," I said, forgetting Joan for now. I cruised through the green and up to the red on Parsons. It flashed green as I approach it, and I turned left without a signal. I always think I'm going to break out in hives after I violate a traffic law. Bill's is in the strip mall on the right. I pulled in.

"I'm just an observer," said Vinny.

"But, if it freaks Michael out, you're in, even though I know the truth."

"Okay. What about Arthur?"

"Nothing freaks him out, except maybe losing his pick."

Sunday November 2, 1975
7:05 PM

The meeting with Michael and Arthur

Bill's is in a building separate from the small strip mall, to the left as you're entering the lot. It has the ambiance of an old diner inside and out, twice the length and the same width. The door opens into the middle. Booths align along the windows extending both ways from the door, and a counter with mounted stools runs across the aisle from the booths for the length of the building. The kitchen is behind the walls across the counter. I assume it's the kitchen. I know tasty food comes out from behind there. I don't want to spoil the magic and see it happening.

I entered with Vinny and looked left. Michael and Arthur are sitting in the last booth. We walked to them. Vinny and I sat without a word. The waitress approached. Vinny got a Coke. I ordered coffee. After telling Michael over the phone the basic idea of what has transpired, I have not looked forward to this meeting. Not in the least.

Michael sat solemnly in a black leather trench coat with the signature big lapels, a gray sweater showing just below his neck. His shoulders, as they often do, look as if they are going to burst through the walls. I witnessed the strength of those shoulders this summer and this fall, that inverted delta of a body, powerfully efficient both in its motion and lack of fat. If God had wanted to assemble the ultimate fighting machine, Michael could have been the prototype. But, Michael is not a machine. He has a soul. Michael is my man for this reason; he knows when to engage in battle and when to lay it down. Very much because of this trait, the contents of the file which I hold in my hand are going to hurt him dearly.

I asked Arthur to come along to take some of the sting. Arthur is dressed in a lined cotton jacket, zipped up to reveal only the neck of a wool sweater, not quite as forbiddingly as his friend. He is the sleek version of Michael, both physically and emotionally. Somewhere in his development he has been blessed or cursed with the ability to allow the storms of racism to roll off his back as if it were water from a bird. He takes it and flies on. I believe he will be able to help Michael, hell, help us all through this ordeal by giving us another perspective.

I started, looking to Michael and Arthur alternately, "Gentlemen, I have to warn you: This is not a pretty sight. As a result of a conversation with a fellow from down in the southern part—"

"We know, Ivy. Lemme see what you got," said Michael softly, referring to the file. I handed it to him and he opened it, examining each document individually and then handing it to Arthur. Vinny and I sat in silence during their discovery. I feel very white, but I possessed the knowledge that I mustn't be the pipeline for Lawson's and McNabb's guilt. It's tough.

Michael, as one might have guessed, spoke first, "This is great evidence for what your friend accused Lawson and this other fucker of doing. The affidavits are it, man. Sworn. They tie it all together." He was a bit agitated in his delivery. "But is this enough to hang Lawson by his balls? In the world of the whitey, I don't think so."

I know, and I think Vinny also knows, that Michael, because he doesn't consider us so, meant no harm to us by calling forth the concept of 'whitey' in this conversation. Before I could contemplate Michael's viewpoint, Arthur stepped in.

"I agree with Michael," started Arthur, "This file comes from four students, two of us black, two of you benchwarmers, with all four of us lookin' like we have axes to grind." That never occurred to me. "It doesn't pack the punch you'd need to bring down a guy like Lawson. He is part of an institution that is much, much bigger than us."

Michael added, "We would bring more harm to ourselves, individually. Runner football is backed by some of the richest people in this state. It might go, but it would be a Pyrrhic victory." He then lightened it up, "I've always wanted to use that word."

We chuckled a bit. But, I'm disappointed in the way the file was received. First, I've got PD wanting to burn it. Vinny's out, then I have Michael sounding like a prosecutor only weeks from retirement, then finally Arthur acts as Burt's mouthpiece. I am ready to nail these mothers and no one wants to go along. "Lemme suggest something to you guys," I said, addressing Arthur and Michael, "The truly injured party here is Lendel—"

Michael interrupted, "—and you, Vinny." Vinny's facial expression didn't change as Michael tried to, as it can be said, put 'cream in the coffee.'

"What do you think, Vinny?" asked Arthur.

The Gunner did not want it to get to this point. So, without moving he replied as any almost twenty year old would, "I think it sucks ass."

Very perceptive, Vinny.

He then moved a bit, and offered more wisdom. "I can see your points," motioning to Michael, "but I think The Cheetah has some pretty valid points himself."

"Do you feel injured here, Vinny?" queried Arthur.

Finally, intelligent life appeared across from me. "Yeah, I'm number two without this asshole with the money in the picture. Head-to-head, I'm the starter in two years when Lendel is gone. That hurts."

"Do you want to do something about it?" Arthur asked.

"I go along with Lendel. If he says yes, I say yes."

Shocked, not knowing why it all looked so differently to him now, and not asking any questions, I avoided jumping up and screaming, 'Go, Gunner, go!'

"As a fellow quarterback, how do you think Lendel will feel about this?" Michael asked.

"I don't really know," replied Vinny. "I know that he has a great attitude about being the backup, but that's Lendel. He accepts the cards he is dealt. I also know that on more than a few occasions he has looked to me in wonder as Bobby finds a new and improved way to choke."

"So, you think we should leave it up to him," Arthur said.

Already much further in this than he ever wanted to be, considering all he holds valuable, Vinny replied, "I think that's true. As a QB and a first generation Italian American, I'll support what he says."

We all looked around to each other. Michael and Arthur sat, two players who had taken similar courses, leaders of a team a wind gust and a Nazi away from greatness in what is likely their last year together. Vinny and I are silent, a bonafide Blue Chip quarterback and his try-out friend who are following their childhood dreams to this team scratching its way out from under the doormat.

The four of us are considering something for which we now by virtue of holding these files have total control. We can put Montani on the same map as Watts and Harlem and anywhere in the Deep South where discrimination was fought. The national media would love this. White people in this country, throwing their support behind guys like our 'old friend' Governor Wallace and our 'new friend' Mr. Twenty-Mule-Team-Death-Valley-Days himself, Ronald Reagan, thought the racial question had in 1975 been resolved. They assumed that since that half-hour segment of television called the evening news showed that the violence had left the streets, everybody's okay. However, any black or anybody who has a close friend who is black knows we are far from 'okay.'

Michael, Arthur, Vinny, and I have the power to rattle their lily-white-ass cages and jump-start the debate which never should have ended. That's a lot to lay in the hands of college students. Months ago, we never imagined we would be considering matters so grave. Hell, we just wanted to play ball. That's all we still want to do, but somebody's got to take care of this stuff.

"Michael, Arthur," I said, "take this file. I have copies. I would be delighted if this would somehow end up with the editor of *The Mail*."

We smiled and asked for the checks.

Thursday, November 6, 1975
6:02 AM

The story runs

I glanced up from my copy of Mein Kampf, *thinking Adolf Hitler was even sicker than his reputation. I then turned my head toward my bath just in time to view Dr. Joan Kissinger exit, hair wet, towel barely enough to cover her copious breasts and stretch down just above her upper thighs. I sat the book aside. That's when the ringing started. "You'd better get that, darling," Joan said. "What?" I asked. She replied, "Get it and get it over with, then do—"*

Bolting awake, I discovered two things: a) the telephone is clanging, and b) so are my loins. Ignoring b) for now, I answered the phone, just what Joan told me to do.

"Yeah," I said, softly.

"Mason, PD," said the voice on the other end.

Flipping through my mind's Rolodex, it's taking me longer than it should to remember who the hell PD is.

"Wake up, Mason. It's PD!"

The voice inside that hook is awake. Wide awake. My clock flipped to six oh two.

"Ohhh. PD. What the hell do you want at six fuckin' oh two?"

"Have you seen the paper?" he asked.

"The paper?" I replied with a little indignation. "Let me tell you what—Oh. I remember."

"Get the paper, Mason," he commanded as I thought it through, "On your front porch, the paper."

"Sorry, PD, the paper. It's six oh two. This is not the time I normally read the paper."

"I usually overlook a man's smart-ass mouth when I just get him from the sack."

I'm now fully awake and very flaccid. "I'll get the paper, PD."

"Thank you." is his reply.

Wearing athletic shorts and a gray sweatshirt, I pulled my stiff muscles out from the bed. Wednesday's scrimmage and the vicious hitting resulting from the animosity between offense and defense had punished me. I found my slippers and stepped into them, every movement reminiscent of that practice where I was bounced around, but by God I got my licks in, too. I slowly open the door to prevent the ever-present creak which I'm fearful will awaken Vinny in the next room. My Italian Stallion had found

it difficult to sleep since a freak shower incident on Monday had left the
backup QB Lendel Ward lying on the concrete floor with a trashed knee,
out for the season. My boy was therefore given a promotion to second QB
behind the erratic-at-best Bobby Kay, just a few days before Pitt. Vinny's
meals are hanging in his throat, I am sure.

I pad down the steps in the early morning's darkness, then across the
living room floor, clean and free of obstructions due primarily to the
influence of the two lovely young coeds who live in the opposite wing.
Finding the crystal doorknob on the old beveled-glass door, I turned it
and pulled it open. I then open the security door in front of the glass
door and walk out onto the porch. It's cold, but I don't feel it. Almost
instantly I spotted the rolled newspaper with its Thursday edition thick-
ness. I reenter my house, shut the doors, and carry the paper bound up
to my room.

Arriving there, I flip on the ceiling light, wincing a little, and unwrap
the newspaper while picking the phone up. "Okay, PD. I have the paper,
I'm unrolling it now, and…holy hell!"

The headline of this morning's *Mail* blared to the world what I had
known: "Lawson Accepts Money to Bench Black QB" with the subhead
"State Businessman Implicated." There is also a quarter page picture of
one of the photographs of the briefcase exchange that had first arrived
in Montani at my house, purported to be Coach and Myron McNabb.

Michael, Lendel, and Arthur had, in a response of frustration both
due to Lendel's injury and the feelings of loss of control associated with
the event, changed their minds about keeping it all under wraps. My
teammates, to avoid tainting the whole thing with what they called "the
bitter taste of the angry black man," and much to Vinny's disapproval
borne from his recurring fear of the consequences, asked me to make
the initial contact with the newspaper. Monday evening I pulled
reporter Tom Brown away from his deadline project to steer me in the

right direction with the evidence. Knowing that stories such as this one walk through the door maybe once in a career, Tom dropped what he was doing and introduced me to the editor, Dale Kitchen. Mr. Kitchen took my box and files and I didn't hear from him again until yesterday afternoon when he called to tell me the story would be printed after Saturday's game with Pittsburgh. And now....

"Jesus H. Christ!" I exclaimed, shocked despite being involved in every step of the way.

"Read the article to me, please," requested PD.

I started. "*The Montani Mail* has discovered that The University of West Virginia head football coach Dennis Lawson accepted money in the amount of $65,000 from Beckley multimillionaire coal operator Myron McNabb to play quarterback Bobby Kay, a white sophomore, over black junior Lendel Ward this season. The newspaper has obtained from a reliable source photographs of a meeting between the two men at which a briefcase presumably containing cash was exchanged, photostats of bank receipts from transactions by both Lawson and McNabb, and a sworn affidavit from a man wishing to remain anonymous tying the meetings with the bank transactions."

"Damnation," is all I can add.

"Is that all?" asked PD.

I scanned the rest of the article. "No. There is more about the photo, and more about McNabb wanting to play, quoted from the affidavit, our boy, end quote. What a couple of prima donna jerks," I finished, almost as if I am hearing it for the first time.

"Does the article mention the paper trying to contact either of the men?" PD asked.

"Yeah—wait a minute!" I said. "How did you know to call me this morning?"

"I have my ways," is all PD would say.

I'm perplexed, "If you have your ways, why did you get me involved?"

"I do have my ways," he responded, "and you're one of my ways."

I accepted that. "Okay, about contacting the sonofa—, er, men, the coach 'categorically denied' it and McNabb's in West Germany, for all I know picking up shower nozzles for his gas chambers he plans on building soon." I'm disgusted with myself for making light of that.

"Well, my boy," PD said with a touch of pride, "You've done it!"

"Oh, no," I said, backpedaling a bit, "we've done it."

"I just bagged it up. You carried the mail."

I wonder if I'm being recorded. "I don't care what metaphor you use, we did it."

"You remember the agreement."

I do. And I truly am excited to be the pivot man on such a story. All I can get out is, "Well…."

"You're Deep Throat," said PD.

"I guess that at least makes you a patriot."

He passed on the remark. "As we discussed, Mason, we have to keep as many levels between my source and the action. McNabb owns the man. He'd have his balls on the platter."

"I don't care if they use the water torture on me, PD, they'll never get it out of me. Besides, up until a few days ago, I had a shower like that," Shower. That brings Joan back into the picture. I like how that feels, but I struggled to concentrate on this matter.

"This whole thing, Mason, I was just testing you as a brother," PD said, tongue in cheek. "You passed. But, really, I can't wait until this story hits down here in Marshall Town. They will absolutely love it. Not that they're above it, but they will get off on it."

"Anything to make the people of Huntington happy," I said face-tiously. "Anyway, PD," I said, serious again, "I guess this whole thing won't damage your career in anyway."

"It shouldn't. I didn't talk to the newspaper, or at least I didn't seek them out. I don't know the name of the newspaper. Well, that's a lie, but I'm out of it because you're the key to the whole thing."

I enjoyed being the Man. "It was a calculated banker's risk on your part, PD, but you're okay. If I couldn't have done it, I would have told you."

"You've done the right thing, Mason. I've spent an athletic career as a young man and a professional career up until now basically selling out my people. We've talked about this."

Yes, we had, but out of respect I let him go on.

"I've got some jack and a nice house to show for it, but it's been bittersweet. My people have been getting screwed for hundreds of years and, with regard to the attitudes of the general populous, it really hasn't let up much. Lendel's unfortunate injury gave your buddies the courage and the reason to give you the green light. I appreciate your contribution. You yourself are courageous. You didn't have to do what you did."

My chest became tingly deep inside. "I don't see it that way, PD. I did have to do what I did. I gotta look in the mirror and shave every three days."

PD guffawed, "Goddamn, I recruit them young, don't I?"

That remark hurt. I instantly thought of Joan, but I continued, "I guess we're the ones who will jump on the hand grenades for you."

"Speaking of war," PD said, "this should be the final communiqué between us for a while. They're going to follow you and tap your phones."

I'm taken aback. "That's paranoid of you, PD."

"But pragmatic, Mason," he said, "You don't know what that one weak link is going to do to you."

"What weak link?"

"The newspaper itself," PD replied. "Football's huge in Montani. You know that. Everybody is in it together. Things haven't changed much since I was catching passes up there. They may not blatantly rat on you, but they could leak it, you as the source, that is."

I sat silently, considering these things which have never crossed my mind. My trust for the newspaper is implicit and strong. Is it all a mistake? Too late. "Oh, you're right. We shouldn't talk. We'll be separated like two passengers on the *Titanic*." I shook my head at the simile as if I had bitten into a lemon.

"Except this time," PD responded, "the water's hot."

"That it is, my friend," I said, feeling like Patrick McNee of *The Avengers*, with Joan as Diana Rigg's Emma Peel.

"I hope you find a good lifeboat," said PD.

"It's been good working with you, PD."

"And you, Mister Bricker."

A lull appeared in the conversation. I broke it, saying one more time, "PD, I gotta tell you I never considered not taking this to the press."

"Well, son, you should have, but I'll accept that and congratulate you for your commitment. So long, my friend."

"Bye, for now," I said, hanging up the receiver of the telephone, feeling brave and haughty.

Thursday, November 6, 1975
6:15 AM

In the shower

This all seemed a helluva lot easier when we were talking only about boxes of documents and photos and possibilities. Now, the fan has been hit squarely and men's reputations are at stake: Lawson and McNabb, namely, although Fat Mac seems to be the type who would enjoy this kind of notoriety, using it to advance his cause. And the school's athletic director, Lyndon Fadden, is definitely involved, left here to pick up the pieces, a difficult situation since race relations is not his strong suit. I gotta wonder: just how much has the newspaper leaked already? Just how much do all the boosters know about me? How long can this secret remain a secret? Like my father in the hole on Guadalcanal, life as I know it is over. I've gotta do what is right. It's going to be tough, but I've gotta do it.

What's everybody going to think? Joan, for one. Hey, why haven't I thought of this before? This may be good. The liberal in her really digs this kind of stuff. First the letter, now a major protest action for the distressed, against the fatcats. Even though she was born into fatcatdom, a leak has to improve my chances with her. It makes me look older to her. I, doing the things they did, she possibly did…no, I doubt that, but even better, old boyfriends of hers did. Or better still, things men did whom she couldn't quite get; the handsome protester, long hair, leather headband, bare-chested except for a vest. This could be the ride. It's 1968 all over again and this is the Chicago Democratic National Convention. I'm like Tom Hayden, or one of those guys, like Abbie Hoffman. I bet they had really good sex anytime they wanted it, with whomever they wanted. Man, this could be good. I may take a bullet on Saturday, but, hey.

There's something to think about. Saturday. Pitt. A major underhanded scandal has been uncovered about our head coach against two of his players, quarterbacks mind you, involving the ignorance of a fair assessment of the facts because one player was black and the other was white. To make matters worse, the head coach received remuneration (read: lots of fucking money) for playing the white guy, even though it was obvious that the black guy could play better and lead the team better. All this crawled out from under its rock two days before we take on one of the best teams to come out of the East in the modern era.

This is not a pretty sight. I wonder how, and if, we can hold together. A coach is a compass and ours is shattered. I don't know if two days are enough to find our way again. What about The Kid? How will he feel when he discovers his tenure as quarterback is a sham? What will he do?

And how will Vinny feel when he in all likelihood will have to at some point replace Bobby; The Kid wounded of spirit, already not possessing the fortitude it takes to lead us against a team such as Pitt? Vinny's first action could be against number one with a team ripped of its potency by a man with no moral bearing, a man whom we trusted with all that is important to us. Man, Godspeed to The Gunner.

Lots of variables there are. Anything could happen today. Should I just tell Joan or wait for her to hear about it? Am I being selfish even thinking about the whole incident in terms of romance and my libido? Dealing with the press over the past couple of days got me through Joan's silence. When the hell is she going to say something about the letter? I don't know.

Who's to know? All I have to say is everything is very dynamic right now. I shouldn't ring the bell louder than needed.

Thursday, November 6, 1975
6:25 AM

Telephone call from Michael

I picked up the ringing phone.
"Mason."
"Mason. Michael. Have you seen the paper?"
"Yep."
"Wonderful! Isn't it a great thing to wake up to?"
"Actually, Burt, I can think of several things I would prefer to wake up to, but yes, I have read it. My man called just a few minutes ago. This

is a great day in my life. I might die by sniper fire today, but it is still a great day."

"You nailed him, Ivy! You nailed the bastard! I can't wait for Lendel to see this. Got damn!"

I could tell that decades, hell, even generations of frustrations are spewing forth. He has to calm down. "Michael—Michael—you gotta slow down!" At the same time, I didn't want to take any sense of victory away from him. But, still—"Enjoy the moment, but stay within yourself."

A less agitated Michael reappeared on the phone. "Sorry, Mason. But this is a great day in my life, too. I'm going to make you an honorary brother, man."

I tried to lighten it up. "I thought you did that this summer when I ran that four three forty."

"That was good, but this is big. You deserve a Nobel Peace Prize for this."

I'm honored, yet humble, "What? For exposing a couple of right-wing rednecks for what they are? And as for a prize, Michael, thank you for your magnanimous gesture, but I would prefer no one find out about this. And that's okay. Let it play. It's got legs of its own." My acceptance speech impressed me.

"Yeah!" Michael said, excitement coming back, "Now Doctor Fadden has to do something. As AD, he can't just let this slide. My men will walk if Lawson is the coach at practice this afternoon."

Sounds like the blacks have developed a plan. Whoa. "Michael, I can't tell you what to do. But we're all injured and defaced to some degree. Lendel the most. You black guys a helluva lot. Everybody on our team. Vinny. Every West Virginia fan more than they realize. Every college football player got screwed by Lawson and McNabb. I can't tell you what to do, man, but I encourage you to just, as I said, let it play."

Michael spoke softly but definitively, "I know how to do that, Mason. You don't have to tell me how to do that. I'm a black man. It's a way of life for me, for all of us. I can be a good nigger."

Acrimoniously, I let him have it, "Now, goddamnit, Michael, you're my friend! You know I don't mean that! You know me better than that! Don't start throwing that word at me! All I'm saying is…is…they've got third and twenty-five, so what would you do? You'd rush three and drop back in a spread two-deep zone. All I'm saying is, Michael, don't blitz. You know what I mean. They're in trouble, in a big way. Let them play into your hands."

Silence prevailed for a few moments.

"Okay, Ivy. You've talked me down, but I'm pissed. I'm pissed."

"And you have every right to be. Just use those smarts God gave you and we'll work this to our advantage, your advantage. They're the ones who fucked up."

"You know, you're cute when you make sense," Michael said, calmer.

"So why isn't there a woman in my shower?" I asked, thinking of Joan for about the fifteenth time that morning.

"Another mystery of the universe," he said. "See you at lunch today."

"See ya, Michael," I said, wondering how long that would last. But, who in the hell is to blame them? I didn't have much growing up until my benefactor down the street left me a little cash when I was fourteen and then, by the grace of God, a financial genius turns it several times over. I've seen both sides, if you can call a buck fifty grand the rich side. I call it not quite enough to retire to Tahiti on but just enough to get a good start in life. Anyway, I've seen both sides, but I have, according to the bigots, always had the proper skin color. Despite my support, for lack of a better word, of all people of all races and all religions, I in no way can imagine what it would be like to be black. I really don't have a clue as to what Michael or Lendel or Arthur or any of my black team-mates are going through right now. I'll stand with them, but I can't in all honesty pretend I know.

Thursday, November 6, 1975
6:50 AM

Vinny

"Enter," I said in response to the knock at my door.

"You got the paper?" asked my friend Vinny.

"There," I motioned to my bed where the newspaper laid front page up.

He glanced at the headlines. With little emotion, he said, "Shit."

"You understate," I commented. "Read it. The story's basic, but it will still be viewed as a shocker."

Vinny read the story, "Damn…Damn it to hell this makes me sick."

"Don't worry. You're not involved," That jumped out before I knew it.

Throwing the paper in the floor, Vinny spat, "You're a bastard!"

Not being able to stop, I retorted, "Isn't that what you want?" That's enough, I said to myself.

"Stop punishing me for committing no crime! You know why I chose my course. You don't have parents sending you money. I'm sorry, Mason, I don't mean to belittle your tragedies, but you don't have anybody to answer to. Just don't get uppity over this. Turning it all over to the newspaper was a helluva lot easier for you to do than for me to have done."

I paused, looking right at him. He's right. I'm letting him have it for no real reason. Vinny and I have always been together, on everything. Now, the biggest deal of my life surfaces and we're in a constant state of Point/Counterpoint. I can't let McNabb drive a wedge between us. "You're right. It was a no-brainer for me. I'm sorry." I extended my hand. Vinny clasped it.

"Not quite a no-brainer, but simpler without Mike Vacca breathing down your neck."

No doubt. Vinny is the number one of Mike's three sons, receiving the full brunt of the father's rookie mistakes. Mike's biggest error was assuming Vinny couldn't think for himself. To Mike, life is one long series of tests, and only one score: pass or fail. After Dad died, Mike tried to take over with me in the same way he had done Vinny. I knew better, and I didn't let him do it. This, I think, gave Vinny the courage to handle his father and try to grow into a man in his own way. Vinny became the negotiator to my rebel, by my admission a better way to be.

Interestingly, The Gunner selected a girlfriend much like his own father. Jean Elizabeth Lopinski, dubbed by me as 'The Jean Queen, She Can Do Anything,' found Vinny and will not let go. She's got it all figured out. Vinny will become a CPA, they will marry, move to her hometown in Charleston, live in Rolling Hills, have three kids, boys or girls, it doesn't matter (if you can imagine that), join a club, Vinny will become partner, and all will definitely be well. As one would think, Mike adores Jean. Vinny merely puts up with that part of her because she is blonde and blue-eyed and built like a brick office tower. Also, he's used to it. After dealing with his father all these years, he knows how to handle the Jean Queen.

"Okay, Gunner, okay. You ready to go?"

"Yeah. I'll pack the paper," Vinny said.

"Gotcha," I said, "Let's see if the girls are ready. We oughta tell them about this."

"The circle's growing bigger," Vinny said as he walked down the steps.

"It's not a national security issue," I replied as I followed. "They do live with us. They've seen the box. Besides, if the house is leveled by a bomb, they'll know why."

"Comforting," sighed Vinny, as we stepped into the living room and over toward Alice's and Judy's wing. I walked up the first steps and to the fire door that we all promised their parents would be always locked. I pressed it open and yelled, "Excuse me…any naked ladies up there?"

"You couldn't handle it if there were!" shouted Judy.

"Go away!" yelled Alice.

"We've gotta talk to you," said Vinny sternly.

"Okay, we'll be right down," said Alice. Alice has a crush on Vinny. Vinny has the hots for Judy. Judy would swear she doesn't, but she kinda favors me. And I get weak every time Alice looks at me. We are a perfectly balanced house, largely because we are simply the best of friends.

"What do you think will happen to Lawson?" Vinny asked me.

"It's difficult to say—," I said, interrupted by the girls' arrival. "Wow! Damn!" I exclaimed. Vinny's silenced. Judy is dressed in a form-fitting midi, black, with a belt to show you just how high in the atmosphere her waist is. Alice's tan woolen knee high skirt held her tight. I don't know anything about her blouse. I'm sure it did its job.

"What's the occasion?" Vinny finally said. Both our friends have dark hair, slightly below the shoulders, full, winged, curling-ironed, ready for takeoff, like just about all sorority babes. Hair for which there must be specifications. Hair codes. Nice looking, but a sign of the conformity of the seventies we all fell back into after a good many of our predecessors tuned in, turned on, and dropped out.

"Sorority breakfast," Judy replied, "We're late. You have one minute."

I, without a word, held up the front page for them to read. Alice grabbed it.

"Christ!" said Alice.

Judy the accountant got to the point. "Sixty-five thousand dollars. Damnit!"

"This McNabb guy really puts it where his bigoted mouth is," said Alice.

Looking up, Judy said, "I'm sorry, guys. Helluva time for this to happen."

I looked to Vinny. Vinny looked back. I said, "You remember that Trans Am you guys saw drive away on Sunday?"

"Uh…Oh, no…" Judy said.

"Don't…no…say it's not so…" Alice pleaded.

"The box…It's so…I found a newspaper reporter and narced on them all," I said proudly.

A long pause. Then Judy, once again, got right to the point, "Mason, how can you be so fuckin' stupid?"

"Yeah, Mason, you've really fucked up now," proclaimed Alice.

"Girls," Vinny stated, "what the hell would you do?"

I shot Vinny a look of pleasant disbelief. "Yeah! Lendel's our friend," I said, "He was getting screwed!"

"Does he know about this?" asked Alice.

"It was his final call, but I delivered the goods," I said still more proudly.

"Who else knows?" Judy asked.

"Michael, Arthur," answered Vinny. "Alice, Judy, from a humanitarian standpoint, you cannot let this slide by unnoticed. Something had to be done." My boy!

Alice tried to speak, "Yeah, Vinny, but—"

I interrupted, "But, what?"

Judy motioned to Alice, "We have to go."

Alice again tried," Look, Mason—"

Judy was impatient, "Let's go!"

Alice held her ground, "It's scary, guys. You're dealing with people with a lot of power. You don't know how they are going to use it."

Judy relented, "This guy Myron doesn't play the game like you do. Now we do have to go. Be careful, okay, honeyboys?" The girls gave a peck on the cheek to each of us then walked to the door.

"Since you put it that way," I said.

Thursday, November 6, 1975
7:25 AM

Vinny and I walk to class

Walking down the bricks in the middle of Wagner Road, Vinny and I seem to enjoy each other's silence. The morning is mostly gray and autumn cool, a signature day in Montani. Montani is very much spoken ill of: Monhole, The Mon Trench, just to name a couple. Sure, the houses are clapboard and old and spent beer kegs are used as porch furniture. But one has to realize, Montani, accentuated by the fog of fall, you either love it or hate it. And when the sun comes out, we really appreciate it.

I decided to speak first. "So, that's six out of seven people who say this is scary."

"Who doesn't?"

"Michael."

"Oh, that figures," Vinny replied, "You'd have to drive a stake through his heart to frighten him."

"Michael doesn't suck blood," I said, continuing the vampire reference.

"He would if he could have Penn State all over again."

"No doubt," I said, then pausing, "You know, Vinny, maybe I should have given this more thought."

As we cut left down Simpson Street, Vinny expounded on my comment. "You thought about it as much as you do everything else in your life."

"What the hell do you mean by that?" I asked curtly, knowing what the hell he means by that.

"You're impulsive. You do what the fuck you want to do at the time because you have no one to answer to."

"You're really hung up on that, aren't you?"

"For good reason. I know you, Michael Mason Bricker. Like the back of my hand. It's like chemistry with you. You are reactive—"

We turned right onto South Hale Street. I tried to speak in my defense…

"Huh-uh, wait," Vinny continued, "Only this time I agree with you and I'm with you. I'm in. I've actually been in since the beginning, but…you've just gotta consider what I'm saying, you know—"

"About being impulsive."

"Yeah."

"But think about this, Michael Vincent the second," I said, "Myron doesn't like anyone straight from the boot, either."

"I know. That's partially why I'm in."

"What's the other part?" I asked as we stepped onto the Hale Street Bridge.

"I don't want to stand back and watch you get your ass hung out to dry."

"So, you are going to get yours hung out with me."

"No," said Vinny, "I'm going to make damn sure you stay out of trouble." He smiled and patted me on the back.

"Now, how the hell are you going to do that?" I asked jocularly.

"I don't know. Pray a lot."

I laughed. "That's the spirit! So, what's your father going to say when you tell him you've enlisted in my war?"

"You are going to tell him Myron doesn't want any wop quarterbacks either."

I examined that as we stepped off of the bridge and up the hill beside the Post Office. "Okay," I said, not really knowing how that would go over.

Looking at my friend as we continued the walk…it's the face. The gorgeous, chiseled, olive-skinned, brown-eyed face with wavy, dark hair. I know, anybody knows, that face, topping the six-two, long-limbed lean muscled athletic frame, not powerful, but nevertheless…anybody knows he is possibly the best looking guy you've ever seen. You know that, and you know that if he doesn't smoke or drink or eat to excess, he will be the best looking groom, the best looking associate, the best looking father, the best looking grandfather, the best looking member of AARP, and the best looking corpse you'll ever see.

Always seemingly in control of himself, Vinny is certainly everyone's idea of an ideal, a man whom men could envision making it through anything, a defense, a snowstorm, gale force winds, pouring cement, a swarm of mosquitoes, anything, and look great at the end. And women…they extrapolate through the span of life because most females can only imagine how glorious it would be to turn out the lights every night beside a guy like Vinny.

Great looking guy he is. Within, however, Vinny at times struggles. He's at his best on the fields and courts and courses of play, away from his autocratic father and controlling girlfriend, able to express his creative soul. Vinny viewed it as his duty to allow them to overstep the boundaries so as not to damage the relationships. This sometimes leaves him oppressed and feeling trapped. He therefore anticipated any chance to get away, taking pleasure even in practices, more so than the average college athlete, definitely more than he would allow himself to realize. So Vinny suited up, spending the first several minutes breaking away from the constraints that sometimes defined his life, flowing through, always in the end playing unbeatable ball, finally free. Super Vinny.

A man so physically appealing, yet so vulnerable; men watch him take command and miss it entirely. Women see it, and it adds to the mystique.

"This is exciting," Vinny said, "Sure beats being on chart detail all afternoon."

"Keep your hat close by," I told him, "Nobody knows anything now."

"What's your best guess?"

"Fadden suspends Lawson with pay pending an investigation."

"Not before the Pitt game!" Vinny exclaimed.

"Precisely," I started, "Look at the attention we're getting anyway. Some guy from ABC interviewed me, for Chissakes! Third team! I can understand you, the QB, but a lotta cases of salmonella have to take place before I play. Anyway, we're on the national stage. Fadden can't just let this slide."

"Mason, we play Pitt in two days. They're number one. We're number twenty-one. They're undefeated. We're on a two game losing streak.

We absolutely sucked ass last week. Fire the coach? Really, not a bad idea, but not gonna happen."

"Vinny, half our players are black. Does Lyndon want the NAACP to lead a protest on national television, fuckin' decimating his football team as America watches? Not gonna happen."

We paused, finding ourselves taking quick steps toward the Hotel Montani.

"God, this whole situation is awful!" Vinny said in anguish. "This is the first time in two years I have felt foolish for turning down Notre Dame. How stupid of me!"

"You had no way of knowing. Ya gotta wonder how this could happen here. But, then again, why not? I mean, West Virginia can be called a pretty racist state in some respects. Hell, in high school, I was blocking for one of my black teammates as he was running down the sideline. We were visitors in a town of all white people. My friend got jacked up along his ankles and flipped onto his head. Guys, coal miners, grown men, came out of the sidelines, screaming, 'Kill the nigger! Kill him!' Man, that's the most frightened I had been in my whole life. I thought they were going to kill him!"

Vinny calmed down. "I guess you get some guy like McNabb with a lot of scratch and a long stretch and he can call a lot of shots."

"And Lawson. Jeez, what a bastard! It all works well for him until we go to Happy Valley. That was it. That game led me to believe PD."

"And last week. It was as if The Kid still had the Nittany shakes. And Lawson gives him the vote of confidence, which in some cases is what you do before you sharpen the ax."

"Except with Kay. He plays. We'd be undefeated and in the top five with you or Lendel in there." We approached Walnut Street and stopped for traffic.

"I can't believe it!" yelled Vinny, attracting the attention of a passersby. He quieted. "This explains it all. All the time I have wondered, doubted. The newspaper makes it so real, doesn't it?"

"The power of the press," I remarked. "Just bites. You gotta consider transferring. Somewhere where they play Italians."

"Saturday the thought crossed my mind. But what happens to our dream, man?"

"Adrift toward the rocky shore of reality, Gunner. Anyway, where would we go?"

"We?" He was surprised.

"Sure, I'll walk on where ever you go," I said as we crossed and continued on our way. "I'd be able to play at a lot of places where I wouldn't have Dhali, Clark, Tom, and Dave in front of me. What about Pitt?" I quickly offered in jest.

"Remembered how mad Dad was about coming here instead of Notre Dame? Multiply that by a dozen."

"The irony would be suffocating."

"What would Joan say?" My man. Always pushing the buttons.

"Probably goodbye."

"Does she know about you and all this mess?"

"No, I really haven't talked to her much since the letter. I'm thinking I'll tell her."

"Why in the hell would you do that?" Vinny asked in an indignant manner. "That would only get more people involved and fuck up the leak situation even more!"

"Look older. More responsible."

"There you go again! Spontaneous human combustion."

I'm almost pissed. "Anyway, back to Joan."

"If you say."

"Terminally gorgeous," I remarked.

"What day is this?" Vinny asked.

"Eleven, I do believe."

"Is it your only plan, that is, to take it by the horns, or are you just in need of getting your horns clipped?"

"Watch it, Vinny!" I retorted. "I'm in love. She can therefore take all the time she needs."

"What happened to two weeks?" Vinny said. "Come on, Mason, call it what it is! You just want to get in her pants."

"Vinny," I said with all seriousness, "don't talk about Joan like that."

The Gunner paused, then backed away. "Okay, that's too strong. I'm just starting to think it is not possible."

"You're the one who said two weeks. Why are you giving in?"

"Because we have three days to go—"

"Four days. Four."

"Okay, four days. And you haven't even talked with her about it yet. Starting to look like your boat has sprung a leak. Why is that?"

After several moments of silence, I came back. "I don't know."

"Mason, goddamnit. Sometimes! Because of your ages, you dumb Mick."

"This is getting personal, dagobreath."

We paused our conversation as we stepped up the incline of Hale Street toward White Street. "Okay," Vinny said, "let's cut the insults while we're even."

"I agree," I said, "But what is suddenly so wrong about this?"

We took more steps in silence, then Vinny began, "This. *This. This* is like…It's like you're driving a car looking in the rear view mirror fixing your hair and I'm the passenger and I see a truck coming right at us head-on and you won't stop combing your goddamn hair."

I contemplated Vinny's simile, not bad for an accounting major. We've made it to the intersection of Hale and White. "So I'm primping my coif and that's represents how this all makes me feel, despite the impending disaster of the truck, Joan's ultimate rejection. To sum it all, I'm in love with the fact that I'm in love with her."

Vinny burst out, "Exactly! I couldn't have said it better myself."

What I said doesn't really make much sense, but it made Vinny happy. "I know you couldn't have," I said," but at least we agree."

"We should," Vinny said, "This has happened before."

"So what happens next?"

"You're going to talk to her about the letter, Maria."

"Exactly!" I shouted, as we continued down White.

"So, you're not going to stop."

"No."

"What about the rear view and the comb and the truck?"

"Very good. I give you an A minus."

"All that brilliance, wasted. What has happened before shall happen again."

"Maybe things will change," I said.

"I read in my psychology class that the people truly sick in the head do the same thing over and over again looking for a different result," Vinny said.

"I promise I'll stop after this last one. Just one more hot, intelligent babe. Okay?"

"You know, she'll want babies in a couple of years," said Vinny astutely. He won't give up.

"Fine. I'm a baby-making machine. I'm up, anytime she wants to procreate."

"Jesus—" Vinny looked up and saw our church, St. Mary's on University, dead ahead. He chose to curb his language. "Louise, Mason. Fifteen freakin' ten on the SAT and you're missing the point. It's her time, not yours."

I looked up to see the Pi Gamma Pi house beside St. Mary's (in the sense of purity, if that isn't irony I don't know what is). Should Jennifer figure into this? Nah. "When was I one to do something because it was one's time? Answer, not at least since Dad was killed. All of a sudden, at thirteen, I'm the man of the house. That's how Mom and Camy and Ron and Junie saw it. I'm fourteen, fifteen years ahead of my time. That makes Joan six, seven years younger than me."

It's safe. We've passed the church. "Mason, you're fucked."

"That is one of my objectives."

Vinny smiled, somewhat wickedly, "Cheetah, my man, she has the ability to make you look damn silly."

"I'll take that chance."

He gave in. "Okay, okay…let's talk about something else. I know you're not going to take my advice."

"Pull down my pants and slide on the ice." We crossed Hodges Street. "Anyway, I am taking your advice. I'm going the full fourteen days. Hey," I said, finally changing the subject, "guess whose birthday is today?"

"Bazooka Frank," Vinny said with respect.

"One of the baddest mothers in the nation."

"That he was."

"Of course," I said, including his father Mike, a Purple Heart veteran of the Korean Conflict, "Mike's pretty tough himself."

Vinny acknowledged my attempt to patronize him, "Mike never crawled out of a foxhole to blow away the enemy."

I countered, "He would have if he had to. Besides, Frank didn't come home from the war on a stretcher, start a family, then build a business from the ground up. That takes a helluva lot of courage itself."

Duly and factually placated, Vinny asked, "You think so?" Then he answered before I had a chance, "I think so."

"Do you think we could have, or will?" I queried as we strolled up the hill toward Milliken Hall.

"I don't know."

"I like to think so," I said in reply to my own question. "My dad was a special man, as is yours. Perhaps God put them in their respective positions because they were just the men for the job. The world's a different place now, though. Still, there are guys like your dad and my dad out there doing maneuvers in a big field preparing for that ground battle in Eastern Europe, preparing for the moment."

"Giving the newspaper the freedom to publish the story."

"Is this where we sing *God Bless America*?"

"We do sound like a couple of Republicans, don't we?" Vinny remarked.

"Vinny, that's possibly because we are Republicans."

"Then why am I so happy we missed out on Vietnam?"

"Whoa! Where in the hell did that come from?" I've never heard him say that. It makes a helluva lot of sense, but….

We stopped at the front of Milliken. "I mean, Mason, your father fought a war. My father fought another war. Why are we so lucky? Or, are we lucky?"

"In the sense that I personally would have gone over to emulate my father to fight the VC and gotten my head shot off and someone would have stuffed the two pieces in a bodybag and shipped them back to whomever would claim them, in that sense, I'm lucky. The Big One, it had an objective, fight the evil imperialists, the two superraces and one's attempt at genocide of Jews, man, just because the asshole with the funny haircut and weird mustache thought they were unclean. Germans have always had a hard time with the bathroom. Hence, they're great scientists. Anyway, that's just a nasty example from his book, the motherfucker. No real philosophical disagreement of which to speak. Not to say that would have justified it. A phobia spread throughout his nation, his nation starving for leadership." Vinny gave me one of those amazed looks he issues when I 'go off.' To hell with him. He's used to it by now. I continued. "Jesus Christ, man, that's sick. More people have been killed in the name of Jesus than…it's pathetic. That was as close to a moral war as you're going to get. Korea, Communism was the issue, and I guess we did so well there ending up in a dead heat that we thought we could kick Cong butt, but we didn't go about it quite right. We loaded refugees on helicopters, retreating much to everybody's delight. What was the question?"

"Two questions: Are we lucky, and what exactly happens inside your brain when you rant like that?"

"Yes, we're lucky and how the hell would I know what goes on in my brain?"

"You're impossible," Vinny said. "Let's talk football. I am the backup quarterback now, you know."

I looked at my watch, a chronograph. It read ten til' eight. "Okay, football."

"Okay, man, okay," Vinny said, kind of agitated, "I found out earlier this year during the airlift from Saigon, from my mom, that Dad had lined up a stint in the National Guard for me if the peace talks had failed and the war would have been still going on."

I stared at him. That face. That beautiful, very upset face. "You act as if there is something wrong with that. What's wrong with that?"

"Okay, so I'm not a frothing good soldier like you." Vinny's breathing had picked up pace.

I had to calm him. "Nothing wrong with that, buddy. You're smart. You and your dad and your mom. Ilie Kuriachan from *The Man From U.N.C.L.E.* 'Run, run, run away; live to kill another day.' You gotta pick your battles. You know that."

Vinny's head hung. "I'm sort of ashamed."

"Don't be, man. It's no big deal. It never happened. And had it happened, it would have been for the better. Concentrate on the problems at hand, like how you're going to get me in the offense when The Kid totally explodes from all the pressure and you are the QB!"

Vinny hesitated, "Let me ask you one question, then I'll leave it alone."

"Shoot."

"Do you have anything you're ashamed of? I'll understand—"

"No, I'll tell you," I said, unsure of what I'm getting into, but wanting to make my friend feel better, "It was Dad. Strange, because he's the source of a lot of my pride. Well, you how he and Mike could hoist the brew. Well, Dad couldn't stop. You know about this. He'd pound away after they would part. Luckily, he was a docile drunk. Loving and kept to himself. Unfortunately, he missed some work because of it. The guys from Guadalcanal would help out. I used to think that made it worse. If they'd cut him off, maybe he woulda straightened up. Who knows? But, Vinny, look, about your dad: you can't blame him. He's a man who's seen both sides: the war is hell side and the fatherhood is wonderful side."

"Sometimes it's hard to see anything good in my dad. He's so fuckin' hard to get along with. But, hey, that's my dad."

"I know about you and your dad. Don't worry, I'll take care of you."

"Now how in the hell are you gonna do that?"

"Just wait and see. In the meantime, let's promise. Let's take it easy on ourselves."

A standing eight count. "Deal," said Vinny, offering his hand amid the eight o'clock class traffic.

"And Vinny."

"Yes, Mason."

"Let's not give up on our dream."

"I promise, Cheetah. We're getting in there—"

"Mark my words!"

"Cool."

"Righteous."

"Bitchin'"

"No doubt."

"Listen," Vinny said, "I want you to know. I think that was a real grown up thing you did with the newspaper this week."

I'm stunned silent

"And, football. You've been hell on wheels in practice lately. Especially yesterday. You got the Big Stick Award for NC State—"

"Probably by default," I said modestly.

"No, you've been firing on all cylinders lately. Your normal is definitely good enough, but, man. I don't know if Joan deserves you."

Warily I said, "Wait a minute."

"No, listen to me: You're a great catch. Remember that with Joan. Don't sell yourself short."

"Thanks, Gunner,"

Vinny continued, "You've really been handling this 'on your own' stuff pretty well."

"What the hell is this? What the hell happened to spontaneous human combustion?"

"Oh, there's always that chance with you. But, you've been doing well."

"This 'on your own' business isn't what it's cracked up to be. Like women, for instance. I really can't blame you for answering to Jean."

"Yeah, you do."

"No, I don't"

"Oh, bullshit, Mason."

"I don't."

"You can't stand Jean."

"You've got it twisted, my friend. I've told you this before. She's the one who can't stand me."

"No, she wishes you weren't so wild. We've been over this. But, I always defend you," proclaimed The Gunner.

"You're a pal."

"I just don't want you to die or look like a fool. So, what about Jennifer?"

"I don't know. We shall see." I hate this subject.

"That's one of the more rational things I've heard you say. You are…uh…."

"Thoughtful in my thoughtlessness."

"Yeah! That's right! Keep her in there. That's a perfectly acceptable woman there who wants your bod."

"Perfectly acceptable is an oxymoron in my book."

"Oxymoron…" said Vinny, searching for a meaning.

"Two conflicting words in the same phrase. Like corporate values. Nixon intelligence. Perfectly acceptable. Since all my relationships with women are agonizing…."

"Okay, I get it. Anyway, perfectly acceptable in a good way, Mason. So, back to Jennifer. Don't wait for the fall of communism or West Virginia beats Penn State."

"I just can't back away from Joan now," I pleaded, "I've got to see it to the end."

"Okay, Ivy."

Pedestrian traffic has died down to a point where Vinny and I are now sure we're late for our eight o'clocks. We wrapped it up.

"So Jennifer's in the equation," I said, hoping if I throw some meat out there, Vinny will chew on it and leave me alone about Jennifer.

"Jennifer's the answer."

"What's the question?"

"The question is: Whose butt hovers high off the ground and most likely looks good in a one piece?"

"See, I never would have said that," I said, voicing my neutrality I hold for a very fine woman.

"But you're thinking it."

"A long time ago, maybe."

"Sure, Mason."

"I stopped thinking about her when I started thinking about how serious I am about Joan."

"I stopped thinking about her when I found out she was thinking about you."

"That probably was the remedy to your nocturnal emissions problem."

"Son, I don't need nocturnal emissions."

"I know. I have a peep hole into your shower."

Vinny's smiling silence finally ended this inane exchange. "Go ahead and give this Joan thing whatever time it needs." Vinny said.

"Joan thing?"

"Day by day, Mason."

"Okay, coach. See you at lunch?"

"Twelve thirty. Michael will be there. Maybe something will have happened to Lawson."

"It's in God's hands."

As Vinny walked to Henry, I headed for Amster, resolute.

Thursday, November 6, 1975
8:00 AM

Resolute. Hell, yeah! I'm ready, just like the first kickoff each Saturday. There's nothing so vehement in the violent world of football as the kickoff. One man tees the ball up to kick it as the other ten line up the width of the field. Upon the kick, they run at near top speed; objective: hit somebody. On the return side, five are spread out over their half of the field to block the human projectiles, two stay back to catch the ball and run, but my interest lies with the four men, arms intertwined in formation of a "wedge" that the return man will run behind. It is my job, my duty, to fling my body into that wedge and bust it like a sledge hammer would a plaster wall, thereby leaving the return man unprotected. If I'm lucky, I'll get the tackle. That, however, is not the point.

Considering everything, there is in my opinion no better man in the state of West Virginia than me to perform that task. I am fast. I hit like a locomotive. And, most importantly, I don't give a shit what happens to the musculoskeletal structure of any of us. If we score a lot, we might kick off five or six times a game. That's five or six automobile accidents for me in each afternoon. Believe me, I feel it, every wedge, every hit. But don't get me wrong. I love every minute of it. I love the anticipation before the kick and during the run. I love the acceleration before the contact. I love the collision. And, I love the stiffness that creeps in Saturday evening, and sets like concrete Sunday morning, a reminder, every step, every genuflection, every kneel to pray, every move, for that matter, a reminder that, because of my father, I play the game as it truly should be played.

Joan doesn't scare me. I'll throw my emotional body at her romantic wedge. It's been five days since the letter. If things looked good, I would have heard by now. But, I've gotta play it out. And, today's the day to do so. To the point. Guys on my team say you can't let a good woman get to ya or she'll scramble your mind. I'm in control of this. She hasn't "gotten" to me. I'm in full control of my faculties. What a pun.

*   *   *   *   *

My English Department is in Amster Hall, a neo-institutional structure over the hill from Woodside, the building which looms behind Ridge Field. Amster is elongated and four stories and in another setting would be easily mistaken for a high school with its spartan, sanitary feel. It's as if it were built by educators who subscribed to the philosophy that a place of learning must be stripped down to its beige and light green essence. And who's to tell them differently? The duck-and-cover generation was educated in such an environment and they turned out okay. Why change it for the daisy-in-the-gun-barrel kids of today? So, here it is.

I walked up the four flights of stairs two at a time because I know I can and not raise my heart rate. It's eight oh five and I'm officially late for my Physics for Liberal Arts Majors class four stories and a building over, so it looks like I won't be there again to watch the prof demonstrate conservation of energy by standing on a chair against one wall and holding a twelve pound shot dangling from a wire connected to the ceiling to his forehead, allowing it to swing across the classroom like a pendulum, then swing back and barely touch him, to the amazement of his cringing students. Ta-da! Tuition, the price of entertainment.

Entering the English office, it looks like it was decorated with wood and tile twenty years ago and dusted occasionally. I find my pal Michele speaking with two of the English secretaries, Kathleen Soski, thirty, strawberry blonde, recently divorced mother of two sons, probably has been always attractive, and Hannah Brown, early twenties, brown-eyed brunette, thinks she's fat, is not, but is nevertheless the resident expert on dieting.

"Mason!" said Hannah, surprised, probably because she was just talking about me.

"Hi, Mason," said Kathleen, too cool to be surprised.

"Ladies," I said.

"I guess you know we've heard," Michele said.

"I could guess," I said.

"I would think you feel pretty shitty right now," said Michele, always hitting it on the nose.

"I'm pissed," I started, "Lendel's a friend of mine. I can't believe he was getting screwed like that. Everyone on the team knew he was and is a hell of a quarterback. But the need really didn't show until lately because we hadn't played anybody." I paused, "I'm-I'm sorry. I'm just rambling."

"Go ahead, Mason," Michele said. "Ramblin' on. Led Zeppelin." We play a lyrics game between us. She was trying to lighten it up. I appreciated her help, even though I wasn't showing it very well.

"What do you mean you hadn't played anybody?" Hannah asked honestly.

"Anybody good," Kathleen snapped. "Go ahead, Mason."

"You know something," I said, "Bobby's a victim here, too. He knew he was third team."

"Third team?" Michele asked.

"Behind Vinny," I said.

"Great place to be," commented Hannah in a sultry voice.

"But we were seven and oh and you can't argue with results," I said, starting the story again. "Everyone felt that way. Until Penn State and Bobby played abysmally. But we all went on because anybody can have a bad game, especially against Penn State. Then N.C. State happened and we all had a bad game, so again no one thought about it. Until now. It answers so many questions. And those answers just plain ol' suck butt."

"What do you think is going to happen now?" Kathleen asked. She is really attractive.

"I think, and this is just what I think, Lawson ought to be suspended. This has the potential to damage the football program and the university now and for years to come, and somebody has to step up and save us."

Michele cut in, "It was so wicked, so sleazy. I mean sixty-five thou. Jesus. And he's in deep doody because he's a public employee, takin' bribes. He's had it."

"We've had it," I uttered, "Think about being a black player right now. Half our team's black. How would you feel? And speaking of money—Lendel should have been a starter for at least nine games and has only eleven, maybe twelve left in his career, left in a chance to impress the NFL. He's got a big league arm and wheels and sense and all he needs to do is show somebody, so think of the money that sonofabitch Myron McNabb is taking away from him. Jesus!" I'm angry.

We sat in silence. Kathleen pulled us out with the obvious, "This does not fare well for the U."

"And all the while," Michele said, "ABC Television is in town prpared to broadcast every avaricious detail."

"Nice word," I said to her. That's another game we play.

"Thanks. I may not have used it correctly, "Michele commented.

"I'll find out later," I said, smiling.

"What can be done about that McNabb guy?" Kathleen said.

"Too bad we don't have the laws of the Bible in our nation," said Hannah, "But otherwise, you'd have to ask an attorney. I know an attorney."

"Is that….oh, forget it," Kathleen said with a smile.

"This is so wild!" Hannah said, ignoring Kathleen. "It's gross. This makes West Virginians look like….like…."

"Virginians," clipped Kathleen.

I roared with laughter, in desperate need of comic relief. And it just about sums up how I feel about our neighbors to the south.

"This is 1975," Michele said. "How could something like this happen at a major institution of higher learning? I thought we had been though all this. Besides, Lawson's a Yankee."

"Good point, Michele," I said. "But, see, you three are Yanks, right? Pittsburghers, all of you. The key here is McNabb. It's not the Mason-Dixon Line separating north and south anymore. The boundary has dropped a hundred, hundred fifty miles to the south. North of that line is like Pittsburgh. South of it is like Dixie. We're North now, but I grew up in the part of Dixie McNabb calls home, and the whole thing really doesn't surprise me. White Protestants as far as the eye could see. I had one of the more melting-pots of a high school graduating class. Out of a hundred fifty kids, there were ten blacks and two Catholics. A good many of my classmates think Catholics don't believe in God. You can imagine the misinformation they have received about blacks. Point is, that's where McNabb's operating from. Look at McNabb's constituents. Look at those whom they look up to. Wallace and Reagan. Most of his neighbors probably think the sixty-five grand was money well spent."

"That doesn't let the coach off the hook," Kathleen said.

"Oh, by no means!" I exclaimed. "It was easy, too easy for the coach to do what he did. Bobby made it close enough to make it a judgement call. But experts of the game saw that The Kid cracked at Penn State. And that's probably what got the newspaper source to think."

"Do you know who the source is?" asked Michele.

I stood silent in reply.

"You just answered my question…..Hello, Joan."

My heart skipped a beat. She was spendid in a grey wool suit and a plain white shell and black tall spike heels, pushing her Laura Petrey bangs and flip up to five-eight. Carrying her Etienne Aigner overcoat in one arm and a purse and a brief case in the other arm, I wondered why I would ever deserve such a woman. I went from lecturer on the sociology of the south to dumbstruck sophomore at the speed of light. This is not where I wanted to be, but at the time I could in no way help myself out.

Thankfully, she spoke first. "Hi," she said to everyone, then to me she said, "How are you, Mason?"

I considered my response. Wanting to be feeling as well as thoughtful, I chose one word, "Disillusioned."

It must have sounded awful, because Michele helped me out, "Seriously bummed." I breathed for the first time since Joan walked in.

"I'm sorry this has happened to you during this your big week," Joan said, professor talking to student, like 'You'll look back on this someday and discover this was not such a big deal.' Fuck.

"Thanks," was all that would come out.

"Where do you go from here?" Joan asked me.

This answer requires more than one word, so I breathed again, "Today, I don't know. But Vinny and I are talking about taking our show on the road." I surprised myself with that one.

"No!" yelped Hannah. "I mean, don't you want to play for the Ridge Runners?"

"I think I know why," said Michele.

"Why?" asked the sometimes naive Joan.

"Blacks today." replied Michele. "Dagos tomorrow."

"Precisely," I stated.

"Why you though?" Kathleen asked.

"Vinny and I have a pact. Where he goes, I go."

"You're very loyal," said Joan, "as juvenile as your agreement sounds."

I became dejected quickly; crestfallen. I stared at Joan as if maybe time could be rewound and the remark would be stricken from the record. Michele, knowing what is at stake, said quickly, "Was that necessary?," after which I had no choice but to leave.

I walked in a fog down the hall and into my office, a closet-sized room just big enough for a small desk, two chairs, a modest bookcase, and a framed autographed eight by ten glossy of Joe Namath, an eighteenth birthday present from Stan the Money Man. The desire to stay in the game with Joan was doing battle with the stark reality that I shouldn't even be a participant. Even the size of my office and its direct proximity to Joan's more spacious digs, connected by a door that locked only on her side, relegated me to the station in life that was becoming more and more apparent to me. Joan's beauty and attention had taken me by the hand and led me to believe the woman could be mine, whereupon it is, despite the real love I feel, becoming obvious that she is the kind of person who can turn the charm on and off. It looks as if she is utilizing, a word which signifies the barest essentials of using, that charm to get the maximum work out of me, for her. In spite of the letter, and despite the feelings that actually by a psychological professional can be explained away as just a teenage crush, after it all, it's time to say hasta luego. This is quickly becoming Dreams Shattered Week and I might as well face it all like a man.

There is a rap on the door glass. "May I come in?" asked Joan.

I had lost the desire that so overwhelmed me in the main office and affected my speech, so I asked her in. "If you wish."

"Don't you have class now?" she asked, like a mother would.

"It's Physics for Liberal Arts Majors. In a loose sense, I guess I do,"

"You're committed to Vinny, yet you won't go to class."

"I'm going to Michele's class. Does that make you feel better?" I said, anger swelling.

"Mason, there's a test. Of course you're going."

"Joan—," I cut myself off, quelling the rising wrath. After a pause that refreshed, I continued, "Joan, I'm having a bad day and it's not even eight thirty. Will you help me out here?"

"Okay," she responded, "how can I help?"

I resisted the urge to look at her agape. Rubbing my eyes, I decided the time is now. "Joan, common sense tells me to leave this one alone for the rest of my life, but it really can't get much worse than this. So, here goes. Did you get a letter from me recently?"

"Yes," was her response, eyes afixed to mine, as if answering the question, 'Will you eat lunch today?'

After a pause, I asked in anticipation, "And?"

"It was sweet, very sweet, Mason, but I don't date students. I am entrusted with their educational welfare. I can't allow that to be compromised."

Date, I thought. I had never considered that. I love her. I don't want to date her. I don't want to date anybody. She's rehearsed this. And that 'welfare' bullshit. After being mentally rocked back, I recovered, and replied, "Date?"

"That's right, I don't date students." she repeated, as if she were reading the tag on an article of clothing. Don't date students, dry clean only.

I squinted and gathered my thoughts. I was taking too much time. Then, it hit me.

"What the hell do you think this is, *The Mary Tyler Moore Show*?"

She's puzzled, "Excuse me?"

"The—" I'm close to exasperation. "Oh, fuck. Forget it." I said under my breath. She's right. It doesn't even make sense to me.

"Mason, you've lost me. What does Mary Tyler Moore have to do with this?"

Finally, I'm more direct. "Joan, did I mention dating anywhere in that letter?"

Confused again, she softly said, "Not explicitly."

"Correct. The letter transscends dating, as do we."

Her three degrees were having a difficult time fathoming that. "Well….that's just how things are done."

"How are things done, Joan?" I asked earnestly.

"Mason, guy meets girl. They have common interests and goals. They like each other. Guy asks girl out, on a date." she said, as if I were to take notes.

'Well, here's what happened….Guy and girl meet. Guy and girl work closely together. Many things are discussed. They have some things in common, and the girl's very pretty and the guy's not too shabby himself. Boom. Guy falls in love with girl."

"I don't date students. You're a student, Mason."

"I'm not one of your students. I'll go to great lengths not to be if my educational welfare concerns you," I spat, "Besides, you haven't heard the last several sentences, have you?"

"And you haven't heard this: I don't date students." Joan crossed her arms with finality.

Go for it, my mind screamed, "And, in spite of that," as I lowered my voice to a whisper in deference to the academic environment, "I love you." I didn't know where it was going, but I got the shot off.

I might as well had said, 'Joan you're sitting on my jacket.' "I'm sorry, Mason. You're a student and you are several years my junior, several critical years."

The trump card, "That didn't seem to matter when you thought I was dead. That's some welfare for you."

She emitted a nervous laugh and said, "I was just relieved to see you."

"I'll say." My treatise is complete.

"You're making too much of that meeting."

I clumsily started over with a different tack. "My gut says no, I'm not. But, Joan, this—we—when I was a kid, I got for Christmas one year this game by 3M called Thinking Man's Football. It impressed me. It took a game with sweat and mud and inserted brains and intuition." 'When I was a kid...' what are you *thinking?*

"First Mary Tyler Moore, now Christmas. Mason, you've truly lost me."

She's right. "Here it is, Joan. Through it I looked at something very familiar to me in a whole new light. It took me to a higher level."

"So, I'm just a new Christmas toy to you. You realize how old I was when you got this toy?"

Bring it home quickly, Mason, or put yourself out of your misery. "You were a junior in college, but we're beyond that now, and here we are, an unusual romance, unlike those in the pasts of yours and mine, but a romance nonetheless. A thinking man's romance. Hearts and souls and flesh, with brains and intuition. A wish list for passion. Definitely on a higher level." Not bad for having shot myself in the foot.

Joan studied me for the longest time, making me feel as if I had pulled it out. "You are full of shit, Mason Bricker. Call your sorority girls and I'll stick with my junior partners."

"And someday when I'm partner you'll wonder whatever happen to the promise that was held on that November day in 1975."

"You excel in soliloquy," Joan said, "And I still don't date students. And—start going to class. Excuse me." She turned and walked. I refused to look at the butt of the love of my life: The beginning of the long road back.

Thursday, November 6, 1975
9:30 AM

Creative writing test

This is the best way to go into a creative writing test: on automatic. I have so much happening in my life right now to actually sit down and try to think about it all would put me that much closer to the state hospital Vinny says he for my benefit has the telephone number to. Well, Vinny's the one who drives me crazy. Every time I pull a boneheader, it's always, 'Fifteen fuckin' ten on the SAT and look what you just did.' So much pressure to be bright, so little time in which to do it. Maybe I try to bring the expectations down a couple of notches by cutting class. That's the quickest way to turn As into Bs. Just don't go to class. A three four three and look at all the spare time I have. I read what I want to read and, most importantly, hang around the English women, with Joan, of course, and Michele and don't forget about Kathleen and Hannah, even though she is a bit flaky. And that also gives me time to be the professional tutor. Half the time I meet with the guys from ALit and talk about the women I see with the other half. Who's crazy now, Vacca?

Regardless, I don't cut Michele's class. One, it's damned interesting. Two, it's my future. I figure I'll be writing for someone somewhere once I get out of here. And three, she's got…And here they are….

"All right, class," Michele said, two steps into the door, "put your imaginations in high gear. Write a dialogue with the divine. You have an hour. Have at it."

As usual, we begin by asking too many questions.

"Divine?"

Long pause.

"Is Jesus divine?"

"Mary?"

"Moses?"

Michele responded in her best Pittsburgh dialect, "God almighty, boys and girls, this is a mid-level class. Can't you think for yourselves? Use whomever, just show me how they are divine to you." Then she switched to hillbilly, "Lordy, Lordy! Ain't 'cha got any sense?"

Michele…what can I say? If I weren't chin high with Joan right now I'd, uh…naa. Sex is the best way to ruin a friendship. I'm sure she feels the same way about me. Sometimes she's dreamy, though, in a mind-provoking sort of a way. She's a 3M woman, a thinking man's woman. But, thank God, for me….

Just write, okay?

*   *   *   *   *

English 111
Creative Writing
Mason Bricker
Torture…uh…I mean…Test #2
Ya Gotta Believe!!!

Thor: Norse god of thunder
Lumen: French god of lightning

Thor-Whoa! Lumen, my man! You're getting away from me! I can't keep up!

Lumen-Stay with me, man! I'm hot!

T: Break time! Whew! Have a seat. What's gotten into you?

L: I don't know. I just feel good. Used to, a zap here and there was all right. Now, I can zap and zing. It's a lot more productive. I just don't question it. I just do it.

T: Well, inform me next time. Look, I'm starting to feel like this international treaty is a mistake. I mean, here I am, the Norse god of thunder, assigned to work with you, the French lightning guy—

L: That's ghee…ghee…

T: Guy…Then, the Federation gets involved and transfers us both to, where's this?

L: The country of West Virginia.

T: Whatever…

L: Mountain mama. Miner's lady. Stranger to blue waters.

T: Okay, okay. You've been listening to AM radio, haven't you?

L: Yeah, but we've taken care of that, huh, pal?

T: Big static. Big static!

L: That's right, Norseman. I'm on fire! Striking farther. Flashing brighter. Just like the god I want to be.

T: Yeah, but you're just going cloud to cloud, Frenchy. You haven't cracked any structures lately. You haven't turned any trees to toothpicks. Is all this really efficient?

L: (pause) I don't want to hurt anybody.

T: In fact, you haven't flashed earthbound since you blew out that transformer at that college. What gives there?

L: Nothing, Thor, I just enjoy my sky shows, especially at night. Watch. (Flash) Wow!

T: (skeptical pause) Wait a minute…you went down there to check on that transformer, didn't you?

L: Oh…uh…

T: You know that's against Fed regs! No fraternizing with the mortals. Mere mortals, Lumen. You could lose your license.

L: That's not always the case, Thor. There are some nice people down there.

T: People being the operative word. (Thumbing through a book) Here it is: Section 26.c.2 "No god shall—"

L: I know, Thor. I know. Look we're buddies now, you know, after all the Fed uncertainty. Can I talk to you, god-to-god?

T: Uh-oh.

L: Look, Thor, if you're going to take the high moral ground, forget it.

T: Sorry, buddy, what is it?

L: Can you listen without rumbling?

T: Sure, friend.

L: Reason why I'm so good lately is because I've met someone.

T: Oh, God.

L: Venus?

T: Whomever. Down there I assume?

L: (nodding the affirmative) She's just wonderful, Thor.

T: (eyes closed) What's her name?

L: Margaret.

T: Sweet name. Once again, she's not a goddess, is she?

L: She's not one of us, if that's what you're asking. But she's better than a goddess.

T: Lumen—

L: I know, I know.

T: Where did you meet her?

L: She's a college instructor and she was teaching in a classroom beside the transformer. I was looking the transformer over, trying to find a way to supernaturally fix it.

T: Did you?

L: Needs parts. Not in stock.

T: Somethings cannot be divinely overcome.

L: So I disguised myself as the power technician to the Montani Power maintenance office over the phone, gave them hell and got a new transformer installed.

T: The netherworld. Now you're in it deep.

L: I felt badly, Thor. I blacked out Margaret's classroom.

T: Lumen, you've been a god for eons. You know that if you think of all of the earthly consequences, you can't do your job effectively. How the…how did you make the call?

L: I used her office phone.

T: Oh, so now Margaret thinks you're a Mon Power employee?

L: No, no. After her lights came back on, and after her class, I told her the truth.

T: I'm sure she believed it. Humans, of little faith.

L: She didn't. So I took her outside and flashed a cloud.

T: That got her attention.

L: It did.

T: What do you think now?

L: I think she's lovely.

T: All the goddesses in the heavens and you go for a human.

L: Thor, as I said, she's better than a goddess. She's just as beautiful, even more so, and she's not nearly as temperamental.

T: We've go to stick with our kind, regardless.

L: No we don't, Thor. We should follow our hearts.

T: Is this really coming from your heart or some diseased part of your psyche?

L: Oh, good point, Thor. Play the crazy card.

T: Oh, Mars. In romance novels, Lumen.

L: You wanna hear more?

T: Go ahead. I'm not reading anything else good lately.

L: After I split the cloud, she was really impressed, but still a little reticent. I, however, was convinced. I hung around the local cafe waiting for her to finish her day.

T: You know what coffee does to you.

L: Just that one time. I was wet.

T: Zeus Louise, Lumen.

L: Listen to me, Norseboy. Margaret came to the cafe. We sat and sipped and talked and talked, about family and friends, likes and dislikes. Then we went to a restaurant and she introduced me to a new food.

T: What's that?

L: Pizza and beer.

T: Alcohol makes us go blind.

L: That's an old Juno's tale.

T: Still, I don't like this…

L: Can't you see, Thor? I'm in love. Give me a break.

T: You want me to turn my back to this?

L: Thor, do what you must, but my feelings for Margaret are real.

T: I guess I really can't stop you.

L: From the first time I saw her she stole my heart.

T: That's beautiful. But, you can't have her.

L: Yes, I can. I can visit her anytime. I can emulate humans. I'll be whatever she wants.

T: And what will that do for her? Lumen, the French god of lightning, dressed as an engineer?

L: Or anybody. A college football player, perhaps. Anything she likes.

T: Lumen, it won't be you. You're Lumen, and any disguise is just that. You've eventually gotta be you. And Lumen can't be Margaret's lover. End of discussion.

L: Well…Thor…I'm up the River Styx without a paddle…What am I going to do?

T: You're going to have to lower your sights and find a goddess.

L: She is a goddess.

T: A real goddess.

L: I don't like this.

T: No one says you have to.

Thursday November 6, 1975
10:45 AM

Jennifer visits the office

Good test. I can still think of the standard post-test obsessions, nevertheless a good B effort. Michele brings out the best in me.

I know I have an A in Creative Writing. Despite being able to recognize but a few students in the class, Physics is a strong A, including the lab. Philosophy and Logic are both Bs. I could push it for the next three weeks for an A in Poetry and thrill Joan by scoring a goddamn ace in a major class. A little bit of work and concentration, along with some charm and class attendance and I've taken a three four three up to a three six three. That's Dean's list material, and if I were averaging seven catches and a hundred twenty yards a game, I might be Academic All-America. Trouble is, Moses couldn't catch seven for a hundred twenty with our offense regardless of how many defenses he could part. It's not a set that develops receivers into game dominators. We never pass on first down. In fact we are so predictable the only way we complete a pass is because Dhali and Clark and Tom and Dave are so athletically gifted they make incredible catches of Kid balls always just off the mark, sometimes actually taking the ball out of the defender's hands. I amaze myself with my ability to completely change subjects in mid-thought.

The test is my swan song with Joan. I wrote her a letter. I confronted her. She gave me the snowball's chance in hell schtick. I'm out. Not because I want to be, but because that's the way nature commands it. Like Lumen with Margaret, I don't like this, but no one says I have to. Wow, not yet twenty years old and I'm quoting my own works. Sometimes I do take myself too seriously.

I saw Jennifer yesterday after her nine o'clock ALit class. She reminded me she is here to help me. I must appear to be in need. She's talked to Jean. The Jean Queen has set me up with a head doctor. Sometimes, I think she could be right. I do have some self-destructive tendencies; hell, maybe an entire structure of internal consummation. With regard to love, I seek only those relationships that have wires attached to cylinders full of nitro and are operated by a ticking device. It bears repeating, there's Jennifer, a lovely, attractive young woman who apparently would do anything for me, but I have to feign interest. In athletics, I am with my normal body fast enough to turn a good, safe collegiate quarter mile, but I spend months hardening it with muscle and fling it at a group of guys with a combined total weight of nine hundred pounds. I use the pursuit of my father's dreams to rationalize why I'm not Ivy League. I lose applications and miss deadlines for academic scholarships. I squander my tuition paid out of my own pocket by not going to class so I can work more and more for the timebombshell with whom I am romantically involved, if only in a one-sided fashion. Love hurts, love burns you like a flame when it's hot; thank you sir, may I have another?

I turn to catch a female shadow at my door. "Enter!" I shout regally.

Jennifer walked in dressed with everything feminine L. L. Bean and Levi Strauss offers. A Pi Gamma Pi dress-down day. Check it and I bet they're all L. L. Bean and Levis this morning. Her hair cascaded long and her brown eyes just about brought me to my knees. Why can't I call up this memory and feeling when I'm thinking of Joan?

"Hi, Mason," she said, smiling like 'I know your secrets.'

"You know my secrets, don't you?"

"Why do say that, Mason?" she responded in a coy fashion.

"I don't know, Jennifer," I replied. "I've never been somebody's project. Most go on to bigger and better things. They just don't bother with it." After engaging my brain, I still decided the best way to take on ol' Jen is directly up front.

"This is an awfully serious conversation for the morning, isn't it?"

"I don't know, Jennifer. I'm just wondering. When you fix this emotional Eliza Doolittle, what are you going to do with it?"

"Fix?"

"Yeah, you're Professor Higgins, here to retrain me."

Jennifer looked shocked, then quizzical, then pleasant. "I saw that movie. I guess...I am the Professor." She smiled.

"What are you going to do with me?"

"What do you want done?"

"Can I make a list?"

"That's your first assignment. Make a list. Have it completed by ten tomorrow morning." She stopped. "Do I sound too much like Dr. Kissinger?"

I considered eagerness, alertness, length of gams. "Not at all."

"Then it's time for the $64,000 question—Do you and Dr. Kissinger have...anything...going?"

I didn't pause. "Nothing except the mutual belief that Arthur Miller's play *Death of a Salesman* is among the most depressing pieces of American Literature written."

Jennifer stared at me, either not understanding my answer or in an attempt to extract the truth by clairvoyance. Probably the former. The next person to speak loses.

"There are rumors..." she said.

"I understand that, and I understand why, but nothing has taken place between us, nor is anything planned for the future." Honesty is most certainly the best policy.

"Do you want something to take place?"

"No." A white lie in the face of sexual freedom is no vice.

"Have you ever?"

"Oh," I replied, "that's a different story."

"So, you have."

"No, it's just a different story."

"You can tell me the truthful story. It won't affect how I feel about you."

This is now a most interesting conversation. Jennifer Pierce and I, in the smallest office on campus, are about to embark on the discussion of feelings. After all the kissing and embracing and talking and dancing around, she is ready to offer hers, and I'd better come up with mine.

I spoke. "Let's take your last sentence one subject at a time. The truthful story." I prepared to tell her the truth, or my version of it, not in honor of the truth, but because I am a latter-day kamikaze and it would be a test of just how much shit she is willing to take. "Here goes, Jennifer. I've had a crush on her, and I've dealt with it. I've realized that it would not be in my best interest to have a relationship with Joan. We've actually discussed it. She's not my type anyway." The truth, or so. Never mind that it has all come to pass within the past hour.

She looked at me and nodded. "What is your type?" she asked.

"Romantic and passionate...like you." Goddamn, Mason. Why the hell did you say that?

Jennifer's face didn't change, but the color did. To a crimson, bright. For some odd reason, I took it home. "Now you were saying...."

She sighed. "I never really considered myself passionate until this semester. I guess you make me that way." Her eyes moistened, but remained fixed on me.

"Well..." I began the reply, "I'm a lucky guy." Okay, boy, you're in, whether you want it or not! "I guess it's okay I'm not greek. I mean if I were we could have had one of those rites where I pin you, or you pin me, or...you get me in a technical knockout...."

She laughed as I tried to make up for making her mascara smear. "I'll get you a tissue." Running down to the office, I found Michele there with Kathleen and Joan.

"Great test, Mason. You're hilarious!" said Michele.

"Thanks." I snared a kleenex. "Later. Gotta go."

I ran back to my office to find Jennifer awaiting me so she could right herself.

"I'm sorry. I just…lost control," she said. "If you weren't so damned sweet…." After dabbing her eyes, she embraced me. "Thanks, Mason," she said smiling, "Thanks for being you…God, that sounds stupid, but it's true. I don't want to change you. I just want to help relieve any pain you have." Her eyes are repaired.

"Frankly, Jennifer," I said with a smile, "I can see you relieving me in many ways." Grab gun. Place barrel against temple.

She smiled wryly, pressing her hips against me, hard, "Funny, Mason, I can see that happening." She then delivered an open-face sophomore kiss, and scored that TKO. We pulled away and laughed just as we heard a knock at the door ajar.

We dropped our hands right after Joan entered. Upon seeing Jennifer and me standing, facing, Dr. Kissinger issued a look of horrified embarrassment on her face.

"I'm sorry. I didn't…."

"Don't worry. Come in." I said, inwardly happy to have broken the chains.

"I was just going to…," said Joan, still stumbling.

"Go ahead." I'm okay with it. It's part of moving on. Jennifer's certainly okay with it. She's marked her territory.

"Go ahead," I said again.

"Michele told me about your test. With regard to content, she found it to be a very touching and funny piece. You're good Mason. Now, start going to class. Bye." Joan then left without addressing Jennifer. Then she popped her head back in. "Hi, Jennifer," she said.

"Hi," said Jennifer. She then after Joan had left turned to me and said, "Must be difficult for her, you not being hers any more."

"Whatever."

Jennifer planted another one on me. I love the seventies. I saw out of the corner of my eye Michele walking in holding a paper. She cleared her throat. Jennifer backed away.

Extending her hand, Michele said to Jennifer, "Hi. I'm Michele Taranucci. You must be the Jennifer Pierce Mason's told me about."

Shocked to hear she had been a subject of past conversation, Jennifer could only respond, "Hi."

"Now, Mason," she said, turning to me, "Here's your test. I graded it first, just for the hell of it. Ninety-two. Funny. I might submit it to the executive producer of *Saturday Night Live*, if I knew him or her. Regardless, start going to your other classes. Bye, kids." Michele turned and walked away.

"You have way too many good looking teachers surrounding you," Jennifer said. "I will be up here more often."

"You are welcome," I said.

"And on that, I'd better go," Jennifer picked up her bag, gave me a peck on the lips for the road, and said, "Call me later." I agreed to that.

After a few minutes, the memory is gone. I can't even attempt to fight the indifference.

Thursday, November 6, 1975
12:30 PM

Lunch at the High Ridge cafeteria

I weaved through the maze of the High Ridge lunch crowd. Since I look the part of a football player, I due to the news attracted a few stares this particular morning, despite being anonymous on the playing field. I walked up to a corner table and found Vinny, Michael, and Arthur solemnly sitting there.

Vinny looked up to me and said, "Almost your prediction."

"What?" I asked sharply.

"Suspended without pay pending an investigation,"

"She-it," I whistled, drawing it out Southern-style. I then looked to the seniors out of respect.

"I don't know if it's enough," Arthur said softly, aware of the eyes upon him.

"Dit-to," Michael said, emulating me.

"Can't fault you there," said Vinny. He paused, then asked, "Have you seen Lendel?"

"He was going to class," replied Michael, "My man Lendel has a 'No comment' for everybody." The size and definition of Michael's physique is accentuated by his square jaw holding firm.

"I really can't blame him," I said. I again felt between my buddies and me the crevasse dividing the black and the white experiences.

"Black players have a meeting at two fifteen this afternoon in the projection room," Arthur announced.

"Fuuuck," I said, again and at least in diction-style true to my Southern roots.

"Can you blame us, Mason?" asked Michael, testily.

"Hell, no. Go for it." I responded sincerely, "I'm serious. This is all so contemptible."

"Do it," added Vinny, "I'm just sorry to see the team go down the tubes." That last statement doesn't help things.

"Why do you necessarily think the team is going to go 'down the tubes?' It could be said we're there already." Michael asked calmly.

"Because we gotta be together to beat Pitt," Vinny said, firmly.

"Vinny, we're not doing this because we want to," Arthur stated.

"And, if you're a black guy, this goes way beyond Pitt," Michael said, not in a retaliatory way, but as if to explain things.

Silence. Then I stepped in.

"I see Michael's point. And Arthur's. And Vinny's."

I can also see Michael began to feel the isolation of a man persecuted. "Who's to say we were ever together, anyway?" he said.

Vinny, holding strongly, said, "I like to think we are."

"Me, too," I said.

"I don't know," replied Michael, noticing the looks and glances Arthur has picked up on. The two are campus celebrities, and considering the events of this morning, it's difficult for them to hide, despite probably feeling as if they wanted to.

I didn't want the undercurrent of the detachment of my friends to gain strength. I mean, we're tight. Vinny, Arthur, and I are the only ones on the team who would submit ourselves to the torture Michael called summer workouts. "It's us," I said, "We four. Summer. Game prep. Games. Lunches. That's us, man. Am I right? I mean, we've overcome this senior-sophomore crap and we're cool. Cool? You NFL guys don't mind hangin' around a couple of scrubs, do you?" I flashed my dimples. They kill men, too.

The two smiled. Good. Arthur hesitated to consider and responded, "No, we don't mind."

"Michael?" I asked.

"Right," said Michael, giving in.

"I mean," said Vinny," if there is anything we can do to help fix this, please let us know." I thought the honesty of his intentions rang true to Michael and Arthur.

The discussion paused for emphasis. I feel the eyes of the High Ridge.

"I think it's gotta run its course," continued Michael.

"We'll be tested," said Arthur," but I suspect others on the team will be tested even moreso for their beliefs."

Vinny and I looked to each other. We know what he's talking about.

"Prejudiced beliefs," stated Michael.

"Who do you have in mind?" Vinny asked.

"Well, for starters," Arthur said, "the biggest redneck of them all."

"Cap'n Teddy," Michael said in his best rendition of a white boy from Dixie.

"Gerlach," I affirmed.

"He's the most outspoken," said Arthur, dangerously closing in on his boiling point, but fighting to maintain control of his emotions.

Even though I know Ted, The G-man he is called, and The G-man made little effort to hide his 'good ol' boy'-ism, I'm still surprised to hear his name. "I guess it's good to get it out in the open."

"It's already out in the open among us," Michael confirmed.

"As are others," Arthur said.

"Mason," began Michael, "you've studied Richard Wright. You know about the three roles the 'Negro' can assume. One, the role of passivity designed for him. Two, the carving out a middle class beside you 'white folk,'" he said irascibly, "And three, the role of a criminal, rejecting and fighting the Southern white system, the role which a lot of white people are scared of."

"We don't really want to be criminals," continued Arthur, "and we don't want to be in service as your 'boys,' so it's like we're gonna move into the neighborhood," he said with some humor. "Howdy, neighbor!"

Vinny and I laughed. Still, this is intense.

Michael spoke to cut the tension, "We know you two are behind us. But there are people, even on the team...."

"Especially on the team," Arthur interjected.

"Who want 'nigger number one' forever, the boy," Michael hesitated to quell a rising resentment. "Still, Mason, Vinny, still here in the mid-seventies, even after all we all went through in the fifties and the sixties, they still want 'the boy.'"

We four sat in silence upon Michael's punctuation, within ourselves, no longer aware of the growing crowd around us, a gathering of student 'civilians' as Coach Lawson liked to call them. 'Civilians,' also concerned with the latest renewal of the racial question, but hoping it'll all blow over before anyone suffers the pain of reaching an answer. The students surrounded us four, four men who intrinsically know that the time for an answer has come, that this time is different, that the day of vindication is nearing with little regard to the cost.

"Terrible," I said.

"Suckin' ass big time," added Vinny.

"Michael and I, as well as Lendel, and others, just want to keep the criminal rejection element down during the meeting," said Arthur.

"It's there?" I asked, fearful for the first time.

"More than you would think," replied Michael, "or even would wanna think. Some guys are just pissed off…they are so pissed, they're on the verge of doing whatever."

"I don't know what's going to come out of the meeting, guys," Arthur said, "My hope is we will follow Lendel's lead, who I think will want to keep it all under control. But, I can't guarantee anything." My fear had floated to my two black friends.

Vinny announced, "I have this aunt in Weirton who goes to communion every morning. I like to think she has a special link to the Man Upstairs. I'll get her to put a word in for us."

"An excellent idea," said Michael, "Great. We're gonna need all the help we can get. In fact, let's start now. Let's us four pray together, now," I could see just that thought lifted a mass from him. "Mason, you're the wordsman. You lead."

Three of them thought that's wonderful. I, however, am a bit apprehensive. I feel as if I would be impersonating a priest. I'm certainly the wrong guy for that. But the looks on my friends' faces urge me, and I started thinking about what to say. Michael and Arthur clasped the hands of their buddies, making a perfect black/white circle of meaty football players with bowed heads, awaiting the word.

Showtime….

"God," I began,"…uh…we've got right around a hundred twenty men, a hundred twenty of your not-so-most-faithful servants. A hundred twenty fighters and drinkers and swearers and smokers and leerers and druggers and guys who have a lot of sex out of wedlock and use Your name in vain every chance we get, but nevertheless men working together toward the same respectful goal, and something…something just terribly wounding, very damaging to the souls and to the dreams that we all hold, has hit us, hit us hard, God. What the coach did to us was not fair, and God, we sit here as mortal men, before You, needing Your help…I know life is just not fair sometimes, and I know You're probably gonna hear from a few of us over the next couple of days, and I know it's just very difficult to give us all what we want…I know…So, I speak for the four of us and pray that You help us all do the right thing. We pray for the men who have violated my friends' souls and trust and the other men who have been hurt. Do what you think is best, God, and help us to accept whatever happens, and we'll do our best down here. In the name of the Father, and the Son, and the Holy Spirit, Amen."

Vinny and I unclasped hands with our friends and each made the sign of the cross.

"You Catholics are pretty cool," said Arthur, smiling.

"Thanks, Mason, that was beautiful," Michael said, "Beautiful. We'll catch you guys at practice after the meeting." He and Arthur stood to leave. I guess they feel better.

I'm a wreck.

Thursday November 6, 1975
1:30 PM

In the English office

"Mason!"

I immediately recognized Michele's voice. Having just walked by her office, I noted she is on the telephone. After the lunch, I had placed her on my 'To be talked to in the near future' list. I figure I should give her 'The Word.' Well, the future is now. Backpedaling, I stepped in front of her door to find Dr. Taranucci holding the phone in one hand and cupping the transmitter with the other.

"Ma—! Oh, there you are. Come in and wait," Michele said as she continued her conversation. "Okay, Rex. Talk to you another time? Okay, okay, hon. See ya. Bye, bye." She hung up. "Now there's an odd one...an attorney who just won't shut up."

"Rex..." I said, like a friend making internal guesses about a person of the opposite gender.

"Rex Hernsen. Old boyfriend from my swinging Duquesne days."

"This I've gotta hear."

"Female grad student on the loose. Rex and I hit the town for a couple of years, then decided to become friends only. Great move. He had heard the news about the football coach and called me. I told him after I interrogated you, I would know more. So, what do you know?"

I paused too long. It's tougher to tell her than I thought it would be. Why? "Just what's in the papers."

"Bullshit!"

I giggled in a masculine way, "What do you mean, Michele?"

"One, today, you were a) too nervous and b) too authoritative. Two, you look like a man who has something to hide and doesn't know where to put it. Three, your phone was ringing off the hook. I finally answered it and it was the *Pittsburgh Advocate*. Why would the city's newspaper be calling a kickoff team guy? You know more than almost everybody thinks you do. Everybody except me, God's gift to inductive reasoning. So, spill it before I have to beat it out of you."

Never a day goes by that Michele doesn't in one way or another impress me. I can't deny her. "Okay. First, those who know are Vinny,

Judy, Alice, Michael Burton, Arthur O'Neill, Lendel Ward, the banker
from Huntington who gave me the info, a *Mail* reporter, and *The Mail*
editor. Now I'll tell you."

"Jesus, Mason, that's no secret!" Michele whined, "I'm insulted! And
now this Pittsburgh reporter knows something, which means your
newspaper has leaked its source. I had to find out from a leak? A leak of
a leak? I thought we were friends."

"We are friends, Michele. It's just that it is very...touchy. Also, when
was I supposed to tell you? We were pretty busy this morning."

"This is academia. The wheels can stop rolling anytime for a good
piece of gossip. Also, when did you find out? Never mind that. Just tell
me."

I took a seat and a deep breath. "The banker from Huntington left a
box with me last Saturday with a promise to visit on Sunday." For the
sake of brevity I sacrificed some accuracy. "He did and explained it all,
just as the newspaper account reads. Then he talked me into taking care
of it from here, being fearful of his job."

"Rightfully so," said Michele.

"I went to Michael and Arthur that night," I said, starting back. "They
wanted to hold. Then Lendel wrecked his knee. Out of frustration, I
guess, Michael and Lendel told me to pull the lever. I called a reporter
that night. He talked to his editor. They dropped everything. Two days
later, it's printed, front page."

Michele stared at me. She took a quick breath, then leaned back
slightly. I waited. I value her opinion. I want to hear what she has to say.

"Several things," she said. "First, call this Pittsburgh reporter. Pretend
you think you're being called about the game. Just call him. The longer
that festers, the uglier it'll get. Deny everything that has to do with this
whole affair."

"What?" I asked in surprise.

"You heard me. Second, if you need a safehouse, call me. No, don't even call. They're going to tap your phone. Just come over. Go home as soon as you can and pack a bag, leaving it by your door ready."

"Michele—"

"Let me finish," she demanded. "Third, call, no, visit your Montani reporter and editor and ask for a list of names of those who know about this. Fourth, get a lawyer. Tell him or her the story, show him or her the list of names, and follow his or her advice to the letter. And fifth, realize you are a marked man and act accordingly. Mix in wealthy fans and racial strife and you've got you one huge motherfucker here."

I stared back. After a few moments, I said, "Look, Michele, I know this is serious, but you act as if I have ratted on the Mob. I just don't think this calls for your drastic measures."

She leaned in. "Mason, the key words here are money and race. You're right in the thick of both of them. I may be wrong, but if you're wrong, you're going to have one bitchin' price to pay."

"I think it's under control."

"I think it's on the brink of a disaster, for you," Michele said. "Whatever possessed you to do this?"

"Duty. Honor."

"Country?"

"Well, yes. Hell, yes!" I exclaimed. "Country. Duty. Honor. Country." I'm proud.

"Mason, look…I really do admire your fortitude. Just realize you have placed your butt in jeopardy. Now, go call *The Pittsburgh Advocate* and call your lawyer. As a matter of fact, call your lawyer first. Even better, call Rex Hernsen. I know he's there right now. Here, I'll dial it for you." Michele did just that and handed me the phone.

Two rings. Question: Why am I doing this? "Hernsen," said the mid-range deep male voice.

"Hi. Rex Hernsen? This is Mason Bricker, Michele's friend." Answer: Michele.

"Mister Bricker! It's a pleasure to finally meet you, even if it's just over the phone. Michele talks well of you. I understand you're Deep Throat."

"How do you know that?" I asked.

"Michele's guess. You should be proud," said Rex, "How may I help you?"

"Michele suggested I call you because she thinks someone's going to try to kill me."

"She's always been so melodramatic. But, aside from the magnitude of the danger you face, she's got it on the money."

Okay, okay she's right, goddamnit. "In short, Rex, what should I do now?"

With exception to packing a bag and keeping it readily available, Rex gave me the same advice Michele offered: return the call to *The Advocate*, call *The Mail* to assess the leak situation, and lay low.

"Physically, I don't envision any danger, yet. If you receive threats, call the police immediately. Then call me. With regard to the team, you might just get your butt kicked off. Are you scholarship?"

"No."

"No trouble there. You'll probably be allowed to remain in school. Probably."

"Damn, Rex. I never thought of that." There are most likely a lot of things I never thought of.

"You've ruffled some pretty powerful feathers, Mason. They'll be looking for ways to get you back. How can I be of assistance, you may ask? First, if the coaches give you trouble about the team with a suspension, I could help you there. Possibly. We'll have to see how and why they do it. If the school gives you any grief about remaining enrolled, I can definitely and will most definitely help you fight that one. For what you did, there is no reason to kick you out of school. Besides, if they do, they may see a backlash from the students that would compare to 1968. But, for the present, Mason, we'll just sit back and watch it unfold."

With little pondering of his counsel, I said, "Rex, thanks for the advice. Here, let me give you my address for the bill."

"No need, Mason. You're a friend of Michele's. If this gets deep, we might, just might, talk about that then. Don't worry about it. I'm proud to help you. You demonstrated a lot of courage doing what you did."

"Rex, thank you, but, really, I can't imagine not doing it." If I say that enough, I'll start to believe it.

"Still, Mason, it was above and beyond the call of the duty of a student."

"Well…," was all the response I could give.

"I'm sorry, Mason, I have to run right now. As things develop, call me. I want to help. And I think in some regards, I can."

"Okay, Rex, thank you for your time."

"And, Mason, if Michele starts telling you wild stories about us, don't believe her."

"Okay, Rex. She has the potential to embellish somewhat. Everything's a story."

"Oh, fuck you guys, both of you!" said Michele.

"I heard that," said Rex, "Gotta run. Keep in touch, okay, Mason?"

"I'll do it."

"Goodbye."

His phone clicked. "Thanks, Michele," I said, "I think you gave me the right advice."

"Go home and pack your bag," she said, "You know I have a guest room. And, don't worry. I won't try to seduce you and take any of Joan's meat away from her." Michele grinned slightly.

"I don't think she'd care," I said, feeling again the stab wounds of this morning.

Michele just smiled and wagged her eyebrows, "We'll see about that."

A power surge lifted through my heart. Seriously? Oh, hell, Mason. You heard the lady this morning. Just drop it. With my circuits about to burn, I decided not to pursue an explanation of Michele's remark.

Thursday November 6, 1975
2:30 PM

Thursday afternoon practice at The Ridge

The horseplay and practical jokes which are common in football fieldhouses and which entertain us before and after our practices have left us as we Runners took one shot after another. We stood together unbeatable amid the mountains in central Pennsylvania and lost to an act of God, then came home and lost again in a commission of mass suicide. And as if those aren't enough, the same newspaper article resulting in the suspension of the head coach has necessitated an assembly of the black guys in the next room, hashing it out among and for themselves. It's not much better out here, as the white guys sit, cursing and guessing. Knowing everything that is going on except for the agenda of that damn meeting has left me very uneasy.

I had been taped by a trainer before I dressed for practice. Sitting still on the bench in my locker area, I await the end of the meeting, headgear on, its hard shell and facemask metaphorically shielding me from that which is taking place at the school of my boyhood heroes: sixties All-America tackle Curt Rush; All-East tight end of a few years later Jack Sinnell; Bernard Luenzo, the quarterback with Namath style from 1970; Larry Hunter, the first black quarterback at The U and, much to the chagrin of the white-fart fans, a damned good one; John Peters, an All-America flyboy receiver with whom I had the pleasure of playing last year; Hayward Stern, John's bookend running buddy; and Mike Andrews, the All-East safety of the late sixties who against Richmond set the NCAA single-game interception record at six. I wonder, what do these Runners of old think about a sell out coach and a team becoming divided? I envisioned them and other Runners of the past swooping into the fieldhouse like superheroes; Batman, Spiderman, the Phantom, and Superman, saving us from the Nazi evil, and saving us from ourselves, from our own bad choices we might make in the name of fairness, preserving the team for the sacred devotion of boys of the future.

Our lockers are assigned by our game jersey number. As you enter, the numbers start from the left with Raj Retnitraj, the kicker and number three, and run down the left side to the end, where they cross over to the right and come back on the right side to the end. Vinny is number twelve, a quarterback number made popular by Joe Namath of the New York Jets and his social antithesis Roger Staubach of the Dallas Cowboys. Vinny's been number twelve with religious courtesy to Mr. Namath since Pop Warner and could make that call here at West Virginia because he was a Blue Chip recruit. I've been number eighty-eight since we dressed everybody for Penn State last year and it was the last jersey available. Therefore, Vinny and I dress across from each other. Today, he found me in contemplation.

"Mason, you there?" he asked.

I shook myself free. "Yeah."

"How long you been here?" he whispered.

"Since the meeting started." I whispered back.

"Anything?" Vinny asked.

"Nothing. No noise. Nothing."

We sat in our respective spaces silently for a while. A few other players, white of course, milled about. The time is two forty. Practice begins at three.

The mountainous Ted Gerlach walked in. Six-six, two-seventy, favorite song, Lynyrd Skynyrd's *Sweet Home Alabama*. He stopped and looked toward the projection room and glanced at his watch. "Goddamn, how long does it take?" he spat out. Then he looked to Vinny and me. "You guys guarding the door for them?" he asked.

Vinny is plain-faced. Ted is a team captain and an offensive tackle, a left tackle blocking on the right-handed QB's blind side. Vinny always treated Ted with respect, knowing that if things went Vinny's way Ted would hopefully be one of Vinny's best friends.

I always handled Ted with ease, knowing that he could and would beat the shit out of me if he deemed it necessary.

"No, Ted," I answered as our eyes met.

"I figured you'd be in there with them," Ted said, walking away with a snort, in reference to my friendship with Michael. I know he considers me a traitor to Caucasians everywhere and talks of me that way with the other white players. That's where Joe Osbourne comes in handy.

Joe is one of my proponents, a friend in his mind. He also claims, and acts as if, he shares allegiance to every race. The white guys are careful with Joe. They know he's killed once and would kill again if he has to. Therefore, with regard to Ted and me, Michael and Joe cancel each other out.

Vinny discreetly rolled his eyes. After Ted moved out of range, Vinny asked, "What's going to happen here?"

I nodded my head in thought. After a pause, I responded, "They don't want to, none of us want to…not play the game. We're…we're all athletes first. I think Michael and Arthur and especially Lendel are giving everybody a chance to air it our. It's also an opportunity for Michael and them to find out where everyone stands on the subject. They're hurting. It's gotta be painful for them. And what does an athlete do when he's in pain? He eats it. And what does that do? It makes the potential for an explosion greater. I just hope we explode on Pitt."

Ted came back to us quickly. "You know what this is? Coach was set up. Maybe by one of the guys in there. That's what I think."

Vinny remained silent. I looked at Ted. "Who's to say, Ted? But, photos, transcripts, affidavits. Someone went through a helluva lot of trouble to take Coach Lawson down. A helluva lot of trouble."

"You seem to know an awful lot about this." Ted said.

"I know what I read." I said as my gut twisted.

Ted stood above me, nodding his head slightly. After a couple of moments, he turned in silence.

Vinny and I sat there, hoping Ted's deductions would go away.

The Kid walked in. I thought about how little I had considered him in this whole affair. As I looked him over, tall, muscular, knowing if he couldn't throw rifle shots he'd just be another frat brother majoring in phys ed, it occurred to me Kid isn't feeling well. His normally placid face is strained and somewhat beaded with sweat. Ted saw it's difficult for Kid to be here and went to his aid.

"Hey, man," Ted said to Kid, patting him on the back of his shoulder. "How'ya doin'?"

"I don't feel good at all." The Kid replied. He shook his head and closed his eyes, then took in a deep breath.

I don't blame him. And I felt guilty. It is pitiful to see him having to face up to his efforts as a twenty-year-old leader, efforts which are now known to the state and the nation as bogus. By and only by money is he the West Virginia QB. I'm embarrassed by him and embarrassed for him. And knowing I got the wheels rolling didn't help. I hope it doesn't show on my face. I can barely do it, but I have to say something to him. I stood, and Vinny stood. We walked to him and I placed my hand on his shoulder, much in the same way Marcus Brutus did Julius Caesar, and paid my condolences.

"We're with ya," I said to Kid. I can't believe I said it.

"Hang in there, Kid." Vinny said as a QB compadre.

The Kid looked at us gratefully, shook his head up and down, then ran to one of the commode stalls and threw up.

*   *   *   *   *

The Kid laid on his back on the trainer's table, in his jock and hip pads, getting his left knee and his ankles taped, complaining of an aching stomach and a fever. One of the trainers took his temperature orally. He was clocked at one oh two five. Doctor McCormick, the team physician, was present, checking up on pre-game injuries. The doctor examined Kid, finding him feverish and with a tender tummy, and ordered him to the hospital for further tests. But Bobby Kay, knowing what's at stake here, wants to show the team that aside from the sixty-five grand he is the man. After the last strand of tape around his ankles was torn, he gingerly hopped up from the table and, holding his right side, staggered to his locker. I, upon witnessing this, turned to Vinny and told him, "Get ready."

At two forty-five, the black players filed out of the projection room, around fifty of them, solemn in their carriage. I found Michael. He nodded toward the field. I assumed this meant he would talk to me out there. Finding Vinny, I walked out of the fieldhouse with him and onto the gridiron we Runners call home.

Today is Thursday. In two days we are scheduled to host the top-ranked team in the nation, a team which is also our biggest and longest standing rival. Our starting quarterback has been, aside from being an unknowing participant in a most awful scandal, ordered to the hospital for tests. Vinny walked to the bleacher seats in the south endzone and pitched his cookies. Bribes. Racial dissension. Nauseated quarterbacks two deep. This is not how I imagined my first game against Pitt would be.

Vinny approached me. "I'm okay. I'm okay. This is the way it is. I'm okay with that."

I put an arm around my friend. He had the odor of an elementary school during flu season. "You've got puke on your chinstrap, buddy," I offered. I then looked around. ABC Sports is not present. The U administration must have gotten to them.

Vinny wiped it off with his left hand as he picked up a football with his right hand. No other players of the so-called skill positions are with us yet, so we did what came naturally to us.

Vinny matured early for a boy, therefore he was a passing QB long before any others could even think about it. At the age of eleven he was throwing fifty yards and could vary speed and trajectory. That's when the dream started for us. Vinny and I got together every other weekend. That's most of the day Saturday and a half day Sunday devoted to pass and catch with the football, either at Madonna's field or Rebel Field, but always dreaming about The Ridge. With the navy and silver in mind, from that age of eleven to age eighteen, I caught, bare minimum, five hundred passes per weekend we were together, thirteen thousand per year, and a hundred thousand passes before high school graduation. Including estimates for college, since we've been together almost every-day, this now involves astronomical numbers. We have always known that we're getting out there, mark our words. But with him as a backup and me languishing with the third team, we just don't know how that's going to happen yet.

We stood twenty yards apart, with the just arriving third team QB David Crikstein at my side on the goal line and the fleet second team receiver Tom Smith on the twenty with The Gunner. Vinny threw the ball to me, then I handed it to David. David threw the ball to Tom, who in turn handed to Vinny. Receivers caught, quarterbacks threw. This went on as the players dribbled out of the fieldhouse

As time elapses, Vinny quickly gets better. During this warm-up drill, my man started out crisp and improved on that. His eyes fixed on me more and more like lasers. His passes came to me more and more like darts from a blowgun. Vinny is the only player I know who can go from yakking to peak performance in a few minutes. Even when Bobby is on his game, and especially now after Lendel is out, Vinny is the best QB. No question about it. We shall see if it comes to realization. When it happens, I'd certainly like to be out there. But I don't see that tree coming to fruition anytime soon.

At three fifteen, late because of the meeting, Coach Robert 'Red' Van Watt, acting head coach, whistled and called us to midfield. Michael then pulled me aside. "Listen, the meeting, we talked about a lot, a hell of a lot, some of it scary, some of the scary stuff coming from yours truly, but we all agreed to a man that Lendel would call the shots. Lendel says play the game. But, Mason, for now. Let me stress that. For now."

Knowing I had ten seconds for a response, I said, "Sounds like a day-by-day thing."

"Hour-by-hour, my man," Michael replied.

"She-it yow, man." I said in Texas lingo.

All one hundred of us encircled Coach Van Watt, blacks on one side, whites on the other. That doesn't look good.

"All right, men, and I call you men because I know and expect you to conduct yourselves as men in light of the circumstances. I've been named interim head coach. Coach Browning will take over my offensive coordinator duties. So, here goes. From this point forward, we will concentrate solely on our game with The University of Pittsburgh. Since they have sets similar to ours on both sides of the ball, we will today run number one offense versus number one defense. We will, since it is less than forty-eight hours before the game, limit hitting. We will also as usual for a Thursday work on special teams. So, as you can see, men, we have a full afternoon ahead of us. We've had our meetings and time for discussions, so it is now time to play ball. Any questions?"

No one dared.

"One more thing. We haven't had good luck with QBs this week. Bobby Kay is on his way to the hospital to get looked at. He's number one until the doctor says otherwise. So today for practice, Vinny will be running the number one offense." Coach Van Watt looked at Vinny. "Battlefield promotions are few and far between, Vacca. This is your chance to show us something."

"Gotcha, coach!" is I guess the only thing Vinny could think to say.

It must have been okay, because Coach Van Watt's response was, "Okay, men, stretch 'em out!"

*   *   *   *   *

The Thursday practice started great and gathered momentum. Considering everything that is surprising. Of the twenty-two starting positions on a football team, West Virginia's blacks have a slight majority. On offense, Montgomery Cash at center, John Pettibone at guard, and Reginald Smith at tackle are on the line. Dhali and Clark are at receiver, and Arthur is the running back. Defensively, Francis Lionel and Tim Seiler are on the line, Michael is the middle linebacker, and Shane Evans, Dougie Roland, and Chandler Childress are the d-backs.

Practicing quietly in a workmanlike fashion, the offense had made the adjustment with Vinny, mostly because my boy is 'on.' He threw precisely into tight coverage when he had to. He scrambled to spread out the defense when nothing was there, something The Kid was unable or unwilling to do. Vinny presented himself as a great decision-maker with a 'gun.' You could see the team's confidence building. Even the defense saw Vinny Vacca, a man who is today cutting them up at times, as the answer to the Runners' lack of point production. Therefore, unlike at Penn State, the offense with Vinny as the leader will do their share in the quest for a victory.

Then it happened. Just at the time when we were becoming reintroduced to each other, when we felt as if we could be a team again, Vinny sent Dhali on a short crossing route with which Coach thought the talented receiver could get yardage anytime we needed it. As Dhal brought the ball into his fingertips, Joe took Sellers into his crosshairs and unloaded on him one of the hardest hits I have ever seen in a college practice during the season. Immediately knowing the ramifications, I thought, 'Why the hell did he do that?' Dhali with some difficulty pulled himself up to his hands and knees, then knees, then ever so slowly to one knee. Trainers came to his assistance as Joe walked away, unconnected to what his hit meant on a larger scale. The white players stood frozen in their tracks as Dhali was helped to his feet. The blacks looked to each other incredulously, their anger, before steeped under the surface, now doing a flash boil. They wanted answers to such an unnecessary act. The coaching staff, sensing revolt, directly jumped on Joe's case, also looking for answers, and wanting to show the black guys they weren't going to with consideration of fairness and of the safety two days before the big game take any crap from anybody.

"What the hell was that, Osbourne?" shouted one coach.

"We said limited hitting, Oz! Watch it!" yelled another.

"We're a team, Oz! That mercenary shit doesn't flush here!" still another piped in, this in reference to his summer job.

Obviously, nothing is going to result from the coaches' mouthings. Dhali is shaken up but all right. The team desperately needs Joe, so there will be no reprimands. He broke his usual vow of silence and, standing in the middle of all of us, coming to his own defense, said, "You run that route, once, twice, but sooner or later the Pitt DB will sniff it out and he'll be after blood. He won't hold back like I did."

After all this I believe two things: a) Joe did hold back, which is a scary thought, and b) Joe set Runner racial diplomacy back about ten years.

Thursday November 6, 1975
8:00 PM

Home with Judy and Alice

I sat silently with Alice on the love seat in our living room. Vinny and Judy have the sofa. The two pieces of furniture comprise a set from the low-to-medium price range, upholstered with an inconspicuous sea foam green print. The color is too light for a college house, certainly unable to hide party accidents. My grandmother used to think in a similar way; I for the longest time thought fine furniture was covered with clear plastic. Anyway, we are fortunate to have a landlord who set us up, and he makes us pay for it. By forking out a cool two hundred per month each, including utilities (the parents didn't mind when they saw the alternatives), we, in comparison to the average student, live in luxury. The sofa and love seat rest among a chair and another love seat, all with the same color scheme, circling the middle of the hardwood floor on which lays a large forest green solid rug. Two other sofas, navy blue in color, not quite matching, sat against the off-white walls in the corner of the house away from the door, which opens from another corner. Laminated tables are positioned with the sofas and seats; coffee tables, a table for our television, end tables, all with appropriate floor and table lamps. Downstairs the basement is finished, with half windows in paneled walls and older furniture. Our place is all well-lit and cheery, with bright modern art framed prints hanging about on the walls, upstairs and downstairs. One part of a wall in the living room is saved for framed snapshot photos of the four of us in various stages of partying to give it our personal touch.

We four are an interesting group. It never occurred to me until it happened that Vinny and I would surround ourselves with such outstanding women without any expectations of sex. Pondering, yes; expectations, no. However you look at it, everything among us clicked. We four have the feeling we have found those college friends you keep for life.

It is unfair that I had earlier talked about Judy and Alice only in terms of their bodies. Since our first group pizza and beer only four weeks into our freshman year, it was apparent to Vinny and me that we should keep these girls around. Sure, they looked good, but in other ways they were damned impressive. Judy is an accounting major, a cutie from Martinsburg who at the time I first met her in an English Comp section I tutored was a sophomore on track to graduate a year early. Her long legs and brains stretched to engulf the class, enticing me to set up that first pizza just to find out what it was I was getting into. We agreed to bring a friend. I brought Vinny, which is always somewhat difficult since there is tremendous potential for me to get lost in his looks. Judy showed up with Alice, a Huntington girl with the aforementioned bod, but also with other redeeming qualities, qualities that Judy said made her one of those rare engineering students who didn't need to study much. After it all, Vinny and I spent half the night wondering what the hell was going on here. The Gunner had just met and fallen head over heels for the Jean Queen, and I couldn't have a woman unless there was little hope for a relationship. So?

As it turned out, Jean was floor buddies with the two of them and staked her claim on Vinny early. Alice and I had a tornado of a romance. She quickly put an end to it with the classic, "Let's be friends." Difference was, she meant it. And Judy came along. Vinny and Mason as Andy and Barney from Mayberry, North Carolina, complete with their Two Fun Girls from Mount Pilot.

Now we sit in our house, our friendships steady and strong. Our house, as CSN sang, a very, very, very fine house, with beer kegs in the yard, life used to be so hard, now everything is easier, you see. If only my head would stop clanging.

Ah, my head. Considering the rancorous tone the black guys felt after Joe stuck Dhali (and I really can't blame them), practice ended with neutrality as dusk began to fall. That of course after I, the fifth receiver in a two-receiver offense, was interestingly inserted in the first line-up to, as the coaches put it, 'give me a few reps.' Only when Coach Van Watt, in my third play, in a tone louder than normal called for a cross did I realize my true purpose this day to West Virginia football. Vinny knew what was going on. Hell, most everybody had caught on, including me, before the two teams approached the line of scrimmage. I, an expendable third team walk-on, and most notably the only white receiver, was being offered as bait for peace by the administration of the university.

It is these situations in which a man's worth is very much tested. Therefore, I psyched myself into believing it was a religious moment, for the team. And, for Vinny; not just another catch of a Vacca pass, performed tens of thousands of times over a decade, but The Moment, coming after all of that time of dreaming of it. The Moment, of course, of our First Completion With The First Team. Never mind I was being set up to get lit up like a Christmas tree. This was special and I wasn't going to do anything chickenshit to fuck it up.

I lined up wide left. On Vinny's count, I as directed took five strides downfield, then cut sharply over the middle, that charged region most receivers love to hate. Not me, boy. Not today. Not any day. Vinny fired a bullet to my gut, being the good friend and not stretching me out for the moving Mack truck that was in line to hit me. I looked the ball in and gripped it tightly. I had it. It was the First One.

The absolute next thing I knew was I was on my back on the turf. But most importantly, I was still clinging to the ball. A couple of guys with defensive shirts gathered around me. "Are you okay?" one asked. Thinking it was Chandler, I responded, "Okay, CC." It wasn't CC. I don't know who the hell it was.

A hand extended to assist me in regaining my footing. I grasped it and stood to find Joe at the end of that hand. He smiled and nodded approvingly, then helped me direct myself back to the huddle. I heard a voice, "That's all for now, Bricker. Tom…." Coach Van Watt approached me. Strange, he never talks to me. That same voice said, "You okay? You took a hell of a lick. That's one of the hardest hits I've ever seen anybody take and walk away from."

"You flatter me, Coach," I said, still woozy.

"No, seriously."

It took some effort, but I gathered the energy to ask, "Who the hell was that?"

"Joe, of course."

Racial discord was relieved, somewhat. The Coach's whistle's shrill knifed through my head.

*   *   *   *   *

Iron City sat askew on the coffee table. I had arrived from the smoker upstairs with a solitary joint of Homegrown, just enough to take the edge off our days.

"I don't want to get stoned," said Alice, warily.

"Same here," replied Judy.

I looked the two over. It must be sweatshirt-with-white-turtleneck-and-flared-Wranglers-with-earth-tone-shoes day in Pi Gamma Pi World. I wonder, is there a calendar?

"Don't worry," I said, "This is mild stuff, cultivated in a bedroom in an anonymous apartment in Pine." Pine is a small town just north of Montani.

"Actually, this is a day I don't want to forget," said Vinny, hoping someone will ask why.

I concentrated on the Bic lighter and the ember.

"What happened, Vinny?" Judy asked.

"I thought you would never ask," Vinny replied, "I led the first team offense today."

"Oh, you're kidding!" exclaimed Alice.

I took a toke and passed it to her. No adverse reaction. Just the right strength. A good Thursday number for four serious students.

"Way to go, Vinny!" exclaimed Judy.

Knowing the girls are too polite to ask how that happened, Vinny continued, "The Kid got sick. I was called into service for the entire practice. Ran against the number one defense, too."

"Ooo, Vinny! We're living with The Quarterback. Is it permanent?" asked Alice.

"His wife of the future might object," I said.

"What?" Judy asked as the doobie passed from Alice to her.

"His wife…you living permanently," I tried to explain. Blank face. Too late. No wonder she's concerned about getting stoned.

"I doubt it. Kid's probably just got the bug," Vinny said.

I piped in, again, this time more conversationally acceptable, "You should have seen him. He looked like he had been with those guys all season. You looked damn good, Gunner, damn good. You're getting in there, mark my words."

"What about you, Mason?" Judy asked as she, too, toked and gave it to Vinny.

"He was in for a couple of series. Did well. Caught a pass and took a helluva shot. I mean one huge hit," Vinny said.

Vinny took a small puff but held it in long for maximum effect.

"But…and most importantly, I held on to that mother," I said.

"That you did," Vinny said, reaching out to slap palms with me. I obliged. Judy moved the joint back to me. It's half gone. So's my headache. I drew on it, possibly my final. It went on to Alice.

"You're moving right along, guys. I'm proud of you," Alice said curling her arm into mine. She has a guy, John, a first year med student. Regardless, I felt it. I propped my boots on the coffee table and placed a pillow on my lap of my Levis, covering it with my cord blazer, which of course was over my blue oxford shirt. I guess I have dress regs, too. Anyway, she giggled. In fact, both girls become a bit more, can we say, casual under the influence of marijuana. Not much more, but just enough to notice. Nothing stupid, just nice.

"Watch it, Alice," said Judy, "Jennifer will kick your ass."

Alice looked directly at me, "That's okay. I'll just tell her what I told Mason a long time ago."

"What's that?" asked Judy. I am the subject of 'girl games.'

Bringing her lips close to my ear, Alice said, "We're just friends."

Playing along, I said, "I need a bigger pillow." The girls cackled. It's not that funny.

Alice backed away to her original position on the other side of the seat. "Tell us, Mason," she asked, "What is it with you and Jennifer?"

I paused, opened my mouth, and paused again. "I don't know," is my answer.

"She apparently knows," Judy said after a swig of her City.

Vinny sat up in his gray and navy ski sweater and Levis, lookin' really good. But, the idiot furrowed his brow and glanced at me. Smooth move, Gunner. I tried to be as inconspicuous as possible.

"Uh, oh" Alice said, who saw the full effect of Vinny.

"What?" Judy said.

"There is something here we don't know," said Alice.

"You're supposed to tell us everything, guys," Judy quickly said in response to Alice.

"That's right. Are you holding back on us?" Alice asked. We all sat silent for a few moments. Alice broke it. "Mason, there's something we don't know."

I shot a look at Vinny. My mistake. Judy saw it.

"Okay," Judy said, "There is a secret. We're not supposed to have secrets, boys." Actually, there is no real agreement to that affect. It's just understood that we as friends are open. It wouldn't stand in a court of law, but why am I now sweating bullets?

"Come on, boys, you're hurting our feelings," Judy said. I looked to Alice, to Judy, then to Vinny, then to a lamp across the room. I'm trapped

"Is it a woman?" asked Alice. Before I even had a chance to answer, she said, "Another woman. You're cheating on Jennifer! Our sister!"

'Our sister!' God, sometimes I hate this greek shit. "All right, now. A couple of things," I said sternly, "First, I'm not cheating on anybody. This…this…other woman as you call her happened before Jennifer. Jennifer happened as I was trying to figure it all out."

"Does it have a name?" Judy asked.

"Yes, of course," I said, but I'm not prepared to get into that. I have to handle the 'Jennifer deal' first. "But, if you're going to evoke this fucking…." I held my tongue, then continued, "I'm going nowhere with this. You've gotta back me up. I don't mean you have to agree with me, but you have to allow me to work this out without running to Jennifer." I then lied. "I really care for Jennifer, but this somebody was there when Jennifer showed up. And I have to work it out. I ask you to give me a chance."

"Why have we never heard about this other woman?" Judy asked.

"I don't know," I replied, like an ostrich with his head in the sand.

"Sounds like you kinda have a relationship with this other woman," said Alice.

"I don't know. Sometimes I wish I did."

"Other times," said Judy.

"Other times I really wish I did." I said.

"Why do you feel as if you have to keep this a secret?" asked Judy.

"You act as if it is one of our moms," Alice said jokingly.

"Close," said Vinny, speaking for the first time in a long time. Great, Vinny….

Alice and Judy glanced at each other.

"Okay, that's enough. It's—"

The doorbell rang. I stopped and froze. Alice ran to dump and wash the ashtray. Judy found the air freshener and sprayed. Vinny located the roach, dashed it out, and ate it. We all took a deep breath, the girls and Vinny sat, and I approached the door. Paranoid? You bet.

The door was opened to reveal Ron Bricker, noted news anchor from Pittsburgh's KDKA-TV. A boyish thirty, Ron shares my Irish facial features, but the resemblance stops there. He's an inch taller than his younger brother, however I had him by thirty pounds of solid sirloin. The girls had met Ron once before, but it was at the funeral of our mother in March. He of course was not at his best, so they could be anxious to meet him again and get to know this brother of mine over whom I am usually spitting when I mention his name.

"Hello, little bro," Ron said.

PD Doughtery, *The Montani Mail*, Coach Lawson, Myron McNabb, Joan Kissinger. The brother with whom I hadn't spoken since the day we buried our mother stood before me and I'm not the least bit moved by it.

"Ron, come in," I said in a nice way. The lack of surprise surprised him, and maybe even hurt him a bit. Good.

He extended his hand for mine. Well, the least I can do is give him a decent handshake. I did.

"How's my bro?" he asked.

"Wondering why you haven't returned his four phone calls and one letter, but otherwise life is peachy." I turned to my girlfriends, who are standing politely to greet him.

"Ron, you remember Alice Calire and Judy Lambert. They're the female half of this house."

"Ohhh…" commented Ron.

"It's not like that," Judy, Alice, and I said in unison. Vinny laughed.

"Hello, Vinny," Ron said, looking for a handshake. He got one, albeit slightly tentative. I have been helping Vinny accept homosexuals. We're just about there.

I love my brother. I truly am excited to see him. I look up to him, admire him. What the fuck is he doing here?

"The aroma," Ron said with a Latino accent, in reference to the pot. "Is that Lysol?" As a Thespian and television personality, Ron has taken being a smart-ass to new heights. Judy and Alice are embarrassed. I think Vinny's more stoned than the rest of us and probably doesn't care. Or maybe he's extremely relieved it's not his father.

"The concept of getting ready for the big game has certainly changed since I played." said Ron, looking at Vinny with the implied message, 'Can you believe a queer played football, handsome?' The Gunner went blank.

"I didn't mean to interrupt here," continued Ron. "I was just in the neighborhood and thought I'd look you up. Nice house. I used to live in what would be your servant quarters, you know, changing the sheets for guys like you and Vinny, bro." Vinny's face reddened.

"How did you find us?" Alice asked, changing the subject.

"I have your address from your letters and I got excellent directions from a friend. Please, I can sense I've jumped in the middle of something. Don't let me stop you," said Ron, sincerely.

I hoped I could further delay what is now the inevitable.

"Well, yes, Ron, there is something. Your brother was just getting ready to reveal one of his secrets…a secret of romance," said Judy.

"Oh, my favorite!" squealed Ron, "Of course, Vinny, that should be of no surprise to you."

"That's it! I've had it!" Vinny slung his IC into one of the navy sofas and fired out of the room into the kitchen and upstairs.

"That reminds me. May I have a beer?" said Ron, pleased with upsetting Vinny so. So thoroughly and so quickly.

"Ron, goddamnit," I said calmly, "You've been here five minutes and you've already insulted my friend and insulted me, for that matter, by just all of a sudden fuckin' vaulting back into my life! I want you to stay a while, but drop the chip on the fag shoulder act, okay? It's not original, and I know how you like to be original, don't you, Ron?"

Ron smiled, having gotten his dig in for the night. "You got me there, little bro," he said. "Okay, I'll be good."

"Good. Now, one more thing. You owe Vinny an apology. I'll call him."

I picked up the phone and punched my line. We each have private lines which can be accessed from the living room phone. Pretty neat. I dialed Vinny. He answered.

"Vinny."

"Vinny. My brother has something to say to you."

"He can go—"

Ron took the phone. "Vinny. Ron. I'm sorry I laid into you so hard and so quickly and with such nastiness and lack of understanding, and I wish you would come back down here and share a beer with me. Any friend of my brother's is a friend of mine…Okay."

Ron hung up. "He's coming. Now, when he gets back down here, I want you to tell us your secret."

"You gonna be good?" I asked my brother.

"Yes. I promise," he replied, as we heard Vinny come down the stairs. Judy and Alice can only hope for good.

Vinny entered the room. Judy said, "You three boys going to play nice?"

Affirmative nods went around the room.

"Okay, Mason," said Judy, "let me rephrase the question for all of us: What woman is keeping you from giving Jennifer the commitment she deserves?"

"Unfair!! This woman was around before Jennifer and in the sense of accounting FIFO, first-in-first-out…and anyway, one cannot account for romance with anybody. It comes from the soul."

"Cut the bullshit, Mason, and get to it," said Alice.

"It's Joan Kissinger," I said.

The women's shock is immediate.

"Who's Joan Kissinger?" Ron asked.

"PhD." said Vinny.

"Bro, you've gone for a professor?"

"Instructor," said Vinny.

"Still…what's she look like?"

"She's an unbelievable fox," qualified The Gunner.

"Bro, you have the hots for a twentieth century fox?"

"I guess," I shrugged, waiting for the girls to escape from their stupor. Judy did first.

"Normally," she said, with excruciating calm, "I would pass this off as a teenage crush. I hope I am wrong about not doing that. Am I wrong? Please tell me I am wrong."

I just looked at her. How do I answer? What's the damn question?

"You are wrong about not doing that," said Alice. "I can just feel it. He's not serious about this."

"Way to go, Bro!" said Ron against the quickly swelling tide.

"Don't listen to him. He's kin, I know, but don't listen to him," said Alice.

"When did you know about this?" asked Judy to Vinny.

Vinny's still trying to decipher Judy's question. "Know what?"

"This!" screamed Judy, venting her flashing frustrations. I know why she is so adamant about this, about Joan. Joan is too…too…too much for them. Her beauty not only doesn't raise cause for admiration, it downright pisses them off. All of them.

"You mean about Mason being attracted to Joan, or about Mason can't stop thinking about Joan, or about Mason skipping classes to work extra for Joan, or about what part of all this?" said Vinny.

Thanks, Gunner, for your perceptive analysis.

"The most recent, advanced part of all of this," said Judy.

Vinny sat still. It is my turn. And that's all right. I've always wanted to tell the girlfriends. I just never knew when or never knew how. Now, here goes.

"I'm in love with Joan," I said. It feels good to live it and say it.

"Teenage crush," said Alice like a homeplate umpire would call a ball.

Judy threw up her arms in exasperation, then cupped her face in her hands.

I looked to Ron. He's been quiet. He usually liked to stir the cauldron. Maybe he's waiting for the right moment. There is a part of me that wants him to jump in here and do just that.

"Let me tell you something about my bro," said Ron, "My bro can't help this. It's as if he has some sort of a transistor misfiring in his brain. It's a bad electronic device that screws up the decision-making process when it comes to women. I doubt if he'll ever have a relationship like you three have, by that I mean a normal one. Don't blame him. He needs medication."

I don't know what to say to that.

"Bro," he continued, to me, "you gotta know, this hot professor is not going to go for you the sophomore split end. But I know you, and you won't give up until the whole thing blows up in your face. This is those college chicks from when you were in high school all over again."

Ron is making me mad as hell. Lawson, Ron, rednecks, the anti-Joan crowd. Everything's going against me. And the discouragement and bafflement of it all is wearing me thin.

"Let me tell you something about your brother," said Vinny, my true friend, the cavalry, "He may have a wire loose. But that wire leads him to do something we should all try every once in a while. He chases dreams. He may look like Don Quixote, but he goes for it. I was there for Roxanne and for Ursula, and let me say to you, I was impressed as they went along, and I was sorrowful at the end, but he went for it, and he impressed me, and my friends and his friends. They were some women, and he went for it."

Vinny finished with his prose only a jock could love, and a red-blooded woman of the seventies could despise.

"Oh, Christ, you're making me sick!" screamed Judy. "Do you expect me to sit here and take that? He went for it? We're not destinations or goals. We're women and people. Jesus, I can't believe I share a house with anyone who actually believes that crock."

"I didn't call you a goal!" said Vinny (I thought he had, too, but you'll never hear me own up to that), "I simply said he seized the moment. And he does it without guarantees. That's what I meant."

"Well that's not what you said," said Alice, "You said men choose women to impress each other."

"No!" Vinny said sharply.

"That's the kind of Cro-Magnon thinking that will keep women barefoot and pregnant," said Alice, "Well, it's not going to happen. Not on my watch, mister!"

Ron and I looked at each other. We're out of the loop.

"Let me rephrase everything," said Vinny, "and say, in one sentence, Mason is brave. Another sentence, without reference to the women of his past, or present: we should all be as brave as Mason."

With deference to the men, because we are men and we will never get it right, the womenfolk let us off the hook, but not before they had the last word. "Okay, Vinny, you've had your last chance," said Judy. "You've had your milligan. One more outburst of primeval thinking with regard to women and…and…well, just don't do it."

It is golf terminology and it means you get to tee up for one extra shot per round after screwing one up and it's 'mulligan,' but Vinny and I aren't about to tell her that. We simply turned our attentions to the original topic of conversation. But, we let them have the first word and will probably again give them the last.

"Mason, sweetie," started Alice, "we're just afraid you're going to get hurt. Hurt badly. Joan has the capacity to do that," Something tells me she was not laying it all on the line.

Judy calmly tried. "Mason, it's like this: where's the commonality? I mean, look at Vinny and Jean. They went through the same things together, even before they met. You and Joan, well, you and Joan wouldn't work. That's partly because, uh, she was probably at Woodstock and you were in junior high. How can you two relate? You have no common history. She got her masters when you were in high school. What would you guys talk about? And her family? How could you go home with her to meet her mom and dad? It would be much easier, very much easier to meet Jennifer's parents than to meet Joan's. Dr. Pierce would accept you, embrace you. Mister or Doctor or Sir Kissinger would wonder how this ever happened."

They just don't like her.

"How did it happen, Mason?" Alice asked.

"Well…uh…" I stumbled, not really having a clear, conversational chain of events, "You know, I worked for her, we talked, she seemed interested, I wrote her a letter—" On that, Alice's face fell into her hands and Judy rocked back, asymmetrical frustration. I stopped to hear what they had to say, but what the hell, I'm taking charge of this conversation. "Look, ladies, as I said, I wrote a letter, we talked, and she doesn't think it's such a good idea."

"Well, Mason, what did you think she'd say?" asked Alice.

"Well, Alice, sometimes she acted as if she thought it was a great idea," I said with some indignation, "What about you and John?"

"I knew that would come up," Alice said, "Big difference between one and three degrees. Between three and ten or whatever years."

"It's eight, and the real question here is the older man and the older woman," I added, deciding to let it ride right there.

The room sat in silence for a short while. My cynical brother was the next to speak, "Bro, why do you keep trying to prove you're older than you are. Accept it, man. Accept where you are."

The fuse is lit. "Who in the hell do you think you are," I started, "to march into our home and tell me what to do? You have no right to tell me how old I am, or should be." And forth it came. "You were derelict of what I think were your duties at a time when we could have used your help. Mom wouldn't do it. Same goes for Juny. But there was shit to do, even though I was only thirteen years old, and guess who did it? Guess who talked to all the lawyers and bankers and insurance men? You were in Pittsburgh starting your career as a fuckin' TV star anchor and there is nothing wrong with that, but there was stuff to be done. Take a look at your investment account. How do you think it got up there? I didn't do it directly, but I was the only one who would talk with and listen to Stan and the rest is history. Now, I'm not trying to hold myself up as a hero, or you as Lucifer, but consider all this when you again ask the question why am I trying to be so old."

Ron is not about to go down easily. He went for it. "I reported your troubles with your football team today. Funny…our family knows Myron McNabb. I walked in on a conversation between him and our father, our illustrious, decorated father in his manly workshop basement. Didn't hear it, but I saw some twenties change hands. How masculine! How else do you think we survived after all the mark-offs and Pabst Blue Ribbon?"

I sensed Alice, Judy, and Vinny wanted to leave right then, but couldn't find an easy way out. Too bad for them. It got worse.

"You motherfucker, you can't come into this house and talk like that. You keep talking like that and I'll plant a fist into that pretty TV face and throw your bony ass into the street! You hear me?"

"Face up to it, Mason. Dad volunteered as the manager of the public swim pool. No blacks allowed. He could have turned the tide on that one, but McNabb got to him first. Dad pleaded no contest. Something like Pontius Pilate, sort of washing his hands of the whole thing."

I was on him quicker than a cat, absolutely pummeling him, crying, fists flying. Vinny jumped on my back and rolled with me away from Ron but not before I got in some good pokes. As I was pulled away, his bloody face was exposed to the girls, one of them emitting an "Oh, my God!" as the other made tracks, I guess to the downstairs bath for a cold compress cloth. When I arose, Ron had the cloth on his face. I hope I broke his nose.

The sofa and the love seat were askew and the coffee table legs had scooted the rug into a fold. I felt a need to rearrange everything, and I did so. Then the anger reappeared in a raw form. It's so overwhelming, I want to rip something apart. My face became hot, my breathing rapid. Involuntary twitches, like sobs without tears, intrude my chest. I have to get out of here. Running upstairs to my room, I collapse on my bed and shout a muffled scream into my pillow.

*   *   *   *   *

The door knocks slice through my deep stupor.

"Enter!" I shouted.

The opened door revealed Ron minus compress but plus Vinny.

"Welcome. Have a seat." Even after a fistfight, I still have my manners. "Beer?"

"I'll get 'em," said Vinny, exiting.

We brothers sat there in silence. "I think you broke my nose," said Ron finally. "The station won't like that."

I wanted to say, 'I think you were begging for it.' But I conceded to a "Sorry, I'll pay for the doctor. I'm really sorry."

Vinny stepped back in with three fresh Cities. "We're getting low. Time for another road trip." We bought our beer ten miles away in Pennsylvania at a place called State Line Market, which is a big, warehouse-type building with coolers and nothing else. West Virginia had a cap on alcohol in beer at half of our neighbors. It was cool in Montani to frequent State Line. They have a hell of a business.

"Where are the girls?" I asked Vinny.

"Studying."

"They must think I'm a real ass."

I heard no arguments.

"Listen—" I said. Then I looked to Vinny. "Do you want to stay for this?" I asked.

"In the name of our damage deposit, yes."

Reasonable. "Ron, I'm sorry. You caught me at a bad time. I've had a lot to put up with lately."

"Yeah, ol' Myron helping your coach take himself down. That's a lot to put up with." Ron said sarcastically.

Quickly, I said, "There are some things you don't understand. First, how I feel about you is an item you are completely missing the boat on. But we'll get back to that. Second, and very important, is you must know that I am the guy who took the evidence to the newspaper. I narced on Myron and the coach." That should shatter a few notions.

Ron removed the beer from his lips in mid-swig. He stared at me for the longest time, blank. Finally, he said, "How did that come to pass?"

I told him the story, from discovery to insult to discussion, and right into doing what I thought, what we thought was the best thing to do. And I told my brother of the aftermath, the divisiveness and the dissension. He still stared at me, finally breaking eyelock to glance at Vinny and ask him, "Were you in on this?"

The Gunner proudly answered, "You betcha."

Ron asked if he could smoke. "Only if we smoke this," I said, as I reached into a box in my nightstand and produced another doobie of Pine. His eyes lit and his face beamed. The brothers are about to burn their first joint together, with Vinny as our honored guest.

After much concentration on the toking and the passing, and after much consideration of the new information, Ron broke the ice, "You know, Myron draws from the ranks of conservatives such as you two to recruit for his cause, his cause of and for the Wasps, in particular the Wasp male, the straight Wasp male. I have friends, homosexual friends, down here in the great state of West Virginia, who have been targets of McNabb."

I'm tired of these 'conservative' tags, like everyone throws me in there with Bonzo's leading man. Still, "Targets?" I asked. "How?"

"He hits our sustenance first," said Ron, "Employment. You're marked gay and you screw up the least little bit, and you're out of a job. And it's tough to find another, because of what is believed by the Wasps who run businesses…they believe you're disruptive."

I can only be empathetic, again. My good friends are black, my brother's gay, and I belong to the race and persuasion which puts them down and pushes them back. There is not much to say beyond that.

"I'm sorry," I said, "I don't know what to do."

"Your deal with the newspaper is certainly a huge gesture. Again, I'm proud of you for standing up for your beliefs, and surprised by your beliefs."

"Thank you, Ron," I replied, "but I'm not sure I'm standing up for anything. I've positioned myself as Deep Throat." The Pine marijuana was just strong enough to give us a mild, a very mild buzz, very gentle, but allowing for lucid conversation, giving Ron and me a chance to lay down the arms and come to agreement. I should ship some of this to Anwar Sadat and Golda Meir.

"You could have just ignored it. But you didn't," said Ron. "I have to admit I am pleasantly surprised. From the way I viewed you at Mom's funeral, I was almost sure you were one of 'them.'"

"Well," I responded, "I don't know what I did to make you feel that way, but it's not true. I'm not one of 'them.' I'm one of 'us.' I don't merely…here they are…I love you, Ron. You're my brother." I cry a lot. It's the Irish in me.

And we stood. And we embraced a tearful embrace. None of our feelings about some things have changed. Feelings and beliefs about football, Dad, why Ron left the family, all these remained. But, new truths are willingly accepted. New trusts are formed. I have always admired my brother as a big brother should be, but I not for the longest time have I ever felt closer to him than this evening. Through all the differences working against us, today almost by luck we have truly found each other.

Ron finished his beer and decided to leave for the home of a friend in Eastern who had invited him to stay. Vinny wished Ron well and went to his room. I walked Ron to the door.

"Damned good of you to come over. You'd better put some ice on that," I said motioning to his nose.

"That's okay. I don't really think it's hurt that bad. Actually, I think things are good after tonight. In fact things are so good…"

"How good are they?" I wonder where he's going with this, a state of mind in which I am often in my dealings with Ron.

"Things are so good, I invite you to the newsroom to watch me at work and find out for yourself why the majority of Pittsburghers can't be wrong by voting me the city's best anchorman." I never catch him on TV since I'm always into something else. Seeing him in action would be great. "But, only if, only if, you can get me a ticket to your performance this weekend."

I'm dumbstruck. Ron hasn't been to The Ridge since just before his declaration of independence from Dad. "You're serious about this new relationship shit, aren't you?"

"Very serious," he said.

"Then, please be here by seven thirty Saturday morning. You can have breakfast and get your ticket."

"I'll do it. Get two. I'll bring a friend. He's like me, if you don't mind."

"You mean he's a fucking jerk?" I asked with a smile.

Ron laughed, "Yes," he replied with a deadpan.

"Then I'm looking forward to it," I said.

On that, we exchanged our goodnights. I watched Ron enter his Datsun 280ZX and drive away, thinking that maybe this miserable week has turned a corner.

Thursday November 6, 1975
11:30 PM

In my room, in bed, in the dark

Ron effectively left the family right after my father's burial, not even wincing during the gun salute, looking distracted instead of dismayed and disheartened like the rest of us. Sure, he went back to the house and made yet another sandwich from yet another cold cut tray. He mixed with the guests, displaying the best of his acting ability, playing the role of the survivor, the elder son, the new leader of the family. The fact was he had no intention of carrying out his dramatic appearances. He simply couldn't wait to return to Pittsburgh and continue the post-collegiate life he had carved out. The family was, as he saw it, on its own.

An hour before he left, Ron took me to my room and laid the news down on me, not of his return to Pittsburgh, but of his secret of secrets. He told me it was difficult for him to tell me, not because the secret was bad or anything, but because he didn't want to hurt me. At that time Mom came into the room and stood with Ron, her hand on his elbow as if to steady him. Then Ron told me: he is gay, a homosexual. It was something he had known throughout his life, he said, but something he couldn't get a real handle on until he was in college. It's almost as if he was born with it but in a sense he had to discover it. But most importantly he hoped I didn't hate him because of it. "I can't help it, Mason. It's my nature."

I saw Mom was with him with her acceptance. That made me feel safe to do the same. Without a word, I reached for him and hugged him, telling him without actually saying it that I was all right and most importantly he was all right, too. On that my brother soon walked to the front door, ambled down the stairs, hopped into his Ford Maverick, and left. He returned for that Christmas and then never again until my Mom's funeral.

I walked up to my room, locked the door, and cried and prayed. In my own thirteen year old mind and soul, I prayed for Ron, not that he needed to be changed or that his homosexuality was an evil curse, or even evil in and of itself. I didn't even feel it was wrong. But I had heard the talk in school, especially among my teammates. To put it mildly, they had no respect for gays whatsoever. That's what I was worried about. I was concerned for my brother and his life in this cold world. And I was concerned about me. Looking into the darkness of the vacuum, I had no father and a gay brother. There was no choice: I had to get into the following day's game.

In ten minutes, I was on the telephone with my coach, pleading my case. "I realize I haven't practiced all week, Coach, but it's the last game of the season. My father would have wanted it that way. He would have wanted me to play. My football games meant so much to him. And they mean so much to me." Joan said I excel in soliloquy. I started early. Coach conceded. And everything I told him was true. I just left out one important part: I only had one game remaining to prove to the world I was not a fairy.

My team welcomed me. And after my maniacal performance on the field, they lauded me. I got home that evening, relieved. We had won. I was a major contributor to the victory. And, I had saved myself. No one who put three of the opposition players out of the game with vicious hits could have ever in my eighth grade reasoning be called a fag. And I have rediscovered tonight that despite that feeling of vindication that evening, and despite my reputation as a hard-nosed football player both in prep and college, a reputation of the highest order on the gridiron, I never really escaped the need I had that Thursday evening in October of 1969 to justify my masculinity. My father and my brother, both always throughout my high school and college years physically absent, drove me to my athletic successes. And as my brother watches me play on Saturday, he will in an interesting way be sitting beside my father.

*　　*　　*　　*　　*

Friday November 7, 1975
6:30 AM

At home, in the shower

I lead a life on strange paths. Ron last night reminded me of my days with Roxanne and Ursula. God, I haven't thought of them for such a long time. I guess Joan has taken their places. Again, three examples of propping up a fragile manhood. Jeez, I need a psychiatrist. Maybe I'll wait until after my college football career is over. Don't want to lose that neurotic edge.

Joan has called it a ball game. The cars are emptying the parking lots and the maintenance guys are sweeping up the rubbish. Why am I still dressed and ready to play? I guess it is just going to take time, time amazing in its duration especially when you consider the nature of the relationship. Sure, there were the mere minutes of that Saturday evening on the porch after the plane landed safely. And there were those occasional furtive glances, stealth shots I caught and passed off as Motown so aptly put it, "just my imagination runnin' away with me."

Until the episode on the porch. No one believes me about this, except maybe Vinny, who would believe me about anything. Everyone is all too willing to cast me upon the pile of men who for over a decade have been so overcome with Joan's beauty that they became unknowingly self-deceptive, leading with the best in candy, flowers, and concert tickets. I bet this Chicago girl has seen some great bands and hasn't shelled out one buck. Maybe that's why I'm getting nowhere. I offered only prose, and I sold it all with the first letter. That doesn't leave much to be said in the second letter. "Dear Joan, Well...I...uh...still love you...and...what do you think of this crazy weather?" In my fervor to not be like the others, I've now painted myself into a corner. As it turns out I am just like them. How did I allow it to get this bad? Maybe I'll just stay in the shower all day.

"Yeeeeow—yeah! Allright!! All right!!" screamed Vinny as he barged into my bathroom and flung the shower curtain open. Luckily I'm not doing anything I would look damned silly getting caught doing.

"I'll be out in a minute, Vinny," I said as if I hadn't noticed his entrance.

Vinny jumped on the toilet with both feet, and exclaimed, "Guess what? Guess what!"

"Jean isn't pregnant," I said.

"Nothing is better than that," said Vinny, more calmly, "But right now, this is sooo much better. The Kid underwent an emergency appendectomy...shit, most of the time I couldn't even say that, but today, I'm on, baby, ON! Because that makes me the starter tomorrow, Cheetah! I'm in there!"

I'm shocked. Naked, dripping wet, and shocked. Then I moved to happy, ecstatic. My man is the quarterback! Wow! This soon as a sophomore, for medical reasons, true, but fuck it!! He's the man!!

"Congrats, baby! You're the QB! Against Pitt! At The Ridge!"

Suddenly, Vinny lost expression and color. He slowly raised his left hand to his mouth, turned, flipped up the toilet lid and seat and as I ran out of my bath with a towel wrapped around my waist, very fortunate since Judy is in my room in a robe along with Alice in a long sweatshirt and shorts.

"He's the quarterback?" Alice asked.

"That's what he tells me, and by his actions," I said as I motioned to the bathroom door, "it is true."

"Damn, our Vinny, the man," said Judy.

We heard water in the sink and the toilet flush. I cracked the door open. "Mouthwash in the medicine chest, Gunner." I turned to the girls. "I'd get sick, too. Weighty responsibilities."

"Yeah," said Alice. "In a big way."

Vinny exited from my bathroom to a round of applause. He bowed.

"I'm glad I was here instead of Jean's place," The Gunner said, "That may have been messy. But, I've kinda been getting myself ready since Lendel went down. But, still it's a surprise."

"You are the man! You're on! Quick, let's take a bag of blood and a sperm sample," I said.

"Let's not," said Judy, still smoldering from last night. "Let's just live in the moment. How does it feel?"

"I can tell you because you're my closest friends, I'd better just eat dry toast and soda crackers today."

"That's okay, Vinny, around the end of the fourth quarter you'll get used to it," I said in jest.

"You'll do great. Just great!" said Judy.

"Yeah, from beginning to end," said Alice.

"My man! I knew this would happen! Mr. Blue Chip! The Man!" I said, poking at his right arm.

"Ah! Ah! Watch it!" Vinny said, smiling, protecting 'the rifle.'

"Let's all get dressed and reconvene in the kitchen," suggested Alice.

"Let's all get naked, in a coed way, and stay in my room," I said.

"Don't you have enough women problems?" Alice asked sharply.

"Potential women problems," I replied. "Potential."

"Potential like a land mine," Judy ripped.

"Damn, this got nasty fast," I said. "Let's not take away from Vinny's day."

The girls' faces turned softer in consideration of Their Gunner. "Okay," mumbled Alice, "Let's take this up after the game."

"Great!" I exclaimed, thrilled at the prospect of buying time with Jennifer and Joan. Judy stuck her tongue out at me as she walked out. "Enjoy your day, Vinny," she said.

Alice reached to kiss Vinny on the cheek, then she gave me the 'up yours' fist salute.

"Wow! They really despise Joan," I said.

"Today's the day to talk about Joan, Cheetah. It'll keep my mind off Pitt."

"It's all been said, pal," I countered, slipping back into the depression from the shower.

*   *   *   *   *

This will give me something to take my mind off Joan: Vinny Vacca, Runner quarterback. The arm. The mind. The legs. The season tickets. What a story. Boy sits on The Ridge fifty for ten years, turns down the big names to play for the team of his dreams, toils on the scout team for almost two years, then is called into emergency service against the Big Rival which happens to sport a perfect record and the top ranking. This is the stuff from which legends are made. Vinny Vacca, Legend. Honestly, that's what it'll be if he can hold us to within ten and make a game out of it. Think I'm pessimistic? Two game losing skid, head coach suspended, racial obstacles, that's a hell of a load for a new QB to haul. If Vinny can keep Pitt guessing until the final gun, if he can lead our bunch and keep all forty thousand on their collective feet to the end, it will be a moral victory.

I hate moral victories. I want Vinny to get the win, the tick in the W column. He has all the tools, including leadership. Maybe, just maybe he can pull us together and together we can get the upset. And what an upset it would be. Vegas had us listed (and listing) as twenty-four point underdogs yesterday afternoon after the press conference. Vinny might shave that down a few points. His uncle's a bookie…bad choice of words! Vinny's presence may alleviate the QB question and cause the gamblers to look more favorably on us. That's what I meant. He might just do it. If I were a betting man, I'd take the Runners and the points. I can see us keeping it close. Fuck it! I can see a win!

The dream of my dreams would be to be out there with my boy. We've got it half right. With a three-receiver rotation, however, I'm two away. Which means I might as well be an offensive tackle. I really can't count on seeing any action with my man. My best efforts would be to bust up a kickoff return or a punt return and get Vinny good field position. That's how I can help him out; do what I do best.

I bet he's nervous as a kid on Christmas Eve. Maybe I can help out by being with him, like a bodyguard. I'll see if he wants to do that. Maybe I should check with Joan first. I'll call her now. I've always wanted to dial all seven digits of her number. Here goes…naa…do it! I don't know…do it now!

5-5-5-4-8-7-6

Ring…I hope Alan's there.

Ring…Time for him to find out….

"Hello?"

"Hi, Joan…this is Mason." My heart's pounding through my ribs.

"Hi, Mason…what a surprise!" More pounding….

"Is that what you usually say when someone has called you at a most inopportune moment?" I'm prepared to telephonically find Alan in nothing but a towel.

"No, then I say, 'I'm so glad you've called.'" She Laughed. I will always die for her Laugh.

"Then, I'm not bothering you…."

"No, Mason, as a matter of fact, I was just thinking about you."

My head spun. I barely got out the next sentence, "So, this is what results when two great minds meet."

"Must be. Now, you were obviously thinking about me because you called."

Then I should be calling you at least fifty times a day. "Yes. I have a favor to ask you. But, first, allow me to tell you why. The Runners quarterback, Bobby Kay, is sick and in the hospital."

"Oh, no! Anything serious?"

"Appendicitis."

"Oh, no!"

"Yes. That's too bad for him. But all is right with the world, because my Vinny Vacca is now the starter."

"Oh, yes!"

"Now comes the favor I want to ask you. I want to be with Vinny as much as possible today to ease his mind. May I please take some of our time together and give it to Vinny?"

"Well, remember I said I was thinking about you…."

"Oh, I definitely remember…."

"Well, I still am, silly boy…."

Oh, Jesus, Joan! Will you please stop driving me crazy?

"Anyway, I thought I would enlist your services today in my opening discussion about Sinclair Lewis' *Babbitt*. I want to try this in the nine o'clock to see how it works. You have a friend in that section, don't you?"

She is referring directly to Jennifer Pierce. I don't know what this means, but my constantly optimistic nature tells me she's at least concerned for Jennifer's availability to me. I don't know why I'm thinking that; it could be a bit of a stretch. I stretch a lot. Anyway, I smiled. "Several."

"You can show off for her," Joan said, ignoring all but one. "Can I take you away from Vinny for that hour?"

"Sure…sure…Nine o'clock; I will be there for you."

"I'll see you in my office at eight thirty for further discussions."

"Eight thirty on the dot."

"Good. You know how I like punctual men."

I have no idea where if anywhere she was going with that one. I think she likes toying with me. To which I responded, "Uh….sure."

"Goodbye, Mason."

No, wait! Oh, hell. "Goodbye, Joan." I didn't want the conversation to end, which is consistent with everything Joan. Good God, please help me.

Friday, November 7, 1975
7:30 AM

To class

"Vinny," I said over wheat chex, carefully keeping the milk from slopping onto my white shirt and gray herringbone blazer with Levis and yada, yada, yada. "I'm free from duties to Joan today after ten."

"Duties to Joan," Judy said, holding her crumpet, dressed in a navy turtleneck and silver slacks, completely different from Alice's silver turtleneck and navy slacks. Greeks…Jesus. "Free from duties to Joan. This relationship needs some balance."

"Listen, woman," I said to Judy. "And also you, woman," to Alice, taking a slug of her instant breakfast. "I'm helping to teach your class today, so be kind."

"Teaching?" squealed Alice. "This is too much. We know. Joan knows. Jennifer doesn't know. Jean…."

"Doesn't know," said Vinny, reaching into the saltine box, dressed like the white Superfly without the lid. I returned with a thumbs up.

"Please, Judy, Alice, no matter how disgusted you are with this and me, please keep it in the house. I know the irony of me assisting Joan in your class may be unbearable. But, please…"

"Okay, no harm is done, except to Jennifer," Judy said.

"Actually, Jennifer does know. The topic came up yesterday when she visited my office," I said.

"What could you have said?" Judy asked.

"I told her it was a crush and I'm over it."

"That's not what you told us last night," Alice said.

"No, it's not." I said, hoping the whole topic will pass. It didn't.

"What do you want us to do about it, Mason?" Judy asked.

"Please just keep it among us in the house. I'm in the process of figuring out an exit strategy. That's what I'm doing." I said, like trying to find a way to make Joan see me as a man with overpowering appeal.

"Why don't you just drop it?" asked Alice.

"It's not that easy," I said.

"Why?" asked Judy, "Do you think Dr. Kissinger cares what you do, beyond calling her at night and prowling around her house? Mason, she sees the same thing Alice and I do. If you think she looks at you as a prospective boyfriend, you are suffering from a misconception at best."

"Let it die, Mason," said Alice.

This is not what I want to hear this morning. By the way, they weren't in on the latest phone conversation. 'Silly boy.'

"Okay, this morning in your nine o'clock you'll see my effective neutrality toward your instructor. And, you'll also see respect for Jennifer." I stood up to rinse out my bowl.

"What the hell is effective neutrality?" asked Alice.

"Kindness without the expectation of romance."

"Whenever you get wordy, Mason," Judy said, "your bullshit factor goes way up."

"Okay, I'll just drop it," I said.

"That's better," said Judy.

"Just do what you told Jennifer you were doing," Alice said.

"All right," I said, without any intention of doing what they said.

"Are you boys driving to school?" asked Alice.

"I don't know, Vinny, are we?" I asked.

"I'd better save my legs," Vinny said. "I'll drive. Besides, if I need to get sick, I'll just pull over to the side of the road."

"Oh, we'll drive," said Alice.

"I'm just kidding," said Vinny.

"No, we need to get home early this afternoon to prepare for tonight. We'll drive ourselves," Alice said.

*　　*　　*　　*　　*

We pulled the doors shut on Vinny's longmobile. "Now, what was that you were asking about being free from Joan?" The Gunner asked as he raised the automatic garage door and turned the ignition.

"Oh, I thought we'd hang out today, you know, I could walk you to class, meet you afterward, lunch, just hang out, you know." One too many 'hang outs' and 'you knows.'

Vinny wheeled out into Donnalley and headed down the hill. "Do you think I need somebody to be with me?"

"I thought you might want somebody like me to be with you."

Vinny drove silently around the curve on Donnalley toward University. He stopped at the intersection, "Actually, I might like that."

"Let's do it. We have spent a great deal of time dreaming of this day. Let's make the most of it." I think Vinny genuinely appreciated my offer, for the reason of just being together and for the reason of being his watchman. Once the word gets out about his start, Vinny will cease being just another student, in light of recent events and with regard to Pitt coming to town. He may need some help out there as his status as a celebrity grows, most likely exponentially. "I'm free at ten. You're at Amster, right?"

"Right."

"I'm downstairs. I'll meet you there." With respect to getting used to the recent events, we rode in silence for a while.

Vinny pulled up to the light at Pleasant Street. "How did Joan know to let you off?" he asked.

"I called her this morning and asked. She was very understanding. She's not the backstabbing bitch Alice and Judy make her out to be."

"Yeah, but I can see why they feel that way," Vinny said as the light turned green. "Even Jean dislikes her."

Why am I not surprised? "Well, sometimes…."

"I know," Vinny interrupted as he accelerated through the green light, "you feel sorry for her. I can understand all of your feelings for her, but that one…."

"How would you feel if guys didn't like you?" I posed.

"If I were a female, gorgeous with large knockers, pardon me, and rich, I wouldn't give a damn if other girls liked me. It simply wouldn't matter."

"I say it would."

"I say the argument is crap," Vinny said as he wheeled down University below the stadium, "because I have the luxury of parking," as he turned the right signal onto Campus Drive, "in the QB's space." Vinny turned up the hill, then turned into the staff/players' parking lot and pulled into the space with the sign that read 'QB' beside the "Captain' spaces. Michael's here. Ted isn't.

"You have arrived, my man," I said admiringly. "You have made it."

"It's so beautiful, I makes me ill."

"You'll be okay. Just don't take yourself too seriously."

"Good advice," Vinny replied.

I dispensed with the 'slide on the ice' comment. "What are you going to do now?" I asked.

"I thought I'd try to make it to my finance class, since I am a college student, although I do know that doesn't stop you from missing a few." Vinny said.

"I have a meeting with Joan in a half hour or so."

"You actually called her this morning?"

"Yeah, I had a real academic reason, so I dialed the number. For the first time."

"From memory?"

"Of course."

"You are sick."

"Probably."

"Let's go to class," Vinny said.

We exited the car and walked toward Brecht Hall. Amster Hall, the building of our destinations, is on the other side of Brecht.

"Today is going to be some day," Vinny said as we entered Brecht.

"Just wait until tomorrow," I responded.

"I'm not thinking about tomorrow."

"Even though you do get better looking every day," I said, continuing my Namath obsession, borrowing from the title of Broadway Joe's autobiography.

"No, Mason, the key is not one day at a time, it is one step at a time."

"I can go for that, Gunner."

We walked silently as the Brecht eight o'clocks filled, knowing that because the newspapers were put to bed before the story hit, we are among the very few who know. Because of my history I most certainly give football at The University of West Virginia an elevated status. There are students, more in number than even I realize, who don't care who the starting quarterback is or if the game even takes place. Then there are those others who are greatly concerned about the instability of the quarterback position. The masses lie between. You play for the masses because those who don't give a damn never will care, and those who know all the intricacies of the football team will never be satisfied.

The fans in the middle are most appreciative. To them, our work is like that of actors. They love the Saturday shows. They phone home about having a football player in their classes. They hang on our words, wanting to hear what we have to say regardless of the topic. Win or lose, they're there with smiles and congratulations. They may not know much about the game, but they want to be with us. Seven and two, or two and seven, they love us and we should love them and give them whatever they ask for. But, they're so good, they won't ask. Whatever we give is just okay by them. I'm lucky to have them.

Friday, November 7, 1975
8:05 AM

My meeting with Joan

Funny how it happened—the closer we approached Amster, the quieter Vinny became, the quieter I became, and the more I came to realize that I wanted to be with Vinny today because I wanted to bask in his glow. I'm a bit envious. A bit envious is a bit of an understatement. This is our dream and it's being half fulfilled by, with regard to me, the other half. I have these feelings, and I have the guilt associated with having them. Maybe, just maybe I'm not cut out to be a receiver. Wideouts, the great ones, have size and speed and hands. I have little of the first and a great deal of the second, but not enough of the third to make up for what I lack of the first. Dhali and Clark have it all. They lead our receiving corps, pulling in five to seven a game. Tom is a merchant; he can really pick them up and lay them down. Never mind he's not big and can't catch water in a bucket. But he does it well enough to find two or three every weekend. And Dave is the hands guy, with enough size and enough smarts to run precise routes and get his couple a game. But as for the Ivy Boy, with exception to kick coverage I haven't been in a game this year. Maybe I should break away from the dream and get real and move to defense, capitalizing on the speed I have and on the fact that I hit like an avalanche. I wonder what that would do to Vinny and me? What's today going to do to us? I mean today is the first day we aren't on the same depth chart teams. And it'll be that way for Syracuse and the bowl game if we get in one. This could suck.

Vinny and I have been the scout marauders every Wednesday, taking our third-teamers against Michael and his men. I'd find a way to get at least five every Wednesday, even during those times we were running the option, the offense *du jour* of the seventies, an offense not prone to pass. Vinny and I and all the others usually gave the first team defense fits. We take pride in that. Now, the marauder QB has been called up to the big leagues, and we are proud of and proud for him; but we, especially I, feel left behind.

We stood at the Amster steps before I knew it. "See you down here," said Vinny.

"Oh, yeah, see ya. I'm sorry. I was thinking of what I was going to do with Joan."

"You and hundreds of other men," the Gunner quipped, slapping my shoulder. He went to Finance on the first. I trudged up to the fourth. I checked my watch. Eight oh five. I walked back downstairs.

*   *   *   *   *

After strolling around the campus killing time, feeling sorry for myself with regard to love, sex, athletics, you name it, I made my way back for the English department. Walking just twenty feet from Joan's door, it finally dawned on me that my problems with Vinny are selfish. I know I have to be more of a team player and quickly. But all was forgotten when I stood at Joan's office and noticed she had chosen today to show me and all others around an inch of cleavage, a long line for a college teacher. There is no better way for a headhunter such as I to prepare for the biggest football game of his life. The things Dr. Kissinger can do with that navy wool suit would shock Talbot's.

"Joan, I'm here. This is an exciting day," I said. I thought about taking my blazer off to expose the rear pockets of my Levis. How childish. Still....

"That's okay, I got here earlier than expected. Now, tell me the story again. I got lost in it this morning."

The things my imagination could do with the last sentence. "Okay, fifty words or less: Bobby Kay, QB number one, gets sick yesterday in practice and leaves early. Now Vinny, originally the number three QB but now number two because Lendel Ward, the original number two, trashed his knee this week and is out for the season—"

"Lendel is out. Bobby Kay is out. What's a QB?"

Good question. A hundred bucks for you to lean into my face. "QB is the abbreviation for quarterback—"

"Oh, Vinny's a quarterback. What are you?"

No frustration here. I'll do this all day. She's a middle fan. A beautiful middle fan. "I'm a receiver. I catch Vinny's passes—"

"And Vinny's the QB because all the others are hurt and now he'll throw to you. Oh, that's exciting! Two friends! I can't wait to see that. I'll be there, you know. My sister Pamela from Chicago is coming in and we're going to visit and go to the game. How will I know it's you? What's your number? I bet you are really looking forward to this. Your friend's going to throw to you. That's great, Mason. What is your number?"

I didn't have the heart to tell her I probably wouldn't get anywhere near the ball. And…why doesn't she know my number by now? And why is she rambling so? "I'm eighty eight, double ochos, double eights," I said.

"Double eights. Eighty eight. I'll remember that," Joan said.

"Against the number one team in the nation," I continued.

"That's incredible. That's…..just incredible," she said, dreamily, or so I dreamed.

"Ain't it?" I replied.

"I'll excuse that because it was appropriate," said Joan, the English doctor of philosophy, "How's Vinny?"

"Excited. Confident. Nauseated."

"Understandably."

"That's why I called you this morning and asked for the time off today. He may need me and it might be kind of fun for the two of us." I didn't tell her I'm driven by envy, but I am working on that.

"What about your ten o'clock?" said Joan the academic advisor.

"I'll have to let it slide today," said Mason the sophomore.

"You let it slide all the time. What class is it?"

"Philosophy."

"What's your grade?"

I glared at her for asking that 'I'm older than you are' question. "B, I guess," I said with indignation.

"You guess! Mason!"

"Come on…."

"You are too bright to ignore your education like this."

"What ignore…it's not like I'm doing mid-morning bong hits and watching Phil Donahue. I've got a lot of things going on here. Your tutor, leading and learning." Joan rolled her eyes. I grinned. "Football, which has some educational value. All part of being a well-rounded college student. Consider that, Joan, before you brand me as a goof-off. Now, let's get to work."

"Only if," Joan said, "you promise me you will go to each and every class next week."

"Joan…."

"Promise!"

"Okay. Cross my heart and hope to die."

"Don't say die before you play Pitt."

"You're a cutie," is all I can get out.

"I know," is her response.

"And…that's the trouble."

"No trouble, Mason. None at all," she said as an ever-so-slight smile sneaked onto her face, "You've read *Babbitt*."

I don't want to think too hard about the last few seconds, "I studied *Cliff's Notes*." I replied.

"Mason!"

"Just kidding. I read it in high school. Tell me you've never studied *Cliff's Notes*."

"Tell me about *Babbitt*," Joan said, avoiding the statement.

"Two hundred words or less," I started, aware I am redundant with the 'words or less' phrase, "George Babbitt is a successful real estate broker who is presented by Sinclair Lewis as a buffoon. I don't go for that necessarily, but hey. Anyway, he is married to a shell of a woman Myra and has three vessels for children. His life is filled with platitudes and double standards like those around him, and that's what makes it all work. He's able to wrestle all this until his buddy Paul shoots his wife Zilla and then all hell breaks loose. His belief structure openly changes and he espouses these new discoveries and tells them to, aghast, all the movers and shakers of Zenith. Then he has an affair with a very un-Babbittlike woman. He rides this until everyone in his circle thinks much less of him, then the relationship with the woman ends, then in finality to his self-destruction, he tells his wife. Thank God, his wife gets sick, all the pillars of the community come to his aid and he is re-accepted. But, his son Ted quits school, gets married, and gets a job in the factory. Babbitt privately tells him that's cool because he's seen the other side and secretly wishes he could do whatever he wants to do." I raise my hands inviting questions from the floor.

Her expression didn't change.

I waited a couple of moments, then asked, "Is there anything wrong?"

"Oh, no," she said in a low voice, kind of sexy and sultry. Then she sat up and cleared her throat, "You could teach this class," she proclaimed, "You're good. And that's why I am going to try you today, the class, I mean."

"But, of course," I said, trying to help her through. This is officially interesting. Dream on....

"As if you didn't already know, we have differing political philosophies," said Joan.

"Hadn't noticed," I said with a smile.

"We can...." Joan waved her hands in a double circular motion just below her chin. I have great appreciation for that.... "play off....work with each other. I'll start the story and you intervene when you see fit. You know the book and know the class well enough to know when."

I get it. It'll be like making love with our minds. That's close enough. Okay. "I'm in," I said to continue the metaphor she started. I know she did. I'm just following along.

"Good," Joan said, "It'll be good for the students, I think, and fun for us."

"Nothing like having a good time at work," I said.

"Should happen to more people," she said, smiling, "If this works, we'll do it again."

"Early and often," I said. Joan laughed that Laugh, the one I'd run through a snowstorm for a mile in gym shorts to hear. "See you there." I retired to my office to consider all this.

Friday November 7, 1975
8:40 AM

With Michele before 9:00 'show'

Sitting in my very cramped office, work to do, gotta get ready, behind closed doors, I am still. The events of this week have brought me to Friday and I deserve a break from reality because reality can still level me. With exception to Ron, it's so much not going my way that Joan's repudiation of me as a potential and proper suitor has become a constant in my life. But, just when I'm about to forget her and pursue the more likely lover Jennifer, Joan acts interested. As certain as I am that I love Joan I am with due disregard of my id becoming equally as certain I'd be better off without her. Well, today's the day I forget about it. Realizing that the mores of life in the seventies would prevent me from having complete love with the woman with whom I am separated by three degrees, eight years, and a load-bearing wall, it is time to forget about it. She was just charming me because I am doing her a favor this morning, tutoring above and beyond the call of duty. Furthermore, how much longer can I be around the brown-eyed Miss Pierce, within sight of convenient sex with a woman so long-limbed she could possibly touch all four sides of my room at once? I have to have a great appreciation for that. However, this renewed rejection of my feelings about Joan has left me in a quagmire, stuck, empty. And just when I thought it could sink no more deeply, Procol Harum's *Whiter Shade of Pale* came on the box, taking me down another notch or two with its swaying organ melodies, imploring me to come up with the names of sixteen vestal virgins I personally know in an attempt to pull out of my power dive. Leaning back on the stick at number three, a knock rapped at my door.

"Enter."

The door opened. A head peeked in. It's Michele. Not vestal virgin number four, I am almost sure.

"You're not making out with any girls in here, are you?" Michele asked, smiling and Sicilian. She is looking healthy in a gray pants suit and a light pink sweater. Why me?

"I wish," readjusting my dial back to Dr. Kissinger.

Michele looked at me for several instants. She said, "I find it refreshing that you actually embraced a female right beside Joan's office."

"As she was walking through my door," I said softly, cracking a soft smile and pointing to Joan's office to indicate she's in.

"Get outta here!" she whispered, taking both of her hands to her diaphragm to quell any laughter.

"Yep," I said, "Right before you came in."

Michele's face indicated that she's happy to see me happy. She knows what I've been through.

"Damn," she said, as I motioned her to my solitary sitting place. She sat and her gaze became that of a junior high girl. "So, you've gotcha a new woman."

I decided to take it for a test drive. "Looks that way."

"How long you been working on that?"

"A week," I said. "My friends did all the front work."

"What are friends for?" Michele touched my arm. I instinctively looked to the door to Joan's office.

"Stop looking there or I'll sit on your lap." I swear she'd do it.

"Sorry."

She decided to raise her voice a bit. "In your test yesterday, even through the humor, it was obvious to me you are...or were...but probably are still packing a man-sized angst for your forbidden love."

I'm beyond fighting it, especially with the Queen of Human Emotion. "I agree," I said, "But the Stephen Stills Theorem kicks in."

"The Ste—oh, I get it. Go for it. You're only nineteen once. Although I think you are a forty year old man in the body of a nineteen year old, you know, selective in your immaturity. Stephen Stills. I haven't applied that one in a long time."

"I was sitting around in the eighth grade thinking I might need that song one of these days.

"The day has arrived, sweetheart."

"So, you're saying I'm not foolish with Jennifer and Joan?" I asked, expecting a favorable answer.

"You're doing okay."

"You know, Michele," I said, leaning forward, "Joan made Jennifer possible. Dr. Kissinger is not going to be my girlfriend, lover, steady, main squeeze, heater…."

"I wouldn't be so quick to dismiss those," she interjected.

I'm surprised by that remark. "Okay, now you're fuckin' with me. Dr. Kissinger is not going to be my lover."

Michele leaned in. The hallway is silent. Joan's on the phone, hopefully. "But wouldn't it be interesting if she were?"

I allowed myself to dream, "Well…."

"Well…," Michele responded.

"You know something I don't know," I said directly into her eyes.

"Maybe," she said.

"Don't tell me," I said, wanting, dying to know.

"It's a theory, but I'm pretty good at this," said Michele with a friendly taunt. She then stood and exited my tiny office, shooting a wave over her right shoulder. Random Joan theories and Michele teasing. I don't need these things.

Friday November 7, 1975
8:58 AM

With 9:00 section of American Literature
Joan and I presiding

"You chicken out?" asked the face of Joan squeezed through my door.

"Oh, no. Not this. Not a chance to go head to head with the Madame," I said with a smile.

"Remember that. Do you want to walk in together?" she asked.

"Do you want to pour gasoline on the rumor fire?"

"On second thought, better not," Joan replied. "Why don't you go in before me and loosen the crowd up, and I think the correct phraseology is 'head mistress.' 'Madames' have to be married."

"Let's not screw up and do that." I said. Joan gave me one of her Laughs. I walked out of my office, shook my head, and turned down the hall to her class.

The room sits eighty, eight rows of ten. There are forty-four in the class. Most everybody already knows who I am. Others know me better. Gerard Fletcher and Don Crozert are old high school buddies sitting next to the row of windows lining one wall. I see them occasionally up here at The U. They will swear on a stack of bibles that I am lying when I swear on the same stack of bibles that Joan and I don't do the 'wild thing,' as they so tranquilly and lovingly refer to it. I've learned it is better to let guys like that have their visualizations. Next are Judy and Alice, who think Gerard and Don are crude beyond respect, and who also think I am falling into their category. Then comes Jean who knows I'm depraved. Finally, Jennifer, my guardian angel, probably possessing the truth about Joan and me, but heretofore refusing to tell me. So far, it hasn't chased her away. Despite Michele and her postulations, I don't believe Jen has much to worry about.

Nine o'clock on the nose and Dr. Kissinger strides in. The men freeze in their seats and women are disgusted. Like Richard Nixon in 1960, split down gender lines.

Joan rested her two files on the desk as I took my position at a podium near the door. I feel my face flush, praying I won't sweat. Resisting the urge to check my armpits, I looked to Joan. She walked to her podium, ready to address the class. I've seen her in class before. She runs the range between formal and informal, but does it appropriately. In spite of how her female students feel about her, Dr. Kissinger is really quite good at teaching. Still, I've never known of a doctorate degree giving one an aura. Right now, Joan possesses one. I'm sure it's just me. What was I just saying about forgetting 'all that?'

"Good morning," she began, "I'm going to try something today because I think our next selection, *Babbitt* by Sinclair Lewis, is fitting for debate, even though this an American Literature class. I'm going to set up a loose format between your tutor and mine, Mason Bricker, and me," Ohhh...hers "This is one of those books that I think could be better understood if we argue about it. And since Mason and I argue a lot, we are the best two people to do this," Joan smiled. "Any questions?"

No response. Do we argue a lot? We certainly had a burner yesterday. "Mason?"

"All systems go, Chief," I said.

"Then in the first seven chapters of *Babbitt*, Sinclair Lewis shows us a day in the life of George Babbitt, the real estate man living in the mid-sized midwestern city of Zenith around 1920 or so. We meet his family, we look into his business, we meet a friend, and so on.

"First, allow me to discuss the use of the word 'Zenith' as the city's name. As you know, zenith means pinnacle, the ultimate. But, Lewis then talks poorly of the city and what it represents, suggesting if this is the best we have to offer, we are certainly lacking."

"Joan," I interrupted.

"Yes, Mason?"

"Joan, what are we lacking?"

"Imagination, for one thing."

"Where?" I asked as the students stayed glued to the challenge of their teacher.

"Downtown. Around downtown. The entire city lacks creativity," is her response.

"Considering the utilitarian aspect of commerce, how much creativity does he want in a business district?" I had her.

"Enough to keep our spirits alive," Joan said. She got me.

Conciliatory, I said, "Good answer, Dr. Kissinger." She's good.

"Thank you, Mr. Bricker." As I gazed at her, I thought about love and…like a horse and carriage…. Uh…wait….

"Lewis suggests man has created a metal forest with enormous 'steel trees' represented by factory machines and the office towers of downtown. Why do you think man has done this, Mason?"

Luckily I had pulled myself away from thinking about how bright and buxom she is and actually listened to the last half of her statement. "Lewis thinks we build this to ennoble ourselves, but we are actually reduced by what we build. But, I think we originally plan to build to make money, which isn't such a bad pursuit, provided we don't get lost in it. Lewis sets up his main characters such as Babbitt as guys who have done just that. They're really caught up in it."

Joan paused, then asked, "Why is that so bad?"

"What Lewis is suggesting," I said, "and I couldn't agree with him more is it is easier to chase money than examine your soul. It's easier to keep score."

"I couldn't agree with you and Lewis more," Joan said with one of her grins.

"You're trying to trap me, aren't you?" I said facetiously. The class laughed. I'm relieved. *I'm* good. But, at least they're paying attention. I also took this time to examine a few faces. Jennifer looks proud to have me her new man up there. My dad always told me brains will eventually get a woman, even if you don't particularly want her. Speaking of that, it's not working with Judy and Jean. They're not entertained or impressed. And Alice looks to be on the favorable side of neutral. All in all, considering there is nothing I can do about the middle two, I am winning.

"You'll know when I've trapped you," said Joan to a chorus of male 'ooohs.' She smiled and winked. Winked...winked! Uh...I think the trapping has taken place. The end of effective neutrality is upon us

Judy saw the wink and openly spat. "Okay," Joan continued, "next Lewis awakens Babbitt. What's the contrast here?"

I'm in love and confused. I thought this is supposed to be an argument point-counterpoint session. Now I'm called upon to answer questions. That's okay, she can get by with it. "The sleeping Babbitt is a dreamer, a romantic. He's human. But, as he awakens, he transforms into the capitalist Babbitt. He has expensive things surrounding him as he enters the expensive things world. He goes from sleepy PJs to looking like a little boy in his BVDs. That image by the way is precisely the reason I wear boxers."

That last sentence surprised me, but not like it shocked the students. Laughter slowly built to a roar, necessitating one of those looks of disappointed but amused femininity on Joan's face. She had not intended to have a discussion of men's underwear styles today or any day, but she is youthful enough to know the humor in it. It is, however, her duty to keep order, and she did so after several seconds.

"I can't believe you," Joan said. Yes, you can. Look, even Jean thinks it's funny. "Is there anyway to re-dignify this exercise?" Joan asked with a smile.

"No," I replied. "But, I'll try."

"Then, proceed, Mason," Joan said with a slight smirk.

"Okay," I said, "Then, Babbitt puts on his battle uniform, the business suit. He gathers all of his stuff, and now he is fully changed."

"Very good," said Joan, "And to think we did it without talking about your personal articles." The class laughed again. You'd like me in my boxers, Dr. Kissinger.... She continued. "Next, Babbitt had to deal with his children. They're dreamers, his eldest daughter, Verona, and his son, Ted. Their dreams run counter with the fully awakened Babbitt."

I don't like her implication. "But, why is this bad, Joan?"

"Why is it not bad, Mason?"

"I'll tell you why it's not bad. Everyone is fulfilling his or her roles. Fathers are supposed to bring home the money, so his kids can dream as they are supposed to. I mean, you have to have an anchor to some semblance of reality to hold down a good job and support a household."

"Good answer, Mason," my ideal of a woman said.

"Then I've trapped you," I said as a female chorus of giggles took over. He burned the bitch, they thought.

"You'll know when you've trapped me," Joan said. The men roared. She smiled. I smiled, face hot, having lost the cool. Just rip my heart out of my chest and hand it to me, okay, Joan?

"Okay, Mason," Joan continued, as the class calmed while Judy and Alice, as if on cue, both squinted a 'fuck you' look at me, "This brings us to his values structure. There is one example concerning foreign governments and our involvement with them. He uttered two phrases that were grossly inconsistent, giving us a look into Babbitt's mind. He thinks he's wise, but his wisdom comes from the simplistic thoughts of others. That's okay with him because he's successful, and that success verifies his values."

That edge into liberal tripe really let me know why I am here. "Joan, I'm concerned with the inability of the citizenry of this country to come up with an occasional original thought, so in that regard I'm in agreement with Lewis. But it's just not that simple. There's a time to think and a time to do. This capitalistic system, which by the way is not dead and working as best as it is able to in this day and age, was built by thinkers thinking and doers doing. We need both." I closed with pride.

Joan stared at me with a solemn face. "You almost sound like somebody's father."

"I almost take that as a compliment," I said. "But, you know, Babbitt's an easy target for guys like Lewis because he's so ominous. However, the Babbitts pay tuition and fees and room and board so we can sit in classes like this one and bitch and moan and reexamine. We're all in this together." I could have walked out of the room right then. Possibly, I should have.

Joan smiled and hesitated. Maybe she liked what I said. Maybe Michele's...oh, bullshit, Mason. "Speaking of togetherness," she resumed, "when Babbitt gets downtown, he is with many other people like him. I should say men like him. Lewis infers they're like multiple carbon copies. Individualism is gone, but this is how America runs."

Here we go. I said, "I don't like the way you said that."

"No, you don't like what I said."

"With all due respect, Dr. Kissinger, that's not true."

It's as if she didn't hear me. "Lewis is establishing Babbitt as a faceless man who will, as the book progresses, seek his individuality," she said.

I'm primed to argue. "And the satire evolves from the fact that he already has his individuality, that he is a faceless man because he has a husk for a soul. Once again, his struggle must come from within."

Joan looked at me like I didn't make any sense. Then she didn't make any sense. "Man's facelessness comes from commerce. The pursuit of money wrings the life out of us,"

I countered. "Only if you let it. Only if you become a slave to the pursuit. Commerce is not to blame. Man is to blame."

Quickly, Joan said, "It's inevitable that a man, or a person, sell his or her soul to chase money. I've seen that happen."

My posture began to assume an athletic stance. "That's not true. The chase puts one at greater risk, but it doesn't have to be that way. I've seen that happen."

We simultaneously reached the conclusion that we are arguing for the benefit of ourselves. Joan suddenly exhibited self-control. I'm ready for a battle. We paused for a moment or two. The exercise now sounds as if it's coming from a political science class. Then, Joan spoke, "We might be getting a little off track here." Her voice of reason reigned. I succumbed to the maturity. But it is also evident that our passions can spark, even in front of a few dozen students. I view the whole incident as a positive.

"Let's continue, Mason."

"Got'cha, coach." One has to care to disagree.

"Lewis leads us to believe," Joan said, "Babbitt is not a happy man. His brain is atrophied, as is his soul, but Lewis does suggest his interest in sex is alive."

"Poor guy," I said.

"Why do you say that?" Joan asked, trying to suppress her surprise.

"If your intellect and values system are about gone, but you still want sex, you're nothing more than an alley cat with food service."

The class chuckled.

"Isn't that what men want to be?" queried Joan. A few feminine ohs and ahs broadcasted from the class.

I stood firm. "Now that you've insulted approximately one-third of us in this room, let me speak for the men and say that we have feelings. Some of us don't quite know where they are or how to use them, but we have 'em."

Joan must have thought that was going nowhere. "Whatever you say, Mason."

I agreed. "Let's drop this subject."

"Moving away from sex…," said Joan.

"…before we have a stand-up, shouting match…," I said.

"Wisely…Lewis presents Babbitt's business ethics. The core of his business values is external. Business is manly and you must look like a man."

"Which," I interrupted, "makes for great satire. I've got friends who I think will do very well in business when they graduate and they look absolutely nothing like a man, not at all."

"Now that's a good point," Joan said, "Even though the book is staged in the early twenties, the story is timeless. And, unfortunately, women are still having a difficult time breaking into the manly business world. But, that's not necessarily Lewis' point."

"You're not going to talk about sex again are you?" I asked in jest. It worked. The class laughed.

"No," is all Joan can say for the time being, but the corners of her mouth turned up slightly. She continued, "Babbitt's core is driven by self-deception and subsequently by the use of dishonesty which, according to Lewis, has been 'sanctified by precedent.' This is well-illus-trated by Babbitt's land deal with the grocer."

I took over. "This is good stuff if the reader realizes *Babbitt* the book is satire and Babbitt the man is a caricature."

"That's easy with capitalist pigs," Joan added. Holy shit, that's strong…there's something in her life…. "Next, we follow Babbitt to lunch and meet his good friend Paul Riesling," Joan had moved on pretty fast. 'Capitalist pigs.' Damn…"Riesling is different than Babbitt in his body frame and his speech, in both of which Babbitt thinks he is superior. But he is Babbitt's confidant, and is so because Babbitt feels superior. It is at this lunch where Babbitt returns to the humanity in which he existed in his baby blue pajamas. He confides in Paul about his feelings of dissatis-faction. Paul then turns the table on Babbitt, complains about his own life, displaying a recklessness which Babbitt experiences vicariously. With this, and also with Babbitt taking care of Paul, Babbitt can return to his world."

"Babbitt maintained his superiority over Paul and got a kick of his own," I said. "But most importantly, Babbitt does realize something is wrong. Maybe he does have a trace of a soul."

"A trace," said Joan. "Then we find Babbitt at home, at dinner, quarreling with his family. Ted wants a new car, showing he's Babbitt's son. How's that, Mason?"

Here come those questions again. But, I'm a pretty smart guy. "Ted wants it all now. He wants a hot new car, hot new job, and money, now, without work. Well, Babbitt was always a man to work hard, but he wants hot new opinions and hot new thinking, without the expense of reasoning. They, father and son, are essentially the same."

"Also, Mason," she said. I've never heard her say my name so often. It's sweet. "You earlier spoke of the Babbitts paying tuition. Well, why are they doing it? Lewis thinks they are looking for a prestige education, not a real one. And for whose benefit? Sometimes it is difficult to say." You and Northwestern versus me and The U? Don't give me any of that 'prestige doesn't matter' crap, darling....

"Babbitt then closes his day by preparing himself for dreamland. He alludes to the compromise of earlier dreams to become what he is now, and he does this without knowing. But he goes to bed resolved of his success, then he turns himself over to the fairy child."

"Joan," I said, "everyone compromises dreams. And not to accept mediocrity, but to accept life on its terms. Sometimes I can't buy Lewis' expectations."

"You're right, Mason," said Joan, "He demands much from his readers. Most satirists do. That's the key here. And also, you can satire most anything. Parents, children, work, school, religion. Football, Mason."

"Academia, Dr. Kissinger," I shot back.

"Republicans," she said.

"Liberals," I said, "Oh, but no, since liberals control the press and literature."

"What a litany! Anyway, our man Mason seems to forget what happened in 1974. I don't think that was a left-wing conspiracy."

"Apparently not." I have long-since resigned to the lurid truth about Tricky Dick.

"That's a good answer, Mr. Bricker. We'll have Mason in our class a couple more times or whenever we need someone to publicly thrash," I heard female laughter. I can only see Joan smile. "But, now I'm going to give him time for some closing remarks. Mason?"

"About *Babbitt*?"

"About anything."

I'm surprised, but the discussion has gotten me well oiled. "Joan, you lead us to believe that guys like Babbitt have steered us toward demise. With regard to Republicans, it surely seemed that way. Nixon and his court jesters made us all look pretty foolish. But his personal failures don't take away from the facts that Keynesians could be on wrong more than they're right. With his wage and price controls, Nixon himself could fall into that category. Sorry, I've fallen off the subject. Where was I?" Keynesians? What the fuck? I can't tell who has more glaze over the eyes, the coeds or me…. "Oh, anyway, less government and lower taxes are better for the nation. Less is more. For the entire nation. Just remember, you'll probably never read satire about liberals since they control the publishers. Where do I stand? I'm a social centrist. And, thank you, my fellow Americans."

Several men stood and applauded.

"I closed my eyes," Joan said, "and I heard my conservative economics professor. But, please tell me, Mason. What is a social centrist?" She laughed and shook her head.

"In my case, I'm against unions, but for blacks and for environmental reform," I said, sticking my tongue out at her after my very lucid answer.

Joan narrowed her eyes and grinned, capitulating to the ribaldry of my tongue. She said, "I'm sure all the proponents of integration and the environment are happy you're on their side." The coeds smiled and nodded their heads. They and their instructor have reached common ground, possibly for the first time this semester. I'm happy to help in any way I can. "And thank you for enlightening us." She raised her chin and nodded to counter her sarcasm.

"The pleasure is *mine*," I said just before more applause.

Joan looked at me pleasantly, "But, seriously, Mason thank you." I guess I gave her what she wanted. Wow! That's a nice thought.

"Thank you again, everyone. And, thank you for the opportunity, Dr. Kissinger."

"The pleasure is mine," she said, winking. Again! I smiled back, then turned and walked out before I almost passed out.

Friday, November 7, 1975
9:30 AM

Michele

I enter my office to drop my stuff off, doin' the double fist pump. I killed them! Joan never nailed me. I always had something to say, and most of the time it was good. Yet another example of meeting her on her terms. There I stepped into her realm and made the grade, baby. It's gotta leave her thinking. "You're just a student, Mason." My butt! My little ol' butt!

It's up to her. I can't do anything else, anything else to prove to her I'm a man among boys. God, I'm really glad no one can read my mind right now.

Just as I'm paying homage to my glossy of Joe Willie, I hear a rap on the doorjamb. "Excuse me, Dr. Bricker?" said Michele's voice.

"Hey, babe!" I said.

"You were pretty scary up there."

"How do you know?"

"I was in the hallway for a small part of it. You were damn good. I think you might have found a profession," she said in all earnestness.

"Well, thank you. If the NFL loses its need and desire for psychotics, small, but slow, then I have something to fall back on," I said with genuine graciousness.

"No doubt…speaking of football," she said, "can I break into your day a little bit at, say, noon today. I have something to go over with you."

"Let's go over it now," I offered.

"I would, but I'm busy and I'm not ready. Is noon okay, or is another time better?"

"Another day might be better. I'm watching Vinny today. Did you know he's the starting QB tomorrow?"

"No lie!"

"Yep, he killed off the other two and they are finally giving him his due."

"Well, bring him by," said Michele. "We'd love to talk with him. Starter! I'll be damn."

"Damn right!"

"I gotta go, so, I'll see you at noon? With your sexy friend?"

"Thanks a helluva lot, Michele. You know how to float my boat," I whined.

"But Mason," Dr. Taranucci said in conclusion, as she motioned down the hall to Joan's class, "*Knowledge* is sexy."

"Power is an aphrodisiac," I replied, "Who said that, Dr. Taranucci?"

"*Henry* Kissinger," Michele said smiling, "And, with regard to *Joan* Kissinger, you may already look pretty powerful."

"You keep insinuating that, and I'm going to ignore you until she gets in my face, if that *ever* even happens, which I doubt it *ever* will," I smiled.

"What *ever*," Michele said, continuing to smile.

I gently placed my left hand on her cheek and kissed her other cheek. I then turned off my light and strolled down the hallway. What a great morning to be alive, despite being inwardly frightened out of my boxers..

*   *   *   *   *

I keep checking myself every ten minutes or so, much like a nurse might read the vitals of a patient in intensive care, and I have lately found that I am not envious of my best friend The Gunner. Or, maybe more accurately, not overly so. After all, I have today's victory over Joan and her young minds. I have Michele's approval, always important. And I have the possibility of getting a stick in on Pitt's Heisman Trophy winner-in-waiting Drew Osberg, who, after Michael and I release on him tomorrow will forever refer to his duties as a kick returner a mistake hopefully never to be made again. All these things are going in my favor and I don't need to be first team to validate them or even augment them. I don't even need Joan. I want Joan. But, I don't need her. There are other women. Maybe if I started going to class, I'd meet them.

Friday, November 7, 1975
9:55 AM

Taking care of Vinny

I'm standing outside the door across the hallway watching Vinny speak with his intermediate accounting professor, Dr. Helmic. Unlike me, The Gunner consistently goes to class. Because of that diligence, he's a high B student (or sometimes a *high* high B student) in the undergrad B-school. He wants to be an attorney. Jean wants him to be a CPA. Fuck her (figuratively). If he keeps going to class and continues to get his Bs, plus throws a couple TDs tomorrow, I'd say he's a lock. I can just imagine Vinny decked out in Brooks Brothers. He's partner material. The rainmaker. At least he'll dress better.

He walked out, kind of surprised to see me. "I didn't think you were serious," he said.

"Joan gave me the day off, but I have to get back up there at noon for a little something. Michele says she wants to see you, so you're welcome to come along."

"I gotta see Coach at one-thirty at the field. Film."

"You're the man in demand," I said as we walked out of Amster and headed up the hill for the High Ridge. Skies are aluminum gray, temp in the high forties. No rain, please.

"It's amazing, isn't it?" he said, I guess referring to what has transpired.

"Yeah, and you haven't been formally introduced," I said.

"I'd just as soon that stay true."

"The word's gonna get around. The Pi Gamma Pis, the English department, radio, the dorm tele-freshman line. It won't take long. You'd better get used to it."

"I guess. How many people have you told?"

I counted on my fingers. "Five. No, six."

"You didn't blurt it out to the class, did you?"

"Well, Jean, Judy, Alice, Jennifer, my boys from Mullens, they all knew. That's ten percent. The word's rampant. It'll spread like wildfire. Why does this concern you? You're the man regardless."

"I just don't want to get caught in a press reporter trap," he said.

"It's gonna happen. Just be yourself, consider your thoughts before they jump out of your mind, and keep walking."

"How do you know so much?"

"Because I'm Mason."

Friday, November 7, 1975
10:15 AM

At the High Ridge

The cafeteria is bustling with its mid-morning crowd. There are a lot of warm jackets since we're coming off an Indian summer and aren't quite use to the cold. A lot of curly perms, a lot of Warren Beatty hair, and a lot of *Charlie's Angels* doos. The tables directly surrounding Vinny and me are filled, with students sitting at them occasionally looking askance at us. As always, I'm sure that's because Vinny is so…you know. Still no rain. My prayers remain answered. Well, most of them.

"People are looking at us. It's like we're gay and we don't know it," I said. I'm creeped out by a personnel change on our football team. Jesus, get a grip, Mason

"You know how I feel about that," Vinny said.

"Yeah, but…."

"Well, what ever you think you know, it's changed," interrupted Vinny. "Ron and I had a good time with you last night, bringing you back to sanity."

"You don't understand."

"Yeah I do," he said, jumping in again. "I've always wanted to cave my brothers' faces in, but you've never seen me do it."

"Try it."

"I know, I'll like it."

"He deserved it," I said, "He was being overly critical, to put it in the best of possible lights."

"That's not enough cause for that effect."

"Okay. He hit some tender areas about my father and that Nazi. I don't take that very well."

"My favorite Aryan," Vinny said, "Because of him, I'm starting."

I closed my eyes to try to hold in a snappy response to such a stupid statement, "Vinny, your scope is about as long as your dick. Myron's kept you on third team, remember?"

"Oh," said Vinny, now with perspective, "The son-of-a-bitch. Anyway, you outweigh Ron by twenty-five pounds. Plus, you hit people for sport. Hardly a fair fight."

"I know," I said, "Okay. I'm sorry."

"Don't let it happen again," Vinny said.

"Who the fuck are you?"

"I am what is known in the species as Starting Quarterback. I tell everyone what to do and I handle every ball. What's a good word for me, Mr. Wordsmith?"

I thought if I played along long enough he'd let up. "One compound word. Starts with an M."

"Mudtrucker? No, seriously, I feel better right now. I'm ready to play."

"Good. Then this is a good time to tell you that you have left a piece of sandwich on your cheek."

Vinny wiped his face with a napkin. "Is it gone?"

"Never was there, Starting Quarterback," I said. "Just trying to humble you."

"I am Starting Quarterback. I am unhumbleable."

That's kinda funny. "Starting Quarterback, butcherer of the English language. SQB, guarantor of victories."

"What was the line last night?"

"Call your uncle."

Vinny leaned in. "Last I heard, thirty points," he said with a whisper.

"But, if you're a true SQB," I whispered back, "true to the cloth, the line doesn't matter. You will still guarantee victory."

"That is true, sage," he said.

Vinny's good and loose. I am happy to see it. Now, if I could just keep him from having contact with his father until the end of the game...Hmm...that'll be damn difficult, but necessary. I'm going to have to figure out something before this evening when The Mike will arrive, flourishing and opinionated and just being a general pain in the ass, no doubt.

"How do you plan on beating the Pitt D?" I asked.

"I don't want to talk about it," Vinny replied.

"What?"

"You heard me. Any thoughts I have right now could just be crap, because you know Van Watt is going to call the shots. He's a rookie. I'm a rookie. My backup just got his home jersey yesterday. The coaches will control this game."

"He's got to give you some leeway. I mean, you're not mentally incapacitated like The Kid."

"Van Watt will direct the game. Count on it," said my SQB.

"That sucks."

"Maybe not. Maybe it'll take the pressure off so I can just execute."

"Pitt won't stand still for you and Red. You'll still have to make some on-field in-the-heat adjustments."

"We'll see what he says about that."

I know my Vinny, and I know he's better when you turn him loose. Red has the potential to fuck things up by being too rigid. "Vinny, you don't beat the number one team in the nation by playing close to the vest. We gotta open up. Tell Red that."

"You tell Red that. In fact, just tell Red you want to coach," Vinny shot, becoming a little agitated. I decided to change the subject.

"Let's get away from that. Listen to this: Michele keeps insinuating our fourteen day plan just might work."

"What? Joan?" Vinny asked, shocked.

"That's what she says. Michele has this heightened sense of things, like a dog's hearing range, or like Chuck Yeager being able to see German fighters from fifty miles."

"Fifty miles?"

"Yep. That's probably why he survived in the friendly skies."

We paused to get the conversation back on track. "Damn. Michele. What do you think about that?"

"I don't want to think about it. I'm already outside of reality with regard to Joan. All I need is to have Michele feed my deluded mind."

"Since when have you started worrying about your deluded mind? Besides, that's what's gotten you so far in life. Here you sit at one eighty-five soaking wet, but you think you can take any man, any size down. I mean, not just take them down, but inflict pain. Most people your size sit in the stands. You, however…and not only that, I know you, and you really believe you can challenge the four receivers ahead of you. I know you, and I know you think…no, you know you're just as good as Dhali and Clark and Tom and Dave. You show it every Wednesday. There are guys on teams on our schedule who can't sleep the night before they play Michael and Joe. Yet, you show up every Wednesday, right after your Poetry class, and you strap on your pads and line up and smile. You're probably the one guy Michael and Joe have hit the most in their lives, and you still line up every Wednesday smiling. Deluded mind? Every Wednesday, first play, like clockwork, you yell, 'You sad bunch of pussies. Today's the day I kick your ass!' If I didn't hear it every Wednesday, I wouldn't believe it. Deluded mind, Mason? What do you think leads you to go over the middle with no regard to what will happen? You say, 'Go ahead, Michael or Joe or whoever. Hurt me. I don't give a flying fuck. I'll get back up and flip the bird in your face and dare you to do it again.' You're crazier than hell, Mason. You shouldn't be here, but here you are. And it's all because you're nuts."

"Don't you think I have any ability?" I asked, wondering where he was going with all this.

"Sure, a lot of people have ability, but very few have your attitude. You don't think anybody can beat you. That's why you're a Runner. That's why you were with Rox and Ursula, and that's why you're going after Joan. You may act worried on the outside, very occasionally, and you may express a few doubts, but deep in your heart, you really believe you and Joan will be together as a couple. I know what's deep in your heart, and I don't listen to any other bullshit. And I think Michele has picked up on that, and I think even *Joan* has picked up on that. I swear to God, if you get in there tomorrow, I'm immediately sending you long."

I'm worried about how it's all going to turn out with Joan. And, I'm afraid. But, after a glowing recommendation like Vinny's, there's only one thing to say.

"Thanks, Gunner. You're my friend. I love you, Pretty Boy." I smiled.

"Think about what I've said," Vinny stated, "Remember: nobody, nofuckinbody knows you like I do." He stood up and walked. "And," he added as he turned, "I bet Joan's daydreaming about your Tarzan body right now." He gave me a GQ look.

Pretty Boy. Tarzan. No wonder people think we're gay.

*   *   *   *   *

Friday, November 7, 1975
10:45 AM

Walking back to class

"Keep it in mind, Gunner…."

"What's that, Cheetah?"

"You've started forty-eight games at quarterback since the eighth grade…."

"I know…"

"You've lost one…a helluva good record."

"I know…go ahead and say it…"

"It's better left unsaid…but there's no way you Madonna girls could have beaten my Hit Men Rebels," I said, referring to the one time my high school played his and we made Vinny's receivers cry. That was fun. It's irrelevant now.

"You're a bastard."

"What class are you going to?"

"Marketing."

"Marketing?"

"Marketing."

"I've always wondered…what kind of a fuckin' class is that? Don't ever again make fun of Poetry."

Friday, November 7, 1975
11:55 AM

After Vinny's Marketing class

"How was marketing?" I asked, not really wanting an answer.

"Good, able to be understood, not like Emily Stevens," Vinny replied.

"That's Emily Dickinson, and Samantha Stevens," I said.

"What's the difference?"

"We think Emily died a virgin. Samantha gave birth to another witch, even though her daughter was conceived by a mortal, an ugly mortal, but a mortal still."

"Remember how greasy his hair always was."

"That's that VO5. Frank used to wear that."

"My mom used to plaster down my hair with Dippity Do. Didn't help."

"She should have known better than to try to contain Italian hair. Still, after it all, it's hard to figure how we ended up so cool," I pondered.

"It's that Starting Quarterback aura."

"But you've gotta ask yourself the questions: which came first, the SQB or the coolness? And when does the SQB give his K. C. and the Sunshine Band clothes to charity?"

"Oh yeah, like the chicken or the egg. And, fuck you."

"Take a guy like Namath."

"I knew you would."

"Now he was probably cool at his circumcision."

"Is Namath circumcised?"

"I don't really know. But whatever, he is cool."

We rose up the stairs to the fourth, standing on the floor just as I heard Michele whisper, "Here they are!"

Something's up. I stepped to the English office ahead of The Gunner. "SURPRISE!"

Vinny walked up beside me. I can speak for him by saying we were both very surprised. Not knowing the cool way to react to the surprise, we simply teared up. Just a little, though. I don't think anybody noticed.

"Surprise, guys!" said Hannah in singsong, as if we didn't hear the first time. "Ah,ha, we gotcha!"

The first thing we saw was a big banner strung across the back wall with large letters, 'GO GIT PITT,' making light of their own grammatical perfection. Under that was 'MASON—VINNY—MICHAEL.' Navy and silver balloons are everywhere, in the corners and strung to the typewriters and telephones. The event is catered, coldcuts with wheat, rye, and pumpernickel, with beer for the non-athletes, Hannah, Kathleen, Joan, Dr. Cost, Michele, of course, and Ellen, and sodas for the guests of honor. I guess they're not aware that Vinny and I will drink beer twenty-four seven.

Typical party? I beg to differ. Below the signs is a table in front of which sat a lower table and in front of which laid cushions from one of the office sofas. Michele asked us to kneel on the cushions, light a votive candle on the smaller table, and pray to my eight by ten glossy of Broadway Joe on the larger table, after which we were to make the sign of the football.

"We're all going to burn in hell for this," I said to Michele.

*   *   *   *   *

Michael finally showed and we football players are quickly on our third sandwiches, eating volumes to the amazement of everyone.

"Eat now, for in thirty years that will not be possible," Dr. Cost said to us and his associates, rubbing his better than average-sized belly, "without putting on the tub."

"We'll worry about that when we get there," I said, to my boss' boss, for Christ's sake.

"That's the best way to look at it. Be young and be merry," said Dr. Cost.

I simply do not care any more if I'm referred to as young. Joan is just going to have to deal with it. I ams who I ams, or something like that.

"We ordered lots of food so you'll be strong tomorrow," said Kathleen.

"Thank you," Michael said, humbly. "We just hope not to disappoint," Michael is very much the gentleman in public, but a trained killer when he's in his helmet looking through his facemask. As I've said before, the transformation is awesome.

The ladies are charmed to have Vinny here. And he does so without trying. He just shows up. I've seen this happen ever since boys and girls knew there was a difference and why. My hometown girls liked me anyway, I guess, but they were always asking about Vinny. 'How's Vinny?' 'When's Vinny coming?' 'Do you want to come up when Vinny visits you?' 'When's Vinny coming back?' Simply incredible. So, Kathleen, Hannah, and Michele have Vinny cornered, while Ellen and Michael are with Joan, Dr. Cost and me. Much giggling is coming from over there, but we're having a good time, too, because Dr. Cost is a laugh riot.

I think I have my career plans made. I want to get on the Ph.D. track and teach. I had a lot of fun today with Joan and her students. While I was up there I felt as if I were a natural. The whole thing just flowed forth.

Joan turned from the others and said to me, "Thank you, Mason. You were great this morning." Great in the morning for Joan…what a concept! I feel admired. Maybe it's just my imagination, again runnin' away with me. "Plus," she continued, "I saw several of my women checking you out."

"Thank you, Joan, but I know of at least three who weren't."

"That Jennifer…her feelings surely shine through," Joan said, with a sly grin.

If Dr. Kissinger only knew how indifferent I am. "Well," I replied, about as noncommittal as I could be. It's not Jennifer who sets me afire, Maggie J. Joan and I can only look into each other's eyes for the longest time. Just say it, Joan, whatever it is you're thinking now. Tell me. I want to know. Is Michele right? Or, are you going to settle for the consolation prize, Alan?

Dr. Cost ambled over to ask about the experiment.

"He did a fabulous job," Joan said. "I'll have to teach him not to disagree with me so much, but when he learns not to bite the hand that feeds him, he'll go places." She smiled and excused herself, stepping over to Michele.

Dr. Cost grabbed my arm. "A little disruption never hurt anyone, my boy. You keep that filly honest." Filly. I never thought of Joan as a horse.

The crowd is having big time fun. And that's good. Better still, no one's talking about Lawson and McNabb and blacks vs. whites. It's a great safe haven from the true existence, an existence we would again deal with in a matter of hours. Or maybe much sooner. When Dr. Cost had the party detained with his own brand of humor, Michael took me aside.

"I understand there is a whites-only meeting at two-thirty today in the projector room."

I sucked in a deep breath. "You had to expect it, but that's all we fuckin' need. I wonder why we hadn't heard about it, you know, Vinny and me?" I answered the question in my mind before I finished it.

"Man, you're one of us," Michael said. Considering everything, we effectively are.

"But, I gotta go to the meeting. Skin color will get me in," I said.

"Beliefs will get your ass thrown out, too," Michael said.

"I'll take that chance. It'll be a good way to find out what's going on."

"Come on! You guys look too serious over there! Let's party, for tomorrow you may die," said Dr. Cost festively. "Michael, you are too young to take on the whole world. Mason, you, too. Revelry, men! You don't realize how much potential you truly have, but to fulfill it, you must know when to lighten up!"

Michael and I stood in silence. I felt my friend's pain, pain for his people, much less for his final season he had so much looked forward to. For wanting to try so hard, so goddamned hard to make things work out for him and for everybody else. For expectations and for the less favored all around the world.

Dr. Cost continued. "I know what you've been through really bites ass, as you fellows are wont to say. I want you to be happy. Do what you can and leave the rest to God. Now, come over here and let us take care of you."

Ellen loves Michael with all her heart. She knows what he needs. "Michael, let us take your burdens off your broad shoulders. Let us help you."

"I'll let you help me," I said, hoping to bring Michael in. "I need your help. This is weighing down on my soul and I want to release it. And I know you, you all can and will."

"We will, Mason," said Joan, with a beautiful smile and a beautiful gaze that turned my gut to putty.

Ellen stood to Michael's side and embraced him. He smiled, too, a smile of release.

I looked to Joe Willie, then stepped over to his picture, picked up the matchbook, struck a match, and lit a candle. "The spirit of the underdog burns. Let it burn with us."

It sounds really hokie. However, I think these folks understand and are somewhat proud to be a part of that spontaneity. Lighting a candle before the autographed framed picture of an aging hero to fend off a Vegas point spread is pretty wild, and no one would had believed it had they not seen it. Still, the candle burns, and if that's what it takes to spark our hearts, then strike a match every week, I say.

"The 'dog is lit," the quarterback in Vinny said, "Let's play!"

"Here, here, my man!" announced Dr. Cost, "Let's play!"

Jesus Christ. I had to leave the room.

Friday, November 7, 1975
2:30 PM

Friday practice

The projection room looks like a large classroom, capable of seating one hundred twenty beefy guys in uncomfortable deskchairs. There are two blackboards on either side of a large screen. A 16mm projector is positioned in the center of the room, its lens trained on the screen. Soft gray windowless walls surrounded the chairs with framed photos of the best of those who have gone before us. The room is lighted by the harshness of florescence. Comfort is not a high priority. The projection room is a place to learn about the opponent's sets and plays. It is also a place where mistakes were discovered and 'ironed out,' not, however, without a subtle question of our worth to the team and a request for commitment, this time. As a matter of fact, Michael had told me of the feeling he has sometimes on the field during important scrimmages and even the games. He says at times he's not motivated by doing well for the sake of doing well, or by beating the man in front of him, or even the opposing team. Michael says he can feel the 'eye,' and he doesn't want to hear any shit in the projection room. The 'eye,' the projector: the silent sentinel.

Vinny is with now back-up but formerly fourth team QB David Crikstein (don't even think of what will happen if Vinny goes down) in the head coach's office now occupied by former-assistant-now-head Coach Van Watt. They are in their second hour of decoding the Pitt defense. Van Watt. Vinny. Crikstein. I think we've had our share of disruption. And speaking of that, it looks like I am on my own in the white guys' meeting.

I entered. My eyes and Ted Gerlach's eyes met immediately. He is standing up front prepared to lead us. He didn't say a word to me, continuing his conversation with Andy Bruzinsky. I moved down the row and toward the middle, taking a seat beside Frank Adams, figuring I would want some beef beside me if this thing got ugly. But, in fact, only six of us were there: Ted, Frank, Andy, Andy Baum, Marty Louisinski, and yours truly. Five starters and a third teamer. I would have thought second team white guys would have been 'influenced' by the starters, but they stood interesting in their absence. Absence is the word of the day. If we're going to set policy, I don't really think there's enough for a quorum.

Ted started. "Because of the black guys' meeting yesterday, I thought we should have our own. Any problems with that, Mason?"

He got right to my point early. Might as well say it now. "This is senseless. Just read the article. We are not victims."

"We have rights and turf to protect. We must stand together," said Ted.

"Stand for what? No one did anything to us!"

"They will," Ted said. "They've already done it to Coach Lawson."

"Coach Lawson did it to Coach Lawson," I said.

"He was set up, I tell you!" Ted exclaimed.

"Then take it up with the newspaper!" I yelled. "Don't come to me in the name of rights! We oughta reach out to the black guys. Lendel got screwed. We oughta be a team!"

"We've gotta do this to save the team!" Ted said, pressing.

"You're fucked in the head, Ted. I'm leaving. I'm going to go do something for the team." As I stood up to leave, Frank Adams went with me. Frank, in the name of curiosity, sacrificed his standing with the blacks. He saw more than he wanted to see and got out of there with me. I decided to spread the good word for him.

"Southern man," Frank said as we stood outside, recalling Neil Young, "do what your Good Book says."

"This is scary," I said to Frank. "Ya gotta wonder how mental Ted will get when no one goes his way. He's not desperate yet, but he's close."

Frank said, "Call him on it. You're headed in the right direction. He's a true Runner, like you. You two just differ on the role of the white man in society. But, he's a good ol' boy. Where's he from? Bluefield? Down state there? He grew up with the U. In his own convoluted way, he's trying to protect them. In a more refined way, so are you. Use that in your dealings with him."

"Not a bad idea, Frank. Not bad at all."

"Well, that's my good idea for the year."

"Glad you waited for me to use it, Cement Head," I said with a grin and a slap on his back. Frank winked. Cement Head…my pet name for the power runner; head down, feet moving. Ya gotta wonder, why do these seniors let me the bench navigator get by with so much?

I walked to my locker and laid out my uniform, stripped and got suited up. During it all, I noted Arthur is strangely light-hearted, and just as strangely most of the team went along with him. Most, except for Michael. My friend Michael has a game face he puts on usually at this time of the week. However, I sensed a bit more of an edge to his demeanor this time. He's jumpy, and kept glancing over the projection room door. I walked over to him as he was putting his head through his shoulder pads.

"Michael, don't worry about those guys in there."

"Why should I worry?" he asked in denial of his anger.

"It's why you should not worry. There are only four of them in there, and I think three of them are there so as to not catch any of Cap'n Teddy's crap he so loves to deal. A fifth, Frank, walked out with me when it got unbearable, which happened quickly. Don't worry."

"I can't believe this is all taking place! What a fucked up season this has been! Here we are, one of the two biggest games of my life and that big ass is having separate meetings. Damn!"

Of course, his meeting of yesterday was different, and I don't say that facetiously. It was. But we as a team are in trouble when Michael starts to lose perspective. I patted him on the back and left him to cool off.

As I was walking back to my locker, Joe stopped me for one of his rare public conversations.

"Did you get me a 'Wallace for President' sticker?" he joked.

I laughed.

"Don't laugh." he said smiling. "This is going to get a lot worse before it gets better."

"Why do you say that?" I wondered.

"The leadership is falling apart." That's not at all a pleasant thought.

At that time, the whites only meeting broke up, all four of them. Three of them looked normal Friday pregame. The fourth, Ted, found Michael.

"Burton!"

Michael heard the voice. He arose from his shoelaces, eyes burning with the fury of a man derided.

"You, you ratted on Coach Lawson!"

Knowing how offbase Ted is, Michael actually relaxed. "No, Ted, I did not. But if I had to, I would have."

"It's a sad day," said Ted, "when you take a man down in his prime."

They're getting dangerously close to me, both physically and with regard to reality. I thought about admitting it all right then to save Michael, but decided at the last moment to keep my mouth closed.

"Prime? How about Lendel? A junior with the skills to run this team, but held back by a man, a man he trusted. Talk about taking a man down."

"Again," said Ted, "tell me how you know this."

"Again," responded Michael, "the newspaper. Ted, you're looking at the wrong conspiracy. Coach Lawson did it, and for this he will pay."

Throughout this conversation, the two slowly approached each other, tightening the tension in the locker room. I kept thinking, if they got into it here, in this relatively small space, that would be close to five hundred pounds of meat on the hoof, horns locked. There could be a lot of collateral damage.

Ted stopped moving toward Michael at about three feet from him, arms length for either man. Still, he offered more remarks. "Burton, you and your brothers start more than half the team. Ain't that enough? I guess you'll do anything for that prized quarterback position. Of course, your boy Mason has his queer buddy in there now, so you should be satisfied."

I looked to Vinny. I've heard some of those who live in the entertainment world say, half in jest, all the best looking men are gay. He's not, but he is a Greek god. The Gunner shrugged his shoulders, then pursed his lips at me with an air kiss. I had to hide my face in my hands, convulsing in silent laughter as our two captains continued to debate, 'Resolved: You're an asshole. One-minute response: No, you are.'

"Ain't that enough, Michael? Ain't Vinny enough? He should be close enough."

Michael must have realized right then he was dealing with a sick man. He backed away. Sensing the frustration he has felt, I knew that was difficult for him to do. That and the fact that he didn't want to give away forty-five pounds in tight quarters, he did the smart thing.

"We want the best man there, for QB as well as any position, Ted. Right now, that's Vinny. This time last week, it was Lendel, but that's a lot of water under the bridge."

"Well, you got your man in there," said Ted as he turned his attentions elsewhere.

Something told me Joe is right.

Friday, November 7, 1975
7:00 PM

We meet The Party

Every home game this year, from the heights of Temple to the depths of North Carolina State, as the calendar flipped away from the heat of the late summer and well into the rains of the fall, every home game the living parents of the residents of the house, after that Friday afternoon having piled their respective families securely into their automobiles and laid the rubber to get here before dinner time, met at the house for an Open House staged by Alice and Judy. Fortunately, Vinny and I are spared from helping by virtue of football and gender and disinclination and inability to do the tasks necessary to put on a party for adults. Party for college kids? Easy. Hop in the car and go to State Line. Vinny drives while I roll the joints, with Grand Funk providing the music. 'Sweet, sweet Connie doin' her act / She had the whole show, that's a natural fact.' We can do that. Parents? That involves fondues and horse ovaries (not original, a rip-off from Archie Bunker) and fifties music. Sorry, girls. We'll be there at seven. Thanks a bunch.

Tonight we are especially happy to be here. At training table, we all suffered dyspepsia as we witnessed three black versus white fights leading to a cascade of more wrangles. After Van Watt dismissed us, Vinny and I got the hell out of there. I can't but help feel as if I fucked up big time. Luckily we aren't all staying in a hotel together tonight. We'd level the joint.

Walking onto the porch of the house filled with laughter and the *American Graffiti* soundtrack, I took one final look at my friend. That made me recover quickly. The face of surety from today and just a few minutes ago has been overtaken by the deer-in-the-Mikelights. I know I have to do something about it, but 'what' is a mystery to me.

"You ready, cowboy?" I asked Vinny, with my right hand on the door-knob. He knows that I know why he's about to get sick.

"Open'er, partner," The Gunner said, knowing that I know why he likes to have a partnership in these situations.

"You're starting. That means a lot to you and to me," I said, "Don't let anybody screw up that feeling." He knows what I mean.

Vinny nodded slightly, then breathed deeply.

I turned the doorknob, slowly pushing the door open, then walked in first.

At or about seven o'clock on the Friday evenings before our previous home games with Maryland, Boston College, Virginia Tech, Temple, and North Carolina State, I had at those times turned that doorknob and walked in first to applause. Those evenings were nothing in any way like the ovation I received today. I'm shocked and blandished. Then Vinny walked in and they torqued it up a dozen decibels. The Gunner couldn't help but smile his biggest smile of the day since he jumped in on my shower this morning. Someone found *"The Fight Song"* (actual title) and put it on my two hundred watt box and everyone sang along:

Fight, fight, (oh, yeah)

The gallant fight, (as if there is any other way)

We are right, (just ask us)

Students of might (the mighty Ridge Runners)

Daughters and grads, (NOW might have a hard time with this one)

Sons and lads, (and don't forget the gay community)

Moms and dads (it really says this)

It's West Virginia, the great state (no argument here)

We'll climb the hills, (just to get to class)

The beautiful hills, (they tried 'beautiful women' but it didn't quite lyrically fit)

Go, Ridge Runners, go! (An asinine name until you consider the shortened and very cool 'Runners')

"The Fight Song" is like an old, worn sweater you pull out every fall, proudly displaying it as everyone around you tactfully asks when you are going to get a new one. I love it, but mostly because I for the past several years have been playing it in my head whenever I catch one of The Gunner's balls. The marching band strikes it up upon the scoring of a Runner touchdown. I wanna hear the band play *"The Fight Song"* while I'm holding the ball in the end zone in The Bowl at The Ridge. It is difficult to convey how badly I want that to happen.

The men greeted us first.

Wayne Lambert clasped my hand, no, ambushed it, with his bright face and his lever arms coming up behind it. Judy got her long femurs from her dad and her gorgeous brown eyes from her mother. We'll get to her later. Wayne's an attorney in private practice in the Eastern Panhandle. In addition, he possesses some qualities I wish to emulate when the time comes. He's a wonderful husband, and great father to his three girls. And I think he likes me, too. I guess he would have to, or he wouldn't stand for me living under the same roof as his Judy.

"Welcome home, Big Hitter," said Wayne. God, he knows how to win me over.

Wayne turned me over to Rob Calire. Rob greeted me as if I were coming home from the battlefield. He's a great guy. Despite being an engineering exec for Ashland Oil, pumping out the Valvoline that keeps my Taz engine slippery, Alice tells me her father refused to climb and claw over the backs of those in front of him in rampant pursuit of The Buck. He was deeply involved in the lives of his two daughters, striking a favorable chord with me. My dad used to mark off when I was playing and sometimes when I was just practicing, just to be around.

I never tried to hide the fact that I admire these two men a great deal. And I guess the fervor the two display with Vinny and me is in part because they each drew from the baby lot and came up with no sons. So,

The Gunner and I served as surrogates. We don't mind, since we could both use a sort-of father figure. That's odd for Vinny, since right down the line from Mr. Calire stands his actual father, Michael Vincent Vacca, the First.

Mike. They made Mike, then twentysome years later they made The Jean Queen and then they broke the molds. Mike greeted me in an authoritative manner, like we're to abide by military hierarchy. He knows, and I know because he, Mike, has told me I could mess up his son's mind. His opinion, of course, because I know he already has. I have spent the last four years applying the salve to the wounds my best friend has received from his dad in the interest of 'Getting The Most From Your Son At Any Cost, Part One.'

Vinny's dad got off the boat from Italy at an early age and moved with his family to the Northern Panhandle to live with relatives in their new country. Mike was instilled with the immigrant ethic and patriotism. He therefore felt it was his duty as a naturalized citizen to become a United States Marine for the Korean Conflict, training as a boot recruit under, in one of the freakiest of life's oddities, my dad the drill instructor. His desire to do so was strong enough to entice him to drop out of The U and pursue the honor of being a soldier.

After getting lucky and suffering only a leg wound, costing him the chance at a stellar career as a Ridge Runner quarterback (which probably drives him to turn Vinny into the player he wasn't), Mike came home with a Purple Heart and quit the whole college scene to return to Weirton. Not idle for long, Mike used his persuasiveness and charm and Italian good looks to land a job selling Fords for the local dealer. He got lucky again, getting caught up in the steelworker-makes-the-steel-from-which-the-autos-are-built-then-bought-and-driven-to-work-to-make-more-steel-which-makes-more-autos cycle, a big driving force of the US economy in the fifties. Mike took full advantage of this opportunity and sold enough cars to buy for himself the Chevrolet dealership across the street, thereby setting himself up to make the huge dinero relatively early. He has it made in many ways: money, wife, the absolutely knock-me-down-and-slap-me-until-I-see-God gorgeous Patricia, and strong sons, three, one right after another.

Trouble is, Mike thinks he alone made his life remarkable. And he thinks he can impart his knowledge and wisdom to his sons and they'll do it his way, the only way. Unfortunately for Vinny, Vinny is first. His father's lack of experience in dealing with matters such as these has made life very difficult for The Gunner. That's where he is fortunate he has me, and where Mike at best thinks I simply impede progress. Interesting.

"Mike," I said.

"Mason," he said, clasping my hand, shaking, trying to grip firmer than I can. No way.

"Your son's ready," I commented, insinuating, 'Don't fuck it up.'

"He was ready a long time ago," saying without saying, 'I'll be the judge of that.'

"I couldn't agree with you more," I said sincerely.

I stepped aside allowing Vinny to greet his dad. The two embraced as generations of Europeans have, and Mike backed away, seeming for a second as if he has something in his eye. He cleared his throat and recovered. Looking directly at his son, six foot to six-two, Mike said, "Why didn't you call me today?" Oh shit…Mike had to hear the news of his son's gridiron arrival on the radio. This is not going to be pretty.

"I tried to call late this morning," Vinny said. I thought he was less than truthful with that one.

"Didn't you even try to call your mother?" the father asked.

"No…I…I had classes and a lot of meetings today. I'm sorry I couldn't reach you."

"The biggest day of your athletic career to date and you couldn't call?" Mike is hurt. That's when he turns the thumbscrews down. There goes the evening. Vinny, you dumbass…

"I'm sorry, Dad."

Mike tried to swallow his pride, but he left enough out there to establish that he will control this party.

"Wayne, Rob, what do you think of a son who did not call his old man upon the announcement of his starting quarterback assignment for the West Virginia Ridge Runners?" Mike asked.

"Well," Wayne said diplomatically, not wanting to be a part of this, "I certainly would have wanted to hear from him, but I'm sure he had a busy day today."

"Did you try, Vinny?" asked Rob, trying to end this.

"Well, yes," Vinny responded as the lie grew legs.

"That's all you can ask," Rob said. He deferred to the son. He knows what's going on.

Still, Mike could not be consoled. He pouted in the fashion of a man in his mid-forties and his stature can only do and turned away from his son to strike the final blow.

Across the room, Patricia Vacca sensed what's going on. She left the hostess assist duties she had offered the girls to try to salvage something out of this, knowing all about it because it was most likely all she heard about during the two hour drive down. The mom is adept at her role as the Good Cop to her husband's Bad Cop.

Vinny has not pleased his father. He quickly blamed himself, as always. I know from the past how these feelings erode The Gunner's psyche. I thought tonight could be trouble, but I'm still surprised by how quickly it accelerated. To save him and the fragile condition of the Runners, my boy needs some TLC, and who better to administer it than his mom.

"Vinny," Patricia said as she approached from his side, "Vinny, Vinny," as she hugged a mother's hug, "I'm so proud of you. That's my boy!"

As he accepts his mother's affection, I can see the tightness in his face release. He has never had to prove himself to her. She will always be proud of him. The mother and son: they are good together. They looked damn good together. Think tall, dark, and handsome standing beside his mother the Venician Donna Reed. This all sounds really wonderful, but as it is for many wives, Patricia often defers to her husband. So, the Good Cop is of some help, but she can only do so much.

"Congratulations, darling," Patricia said to her eldest son, "I am proud of you. You'll do very well. Why didn't you call?"

"Classes, meetings, college." Vinny said, continuing with a more honest version of the original excuse.

I can tell she knows.

"Don't worry," said the mother, "I'll take care of him." She patted his cheek and smiled her Miss America smile; Miss Ohio, 1953, to be accurate, and fourth runner-up in Atlantic City.

"Hello, Mason," she said. "What do think of my man Vinny?"

Aware that she knows how important Vinny and I are to each other, but also guessing correctly that she is concerned about how reckless I can be, I replied, "I think he's our key to victory. He's the man to turn us around."

I'm the only one here who knows what exactly is at stake. For many reasons, the outcome of the ballgame tomorrow is up to The Gunner, and his mind is getting screwed up. It's my responsibility to pull him through. And right now, I still don't know how. I need to talk to my fine female friends.

I found them in our kitchen reloading party trays with cheese things and other stuff served at these Friday-before-the-home-game parties. These events are good to have, but I this time as every time urged Judy and Alice to have it catered, thereby freeing them to enjoy. It must be some sort of a woman thing, as it is some sort of a man thing to make a suggestion that involves less work. It's good that their mothers are here to help, because I'm obviously not about to.

Their mothers. Now there's a pair. Geri Lambert, petite, dark-eyed, the one who has made me break my rule about lusting after…the best way to describe her: oh, no, huh-uh…And Pauline Calire: Alice's twin sister. Imagine 'Calire Cut-Off Days' to the power of two. It could happen. But most importantly, Geri and Pauline are two extremely nice ladies. They with my deceased mother in mind do their best to take good care of me.

"Mason, sweetheart," Pauline said, rushing over to apply a peck on my cheek. I saw her just last week, but hey….

"Mason!" exclaimed Geri while pushing Pauline away to give me a big hug.

"He's mine!" said Pauline.

"But I've got him now," laughed Geri, holding on tightly.

"Moms," said Judy, "trust me, the last thing Mason needs right now is two women fighting over him."

"An overabundance of girls, Mason?" asked Pauline.

"You want to tell us about it?" asked Geri.

"You wouldn't believe me, and you wouldn't respect me," I replied.

"Well, do them now while you're young, whoever they are," Geri said with laughter.

"Mom!" Judy yelled in disgust.

"Just as long as they're of age and it's consensual," cracked Pauline.

"Okay," I said looking over at Alice and Judy. They caught my glance. "They are."

"Go for it," said Pauline.

"I just might," I said, as Jean and Jennifer walked in.

"Ladies," I said, looking at Jennifer. Jean looked around, said her greetings, and left the kitchen. Jennifer made her way to me and planted a big one on my lips. Geri and Pauline exchanged smirks of satisfaction.

"Whatdayasay, muscle man?" Jennifer said.

She's approaching Joan's record for number of times leaving me ga-ga.

"Hello, Mrs. Lambert. Hi, Mrs. Calire," Jennifer said with that satisfied look one has after marking.

"Hi, Jen," the moms said in staccato.

Geri picked it up. "I respect you, Mason."

Pauline laughed. Everyone but Jennifer was in on it, but she didn't care. It's getting around: I am officially her man.

It's not that simple.

The womenfolk filed out to perform various hostess duties, still without me even offering to help. Funny how that part of women's lib, the part involving men as hosts in front of other men hasn't quite caught on. Regardless, it left Jennifer and me alone long enough for her to drop the bomb.

"My parents are coming over tonight around eight. I've told them all about you. They're looking forward to meeting you."

As the shrapnel bounced around inside my torso and my brain, my mouth said, "Well, that's great, Jennifer. Gee, I hope I meet their expectations. I would imagine your father the doctor would want only the best for his girl."

"He's got it," she said, then laid a kiss on me no father would ever want his daughter to lay.

After things settled down, my brain began to race. I'm trapped, a prisoner of football policy. I can't even go out for a beer and stay a couple of hours until they become bored. I have forty-five minutes to think of something and execute it. This is going to be very difficult to figure out, even for me.

"The Lopinski's are coming over, too," Jen said.

Great. Jean didn't become Jean by some social experiment gone awry. Her genetic pool will be here, just in time to see the other captive, Vinny, already about to explode.

"Super," I said.

Alice and Geri came back in and told us to go make out somewhere else. I laughed. I walked. Jennifer stayed to help. Yeah. I need to check on Vinny.

Oh, shit. The men had apparently made their rounds with him because it's The Gunner and The Mike on the navy sofa having a father-son chat. Neither looks happy. I walked over to hear what there is to hear. I know whatever I would catch would be germane to the conversation, since Mike never thought it was necessary to change subjects when interrupted by me.

"Hi, guys," I said.

"Mason, we're talking strategy. I've told Vinny to throw under the coverage every time they give it to him. It'll open up downfield. What do you think?"

A couple of things here: a) The Runners don't throw under, meaning we don't throw five yards or so 'underneath,' or in front of the defenders. We throw, when we throw, outs and hooks. Outs and hooks. Ten to fifteen yards toward the sidelines. If it's not a hook, it's an out, miserably predictable. The only reason why we have been as successful as we are is because, as I've said before, Dhali and Clark and Tom and Dave are remarkably gifted athletes who make anything look good. Things will work still better with the talent of Vinny, who actually can combine with the receivers and make a downfield offense work. b) Mike doesn't give a diddly-damn what I think or anybody thinks. But he holds sway in his son's mind and, knowing this, he will press his point *ad nauseum.* Nevertheless, I decided to challenge him.

"Mike, why go under and chip away and make Pitt stack up against Arthur?"

"Arthur's a football player," he responded. "He's supposed to be tough. And he's supposed to do what the team requires. And this team needs them to go under. It's like a run-pass." What the hell is the 'Arthur is supposed to be tough' supposed to mean? Mike's crazy.

"I know what under is," I retorted. "And I know what it does. But a passing offense structured on the short underneath pass against Pitt's outstanding athletes will fail." Actually, it may be the best way to bring 'em down, but I'm not allowing Mike the satisfaction of thinking he can tell our QB what to do, even if he is his own son.

"What are you going to do?" Mike asked.

I'm equally unmindful, as well as tired of the topic of conversation. Just like Vinny at lunch this morning, "I'm not going to talk about it."

Mike laughed a hard laugh that grabbed the attention of the men in the living room, but he kept his voice low. Leaning forward, he let us have it. "What's the big deal? Anyway, do you think Pitt doesn't know what you're going to do? They probably know your offense better than you do. And if Lawson is a joke, you can only wonder what his assistants are like. Just look at what Dennis has done. He's taken a team of great athletes, how he got them I'll never know, and he choked Penn State, was obliterated by NC State of all teams, then was caught with his hand in the cookie jar getting money playing one of the most pitiful excuses for a quarterback in the NCAA. Sure, he's gone and that may be wonderful for you guys, but losers begat losers. I'm a West Virginia fan and I'm navy and silver through and through, but enough is enough." Then he spoke directly to me, "I don't know why I stood by and let you drag my son away from Notre Dame to this sorry excuse for a football program. Now, I'm going to go talk to the men."

The message is succinct. He's pissed off at his son for not calling and thereby landed a few direct hits to him, showing him who the man is. And he simply doesn't like me. But I can take it. It's Vinny I am now worried about. My man looked as if he had seen the devastation of a B-52 attack. However, this is not the time for blows to The Gunner's confidence. I only have a few hours to turn it around. Therefore, I decided the best approach is a counterattack. After a few moments, I patted Vinny on the knee and left him to heal with his mom who had heard it all and is on her approach.

Wayne and Rob are yukking it up with Mike on the sofas in front of the TV. There is a space beside Wayne directly in front of Mike. I took it. The current topic of conversation is Ronald Reagan. The three men supported him. An actor for President. Hell, let's elect Jill St. John. At least it'll be great looking at a very attractive Commander-In-Chief on the news night after night. I let that cool off, then I asked Mike, "Could you, uh, step aside with me?"

"Go ahead and say what you have to say right here, Mason," Mike replied.

I paused a moment, and said, "All right." I'm nervous, but I'm trying very hard to not show it. Finally, I said it. "Why did you say those things about our team?" I exhaled.

"Easy," Mike said, talking to me, and Wayne and Rob. "You have a team loaded with studs, and all you have to do is stop four plays at Happy Valley, then play your normal ball here on The Ridge against God's gift to victories. Your team blows both of them. Then the coach is shown publicly to be a fool, putting him in the same league as Lyndon Fadden, a man whom I've never had any respect for. I was just pointing out that there are better places in the nation to play football." That's the first public party mentioning of Lawson's pay-to-play. It made me very uncomfortable.

Mike has the uncanny ability to say the same thing to different audiences and come out on top. Under no circumstances do I want to get in an argument with him before men of his generation. But surely, for the sake of the team and its performance tomorrow, for the sake of Vinny, and to keep me from getting into a fistfight, we've got to get out of here.

I quickly weighed several options on what to say. 'Fuck you and the horse you rode in on,' ranks up there, but it doesn't play to the crowd. 'I agree with you, Mike, and I'll do what I can to make it better,' parleyed to the men, but it makes me ill. I decided to go with the compromise.

"Mike, a few bad things have happened to our team in a short amount of time. Despite them, we're still going to show up at breakfast tomorrow morning at eight. And if we beat Pitt, we can get it all back."

Rob and Wayne looked at each other and nodded their heads in the affirmative. Mike rubbed his face with the palms of his hands and said, "Whatever you think, my boy, whatever you think."

We definitely have to get out of here.

*   *   *   *   *

I walked up to my room to think about all this. When I get anxious, I begin to feel all alone, just like that midnight drive around town last week. Sure, the families work to include me, all three of them, but when it is time to circle the wagons, I've got but one Conastoga and I'm as wide open as I look. This anxiety has come at a most inopportune time, the night before the Big Game. Hell, I'm sure it is in part related to it, but I'm not about to analyze it tonight. I don't want to hear it. But, this is not about me. This is about Vinny. I simply want to fix it for my buddy Vinny. He's down there about to pop. Just a mile and a half away, he was Dr. Joyce Brothers in a jock strap. Damn that Mike, goddamn him, that narcissistic son-of-a-bitch. Kicking his son while he's down. I can't believe he's still dragging that Notre Dame thing out. Nobody can help what Lawson did. And there's Mike; instead of being supportive, he's beating his own son over the head with his twenty-twenty hind-sight. He doesn't want a football player; he wants a sycophant. He used sports to try to create his Stepford son. Damn thing about it is he's half there. When Mike's not around, Vinny is his own man. Otherwise, the man owns his boy. It's bad.

I've got it. I'll call Michele. She's said by virtue of being raised in her family, she's an expert in abnormal psychology. And there are fewer things more abnormal than that megalomaniac Mike Vacca.

I can feel the stress relieve as I sit in my room. Looking around at my walls, I wonder: What would Jim Morrison do in this situation? Bad choice. How about Jack Tatum? He'd face-tackle the bastard. There's a thought. I picked up the receiver and punched in Michele's number from memory. Two of the hottest faculty women in the East and I know their numbers by heart. What does that tell you about me?

One ringy-dingy…

"Hello." Even her phone greeting is Pittsburgh.

"Hi, Michele. This is your ol' buddy Mason."

"Mason! For God's sake, this is the night before the Pitt game! Aren't you supposed to be ramming your head through a wall or something?"

"We're not animals, Michele. We have feelings, too. We just can't find them."

"You got it there, bub. Why are you calling me?"

"I've got a big problem."

"It's your dime, sweetie"

"In fifty words or less, Vinny was doing great until he got home and his father started screwing with his mind. He's the QB tomorrow, Michele. He's got to be free and very easy. He's got to be the man. Thing is, down here he's being reduced to a gerbil."

"Come over."

"Thank you, but we are curfew captives."

"Curfews. What is this, wartime?"

"I didn't set them, honey."

"Give me fifteen minutes. I know what to do."

"What are you going to do?" I'm very perplexed.

"I can't say now," she said evasively.

"Damn it, Michele, before you do anything, you have to tell me," I said, not really knowing why that's true.

"I can't this time, darling, but I'll get you boys out of there. I'll call in fifteen minutes. Okay?" She sounds at ease with the whole idea.

I'm not. "Michele, I'm putting my trust in you, completely. Thank you in advance for fixing it. Otherwise, we're walking toward the brightest star in the sky and finding accommodations in the nearest manger."

"Which one of you is the virgin?"

"These are the seventies. Some allowance has to be made."

"You're funny for a mindless ball-seeking robot."

"Thanks, Michele."

"I'll call."

Just as I placed the receiver in the cradle, the phone rang.

"Mason."

"Mason. Stanley here."

"Stan! Nice surprise."

"Are you sitting down?"

"Great, Stan. I get a call from my moneyman and he asks if I'm sitting down. Just tell me. Do I need Valium for this?" Numbed deadpan.

"Sit. This is good."

"Okay." I obediently sat.

"Nashua and North Allegheny were both bid on today for buyouts; Nashua late morning and North Allegheny a couple of hours afterwards."

After this week, I am beyond shock. All I could say was, "Fuck, Stan."

"Fuck is the wrong word," he said, "I'll keep this short since I know we're both very busy right now. Bottom line, you're doing fine."

The circuit breaker in my brain went off. Instincts led me to say, "What do we do?"

"Give me the weekend to study the deals. It may be good to take the market price as offered right now and get the hell out. I don't know. I'll have more for you on Monday. They both went out at around three times book, an unheard of valuation. They're both selling for just about two-and-a-half right now. I don't want to get greedy, so we'll see. At closing prices today, after taxes, each of you, individually, you, your mother, your brother, and your sisters are sitting on one hundred eighty-five thousand."

"Christ…well, Stan, once again, thank you…thank you…I know you have to run, but thank you. What a great idea this was. I bet you get a lot of good scotch after this one."

"I might even get laid after this one."

"I admire you and your abilities, Stan, but I'll just send scotch."

"I would hope. Anyway, talk to you on Monday. I heard about your coach. I'm sorry."

"Yeah, it's never good for that to happen, but his timing sucks."

"Gotta go. Good luck tomorrow. Hit somebody for me, okay?"

"It's the least I can do."

"Bye, Mason."

"Thanks, Stan." I hung up after his click and dropped my face into my hands, in a torpor. Of all my worries, I can thank God and Stan that money's not one of them. Respectful of Guadalcanal and scrounged Japanese weapons from dead Japanese soldiers and Leonard Myers and how I got lucky, how it all got started, I after a few minutes for recovery decided to put it out of my mind and do the good deeds that have been done for me. Pass it on. Take care of Vinny.

Friday November 7, 1975
7:30 PM

The escape

I remain in my room. Temptations abound, all driven by anxiety: a) Flight…Let 'em all work it out for themselves, go to Michele's, and to hell with the risk of getting booted from the team for curfew violations.

If I think about this one too hard it becomes very plausible. Mike's impossible to deal with, the dynamics with his son are difficult to overcome, and the team's about to implode. The only things that keep me here are my love for Vinny and my penchant to not quit. Therefore, I stay and…. b) Fight…Nobody; I say nobody treats my friend like shit and talks about my team the same way. The path to Utopia, that's Mike's, not Sir Thomas More's, goes through me and I don't go down on this one because his ideas are purely screwed up. While I'm here fighting, I might as well…. c) Coax Jennifer into a quick consummation of our relationship before her parents arrive. Pitt has my hormones raging in a fire. I haven't had sex since right before Ash Wednesday noon mass. And I think she just might agree to it. Besides, it will exorcise the Joan demons ruling me and I've got a five minute window of opportunity so I'd better get to it…there's the phone…damn it, who in the hell could be calling at this stage of rapid seduction!

I picked up the receiver. "This better be good."

"Whoa! That's no way to address the woman who has the answers to most of your problems," Michele said.

"I'm sorry. I'm just frustrated in a lot of ways and they're not your fault." I'm as deeply conciliatory as one can expect me to be considering all of the circumstances. I looked at my watch, again thinking about Jennifer and cyclone sex.

"Apology accepted," said Michele. "Now, about your captivity problem, I went straight to the top and you and Vinny are free to get over here as quickly as possible and spend the night."

I'm so astonished I can barely speak. Dr. Taranucci recognized this possibility and proceeded to explain further.

"I am a personal friend of your coach Red Van Watt and I offered to barter one thing he wants for one thing I want, which in this case is your freedom from the punitive curfew that keeps you two caged like animals."

Now more astounded than before, I remain silent, trying to figure it all out before I spoke. Anticipating this, Michele gave me room to do so.

So, I pondered how could she know Coach Van Watt…why would the coach deal with her…what is it…OH, NO!

"You're not…I can't allow…Michele!"

"He said I will then find out why they call him Watt."

"I can't do this!" I said in an exasperated fashion. Michele and Red…this is purely animal satisfaction for her…ughh…I don't want to think about it. What the hell's gotten into her?

"Will it make you feel any better that it would have happened in a couple of weeks anyway and that I just saw an opportunity to help you out and that I being the woman have the highest order of bargaining positions known to mankind? Take advantage of it, Mason. Red said you can tell whomever you are staying with him, the starting quarterback and his friend, in his house."

She must have sensed doubt, so she offered, "Look, call the Redman yourself."

She got the nickname right. "Okay, I'd feel better checking in with him." I'd rather see Michele with a priest than with Red. She'd be vaporizing his vow to God but at least they could have an intelligent conversation afterwards.

"I think," Michele said, "he'd like to talk to you anyway."

"I've got his number."

"He's expecting your call. Oh, by the way, don't let on about the big payoff."

"Huh? Oh," I said. "Of course not. I don't talk to the Coach about anything but football related matters."

"You don't have to be that restrictive," she said, "Just check in with him."

"Thanks. Jesus, I don't know how to thank you."

"I have a father. I understand."

I looked at my watch. Maybe it'll be another time with Jennifer.

"Bye, Michele. I'll call you soon."

"Bye, Mason."

I hung up. I punched in 555-1012. In three rings Coach answered.

"Van Watt." Red and Michele...oh, I'm sick

"Coach, this is Mason Bricker." I ignored the fact that I'm a lowly third team acolyte and I am calling the interim head coach of a top twenty-five program with little pretense in regard to his soon-to-be 'score' with the player's female friend and instructor.

"Hi, Mason. I understand Vinny is under duress."

He may not have used the word correctly, but I certainly appreciated him taking the heat off of me. "Yes, Coach, I've seen this happen for so long. I just feel like Vinny and consequently the entire team would be better off if the he and his father were to part."

"Why can't you just kick the son-of-a-bitch out?" Red said, asking the obvious question.

"Oh, no way would he stand for that."

"Well, I understand. I used to go to great lengths to get away from my father. We finally came to an agreement to stay the hell away from each other twenty-four hours before each game."

Really, I thought. Damn. Good idea. "Coach, I'd say it's too late to strike a deal for this weekend. Thank you for agreeing to have Mi—I mean Dr. Taranucci take care of us."

"Don't worry. She'll take care of me," he said laughing.

I have no response to that.

He sensed that. "Just have Vinny give me a call when you get there. And don't go anywhere else."

"Gotcha, coach."

"I'll talk with you tomorrow. Goodbye, Mason." He hung up.

Oh, Coach, could you put me in for a few plays tomorrow? Too late.

I called Michele back. "Hi. We're all square on this. I'll talk to Vinny and we should be over within the hour."

"Groovy," she said, "I've always wanted to spend the night with the star quarterback."

"That's completely unexpected, but it's up to you and Vinny." I'm not about to stand in the way on that one. A night with Michele and The Gunner might throw for six hundred yards.

"Nah, I have my sister Mary Josephine with me tonight. My married sister MJo, although she has the eye of the tiger right now, if you know what I mean."

I heard a feminine voice in the background cursing. Michele laughed. I've gotta get over there as soon as possible.

"Let me go and work on Vinny. I'd say with regard to his fragile state he'll go for it."

"Good," Michele said, "Call me if you need me."

"Good deal. See ya. And thank you."

"Don't mention it."

"Ahhh…."

"No really, don't mention it. Can you imagine what Joan would say if she found out I was this fervently an athletic supporter?" She caught herself, "Don't say it!"

I laughed and laughed. I have to make sure I have her telephone number close at hand for the rest of my life.

"See ya soon, baby," I said.

"Drive safely."

The game preparations begin now. I looked at my watch again. Seven fifty. Well, Jennifer…Maybe I can get out of here before Doctor Pierce and his wife show up, thereby in her mind sealing my fate. That's enough to scare a man limp.

How do I do this? I think it will only be right to approach Judy and Alice first. They go through so much trouble every home game weekend. It might otherwise be rude to just jump from their party without a good explanation. Then, I take Vinny upstairs and help him pack. Or maybe I should lay the staying-at-Van-Watt's-house lie on The Mike. Boy, he's not going to like this at all.

I walked from my bedroom to the kitchen, stationing there in hopes of catching one of the girls making an ashtray run. I'd insist on letting our smoking guests, Geri and Pauline, a turn on, in a lines-along-the-lips-and-cancerous sort of way, merely flick their ashes on the window sills, but the females of the house wouldn't stand for that. And, wouldn't you know it, here Judy arrives, headed for the sink with two large ashtrays. A lucky guess....

"Hi, sweetie," I offered.

"What do you want?" She knows me all too well.

"Well, since you put it that way, I've talked with the coach and he suggests I get Vinny out of here, and, because of his...sour relations, to put it one way, with his dad, in order to give him, Vinny, a chance to relax before the game by getting out of here for the evening."

Judy's gaze did not waver during my entire rambling sentence. She stood for a while, silently contemplating. Finally, she spoke.

"You're crazy."

"No, it's real," I said, "Vinny's about to pop. He's bug-eyed out there. Plus, I heard his dad verbally attack him. It's no way to get the quarterback of an NCAA Division I school ready for a game."

"I really haven't noticed," she said, face unwavering. I know what Judy thinks. She thinks this is another one of my schemes.

"Can't you see it in Mike? It's a pressure-cooker out there!" I pleaded.

Judy cracked the kitchen door open. "All I see are a bunch of nice people."

"Shit!" I exclaimed. "On the surface!"

"Looks okay to me," Judy said. The best way to deal with the mentally ill is to remain calm and not react to them.

"Listen, Judy," I said, calmly myself, "I just wanted to tell you because I respect you and your hard work behind this get-together. I don't need your rubber-stamp on this. We're going."

She finally showed a little emotion. "Oh, hell, Mason, this is no time for conspiracy theories."

"This isn't a theory," I argued. "Vinny's dad drives him crazy. Jean doesn't help."

"Bullshit."

"Look at Vinny's face. Tight jaw. He's about to explode. He needs to be loose."

"Damn it," Judy said, "All right, Mason, let's suppose you're right. Considering the half-dozen or so reporters lined up outside our house, a group I'm considering inviting in, what's your plan?"

Reporters? What reporters? I ran out of the kitchen and opened the front door to find a gathering of several guys, some with cameras, on Wagner Road just beside the retaining wall that is below our porch. I shut the door quickly, and thought still more quickly. How in the hell are we going to get out of here? Finally, after a few moments of panic, I decided I have two choices, a) call Jacqueline Kennedy Onassis for advice, or b) convince someone that it is their duty to the great state of West Virginia to drive Vinny and me undetected to our safe house. The problem with this is it would involve telling that certain someone the truth about going to Michele's, which could present a bigger problem as that driver, probably intelligent and independently thinking, probably Alice and/or Judy would wonder why an interim head coach would agree to allow his starting quarterback and his designated wedgebuster to spend the night before the biggest game in the school's history at the home of an instructor of English. Again, why am I doing this?

Vinny walked into the kitchen. His face; he was the definition of death warmed over.

"Grab a couple of cigarettes and join me on the porch," he said to me. Vinny's smoked a half-dozen times in his life, all as a result of dealing with his father, all at the last resort. I looked to Judy with my hands palms up, the universal sign for 'see, goddamnit!'

I looked to Vinny. "I've got a better, healthier idea."

"I'm listening."

"You wanna get out of here for the night?"

"Right!" was his immediate, sarcastic response.

"No, really, I spoke with Van Watt just ten minutes ago and he said get out of here."

"Sure, Mason," said the ever-skeptical Judy, "Try finding a hotel room within fifty miles of here."

Alice came in with dirty glasses. "Hi, guys. Who wants a hotel room?"

I know we are going to need their help, so it's time to come clean. As I paused upon Alice's entry and reviewed what had taken place in the past half-hour, it is apparent to me I probably wouldn't believe me if I heard me. But I have no choice. And away we go…

"Here goes," I started, "from the top," All eyes are upon me. First I qualified their skepticism. "This is going to sound like the wildest thing I've ever come up with, but it is all the truth and if you let me finish, I think you'll see why we have to do it and why it'll work." They stared at me. "Okay, I'm really worried about Vinny, and I'm kinda losing it myself. I called my buddy Michele—"

"God, I thought you were going to say Joan," Judy spat.

"Why didn't you see us?" Alice asked.

"You were busy," I said.

"You got us now," Judy said.

"I know," I said, in placation, "I should have come to you earlier, but I've got you now and you'll soon see why Michele is important."

"You're going to stay there," Judy said.

"Well…I…"

"I knew it!" said Judy, slapping her hands.

Pauline walked in. "What did you know?" she asked.

Without breaking stride, Alice said, "One of Mason's professors is a lesbian. A young one. Pretty."

I quickly came to Michele's defense, "The hell she is!"

Pauline added, "You'll find that among your academic types, dear," she said to Alice. "Listen, honey, do you have the ashtrays in here?"

Alice showed her a clean one and with the appropriate thanks, her mother was off, back to the party. I continued my explanation, hopefully without this growing number of sidebars.

"Not that it would matter, but Michele Taranucci is…a…regular woman."

"That's not what we've heard," said Judy.

"Well," I continued, "it turns out she's Van Watt's girl and that's where the coach comes in." I decided to bring it home. "Michele talked him into letting us out of our house and into hers. It's good to have friends in high places." There. That is my summation.

Judy and Alice looked down then to each other, then to me. Their faces are sad, like kittens in need of a lot of strokes.

"Look, guys," Alice started, "I understand why this is taking place, but you've gotta realize we really dig being a part of this, and your leaving takes that away from us."

I glanced at Judy. When her eyes well up with tears she resembles Patsy Cline at her finest. And she gets me every time. Damn, I'm too much of a softy. This has to be The Gunner's call. Vinny took Judy in his arms and held her head to his chest. Alice moved to me for comforting. We four stood there in silence, seldom any closer. I had not realized that our football, a game of boys and men played in a semi-idiotic state, meant so much to them.

"I'm sorry, ladies, it's not you," Vinny said softly, "but I've gotta take the coach up on his offer and get out of here."

Good choice. Mike's got a good two hours of torture left in him tonight.

"I'll go to take care of you," I said

"Damn straight you will," Vinny said.

"So, I guess you'd better go pack," Alice said, sad.

Judy raised her head and asked sheepishly, "Can we see you tomorrow morning?"

Vinny and I looked at each other, "Yes, I don't see why not," I said. I then remembered the press out front. "Oh, shit, Judy," I said, "How in the hell are we going to make it by the horde of reporters and photographers?"

Vinny's eyes widened and his jaw dropped. Judy stepped in. "Hell, Mason. Six doesn't qualify as a horde. You exaggerate so much!"

"Two's bigtime to me," Vinny commented.

"We've got to sneak by them," I stated, "or Vinny and Michele will hit the papers in a tabloid fashion." Jean would love that. I wouldn't mind it.

"Oh, damn," Alice said, "Oh, damn, what can we do?"

"You guys pack," said Judy, "We'll think." We stared at her. "Go, go upstairs before somebody comes in and asks what the hell is going on. Go!" We moved quickly.

Halfway up the stairs, it hit me. I ran back down and caught the ladies as they were getting ready to go back out.

"As you know," I explained, "it is Vinny's week to park in the garage." Only one car at a time fits and we took turns. I continued. "We simply slip into the trunk and one of you girls will drive us out and away. It's been done before in many movies and will certainly work here in the quaint college town of Montani."

The faces of Judy and Alice showed wonder, then skepticism, then resignation and acceptance of my plan.

"Pack," said Judy. "We're all going."

I ran back upstairs, wishing it were Judy in that trunk. For a long time I have known that what separates me from the lower forms of life in the fraternities and on the football team or really any athletic team here and across the nation is that my desires, after being stirred first by physical attractiveness, are honed and struck in finality by a sense of daring, either hers or mine. Joan's stage in life nailed me in those regards, and the audacious Michele's keeps me thinking. Now Judy wants to drive the getaway car. It's all almost too much. Most guys want the girl next door. That's great for me, if she's a skydiver.

Packing tomorrow's clothes, sleepware, and essentials into a small duffel bag in record time, I walked to Vinny's room. Jean is there. The Gunner's explaining the new agenda for the evening.

"Jean, I'll say it again, Coach called and wants me to stay at his house tonight and talk over game strategy." The interrogation had started.

"I didn't hear your phone ring," she said.

"He's friends with Dr. Taranucci and was over at her house. She called Mason, and the coach asked for me," he replied.

"What are you doing tomorrow morning? Are you riding to the game with the coach?"

"No, he's bringing us by here early, and Mason and I will take our regular walk to the game."

"Why's scum Mason going?"

"Wha-ho!" I responded. That's strong, even coming from a woman who thinks I'm the human incarnate of Lucifer

"It is kind of strange," the Jean Queen said to me, backing away somewhat, "It's easy to understand my Vinny, but you…"

"Crikstein's going to be there," Vinny explained. He can lay down the lies deep and wide, even when they're not entirely necessary. That's frightening. "So's Arthur, representing the seniors." Jesus, Vinny, cut it out! "I guess he wants me to bring Mason because he understands me or some bullshit like that, Jean. I don't know. I just do as he says." He continued to stuff clothing in his bag, not knowing what he is cramming in there. My guess is he's right on the verge of exploding into a madman as his girl plays the kind of twenty questions she would ask if she thought he was going to a strip bar. The price of undeviating nookie.

I found Jennifer looking for me in my room. She bit my explanation,
Vinny's version of the truth. Understanding and harmonious, she never
looked less sexy. That says a lot more about me than her. I need challenging women, ones who stand in defiance of my nonsense. She kissed
me and wished me good fortune in a way only her beautiful eyes can.

We lugged our bags downstairs, Vinny's looking as if he were going
away for a week. I wouldn't mind it at all if Michele kept him as a sex
slave chained to her bedposts turning him loose only for football and
class. Vinny would like that and would dutifully report at the end of
each day, there to do anything she says. Anything. My imagination is
dangerous.

The Gunner found his dad and his mom and gave them the news of
The Coach's orders.

"I'm sorry. I wanted to hang around here with you two. Sorry." The
conciliatory son. I'm sorry he has to lie to the ever-supportive Patricia.
She just got caught in the wake. The Mike, however, the bastard doesn't
deserve the respect other fathers get.

Mom is fine with it, and proud of her son, looking at the coach's special attention as one of the advantages of leadership. Dad, however, is
surprised and wounded, his power over his Vinny having been seized by
a man who represented an organization for which he has little regard.

"Well, son," said Mike, standing stoic, "what do you want me to say?
You're free to go."

What do you want me to say! To say? Holy Mother of God, Mike, try
'I'm proud of you.' or 'You're the greatest!' or 'I know you're going to
win it for them.' You've gotta work at this fatherhood stuff, man! You've
got some man in Vinny as your son and he'd like to look up to you.
Instead, he spends his time figuring out how to fit his well-rounded life
into your square rules and regs. It doesn't work that way, my man.
You've gotta ease up.

That's what I wanted to say, but I'm stuck in the impasse of not having much credibility in most adult's eyes. I simply stood, enduring it all, waiting for the time to get out of there. Maybe, with any luck at all, we can get here tomorrow morning and leave before The Mike arrives. The longer Vinny is away from his father, the sooner he plays championship ball. That's not the way it's suppose to be, but it is the way it is. Saint Jude, patron saint of lost causes, please pray for Mike. And throw one in there for me while you're at it.

Patricia silently understood, as did the other parents, I think. The five of them wished us well and told us how proud they are of us. Vinny's mom squeezed him, a look of delight on his face, then passed him around for hugs and handshakes. Nobody understands my role as a wedgebuster, but they all treated me the same, including Mike, who after losing control of both of us just let us go, probably with a 'They'll be back.' Fuck him.

I found Jennifer and embraced her, feeling an almost overwhelming need to confess all to her, a need to be truthful, to stop screwing with the mind of a truly fine woman. I've lied to her and purposefully avoided her parents. She wants me to be the good man she deserves. Why not I?

Maybe next life.

Alice and Judy passed off the hostess duties to their moms and we four walked downstairs to the garage. Closing the door, only the streetlight outside above the reporters filtering in through the windows on the garage door guided us to the trunk lid lock on Vinny's Caprice. He must be desperate. Nobody but The Gunner drives Big Red.

Judy has the keys. She made a move toward the trunk, then stopped. "I really wanted you guys to stay home tonight. You're special to us. Damn." she said. Judy seldom pours it out. This must be getting to her. Alice put her hand through my arm. She, too. More causalities of The Mike.

"Come home for breakfast," Alice pleaded with a whisper.

I said, "We have to be at the High Ridge by eight. Have something ready for us by seven and we'll be there."

"Deal!" said Judy. Her dark face jumped into mine with a kiss. Wha-ha-ha-ho!

"Just as long as we eat and dash before my dad gets here," said Vinny. He's thinking straight.

Judy finally opened the trunk. Because of the trunk dome light possibly attracting unwanted attention, we hadn't much time to load us two in. That's when Judy said, "This is going to be fun! I haven't told you guys this but I'll be able to shake to press if they run after us. I once lost police pursuit."

"Fu—," was all Vinny could get out before I shoved his head in and climbed in after.

"Close it!" I exclaimed.

The trunk lid slammed, then was followed by the two car doors. We heard the garage door open and the ignition fire. Goddamn, I hope they hurry. Now I know what it's like being buried alive.

We felt the Caprice move out and turn left. Judy pulled it up a ways then inexplicably stopped. She's talking to the reporters! What the hell is she doing that for?

"Damnit! Damnit!" Vinny whispered.

The car started rolling again and turned right. We're moving at residential speed. Oh, shit!

"I don't know whether to wind my watch or kiss my ride goodbye!" Vinny said softly.

"Which ride?" I asked in reference to either his car or his scholarship.

"Both, goddamnit!"

"We're okay, Vinny. Trust me."

"I've been trusting you all week and you haven't screwed up yet. But when you do, it'll be a big kaboom!" My man is tense.

"You're going to find out that going to Michele's will be my best idea ever," I said with confidence.

"When am I going to discover this?" Vinny asked.

"When you hit your tenth consecutive completion tomorrow," I replied.

"So, Dr. Know-It-All, when will I stop feeling the pressure, you know, from The Mike?"

"Tomorrow morning. As we're crossing the South Hale Bridge."

"No, dipstick. I'm talking long term here."

"I can't answer that question. All I can say is, I'll be there with you."

"So, I'll be a young attorney, you'll be working on your first novel, and you'll be, like, down the street?"

"If Jean will have me."

"Who will be your bride?"

"I haven't the faintest. This could be the furthest I have ever been from the female gender."

"How can you say that? What about your ideal woman Joan? What about everyone else's ideal woman Jennifer?"

We hit a chug hole.

"Goddamnit!" shouted Vinny.

"Sorry!" yelled Judy.

"Anyway, what's this with you, November 1975, and women?" asked Vinny.

"Joan's ignoring my logic and I'm ignoring Jennifer's. It's classic," I responded.

"You have two days left with Joan. How can you give up now? Are you starting to believe her crap?"

"I don't know. I've done all I can do to prove my point. You should have seen me today in her class. I withstood her generational test she was unknowingly giving."

"How do you know it was unknowing?"

"Nothing resulted from it."

"You haven't given it a chance."

"Listen to you! You're planning my wedding, already!"

"No, she hasn't been around you enough today, or maybe it took a while for it all to settle, or maybe it's still settling—"

"What are you two talking about back there?" came the muffled shouting voice of Alice.

"Not sex," I screamed, "We're too close together." I could hear the girls' laughter over the road noise.

"No, Vinny. It's this," I continued, "I'm trying to protect myself from getting slapped around."

"When the hell did you start doing that? I told you today, that's you, man! That's the way you are! It's great!"

"I guess today...football's one thing...getting hit...you know, Gunner...it's...scary how I feel about her."

"And you've been slapped around before—"

"And I don't have good memories of that feeling."

My fears rendered us quiet. Maybe the unloading of my heart is because of my physical closeness to my closest friend. I've never laid beside Vinny for this long. He smells good. Maybe being boxed in a trunk of a car impels me to find my way out of the box I've put myself in with Joan. Maybe the absolute darkness cancels one of my five senses and forces me to examine her with my sixth. Sometimes I wish I were as simple minded as most college football players so all I would be able to think about is television and tits. Well, with Joan I guess I do half of that.

The car stopped as it had several times during the trip, but this time the car doors opened and slammed closed. I didn't have any more time to get into the philosophy of Mason and romance.

The girls opened the trunk to discover Vinny and me face-to-face, he on his right side and I on my back.

"Good thing I didn't find you two in the sixty-nine position," Alice deadpanned. Judy laughed.

"Tell me, boys, are we here?" Judy asked in a cocksure fashion.

I raised up, stiff, and looked. I saw Michele's house.

"We're here, Kato," I said.

I climbed out, then did Vinny as Michele stepped onto her porch holding a beer in her right hand.

"The trunk? My God, this NCAA football is serious," she bellowed.

"Michele, you remember Judy Lambert and Alice Calire?"

The three exchanged greetings. I became edgy. "We'd better get inside, Vinny. The press crew may not be far behind."

"Press?" asked Michele.

"We've gotta get back," said Judy, "We left a party we're hostesses for."

Michele tracked back to the matter at hand, "Come back another time," she said, "sometime when Mason doesn't have his Agent 86 complex kicked in high gear."

The girls laughed at that one. I gave them hugs of appreciation anyway.

"Tomorrow morning, seven sharp," commanded Alice.

"Yes, ma'am," replied Vinny.

Alice and Judy jumped back into the car with Judy still driving. She cranked it up, dropped it in drive, and squealed out. Vinny cringed.

"Who's pimpmobile is that?" asked Michele.

Friday, November 7, 1975
8:30 PM

At Michele's safehouse

Michele's house is an old turn-of-the-century mid-sized brick two-story with a full front porch. Located only five minutes from us, it's one of the classier old homes here in Montani. The Professor got lucky; the home actually hit the market this summer the hour she called the realty company. With help from her U. S. Steel assistant VP father, she had enough money to get a mortgage and closed within a week. Everybody was happy; the seller for moving so quickly, the realtor for garnering the commission, Michele for getting what she wanted and not having to endure the pain of looking and looking, her dad for making the apple of his eye smile, and the bank, well, just for being in a business in which if the world explodes and there are survivors, the banks still make money.

Interestingly, Michele's house was a speak-easy during Prohibition. That's a bullseye on her personality. And as the house tonight continues to re-live its history as a haven for those seeking to make sense of authority gone mad, Vinny and I turned to the open door. I have been here before and therefore know of the mahogany trim and the hard-wood floor and the antique mirror over the working fireplace, stoked for our warmth. I already have seen the contrast of the modern living room furniture; a sofa and easy chairs looking out-of-place in a strict sense, but knowing that's okay because most anything with Michele is not strict. I know of the old kitchen modernized with a dishwasher and garbage disposal. I have seen the dining room suite she scored for a hundred dollars at six o'clock in the morning at a yard sale. And I know of the steep stairwell going up from the living room, refurbished before she had moved in. All these things I have seen previously, and it's a good thing, because I would have definitely missed them this trip. As I walked in the door, my eyes and my mind and my soul were precisely focused on the beautiful woman sitting on the sofa. Joan is here.

She is dressed in a black long-sleeved top, probably cotton, probably soft, probably inviting, tucked into straight leg Wranglers over black leather boots, all accentuating her hour-glass (for lack of a better description, indicative of how difficult it is for me to think on my feet) frame. Her dark, dark brown hair did its flip. You're going to make it after all, Maggie J. Holding the brown bottle of a Miller Lite, she stared at me, very much I guess in a relaxed state.

"Why don't you go meet MJo then come over here and sit beside me," Joan said. She has to be at least slightly inebriated. I'm not prepared for this. I glanced at Vinny.

"You heard the woman," he said, grinning, "Go meet MJo and get over there."

Always obedient, I turned my attentions to Mary Josephine. She looked as Michele might look after her future babies, and that rests fine with me. Same everything, including the disarming smile.

"Hi, I'm MJo. I've heard so much about you. I think that qualifies you as Michele's favorite student."

I can feel my face flush. Too much attention from too many women. No, there can seldom be too many. Perhaps ultimately, but we're not there yet.

"Hi, MJo. And thank you. And this is my friend, Vinny Vacca." It's as if God found a bunch of great-looking Italians and sent three of them here.

"You're excused," MJo said to me, laughing.

"Thank you," I said, looking alternately at the sisters. Michele donned a black leotard top with a dark red mid-length skirt and black boots, a babe. Mary looked as if she had just left work, sporting well a white shell and a purple suit skirt, pumps, and a beer.

"Okay!" I said. "I'm coming, Miss Joan." There is a spot beside her left on the sofa as she rested against its arm. I took it.

"I thought you'd never get here," she said, eyes away from me. She is stunning and has alcohol on her breath. The ideal woman.

I got to the point. "Everybody here has a story, Joan. What's yours?" I asked.

Looking to me askance, she said without hesitation, "I needed company, so I called Mickey and she insisted I come over."

Mickey! Turning my head to Michele, I saw her smiling in a big way. Oh, I think I get it now. Oh, no, no, no…this can't be a set-up. No.

"What's your story, Mason?" Joan queried.

"Well," I answered, but not before I shot Mickey another 'fuck you' look, "Vinny and I were getting uptight, so I too called Mickey, and she insisted we come over."

"Why didn't you call me?" Joan asked as she pulled on a swig.

The other three are involved in their own conversation and are probably ignoring us. "I don't know," I replied, "I just don't know. I didn't think you wanted me to."

"You called me this morning."

"Yes…yes…but that was about school and this is the weekend, so I'm…I was trying to respect your privacy," I stammered out, nailing the truth and shaking on the inside because of it. "If you give me more time, I'll come up with other reasons." I have no idea why I said that.

"Don't take too much time," she said, "but, always remember, you can call me anytime you wish."

My brain is filling up with questions at a rapid rate and my abs are squeezing my gut, but I have to remain calm. Often, Joan by herself sets up within me the 'fight or flight' fear-reactive stress I felt back at the house tonight. However, with her there's a third, more correct, choice: do whatever she says. I gotta find out what's going on here…okay, here goes. "Mickey," I said toward Michele softly, "Let's get a beer." I then stood and walked to her kitchen. I turned around and there is the ol' Mickster. "What the hell is going on here?" I whispered. "What the hell is she doing here? And why didn't you tell me?"

Michele wouldn't rid herself of the grin. She softly said, "The last time I talked with you, she then called. I invited her over. It wasn't but a few minutes before she was at my front door. The rivals, together, partying on a Friday night. She had a beer in hand when she showed and has had two since she's been here. Who knows what happened before?"

"God, she's sloshed," I said in the same low tone.

"Then, that means your prayers have been answered. Just quarantine everything in that room," Michele said, motioning to the guest room/library across the hall. "And, also, Mason, don't forget, 'beware of prayers answered.'" She smiled, pecked my cheek and led us back to the living room.

Vinny and MJo sat across from each other, talking and trying to include Joan. It looked to be difficult. Dr. Kissinger has for the night given up that polish her parents had spent many years and many dollars perfecting. It's curious; I've never seen Joan like this. As I walked to her and once again sat beside her, I deliberated on the difference. Joan turned to me and smiled at me, giving the most sultry, artful visage I have ever been on the receiving end from any woman in my short but rapidly accelerating career with females. Then, it hit me: that's the difference between a First Family's finest and a five hundred dollar prostitute. It's merely in the way they carry themselves out of the eyes of the public.

I don't like that disparity, but not because it threatens me. I don't want roles. I want honesty and candor, between the woman and me, in public and private. This isn't theatre, honey. Just show me what you got, and what you're truly willing to give. And, I'll do the same.

If I have any one problem with Joan, it is exactly that. Is she just playing to the function, or is this the real her? Or does she even know who the real her is? Or is there one? And, if Miller Lite is indeed hops aged and brewed to yield sodium pentathol, then is this the true Margaret Joan Kissinger I'm seeing now? Or is it: Thursday, practical; Friday, practically out of her mind? And am I The Guy, or just a convenient bag of muscles, a brawny man she knows she won't have to sell on the idea? And if she does sell me, will I be able to live with myself the next day? It is in my best interest to remain skeptical.

Oh, hell, look at her here. Let's just see what happens. It is her call.

Joan turned and looked at me with a most unlikely combination of sensuality and detachment. The conversation then took a lull as the three women drew from their bottles and Vinny and I sat there empty.

"Oh my God!" exclaimed Michele, "I'm such a piss-poor hostess! Can I get you two something to drink?" She's appalled with herself, but she has a humorous way of showing it. Michele would probably make orgasms funny. Ron's right: I need medication.

The Gunner and I looked to each other. In our shorthand that sometimes is freaky, we decided without consulting to respectfully yield to our status as athletes in training getting ready for The Big Game: two beers each, one at a time.

"A beer each, please, you pick'em," I said to Mickey.

"Do you always order for Vinny?" Michele asked.

"Oh, no," I said. "Sometimes he orders for me."

"Sounds like marriage," MJo quipped.

I want to bring up the subject of soulmates, but I decided to wait until they have much more to drink.

Michele left to fetch the beers. MJo smiled. Joan looks less detached. Upon her return, Michele served the beers and took her seat. The silence is becoming awkward, so Vinny broke it.

"Thanks for having us over. I just hope I don't get weird tonight. It's been a strange evening to top off a strange week."

"I've told you about the football team travails," Michele said to MJo.

"Yeah, I'm sorry about that," MJo offered. "Not a good time for it to happen."

"No, and it's nice to be here in your little decompression chamber," I said. "This is just one in an odd series of events. But to be frank with you, as nice as it is to be here, preparing to play Pitt with three women never occurred to us. Right, Vinny?"

"We couldn't have planned it better," Vinny said. We laughed as a group.

"Well, this is your lucky day," Joan said, halfway through what at least is her fourth beer. "We're not just any women."

She's got me there.

"Yeah," said Michele, "Twenty years from now you'll be telling your children, '...and that's how we beat Pitt. Now let me tell you about the night before.'"

"All right, the night before...." mused Joan.

"I don't want to hear your night before, Joan," Michele snapped, smiling. Joan stuck out her tongue at Michele. Odd behavior. I guess they don't really hate each other. They seem to be like sisters in competition rather than rivals. Still, Mickey has been hinting and I...damnit I wanted to hear Joan's night before.

"Vinny," Michele asked as she turned to The Gunner, "how about your night before?"

Vinny sat up and took a deep breath, "Oh...it has something to do with...with...you know...doing whatever it takes to have a great game tomorrow." He is satisfied with his very covert answer.

Michele's not. "What do think that would be?"

Vinny held his palms out and nodded his in the negative. Michele responded, "Don't feel pressed. I just want to know what makes you tick. I find you...." She held it right there.

Even after that, Vinny could only get out, "I don't know. I just know I would do it, whatever it is." Sometimes my Gunner is just not imaginative enough. But, Michele has high standards. Trying to help him out, I stated, "Whatever it is, I, too, would do it."

"Works for me," MJo said.

Relentless, Michele continued to probe, "Now, gentlemen, does this 'whatever' include felonies, high crimes and misdemeanors?"

"You betcha!" I exclaimed.

"Whatever's reasonable," said Vinny, "Where's this going?" He's concerned.

"Don't worry, my man," I said, "She's just messing with our heads. I'm used to this."

MJo and Joan continued to yield the floor to their sister and colleague. MJo stroked her beer bottle and Joan pressed her leg against mine. I took it all like a man.

"*O contraire*, my Mason, I am interested," said Michele, "For instance, what does it take to be a high performance athlete? When you 'sell it,' as they say, what do you sell?"

"I need a beer," said Joan as she stood, "Beer, anyone?" Knock 'em down, Maggie J!

Michele hates to be interrupted, especially by Joan. "I'm about ready to cut you off," said one Doctor to the other.

"But, Mickey, I really need a beer," pleaded Joan, "It's high priority."

Michele paused, then said, "Okay, but we're going to monitor you bottle-by-bottle. Now, gentlemen...."

Most of me is elated Joan wants another beer. What was the question?

Vinny started, "Okay, look at this summer...we lifted weights and ran and..."

Oh..."And sweated and grunted a lot. But...."

"But?" asked Michele.

"But anybody can sweat and grunt. What we give up is our souls." I concluded.

"Yeah," punctuated Vinny.

"Yeah, Vinny?" asked Michele again. She wanted in his mind.

Vinny tried to start it, "Yeah...." then I think he just wanted to relax his brain; that or he's afraid of giving the wrong answer. I have no such fear, except maybe to the question, 'In three seconds, where is this thing with Joan going?' "You take over, Mason. She's your teacher."

Michele visibly displayed her disappointment. She hears from me all day, every day.

"What do we sell, you ask," I began, in a manner in which I had decided will be blatantly honesty, "Football is demeaning. Some say it's a contact sport. Other go beyond that and call it a collision sport.

Actually, it's worse than that: it's an attack sport. In front of forty thousand witnesses you can do things that would get you locked up elsewhere. Take the helmet, for instance. Protection? Yeah, but it could be more accurately described as a weapon. I run forty yards in four point four seconds, fast but not blazing. That's nineteen miles per hour average. And I get up to that speed pretty quickly. At a hundred eighty-five pounds, that's a lot of momentum behind the rock-hard helmet. Take my word for it, I dish out a lot of pain. And, forget me. Think about Michael Burton, big, fast, and irate. And Joe Osbourne, big, fast, and intent on extermination. Each top twenty team has a couple Michaels or Joes. Top ten teams have several. It's hit and be hit, kinda like a combination of the movie *Roller Ball* and the real demolition derby. That's why it's so demeaning. And that's what we give up."

Joan repositioned herself, turning toward me and placing her left arm behind my head. I guess she likes something I said.

MJo is the next to respond, "Why do you do it?" Michele leaned forward, very interested in this answer.

"I don't know," I replied, "but the night before facing the number one team in the nation is not the time to ask that question." The Taranuccis nodded to the affirmative. I didn't look at Joan. I assume she is stirred by my insight.

"As I expected," Michele said, "you're very eloquent in your discussions of such a brutal sport, a game so devoid of feelings."

"Oh, we have feelings," I said, "We just turn them into the energy it takes to rock someone's back teeth. Everything in football is hit, everything, that is, except for most of the quarterback play."

"What do you do, Vinny?" Michele asked, "What do you do with your feelings?"

"I've got to keep my head," Vinny responded, "I usually end up eating my feelings."

"Not good!" MJo said, "Does this describe your life?"

Vinny inhaled through his nose, "Yes, and that's why I'm happy to be here."

"You're welcome anytime, Vinny," said Michele.

"Just get me through the night," The Gunner said. He's calmer already.

"Deal!" said Michele, "Another round. But first, Joan, walk this line in the rug here."

She refused with a smile.

"Aw, I'm just kidding, anyway," Michele said as she headed for her refrigerator, "But, at this pace…well, we'll just keep an eye on you."

Joan smiled again. I'm in love. Somebody better keep an eye on me.

MJo quickly turned to Vinny, "I've always wondered: What do you guys say in that huddle?"

That is a good factual question for my boy. I know Vinny will respond thoughtfully. "Keeping in mind that tomorrow will be the first collegiate varsity huddle I will have ever been in and can only guess from comparison with the lower-grade huddles, there is first a lot of swearing at each other, a lot of use of the f-word, then I shout everybody down and call the play."

"Give me an example of a play," MJo requested as Michele brought the beers. Is MJo just being nice, or…

"Uh….uh….here's one I might call tomorrow, 'Red formation right, flanker X, CI sucker double bow out," said Vinny, "Oh, on one."

"What the hell does all that mean?" asked Joan, in what could be her first question ever for Vinny. But, her reaction is right. For some reason, football coaches, most of whom have a hard time getting through a Louis L'Amour novel, make plays as complicated as the Dewey Decimal System.

Being diplomatic, since he loves me and despite providing me with Joan pep talks doesn't particularly like Maggie J, Vinny explained, "Red formation puts the tight end on the left and the split end and the flanker on the right. The tight end and the split end each run a bow out, which is a curve in then out. The flanker, after the ends sucker in the defensive backs, crosses over the middle."

"Then what do you do?" asked MJo.

"I throw the ball to the open man, probably the flanker."

"What if nobody is open?" asked MJo.

"I throw to Arthur O'Neill, the running back."

"What if he's not open?" asked Joan.

"I run for my life," Vinny concluded with humor.

The three ladies looked around at each other. "You guys need more women in football. That would certainly improve communications," Michele said.

"Plus, we wouldn't curse in the huddle," said MJo. "We'd just whisper to each other catty comments." The girls giggled to that one.

Vinny and I stared at each other. Point missed. Change the subject.

"Vinny," said Michele, "and I ask you this question not trying to pin you or harass you, but because it is my nature to ask these types of questions, I'm not looking for any one answer, or any answer if you so wish—"

"Jesus, Michele!" I said.

"She's been this way her entire life," laughed MJo.

"Okay, I'll get to the point—Vinny, are you nervous?"

I've taught Vinny enough about being open minded and about considering things beyond the jock world, and the thoughtful look on his face showed that he's not going to give the simple man-stud answer.

"I'll tell you ladies," he finally started, "I am confident that I will do my best tomorrow. I can say that. But, the lingering doubt that all football players have, and only Mason I know of, and probably me, who has been shown by Mason, only we will admit to…Jesus, I sound like Mason." The girls laughed. Vinny continued, "is the fear that our best will not be good enough. And that's the problem."

Wow, Gunner! You are miles ahead of your father, my man. The room sat silent. Kung Fu, baby! Snatch the pebble, grasshopper.

I decided to pick up where he left them. "That's where the real nerve-racking nerves come from," I said, "You don't wanna look stupid and spend the day on your butt. And it also stems from failing somebody. If you give your best, you can't fail yourself. But if someone expects you to do a job, and you respect that someone, and you don't get the job done, well, the potential for that disappointment makes for a lot of jitters as kickoff approaches."

"Because of all that," Vinny added, "I am proud to say I have prayed to the porcelain alter a couple times today."

The women aren't grossed out by that last remark, probably because Vinny is so handsome he can say anything he wants. I would hope that they're impressed by our worldly ingenuousness.

"Wow!" MJo said, after a pause. "Thanks. Thank you for not being the typical jocks. I feel like I've just watched *60 Minutes*." All the women nodded in approval.

"Can he, the coach, be gotten for anything really serious?" asked MJo. "Isn't this some kind of crime?"

"It's at least tax evasion, although since he recently received the money he may not get nailed on that," I answered. "I don't know. As Michele said, there has to be some kind of law against state employees receiving money…I don't know, the son-of-a-bitch."

Joan has been silently and to my delight draped on my right side for sometime now. She chose this time to speak.

"Follow me, Mason," she said, as she stood and walked through the party, down the hallway and toward the guest room/study. I blindly followed, walking by Michele, who commented, "Remember what I said." I do. I most certainly do.

Friday November 7, 1975
8:55 PM

Joan and I, together, alone, sort of

Joan walked to the open door of Michele's spare and stopped. She turned to me. I knew what to do. Chivalrously, I swept the damsel into my arms, turned quickly and glanced to Vinny who has his face in his hands in semi-disgust. I then turned back, carrying my woman through the threshold. Kicking the door shut louder than I had wished, I walk the three steps to the bed, laid Joan on it, and then placed a chair beside the bed, sat in it, and propped my booted feet beside hers. More Jerry Lewis than Dean Martin, but it's all I have to offer for now.

The room functions as a both a study and a guest room. There is the bed, of course, but also two bookcases filled with the classics as well as contemporary novels. A desk made of dark mahogany, the same wood as the bookcases and the trim, sits beside the bed and in front of a window with louver blinds. For added measure as well as punctuation, Joan reached to her left and closed the blinds. Only the eyes of the Dutch masters with which Michele interestingly has chosen to decorate the walls can now see.

Lying on her left side and propping her head with her left arm, Joan looks like a woman who owns her destiny. I just want to make certain she doesn't sail that yacht through me.

"Mason, Mason," she said,

"Joan, Joan," I replied.

That which has transpired tonight, the drinking, the flirting, and now the bed lounging, all out of character for Joan as I know her, almost crowds me out of the room. Believe it or not, the fear of love-making is present. I know if I do anything it'll look awkward, so I just sit here.

She quickly sat up, then caught herself to her right and giggled a bit. Yep. She's drunk. I've got a good-lookin' drunk chick on a bed behind closed doors. Referring to my rule number one, I'm trying not to freak out.

"So," Joan said, after which she took a deep breath, "how's Jennifer?"

"Fine," I answered, "I saw her right before I left. Why do you ask?"

"I care about my students," she said.

"I know you care for the welfare of your students. You've told me," I said, a dig. I am however comfortable enough to let her steer the conversation for now. Jen? What exactly does she mean by that? It's at least the third time today she's mentioned Jen….

"Is she taking good care of you?" Joan asked in a coy manner, probably missing my 'welfare' remark.

"What do you mean by that?"

"You know what I mean. Taking care of," she said, head weaving a bit, pausing, then continuing, "In the sense of…animal needs." She leaned in on that one.

Wow! Whoa! Why? Well, let's just be careful and have some fun with this. "In the sense that Jennifer and I have congressed and exchanged genetic material like protozoa, no. And with regard to relationships between men and women, I don't discuss those."

"Ah, bullshit! I'm sure you and Vinny don't talk. And you're in a locker room everyday. I'm sure you guys only talk about your cross stitching," Joan said with the grin.

"They may talk, but I don't. And as for Vinny, we just assume it is given unless otherwise stated."

"What have you told Vinny about Jennifer?"

"I have told him the truth. Nothing has happened."

"Bullshit, again!" Joan slurred.

What's her problem? "It's only been a day and a half. She really hasn't had a chance."

"Good!"
"What?"

~ ~ ~ ~ ~ ~ ~ ~ ~ ~

The three remaining in the living room huddled. Michele started, as always, "Okay, Vinny. Mason talks to you more than Joan talks to me. What the hell is going on here?"

"I really don't know," Vinny replied, "but I don't like it because she's drunk. She's manipulative, and she's drunk, and she's beautiful and I don't like it at all."

"Good read," said Michele.

~ ~ ~ ~ ~ ~ ~ ~ ~ ~

"What I mean is," Joan said, "she'd better take care of you somehow or I'll kick her pretty little ass."

"Why?" I'm astonished.

"Because I care for your welfare," Joan said, Laughing.

Just great! Now the professorial back-pedaling. I thought this all could have been something, but I guess you can never be sure with Maggie J. It's still in my best interest to give her room. Therefore....

"What about Alan?" I asked, turning the conversation. "You're crazy about him."

"Nah..."

"He's all you could talk about for two weeks now. And, you have to admit, he's rich, handsome, he's got that movie star tan. He must be a sight naked."

Responding without questioning my sexual preference, Joan just re-emitted a, "Nah..."

"There's something to talk about," I said, "Subject: Jennifer and Alan. Why Don't They Work For Us?"

"I didn't say that," said Joan in a shift, "I simply said 'Nah.' "

"Nah," I retorted, "Nah, nah, nah, nah," I sung in the familiar rhythm and blues song, "Nah, nah, nah, nah."

Joan and I brought it home it together, "Hey, hey, hey, goodbye." We laughed and laughed, though you have to have at least one drunk person to make that really funny.

~ ~ ~ ~ ~ ~ ~ ~ ~ ~

Michele, MJo, and Vinny heard the muffled singing and laughter. "Should we check on them?" asked MJo.

"Nah," answered Vinny, "I know Mason. He's holding his own right now."

"I think I know what you mean by that, and I hope it's true," Michele said, "I hope he hasn't capitulated to the Eyelashes."

"What the hell do you mean by that?" MJo asked.

"It's Joan," answered Michele, "Her bod sets the hook but her eyelashes reel them in."

Vinny thought for a while, "I can see that."

"Yeah, it's pretty easy to figure out once you've seen her in action," said Michele, "She maintains eye contact, and it's as if she zaps them with a laser death ray."

"Avert your eyes, Mason!" cried MJo in a semi-shout. Michele gave her a weird look. MJo just smiled.

~ ~ ~ ~ ~ ~ ~ ~ ~ ~

"Oh, Mason, you could have any woman you want by simply hanging around the cosmetics aisle at the supermarket," Joan said. "Can I get you a beer?"

"Thank you, Joan," I said in reply to her comment and to the mystery of it, "And, sure. I'll have another. And that will be my limit for the night."

"We'll see about that," she said smiling, lifting herself from the bed, then opening the door and exiting the room.

I don't want think about this too much, you know, like developing a strategy or something. Things seem to be going well. I surmised she has something to tell me or she wouldn't have dragged me into this room. Let her tell you, then take it, whatever it is, from there.

I could hear Joan asking Michele for two more beers. "Okay, but one of these sober people, of which I do not intend to be, is going to drive you home tonight," said Michele.

"Don't worry, I'll straighten up by the time I leave," Joan said. I'm sure Michele believed that.

Re-entering 'our room' with two bottles of Miller Lite, Joan handed me the bottles, then took her place back on the bed as I remained in my chair. I cracked them open, handed her one, and we clinked bottles to a toast. "To our time together," she said.

"On earth and intergalactically," I added.

"See, Mason, you know just what to say," she said in a complimentary manner. "Women love that."

Oh, I get it now. This is her 'Go Find Somebody Else To Write Letters To' speech. Well, I'm going to play dumb until she has to blurt it out her own damn self. Shit.

~ ~ ~ ~ ~ ~ ~ ~ ~ ~

"That, uh, that tall girl in her class..." stated Michele.

"Jennifer," Vinny responded.

"Yeah," Michele said, "Jen. She really threw Joan for a loop."

"Ya think?" Vinny said, "How's that?"

"Yep," started Michele, "Things changed after yesterday morning. Suddenly this young man whose affection she had in her hands has found somebody new. Very suddenly. I saw it. No more talk of that pretty boy

Alan. And it happened just like that. Joan would hate to know this, but I can read her like a cheap novel. She's scrambling now."

"Now, Mason looks much more attractive to Joan," MJo said, "That probably explains why she called you a little tipsy. She wanted to talk about it. Then, she runs directly into it."

"Exactly," said Michele, "Vinny, you're the Mason expert with the most seniority. What do we do here?"

"Let it play," Vinny said, "Let it play. I've seen this twice before and you can't tell him anything until he hits the rocks."

"We can't just sit here, can we?" asked MJo.

"I agree with Vinny," Michele said, "His history. Her history. This could be the time they come together. But, maybe not. It's difficult to interfere, even when you consider the jeopardy in which Mason has placed his heart."

"That doesn't mean I have to like it," said Vinny.

"What don't you like about it?" asked MJo.

"The obvious," responded Vinny, "The age thing."

"Let me play the devil's advocate here," said Michele, "if they truly love each other, what's the problem?"

"Mason should be with Jennifer," said Vinny, "or some girl like Jennifer…. Maybe not Jennifer, because I don't really believe…she's just not very bright."

"I can understand why that would be important for your boy," Michele said.

"Anyway," Vinny continued, "the ages are important because of the basic…commonness, I guess…you know, like both being in school together during the Middle East crisis, for instance. Mason and whoever that girl would be can draw upon that, and build on it."

"Interesting," Michele said. "Sounds like a romantic version of Meet The Press, *but interesting nevertheless."*

"*I don't really know. I'm just guessing,*" said Vinny.

"*No, really, I see your point,*" said MJo.

"*I've had a lot longer to think about this. Besides, I think Jennifer could strangle Mason with sweetness,*" said Vinny.

"*Yeah, you have to kind of slap him around to keep him in line. But, I've seen Joan and him go at it for a while. There's something there, I'm pretty sure. She's just having a difficult time getting to it,*" said Michele, "*I've always thought it was okay, but dangerous. For the Brick. I also thought Mason was strong enough to take it. Again, I'm not too quick to hop on the age wagon. If neither one sees a problem, I don't see a problem.*"

"*Maybe not for some age differences, but in this case, in our cases, Vietnam calls the shots,*" Vinny said.

"*How's that?*" MJo asked, wanting to hear more.

"*Because you had people your ages getting shot and dying, whether you knew them or not. The war was much more real to you,*" Vinny said. "*We were several years behind you and just didn't see it the same way. It was one of those life-shaping experiences that you had to be there to understand. You two and Joan were there. Mason and I weren't.*"

"*Pretty wise for a quarterback,*" said MJo in a very complimentary way.

"*No, really, I've just had a while to think about this,*" he replied.

"*Yeah, for a guy who looks like a male model, you're pretty much on top of it,*" Michele said.

"*Thank you, Michele, I think*"

~ ~ ~ ~ ~ ~ ~ ~ ~ ~ ~

"You think I'm a real bitch, don't you, Mason."

Oh, hell, it's self-effacing time. She's pulling out the big guns now. I always thought if I had ever gotten into a room with a bed with Joan, I'd be uncontrollably aroused. Well, her attitude sucks and that's a big turn off.

I answered, with my new information less-than-truthfully, "No, Joan, far from it."

"I don't want to be a bitch," she said with a pouty face one might think a bitch would have.

"And you're not being a bitch."

She squirmed back and rested upright against the headboard. She did look luscious. I take it all back. That turned my crank. "I have all of the requirements for bitchdom," she added.

"And those are…," I asked.

"You tell me," Joan said playfully.

"Oh, no. I'm not getting anywhere near that answer."

"Long eyelashes, bod," she recited in list format, "attitude. You know."

Okay…oh…trying to change the subject with dignity, I said, "You are gorgeous, Joan."

"An old boyfriend of mine once said I am drop-dead gorgeous."

"I'll be more creative than that and call you walk-into-a-parking-meter gorgeous," I said, one side of my brain wanting to stop talking about this ridiculous subject and the other side hoping it might get me somewhere by feeding her self-absorption.

Joan Laughed. "I like that one! And, thank you, Mason. You are a gentleman's gentleman. To you, I say something I never say…"

"And that is?"

"Come sit on this bed with me."

Thankful for this opportunity and for the fact I'm wearing heavy denim Levi's and a blazer long enough to cover me, I moved from my lowly seat to my place of honor beside the woman whom has been entrusted with my welfare. She must be what one would call 'full service faculty.'

Having to turn to my right to talk to her, it is more uncomfortable up here, but who's complaining? I restarted the conversation with some topspin. "A gentleman's gentleman. I accept that as a high compliment."

"I've been around you enough to know that you do everything with class, especially surprising since you are a vicious football player." Shoulder to shoulder. Eyes to eyes. This is the closest I have ever been to

Joan without having to almost ride a skidding passenger jet off the edge of a hill.

"I accept both as compliments, for reasons that are hard to explain." I'm maintaining, but at the same time I'm becoming lost in her brown eyes.

"How can you do that, Mason? Football? I have a difficult time seeing it." Our eyes remained fixed. Maybe now she can see how I feel about her.

"Not just football, but playing football and living high social standards." Back off, son. Get humble. Deep breaths. "I had good parents. My mother taught me the mannerly aspects of life. My father taught me how to hit. Playing here in Montani is something I have always dreamed of. I like living my dreams. For that, I'm a lucky man." Is that as humble as it gets? Jesus, Cheetah.

"So, you like living your dreams," Joan repeated. I can't break myself away from her eyes. We're so close. Everything above my waist tightened.

"Yes," I said softly.

Joan took in a breath. "Mason, that's a beautiful letter you wrote me."

I quickly glanced at her lips. That made it worse. "I don't know why you look at it differently today than yesterday, but thank you. I put my heart into it." How I ever said that, said anything, I'll never know.

"I certainly could tell. You referred to me as every nice thing but a goddess."

"Damn it to hell, I knew I left something out." I said by instinct. Joan Laughed. Humor gets them. Whew! Thank God! I need a break.

~ ~ ~ ~ ~ ~ ~ ~ ~ ~ ~

Vinny drained his second one and is close to, despite everything he as a jock has been trained against, talking himself into a third. His degree of relaxation is remarkable to him. The Taranucci sisters have risen to the occasion.

"I can see what you're getting to, Vinny," said Michele. "The war was very real to us. Our family had a friend killed over there. Joan, on the other hand…well, it should have been renamed the Upper Class National Guard."

"I'm sorry," Vinny interrupted, not wanting to uncover his secret, thereby comparing himself to Joan, "I didn't mean…."

"Not to worry, Vinny," MJo said, cutting in, "Vietnam makes our sub-generation within the larger Baby Boom generation, if you can call us that, much different than the others. We challenged a government action that in the past had seemed so natural. I mean, every generation has a war, right? We said 'fuck that.' "

"I can see your point, Vinny," Michele started, "I understand why you are concerned for your friend. She has gained a helluva lot of experience from nineteen to…to…however old we are. That combined with her general nature and she could puree Mason's heart like Christmas yams. You have every right to be wary."

"Then, I ask the question again, what do we do?" asked MJo, now involved like her sister.

"Let it happen," said Vinny, "Not because I want to see him in pain. Far from that. It's just because…"

Michele finished the trailer, "There's nothing we truly can do. I've talked with Mason a lot. I can tell from his life story that he seeks pain. It's the manifestation of what he's been through. And even though he's a good man, his actions on the football field, the way he punishes people all the while sacrificing his body, is cathartic. It's his way of dealing with what he's been dealt . Pain is familiar, plus just as importantly, he takes out his anger on those he hits. As long as he plays football, he's okay. After that, who knows?"

"Yeah," said Vinny, "The way he is now is okay, for now. But the future Michele, you're right."

~ ~ ~ ~ ~ ~ ~ ~ ~ ~

In a fit of drunken female laughter, Joan repeated my name, "Mason, Mason, Mason…."

Still feeling the relief from the comedy interlude, I answered, "Joan, Joan, rhymes with moan…."

She missed it. Losing equilibrium for a moment, more laughter came forth. "Wow! I'm spinning! Hold onto me, Mason! I'm outta control!"

She is, so I held, despite the fact I'm still a bit irritated with her moderate state of besottedness. Is this the only way I can get close to her? Does she have to slam down a few brews to let her passions for me shine through? Must all her inhibitions be overcome by alcohol; the constraints with which she represses our love while she is sober subjugated by the effect a little bit of fermented barley, a legal drug, has on her brain?

I'm at her mercy.

"Whoa, that's better," Joan said as she steadied. "Whew." She held me snug. "Wow, you have a nice body. You are tight." She caressed me under my blazer and looked me over. I'm an absolute sucker for any observation she is willing to make.

"Thank you, Miss Margaret," I replied, this close to her lips.

She jerked back. "No one ever calls me Margaret!" she exclaimed. "You have the guts to go where no man has gone before."

Despite thinking that merely saying a name doesn't put me in the same class as Sir Edmund Hillary, I helped her run with it.

"And where would that be, Miss Margaret?"

Joan jumped over me and off the bed, very agile. That's something to think about.

"I'll be back," she said as she opened the door and exited the room.

~ ~ ~ ~ ~ ~ ~ ~ ~ ~ ~

Joan eased down the hallway, primping her hair and smoothing the wrinkles on her top. Entering the room Masonless, all eyes are on her. She looks guilty and still drunk, especially to Michele, who said, "Thank you for keeping the noise down."

"Michele," Joan began, "it's not what you think. Besides, I'm here in search of my purse."

"What do you carry in your purse that you so desperately need?" asked Michele, the question on the minds of the other two.

Fishing though her bag then finally finding something, Joan ceremoniously pulled it out and exclaimed, "Nailpolish!"

"Whatever you intend on painting, my dear Joan," said Michele, "have some respect."

"Yes ma'am," said Joan like the obedient teenage daughter, nodding and turning away back down the hall.

"And be in by eleven!" Michele yelled behind her.

"She is in," Vinny said.

"Oh. Yeah," she answered. "Anyway, more importantly, now what happens to our friend?"

"I've seen him fall twice before," said Vinny, "It's a bit ugly, but he gets back up."

"Our boy Mason is a passionate soul," said Michele.

"He seems to be years ahead of his time," said MJo. "Oh, Vinny, I'm sorry. The present company thing…."

Vinny waved it off. "One of these days he'll make some girl a lucky woman. Until then, he's going to get jostled around." he stated.

"You really love him," said MJo, very impressed.

"Yes," Vinny replied, "We have history."

The three sat silent with respect to Vinny.

Michele always breaks these moments, "So, we're just going to let him subject himself to Joan d'Arc, the conqueress of men…."

Vinny said, "We'll just have to let him figure it out for himself. And…be there to help him pick up the pieces."

~ ~ ~ ~ ~ ~ ~ ~ ~ ~

Joan reentered the room and closed the door. If I just a few weeks ago could only have known I would be here…or anywhere…with her, I would have been a happy man. Incredible.

She smiled at me, that of a beauty, and held up her left hand. "Red? Or red?"

I gave it a few seconds, but I don't get it.

"Look, silly! Red, or red?" Holding up two small somethings, she continued her explanation, "Don't you see?" Joan then walked closer to me and bent down to me sitting on the bed. She softly kissed my face. That drove it home. "I want you to paint my nails. My toenails."

"You're really not kidding, are you?" I asked, not knowing whether to apply the nailpolish with my tongue or run for the door.

"Please?" Joan pleaded, "Of, course, you have to want to." She looked fine. Okay.

"I want to," I replied, "I just can't believe I'm doing this. If my father…knew I did this the night before Pitt…"

"He'd say, 'Well done, son.'" emitting a drunken cackle that took years off her age. Getting the feeling I would lay it all out for her, I decided being in love with Joan is like running the crossing route of romance. It takes blind focus to pull it in as you wait to get jackhammered.

I then saw this as an opportunity to gauge the situation. "Are you sure you're not getting me to do this because Alan won't?"

Joan didn't bat an eye, "No, and he is the furthest man from my mind."

Initially seeing this development as nothing but positive, I responded with the at best quasicool, "Oh, really?"

"Actually, I'm in a one man universe right now."

The cool collapsed. "Oh, really?"

Joan slipped the boots and the little quarterstockings from her feet quickly, leading me to hope anything can be slipped quickly from her. Her feet are in my lap before I knew it, barely missing the Not There,

Not Yet spot. "Yes darling," she answered to my 'Oh, really?' Then she threw the red bottles toward her feet, this time hitting the mark and causing me to wince. "Paint," she ordered. Is nothing sacred?

I twisted myself into a comfortable position and proceeded to unscrew the cap and brush from the tiny scarlet bottle. Feeling like I'm losing it and therefore compelled to say something that sounds like something James Bond would say, although Mr. Bond would never find himself here but possibly for the honor of the Union Jack, I quipped, "Now that we have each other exactly where we want each other, where are we going with this?"

"Well, sweetmeat," the recovering Joan said, "I'm simply going to sit back, get my toes painted, and enjoy it immensely. But your question begs another question: Where were you going with that letter?" She gazed smugly.

I decided to counter with the starkness of the truth. "Oh, Joan, that's obvious. I'm in love with you. Sincerely yours."

Bouncing from the ropes, she came back with a haymaker of what she considered to be reality, "How can you ever know what love is?"

I swung. "Shall I start from the beginning?"

"No better place," Dr. Kissinger said.

"First, I, a high school sophomore," I offered. "She was Roxanne."

"Great name."

"Thank you. We went on for a year or so. She was some woman—"

"Really, Mason, a tenth grade woman?"

I paused to apply the first brushstroke. "Roxanne was a college freshman."

Joan had nothing to say to that.

I continued. "She was wonderful. Spontaneous. Never knew where she was taking it. Then she finally got used to college and her coed social life and didn't need my anchor any more. You of course know what happened next. I saw it coming. Everybody saw it coming. I'm surprised she took it as far as she did. But, it was most certainly worth it."

"Ah, Mason, your first heartbreak…." Joan said, reaching for me but kept beyond arms' length by the rest of her body.

I probably looked pitiful in the application of my second brush stroke. "I rallied," I said, in a show of strength.

"Where's that hussy now?" Joan said in sincerity.

"Manhattan. Modeling," Maybe it's a blow to her that there is somebody before her who might still be prettier.

"Wow," was all she could say.

"She's very bright," I offered with a twist, "but she also has the look, you know, long, lean, white teeth, smooth complexion."

"What would she say if she walked through that door?" Joan said, testing.

"She just might do that," I said, "She's in town for the game."

~ ~ ~ ~ ~ ~ ~ ~ ~ ~

In an attempt to be a part of the conversation and not to be shut out by her perennially loquacious sister, MJo had been asking Vinny questions about him and football.

"How does it feel to be a quarterback, Vinny?" MJo asked.

Vinny paused to ponder, pleased with the stature he had created between the women. He's done it through words, a realm he had always conceded to Mason. And…he thought…there is life beyond Jean. At the risk of pontificating, but then again not caring if he did, he spoke. "I've never done anything else, so it might be hard answering that question…but, here goes: You're in charge. You handle the ball every play. All eyes are on you. Everyone on the other team is trying to nail you, and I've only gotten sick twice today."

That's the second time I've said that; they're probably sick of me, thought Vinny. Nothing could be further from the truth. The ladies' laughter surely could be heard in the next room. They're having fun, thought Michele, and it's being done without illicit sex, illegal drugs, and rock and roll as she knows it. "Well, let me tell you," announced Michele, with a nice beer buzz, "*From the way you answered that question, I can tell you're ready. You may need some sort of machismo around men, but we girls, we know. You're being honest with yourself. And that's good. And you're ready.*"

"Thank you," Vinny offered humbly. "*I feel like I'm nervous because I'm anticipating it. It's new territory for me. I've never quarterbacked a college play, much less a game. But, once I get in the game and get into the game, I know I'll be all right. I won't have time to think of anything else.*"

~ ~ ~ ~ ~ ~ ~ ~ ~ ~ ~

Upon doing the mental processing about Roxanne and models and Montani, which only took fractions of a second, Joan shot me a glare. I love it! "Not to worry, Twinkle-Toes," I said, "Rox and I are just buddies." I expertly laid down another stroke.

"Okay, lover," Joan said, thinking someone threatens, "who was next?"

"Ursula."

"Where do you get these names?" Joan asked, becoming irritated.

"From the women themselves. Joan, the key to a good toe painting is that all parties, the person with the toes and the person with the brush, enjoy it. Now, I'm having a good time," I responded.

She calmed. "Sorry. I'll start over. Another college student?"

"Not quite. I was a high school senior. She was cum laude from Smith in letters."

Joan went wide-eyed, again. "Considering everything, this has to be a story." The peeve is coming back. Is it too early for her to express real jealousy? Nevertheless, I'm flattered.

I began. "Ursula left straight from commencement in '73 to take a year away and work in her uncle's diner a couple of miles from my house. We hit it off really well. We talked a lot, read to each other, I drank a lot of coffee, probably stunting my growth. I was enamored with her. She liked me, too." I paused to deliver a brush stroke.

"What happened?" the expression on her face not changing since I said the sentence fragment 'Smith in letters.'

"Kind of a contrapositive of Roxanne. She left for Massachusetts, turning me loose against my will two weeks before I took off for my freshman year up here, in the name of my college experience. In a very poignant scene, the last time I spoke with her was from a roadside pay phone in front of the diner to her new apartment in Chestnut Hill in the high middle of an August thunderstorm. I got soaked, in a few ways. That was potent."

"Damn," Joan said. We sat silent for the longest time. I painted a couple more toes.

"This is interesting," she finally said. "I've just had your standard queenie sorority relationships. I mean, no one's ever hurt me. And I didn't hang around long enough to see if I scorched any of their earth. I can't even remember two of them. You, however…"

Joan's words are still from a pickled brain. And, amazed to have been on the receiving end of such a confession, I strangely chose not to address it. "I didn't seek odd relationships," I instead said. "Well, I guess I did in the sense that I didn't go for school girls."

All the while, Joan stared at her toes. This has officially become a sensuous experience.

Breathlessly, Joan said, "You're doing a great job down there. I know you've done this before."

"You've got me pegged on that one."

"Ursula."

"How did you know?" I replied with the cockster's smile.

"Fuckin' lucky guess."

Sensing more fear of supplantation, I remain elated. I feigned wariness. "I hate to think you can read me like that."

"Mason…"

"Yes, darling."

"Am I your Ursula?"

I then said deeply into her eyes, "No. Not at all. You are my Joan. You will always be my Joan and no one will ever be able to take your place. Ever." Her body twisted ever so slightly.

"Damn, you're doing this well." she emitted. Then she addressed, "Mason…"

"Yes, babycakes?" I replied as I applied my final stroke.

Laced with mild laughter, she asked, "Where does Jennifer fit into this picture?"

I inhaled deeply and looked directly at her before I offered my answer, "She is my attempt at normal. After our, yours and my, conversation, very soon thereafter, she came into my office and basically said, 'Let's party.' It felt good and still feels good to be pursued."

"She knows we've talked about her, doesn't she?"

Choosing to answer a different question, I said, "She asked about you."

"Ah!" Joan exclaimed. "What did you say?"

"I lied."

Squirming slightly, Joan said, "What I'd give to have two more feet."

"Now, that would be something."

We sat without a word for a while. I promised myself not to speak next. And I didn't need much help.

"Where do we go from here?" Joan wondered aloud.

"I don't know," I said. "That's really up to you."

"You're the one with the girlfriend." A desperate stab.

I thought that maybe, after all this time, after days of contemplating then ignoring then reconsidering the possibilities, Joan is presenting herself to me, despite her very intrinsic need to remain in control. She continued to probe.

"So, you were in your office passing out random kisses?"

"Essentially," I responded, "since only an hour before I had told you I love you."

Another pause.

"Mason…"

I didn't give her a chance. "Joan, you are of course concerned about the age difference, and whatever other differences there are. You said it then and you are showing it now. It's okay if you can't. I really want you; really, really want to be your man. But I'll understand. I can't do a damn thing about the circumstances or how you feel about them. I do love you, and that's all I have to offer. I think that's more than enough, but that's up to you."

"Mason, just promise me one thing…"

The tolling of the knell. So, I took a shot at it. "I won't paint her toes."

She shot up and squealed, "How did you know?"

"Because now that's us."

After a short time to calm, Joan continued, "One more thing: you had my feet and whatever else in your hands. It would have been very easy to…."

I answered with confidence, "A couple of reasons: I'd like to say it's because I respect you so much, and it's that, but I also go to great lengths not to be like every other guy. And also, I want it to be both ways."

Another long pause as we continued to sit there, feet to face.

"Will you ever be able to handle a normal relationship?" Joan asked of me.

"I don't know, but if you are referring to Jennifer, it may be just that normal, which scares me. Something tells me she would not be the kind who would, say, drive around in her car in nothing but a trench coat and pumps."

"Who did that?"

"No one I know of. I just have an overly active imagination."

"Did you ever imagine this?" Joan asked, sitting up and crawling to my end of the bed to surprise me with the most heartfelt and sexiest of kisses directly on my mouth. It's as if she is competing, and I think she won.

She then nuzzled herself between my right arm and my chest. I throbbed all over. I know it's my turn to speak, but I can't come up with anything intelligent to say.

"Well?" she asked.

"Yeah," I said, inwardly fighting for air, "That's the one. Precisely."

"I hope you don't feel like you're cheating on Jennifer."

"I didn't feel anything but the lips of a goddess," I said, pulling her face to mine, returning the kiss. I didn't dream it was possible to break all the armor I had recently built to defend myself from her, but she did and I just had to lay back and accept it.

"Damnit, Mason, if you were just a few years older," she said just inches from my mouth.

"Then what would happen?" I asked, my heart racing.

"You would have been the one to break my heart." Her eyes moistened.

Voice cracking, I replied, "I would never hurt you. Never."

"You're the only one who can." And as our lips met again, then came another wave, snapping any residual manly resolve of control I have in me. Anything, anything to be yours for now and time infinitum.

"Why don't you stay here tonight?" the teen within asked.

"My sister is flying in early tomorrow," she said. I knew that, and I believe her, much like I will concede if she wants me to burn all my belongings.

"Well..." the disappointed man responded. "I'll miss you all night."

"Then let me wish you the best of luck in the game."

The game. Oh, hell, the game. "And how do you want to do that?" I asked softly.

"With an open face, heavily-panting, wet kiss—" she said right before she made good on her promise, "—that will fall woefully short of what I really want to do."

I could resist no longer, "I love you, Joan, so very much, more than I can ever write or say."

"Woefully short," she added for good measure as she kissed me again. My basic optimistic nature got the message. The romance in me drove it into my heart. There is now no other woman. No other.

I laid beside my love and stared into her beautiful face. Totally content with that and kisses and occasional conversation, I have achieved a state of freedom from the pain of my life. It is Joan and me and that's about it. "I don't have much else to say, Joan," I whispered, eyes to eyes, mouth to mouth, "except that I do indeed love you. I can guess you have heard that before," then I went for it, "but never from a man like me. Never from a man who will treat you like the marvelous woman you are." I quickly realize, despite my sincere intentions that came out hackneyed. But…"It's true, Joan. Give me a chance to prove it to you." I kissed her again. She received me well.

"Mason," Joan said softly, "even as I am here with you and enjoying it incredibly, there are so many obstacles for us to overcome."

"Love will overcome, Joan," I said, surprising myself with my boldness, "Darling, I sense your apprehension; hell, I mean, you've told me, so I guess it's beyond sense. But, I also sense you care on some level, some planar space…to put it extremely poorly."

She giggled. I laughed along with her at how foolish that must have sounded coming in the midst of some serious courtship.

"I sense you care for me," I said, back to my wooing, "Beyond friendship, tutorship, every ship in the sea…" Joan laughed again. At least that's working…. "Because you can see from where we are right now the letter has been fulfilled…you have indeed found your way to my arms." We kissed long and softly.

"Oh, Mason you take me for a spin like never before," I am thrilled to hear that. But…"However, I can't see…it would be so difficult."

Joan's rejections drifted over my head as I can only hear Neil Young in the background, 'I wanna be with a cinnamon girl. I could be happy for the rest of my life with a cinnamon girl.'

"Mason, I wish I could, could just stay right here, but…."

'A dreamer of pictures, I run in the night. I see us together chasing the moonlight; my cinnamon girl.'

"I'm just afraid," said Joan, "afraid of everything that goes against us…."

'Ten silver saxes and a bass with a bow. The drummer relaxes and waits between shows for his cinnamon girl.'

"Oh, Mason, sweetheart…I'm so normal and tied to my background and all that goes along with it. You're so adventurous and daring…."

'Ma, send me money, now I'm going to make it; somehow I need another chance. You see, your baby loves to dance, yeah, yeah, yeah.'

"…and romantic. Mason, it wouldn't be fair to you. You've got to find some woman who can accept, who can thrive on your love. Because of everything, I don't think that's me."

"But, Joan," I replied, "I don't exactly know what Neil Young meant by this, but it surely is pretty, and it reminds me of you. You're my cinnamon girl. A dreamer of pictures, we run in the night, I do see us together, chasing the moonlight. You, my cinnamon girl. We can thrive on each other. We can be alive with each other."

Joan melted into my body. She kissed me hard; her hands are all over me. "Can we find some way to get over to my house for just a little while?"

I'm hot with desire for her, but for the first time in my life my mind overruled my libido, "No, Joan, no. Not until you're sure, you're positive I'm the man. When I get the chance to make love with you, I'm going to be a goner. I mean a rocket to the outer reaches of the universe. I won't be coming back. I'm not going unless I can take you with me." My statement to Joan Kissinger, of all women, shocked me. And I do feel as if I made the right decision.

"Mason, damn you," Joan said in frustration, still welded to my frame, "What the hell am I going to do with you?" Her breasts are heaving ever so slightly. Her eyes are half-closed, "Oh, just lay here and hold me."

"Let your real feelings out, Joan," I said, "Let them go. I'll take care of them. I'll cherish them."

"Just hold me," she whispered.

That I did. The others, only a wall away, must be wondering about us. Well, in no way could they have guessed that I finally have bared it all to my lover, person to person. Now, there is nothing more I can do. I feel great satisfaction, even after considering Joan and I aren't going to be a pair. She, however, unequivocally knows, certain, without a doubt, has to know I love her more than she may ever again experience from any other man.

My only hope is she cares.

Friday November 7, 1975
11:30 PM

Lights out at Mickey's

We stood on Michele's porch as if it's a platform at a station, lovers parting for who knows when or where on Michael Nesmith's *Last Train to Clarksville.* I can do bubblegum pop when I have to. Besides, it's a good way to describe Joan's forty flavored kisses and a bit of conversation, oh. Oh, yes. I only had to wait several weeks for my dream to come true, the clothed part, that is. It looks like that's all, folks. It bears repeating…she's got to go with me. The painting of the toes is I'm sure an allegory to making love. It's what she needed to have as a memory of me until it wears off and another Alan with another hot car and another hot wallet comes by, ready to entertain as she expects. As lovely as it all is, as we come to the close of our time with each other, it all means…

"You seem distant," Joan said, standing in my arms, nuzzled in my chest.

I caught myself quickly. "I'm sorry," I said, thinking for just a moment to tell her all about my fears, and while I'm at it, the team, the press, and me. "It's been a big week, and I can't believe I'm letting that spoil this, what we're experiencing now, I mean."

"What are we experiencing now?" Joan asked, running her hand softly over my fanny for the second time. I can't wait to lose count.

"Why, we're making out like muskrats," I said with a lightness I deserved.

She giggled, "You kill me!"

I allowed myself to enjoy it. Maybe I can win her over that way, laughing all the way to the altar.

Altar? My God, don't lose it, man!

"And as this muskrat making-out progresses," she presented, "it would then be called…"

"Oh, that's like minks," I responded quickly.

Another cackle, still slightly pickled. I'm on, baby.

Afterwards, a pause, during which we stood there gazing at each other like we're on the slow dance floor at a high school hop. I am completely incapacitated in love. Just look at her, will you? I can't believe I still have Joan in my arms, there in broad nightlight. After all those days together, next to her, staring at her without getting caught most of the time, catching her scent, dreaming of her; after all that, here she is.

It is time to seal our fate. Time to lock myself into her heart. Time to do what any nineteen year old in my situation would do. It's time to impress the hell out of her.

"Joan."

"Yes, sweetie?"

"There's there's something I have to tell you."

"What is it, darling?"

Darling. The terms of endearment are melting me.

"Mason, are you okay?" I guess the hesitation took too long because she sounds concerned.

"Yes. I just have to tell you. It's about the coach and the accusations he's facing."

"Yes?" she asked with confusion. She's probably wondering why I'm bringing this up at this time.

I got directly to the point. "I'm the guy who turned in the information to the newspaper. As Jimmy Cagney would put it, I'm the rat fink."

Stunned, her eyes are fixed to mine with a lot of questions in their dark brown irises. I attempt to provide more explanation.

"Last Saturday, a box was left at my house containing photos of the coach and the other guy who turned out to be the bigot with the money. It also had photostats of deposits in the coach's bank account and affidavits from an employee of the bigot swearing to his boss' intentions. Very incriminating. The guy who left the box stopped by the following day to explain it all."

"Sunday," said Joan, "The day of my letter."

Good. She still remembers the letter. "Yes," I said, "A big day in my life. The letter is a great thing. The evidence…sickens me."

"Me, too, Mason. Me, too." Our bodies squeezed in more tightly.

I continued, "That evening I checked with Michael. He was understandably pissed, but he wanted to hold off for then. The next day, Lendel, the black QB benched by the money, was injured and out for the season. All this together made Michael incensed and wanting to strike. We decided I would take it all in to *The Mail*."

"Why you?"

"Because I'm white and sadly to say would therefore be believed. Anyway, the paper jumped all over it and you know the rest."

Silence. Then, "Mason…."

"Look," I said, interrupting, "I wanted to tell you because it's such a huge event, the biggest thing that's ever happened to me outside of you. I feel like it was the responsible thing to do, but it hasn't come without a price. Our team is suffering because of the newspaper story and because of what I dredged up."

Joan moved in closer still. I didn't think that was possible unless she climbed inside my blazer, which of course I'm not averse to.

"Mason, honey, your team was suffering anyway. Oh, don't you see? People have a way of knowing those things are going on without anybody saying anything. It's not your fault. You're just the messenger. Your 'ratting' to the paper, as you called it, sometimes the medicine hurts before it makes you better. Oh, Mason, baby…," she concluded. Here I am trying to snare her and I myself end up falling harder and more deeply for her. I didn't think that was possible.

"Mason, what am I…that was a very courageous thing you did. You're something else, to say the least…You know, bravery is a major turn-on." My legs turned to warm butter as she kissed me. Why do you think I told you this, hon?

Our earlier fun had brought Michele onto the porch. "Let us in on it, damn it," she said in mock anger, or so I thought.

"We're musking out like makerats," Joan informed Michele, switching back to playful. I allowed myself to giggle.

"That's cute, kids, but time draws nigh," Michele informed us.

"Yeah, you're right. I'd better go," Joan said, still draped on me but conversing with Michele. After spending an hour or two or who cares in the guest room of her colleague, maybe she's becoming a bit self-conscious. I guess she's sobering up, sobering to the fact that she's back to being eight years my senior.

"You said that fifteen minutes ago," Michele countered. Damn, Mickey. You're really upset…

"I'll tell you about it later," Joan said toward Michele as she looked at me. "You'll understand."

"Anyway, your boyfriend has a game tomorrow. Now get his letter sweater and let him sleep," Michele cracked, easing up.

"Hmm…." Joan said, sizing me up for about the eighth time that night. I absolutely do not what know what to think of this, nor about how the letter sweater wisecrack didn't bother me. Hmm, yourself.

"I'll go, Mom. And to you, my dear," Joan said to me as she motioned to Michele, "don't go Oedipal on me." Not bad. But, as I've forgotten for a great deal of the night, she's a PhD.

With that, Joan planted another one on my lips, unlatched herself, and strolled down the steps. She made it to her BMW without displaying the effects of her state of just an hour ago, opened the door (the correct one), turned the ignition, started the car, and rolled down her window, yelling, "Score one for me, baby!" Successfully backing out, she aimed it toward the street.

I panicked. "Wait!" I shouted, not wanting it to end, running to her. I leaned to her window, "Don't forget. I love you." Joan looked at me, smiling, with soft eyes, but like she didn't know what to say. "Just don't forget," I repeated. I felt my eyes water. Damnit….

She patted my hand, "See you Monday, Mason," she said, still grinning. And, just like that, she drove away.

"Well, that was a good time," I said aloud to myself as I waved, my heart sinking like a boulder in a lake.

I turned to find Michele looking in Joan's direction, motionless. Walking to her, I felt an overwhelming need to apologize.

"Apology not accepted," Michele said before I could speak. I stood in silence. Finally explaining, she added, "No apology required."

"I feel badly," I said, actually feeling better, "I haven't used another person's house to be with a girl since junior high."

"Don't apologize, goddamnit. For you or for her. You two had no idea or even a dream that things would turn out this way here, tonight. She didn't know you were going to be here, and the same goes for you. Chance of a chance."

Michele and I quietly reached an agreement. For the first time since Joan and I stepped out here, I noticed my surroundings. My breath fogged when I exhaled deeply. A stream of cars motored by, with an occasional party being transported. Sometimes I get so involved I fail to see these things. Joan and football have my mind occupied. Joan and football. What an Odd Couple.

"Michele…"

"Yes, hot blood?"

"Watch it, I'm still hyperhormonal." Michele liked that one. "Anyway…well, let's go in. Maybe we'll catch my best friend and your married sister kissing or something."

"Or something…" Michele and I turned and walked across her porch and through her front door. We found Vinny and MJo engrossed in a conversation. No such luck.

"Casanova," said MJo to me, "you're back."

I took it on the chin. I deserve it. I love it.

"No rain?" Vinny asked me in a instant transformation from cool to worried.

"Overcast, but no rain," I passed on to The Gunner. He nodded his head and held his right fist up chin level.

"Mason has a concern," Michele announced.

MJo said in anticipation of something juicy, "Tell us what you're worried about, hot lips."

"Yuk, yuk, MJo," I said, "My question runs deeper than sucking face."

"You were pretty deep into it on the porch," Vinny said.

"Okay," I said, "Get it all out before I go on, okay?"

The three laughed heartily. "We love ya, Mason," Michele said, "Don't take it so seriously."

I let them giggle on before I put a Band-Aid on my heart and eased up, seeing the humor in it all. Joan and I aren't your regular pair. I hesitate to think that we're really a pair at all. Only now am I able to address the audience. "All right, here goes: what's going to happen on Monday?"

"Good question, Mason," replied Michele. "A damn good one. One that you refused to consider in your pursuit of Joan, the Maid of Northwestern. How do you act afterward? What does it all mean to her? What does it mean to you? The tension in the office: everyone will know something's up without exchanging one word. All the women, I mean. How will you handle that? It was one thing to muse about the potential. Now we all have to deal with it. Kathleen will be okay. Don't talk to Ellen. She's into that traditional stuff, and can back it up since she and Michael are the same age. And for God's sake hope Hannah doesn't find out. She'll take it personally, like a slap in the face."

"In fact," Vinny said, "considering everything, you just might want to hope you die tomorrow." The Taranucci sisters laughed. I'm still stuck on Michele's first question.

"Sorry I'm leaving you with this mess, this huge fucking mess you and your romantic soul has gotten yourself in," Michele said, grinning, squeezing my arm, "but I'd better hit the sack."

'Don't go!' my brain screamed. But I had to maintain cool. A couple of quick cleansing breaths and then "Michele," I said, trying to avoid pleading, "I will need some help with this. Will you consider…helping…me?"

"Consider it done," Dr. Taranucci answered. "Now, unless you want to see me in my nightie because you'll have to carry me up to my bedroom and undress me, I've got to go to bed. But, you're so Joaned-out the sight of me naked shouldn't faze you." Everybody laughed, except me. I think she's right. "Tomorrow's an early morning and I'm drunk. And since you've already gotten that bed hot in there, the study is your room. Vinny and MJo are upstairs, separate for the early part of the night. But if I hear somebody padding across the hallway, I didn't hear a thing. Okay, kids?"

"Sounds like a plan," I said. The others nodded.

"I'm with ya, Mick. I've got to get away from this homewrecker Vinny," MJo said, followed by a friendly punch on the arm. The right arm. The Gunner winced. I don't know if it was from the overprotection of the gun or the loss of a chance with Mary Josephine, last name unknown.

"Good night, ladies," I said. "And, Michele, once again, thank you."

"Yes, thanks, Michele," repeated Vinny.

"Don't mention it," said Michele as she turned and took a few steps up. "Consider it my contribution to The University of West Virginia athletics."

"You don't know how big it is," I said, thinking of the talents of my man Vinny.

Michele stopped, turned back toward us, and spat a laugh. "I guess that does remain to be seen."

Deciding not touch that one, I stood still and smiled. "Good night, girls." Vinny and I rang out together.

"Good night, boys," They retired upstairs. My friend then turned to me and said, "Let's call the limit five, go to the refrigerator, and max out."

"Excellent suggestion," I offered.

~ ~ ~ ~ ~ ~ ~ ~ ~ ~

After cracking open the Miller Lites, we toasted. "To women," I said.

"May almost all of them not become our relatives," he said, interestingly.

"Here, here," I replied, knowing when not to try to top a remark. We guzzled.

"Okay," I started, "Let's get to the most important thing: how do you feel?"

"Man, never better," Vinny responded, without a trace of consideration or doubt. "Never better."

"Michele's the greatest, isn't she?" I said. "And that married chick isn't bad herself."

"That does get in the way," said Vinny, "But, I think we in an unspoken and nice way decided to part wondering what could have happened."

"Watch it, Gunner. That sounds like me."

"No. She's older and unavailable, so you would have written your phone number on her panties."

"Pardon me, my man, but I think I have much more respect for the institution of matrimony."

Sitting in silence, we for a while looked away from each other. Our next gazes brought a laugh from Vinny. Four more counts, then he finally said it, "You've done it. You've done a married woman, haven't you?"

"No," I replied firmly. "I would have told you. Well, almost," I responded, truthfully.

"Sounds like a good story to me," The Gunner said, asking me without asking to tell it.

"You know the Little League coaching position I took over back in May—"

"Oh, God," Vinny groaned, "every Little League team has one of these stories."

"Well, you're right," I said, "It got close, really close."

"What put you back on the straight and narrow?"

"I went to talk with Father Al. After he heard my side, he filled me in on the church's position on sex outside of marriage, especially mine or hers or both of our own. He got the point across very well. Then he told me how he felt. 'Just be wise, Mason, be as wise as you can be. There are plenty of single women. Before you pick your wife, stay single and with singles.' He's a helluva guy. Then do you know what he said?"

"I know you're going to tell me anyway, so go ahead."

"He said, 'Beautiful women abound, but a man who can block and catch is hard to find.' Cool, isn't it?"

"Your amazement with Father Al is well documented, Mason. Now, tell me exactly how close you got to this married woman who entrusted the baseball life of her son with you while almost dropping her underwear."

I laughed. Good memories. "We talked at the field one day after a game when her husband took her son and some friends for sodas. She just laid it on the line for me. I must say, I was very tempted. She was attractive."

"Not to mention at least fifteen years older than you." Vinny said in a scolding fashion. "Did anything happen?"

"Nope," I replied, "No touchy."

"Incredible. Ursula. The Baseball Mom. Now, Dr. Kissinger. What gives, Mason?"

"First thing, that's just two out of three not even that considering Joan and I didn't—"

"Still, a three thirty three. A helluva of a batting average, mind you."

"And where do you get off on your Joan flip-flops you do? I don't know where you stand! Pick a side and stick to it." Almost all of the spats Vinny and I have had lately have involved Joan, but I've never asked him to lay it on the line as I have just now. The second hand swept one side of the clock. I thought he was simply ignoring my request or didn't understand it.

"Okay," Vinny began, "You showed brains and soul with the married woman. I'm proud of you for that. And…I don't know why you are ignoring the lay-up Jennifer for the long shot Joan, but you're my best friend and I'm with you. Just keep your dignity."

"Well, one thing is good," I replied, "I've taken your mind off Pitt."

"Thank you, but I don't want my mind off Pitt. We're going to beat those fuckers."

"Now that we've finally got you in there, I believe," I said, beaming. "Do you think you can you run the felon's boring offense before it puts you to sleep standing?"

"Easy as pie," said The Gunner, "Easy as pie, my man."

I'm not stunned by his confidence. Vinny, my man. A sophomore constantly berated by his father Mussolini thinks he can step in there and do a number on number one. It's Vinny. I know he can. There is only one thing left to say: "I believe, baby. Ya gotta believe! But, tell me, Vinny. What did those women do to you?"

Vinny shifted in his chair. "Nothin' Mason. I stand consistent with everything I've told you. All we did was talk. It was very refreshing and very relaxing. I thank you for setting this up. You are wise beyond your years. Just be careful with Joan." For the eighth time.

"Gotcha, Chief," was my response as my mind flashed back to the 1963 Navy game and the girls of our teen years. Now we sit in the living room of some faculty member we didn't know two and a half months ago getting ready for our biggest game. Wow, man. I inadvertently shook my head.

"What, man?" he asked.

"Nothin'."

"Spill it, man."

"Ah, you know what it is."

"No, I don't, but I will when you tell me."

"Okay," I started, "We've done some pretty crazy things together, you know?"

"Yep, like this."

"Yeah," I said, leading into something. "Vinny?"

"Ask away."

"Will I ever be able to grow up?"

He paused and contemplated, too long.

"All right, I know the answer," I said, "Just let it out."

"The answer has three parts," Vinny said, "First, you think you're grown up already, but you ask the question. Second, if you're, if we are able to give up pot in due time, that's a big part of growing up. But, third, is the part that I hope stays with you."

"What part is that?"

"The, uh, I'm at a loss for words...there's just a side of you that would, uh, not ever consider not taking the box to the press. It's a risky side, but it in some way makes me feel good because I feel like you'd take the same risks for me, for my benefit. I....that's the best way to describe it. It's almost as if not taking the box in was not an option with you."

At that time, the wall cuckoo clock went off, announcing the midnight hour. Like a B-grade Ronald Reagan movie.

"And on that," I announce, "It's time to go to our separate guest rooms."

Vinny stood. "Good night, Cheetah."

"Good night, Vinny. You and MJo keep it down up there, okay?"

Vinny laughed, then scurried upstairs as if Mary Josephine and he have a plan. I have nothing to say to that.

~ ~ ~ ~ ~ ~ ~ ~ ~ ~

I am under the covers in a cotton sweatshirt and wool shorts. As the phone rings in real life with Michele answering it on the second clang, I imagine the bed is still warm with Joan as I lay here, feeling her from her pate to her newly painted toes. Okay, I'll play everyone else's game and publicly be careful, but to myself I'll let it all run away with me. Never have I ever felt this way about a woman. This is a magnitude worse, or better...yes, much better than Ursula. Joan has my soul in a way that I can't think of anything without it being in her context. The big game, for instance. I line up wide left facing The Bowl, in the game by some wild set of circumstances in which no one did poorly or was hurt, but Coach put me the third-teamer in because…oh, the hell with it, this is my fantasy…Vinny hits me on a slant over the middle and I accelerate for the flag, outracing all my opponents for the score. Joan bounces wildly, knowing it is her man who is the hero. Her sister gushes in appreciation and approval of Dr. Kissinger's man-choosing capabilities. They make plans to find me after the game so Joan can set up a time to take care of some unfinished business. Anyway, I make several more big catches, we beat Pitt, Keith Jackson interviews Vinny and me, and I clean up. Dressed in charcoal gray worsted wool slacks, a blue oxford cloth shirt, a narrow rep tie tied loosely, and a wool navy blazer, I head for All That Jazz, a trendy club where you'd expect Joan and her sister to hang out. Joan spots me at the door, she wearing black tight slacks and a black mohair cardigan. She approaches me as only she can, embracing me with congratulations. Joan says, "Whatever I have to do tonight to conceal us, please think only of the possibilities of later. It will happen. I guarantee you. All of it. We, you and I, are going to the outer reaches of the universe." After that I manage to hold on as I meet her sister Pamela. They comprise the two best-looking women in the joint. I have their undivided attention. Not wishing to wear that out, I turn to Joan to say, "So, you enjoyed the game." "Yes," she responds, "you were marvelous. I just wish you could kiss me here as you did last night. Hell, why not just place me on the bar and make love to me as we didn't last night. I love you, Mason. Make love with me. You will get yours. And, just as importantly, I will get mine." I let this pretend world do a freeze-frame right there, as I enjoy what all this, the chase, the letter, the argument, the class, and the impassioned kisses, what all this is doing to me. My eyes are closed as I lay here stoned on a capacitance charge unequal to any other feeling I have ever experienced.

As I'm in this state of electrified slumber, the doorbell sounds. I ignore it. It went away. It came back. Being the only resident of the first floor, I decide it is my duty to take care of it. I crane myself out of bed and, not wanting to frighten our midnight guest, pull Myself against myself with a blanket. Foolishly, I open the door without examining the peep hole. I got lucky because it is not a bad guy but only Jennifer. As an indication as to how I lose focus around Jennifer, I'm extremely concerned that it is raining a steady sprinkle and to how that might affect Vinny tomorrow. My female friend stands before me in her dark olive double-breasted London Fog raincoat with black stockings and pumps.

Jesus Christ, it's Jennifer!

"Well?" she pleaded.

"Oh, pardon me! Forgive my bad manners! Come in! Come in! Get in out of the rain!" I said, not wanting Vinny to play his first start in the rain.

"This is a nice house. Teachers live nice. Or nicely. I don't know. Mason, why didn't you tell me you were coming over here?" she asked.

"We were trying to hide Vinny," I replied, giving her the truth for once.

"What's wrong with where he was?"

I rubbed my face. I need sleep. That's a good question, but it takes effort to talk with Jennifer sometimes, "His father, Jennifer. He's a primo jerk, and it was messing with Vinny's head. Vinny's got a big performance tomorrow, and he needs everything going for him."

"I'm kind of chilly," she said, "Where's your room?" Did she even hear me?

Not wanting to tell her that the room is our room, Joan's and mine, I led her there anyway. We enter the room, where I turned on a desk lamp for soft light. She didn't offer one crack about the Dutch masters. It hit me again. It's Jennifer, stupid! Thinking that she probably has been reading my mind for the past several minutes, something at which she is so adept, and something which I am so afraid of because I've never been up front with her, she sat on the same bed while I perched on the same chair. My feet were next to her pumped up shoes, similar to the feet that had been here only a couple of hours ago.

"Can I take your coat?"

"No, still warming up."

A conversational hole seemed to pass for minutes. Mr. Words is at a loss for anything to say to this very pretty girl sitting on my assigned bed at this very late hour. Next one....

"I didn't realize how ugly it was outside when I took off, but I just had to see you, and when I found out where you were I just threw on my coat and here I am!" Jennifer is pleased with herself.

"Glad you're here, Jen," I said perfunctorily.

"I called ahead to ask Dr. Taranucci if you were actually here. She said to call her Michele and yes were indeed here...I love that word, indeed. You English majors are sexy," she said as she massaged my slippered foot. "Anyway," she continued, "she insisted I come over to see you. I drove through the rain," (again I thought of the rain and Vinny) "and boom-teedy-boom" (I thought of Joan) "I'm here," finally finishing, presenting herself with outstretched arms.

"I hope I'm worth all that trouble," I remarked without much else to say.

"Well, let's find out," Jennifer said as she lifted herself from the bed, stood, faced me, untied her trench coat and slowly opened it to reveal her slender body, Julie and Lee in underwear. Garters and stockings. An extremely nice touch. She's willing to stand there for me, wanting me to take the opportunity to survey her. Not Joan, but I have to admit I always wondered how she, and Judy for that matter, would look with her long thighs extending from a really good pair of panties. Well, Judy's not here and I'm not hunting after her for any comparisons. Jennifer's doing just fine, thank you. And as I imagined what the flip side would do for me, and as any thoughts of Joan are now being seriously challenged, only six words came to mind.

"Now may I take your coat?"

Saturday, November 8, 1975
6:00 AM

Waking up at Michele's

"Jennifer…."

"Yes, studmuffin…."

Lying awash in the lamplight on Joan's bed, enjoying the quivers of the aftermath of number…happy Jennifer brought a half-dozen condoms, happy I made her happy, trying extremely hard to open the empty space Joan has left in my heart to the Catwoman, not succeeding, I laughed and said, "Jennifer, I feel as if we know each other well enough—"

"I'll say," she said. Again, I laughed.

"We know each other well enough…."

"I lost count at three."

"You're embellishing, but, I, a man of relatively little experience in these matters, am glad to serve you in any way," I said, puffing with primal pride. "Anytime." Jeez, Mason, just sign it all over to her, you idiot…joint custody with rights of survivorship.

"You just read my mind."

"What is it I'm going to tell you?"

"It's about Joan."

My face fell flush, I'm sure a bright red.

"Mason," she said, "I want you to know, especially when you consider the last few hours, that I'm not scared of Joan. I can match her and beat her. I've got things she in her wildest imagination doesn't have. One of them is you, naked, right now," Jennifer concluded, homing in.

"Naked to the world," I sang with Edwin Starr in mind. "In front of, every kind of girl. There were tall ones—"

"And tall ones, and long haired ones."

"And lovely ones, and did I mention tall ones?"

"Just as long as you've got me in mind."

"Yes," I said, and then pausing, again duty bound to Joan, and smelling like Jennifer. Now is the time to come through with the truth, as partial as it will be. "I left you at my house and I got here last night in Vinny's trunk, with Vinny, if you can imagine that."

"That's okay, Mason. I know you're all man."

What the hell does she mean by that? "Well, I like to think so, but we arrived that way. I walked into the house, and there was Joan."

"Unplanned, I assume," Jennifer said, maybe a little pissed. I reacted to that.

"I was totally unaware she was to be here. I spoke to Michele. She said she hung up, then Joan appeared at her door. Very much unplanned," I said, "You gotta go with me on this."

Jennifer paused. "Okay. We've gone this far. I don't see any reason not to trust you, especially when you consider I have her prissy ass."

Deciding not to think of Joan's ass or react to a Pi Gamma Pi calling another woman prissy, I continued. "She was…she had been party-ing…and no one knew why she was here. She and I talked for a while."

Jennifer listened with restraint. I decided to withhold some infor-mation, noting to myself that I was foolish to have ever started this conversational topic.

"What did you two, the ALit queen and her prince, have to say?" There's a punch.

"Uh…school, you," That was probably too much for my Jen to handle. I decided to bring it on home, "her man Alan, our pasts, football….you know…."

Jennifer's silence rang in my ears.

"She wasn't here that long. She probably had to run out and find Alan." There. Jesus, how stupid. I didn't care before. Why now?

But I do care. I care for Joan. I have violated her. I love forever, or until the woman tells me to get lost, whichever comes first. I could rationalize Joan effectively ended it when she had no response to my proclamations, as numerous as they were. I can't do that. My love remains. My cheatin' heart remains with Maggie J. And, boy, did I ever cheat. I made up for missing out on the Baseball Mom this spring and Joan last night. In a couple of hours. I don't want to think about it any more.

Apparently having nothing to say, Jennifer sat, still nude, staring at me. She heaved and sighed, assessing the facts and weight thereof with regard to how she viewed the truth. After some silence, her body language read that she has come to a conclusion.

She spoke. "I'm jealous, jealous as hell, but you work for her and I should learn a way to deal with it. Now come here and kiss me."

After that, she asked, "Now, what's the other one you had for me?"

I'm flummoxed, "How the hell do you know that?"

"I'm a woman."

You bet. "I give up, so I'll just tell you. It has nothing to do with Joan or any other woman. The subject is football."

Jennifer paused. "Football. Whatever could it be?"

Time is elapsing and I have to get ready for this football game for which I've spent most of my life anticipating, so I gave Jennifer the condensed version.

More silence.

"Who knows about this?" Jennifer finally asked.

"Those who aren't directly involved, you now, Alice and Judy, because they took the box to my room, Michele, because she answered my phone and it was *The Pittsburgh Advocate*, which made her wonder and surmise, and that's all."

"Joan doesn't know," she asked.

"There is no reason for her to know," I replied. True, there is no tangible reason for Joan to know.

"Well, good," Jennifer said as she plopped herself onto my lap. "Because this makes you sexier than you already are. Fighting the forces of evil, Mason. Selflessly standing up for what's right. How am I ever going to pull myself away from you this morning?"

"Jennifer, it's no big deal. It had to be done. There was nothing else to do. I just happened to be the guy with the box."

"Yes there was another way, Mason. You could have just sat on it and not troubled yourself. Oh, I—I—am so…. Now get dressed before I tie you to the bedposts."

Never before given an appealing alternative to football, I almost took her up on it.

~ ~ ~ ~ ~ ~ ~ ~ ~ ~

Saturday November 8, 1975
6:30 AM

In Michele's kitchen

Jennifer exited the room first. "Good morning, all" she said. Michele, standing in the kitchen, returned the greeting. Vinny, sitting at the bar with breakfast before him, spewed his coffee. I guess he's happy to see her.

Michele looked the part of the young faculty. She wore in preparation for watching the Runners during a cloudy day in the mid 40s a Columbia blue wool turtleneck sweater under a wool navy form-fitting blazer with tan slacks and those waterproof boots L. L. Bean sells.

Jennifer had slipped into the tan woolen sweater over a thermal top and long, long dark denim Levis she brought in her bag last night, much to my unawareness, along with a nice seventies coed touch of a forest green down vest. Why Jen didn't go for the sorority Saks Fifth Avenue game casual dress code I'll never know. Could she be her own woman? I hope not. That would confuse me.

The women are ready, with the exception of MJo, who is surprisingly hung over and is trying to catch as many zees as possible.

Vinny and I dressed alike. "Where the hell did you get the nice clothes?" I asked.

"My mom. She said she likes the way you look. Dominic is my size, so she fit them on him and mailed them to me."

"So, that's all the shit you were packing last night," I commented.

"I wanted to surprise you, Ivy,"

"You did it."

We wore navy blazers, worsted wool charcoal gray slacks, and rep ties. Thankfully we had on different shirts, Vinny's white pinpoint to my blue Oxford button-down. The reps weren't the same, and his tan overcoat contrasted to my gray. Still, it was enough to raise humor among the womenfolk.

Michele: "Do you guys pack for each other?"

Jennifer: "Do you share closets?"

Michele: "Do you wear each other's clothes?"

Jennifer: "Do you shop together?"

Michele: "Haven't you taken the concept of 'date mates' to new levels?

Jennifer: "Stop us if you've had enough."

"I had enough at the pack remark," I said. But that's okay. I'll let these two go on for as long as they want. Jean? That's a different story.

Michele offered me pastries and coffee. I took handfuls and cupfuls. Sex makes me hungry. Really? I went halfway through the liturgical calendar. How the hell would I know?

"Oh, hell," Michele said, "I don't have the paper. I'll bet you're in it, Vinny."

Saturday, November 8, 1975
6:45 AM

The newspaper story

Michele stepped out of her kitchen for her front door. As she opened it, we three sat in silence. Jennifer smiled. Vinny has stress all over his face. And after everything that has happened, I'm numb. It's gameday and not even seven o'clock, and I can't feel a thing.

Standing perfectly still on the front porch, Michele read the paper. Must have been something interesting. I took a sip of coffee. Jennifer bit into her pastry. Funny, I've never seen her eat. Now we are complete. I heard the door close. Michele stood in her living room and stared at me. I noticed the roundness of her breasts pushing out her blazer. Haven't I had enough?

"I think you're going to want to see this, Mason," Michele said. She didn't move, just handing the paper toward me over the ten or so feet between us. I got up from the table and walked to her, taking the newspaper from her. On first glance, I found nothing.

"Look on the bottom of the front page," said Michele solemnly. I did. Within a border in the bottom left-hand corner read the headline, "Pittsburgh Paper Reports: U Player Is Informant." Blood rushed from my head to my knotted stomach and I became dizzy. This isn't possible. Not today. Not any day. After a couple of moments and a few deep breaths, I steadied myself and silently read the article. "*The Pittsburgh Advocate* reported this morning that its editorial staff learned from a reliable source that Mason Bricker, a sophomore on the University of

West Virginia football team, passed on information to this newspaper implicating Dennis Lawson in the pay-for-play scandal that has led to the head coach's indefinite suspension. Also mentioned was Beckley businessman Myron McNabb, who allegedly paid $ 65,000 to Lawson to play Bobby Kay, a white quarterback, over Lendel Ward, who is black.

"Lawson was contacted late last night by this newspaper. He had no comment. McNabb and Bricker were not available.

"The editors of *The Montani Mail* neither confirm nor deny Bricker's involvement with the story."

"Those bastards!" I said under my breath, thinking of *The Mail* reporters, absolutely seething. "I can't believe this! This can't be happening." Then I scanned the section of the paper I'm holding. I thought I had lost my coffee when I saw the story to the right headlined, "Huntington Banker Accused of Embezzlement." I quickly read, "A senior vice-president of First National Huntington Bank has been accused of pilfering an estimated $125,000 from his trust clients' accounts. PD Doughtery, a West Virginia alumnus and ex- football player has been dismissed without pay pending an investigation."

That's all it said. And that's all I need to know. A double whammy. The world knows I'm Deep Throat and the whole thing may be a sham if PD turns out to be the lying motherfucker he is depicted in this article. Either PD was out to get Lawson or McNabb was out to get PD. Either way, I'm screwed. Man, this can't get any worse.

"What is it, Mason?" asked Jennifer.

I dropped the paper to my side and held my face in my right hand. This is just great. I am doubly concerned, wondering what this meant to my football career at the U and also hoping some redneck with a pistol doesn't try to plant one between my eights today.

"What the hell is going on, Mason?" Vinny asked.

"*The Mail* says the Pittsburgh paper found out about me and the evidence." I know that's only part of the problem, but I have to contain the damage by not telling anybody about PD. I'm in enough trouble already.

"Lemme see!" Vinny said, standing, walking, and grabbing the paper from me. As he read, a whistle leaked from his lips. Jennifer walked over to Vinny and also read. Reaching for me, she embraced me, stroking my back. "This is all right, Mason," Jennifer said, "I mean, it doesn't take away from the fact that you were right in what you did. You'll be okay, I promise." She kissed my cheek. Sweet.

I glanced at Michele. She rolled her eyes, apparently not agreeing with Jennifer's rosy assessment.

"Buddy, I thought I had it tough today," said Vinny.

"I can't believe *The Mail* would sell out like that," I said, the closest to total panic I have been in a long while. "'Neither confirm or deny?' Why don't they just fuckin' write it in the goddamned sky over the stadium? What ever happened to protection of the sources? I can't believe this! I thought I was safe. Christ, what's going to happen now?" I stopped myself right there, recognizing the potential I now have to babble incessantly.

"And why would they print that article, today of all days?" asked Vinny.

"To cover their asses," said Michele, "But if they did tell *The Advocate*, it's so obtrusive, so wide-open. It's hard to believe they would print anything at all."

"What the hell were they thinking?" I asked. I began to shiver.

"Do you know where the reporter is right now?" asked Jennifer.

"Heavily guarded, if he knows what's good for him," said Vinny.

"Do it, Mason," said Michele, "Call the reporter. He may know something. Here." Michele handed me her phone.

"Tom Brown," I said, "it's time to get your ass out of bed." I picked up the transmitter and dialed Tom's number from memory. After three rings, a very sleepy voice said, "'Lo?"

"Tom, this is Mason Bricker."

"Mason?" he said.

"Yeah, Tom, I'm sorry to bother you, but I just read something disturbing in your newspaper."

"There are a lot of disturbing things in our newspaper, Mason."

"Quit fuckin' around, Tom. You know what I'm talking about."

"Well, Mason, no I don't." Yes he does, the lying geek.

"Well, Tom, on the front page of your paper, it is disclosed that I am the informant for the Lawson-McNabb crap."

There is total silence, then a deep breath. "I thought Dale Kitchen was going to call you about this."

"What the hell have you guys done, Tom?"

"We haven't done anything, Mason. That's what Mr. Kitchen was supposed to call you about."

"When did he try to call?"

"Late last night, he told me."

"Well, he didn't reach me."

"He wanted to talk to you about it before the story ran. Where were you?"

I was here painting my boss' toes, Tom. Damn, the trouble unadulterated lust can get you into. "I wasn't at my house."

"He couldn't find you, so I guess he decided to run the story anyway."

"Why in the holy hell would he do something stupid like that? Don't you realize nobody's gonna wanna tell you guys anything any more? Jesus, Tom, that was dumb."

"Calm down, Mason. All we were doing was reporting what another newspaper published. We didn't tell *The Pittsburgh Advocate* diddly. They approached us with the news."

"Then what's this confirm or deny shit?"

"We had to say something. If *The Advocate* ran the story and we didn't say anything, we'd look like we leaked to them."

"What the hell do you think you look like now?"

"We couldn't confirm because that would be revealing a source. We couldn't deny because that would be lying."

"So, the source was revealed anyway."

"And we didn't do it. You got caught in a classic *Catch-22*, Mason."

I detest the shopworn use of the title of Joseph Heller's classic as the ultimate explanation for events. "This could have been avoided, Tom."

"Mason, I hesitate to pass the buck, but you'll have to take it up with Mr. Kitchen. He's the one who made the decision."

I took a cleansing breath. "Tom, if you guys didn't tell, who did?"

"This is a very touchy topic, Mason. Anyone could have gotten a hold of this one and looked upon it as their duty to the university to muck up the works."

I can't believe I'm going to say it, but I did anyway. "Tom, I'm going to have to consult an attorney. This has left me very exposed. In many ways." I could see in my mind an ardent Klansman loading his weapon.

"Well, leave me out of it. I'm probably not even supposed to be talking to you right now."

His twist on this is stifling. 'Leave me out of it.' The son-of-a-bitch.

"Okay, Tom, I understand. Well, not really, but there's nothing left to do but seek counsel."

"I'm sorry, Mason."

"You're sorry...."

"Good luck in today's game."

"Thank you, Tom."

"Good bye." On that, he hung up. And, as Vinny alluded to a few days ago, I am hung out to dry.

No sooner than I had placed the receiver in the cradle, Michele had advice for me. "Don't call Dale Kitchen. You'll only dig your hole deeper. Call my buddy Rex Hernsen. He's interested in helping anyway he can."

"I'm sorry, Mason," said Jennifer, "I'm still very proud of you."

"Ivy," said Vinny, "it'll be tough, but the best thing for you to do right now is to put it away and do what you're made to do: abuse people on kickoffs. That's it. Take it out on them."

"You're right, Vinny," I said, although not knowing how I was going to do that with the Vaccas, the Lamberts, the Calires, the Runners, the coaches, and anybody else who wants to take potshots at me. Potshot. What a poor and horrifying choice of words. I scanned the room: Jennifer, Vinny, Michele, and then MJo slowly walking down the stairs in nothing but a long tee shirt. I have to get out of here. "Folks, I think it's time to go." I said.

"But I just got here," MJo said.

"Pitt awaits, Mrs. Franciosa," Michele said. So that's her last name.

I hugged Michele and passed her on to Vinny for the same treatment. Jennifer is immediately on my arm. "Mickey," I said. She smiled at the offhanded reference to Joan. "I thank you for your help last night and this morning. Let Rex know I'll be in touch with him by Monday."

"I'll do that," Michele said.

"Michele," Vinny said, "I couldn't have made it through the night without you. I think I'm ready to play."

"You spent the night with two hot women," MJo said, "If you're not ready, I don't know what else to do."

Michele interjected, "Jennifer, in light of my sister's last comment and her pornographic brain, everyone slept alone last night. Please pass that on to Vinny's woman."

Jennifer said, "I know everybody was good." She reached back, out of sight of all, and pinched my butt. I felt my face burn. "And thank you, Michele," continued Miss Pierce, "for helping me locate Mason and inviting me over. Thank you for your hospitality. You are very kind."

That impressed me. Jennifer is class. What the hell am I doing chasing Joan? I'd like to be able to hold that thought for at least a half-hour or so.

"Let's hop in the car, Vinny Wonder," I said, "To the Batcave." On that, we three moved outside and to Jennifer's boxy steel blue Volvo. Vinny got in the back and I rode up front with the driver as Michele and her sister waved from the porch.

"Good luck, Vinny," MJo yelled, "I won't tell my husband how I know you."

Michele punched her. "Girl, good God, I have to live in this neighborhood!" I glanced at Jennifer. She's still not pissed off. She's either very understanding or has a high shit quotient.

"Knock 'em dead, Vinny!" Michele shouted. "You too, Mason!"

We waved as Jennifer put 'er in gear and took off for our house.

Saturday, November 8, 1975
7:05 AM

To home and a reunion with our loved ones

You wouldn't know Vinny and I are about to play the biggest game of our young lives. I glance in the back seat to find The Gunner in near catatonia, still life in three dimension. I don't have much to say either. We each bear the burdens of the moment. My battles with the newspaper are just beginning, and that's without serious regard to the side skirmishes with everybody connected, which, in the small and tight state of West Virginia includes just about everybody. Then there are PD's troubles and what that all means. Christ almighty! I looked back to Vinny again. It isn't much better for him, leading his eviscerated team against another. Not just any other team, mind you, but arguably one of the best in recent history. And if that is not enough ballast, with regard to last night's disappearance of Jen from Jean the time is quickly approaching for him to face Mike and Jean and explain his evening to their satisfaction.

"Jennifer," I said, the first words uttered in the short trip across the neighborhood.

"Yes, dear," she responded. I guess she figures she now owns me.

"Who knows about you coming over?"

"Just Judy and Alice and Jean."

I paused to emphasize exactly what that meant. She didn't get it. Vinny, exhibiting vital signs, sighed. He understands.

"Vinny, I guess this means we have some 'splainin' to do. So here's the story: I stayed at Michele's because Van Watt decided he didn't see a need for me to be there with you and him and the other quarterbacks, all two of you."

"What about me?" asked the Catwoman, "my family will be at your house."

Why is this not getting any better? What the hell's going to happen now? Do I have to marry this woman? Can't we be casual, at least until Monday when I talk to Joan again?

"Oh, that's good, Jen," I said cheerily, "I'm looking forward to meeting them. I'm sorry I missed them last night."

"I know," she said with a grin, "you had to go." Why do I get the feeling she's intent on getting me about this weekly?

"Okay," Vinny said. He speaks. "that's the story. Okay, ladies and gentlemen?"

"Gotcha," I said.

"I'll take care of you, Vinny," Jennifer said, squeezing my hand. Is she a trooper? We have to find out.

"You mean, Jen," I queried, "You don't feel any anger toward Vinny about running out on Jean and spending the night in the house of two women, three counting you?"

"Mason, there's something you have to know," Jennifer started, "I'm Jean's best friend. I love her, but I know how she gets sometimes. I don't like the way she feels about you two, and as far as I'm concerned, you two are each the best thing that ever happened to each other. You're a fantastic team, and I'm not going to do anything to jeopardize that, even if it means not being exactly truthful with my best friend and sorority sister. Don't worry about me. Vinny's secret is safe with me."

We're stopped by the only red light between Michele's house and our house.

"Jen," Vinny said, "you don't have to sell out. I can take care of myself. I just don't want to take you down with me."

"I can make this a lot better, Vinny, if I join the team. We're like the Mod Squad, except Mason gets all the fringe benefits." She then reached across her console and kissed me on the cheek. The light immediately turned green. In spite of all that, a familiar feeling is coming on. My indifference is accelerating.

"Well," said Vinny, "that's all right with me. Can I be Linc?"

"You're Linc, Vinny," I said. He laughed. Jennifer squeezed my hand again.

We're quiet again, but a lot looser now, although we were riding directly into Vinny's double storm, Hurricane Mike and Hurricane Jean. And as I rode beside Jennifer, I looked her over, even though I have already seen every square inch of her tall, lean machine. It would be so simple to just give in to her. She seems to be in love with me, although I'm thinking she's waiting for the right moment to tell me, like right after I tell her. Jennifer's trying really hard to win my affections, possibly for our lifetimes, which doesn't quite fit into my plans right now. That is, unless your name is Joan Kissinger. Then you can have me whenever you please. I hope she knows that, and I hope she is considering it for all I have to offer. We got off to a great start last night, to say the very least. I wonder what Joan's doing right now? Whatever it is, I hope she's alone.

The house appeared up the hill. Oh, hell, showtime, part one.

Jennifer wheeled in front of our house. A quick scan down the street revealed the Vacca's bronze Caddy, the Lambert's white Impala, the

Calire's red Camaro, the Lopinski's blue Caprice, all sold by The Mike, a real refrigerators-to-eskimoes type of guy. The silver Mercedes most assuredly belongs to Doctor Pierce. Ron's 280ZX is a half block away, and that rounds out the players for The First Round.

As Jen turned off the ignition, Vinny said, "I'll leave you two kids alone. Wish me luck."

"Good luck, Gunner," I said, "Don't get into any fist fights until I get there."

"Okay, that covers Jean. What about my dad?"

I winced and laughed, but it's good to see he has a good attitude about this.

Just as Vinny's door slammed, Jennifer turned to me, "I've got a couple of things to say. First, as far as winning you, all of you, as my man, let me remind you, not literally now, but in the sense of love, I'm going to kick Joan Kissinger's ass."

Huh? First, Jen's going to have her ass. Now she wants to kick her ass. I wish she'd figure out what it is she's going to do with Joan's ass…I have. And, second, the ass kick? Where have I heard that before? Still, I sat motionless, not knowing what to say, only able to emit, "Okay."

"And, second, as far as last night goes and meeting my parents, you slept on the sofa and I took the guest room, if it comes up."

"Okay."

"And, third, before you leave for the game, if anything else comes up, just tell me and we'll go up to your room and I'll take care of it."

"That would make it the most interesting pregame I ever had," I said.

"And, fourth…I love you, Mason Bricker. I'm going to make you forget you ever met Joan and make her envious as hell."

I love a woman with confidence. But I'm not ready to tell her yet."Oh, Jennifer," I said with a smile on my face and a stirring in my slacks, "I guess this means we have a lot to talk about. I have so…much on my mind right now I think this evening would be a great time to do that. Until then, I want you to know…." God, I almost told her I'm playing the game for her today. I've got to get a hold of myself..."until then, we'll do just that."

"That's all I can ask," Jen said, "So shall we go meet my parents? They're just going to love you. Not quite like me, though, even though you'll soon discover my mother is still a looker."

Just like everybody else's mother up there.

We kissed hard. Give it up, Mason...no, don't!

Alternately, we opened our respective doors and walked up my steps to my porch.

Joan's porch....

My gut is grinding....

I open the door. The breakfast party is stuffed over on one side of the living room trying their best to have a good time, while Vinny and Mike are by themselves beside the blue sofas. The father is animated and the son is looking down wishing he were somewhere else, like the Bataan death march. The first thing I heard Mike say was terse, "You didn't go to your coach's house. You went to some floozy teacher's house. Goddamned it, boy, don't you have any respect for anything?"

"I did go to Dr. Taranucci's house. Coach was there. They have something going, Dad. Then we went to his place to talk over the game. Mason and Jennifer came by to pick me up this morning." That's true. Jennifer and I stopped by the kitchen on our way out the front door and picked Vinny up.

"You lied to me. You lied to your mother, your brothers. You lied to Wayne, Geri, Rob, Pauline."

"Uh, keep me out of this, Mike," said Wayne.

Mike looked up at him. He didn't give a shit who he included in his tirades or even where he held them. I can't tell if it's poor judgment or total arrogance. I leaned toward the latter. Then I saw Patricia move in to the fracas. "Mike, you men move it up stairs, okay?" She could take a lot, but this morning her husband embarrassed her. Kick him in the balls!

Vinny and Mike quickly scurried up to Vinny's room. Jean followed, not about to count herself out of this, her man and my floozy teacher. The tension immediately eased when the three left the room.

"Hello there, Mason!" Geri Lambert said with a big grin. "Hello, Jennifer!"

"Whatd'ya say, Mrs. Lambert?" I replied, leaning to move in her direction. I then froze, because out of the pack appeared a tall man, six-four at least, wearing a navy blazer, a white turtleneck, and silver slacks. With him is a tall woman, just about Jennifer's height, lovely and slender in a silver wool sweater and navy slacks, and towing a girl, maybe sixteen, a tall willowy wisp of a child, very pretty in faded denims and a navy sweater. They are all smiling that Jennifer smile, nice but out there somewhere.

"Is this the young man you've been talking about, Jennifer?" the lady asked.

"Mom, Dad, Debbie, this is Mason Bricker," Jen said. "Mason, this is Charles, Eliza, and my sister Debbie. My family." Eliza grabbed my hand like we're going to go into next week together, the smile not fading in the least.

"We've heard so much about you, Mason Bricker, and I for one have been waiting and waiting to meet you. It is so nice to meet you."

Judy's standing a few feet behind the Pierces, staring at me out of Jennifer's sight, about to spew a huge laugh for some reason, well, for many reasons. She knows how goofy the Pierce family is. Considering Jennifer, it makes sense.

"Uh-hum," Charles said, clearing his throat.

"Oh, I'm sorry, dear!" Eliza said.

"Son, it's always great to meet one of my little girl's friends," Dr. Pierce said.

"Oh!" I said to Jennifer in jest, "So you introduce a lot of boys to your family!"

"No! Silly!" she shouted back. The whole family roared. Alice faked a silent Santa Claus belly laugh just over Eliza's shoulder. I placed my hand behind Jennifer's back and flipped her off.

"No, I'm sorry, Dr. Pierce, I shouldn't have made light of your daughter," I said in apology.

"Think nothing of it, my boy," the doctor said, "We're a fun-loving family. We kid and joke all the time." The Mrs. hadn't yet put that smile down, and Debbie wouldn't stop staring at me. Jennifer noticed that.

"Watch it, Deb," Jen said. Oh…this has happened before to Jen and Deb.

"You're cute! I want a Mason!" Debbie whined. "Do you have any football player friends for me?"

"I think you'll have to grow up a little more, sweetie!" said Eliza. Another family laugh. All together now…one, two, three

"Son, let me say to you," the doctor said, "I read the paper this morning. I am very darned proud of you. I've heard some bad things about your coach in the past, but I always put them away, trying to have a positive outlook on the Runners. Well, I think he's overstepped his bounds, way over! You have a lot of guts for standing up to him, that is, if the article is factually correct."

I sucked in a quiet deep breath. "It is."

Wayne and Rob quickly stepped over to me. "Way to go, Mason," Wayne said, "You're a brave man."

"Good job, Mason," Rob said, "You showed 'em."

Suddenly, the entire party was around Jennifer and me. Mike's wet towel had been removed and burned. The father and the son had taken it elsewhere, even though I could catch a loud word or two coming from Vinny's room. Patricia remained with us and she made her way to me.

"Mason, I, too, am proud of you," she whispered. "I just think it is time for this racial animosity to stop. I've got something I want you to read sometime. It's the transcript of my interview in the pageant. It was a long time ago, but I talked about the races just getting together and becoming one. Things were a lot different then. Someone said the interview was the reason why I lost, and if that's true, to hell with them. You've done well, Mason. Frank and Colleen, I'm sure, are beaming right now."

I'm moved. "Thank you, Patricia. I'd love to read your interview. Thank you."

I wondered if Frank would indeed be proud if he found out his son was duped. I have to call PD this morning.

I heard a door slam and quick steps from the top of the stairs down. Mike reappeared. He is not happy. We all tried to ignore him and continue to have a nice breakfast, but the longer The Mike stands there, the more oppressive he is.

"So, you're the man, Mason," he said, not privately, with a touch of venom. Well, possibly more than a touch. "You're the big man. It's one thing to stand up for your beliefs, but your timing is terrible. You're ruining my son's first game and I don't take that very well. Neither does my son."

"The wheels were rolling before Bobby Kay went down," I said, already weary of The Mike "And you're wrong about Vinny. We've talked this over."

"No, you're wrong, Mason," he replied, "You're wrong a lot more than you're right. You're a loose cannon and you don't have the welfare of your friend in mind. You're selfish."

If I hear the word 'welfare' again, I'm going to kill myself. While I was stewing on that, the party moved back toward the dining room and the kitchen. Mike's a lot of fun.

"And you're sad," I said, "You're calling me selfish? A loose cannon? Just because you can't run my life? You oughta know about it. You're always looking out for number one. In fact, you've taken it to new pathological heights, Mike."

"You're foolish, Mason," said Mike, "You can't get your recognition on the field, so you sacrifice the entire team so you can get a little ink. Then you put my son at risk so you can hop in the sack with that whore professor of yours. A woman's got a lot of problems when she lures two young men into her web just for her sick pleasures. I hope you had a good tumble, because everybody is paying for it."

This is the closest I have ever come to taking Mike to the mat. If he wasn't my best friend's father and the best friend of my late father, he'd be a bloody fuckin' mess.

"This is getting ridiculous, Mike," I said, the tremors of anger in my voice, "You don't even know Dr. Taranucci and you have no idea what happened last night. I'm finished here. I know the truth. And your assumptions are way off base."

"You ever consider seeking professional help, Mason?" he asked with a foul tone in his voice, "A psychiatrist, perhaps? Think about it, boy, because you're screwed up in the head. You had nice parents. I don't for the life of me know where you went wrong."

Now he has the gloves off, trying to pull me into his squalor. "Can it, Mike," I said, doing my best to not sink to his level. I turned away to find Patricia and Vinny standing near my side.

"Dad, you're way out of line," Vinny said, voice calm in deference to the others, but still stressed, "As usual, it's always been your way or the highway. It may have worked when I was younger, but now I'm twenty years old, Dad. I can vote, drink, and die for my country. And I don't have to take any of your shit any more."

Damn, Vinny, in front of God and everybody! Oh, yeah!

"You don't know what the hell…," Mike tried to say.

But Vinny interrupted, "I'm not finished. I stood upstairs and listened to you go on and on about how big of a screw-up I am. Then you come down here and say you have my best interests in mind? Ha! You sure have a weird way of showing it. Something you oughta know, Dad. It was my idea to leave last night, just to get away from you."

"Vinny!" Patricia said in shock. This is a surprise? Where in the hell have you been, honey?

"I've got a big job today, Dad," Vinny continued, gaining momentum with every sentence, "and you're doing nothing to help me. You bad-mouth my football program. You bad-mouth my friend. You bad-mouth my decision to come here and play ball. You have your foot in everything and not a good word to say. I've gotten a hell of a lot more from Mason this year than I could ever hope to get from you."

Mike is truly hurt by that remark. He did his best indignant puppy dog and replied, "Does Mason send you any money? Has Mason built a business, a profitable business, for you to cash in on?"

"If you want to reduce us to dollars and cents, Dad, go ahead. The point is, you've done little to prepare me for this game. Dr. Taranucci did me a big favor last night to calm me down and get my head straight after you screwed it all up. But you can't see that. All you had to lean on was to call it sex with a whore, to just discount the hell out of it. Wake up, Dad! You've got to rethink our relationship, because I'm not continuing like this."

Vinny is shaking and his mom is crying. All the while the others in the next room are laughing and carrying on as they should do. Mike took one look around and turned to walk out the door.

"I'm sorry, Mom," Vinny said calmly despite being visibly upset, "I'm just not taking his shit any more."

Patricia opened her arms for her eldest son and held him for a while, then released to also walked out the door to find her husband. It must be very difficult for her to watch that incorrigible bastard tear down her son and then have to be his partner.

Vinny and I moved slowly into the dining room where they're all packed in like Spam in a can. The Gunner spoke to our guests. "I'm sorry, everybody," he said, "This is supposed to be a good time and I've ruined it for all."

"Vinny," Rob said, "think nothing of it. You just do what you have to do to get yourself ready to play today."

"Yeah, Vinny," Wayne added, "That's number one right now. Don't you worry about us. Soon we'll all be at the game screaming our heads off for you."

Pauline came through the door from the kitchen with a dozen tall empty glasses on a tray. Geri followed with three big cans of tomato juice in one arm and a gallon of vodka in the other.

"Bloody Russians for everybody!" said Judy.

Geri placed her load on the table and turned to Vinny and me. "You boys get ready for the game your way. We get ready our way." The prospect of alcohol before eight o'clock in the morning could repulse a lot of people, but this crowd needed a tension-easer. The two ladies started mixing and passing the drinks around, skipping the traditional celery because they're not serving omelets. Soon, everyone of majority age, even the plastic Pierces minus Debbie who had joined the children downstairs, had their elixir in hand. The air's clearer already.

"You boys haven't eaten," said Judy, "Dig in. You need your strength today."

The trays of breakfast food, scrambled eggs, link sausage, bacon, toast, hash browns, looked very much inviting. "Wouldn't want to see this go to waste," I said, "C'mon, Vinny, join me. You got to get some energy for your wheels."

I glanced at my friend, and did a double take. His face, his extraordinarily handsome face, has something. I couldn't figure it out at first, and I didn't want to stare, so I thought as I shoveled eggs and loaded potatoes onto my plate. Vinny followed me as the spectators commented on the ladies' ability to make a perfect Bloody Russian.

"Great, girls," said Rob, "This is hitting the spot."

"I must say, I don't usually imbibe," said the Doctor, "but this is good."

"Watch yourself, Charles," said Eliza, still smiling, "You don't want to fall asleep at halftime."

"Oh, no, dear," Charles said, "I don't miss Pitt games for anything. This is my thirty-sixth consecutive year in the stands for this rivalry."

"Hey, that's tremendous," said Wayne, "I bet you've seen some great football in those years."

"I have indeed," Charles said.

"Well, I'm sure today will be no exception," said Rob, standing beside Vinny and squeezing his shoulder. The Gunner smiled, a grin I've rarely seen on his face, and never near his father. Not the detached male model look at which he is so adept, but an honest-to-God happy face. A smile and a nod, loose. He's going to take his first college snap in a little over five hours, and the boy's loose. This could be the start of something wonderful.

I think I know what's going on here. Vinny standing up to his father and the farcical way in which he treated his son today, and every day for that matter, has exorcised an iniquitous portion of his soul, a painful but necessary inception of the healing process. Mike's unrealistic expectations and his rebuking when they weren't met chipped away at Vinny. I have to provide constant reminders of his successes and, more importantly, his value and worth, but the father is always the hero. By that I can only do so much. When my school beat his school in the championships, Mike had an entire list of things that could have gone better, even though I thought Vinny performed admirably with little help against a group of young men who just weren't going to be defeated. And the next year, when Vinny played the entire season nearly perfectly and led the same team to the title, Mike discounted it all with that one loss. Vinny was thirty-one and one as a high school quarterback, a prolific career, with the major colleges clamoring for his services. Still, Mike couldn't get past that one defeat. Then nothing in the recruiting process could go right. He trashed Notre Dame and their run-oriented option offense and how they would waste Vinny's passing talents and physically beat him senseless. Mike degraded Ohio State and their concentration on the run, predicting Vinny would just be handing-off to tailbacks for four years. But, when we struck the deal with the U and Vinny signed on his own, which he could do because he was eighteen at the time, and which he did as an act of defiance, Mike hit the ceiling. He admonished Vinny for turning down two great football programs for one dinky school.

Whatever Vinny did was wrong. It's going to take a while for my man to become his own man, since nothing like this happens in one morning. But Vinny's stand got it started, and I think he's a lot better off now than he was last night. And this can't be anything but good news for the Runners.

Ron approached Vinny and me holding a bloody Russian. No bruises. Good. He turned to his friend. "Jimmy, this is my brother Mason and this is his friend Vinny Vacca." I like how he said that.

"Hello, Jimmy," I said. We shook hands and greeted each other pleasantly. Jimmy looked something like Ron, same carefree smile, except Jimmy is packing a lot of tanned beef atop what couldn't have been any larger than a twenty-eight inch waist. What a guy! Still, the blond-out-of-a-bottle hair tells the story. Fine with me.

"Vinny's the quarterback today, Jimmy," Ron said.

"Oh, good! Jet 'em, Vinny!" Jimmy exclaimed.

"I will," said Vinny, smiling, in all likelihood wondering what the hell 'jet'em' means.

"Hey, boys," Ron said, "Great party. Booze. Food. Cute guys. Family squabbles."

Another time, I thought Vinny just might go against his advice to me and deck my brother. Instead, he placed his hand on Ron's shoulder and said, "Fuck you, Ron." The two looked at each other and cracked up. The new Gunner. The new Ron. Thought I'd never see the day

"Good eggs, Judy, Alice," Vinny said.

"Thank you," said Alice, wondering if Vinny, who usually bolted his meals down like there's a race, ever commented on food.

"You eat what you need," said Sam Lopinski, the father of the chairwoman of Vinny's planning committee. Sam is the oldest dad of those present. He says he didn't marry until his mid thirties and had his accounting practice rolling along nicely. Then he picked a young one. If Lucinda Lopinski in her silver jumpsuit is indicative of how Jean will turn out in twenty years, that explains why Vinny concedes so much in their relationship. Another explanation could be that Lucinda didn't marry Sam, she took a prisoner. Jean has seen it work for her mother, so why can't it be the same way for her? In only one Sunday meal last fall with the Lopinski's at The Dining Room I figured it all out. Maybe that will work for Vinny and Jean. Maybe Jean will be the target of liberation such as what happened to Mike. Where the hell is Jean, anyway?

While Vinny's the center of attention, I slipped into the kitchen to discover the young Miss Lopinski outside drawing on a Virginia Slim with her mother. There never was a more opportune time to piss them off. I have nothing to lose. They loathe me, anyway.

I opened the door. "Uh, ladies?"

The bouncy, wavy blonde locks flowing down to her shoulders *a la* Farrah Fawsett, the sky blue eyes, the deviation from planarity of her bosom, hips and buttocks. Lucinda looks incredible.

"Go to hell, Mason," Jean said.

"Jean…," I tried to say.

"Mason," said Lucinda, "my daughter and I are discussing a private matter. We'd appreciate it if you would rejoin the party."

"Ladies, Vinny and I are leaving soon. We'd like to see you before we go."

"We'll be in there," Jean said curtly.

"Okay." I closed the door and shuffled back in, duly chastised. If I were the kind of person who had to be liked by everybody, those two would drive me to hard drugs.

Alice and Judy walked through the door from the dining room. "My God, we're going to need more booze for tonight."

"You'd better get it soon, because when we beat Pitt, there won't be any alcohol left in Montani. You'll be baking pot brownies for everyone. Hey, that's not a bad idea. Wouldn't you like to see your parents stoned?" I've brought this to the table before. Always no response.

"And, Mason," Judy started, "to think we were trying to find you to wish you a good day and a good game. That's okay. We can put up with your smart-assed mouth, but just today." She's smiling and tugging at my lapels.

"Looks like you and Jennifer have come to an agreement," said Alice, straightening my tie.

Why is it women do things like discuss the absoluteness of relationships with other women while they're doing other things that signal sex? They seem to take pleasure in setting up perplexities. I guess I'll have to ponder that another time, because now I've got to give satisfactory answers to their questions.

"Yes, we have," I said. I am going to gag.

"Oh, I just adore new love!" Alice exclaimed.

"I think I'm going to cry!" said Judy.

"Don't carry this too far and get us married with little Jennifers running around."

"And tiny Masons listening to The Doors and banging their heads against the walls!" said Judy. Always at my expense.

"Ask Jen about it," I said, "You won't believe me anyway."

"Tell us, Mason," Alice said. "We won't make fun of you or think you're bullshitting us or anything."

"Yeah," said Judy, "c'mon. Tell us."

I'm a little vacillant on what to tell them. In the final analysis, it's 'I love you, Mason' and 'Gee, I don't know, Jennifer. I mean, we did wake up together this morning and junk, but Joan has awfully nice….'

"Mason," Judy said, in all seriousness, "if you can't tell us, who can you tell?"

Well, Vinny, for one. "Okay, Jennifer said she really likes me, and I told her we have a lot to talk about. That's where we have to leave it for right now because I've got a ton on my mind this morning with the newspaper and all."

"All?" asked Alice, transparent about digging in for today's feelings about Joan. I'm not telling them yet.

"Yes, Alice, I have a football game today. And I have a team to answer to now that the proverbial cat is out of the goddamned bag."

"Mason, you take care of Jennifer," Judy said, as if the paper and the team and Lawson and the attitudes of the citizenry of the state have all blown away and life is reduced to a college romance. "She's laid a lot on the line for you."

I'll say.

Jennifer walked into the kitchen, the long tall woman and her sixth sense, just knowing we're talking about her. She looked at me, pointing to the watch on her left wrist.

"You are checking the clock occasionally, aren't you?" Jen asked. Now if that's not a wifely question….

"I mention that," she continued, "because I have to talk with you before you leave. It's very important." Alice and Judy made moves to get out of the kitchen. "No need, girls. I'll take him upstairs."

"Ooooo…," said Alice.

"Give me a minute, Jennifer," I requested, "Then, I'll meet you upstairs."

Jennifer smiled and twitched her nose. "You're not going to call your boss, are you?"

Not a bad idea. "No, Jen," I said, closing in on her face, "Now, why would I do that?"

"I can't think of any reason," replied Jennifer, "since I'll do absolutely anything for you. Absolutely, Mason," Her face got even closer.

Stymied is the best word to describe me. Dr. Kissinger and 'why Dr. Kissinger' flashed in my mind. Judy and Alice stood there. I turned to them. "Get you minds out of the gutter," I groaned. Time is necking down. Necking. Now there's a word for you. I spinned to go up to my room. Jennifer disappeared. I excused myself from my housemates. Jennifer and me. Made 'em really happy.

Arriving in my room, I quickly grabbed the telephone. Dialing information, an operator answered. I spoke. "Could you please get me the number for PD Doughtery in Huntington?"

Silence. Then, "I'm sorry, sir, his number is unlisted."

"Fuck!" I exclaimed.

"Sir! That was unnecessary," said the operator.

I apologized and slammed the receiver onto the cradle. This is just fuckin' great. I may never know until the FBI contacts me.

Jen entered my room without knocking. "You okay?" she asked. I nodded yes. She softly closed the door and locked it. Moving quickly in front of me, she hung her arms around my neck and shoulders and kissed my unsuspecting lips. Her hands dropped with alacrity down to my butt as she pushed her pelvis against mine, kissing me again with an open mouth, grinding and pulling, leaving me no choice but to reciprocate. This…this, this is an instant turn-on, and as I arose I felt the twinges of soreness residual from the ups and downs and all arounds of the previous twelve hours. I'm about to lose my mind, not really knowing what I'm doing or saying. Inebriated faculty with her bare feet and a promise in my hands. Scantily clad coeds driving across town at midnight. It's all so crazy. I can't even remember the last time before last week I was kissed. I'm just not used to all this attention.

OK, Jennifer, you've got me…the phone…who the hell's calling right now?

The phone is on the nightstand to the left of my bed. I laid down there to reach it, with Jen following me, all over me. Managing to pick up the receiver, I placed it to my ear with some difficulty since the long girl had her face on my neck.

"Mason," I said pleasantly.

"Pretend I'm your sister if you're not alone," Joan said on the other end of the line.

My heart came to a halt, then jumped up to my throat. In fact, most everything on my body stopped; respiration, perspiration, eye blinking, digestion. I'm operating on the basics, as the right side of my brain is buzzing coded signals and the left side is trying to maintain order by aligning my priorities. What the hell do I say? Can I pull this off? Do something, even if it's wrong!

"Junie! How are you?"

Jennifer's legs are wrapped tightly around mine for life. Ten seconds ago, I would have…Right now, however….

"I'm wonderfully well," said Joan. "Maybe I should do most of the talking here."

"That's great. Things are going great up here in West Virginia. Today's Pitt day, you know."

"Pitt, schmitt. This is the best time I've ever had in West Virginia," Joan said with a simmer in her voice, "Mason, I just had to call you because I am thinking of you and looking at my feet."

"No! You're kidding?" I said, continuing to send code.

"No, I'm not!" Joan exclaimed. "This is better than any pro in Chicago could do. I think you've found your life's work, that is, if you promise to only work on me. If you do that, I think we've got what you might call an agreement."

I reflexively squeezed Jennifer. An agreement? What the hell?

"Well, you'll have to come to my house sometime, Junie."

Joan laughed The Laugh. I closed my eyes and took a deep breath. "Can you imagine?" she said.

I have many times, Joan…"Vinny says hello."

"Vinny doesn't even like me," Joan said right before another Laugh.

"That's not entirely true. But, it doesn't matter," I said, "Let me tell you: you know that woman I told you about a few weeks ago?"

"You mean Jennifer?" replied Joan with a giggle.

"No, Junie…sometimes you make me groan."

"Oh, that is slick. Your Joan is one big groan. Oh, you're good. At a lot of things."

"Thank you," I said. I'm glad I'm lying down "Well, we had an interesting night last night. I talked to her just a second ago."

"Oh, you're making me moan, Mason!" Joan is cracking herself up. Meanwhile, Jennifer showed her appreciation by unbuttoning and unzipping her Levis and trying to place my hand under her panties. I resisted, drawing the line right there. Nevertheless, she's enjoying the conversation. "I'm calling to ask you if you can meet Pamela and me at All That Jazz after the game. Will you, please?"

My world again froze. All That Jazz. From last night's fantasy. This is almost too much for a young man of my relative inexperience. The only thing flowing is the connection between my brain and my mouth, and even that is impeded by the sludge of trepidation. Jennifer again pulled on my hand as I tried to come up with an answer for one of the more important questions Joan has ever asked me.

"Uh…yeah…of course," is all I can think to say.

I glanced at Jennifer. Her parents are downstairs and my sister's on the phone. She's in her own world of an attempt at risky sex. The excitement is too much as she pursed her lips and breathed hard. All the while my relationship with Joan has soared to a new frontier. There is no way even with my acutely developed imagination could I have come up with this one. Never.

"Uh, Mason," Joan said in singsong, "I'm losing you." She laughed. I sighed.

"I'm back. I'm back," I said, my system overloading and crashing. Jen gazed at me with her almonds and mouthed, 'I love you,' then closed her eyes and laid back.

As if she just knew, Joan said, "It sounds like I've called at a bad time for you and Jennifer." This time I didn't detect a smile in her voice. I really don't want to hurt her. I have no commitment from her, but I still don't want to hurt her. I'm strange.

"Oh, no, Junie, no! Let's talk away!"

The clock ticked slowly to her silence. Then, "Well, Mason, just to tell you," I'm relieved to hear the warmth of her voice come back. "I'm in a navy silk robe, and that's about it. If it had silver bells hanging from it, it would be better than Christmas and your Thinking Man's Football."

Holy fuck, Batman! "Well, you've made my day, sis," I said, waiting to breathe again.

"And you mine," Joan said, "You made my yesterday. You made my today. And it's barely daylight."

"Bare being an operative word here," I said, gambling Jennifer wouldn't suspect a thing.

"Sounds like a good conversation for tonight," Joan said with seduction.

"Yeah!" I said, flutters of excitement running up my spine. However, despite that excitement and the robe and last night, I found a way to hold my ground, "But, remember, you've got to ride that rocket with me." Jen smiled, maybe thinking of her own red glare.

"I know, Mason. I know," Joan replied with a softened tone, "I just don't know what to tell you."

"How about the truth?" My mouth went dry.

"The truth?" Joan asked. "How about I admire you for your convictions. In everything, you bastard." I heard a hint of a giggle.

From definitive to doubt. See what a good night's sleep can do for a woman? "It's self-preservation," I said. I didn't care if Jennifer had picked up on the last few comments. Knowing Jen, she probably hadn't.

I heard Joan take a deep breath. "Good luck today, Mason. I'll be watching. I saw the paper this morning. Are you going to be all right?"

"Right now, there is no way I could be better." I hope Dr. Kissinger got that code.

"You did the right thing, Mason. You always do the right thing." She clearly doesn't know I let Jennifer screw me near submission after she left last night. "That's why...," Joan continued, "That's why...."

"Yes?" I shook in anticipation. God, make her say it....

A pause. "That's why I admire you so much." Admiration. That's the best I'm going to get this morning. I'll take it. "It may get tough, Mason, but nothing can take away from the fact that you did what you had to do."

"Thanks. Thank you. I love you, Junie. More and more everyday," I'm near tears. Would somebody please put a George Carlin LP on?

I heard Joan draw in another deep breath, Then, "And Mason...."

"Yes?"

"I'm untying the robe...."

I shot back to life with a laugh of my own. "That's wonderful. Just wonderful."

"Bye," Joan said, her special Laugh trailing before the hang-up. I laid there paralyzed, but smiling.

Jennifer grabbed the phone from my hands and hung it up. She then kissed me, jutting her tongue down my esophagus. "Golly," she said, allowing me to suck in a breath, "I've never had a better time with a telephone."

"Oh, Jennifer, me either."

The phone rang again.

"All right! Let's do it again!" she said with an extreme giggle.

And again.

"Mason," I answered.

"Time to go, Cheetah," said Vinny's voice in the receiver.

I snapped out of it quickly. Time for football. Unlike the past ten minutes, this was very familiar. I always know how to act when it's time for football.

"All right!" I exclaimed as I hung up. "Jennifer," I said directly into her eyes. "Uh…." I am at a loss for words.

"Football," she said, adding, "Kiss me." I obliged.

"I love you, Mason."

I stared, smiled, and dropped my head.

"Don't worry. You will when you're ready. In the meantime, you keep taking care of my womanly urges and everything will be a-okay. Okay?" Jen is radiant.

I don't take love and sex lightly at all. I didn't set out to get two women. Circumstances brought all our stars in line. Still, I have responsibilities here, to all involved in that three-way conversation Bell Telephone has never thought to offer. I have to do what's right, whatever that is, before this train runs out of tracks and somebody gets hurt.

Saturday, November 8, 1975
7:25 am

Leaving the house for the game

Jennifer and I walked out of my room to meet Vinny and Jean standing at the top of the steps. The girls grinned at each other, saying more non-verbally than we boys could ever hope to understand. I glanced at Jean, who at nineteen brings voluptuous to life. All Vinny has to do, I am sure, to justify why he takes all her shit is to sneak a peek under the sheets.

As always, Jean averted my eyes. Boy, I get the feeling she would rather I transfer to Brown or something. But, her man is the starting quarterback today and nothing, nothing can take that away from her. She's now at his side and certainly feels she had a lot to do with The Gunner's recent success. With regard to my friend and the effect manhood can have on his game, I'm sure she has.

I felt a squeeze on my upper right arm. Thanks to Michael and his summer boot camp, it is ample. I get the feeling girls likes that. I looked over to Jennifer. It looks as if she's up for this game. I have never been able to consider Jennifer without first thinking of Joan. This morning was the climax. Something's got to give. Maybe something's already given.

Ritualistically, the cheers start from downstairs. 'Here we go, Runners, here we go! Here we go, Runners, here we go!' On and on, from the men and the women who pay the rent, and their offspring, enrolled and preparatory. On and on, waiting for Vinny and me to make our appearances as we do every home game Saturday. Today, however, the yelling is louder and the claps and stomps are harder. This is just not any game. It has national championship implications and one of their own is going to play a major role. I can feel the electricity sparking up and around the stairs.

On some silent cue, the ladies start down the steps and turn left to the stairwell that leads to the kitchen, from where they will join the crowd. Jean does it every time, holding on to Vinny to the last possible moment. Today, she showed Jennifer the ropes. Vinny and I after the girls disappeared waited a bit, nodded, and proceeded down to our number one fans.

As we appeared through the fire door, our living room erupted into just about as much wildness as adults in their mid forties can withstand.

It's crazy. Crazy! Every home weekend, I like to stand up here and wave and absorb it all while picking out the faces. There they are: Wayne, Geri, Rob, Patricia! Back from exile! Also, Pauline, Vinny's brothers Dom and Sal, a classic ethnic family, Judy and her sisters Sheila and Joyce, Alice and her sister Liz; and Ron and Jimmy! Jesus, I saw my brother earlier, but the surprise remains. The stadium may fall in today! And there are my new best friends the Pierce family, yes, still smiling right beside Jean and Jennifer. The stalwarts, our always-faithful faithful. This is college football at its finest. With Vinny in there, I have a feeling I'll be saying that a lot.

"Speech!" came the staccato urgings.

"C'mon! Speech!"

I motioned Vinny to take the stands. As he moved up, the folks roared again. He's their man. He's their man!

"...." They wouldn't relent. Vinny stood patiently, I sure enjoying the hell out of this. Finally, the fans gave him the floor. "I want to thank you for your support. Today's a special day for me and I'm glad I could share it with you. Now, just let me hear you when I'm on the field. I need you. Thanks!"

You would have thought it was 1960 and JFK just got the nomination at a high school gymnasium. Ear-splitting screams flooded the house, female-originated, like the Beatles had walked out of *The Ed Sullivan Show* into our living room. I thought the windows were gone those five teenage sisters are so loud. It's a combination of Vinny's humble confidence and matinee-idol looks that drives them nuts. I decided then The Gunner is either going to be a ladies' heartthrob screen star or President of the United States in 2000. He's a tough act to follow. But follow I did.

I stepped up. The girls didn't yelp as loudly, but their parents and Jennifer are more than kind to me. I stood there and received it until a couple of seconds later when it died down.

"We are going to give you a game today, folks," I said, "We've got it all in place. For the first time in several years, we've got a quarterback."

More girlish screams. "Actually, we've got Pitt right where we want 'em." The men groaned and laughed. "Don't laugh," I urged, "They're getting on the bus right now up in Pittsburgh thinking they've got a really easy job today. Well, I know our guys. And I know that once the coin is tossed, all the newspapers and discrimination and coaches won't matter. It's just our eleven against their eleven. And they ain't seen nothin' like our guys." More cheers. "Guys like Michael Burton, Arthur O'Neill, Joe Osbourne, Dhali Sellers, Ted Gerlach. Do you seriously think these guys are going to cower to anybody?" No! shouted the audience. Oh, yeah…"I guarantee you, this game will go down to the final minute, and they're going to freak out under the weight of watching national championships and Heisman Trophies fade away and we're going to take it from them. And Pitt's gonna get back on that bus and wonder what in the hell hit them."

I got immediate hoots and applause, either for what I said or for finally drawing it to a close. On that, Vinny and I walked down the steps from the landing to the floor where the masses parted and stood and cheered more as we made our way for the front door. As is custom, Judy and Alice flanked the door and offered us our final kisses before sending us off for battle. We descend the stairs for the street sidewalk and wave our goodbyes to the crowd now on the porch to wish us well one more time. To the sound of 'Here we go, Runners, here we go,' Vinny and I head for the campus fifteen minutes away.

Walking down the hill to our right with purpose is Mike Vacca. He's looking directly at his number one son as he strides up to him. Standing before him with a military posture, he extended his hand and said in a firm, true voice, "Son, today is the day we've been working for. Good luck to you. I know you'll do well." Then, with a wink, he said, "I know you will. You're my son."

"Thank you, Dad," is all Vinny said. They stepped back from each other. I swear to God, I thought they were going to salute. Vinny turned to his left and continued down the sidewalk. Mike turned right and walked back to the house. I'm left there, astonished at the fact that the confrontation was so civil, and because it was so formal.

Catching up to Vinny, I found him walking fast and crying, tears streaming down his fine-looking cheeks. Even after all these years, I don't know what to say.

Vinny helped me out. "I don't want to talk about it. I don't want to talk about Dad, past, present, or future."

"Vinny, don't worry, man," I said, searching, "You're going to have a helluva game."

"I don't want to talk about football. I don't want to talk. For the next few minutes, you talk. You're so goddamned good at it."

"I don't know, Gunner. You're the one who had the teenagers almost throwing their bodies at you."

"I said I don't want to talk. You talk. How was your morning, Mason?" Stressed. My man is stressed.

"My morning? You wouldn't believe my morning."

"Try me," Vinny said.

Here goes. "You ever read Penthouse Forum?"

"Of course."

The walking pace hadn't slowed. "I had an R-rated Penthouse Forum moment."

"With Jennifer? I don't know if I want to hear this."

"You'll want to, believe me."

"Try me."

"A few minutes before we left, Jennifer and I were in my room, intimate with our clothes on."

"Big deal."

"The phone rings. Jennifer gets me in a leg lock. I answer the phone. It's Joan."

He glared at me.

"She tells me to act like it's my sister. Jennifer is writhing on my bed as Joan tells me she's wearing a silk robe."

Vinny comes to a dead halt, still glaring, "Did she know you were with…."

"No, neither one of them knew. Jennifer thought I was talking to Junie, which I swear is the reason why she had so much fun."

"Why?"

"I think she likes to almost get caught. And Joan…she thought I was with the party."

"Joan called you…What's her story?"

"I don't know, but I'm going to find out more at All That Jazz after the game."

Vinny continued to walk. I followed. "But Jennifer is expecting you after the game. She and her mother June Cleaver."

"I'll have to find a way out. I'm going to see Joan. I love her, Vinny."

"You're going to fuck everything up, that's what you're going to do."

"Vinny, how long have I been at least wondering about Joan?"

"Since you met her, but, man, you're laying a lot on the line."

"It's a chance I have to take."

"And if it's taking chances, you're the man."

"You could say that."

The Gunner slowed the pace a bit. "Damn, Mason, you had the sorriest love life of 1975. I mean, I was really concerned about you. Now, you have one righteous looking babe on your bed while another even more righteous looking babe tells you over the telephone that she's barely dressed. I'm very jealous."

"Another victory for clean living," I replied.

We continued on our way in silence for a while. I have nothing else from my life to top that story, and if Vinny had I would have heard it by now. My thoughts wandered back to the events of the morning, not those involving panties and painted toenails, but those concerning Vinny. He said not to mention anything about it, but I had to know. I'm his friend, and that in my mind gave me the right to know. It's danger-ous, but I'm the risk-taker, right?

"Tell me, Vinny, what did Jean have to say about last night? Was she understanding and supportive?"

Even though I'm being a smart-ass, he answered the questions, "She damned near squeezed my head off. I knew that was going to happen, goin' to Michele's. I knew she'd find out, or figure it out, or interrogate someone until he or she broke down and told her. In this case, though, it was Jennifer and Alice and Judy. I guess I couldn't expect them to keep it shut."

"That's okay, Vinny," I said, "This evening you'll handle it just like you do your other transgressions, as minor as they always are. All will be all right, as it always is."

"I'm going to take your advice," The Gunner bravely said. He's cooling off. "We've got more important things to do. Just like your newspaper problem. Most everyone at the breakfast this morning congratulated you on what you did."

"Except your dad."

"I told you, we're not talking about him."

I quickly changed the subject. "How do you feel, man?" Stupid subject.

"Great. We'll be able to talk about the game in a couple of minutes."

"You're awfully rigid about these moratoriums. You get like this when you are nervous," I said.

"Now, why in the hell would I be nervous, genius?" Back to stressed.

"Well, if it makes you feel any better, I'm nervous with you."

"Oh, thanks," Vinny said sarcastically.

"Not about you. I just want you to do well. Don't call it nervous, as in I'm worried about your performance. Call it full of anticipation. I love you, man. I can't wait to see you out there kicking their ass."

"It's a big game for you, too, cowboy," Vinny responded, "I can't wait to see you get your big hits in."

"Man, give me one shot at that prima donna Drew Osberg. That's all I ask." The adrenaline is already coursing through my veins just thinking about nailing that Heisman dickhead to the cross. But, it's a few hours yet. I've got to calm down. I decided to defer to my friend. "You're in a great situation. Pitt knows nothing about you. And that's good, because you're good. You're going to chop them up and they won't know what to do."

"I know," The Gunner said, "I can't wait to get out there. The only variable is will the team, which is already divided, follow me."

"To hell with them," I said, "Just throw your darts and your rainbows. Dhali and Clark and Tom and Dave will be there."

"Mason, being a successful quarterback is not about throwing for five hundred yards and five TDs. It's about command in the huddle. It's about looking each and every man in the eyes and letting them know I'm their leader and I believe in them, and I will take them down the field. Then it's about execution. It's about doing it. It's about showing them I will do anything to keep the drive alive. About doing anything to win. That's my challenge today. If what it takes to win is grind it out on the ground with Arthur and Frank and I don't throw one pass, well, Dhali and those guys won't be happy, but if we end up with more points than they do by my handing off every play, then I am a successful quarterback."

I'm deeply impressed with my friend. He won't admit it right now, but I do think his stand with his father pumped him up. "I'm with ya, Gunner. You'll be that successful quarterback. You've done it many times before."

"Yeah, but that was high school."

"Yeah, but you've got bigger, faster, meaner weapons now. We can match Pitt man for man. Do you honestly think they'll be able to go man on Dhali and Clark and load up on Arthur? No way. No fuckin' way."

"Yeah, but I'm a little concerned about not having a tight end."

"I happen to think you have a very nice butt, Vinny."

"You would. You've been getting so much sweet love lately it's starting to spill over on men. I think you'd better dress by yourself."

"Just because I've noticed your ass you paint me with the broad homo brush? I think I've demonstrated my exclusive interest in females over the past half-day. Don't you agree?" Smug. The prospects of endless sex do that to you.

"I can't believe you have two women. You spend most of your life with no women, then all of a sudden, bam! Bam!"

"All it takes is patience, my friend."

"Yeah, that and a lot of luck."

"And that, too."

"What the hell are you going to do?" asked Vinny, "I ask you again, how the hell are you just not going to show up at your own house tonight? Jennifer knows of this Joan obsession you have. She'll sniff it out right away."

"I'll think of something."

"I heard only one shower run from your room at Michele's this morning. Then two people walk out. Wow, Mason, you're ready for Calumet Farms"

"No details, man."

"How do you feel about her?" Vinny asked.

"I don't want to talk about it."

"I know you, Mason. You don't do the wild thing unless you can back it up."

"Well, Vinny, this time I can't back it up. I love Joan. I woke up this morning. It was dark. I thought it was Joan beside me. I love her so much." We allowed my trailing voice to lead us to silence. "I do wonder what she's doing and what she's wearing every minute of the day," I said, "Does that satisfy the condition for love? I say that and more."

A poignant pause, then, "I'd say I agree."

"That's about all that can be said," I replied.

We're silent for twenty paces, not looking or sounding like football studmen ready to play in The Biggest Game Of Our Lives, Chapter Two. In fact, even after the silence, neither of us could drop the subject of romance.

"That still doesn't mean that you have done anything about Jennifer."

"Up until this morning, I thought it just might go away."

"Then what happened?"

"It actually happened last night. She opened her raincoat to display very nice lingerie."

"Oh, wow!" exclaimed Vinny, "Don't tell me any more, dude. I assume she was in them, or carrying them, or something."

"'Something' is right. Honestly, Vinny, I feel like shit. Jennifer will eventually recover from what I'm ultimately going to do to her, Joan or no Joan. But Joan...what I did was wrong."

"Oh, Mason, don't feel bad. Really, man. It's not your fault. What else could you have done?"

"You know Stephen Stills? I don't want to do Stephen Stills anymore. I don't want to do it again. I'm going 'suicide' for Joan. It's either her or I'm becoming a priest. But that's how I live my life, my man." I said, going from lovesick teenager to fighter pilot, thinking that made me like my dad, a feeling I like to have on fall Saturdays.

Again, we walked in silence.

"One of these days, one of these days, when I'm forty," Vinny started, "and you're thirty-nine, and Jean and I have two point five five kids and I'm driving Chevrolets and living the Darren Stevens life because I know my mother-in-law is a certified witch—"

I interrupted with laughter. She is.

The Gunner continued, "I'll have the attorney house, the attorney club, my kids will be going to the attorney schools. I'll be partner; and in the middle of all of this, I remind you, you'd better be down the street, or I'm gonna come looking for you. I need you to pull me away from all that madness I will call my life. Not forever, but just for an afternoon. Or a day, or maybe we'll sneak a weekend in, and we can play golf the way you like it, where you bet art treasures and entire civilizations on one single putt; and see who gets Kamchatcha. And, as always you'll lose because I'm a great golfer and you suck. We'll drink beer and smoke pot and you tell me stories like you always do, except this time new stories from the incoherent life you will lead. And then it'll happen. We veg in front of the TV and watch college football and remember the day, twenty years ago, when we, when everyone said we couldn't, beat Pitt. That's what I'm looking forward to, my man. So you'd better not do something stupid like follow Joe Osbourne into some hotspot on the Map of the World—I know you're thinking about it, man, I know you— or harass Joan just enough to have her lean your way, because that's wrong because she's so staid she's supposed to be the wife of some attorney, like Jean…and Jennifer, for that matter because I need you to lead the…what do you say…"

"The bohemian life—"

"Yeah, I need you to find some exotic woman who wears all black and will understand that you have to take care of me and write and publish and keep me sane. Keep me sane, man. Just like you've been doing for about a decade now. Keep doing that for your old friend Vinny, huh?"

"You've got me, my friend." I am *deeply* touched.

"Then, your first order of business is to get me through today," Vinny said. I knew it. It would happen to anybody. His confidence is slipping. Slipping. I decided to fix this. I know just what to say.

So, here goes. "Vinny, the first thing you have to remember is you don't have to do it by yourself. First, you've got the line, with the G-man himself. A bigoted son-of-a-bitch he is, but he and his big boys have been doing it all year. Next, you have Arthur and Frank. You feeling a little down? Hand off to Frank behind the G-man. You got yards and you barely moved. Then, there are Dhali and Clark. If they can catch the

Kid's passes, they are going to love to see yours. We've talked about this before, Vinny. This is different than those pencil-necked sheilas you had to win with in high school. You've got Tom with sprinter's speed. You've got Dave with hands as soft as angel tits. Speed, possession, athlete, height. You've got it all. And you, I haven't even talked about you. I've always known our dream was there. But, watching you lead against the first team defense every Wednesday, you've got the goods, my man. You are the Real Deal. Case closed."

I gave it time to sink in. Vapor blew from our mouths around our heads, more and more as we picked up pace. My overcoat had gone from tepid to almost too hot. I slowed to a more moderate stride, hoping he would follow. No way. He is mission-ready: Get to breakfast, scarf down a few eggs and biscuits, get dressed, and kick major butt. The only problem with how he feels now is how he will feel in a half-hour. Football is a game of fills and backs. One play, Vinny will rifle one for twenty. Next one, he'll be thrown on his head. Happens to everybody. Question is: how will he handle that? Now, in civvies and without the roar of the crowd and the rush of adrenaline, he gives in to the head-shots. After watching him this year leading the scout team, come game time, he won't succumb. It's time to say something else.

"Vinny, all year you've been playing against a top ten defense. They stopped the Nitts cold. They never held sway over you like that. Never. Never, Vinny. And, that's without the big boys and the fast boys."

He was ready to respond. "Yeah, but I won't have you."

I'm flattered. "With regard to that, I have in my coat pocket a vial of botulism, with which I intend to butter Tom's and Dave's toast. I figure number three will put me close enough."

"You get in there, man, we're going big. You got that?"

"I'll make sure I'm limber."

At this time we actually believe it's possible. I don't know if it's our ages or our approach to the blind reality of kickoff in five hours or so.

We have quickly tried to assume our roles. And I can tell Vinny is still having difficulty with his.

"I'll be there for you, Gunner," I started, "I'll be on the sidelines following the game like you QBs do. I'll be there, but I won't be too close. Just dial me up if you need me. I know you, man. I'll be able to help you out. You decide, but I'm there."

"All right, man," Vinny replied, "I gotcha."

"You know, like that James Taylor song. I'll be there, or something like that. I'll be around, no, that's not it. That's Motown—"

"Okay, Cheetah! I got your point. Now let's talk about this game, or something."

"This is the game, man. I'm on the sidelines. Not in the way, but I'll be there."

"I know. Like James Taylor or Carole King—"

"Or, whoever sang that insipid song. They were lovers or something, but I think it was James—"

"All right, Mason, you're driving me crazy with this. You're there, I know your number and what you look like. And that's all I need. Okay?"

"Just don't forget, man."

"How can I with your constant reminders."

I get the point. I guess I'm coming on a little too strong. Vinny needs his space.

"I gotcha, man. You need your space."

"Don't take this personally, but I have to breathe."

"I'll let you breathe, Vinny, but just remember—"

"Let me guess…you'll be there."

"You got it, brother man."

I looked up to see St. Mary's just a couple hundred yards down the street, a sanctuary surrounded in glass, the altar in clear view. We always pass by St. Mary's on the way to our home game breakfast. And, now, as before, we stop in to Her house to talk to God.

I led Vinny through the double doors to the holy water font at the beginning of the aisle. I dipped the tips of my right fingers into the water, and placed them on my forehead to make the sign of the cross. I then walked up to the last pew and genuflected before the altar several dozen feet away. Scooting in to give Vinny room, I pulled the kneeler out, knelt, made the sign of the cross again, and silently prayed.

"In the name of the Father, the Son, and the Holy Spirit. First, God, please forgive me for all my womanizing last night. My full intentions were to be with Joan, but Jennifer came by almost nude, if you don't mind me saying nude in church, and I just gave in to the temptation. A few times. I don't know what I'm going to do about Jennifer. Well, yes I do. And, I know what I want to do about Joan. But, you might just serve me my head on a romantic platter, if you can call what I did romantic. Anyway, God, I ask you to please take care of the two women, and take care of me, too. From the way I've set myself up, I think I'm going to need it.

"Oh, and God, about the game; I know you don't take special requests for outcomes. I know this because we talk about this every week, so please just let us play up to our potential. Play up to our potential, and safely, and help us to accept whatever happens, and move on from there. Use Your hand to guide Vinny. I think his lack of experience will cause him to get into some jams. Help him out and show him that he can play with the best of them, a fact that I am sure of and I think he is, too, in his better moments. Help our teammates play as they should, and help them maintain that confidence they have in my buddy Vinny. As you can see, God, we're just going to need Your help all the way around.

"I pray for Pitt, too. Provide for them Your care, and forgive me for not thinking of anything else good to say about them.

"Father, I pray for the bigots and the Aryans. I think they know not what they do. I know they've wrecked the team, and I don't respect them much, so please help me to forgive the bastards, for I'm not too perfect myself.

"And, Father, let me take this time to put in a good word for all my friends, for Michele and her sister MJo, for Judy and Alice and their families, for Jean, for Joan and Jennifer, and Joan again, especially Joan. There's one outcome I pray to you for, God. Bring Joan my way. Please help her to love me like I think she does. And, back to everybody Vinny, again, and his family, and Michael, and Arthur, and Lendel, and Joe, and all my teammates.

"And speaking of the team, hold me and protect me as the team finds out and confronts me with what I have done. Help them understand that I did my best. Please help PD out of whatever mess he has gotten himself into or been set up into or something and please help me to eventually understand what went on with him. Help me so that I haven't screwed up and made everyone mad at me. Especially about Joan. There I go again. I guess you see by now how important she is to me. You should know since we've talked about her every night since mid-September. And sometimes during the day. Often.

"Thank you, God, for this wonderful life you have given me, and please turn your head as I do everything I can possibly do today to beat Pitt, including inflicting painful, non-life threatening injuries."

I crossed myself. "In the name of the Father, and of the Son, and of the Holy Spirit. Amen."

I found Vinny standing by the font. I approached it, placed my fingers in the water, and made the sign of the cross for the fourth time.

"Golly, Mason," Vinny whispered, "I thought you would never finish."

"It was a big week," I said. We exited and continued our way to the breakfast.

~ ~ ~ ~ ~ ~ ~ ~ ~ ~

Saturday, November 8, 1975
7:45 AM

Arriving at the team breakfast

"So, you talked to God for a long time," Vinny said, "Do I have a chance?"

"The question is," I responded, "does Pitt have a chance?"

"That's my boy!"

The fog hangs steadily and our breaths are visible. Butterflies fluttered about in my gut. Is it the Panthers or the Nazis? The Panzers, maybe? I feel if I make it through breakfast with my head intact, Pitt will be a veritable piece of cake. Warning of the day: beware of teammates offering a handshake and a pat on the back. *Et tu, Gerlach?*

Vinny must have been reading my mind. "I don't envy you right now. I'm proud of you, but I wouldn't want to be you."

"Ah, I don't mind being me," I countered, "It's like it's in my genes to get into scrapes. Kind of like holding up the legacy of ol' Frank. Ultimately, he only screwed up once. Ran a green board. The railroad inspectors think he was somewhat impaired, as in drunk."

My friend found it difficult to say anything after I sprung that on him. He finally uttered an, "I've never heard this. What's come of it?" I'm sure he's wondering if his dad knew and just didn't tell him, or what?

"Blood tests and the autopsy were screwed up. So, nothing came of it. So, I didn't tell anybody. Only Mom and I knew. Not even Ron knew, although he would have loved to gotten a hold of this juicy tidbit. Mom swore me to secrecy. Therefore, I couldn't even tell you. Now, you and I are the only ones who know."

"Jesus Christ, Mason. I'm really sorry."

"I hope you don't feel badly about keeping you in the dark."

"No. Your mother said not to tell. Why are you telling me now?"

"It's kind of the full truth answer to our conversation of Thursday. Besides, I just want you to know." My intention is to show him that no matter how screwed in the head he thinks his dad is, and he surely is, he's not alone.

"Oh, yeah," replied Vinny, "Still, I didn't need to know."

"You're my best friend. I want you to know. Remember, no secrets, Carly Simon and the album cover."

"Who can forget those? But, why are you telling me now?"

"It's a Pitt kinda thing. Today, our lives will change. This will be our tie to the past."

"You're a lot more philosophical about football than I am."

"I have to be this way to justify my attempts to maim people. Besides, that's why you're Vinny and I'm Mason."

"And, Mason, my man, welcome to breakfast."

The concrete, traditional steps outside led in contrast to the first level of the High Ridge, student center for the seventies. The building itself is decades old, but a recent refurbishment brought it to the current times. The High Ridge serves as a showpiece for visiting high school kids and their parents. It is the pivot point for the convergence of the academic and social aspects of college. Inside are a huge cafeteria to serve as a base for the students during the day, recreational activities, such as the staples of bowling and billiards, and The Pine Tree Lounge, the only on-campus site where beer is served. On the second level are rooms of all sizes, including the large ballroom where the football team meets for the first time during game day to eat breakfast, the last meal before going into battle.

As alums and other fans mill about hoping to catch a glimpse of the players going to their meeting, I feel as if a rope has been tightened around my neck and tied to my groin.

"You want to join me at the vomitorium, Gunner?"

Saturday, November 8, 1975
7:55 AM

Eggs and issues

I look at my watch. I always look at my watch. Five minutes to spare.
Eight o'clock says you play. Eight oh one: try again next week. Those are
the rules applying to me. I don't think Vinny would suffer any ill consequences since we've had more than our share of QB problems this week.
He could show up just in time for the coin toss and still line up under
center.

We stand at the door. Strange. Whites are talking nervously. Blacks
are eerily quiet. All are among our 'own kind,' as we had left each other
yesterday evening. In spite of this, Michael and Montgomery saw me
and approached us like they are closing in on us.

"Oh, shit," Vinny said. "Ohhhh, shit. Don't look, Mason."

I thought he was referring to Michael. "I've already seen him, man.
He's coming this way. So what?"

The two rather large men bounded up to us. "Can you believe this?
Can you fuckin' believe this?" whispered Michael.

"I can't believe the motherfucker's here," Monto said, obviously disappointed about someone being here and not afraid at all to express it.

I am clueless. What's going on is not in my cognizance.

"Have a seat, gentlemen," a familiar voice uttered. Michael, Monto,
Vinny, and I grab the empty table near the door.

"It's closing in on eight bells, and time to start this breakfast."

Son-of-a-bitch! It's the man himself, and I don't mean Amos Alonzo
Stagg. Dennis Lawson is back with us and he's speaking to us!

"Coach Van Watt, would you please lead us in prayer."

Red stood and caught my eye. This is the first time I've seen him since he allowed us to stay with his soon-to-be-heater Michele. Lawson, Michele, Red, prayer. Damned weird, this is.

"Lord, thank you for bringing us together to break bread. Help us play fairly and as teammates…" Ya-ya-ya…I hate to interrupt any prayer, but I can't help noticing Michael is looking at Lawson like he'd like to have a scope trained on him right now. This is not good.

"…once again, help us play fairly and play to the best of our abilities so we may have the best chance to bring home the victory. In Jesus' name we pray, Amen."

The team recited an "Amen" together, then looked up, waiting instructions or further developments.

Out of some space behind the head table, Lyndon Fadden appeared. "Gentlemen, may I re-introduce to you, your head coach, Dennis Lawson." Lawson stood amid silence interspersed with an odd combination of low-volume catcalls and applause.

"What the fuck is Goering doing back here as head coach?" Michael asked.

"Maybe he can be our human sacrifice," I stated.

"Only if we're very lucky," Monty said.

At the next table sat among others Chandler Childress. He leaned into us and said, "Burton, what the fuck is going on here?"

Michael stared into space for a while, then snapped, "Let him start to speak, then watch for me. Pass it on." Chandler nodded, then turned to the others and laid down the word.

Lawson took a few moments to allow the team to calm down. "Good morning, men," The Coach said before such silence I thought I heard crickets. "I repeat, good morning, men."

There are mumblings of half assed greetings mixed in with a few expletives.

"It's good to be with you," Lawson began again, always finding it difficult to lay off the politico schlock. He usually left the raw coaching to his assistants, while treating us like the future voters we are. "I say again, it's good to be with you and what a wonderful day it is to beat the hell out of Pitt!" It's as if the past two days haven't happened.

At that moment, Michael stood. I saw the life of Runners football pass before my eyes. The nationally prominent teams of the mid-fifties. The always-dangerous squads of the early sixties. Nine-and-one and Gator Bowl-bound in 1967. A vapor movie running through my mind. Everything I worshipped as a boy, all that carried me away from a sure education as an Ivy to take a chance at the navy and silver worn by my heroes; all that and then some is coming and going. Looking out over his black brothers, Michael implored them to rise and gaze upon their coach, the man who defiled them. I know it's now inevitable. And horrible. It's one thing to have a coach violate the credos of his sport. That's wicked. Players, players quitting, players not playing, for any reason, that hurts the young boys.

"That's it, folks," Michael shouted, "We're not standing for this. You can coach if you want to, hemorrhoid, but without us. Come on, men!" The black players to a man faced the door and began to walk.

No! Not Michael! Not my hero! Not any of them!

I vaulted to my feet. "No! No!" I exclaimed, "Stay! Everybody stay! Let's talk this out!"

"You took it to *The Mail*, Ivy. You got it started," said Michael, "Let us bring it home," Turning to Lawson, Michael yelled, "Now let's see you beat the hell out of Pitt!"

Lawson had no choice but to launch threats, "Sit down, Burton, or you're suspended. And you can kiss law school goodbye, too."

I know how much becoming a lawyer meant to Michael, but his pride and the pride of his brothers meant more. He just kept marching and closed in on the door. Depending upon which side you're looking on, the blacks, the coaches, or mine, this whole thing is going great, under control, or not going well at all. It got worse.

"He gonna take law school away from you, Michael, he's gotta go through me," Montgomery stated.

"Same here," John Pettibone said, standing proud.

"I'm outta here, too, muthafucka," Arthur launched.

I panicked. Don't go into the water after a man who's panicking. "NO!" I ran to the door and got in Michael's face. "You don't leave, Michael! You, too, Monto, John, Arthur. We're a team. We're THE team. We stay."

I turned my attentions to Lawson. Despite the recurring doubts about PD, we have reached a point of no return. I can't believe I'm going to say it, "You coaches. You go. With all due respect, you go. It's time for a players' only meeting."

"You're crazy, Bricker," yelled Lawson. "I'll barely tolerate your crap with the newspaper because I think you were set up, but you're not taking over my team. No way, young man. Not now, not the morning before kickoff! Not anytime. Besides, for your act of insubordination, you've been indefinitely suspended!"

Saturday, November 8, 1975
8:05 AM

The team meeting

I ignored his threat. "You're going to have to give us a chance to talk if you want to play today's game."

"You're fucking mad!" spat Van Watt, who's probably by now thinking I played him like a Cajun fiddle.

"No, son, we're staying," said Lawson with an excruciating calm.

"You stay," I said, willing at this point to say anything, "you lose half your team and any chance of winning today, not to mention what a boycott will do to your already shaky reputation." I still can't believe I'm talking like this to a dean among coaches of the college ranks. Must be the frustrations of a high schooler stood up coming out in me. I closed. "Now, what is it?" My teammates are at a standstill, more than willing to let me the walk-on put their football futures on the line.

"The nuts have taken over the nut house," yelled Van Watt, "That's what I think it is." I'm not doing much for Michele's love life, but I never really liked the bastard. She can do much better.

"Then what will it be?" I repeated to Lawson.

He took a long time considering everything in what I think is his devious mind. Finally, motioning to the other coaches to follow him, he said, "You've got ten minutes."

"Twenty," I shot back.

"Ten, and that's final," he said.

"Twenty, or they walk now."

He turned and led his men out, shooting a stare at me over his shoulder.

Any satisfaction I felt as a result of my victory in the power play was swept away by the six-six monster jumping immediately in my face.

"The Negroes are fuckin' things up!" shouted Ted, "And, you are, too! You're the fucker who did it to Coach!" I'm a dead man....

"We, asshole?" the most appropriate question came from John, stepping to my defense, "I seem to remember it was your man who took the money."

"The man's gotten his punishment," said G-man of Lawson, conceding for the first time that the coach actually did it. "He's not being paid for this game. Lawson just wants to help us win."

"Sure, Ted," said Michael, "He's already been paid. Lawson wants to help us so badly that he pocketed sixty-five K from a racist willing to do almost anything to buy his superrace back into existence."

"Kay was the best quarterback," pronounced Ted, spanning from the outrageous to the sublime. "We're seven and two and number twenty-one because of him." He certainly hit the truth there without even knowing it. "Results don't lie. We owe a lot to Bobby layin' up in the hospital up there like he is."

"The way you're missing the point here, Ted, is remarkable," argued Michael, "Problem is we'll never know who the best quarterback is because your man Lawson took a shit-ton of money to play Adolf's choice. That's not quite fair, cracker boy!"

"I'm not your boy, boy," G-man countered hard, "Anyway, it would be good for us, for all of us if we all know Mr. McNabb. He's not Adolf. He's a successful businessman for a lot of reasons. One is he knows his place in society." Michael and a few others as well as I are shocked by this statement, appalled by the depths of Ted's racism. I'm not so sure I want him for a teammate, even though he can block a charging bull.

After a pause, Michael came back, "You're incredible. You are so fucking programmed to spit out your white bullshit. You're hopeless. The second thing I'm going to do is lead my brothers out of here. But first, I'm goin' to kick your fat honky ass." Michael squared off, prepared to take on a man almost fifty pounds his senior.

"Bring it on, nigger!" Ted yelled, smiling. On, no, not that....

The whites and the blacks circled the two. I knew Runner football had plummeted to no further depths in its eighty-nine years, but I also knew Michael and Ted could be trumped by the other ninetysome heating up their own melees of hatred.

I picked up a nearby table for six, which I can do because I'm pound-for-pound the strongest guy on the team. On the outside chance that anyone is paying attention, I launched it though the closest windowpane, a rather large one. Maybe no one in this room cared, but it surely made me feel better. I heard the noise slice through the ballroom. I watched as glass shards crash out and down to the courtyard below. Considering everything going on in the here, I saw no reason to check if there were any early fans lying below under the table.

Remarkably, quiet and stillness captured the room, as if Jesse Jackson had swung in with pistols cracking to save the world from itself. At this time I'd welcome Jesse and any input he might have, and he may be here later, but he's not here now. I don't know if I want it, and I'm not sure what I'm going to do with it, but I have the floor.

All eyes are on me. If I'm going to say anything, the time is now. To Michael and Ted, I yelled, "For the love of Christ Almighty! Can't you see what you are doing? Both of you!" I let the pause draw, then I continued. "Some dickhead with a lot of jack has bought his way, hell, no, forced his way in to our team through our fearless leader and has told us how to run the show! Aside from this, Ted, you know Kay may have been a little too immature for the job. I've heard you say it. And Michael, you're going to lead a walkout? From whom? We white guys? Why punish us? We didn't pay to play Kay. This summer you said you'd do anything for this team. Maybe staying here could be one of those things. Huh?"

I confessed, "Yeah, I'm the guy who turned in the coach. I was given all the photos and the transcripts and the affidavits by a man who got it somewhere." Upon reconsideration of the evidence, my flagging faith in PD is somewhat renewed. I continued. "Why me, you might ask? How the fuck would I know. But, there it was, in black and white, with numbers and pictures." Silence, then, "What the fuck was I supposed to do? Frankly, I did what I should have done, and I don't give a goddamn what any of you think about this. So, there. There's nothing else to say about that."

Another pause, then I got worldly. "We won't be able to change beliefs and feelings backed up by generations of misery and misconceptions this morning. Probably not this year. But, one thing's for certain, damnit. We are all we got. We are all we got and we've got a game in less than five hours. We're a football team, goddamnit! Football brought us together, and we've got a job to do. The Pittsburgh bus is rolling down the interstate right now, and it ain't stoppin' until it gets to Ridge Field.

You know what that means? We've got just a little time to find some togetherness, some common ground. To become a team again. Michael," I said, walking up to my friend, "Lawson and McNabb are white, and so are we. So, what? If you'll remember, Michael, we were just two short weeks ago together playing the best ball in the nation. It took God to beat us. We were that good. Black and white. And Ted," I said, turning to him, "I can't believe you'd back up Lawson. For money, Ted. He did it to us for money. I know, Ted. I saw the paperwork. C'mon, Ted, you and me, fellow walk-ons, man! What if someone had paid Lawson to play only scholarship players? You'da had a helluva time getting out of the box, much less become captain." I paused. Their eyes are glued to me. They're still with me. They're still with me! Damn. "And let me say it again, Mr. Aryan, lots of money, fucked up soul, never himself, and here's the key, never himself played one stinkin' down of college football. Yet he determines who plays on our team? This is football, man. Head-to-head, pads crackin.' Remember Challenge Days of junior high? Who in here moved up on a Challenge Day? The best play, not the one with the biggest wad of legal tender backing him up. This is our game! What Lawson did was acrimonious, goddamned sick, Ted, so vile, you and I and everyone else in this room should be lined up behind Michael to...walk...out...on...them."

I thought...no, this can't be possible...yeah, it can I thought and as I thought, the team sat and stood motionless, thinking with me. They're football players, though. They can't think for themselves. They're awaiting some sort of decree. And at this point I don't care. I've spent this week on my back. What the hell else can I do to make it worse? I want to do it. I want to. I'm crazy, but I have the solution. Of all people, I have the solution. It's a solution so outlandish, calmer minds would see it and try to stop it in its tracks.

"No, Mason," said Vinny, reading my mind with that special connection we have, "No way."

That's never stopped me. "That's it!" I proclaimed, "That's the way! We stay together. The coaches take a well-deserved day off."

"Keep going," Michael said with a half smile, "You don't quite have me."

"Who organized all those sandlot games we all played in as kids?" I posed, "We did. This is just like a big pickup game, except the sides have already been chosen and we have invited forty thousand of our closest friends to watch."

"Don't, Mason," Vinny muttered.

"Almost, Mason," said Michael. I looked around. I saw some nods to the affirmative, from both the brothers and the white guys. And why not? The trust of our coaches has evaporated, but we're still football players. Today's Saturday. We want to play.

"Here's how we do it," I started, ""Defense…Michael calls the signals on the field. Uh…uh…Timmy's in the box. You know Pitt pretty well, Timmy." Timmy Smythe is a linebacker low on the depth charts but high in the classroom. The look on his face said that he welcomed the contribution. "And David's on the sidelines connected by headset to the box and helping Michael out." Crikstein, the backup QB. He's got to keep his head in the game in case Vinny…oh, that's an awful thought.

"What about the offense?" asked my best friend the naysayer.

"You call the plays, Vinny, with help from the box and David. Ted's the captain and calls the line, as usual. Yeah!" I'm getting excited at the prospects.

"You're crazy," said Michael, "That's a fact. But, it's okay by me." I think he'd do most anything right now to let the coaches have it.

"Ted?" I asked.

The big man stood and thought, and thought some more, finally saying, "I dunno. I hate to leave Coach Lawson hanging out like this." Lawson did take him from a small town big kid to the NFL prospect he is now. What's more, they share the same philosophies.

"Ted," I said, "Lawson would sell your soul if the price is right." It's an awfully strong statement that took Ted aback. "I mean, it's good to be loyal, but project your loyalty to those who deserve it: your teammates. All of your teammates."

"I don't trust some of my teammates," said Ted. No apocalypse here.

"Excuse us," I said to those around me, pulling Ted aside. "But they're starting to trust you," I said to Ted, my bullshit generator running hot. "Ted, I'm not asking you to change your beliefs. Believe what you will. I'm surely no one to judge you. But, Ted, you, Vinny, and I, we're state boys. We're the only ones who fully understand this game today, the bitter rivalry. Don't you want to play Pitt? You haven't beaten them in your four years here. Today's your last chance. Don't pull out because of some disagreement. Accept them. They're ready to accept you," I almost choked on that one, "Accept them so you can play winning college football with them, beside them. Then you can be whatever Ted Gerlach you want to be. Be teammates. Be friends through football. And let's beat the shit out of Pitt, man!" I got him. I don't know what I want to do with him....

G-man thought and cogitated and thought still more. I can just about see the teachings of the Gerlachs of the past breaking down.

"I wanna play and I wanna win," he said through a strained face, possibly expressing feelings in a way he never had before. "This deal you've come up with, it could be our best chance to do both. Between me and you, I've got some problems with the way the blacks handle things. They're so uppity now." I tried to pass over that remark. "But, Bricker, I'm in. I wanna beat the shit out Pitt!" We shook hands on it, mine to his meathook. He's actually smiling. Great. He is critical to this whole operation, especially the game. Ted's a helluva player.

Here comes Vinny. Now a word from our quarterback.

"Excuse us, Ted," said Vinny. Ted gave me a thumbs-up and walked. "Mason," Vinny said softly, but with poison, "of all of the fucked up ideas you ever had, this is...this...are you out of your goddamned mind?"

I'm ready for him. "Vinny, if we don't do this, Lawson coaches, the brothers are gone, and you throw to me and only me all day long, that is if you can get a pass off. We'll lose seventy-nine zip and that's how your first game as a Runner quarterback will forever be remembered. I'm sorry, man, I'm sorry this all happened on your day, but this is where we are."

Vinny stared at me intently. I have no choice but to stare back. Throughout our lifetimes of Runner devotion, we in no way could have thought our big chance would be wrapped in such tumult. Vinny throws it. I catch it. We win. Simple. Never did the riddles and troubles of American culture enter into our dreams. To us, football was always pure, immune to the disorder with which we came of age, broadcasted every night on *The CBS Evening News* with Walter Cronkite. Not today. Resigned to that, my glare held. His gaze rose to the ceiling then dropped. After a several moments, he snickered, and shook his head.

"Look, Gunner, we'll take care of you," I said, patting him on the shoulder. "I have some ideas. We'll talk more later."

Vinny turned to an approaching Michael and Ted. "Let's do it," the Italian Stallion said, "Jesus Christ, Mason, I must be crazier than you are."

"Righteous!" said Michael, after listening in, pumping a fist.

"You won't be sorry, man," said Ted to Vinny. Ted looked like he's finally being a true leader. I hope it sticks. "No one's gonna touch you."

We stood there silent, the three men who will lead us onto the gridiron and take us to victory, and me, buried on the bench with exception to an occasional bloodthirsty mad dash down the field. Kind of amazing, though. Just minutes ago, Michael and Ted were about to wail on each other. They're looking at each other, smiling. Now they're looking at me.

"What's up, guys?" I said.

Michael got right to it. "We need a head man."

"Why?" I asked without really knowing why I asked. It makes sense, but they obviously have a point to this.

"General leadership, critical calls, dispute settlement, go on fourth, go for two," Michael listed, attorney-like.

"You're the man, Ivy," Ted joined in. Vinny is silent in his shock.

"What?" I asked, truly surprised.

"The newspaper. That impassioned speech. You got us going in the right direction," said Michael, "It happened then. You became our leader. Telling you to do so is just a formality."

"Yeah, Mason," said Ted, "You and your box and your newspaper got us into this mess." He seems happy, thankfully. Just minutes ago he was ready to turn me into powder for the same thing.

"Now get us out of it," Michael said, "Be head coach."

"Why can't you guys do it?" I asked.

"We're going to be busy enough taking care of our squads," said Michael. "But, once again, Ivy Boy, you're already our leader. Just accept it."

"Gentlemen," I said, "I'm a sophomore walk-on. I'm a kickoff soda jerk. I'm the smallest guy on the team. Women try to avoid me." Well, the last one's a stretch, but I'm desperate.

"Yeah, but you got that high college board score," Ted said.

"In fact, you may be one of the few guys on the team who took his own SAT," Michael added, tongue-partially-in-cheek.

"He's got you there," said Vinny.

"And, you're strong," Ted said, "You heaved that table through the window."

"I want to talk to you about that," Michael said, "It's awfully cold in here."

"Yeah," I said, capitulating, "but if I hadn't done that, you'd both be dead."

"See?" said Ted, "You're the only guy who knew to do that." Ted's smiling. Michael's smiling. Even Vinny's smiling. I'm stunned, and cajoled.

"Fuck," I said, "All right. Okay." I don't want this. But…I do…I need medication.

"Will you do it for free?" asked Michael.

"You guys owe me breakfast at Bill's. And I'm coming hungry." I said.

"Deal!" said Ted. "We'll be a good team." This is the most positive and least cantankerous I've ever seen the big man.

We four shook hands and thus became the most singularly bizarre coach-captain-quarterback combo in NCAA history.

Saturday, November 8, 1975
8:20 PM

I, the Head Coach

My first directive as the head coach of the Renegade Ridge Runners: "Ted, Michael. Get your teams together, offense and defense, and tell them about this. Get them to go along with this. Stress acceptance. We're not trying to change anybody here. We just want to play football. That's it. And to do that, we just have to be a team. Do it, and keep them together. And, if we want a chance to beat Pitt today, we four have to stay together. We got it?" That sounded okay….

"Got it," said Michael.

"Gotcha, Chief," said Ted.

The big guys split. It looks like it may work. It has to work. It better work.

Vinny turned to me, "You've gotta tough job."

"If I keep Burt and G-man working together, it won't be so tough." I'm trying hard to believe that.

The Gunner smiled, "Of all the times I've imagined us playing here, it never occurred to me that you might be Pappy Boyington."

Oh, damn...We're the poor little Runners who have lost our way / Baa baa baa...Hell's bells. I'm Pappy and these guys are my Black Sheep Squadron.....

I can only hope to be Pappy.

I looked down and nodded, "At St. Mary's this morning, I prayed for a lot of things, but I don't think I slipped up and asked for this. Is this God talking?"

"Maybe," Vinny replied, "But, just in case, I'd keep an open line to The Big Guy."

"Good advice," I said, "You'd better go meet. Remember, you're the man."

Vinny slapped my back and walked away. I thought about his open line comment. I'm going to need some help.

Father Al Kolski is the priest at the Newman Center on campus. He works his soulful trade through St. Mary's. I see him often, although I haven't talked to him at length since just after Penn State. We met briefly when the story hit the papers. As a result, Father Al was worried about me and advised me not to be the hero.

He ought to know what hero means. In the spring of 1968, when all hell was breaking loose all over the college campuses of the nation, Father Al, then just Al, was a senior at Boston College. He was doing the unusual-for-the-sixties double duty as an All-America football player and a concerned student. Leading a demonstration against Massachusetts companies and their hiring practices, specifically their negligence to hire blacks, he was arrested. He ended up in so much hot water that the New York Jets, after having drafted him as an offensive tackle in the first round, almost didn't sign him. Al pleaded his case to the Jets' management, coaches, and captains his desire to play in the

American Football League. Noted for being a team and an organization that thought progressively, the Jets decided to land Big Al.

Their decision would pay off right when they needed it. Injuries left the spot at left tackle open at a very inopportune time, only three days before the Super Bowl game to be played against the heavily favored Baltimore Colts. Coach Weeb Eubanks asked Al to step up and play the man who protected the blind side of The Man, Vinny's Man and my Man, Joe Namath. Al had to face the hard charging rush of the Colts' defensive end Marty Nuckols all day. To make a long story short, which of course I have a hard time doing sometimes, Al punished Marty. Nuckols barely figured in any plays and walked off the field with his teammates as losers of a game they were supposed to dominate. Joe Willie Namath was the leader and the game's most valuable player, but my buddy Al played his silent role to perfection and certainly did his duty for the team that stood by him while he was in jail.

He then heard the calling. Al left the AFL at the top of his game and entered the seminary in Boston. After his time there and after some time at a Massachusetts church, Al was looking for a way to get back on campus. He found us here at the U, and all is well.

If you can't locate Father Al at the Newman Center or the rectory, check out the weight room. As a former professional football player, his lifting is prodigious. I've seen him bench four eighty-five twice, that's down then up then down again then up again. He can squat a Chevy truck. Father looks like The Colossal Priest in his vestments, a walking, blessing, praying Bessemer furnace. I love the guy. That's why I'm going to check in with him about the latest developments.

During the meetings, I found a telephone. I dialed Father Al, catching him before he was about to step out to do a little pre-game iron shoving.

"Father. Mason."

I surprised him. "What are you doing? Do the coaches let you on the telephone as part of the pregame now? What are you doing?"

"We've had some strange happenings I want to tell you about."

"Shoot." Father, like all good priests, is in a constant state of readiness.

"Seems that the head bigot Lawson was hired back this morning by Dr. Fadden."

"No!"

"Yes. As expected, Michael and his guys didn't like it, and they started to walk. By grace, I stopped them, but only before sending the coaches out so we could have a players' only meeting."

"On the morning of the game? I thought I was crazy when I was in college."

I got to the point. "Now we've decided we're going to run the game ourselves."

"Uh-oh." Silence. Then, "But, tell me, Mason, who decided this?"

"Well, I kinda talked them into it."

Father Al paused for the longest time. "I guess you decided not to listen to my advice."

"I listened, Father, but the black guys were going to walk and we had to do something."

He got to the point. "And, you're calling me for…."

"You're faculty, right?"

"Oh, no, no, no. Yes, I am. But, I don't think I can do what you're thinking."

"C'mon, Father," I pleaded, "It'll take you back to your protest days."

"Yeah, and end up in the slammer again?"

"No! We're just taking over a football team. Besides, we need moral bearing. And, we may also need special offensive line coaching."

"Why's that?"

"A tackle, a captain, Ted Gerlach, has agreed to play, but he has problems with blacks. Like, he hates them. He's key to our efforts, and you could provide a positive influence. What do you say?"

"I know Ted. I can tell he could be trouble in that regard. I could get fired."

"Just as I'm going to tell the team: don't worry about tomorrow. Father, this is your chance to have an impact, again. What Lawson has done is reproachful. We've gotta stand up for what's right and frankly we need your help. Besides, who's going to fire a priest for siding with good against evil? It's just like another day at the office."

"Give me a chance to go to God on this one, Mason," he said.

"Make it a quick visit," I shot, a comment borne from coach's anxiety.

Another long pause. "I might as well write my resignation letter right now, but I'll do it."

I'm elated and relieved. "Thanks! Thank you! You really won't be sorry. Plus, we're going to win. You're going to preside over an ecumenical victory against the number one team in the nation. What an opportunity!"

"Can't turn that down. Nor can I argue with your bull."

"We all have to have a talent."

"I'll be there in a half-hour. Don't do anything rash without me."

"Can't get much more rash than this."

"You'd find a way, if anybody can."

"I'm looking forward to it, Father. It'll be an honor to have a Super Bowl man on our sidelines."

"You're very persuasive. Have you thought about the priesthood?"

"I have women problems."

"This could be your answer."

"Maybe I don't particularly want an answer," I said, thinking only of Joan. "Besides, I don't want to think about that now."

"Right. Football."

"Football. See ya."

Father Al said goodbye and hung up. I said a prayer of thanks. Joan hadn't surfaced in my mind since we stepped foot in the ballroom. Maybe I will end up being a priest

The offense and defense are getting antsy. Time for the meeting.

"Gather around, men!" They did. This, too, is scary. "All right, here we go!"

My men broke into applause, then a chant. "Here we go, Runners, here we go! Here we go, Runners, here we go!" They kept up, and got louder, then, to my surprise, the brothers changed 'Runners' to 'Ivy.' "Here we go, Ivy, here we go!" I held my head high. Within, however, I lost it. My throat became very dry. Bad or good, I don't deserve this, and I have no fuckin' idea what to do. But I have no choice. I have to lead. PD, damn you, you lying bastard…or not!

"All right!" My voice cracked. Regaining composure, I tried it again. "All right!" Better. Here goes. "Okay, team!" The clapping and the hoots stepped up. I let them go. Right then, given the opportunity, I would have gone after Jack Tatum.

"All right! Okay, team! Let's go, team!" We seemed intent on letting the coaches outside know we don't really need them. After a minute, they let me address them.

"All right, team! And I do stress team!" I don't think there are any problems with this arrangement, so I continued. "I stand here ready to do anything necessary to beat The University of Pittsburgh." Cheers took over again. When they died down, I said, "Anything. Anything to make sure we work as a team toward the same goal. It's really as simple as that. We've got the steeds to do it. We just have to stay together. Now, I'm not asking you to become blood brother best buddies with every-body in the room. All I'm asking is that we play and win as a team. Today. Our only concern is today. No one knows what's going to happen tomorrow, and, frankly, I don't give a rat's ass about tomorrow. The focus is on today. I just want to play winning football with my team-mates today. Look to your right, and look to your left and that's who you've got. That's who you're going to work for today. Accept your teammate for who he is, come together, and let's beat the mortal hell out of Pitt."

The roar of approval engulfed me.

"All right! All right! Who's hungry?"

"YEAH!"

"Then let's eat!"

Breakfast had been ready for a half-hour or so, but the caterers had been very concerned about entering the room. As we began to look less harmful, my teammates dashed for the chairs right in time for the wait-ers to bring out the eggs, sausages, and biscuits. It's a mad rush and a mad house, but I love it.

In the past three days, Ridge Runner football has taken a lot of body slams. There are those who have, in light of the coach's indiscretions, used this time to call for the team's disbandment, thereby punishing the players for what they had no control over. It is during these times that fired by a subterranean but basic unpopularity, the opponents surface and strike while support for the program weakens. They cite high injury rates and higher insurance costs, low graduation rates, and even the dis-ruption of the typical student by us, the normally crude and unrefined and often out-of-hand players. They open the file cabinets and reissue reports on how the money spent on football can be better used for the education of the student body. They even attempt to push a dogmatic view against the University supporting and subsidizing the brutality that they say so defines the sport. This has not been a good time for the Runners, but looking over my men chowing down with no table man-ners, I feel the glow. Our team's pep rally has given me the confidence. Despite all that has gone wrong, The University of West Virginia Ridge Runner football is approaching its finest hour.

And we haven't even told the coaches.

Saturday, November 8, 1975
8:45 AM

Dealing with the Coaches

There is a pounding at the door, constant, vigorous, repeated blows to the wood dividing the coaches from their team. Well, of course, their team not for today. I guess the time has come to let them know of this latest development.

I stand up from my breakfast and walk the ten paces to the door. Leaning out, I open it just enough to see a wide vertical line that represented Lawson's face.

"Yes," I said.

"Meeting's over, Bricker. Let us in, now!" the vertical line said.

"Uh, I don't know how to tell you gentlemen this, except by just blurting it out, but your services won't be required today."

Silence, then, "What the fuck are you talking about?"

"Just what I said. We won't need you today. We'll take care of the coaching duties."

"How—You—Why, you simple son-of-a-bitch. You can't hijack my team like this!"

"Yes, we can. We just did. We don't want to play for you, but we'll play for each other. We've got forty thousand ticketholders and a national TV audience expecting a game, and we're going to give them one."

"I won't stand for this, Bricker!"

"And we won't stand for anybody on our team getting bought out by anybody!" I then shut the door and walked back to my table. I surprised myself with how efficiently and how unemotionally I handled that. The pounding started again. It's better that they know. I just hope I didn't execute an innocent man.

I had been sitting beside Michael. I returned. "How did he take it?" Michael asked.

"Not well. I tried to tell him that one day he'll look back on this and laugh, but…."

"You're cold hearted," said Michael with his own hearty laugh.

"Maybe we oughta take them some food," I proposed. Michael laughed so hard he spit scrambled eggs through his nostrils.

While Michael is cleaning up, Joe Osbourne walked up. I'd hate to run into him in a dark third world country.

"Mason, my friend, allow me to approach you with a thought."

"What is it, Joe?" I'm immediately concerned. Oz doesn't mess around.

"Mason, have you considered how you're going to get us over to the field house? I ask this because I witnessed your conversation with Lawson, from afar. It doesn't sound like they're going to go down easily."

No, it hadn't occurred to me that I'd even have to devise a plan. I thought we'd just open the doors and walk over there. I guess it'll be a bit more complicated than that. "Well, Joe, you're pretty good at this stuff. I'd welcome any idea you might have."

"Is there a phone I can use?"

"Of course," I said, "Over there in the caterer's kitchen. It works. I used it already this morning."

"Thank you."

"Let me know what you find out," I requested of Oz as he took off for the kitchen.

To consider Joe Osbourne's mind is at times spellbinding. Here in 1975, the year we shamefully bugged out of Saigon, there are precious few warriors. Joe is one of them, as was Bazooka Frank. Maybe that's why I'm drawn to him. I can see in him some of my old man. To think Joe is on track to graduate summa with a BA in history is interesting. He'll have to be a spy; that's his only career option. To watch Joe play defensive football is frightening. You get the sense that he harbors the old Dick Butkus wish, that of dreaming of dislodging the ballcarrier's head from its neck and watching it roll down the field. Michael and Joe are equally cruel on the field of play, but are different in one regard. Michael is the trained killer. His objective is to effectively eliminate the corpus, doing so, of course, with organ-jarring hits. Joe oddly goes beyond that, seeming to be even more personal and still more punitive. I like them both. They're good people.

"I bet Oz has said more to you this year than he's said to anybody his entire Runners career," Michael observed. "What is it about you?"

"You like me and you're an assassin. Take that a couple of gruesome points further, and you've got Joe."

"I guess you're right," Michael said. "Besides, I'm glad you think I'm an assassin."

"If you want me to put a bounty on Drew Osburg, I'll do it."

"Don't worry. After four years with that motherfucker, he'll have hell to pay."

I smiled. Great. I'm happy he feels that way about the Pittsburgh Heisman man. Damn, I must be thinking like a coach.

That's good, because by no fault of my own, I am the head coach. Michael and Ted are right: every team needs a head man. It was wise of them to relinquish the duties on to somebody else. They could have easily gotten into a turf battle over it. I'm still a little shocked it's me. But, the two men are getting along. That's good, too, but we are in the relative calm of the pregame. Once we get into the heat of the war, things could change. That's one of the reasons its good that Father Al is coming up. I think he can keep the Big Redneck on task. God, I hope. Ted's my biggest fear for today. For now, of course. Football players are a crazy bunch. I'm sure some other shit will surface. I pray I can handle it all. I hope God doesn't pick today to punish me for lying to Joan. And Jennifer. But especially Joan and the breaking of my vows to her. You hear me, Big Guy? I'll take all you can dish out tomorrow. Just spare me today. Please, just get me through the day.

It's eight fifty and breakfast is winding down. Damn, we can really wolf down massive quantities of food. That's what happens when you get a lot of meaty, hungry, passionate men harboring rage and wrath. And, speaking of which, the State Police are walking in.

In the ranger hats and the form fitting forest green uniforms, these three men, some of whom come from our ranks, are ominous. There's one, a big, muscular guy with stripes, his nametag reading 'J. R. Willis.' He is a black man.

"Excuse me, Mr. Bricker, sir, I'm Trooper Willis from the Montani Detachment," Trooper Willis said, introducing himself, very well-spoken, "I was told you're the person to speak with here,"

"I am the spokesman," I said with little fanfare.

"I've been sent in by Mr. Lawson to inform you that his men intend on remaining the coaches for the team, and to escort you from the premises."

Michael and Ted walked up, as well as most of our players who tip the scales above two thirty. It's a silent power play with the West Virginia State Police. Awesome. I spoke again.

"Well, Trooper Willis, a couple of things here. First, we are peaceful in our demonstration against our coaches. This is no illegal assembly. There is no such thing as an illegal assembly. You can't get us for anything there." At this point, I'm on autopilot. "Secondly, if Mr. Lawson and anybody else involved with the situation would really think about it, they'd discover the best course of action is to let us have our football game today, mostly because we all refuse to play for Mr. Lawson. Am I right, gentlemen?"

There are manly affirmations from what I thought to be just about every Runner in the room. We're all together. God, I hope that lasts.

"Moreso, Trooper Willis," I said, pleading to his race of origin, "how, personally, can you expect us to play for a man who took money to bench the better player, a black guy? You look like you played the game, Trooper."

"Yes, I did," Trooper Willis replied. "West Virginia Tech, 1970."

"Then you know you have to have a basic, absolute trust in your coach. If your coach violates that trust, the entire team is destroyed. Right?"

"I'll swear I didn't say it to you, but I whole-heartedly agree,"

"And that's why we're playing this game ourselves and that's why the coaches are out there. There's no malice intended. We're just trying to protect ourselves, but most importantly, we are trying to save the game. And that's the most meaningful part, Trooper, it's the game. The game that you gave and all my teammates give a hundred percent of their souls for. Now, Trooper Willis, in your own way, please pass that on to Mr. Lawson."

"Well, sir, before I do that, I have to ask, who knocked that window out?"

"I don't know," I said. The trooper looked around the room. There are a lot of shrugs, some blank stares, and nods to the negative.

"That's destruction of government property," Trooper Willis said, "and if I ever find out who did that, I'll have to arrest him."

"We understand, Trooper, but we just don't know who did it."

"It's a serious offense," the trooper said.

We all stared at him. If any one of the guys wanted to hang me, he had me right now.

The trooper took one more look around the room, then said, "I'll talk to Mr. Lawson." He crisply backed away, "And, Mr. Bricker, I'll once again deny I said it, but good luck to you and your men."

The troopers turned and walked away. I'd love to see Lawson's face now. Mr. Lawson, my ass.

"You are one silver-tongued mother," said Michael with pride. "I think this is going to work. I really think it is."

"Way to go, Ivy," said Ted, "You saved us. I'm with you, man."

"Thanks, Ted," I said, as more congratulations rolled in. I'm awash in relief. I could be on my way to jail right now. Thank you, Jesus.

Addressing the team again, I said, "Okay, as time ticks away, we're more and more invincible!" Cheers, then, "Once we see Pitt across from us, they won't be able to stand us." More cheers. "Now, we've got forty minutes or so before we head to the fieldhouse, so let's have our position meetings and get ready for these bastards."

The players, my team, applauded as we broke up into our groups. It is time to talk to Ted again.

"Hey, G-man," I said. The huge dude turned around. "Just want to tell you, our faculty rep today is going to be Al Kolski."

He had a face like a kid, "The Al Kloski! Wow! I've lifted with him. He's a monster."

"Yeah, I've seen him. He's my priest."

"I'll try not to hold that against him," Ted said. He's serious. "But I won't say anything to him about it. He could probably throw me though that hole you put in the window."

And he will if he has to. "I thought it would be nice to have a Super Bowl champion with us today."

"Can't hurt. I'm looking forward to talking with him."

"Yeah, he's a pretty big fan of yours, too." At this point, I'll say anything.

"Hey, that's something!" said Big Ted. He beamed. Turning and walking to his offensive linemen, Ted threw over his shoulder, "Maybe your priest can show me a thing or two."

"Maybe." I turned away. Please, oh, please!

As all the groups gathered together, I walked to mine, the receivers and the backs, with Vinny. Arthur and Frank are there, with their understudies Danny Brown and Lucious Jackson. We had planned on moving a tackle, Johnny Mueller, over just to fill in the tight end spot, not a good situation. All teams need a big guy who can both block and catch. I don't know about Johnny's hands, or if he even has any. With all that, the wideouts Dhali, Clark, Tom, and Dave joined in and yours truly rounded out the bunch. They didn't know it, but I thought we had a helluva lot to talk about. I've been thinking, and it's dangerous when I do that....

Passing is less than half of our offense. Lawson has spent the season establishing the run, sometimes to the detriment of just getting the ball down the field in the best way. Well, that was with The Kid and his basic but definite ineptitude. Today, however, we have Vinny with his solid, accurate arm and an intuition for the game. He has at his disposal an extremely talented corps of ends and flankers and backs to throw to. My idea is this: Vinny orchestrated a passing offense in high school like a maestro, and that was with a bunch of girlie boys at receiver. Since Pitt expects us to come out running, and since Dhali, Arthur, and company would just love to throw more, and because of Pitt's expectations they would be surprised as hell and might not be able to fully figure out what we are doing, for all these reasons, I am going to propose a total upgrade of our offense. I mean, they already think I'm crazy....

It's as if they knew I'm thinking demented thoughts. All turned to me when I arrived to the group. Dhali spoke first. "Say it."

I surveyed my teammates. After this week, they look as if they could handle anything. Dhali's right. Just say it.

"I think we should scrap the offense, run three receivers, move Frank to tight end, and throw to everybody, including Arthur slipping out of the backfield."

The receivers grinned from ear to ear, Frank looked confused, Johnny stayed blank, and Arthur threw his milk carton across the room. Vinny held his face in his hands, a position reminiscent of when I was with Joan last night and something he does whenever he thinks I'm being ridiculous. I'll get to Vinny later, because I know whom I have to address first.

"Arthur, you are a great runner and an outstanding running back, but you've gotta anticipate. Pitt's ready for you. They're going to meet you coming out of your locker today. And as things are now, we have an inexperienced tight end, sorry, Johnny, and that leaves us with only two receivers to unclog things for you."

"Ivy, you've been fucking with things all damn day, and I know why and I agree and that's okay, but now you're changing my game? I don't know, my man. I'm not going to stand here and take it." Arthur is steadfast, just like I thought a man confident of his outstanding abilities back would be.

"Arthur, I think Lawson's scheme is a remedy for disaster today," I said.

"What about your idea, man? You're taking my blocking back away from me and putting him in the passing lanes. I'm naked back there. How's that going to benefit me?"

"It's a hunch and chance, Arthur. I just think the three receivers and Frank in the tight position are going to open things up for you in ways we don't really know about."

So far, everyone else is silent. I take that to mean they looked favorably on it, with the possible exception of Vinny, who can be wary of my ideas. Still, he isn't saying anything, maybe because he wanted to see if Arthur burns me out.

"What's this sudden problem with Lawson's offense? I mean, true, he's a pig, but he won seven in a row."

I let the implication of 'who the hell did we beat' hang for a while. Thankfully, Frank spoke up.

"Arthur, I'm not moving up on the line and stranding you back there. I'll still be able to block. And block hard. Damn hard. I think Mason could be right. We'll still get you your yards. Maybe even more since Pitt doesn't know what the hell we're doing."

Arthur laughed hard. "Pitt? Pitt ain't the only ones, my man, if we do this new offense."

I saw it's going to be impossible to talk Arthur into this new thing, so I laid off. Maybe Arthur will spend the day on his ass. Maybe Lawson will be a genius in absentia. We shall find out.

"Okay, Arthur," I said in resignation, "We'll do it your way. But keep it in mind. You never know the directions this game will take."

Saturday, November 8, 1975
9:00 AM

Joe's recommendation arrives

Vinny took over. He addressed Lawson's passing game: two receivers, the tight end, or in this case a tight tackle who hasn't caught a pass in a game since midget ball, and a scheme which was designed to cover the weaknesses of The Kid so the Coach could pocket sixty-five grand while advancing the white race. That's a lot to ask of an offense, but for a while this season it performed beautifully.

We don't have to hide Vinny. With him, we can play rock and roll football today, but we've got to take some chances. So, how can I do that and placate my friend Arthur? Mason, my boy, you always set yourself up for the tough choices.

The Gunner's leading the group through some possible plays for the first few series. He's spreading the ball around to everybody. That's my Vinny, the peacemaker. Zone floods (sending all the wideouts to one side of the field), routes to take advantage of Clark's height, sweeps for Arthur, power runs for Frank. All of it sounds good and makes one and all happy, but I can tell there really is no true direction. Hmm….

"Lemme ask ya, Vinny," I piped in. They yielded to the young buck from the coalfields. "What are the first few plays?"

"I'd figure I'd pull them in with a few off-tackles to Arthur, then hit Clark on a hook," said Vinny, ready with an answer. He's good at this.

"Great," I said, "Great choices. Allow me to suggest making that the second series."

"Uh-oh," said Dhali, smiling. Standing, he looks like a tensile spring, six-two, one ninety, four-three forty, hands, leap, instinct, competitive spirit, the total package, by far the best athlete on whatever field he steps. I see it in his eyes. He wants the ball. And I'm going to propose we give it to him.

"What are you thinking, Mason?" Vinny asked, simultaneously wanting to know and afraid to hear.

"First play of the game," I said, "Arthur off-tackle. Second play, no huddle."

"Ohh," commented Clark.

"No huddle," I continued, "and glance at Dhali. If the corner's within five yards and the safety plays off, check for a three step drop soft liner. It could be six." What all that foreign language means is if Dhali is being played close one-on-one, which could happen in the confusion after a no-huddle, Vinny is to take three steps back and throw a soft one over the cornerback's head, hitting the streaking (not naked, of course) Dhali in the hands with the ball. A well-thrown pass would allow Dhali to catch the ball without breaking stride, roasting the corner and putting us in the endzone early. We have the horses to do this. The Runner fans would love it.

There is quiet, intermixed with a lot of looking down and all around. Sometimes I think I'm an embarrassment to these guys. But Vinny's eyes met mine, and it's like one of our Vulcan mind melds.

"What if it's incomplete?" The Gunner asked. I can tell when he's almost sold on something

"Go back to your original game plan of the inside-outside running game with floods and outs." Not that I think it'll work....

"Well, you know I like it," said Dhali.

More silence.

Arthur sat up, "May work. I suggest we try it." Damn...where did that come from?

"We've been following most of your hare-brained ideas all morning, Ivy Boy," said Clark with a grin, "but this could be the ticket."

"Be great to get on the board early," said Dave, "Or at least downfield."

Vinny had it confirmed by his men. "Then let's do it. Dhali, we've run that route before, not no huddle, but Thursday, so if I signal Clark on the other side with flapping arms, it's a go."

"Flap your arms if it looks anywhere close to working," said Dhali, "I'll take it from there." Dhali knows what he can do.

That's a good idea by Vinny with the hand signal. The fans should be cranking that early in the game. There's no way anyone would be able to hear him. Also, a signal not directed at Dhali so as not to tip our hand. Nice touch, Gunner. You're a natural.

"Let's work on it in warm-ups," Vinny said to Dhali. He turned to me. "Way to go, Coach."

"No congrats yet," I said, despite feeling the early play will work. Michele and MJo got Vinny loose and his dad and Jean didn't inflict too much damage this morning. The Gunner held his ground very well and left to go to work just in time. I can see it in him. He's got the 'eye.'

And look at us, will you? Dhali, Clark, Tom, Dave and Arthur are black. Vinny, Frank, Johnny and I are white. In our microcosm of receivers and backs, where egos are running full bore and there is only one ball, we're working together as a team. We have put the happenings of the past couple of days behind us. True, in the heat of the game this runs the risk of changing, but I'm impressed with how we have become brothers in the midst of so much tension. I truly think our state of togetherness is due to Vinny. He's a leader. He doesn't see skin color. He sees the ball moving down the field and a win. We've caught on to this. And there is hope for us all.

Despite Arthur's veto of my pet project, there is a good chance whatever we do will work. We've got the studs in the backfield and the finely tuned athletes at the receivers. Only a few colleges wanted these players four years ago, so they fell into the Runners' lap. The Wallflowers of high school have grown up. Pittsburgh does not intimidate them. How fortunate. The Panthers are probably stepping off their buses right now thinking of all the problems we've had this week, thinking they'll just fire up the steamroller. I feel otherwise. We're ready in more ways than Pittsburgh can imagine.

On the other hand, I wonder how far I this nineteen-year-old borderline illusional book-smart savant can take this head-coaching gambit. The team didn't elect me. Michael and Ted appointed me, then sold them on the idea. It leads me to ask: how strong is this *coup d'etat*? At what point in the game will these college students realize that they don't have to do a damn thing anybody says? Coaches have always had the ultimate authority. In every one of our players' football lives, that was true and never questioned. Until today. Jesus, this thing that sounded like such a great idea only an hour ago now looks very precarious. I don't know how many more mutinies our ship can take. Please, God, let Father Al get up here and come in swaggering with his Super Bowl ring and his four eighty-five bench...twice. He's key. Christ, there are so many keys: Father, G-man, Joe and his idea, Arthur, PD and his trustworthiness. There really is no turning back now. We're on a course for some fate unknown. We're like some new South American government dealing with sky-high unemployment and hyperinflation. How long can we go until the countrymen get restless? How much can they take? The key is staying in the game, staying close on the scoreboard. If Pitt starts to run away with it, we're going to have a hundred different coaches with a hundred different ideas.

Maybe I shouldn't think about it so hard. I could use a bong hit.

"Mason," Ted said, coming up behind me, shocking me out of my despair.

"Yes," I answered, touchy.

"Uh, I think we're done meeting."

"I looked at my watch. Nine ten. Plus the place is turning into a meat locker with that gaping hole I left in the window. It could be time to move on. Earlier than usual, but these special circumstances demand special consideration.

"I guess we'd better start thinking about getting over to the field-house," I said.

"Yeah," Ted replied, "How's that going to happen?" The coaches are right outside that door."

I didn't want to let on that I have absolutely no idea how to do that. Searching around for Joe, I thought and hoped he would appear and save my ass.

Michael stepped up and stood without a word, strangely looking like a freshman at a fraternity rush party. That's odd. Odder still is the baseball that bounced toward us on the ballroom carpet, landing at Ted's feet. We three shot wide eyed glances at each other, wondering if this was a prank or a throw from the plaza gone awry. Michael bent down to pick it up. As he rose, he gazed at the ball intently, then handed it to me. "It's for you," he said. I took it from him and examined it. The ball had handwriting on its leather cover. It is as difficult to read as obviously was to write, but I thought it read in scrawl, 'Bricker, let us in the back door.' Looking over to the broken window, I walked there and peered down at the garden below.

This is college and you at some point get used to strange and incredible things, but anything that happened in my previous life had not prepared me for what is in the garden. I couldn't believe it, and had to allow my eyes to soak in every detail before I would let my mind confirm it all. There are around a dozen and a half men dressed in battle fatigues, combat boots, and red berets. They are each carrying a rifle, although having no experience with guns I don't know whether they're standard issue military rifles or anti-tank weapons. I guess it doesn't matter, because to a football team on game day, a gun is a gun and is normally just not around. Today, however, is an exception.

But why? Are we being taken over by the National Guard? Are the guns loaded? Is this going to be the Kent State of the sports world? Is Lawson behind these drastic measures? Is this his answer to the State Police making no arrests? How can he call out the National Guard on student athletes peacefully having a meeting? What in his mind warrants such action? Is this the means that justifies his end, the propping up of his flimsy administration, one based on being named coach of the year and schmoozing with politicians? Can this man ever be trusted again?

I find Joe at my side. He wasted no time getting to the point. "My men are here."

Turning to him quickly, I shot a gaze of disbelief. "Your men?"

"Yep. The Mighty Montani Militia. A company of patriots bound together to do God's work. I called the major, Andy Wilmore, this morning and told him we could use some help. They certainly responded. They thrive on coming to the aid of those who side with right."

Still unable to fathom what is before me and what it all means, I asked the question, "You mean they're here for us and weren't sent by Lawson?"

"That's right," Joe replied, "They're here for us. This is our best chance, hell, even our only chance to get to the fieldhouse. Talk about leveling the playing field. Now we've got might to match whatever peace action they want to take. It's a beautiful day for the Constitution."

I thought Joe had overreacted. Had I known he was going to do this, I would have at least discussed it with him. Now we've got eighteen militiamen primed for action. How do we know how disciplined they are? How far will they go to carry forth their orders, much less their individual beliefs? What the hell are their individual beliefs?

"Joe," I said, "who are these guys?"

"Farmers. Factory workers. Businessmen. There's even a lawyer. All are brought together in the pursuit of freedom."

Sometimes, that's the trouble with Joe. He makes everything sound so goddamned noble. But he still didn't answer my question. My concern is, and I hesitate to ask this directly in the midst of eighteen unknown West Virginian entities brandishing weapons, exactly how safe are the black guys?

"Joe," I said again, "do they know why they are here? Do they understand the problem here?"

"I think so," is all Joe said. We then stood quietly for a few moments. I guess my point finally sunk in with him. He continued, "You don't have to worry about the black guys with my men. Look, two of them are black." I looked. He's right. I found that surprising, but maybe not enough.

Still searching for that level of comfort I so desperately needed, I said, "Joe, before we can proceed with this, I need assurance, your word, that our teammates will be safe with these guys. We can't have it any other way. We can't risk anybody."

His word. Joe subscribes to a code of honor that basically faded from the soul of our nation during the Saturday Night Massacre of 1973. He sees it as his duty to get everybody to the fieldhouse safely. That's good, because I'm at a loss on just how to do it. "Not only will they be safe with them," Joe immediately replied, "they'll be safe because of them. You've got a really nasty element out there who is used to getting what they want. We've got to show firepower to let them know we are serious."

I thought. At the risk of this just being another war exercise to Joe, I had to put my faith in him. Lawson is a desperate man. He'll do anything. Joe knows how to handle that. I decided to hand it over to Joe Osbourne and let his experience in Angola, how fabled it may be, make this situation work. God help us. God, I've been saying that a lot this morning.

"Okay, Joe. Get them up here. Then we'll get moving."

He smiled, "Yes, sir," cracked a turn on his heels, and headed for the open window. I didn't want to be a part of any military actions, but the team, a hundred hormone-laced college boys, are bored and getting rowdy. It's time to play some football and this Andy Wilmore is going to help us.

The gravity of it all is becoming nearly unbearable. I find myself thinking how easy it was just to be a kick-coverage hack who drank beer, smoked pot, and cut class. Hell, juggling two women is much easier than this. Much. There are only three egos involved, none of which are inflated to the zeppelin-sized proportions of Dennis Lawson's and Ted Gerlach's. And they're not the only worries. I've got ninety-nine others who will undoubtedly expect as a result of this overthrow of the throne to be promoted over everybody else. Everyone will want playing time and the ball. I've already seen that from a senior leader, Arthur. One hundred turf battles and because some trust officer sets a box on my doorstep I'm expected to ask God to part the Red Sea. And the box just may be bullshit.

Speaking of God, there must be some reason why I'm in this position. The Man just hasn't unveiled the Grand Plan to me yet. Not that He has to, but there is one thing now very clear: I'd better learn to deal. It's mine to handle because it doesn't look like anyone else is willing to step up to the plate. It's like my dad. He had to save his men. No one else was going to. Fortunately, before he found his company, he happened upon a cache of armaments. That has to be my mantra: God will provide. Besides, I've got to keep this team together for Vinny's sake. I thought yesterday of the ways I could advance my man's cause. This is The Gunner's golden opportunity and it's up to me to deliver to him a team that can work with him for a victory. I want Vinny's first start to be a successful one. It all comes back to God. He's on the side of good. We're trying to affect equal opportunity for all regardless of race or religion, equal opportunity based on ability. So, we're on the side of good. God will provide. Therefore, Ivy, stop feeling sorry for yourself, earn your place in heaven, be Pappy Boyington, and show your men the way.

I wish Joan were here. Last night, the feeling; there was none better. I'm sorry to say this and I may burn in hell for it, that is if I believed in hell, which of course I don't and may itself put me in hell, but I got more from the couple of hours with Joan than I could from an entire lifetime with Jennifer. It's too bad. Had I never met Joan, it could have been Jennifer all the way. No…anyway the lingering warm fuzzies from the Miss Dr. Kissinger surely didn't make me think twice about not pursuing the possibilities with Miss Pierce. I guess I'm a sucker for an underwear show. It instantly realigned my priorities, if only for the time with her. It's really not right. I was wrong. I wronged Joan. I'm expecting Joan to commit, but I fall into the sack with Lee Meriwether. The steam hadn't stopped rising from the pedicure and the next thing I know Jennifer's sprawled naked. I've got to stop this self-flagellation. What else would any nineteen year old filled to the brim with the juices of life do? That's really no excuse, but it'll have to do for today. I need assurances from within today, man, because I won't be able to count on anyone to give them to me. Don't second-guess yourself, especially over women. Be cool.

I handle adult situations best in English with Joan around. I handle everything better with Joan around. I'm not the tongue-twisted boy. I'm a man! I was a man with Joan last night. I can do this! If I simply imagine her watching me today, observing my every move, maybe that'll give me the edge I need. Really strange, Mason, but it just might be what you need. It used to work in junior high when I would pretend I was under the constant supervision of Lou Ellen Carter and her 34Cs. The psychology is simple, you know, taking advantage of natural mating rituals. Great. I can see her now. Should she be wearing casual like last night or would her teaching attire work? How about a two-piece? No, too distracting. I'll go with that black dress with the simple subtle leopard pleat and leopard buttons. Yeah, that will do it.

Joe's leading the troops in now. Oh, shit, I spent this time performing individual counseling on myself when I should have been informing the team about the militia.

"Mason!" Michael bellowed from across the room as the Mighty Montani Militia took their positions in the ballroom. "Mason, what the mortal fuck is going on here? Who are these soldiers and who the fuck ordered them here?" Michael is shaking mad.

I walked quickly to Michael's side, hoping to calm him, knowing exactly why he's going ballistic.

"Michael, Michael," I pleaded, "They're on our side. They're here to help us."

"Why do we need men with guns? Goddamn it, Bricker, have you gone mad?" Boy, is Michael pissed.

In reality, my idea of taking care of a problem and Joe's idea of taking care of a problem are very much different. But it's not Joe who's getting the looks to kill from our fifty black friends. Jesus. Where's a six-four, two hundred eighty pound priest when you need one?

Well, he's walking in the door, eyes and mouth wide. I forgot until now, Father Al's last encounter with men in green carrying rifles was a memorable one but not pleasant. Luckily, he is not prone to scream from thirty feet. He waited until he got directly in my face. Then he let me have it.

"Mason, who are our guests?" Father said very deliberately, masking what I'm sure is the undercurrent of a football player's temper.

"Father," I started from the beginning, "they are members of the Mighty Montani Militia. Joe Osbourne and I talked it over and we decided we were going to need help getting to the fieldhouse."

"So you called a bunch of guys with guns?" Father asked, the timbre of his voice rising. "What were you thinking?" I have the feeling he thinks he's being kind.

I sincerely believed, with regard to Lawson and all the other coaches and to Lyndon Fadden, whom I haven't seen yet but I am sure has his hands in the pizza dough, we need the Militia. My problem now is I am confronting a few dozen irate blacks whose distrust of the system, any system, is right now running cherry red, as well as one larger-than-normal Jesuit priest who used to head-butt defensive ends for a living.

Oh, Joan....

Saturday, November 8, 1975
9:15 AM

The Fight over the Militia

Bravely, I answered. "I—I—well, it made sense to me."

"Jesus Chr—Sorry, Father," apologized Michael. He then proceeded to ream me a new one. "Don't you know who these guys are? Don't you?! These are," lowering his voice, "backwoods country boys who probably have their basements stocked full of provisions and deer meat getting ready for Armageddon, you know, Mason, when the niggers take over the world."

"I've told you: don't use that word around me, Michael!" is my only response. I took a breath, regathered my thoughts and continued, "Then, how come there are two blacks in their company?" Manly groans emanated from the black guys, with, in spite of the presence of a Roman Catholic priest, an occasional 'shit' and 'fuck' interspersed.

"That's not good enough, Mason," said Arthur, surprisingly calm. "They're tokens, there to pull us in."

"Damn straight!" yelled Clark Nestor.

"Aw, c'mon, Arthur," I exclaimed, "give them a break! They're Joe's friends."

"Oh, God!" exclaimed John Pettibone.

"And that's supposed to reassure me?" asked Michael, the only one in a three state area with the courage to say that directly in front of Joe standing beside me.

Without altering the look on his face, Joe said to Michael, "Don't accuse me of harboring the petty racism you associate with other white people. I'm not other white people. I'm above all that. Besides, you're my teammates, you're all my teammates, and I take teammates for life. I'm a very loyal person, Burton, much to the contrary of my reputation that has followed me around for the last four years. I'm loyal to my team, my teammates, whom I consider friends, and my country. I would never, and get this straight, would never do anything to harm those to whom I am loyal."

Most would agree that is the most Joe has said in one conversation during his entire career at The University of West Virginia. Despite that, and despite his emotional affirmations, well, emotional for Joe, the dissenters still are not swayed.

I can see their points. We're not far removed in time or proximity from the lynchings and cross burnings. The Mighty Montani Militia represents the enemies of those horrible days. But, my trust in Joe, earlier wavering but now returned after his speech, held me steady in the Militia's corner, although they did at times look pretty stupid in the red hats.

"I see this from your standpoint," I said to any black who would listen, "so please listen to mine. You saw the State Police come in here. Fortunately for me, he was a nice, understanding guy. The problem here is not with him personally, but with the fact that Lawson is right now a desperate man. He's not out there biding his time waiting for us to tell him what we're going to do. He's figuring it out—

"But, Mason," Father Al said, finally speaking up, "is this the answer? Is a bunch of guys in battlegear and rifles the way to go? What are you risking?"

"With all due respect, Father," I said, "we're risking the collapse of this whole deal. Do we want to see that, Michael, see it all fall at our feet? We've worked pretty hard for this, and, by God, we're right!"

"We're right, Mason," replied Michael, "but what about the tin soldiers? What the hell are they going to do when while were walking over to the field they see a chance to take a couple of shots at some spooks?"

"Shit, yeah!" came a cry.

"Goddamnit, Michael," I said in anger, "I hope you don't think we all feel that way!"

"No, Christ!" Michael responded, "Not you!" I guess we have abandoned our attempt to curb our language around Father Al.

"Then hear this," I said, "Lawson's and his cronies' lives depend on it. He is a person in a high place and he knows others in high places. He thinks he knows just how to fix this. Either he or Fadden, who could be the biggest racist of the bunch, makes a phone call or two, like to the governor, and we could be taken over by the National Guard. They're threatened, guys, all they believe is threatened, and they'll do whatever they can to save face and blame it on us."

My logic silenced the crowd. Except, that is, for the big Jesuit.

"I see, Mason," Father Al said, "You certainly have a quandary here. But violence is not the way. You can't fight violence with violence. I realize how ironic it is for me to say this before a contest of the most violent of American sports, but football has redeeming value. Carrying guns in the street does not."

"Father," I said, listening but not paying attention, "all this flack I'm getting here is presupposed by beliefs that these militiamen are nothing but a bunch of redneck goons. So, let's get their leader over here and let him offer us some defense."

"Yeah, get his lily white ass over here," remarked Chandler Childress, smirk on high.

Joe turned smartly on his heels as if he is under orders and proceeded across the ballroom to fetch Major Wilmore. The comments didn't stop there.

"Redneck goons," Tim Seiler commented, "Yeah."

"Ain't nothin' that Frenchy dude is gonna say to turn me around," John said. "He's the major. That makes him the biggest redneck of the bunch."

"And in this case," Montgomery added, "redneck is spelled b-i-g-o-t."

"Yeah," replied the crowd in staccato.

"Damn right," said Shane Evans.

I have had about enough, but I let them vent, they'll be more open-minded when it counts. I know that doesn't make much sense, but it's all I have.

"Look," I said, finally speaking up, "give this guy a chance. Let him sell himself. If you don't like it, we'll find another way to get over to the fieldhouse."

"Yeah," said Michael, "like possibly cracking heads. I believe we can take care of ourselves."

"Michael," I said, "it's not a question of being able to take ourselves. That's not it. It's matching might for might, or more importantly, the perception of might for might. I swear to you, Lawson and Fadden and the governor have the National Guard coming and—"

"I think you're out of your mind, Mason," interrupted John.

"Goddamnit, you guys, I—I—"I'm flustered. Leadership is getting to me. "Just listen to him, then decide. Jesus Christ!" I wanted to turn and run, find Joan, and go to The Dining Room, drink coffee all afternoon, and talk about the possibility of her falling in love with me. The odds of that happening seem much greater than getting us out of this fucking room.

We remained silent and civil until Major Wilmore arrived. He's an average sized man, mid-to-late forties, in shape in the best way he can be. Or maybe it's because those uniforms are in no way flattering to the male form.

"Gentlemen," the major addressed us, very military-like, "Mr. Osbourne tells me you have some concerns about my men."

Michael spoke for the group, "Yeah, Major, it's like this: except for two of you, your men are white. We're black. That's a problem. We're black, you're white, and quite frankly, we're gonna spend most of our walk to the fieldhouse with our backs to you. No offense, but we don't know how your men are going to react to us, you know, being black. That's it in a nutshell."

"Excuse me, Michael," said Father Al, "Major, I'm Al Kolski, pastor at St. Mary's Catholic Church." Father extended his hand and the major clasped and shook it. "Allow me to ask you, Major, are your guns loaded now?"

"No," replied the Major, "no weapon is armed when we come in peace. This is not battle, Father. We don't anticipate much resistance, actually. We think when whomever out there sees us, whether it's the coaches by themselves, or the police, or even the National Guard, which young Mason is having some bad dreams over, I understand," the Major smiled on that one and patted my shoulder, "they will surmise that we can take care of ourselves, and you. But, as you can see, we're carrying blackjacks, for crowd control."

"I liked it all until you mentioned the blackjacks," remarked Father. Maybe he had a bad experience with a blackjack and the policeman on the other end of it in Boston in '68.

"Major," Michael said, calmer, "with all due respect, you say the guns aren't loaded. But the way I see it, each man is responsible for his own gun and can load it with some ammo he brought that you don't know about. Am I right?"

"Well," Major Wilmore answered, "theoretically, yes. But my men are under strict orders to load no weapons."

"Which means," Michael said, sounding more and more like he's cross-examining, "they can be ordered to load, by you, correct?"

The major paused, then replied, "Yes, but I don't see a reason to do that."

"Nor do we," said Montgomery, "Nor do we. Where's the ammo now?"

"In my backpack," the major replied, swinging a big, heavy pack around from his back. "All of it is here."

"Now this brings me back to one of the original questions: what about ammo they brought that you don't account for?" Father asked.

"I assure you, they don't have any," the major replied with no animosity in his voice.

"Major, I ask this question at the risk of insulting you, but your men are under your orders. Whose orders are you under?" Father asked astutely.

After contemplation, the major said, "We have a financial backer, a wealthy man, a farmer and land owner from Greenbrier County who would prefer to remain anonymous."

"I would prefer to speak with him," I said, having my fill of wealthy West Virginians and their purchases of influence.

"I don't know if we can reach him," the major said, not wanting to drag his sugar daddy into this. I however have decided that the militia stays here until I talk to that man.

"Let's try it, Major," I said.

"Wait, wait, whoa!" exclaimed Michael, "My original concern has not been answered. What about your white dudes and my black men?"

"Your men are safe, Mr.."

"Burton. Michael Burton."

"Yes, Mr. Burton, the major continued, "My men are professional soldiers. They served their country; all of them were in Vietnam, fighting alongside men of all races, religions, and persuasions. I know what you've heard about groups such as ours, and in some cases you're right. But not here. The men of the Mighty Montani Militia are true to one, and that is God Almighty. Once again, I can assure you, you and your men are safe. If any one of my men steps out of line, he will be dismissed."

Michael responded quickly, "Major, in the US Armed Services, it's a disgrace to be dishonorably discharged for any reason. But here, if one man steps out of line, as you say, what's the real penalty?" The other black guys are quiet. My basic optimistic nature wants me to believe this is an indication of a breakthrough.

"They will be ostracized by their friends, the other men in the militia, plus they'll lose their jobs, their income. Mr. Burton, mine is a very tight unit. We have a lot of pride and brotherhood, a lot like your team"

The gathering is silent for a while, perhaps reflecting upon a desire to have the old team and pride and brotherhood back. Michael broke in, asking the Major, "My brothers and I want to meet alone with your two brothers."

"That can certainly be arranged," the Major said. Joe turned and walked toward the two blacks standing with each other in conversation.

"In the meantime," I said, "let's try to call Greenbrier County."

"Well, Mason," the Major said, "we may not be able to reach him, but if you insist, let's try it."

Father, Joe, the Major, and I left the blacks alone to talk with the two militiamen. The Major and I found the telephone as Father approached Ted with a handshake. Joe talked to a few of the others. I can see my Runners are getting a bit…how you might say…anxious. The details on this walk to the fieldhouse have to be resolved soon before my men explode and rip the ballroom to a shambles. My plan is to talk to the money dude and then if that's okay, let Michael decide. If he comes in with a thumbs down, we'll go anyway and take our chances. Hey, we're big and bad. No one in their right minds, not the coaches, not the administration, not even the State Police and even West Virginia's own militia, none of these organizations, together or individually, will fuck with us. We're young and mean and we've had our chains jerked too much already.

The Major dialed the phone. I really want to talk to this guy, sort of an anti-McNabb. God, the things I've learned this week. If I become President of the United States and get my own library here in Montani, I'm going to devote a section of it to what happened here over the past week: books on racism, money in sports, the evils of money in sports, money in general, sons and their fathers, and beautiful members of faculty.

It seemed like an eternity before the major spoke into the transmitter. "Sir, this is Major Wilmore in Montani…Yes, sir…Sir, we're involved in a situation with a potential confrontation with the National Guard on the college campus here It happened when the young football players took over the team from the coaches who they say are no longer worthy of their trust because of…Oh, you know of it, sir…Yes, sir. The team wants to play the game and run it themselves, but they have to get from the High Ridge, where they are now, to the fieldhouse. They anticipate trouble and that's where we come in Joe Osbourne called us…Yes, sir…No, sir, the guns are not loaded…Well, their new leader is right here and would like to speak with you." Major Andy glanced over to me and handed me the phone.

"Sir, this is Mason Bricker."

"Yes, young man," the unnamed man said, as I tried and failed to imagine what he looks like.

"Sir, I'm sorry to bother you this morning, but I have a few questions about your militia up here in Montani."

"Proceed, son."

"We've thrown the coaches out for the day and intend to handle the game ourselves. I understand you've read of the troubles we have encountered here lately."

"I have, son, and I might add, with regard to money and power struggles, you've really stepped into it." I keep hearing that, but cognitive dissonance kicks in and sweeps me away. The man continued, "But, maybe we can still help you out. I understand you are requesting safe escort to your fieldhouse."

"Yes, sir."

"Son, you have that and protection for the remainder of the day if you wish. I know Myron McNabb. He's a mean-spirited son-of-a-bitch. He knows no bounds and, including today, you may not have seen the last of him. Mr. Bricker, you know as well as I that The University of West Virginia football is a power brokers' game. They like the way it was played in the early sixties before all the protesting and influence of the blacks."

Oh, shit. "Sir," I said bravely, still not knowing his name and just pretending he's that dude from *Charlie's Angels,* "speaking of blacks, that's where we have a big problem. Frankly, sir, our blacks don't trust your militiamen."

Quiet. I'm afraid to think what that means.

"Do they have a leader?" the mystery man asked.

"Yes, sir. Michael Burton."

"Oh, Burton. What a player! Ask him to speak with me."

Excitedly, I looked over to the black guys, finding them with the two militiamen just yukking it up. Is this falling into place? Remember the chicken thing, Mason. Better laid plans have fallen apart, like the League of Nations, the World Football League, the Corvair, Watergate, guns and butter, and Judy's and Jean's and Alice's set-up of Jennifer with me. Get Michael over here and keep praying.

I stepped over to the black guys and got Michael's attention, summoning him to me. "The militia's Big Cheese wants to speak with you," I said.

"Me?" Michael asked, surprised.

"You're whom he asked for," I said.

"Whatever for?"

"Go find out."

Michael ambled over and took the phone. "This is Michael Burton." My good friend's manners lead one to believe he couldn't possibly crush skulls on autumn Saturday afternoons. As Michael is attentive on the phone, I can't help but wonder what the hell is going on between the two. Finally, Michael spoke, "I see," Well, hell, Burton, that doesn't tell me anything. "Okay," he said, then he started, "My men and I are really nervous about the guys in fatigues with rifles. I've been through enough racial hatred for a lifetime. My father was killed in Alabama by a bunch of thugs. Dragged behind a pickup truck until there was barely enough to send back to us in Pennsylvania."

I thought I was going to be sick. I knew Michael's father had like mine met a sudden end. He never said anything else about it. I didn't know this. Oh, God, this is too much

Michael continued, "You're assuring me everything will be all right. Well, sir, I'm going to hold you to your word and hold you accountable. Even though I don't know who you are, if something happens to one of my brothers, I'll hunt you down and you'll pay. I hope you understand." More silence. "Yes, sir. Thank you, sir," and my buddy hung up.

Michael looked at me. I'm in pain. "I'm so very sorry, Michael. I didn't know."

"Few do," he replied, and I think that's all he wanted to discuss on the matter. "The mystery man gave me his word nothing will happen. He says these men are employed by him and if there are any 'shenanigans' as he called it, the man will be ruined." So, that answers the income question. "He says he knows his men and nothing bad will happen."

I paused a bit, still feeling the effects of Michael's admission. I thought after the past couple of days I had a good handle on where the brothers are coming from. My father's death was tragic enough, but Michael...the ire he must feel toward my race; and the fact he keeps it bottled up. Every minute I spend dealing with this issue, from PD to Lawson, awakens me more and more to the fact that despite the enlightenment of the decade of the sixties, there's still enough hatred to go around here in the seventies. And every minute I spend with my black friends, the more determined I am to end the superiority of whites. I can't save the world, but I can have a big effect on changes in my own little corner of it.

"Okay, Michael, here's the plan," I announced, "if your men agree, and if I can talk Father into it, and if the Major agrees to continue carrying the ammo, and most importantly, if there is a need, meaning if the coaches are armed, then the militia will escort us to the fieldhouse. Now, let's you and I take a peek outside to check the situation."

"How are we going to do that?" Michael asked.

"We're going to go out there in the name of negotiations. Of course, there is no negotiation. We'll take Father with us for big firepower and to make it look real."

"You're devious," said Michael.

"Innocence is the first casualty of war," I said. I glanced over. Father had Ted in a good mood. Praise Jesus. "Father," I called, "let's go talk to the coaches. You, Michael, and me."

"Why?" the big man asked.

"We're going to give them one more chance," I said, "and I need your support, if you please."

"I don't really know what I could say at this point, but I'll go along," Father said.

"Don't worry, Father, I'll do all the talking," I said, brazen for nineteen.

Father Al nodded, "Michael, let's go," I said. I gave one final check to the black guys. They're having fun. I wonder if Knute Rockne ever had these problems.

We walked to the door, a twentieth century Triumvirate. Or possibly the Father in Al, the Son in Michael, and me, the Holy Spirit, very presumptuous, almost blasphemous. Maybe I'm not too holy after that telephone conversation with my women this morning. But, I am enough of a spirit to try to get a hundred hellcats pointing in the same direction. Forget the allegories. If we get to the coin toss, I'll drop to my knees and promise God anything, anything except becoming a priest. Well, I've already made a deal about that. But, it'll be tough. I think I'm way too libidinous, which in nineteen-year-old terminology means really horny.

Arriving at the door, we all gave each other a glance. Father Al quickly made the sign of the cross. I joined him, because I need blessed for misleading him to think we're here to talk. He'll be mad as hell if he were to ever discover my true purpose: reconnaissance. Michael opened the door. Father, Michael, and their physical stature. We had to look imposing. Well, except for me.

A staring battle ensued. Whatever you do, don't let on about the militia.

All the coaches, ten in number, were present, oddly positioned like bowling pins. I find this humorous, but this is no time for laughs. Lawson is the kingpin. Van Watt's in the number two position. I couldn't care less about the others because I am surveying the scene. Not good. State Troopers, six of them, are stationed behind the coaches. I quickly scanned down the steps to my left leading to the outside. I saw several National Guardsmen in riot gear, for Chissake! We really could be in for a fight, but we're fighting men. The way I see it, judging from the reactions at my house this morning, we have public sentiment on our side. The campus will burn if we're harmed in any way, with film on the national news.

That I don't want. I want to play this game. It's still a risk, but if we walk out here under the guise of being armed to the teeth, I'll take that risk.

"Coach Lawson, or Mr. Lawson, I mean, it's time for us to get taped and get dressed, so we're headed for the fieldhouse. Just to remind you, you're not welcome," I said. Damn, Mason.

Father Al pinched my upper arm, "Coach, what he means is, if you step down, your men can coach."

No, damnit, that's not what I mean!

"Father, with all due respect to your collar," Lawson said, "I stay. The administration is behind me. My coaches stay, and your services will no longer be needed."

"Lawson," Michael said calmly, "if you or anybody on your staff or any other member of the faculty or the administration without our prior approval steps foot in the fieldhouse with intentions of stopping us from running this game ourselves, you're going to have to recruit from the intramural ranks to field a team for this game because my brothers and I aren't going to do it." Wow. The law firm of Burton and Vacca, my counsel for life.

"Lawson," I added, "that goes for all of us."

"Mason, you two are making a mistake," Father Al said calmly.

"No, Father, join us or join them," I shot, quickly realizing I was too confrontational with our biggest ally. "Lawson won't back down, so we're on our own. I'd like to have you with us. Actually, we need you. And I think if you think about it, you'll see that we're doing the right thing."

The pause seemed to last hours. Father finally spoke, "Okay. Last chance, Lawson." Oh, yeah! Here come the Big Man!

"I am the coach of this team," Lawson said defiantly.

"Not today, Lawson," Michael said with a sinister smile.

"Let's see you get through here," Lawson said. I take that to mean he doesn't know about my militia.

"Let's see you stop us," I countered.

That exchange is indicative of the difference between men and women. We as a gender are much more hostile. Women would have sat down over white wine, worked it out, gone shopping, then talked about each other behind each others' backs. I hope I never say anything like that around Judy and Alice. Moreso, women wouldn't even be playing football. We are Runners. Hear us roar! In numbers too big to ignore! We're fuckin' going to battle, Helen Reddy!

The three of us stepped back inside and had a confab. "I thought you were going to try to work it out with them, Mason!" Father exclaimed, letting his guard down.

"No, Father, I said one more chance. That's what we did. They didn't take it. Michael, check with your men. I'll get the others ready, and if all systems are go with you, we'll talk to the Major."

Michael excused himself to meet with the brothers. Father Al is looking downward, eyes closed. I started to give him the space he needs, but he shook himself out of it and turned to me.

"Mason," he began, "I have a problem here. First, as a Jesuit, I abhor violence. It's just not an option. Second, I'm the fully-fledged adult here and therefore responsible for anything that happens. Third, I've seen first-hand what can happen during a protest. This is now honestly a cause for police action. You and your teammates are violating team rules, school policy, and possibly a few laws when you called in the militia. As I said, from my experience, anything can happen here."

Father hesitated. Next to speak…

"But, I am most certainly one hundred percent behind your cause. This act of racism and bigotry is an atrocity, and for this reason I can't turn my back to it and just walk away. I've got to stay and see this through, all the way to the end of the game and beyond, if you need me. I'm in, Mason. But, I have to tell you, the big risk is the Major's men. If they are professional as the Major says and they remain well-behaved, we can call this civil disobedience and call ourselves lucky."

I'm ecstatic. "Welcome back, Father," I said as I embraced him, beaming. "Let's check with Michael."

As the Father and I walked to the black guys, I realized I had been so caught up in everything that I had completely forgotten about the white guys, including my boy Vinny. I searched for The Gunner and found him engaged in a card game with Ted and a few of the offensive linemen. As I scanned the room, I saw other white guys conversing, bullshitting, some looking bored. Joe came over to me. "Mason," he said, "we're holding our own here, but there's a growing sentiment that this long wait is all the fault of the brothers. If you don't get this ballgame rolling, you're going to have an irreversible revolt on your hands."

Jesus, Joe, spit it out. Don't sugarcoat it for me!

"Okay, here we go, Joe," I said as Michael stepped up.

"Mason, we're ready," he said, "We've talked it out, and as long as Joe inspects the rifles and searches the militiamen for ammo and finds nothing, we'll take the walk."

Relief overcame me. I, too, am becoming impatient, but I have enough sense to know that the search is the only safe way to get out of here. "Joe, please ask the Major to line up his men and you do your thing. You know what you're looking for." And if you find anything, load it in a rifle and just shoot me.

Saturday, November 8, 1975
9:30 AM

The Walk

During the search, the white guys are getting their game faces on, sure they would be on their ways shortly and getting dressed for battle in no time. But the animosity with their black teammates picked up again, an impatience for not following along. The whites are ready to play. But the blacks are intent on the search, preparing to start the whole walkout process all over again if so much as one bullet is discovered. And who the hell can blame them? I went to high school with guys like these militiamen. I always had the feeling they'd take out a 'coon,' their word, whenever they were given a good chance. "Take your time, Joe. This is the last I want to be concerned with this today. We've gotta ballgame to play, but only after everybody is satisfied of his safety."

I can see the perturbation sneak onto the face of the G-man, and I know it's directed at me. He has been a very understanding, if not a changed man over the past hour or two since his and Michael's near clash of the titans. But I know Ted. I know where he's from. I've met his family, his father, who makes Ted look like a McGovern liberal. I also know Ted has a political science class from Professor I. M. Nu, a PhD of Chinese descent who as a matter of standard course in his class gives the floor to all minorities as a forum for anything they wish to talk about, at times just letting them teach the class. You can only imagine how the good ol' boy responds to that. I'm surprised he hasn't dropped, but I have heard him boast that he'll 'have them all converted to the natural laws of the Lord by December.' Tolerance is not his forte and my only hope is for Father Al to provide a positive influence. Or jerk a knot in his head.

"Mason, Michael," Joe called, "No ammunition was found among the militiamen, neither in the packs or their weapons." The assumption is 'let's get the hell out of here,' but as always, that's Michael's call.

Father Al's behind me. "Father, no bullets," I said.

"Michael. Whaddya say?" Father Al asked.

Michael looked at Arthur, then at Lendel, who had just shown up from a draining session on his knee just in time for the festivities. Burt glanced at each of his men, surveying them again for dissent. None is apparent, but then again I'm not privy to all the body language.

My friend Michael looked skyward for a moment. He takes on a lot, but that's Michael and I would have him no other way. "Mason, Father, get us the hell out of here."

You'd think we had already won the ballgame. One hundred men at the top of their lungs rejoicing a victory, not a small one mind you. It's a victory of the spirit. For the first time since Ernie Ernst's kick, I think we definitely are a team.

It took a few moments to allow them to let it out, but I had to speak with them because my job had taken on a new tack. I am now a Scoutmaster and I have to take my Eagles on a walk through the woods. If I can just keep them away from the snakes…

"All right! All right!" I started, "Hey! Let me talk! We gotta talk before we go!" I'm getting a lot of resistance.

Suddenly, as if all of his rowdy past was funneled into one major bellow, Father Al shouted a terrifying, "QUIET!!!" And there is quiet. The hand of God cupped over the mouth of one tough ex-pro football player.

"Thank you, Father." Little he does surprises me. "All right, Runners, we're going to take a walk over to the fieldhouse so we can beat the shit out of Pitt. Now, I've thought this out, and here's my plan: Major, take a third of your men with their empty guns to lead us up front. Behind them will be, listen, half the seniors, and half the underclassmen. Then, Major, another third will be in the middle, then everybody else, and Joe, if you will, grab a rifle and bring up the rear. Any questions?" I probably confused them, but the most important part to this march is the placement of the militiamen. I think Major understands what to do.

"Questions? No? Father, please walk up front with the Major."

"Got'cha," he said.

They are still attentive, and that is good because there are more things to go over.

"Okay, listen up! Just a couple more things. We've checked out the place outside, and there are State Troopers, National Guardsmen, and ten very pissed-off coaches. Some things ya gotta remember. First, the purpose of this walk is to get to the place where we'll play football. That's the key word here: football. Don't do anything, I repeat, anything that will keep you from playing football today, anything like getting hurt or getting arrested. Now, on the subject of arrest, we're not breaking any laws as long as we remain peaceful. And I think the presence of the militia will surprise everybody and keep them all honest, probably leaving us alone. Just use your head and get to the fieldhouse in one piece as one team. Okay? Any questions?"

"I gotta piss like a racehorse!" yelled voice in the rear. Laughter took over. I sighed. Father tapped me on the shoulder and said, "This isn't going to happen perfectly, Mason. Let's go."

I took his advice. "All right!! Let's line 'er up!"

With notable exception to the militiamen, the whole thing resembled a clusterfuck. At this point, I don't care. Father and Major are at the door. I'm in the middle of the first pack, near Michael and Tim Sieler. Someone came up from behind me and goosed my ass. "Hi, handsome. Can I walk with you?" It's Vinny, letting his gander meander. Tim said, "I always knew that about you two."

We're moving. It took a couple of minutes to get us to the first set of the doors, during which time things remained rather peaceful and even playful. Lots of cutting up took place until reality struck. There're the coaches, and they're surely not in a Welcome Wagon mood.

"Bricker, you're a rabble-rousing fascist," Lawson yelled directly to me, "and for this you will pay, young man."

"Fascist. My Uncle Benito was a fascist," said smart-ass Vinny.

"Look the word up and try again, asshole," shot Michael to Lawson. Burton's probably right. I'll lay money on Michael's vocabulary. He burned the LSAT.

Red Van Watt is burning a hole through me, "You son-of-a-bitch viper. I stuck my neck out for you last night. You bastard."

Other catcalls and expletives most coaches don't emit in public came from group, the cradle of shitheads. But once we were past them, we're suddenly flanked by the Troopers, possibly each one of them among the biggest ever graduated by the academy. They did nothing but stand there and silently intimidate. It's not working so far. But, by God, with anyone else besides football players, it could have been very effective.

Thank goodness that's over, but just outside the glass door on the large patio leading to the street the gauntlet continued with a serious edge. A bunch, seemingly a battalion of Guardsmen, all in riot gear, more awesome than the police, stood in single file on each side of us. For maximum effect, the files converged slightly, with the intent of engaging one or some of us young bucks and give them due cause to bust heads. Vinny's scared silent. I prayed and prayed like never before, and it must have worked because we're maintaining good behavior. At least those in front of us. Behind, God save their souls.

One thing I congratulated myself for is not underestimating the fire-power the state had assembled. Public sentiment disallowed them from taking any overt action, but they thought we might crack. And even though the enlistment of the militia was almost instantaneously unpopular with everybody but Joe and me, I think their presence gave us the confidence to be a team and take this walk. That's good, because now we are rewarded.

Interspersed with a smattering of Montani police and men from the county sheriff's department is a massive, throbbing, wild throng of fans who must have collectively taken upon themselves to treat us like the men we are. They knew we had it tough lately and they are doing everything possible to let us know they were with us, that we're the kings. I saw them and heard them and standing among them, they got to us. Many of my teammates and I shed tears. After not holding Penn State for a final few seconds and totally blowing it to a bunch of losers like North Carolina State, and when considering the overall petulant nature of the spoiled athlete of the seventies, you'd think they'd just let us die. But, not this morning. The beloved Runners' fans are out for our walk in numbers I have never witnessed. The morning is foggy, high forties, a typical Montani mid-fall morning, the beginnings of great football weather. To add to this ambiance, the fans, our fans are stacked six or seven deep to get a look at the procession of large men in overcoats and parkas. Cheers and individual names rang out, reminding me of why I turned down Princeton, a thought that has escaped me since the monsoon at Happy Valley. They urged us on, as if we had already derailed Pittsburgh's run for the national title. I recognized some faces, but the sight that really choked me up was Dr. Leo Cost, English department head. There he stood in front of the pack on the left in his middle-aged chutzpah. The consummate sixties intellectual liberal, once an assistant speechwriter for JFK, saluted me. He must have read the papers. I stopped, returned the salute, and embraced him. "Well-done, my boy," he said.

The women, they are going nuts, a frenzy of sociobiological significance, all possibly wanting to have our children. Maybe I took that a little too far, but it's a nice thought. Case in point: I had just walked past Dr. Cost when out of nowhere appeared Edie Loden, a senior art student I sat beside in my Physics for Liberal Arts Majors class. As she grabbed and hung onto my left arm, I wondered what the hell this is all about. Recalling several conversations I had with Edie before the several classes I had attended, I then knew.

"Mason Bricker! Mason! Thank you! Thank you for what you have done!" I looked at her. Really looked. She has short black hair, with cowlicks and wisps just touching her forehead and above her ears, dark eyes, a gorgeous, I mean gorgeous face, as if Raphael had painted a raven-haired 'Madonna of Foligno' or something, with a smile that would either disarm you or drive you wild depending upon the mood. This is football, so I'm the latter. She's shorter, with a cute little cuteness of a bod, today wearing a black cowlneck sweater and faded straight leg denims. In spite of everything and everyone last night, she has my full attention.

"Mason," Edie continued, oblivious to all around us, "a group of us at the temple have been trying to get that bastard McNabb for a long while. You did it! Mason! You got him!" We walked together. Our eyes locked. "Oh, Mason, thank you! I love you!"

My jaw dropped and she quickly covered her mouth with her right hand, eyes surprised. She dropped her hand and said, "Well, maybe not…but maybe I could." I'm still agog. "Oh, just call me!" Edie exclaimed.

I could think of nothing to say but, "What's your number?"

"555-2468. Easy to remember. I'm looking forward to it."

Still in shock, I upgraded Edie to a near-Joan-like extremely beautiful rating. "Me, too, Edie. Me, too," I said smiling. She did also, ringing my bell.

It took a couple of seconds, but I pulled myself away from Edie Loden. I felt a grab on my right arm. "Hey, buddy," It's Vinny, "I was there for that. Whatever you're eating, I want some."

"I…I…," I stammered out, still overwhelmed by Edie Loden.

"Who is she?" Vinny asked. "She's fucking gorgeous!"

"Edie from my Physics class."

"How do you get all these gorgeous women to tell you they love you and follow you all over town and stuff? I thought you never went to that class."

"Maybe that's why she likes me," I said, eyes darting through the crowd, looking for Joan, again feeling guilty.

"Well, hell, she likes something about you," Vinny commented.

I brought myself back to the walk. It is game day and I don't know if it's the thick atmosphere of hormones but all the coeds are glowing and pretty. That's entirely likely because I'm always positive about women, looking for the bright spots in what they often consider their drab features. I like my way better. And apparently, so do a majority of my teammates. There is no concern for race in this public display of the admiration of our sexual potency. White women are swooning over the black guys, pissing off a few of my Caucasians, and thereby perpetrating the old Southern myth that the blacks were here to steal our womenfolk. That's absurd, but whatever, it's not malicious on the brothers' part. The attraction is understandable. Our black players are for the most part athletically handsome men, well-groomed, broad shouldered and narrow hipped. And there is the potential of the coeds acting out fantasies of independence against their bigoted-by-generation parents, a Sidney-Poitier-Guess-Who's-Coming-To-Dinner scenario. I consider it harmless and natural. Much unlike almost all the people I grew up with and around, I know our kinds can mix, and that includes Catholics and Protestants and blacks and Jews.

Michael remained with Vinny and me through the entire walk. He has to be one of the more admired college students in the history of the University. To call him a fan favorite is a gross understatement. It is no secret among our team that I want to be like Michael. It goes further than that. I want to be Michael. He, and my best friend Vinny, too, let's not forget about him, have had a profound impact on my life. I am a better person for being in their company, and it isn't enough to say that I am proud to be their friend.

Saturday, November 8, 1975
9:50 AM

Finally home

I realize I risk sounding maudlin when I express such admiration for my two men, but it's Saturday and the team is lean and mean and the crowd is burning like a brushfire. It's the proper mixture for a sudden release of emotions that I hope gets directed into the planting of my helmet through somebody's sternum. Maybe I'm coach, but I'm a player-coach and any Pitt return guy will have to contend with the man who's going to take out his frustrations of the week on whofuckinever gets in the way.

All these things ran through my mind as I look over the hill to the entrance to our fieldhouse. Fans are thinning out only somewhat, but their enthusiasm remains. I saw Father Al and the Major turn left onto the sidewalk that led to the double doors, my teammates following behind, fists pumping the air to the crowd, a general whooping it up. This walk, these people on the throes of undying dedication to us, each of us a Lucky Man of Emerson, Lake, and Palmer fame, is our best prescription. Well, maybe Lucky Man is a poor metaphor since his blood ran and he laid down and died, but you get the point. We're the heroes, and we're not even really sure if our managers made it down here to hang out our jock-straps in our lockers. That, however, doesn't matter right now. As I turn the path to the doors, I look back and realized that for a few moments I had again forgotten McNabb, Lawson, and The Big Kid, seeing, hearing, and feeling only the screams, the colors, the banners, the snap of the nip in the air, everything essentially college football. Never at my wildest times could I have ever dreamed of it being better.

We the Runners and The Runners' faithful stand in this humanity, none of us moving an inch away from it all. An impromptu rally is staged, urging all those who stood along the early parade route to join us in the natural amphitheatre that formed to the north of the stadium. There are no cheerleaders, no band, just thousands of students and alums with us and extending up the hill we just walked down, all joined together by all the noise so many human voices can emit. The energy is electrifying, bordering on frightening. If Pitt or the Pittsburgh Steelers or even the 1974 NFL All-Pro team would show up right now, we would beat the holy hell out of them.

It was wonderful to watch Michael manhandle Penn State. Drilling that hapless NC State returnman to the turf is a personal best. But heretofore the last ten minutes had been the most magical of my life, almost comparing to when Joan's lips first touched mine. This has been a big weekend. It's going to get bigger still, and I, we, don't want it to end. With no coaches to say otherwise, including yours truly who is not about to step in and tell everyone to get dressed, it didn't end. Each crescendo was topped by another. It's a runaway semi with no air brakes and straight road to the horizon. I get the feeling the University community has been stewing on this since Thursday. There is no better way to get us pumped up for the number one team in the nation, but the crowd, the fans themselves are also well-deserving. So we just stand out there with them and feed on each other, exponential to an endless degree.

After what seems like a glorious eternity of infinite noise no other college can ever dream of topping, Michael himself looked ready to burst through the pillars that held up The Ridge. He's sobbing, not with the sadness and frustration he experienced at Beaver Stadium, but now with a nearly uncontrollable chemistry, both impelling and narcotic. As the leader, he has decided in the rational mind he has remaining that it's now time to play football. Opening the doors, he let out a banshee scream that cut through the thousands and led his team in a charge of the fieldhouse locker room.

Inside, we are still too cranked to notice there are no managers, no trainers, no uniforms, and no equipment. We don't give a damn. The parties continued both inside and outside, our rhythmic clapping sustaining us, our adorers yelling at us through the walls. The relief of being here in the familiarity of the house further released us.

Alas, as we hear the fans die down while they're moving their celebration to their seats in the stadium, our mood became more subdued. Emotions cycle rapidly in athletics, with the settling-in of the reality of the impending sixty minute job. That would concern most football players afraid of losing it before the biggest of contests, but we're just fine. We haven't broken out the drugs yet.

There's a gentlemen's agreement among us in a world of the anti-gentleman that we will all do anything we can to keep this aspect quiet from the authorities. Any other Saturday, that would be the coaches, trainers, and the doctors. Today, the doctors and trainers if we get any, but most importantly the Major and the Father. Out of a sense of respect for each other, but also due to that fuzzy region known as paranoia, the 'speed,' the 'uppers' are the Runners,' all of the Runners,' own game. Even if you don't take the pills: your teammates do it, you know about it, therefore you do it.

There was one day, the game against Virginia Tech when I first became wistful about Joan and had a hard time 'getting it up,' I took solace in a 'black beauty.' The pill provided, no, forced upon me a very real sense of superhuman capabilities. Black with the yellow numerals 18-875 etched on the side to indicate authenticity, the tiny capsule elevated my thought processes, heightened my optimism, and lended to my muscle reactivity and strength, all allowing me the ingestor to closely approach the asymptote of invincibility desired and required to take part in a game of crashing bodies and grinding bones. I rationalized the need of the black beauty that day, borrowing it from Andy Bruzinsky, the Candy Man. In short, it worked, although I paid the price later that afternoon when my body was depleted of the chemical and screeched to a dead stop. Anytime you take drugs you live for the moment. For all obvious reasons, I was pretty disgusted with myself for doing it and vowed to make it on my own in the future. It's just not for me.

It is, however, for a lot of others. I am knowledgeable of the chain of acquisition due to my inquisitiveness, or you could also say my persistence in knowing what it was I was putting in my body. A pharmaceutical company representative, her name and the name of her employer withheld because you could just imagine the hypertrouble she would get into, her intentions to meet good-looking football players well-known, got the sample diet pills by the boxload and fed the team. Andy is her contact here at West Virginia by virtue of the woman being a long-time family friend. From there, Andy, under the table or from the dark corners of the fieldhouse or for the more cautious in the comforts of their own apartments, sells the pills to those of his teammates who want them. Others who have to think straight, like Vinny and the quarterbacks, and the superstars like Michael, Ted, and Arthur, and others who for various reasons subscribed philosophically to the desire for a clean body like Joe, steered away from the black beauties, although they are aware of their use and for the most part issued no judgments. However, the Runners who are with The Program are those who are factually or by their own perceptions marginal, the athletes who exist in constant fear of losing their positions and playing time to their understudies and need that extra push.

Andy's clientele are in a big part white guys, looking for any way to get the edge on the more athletic blacks. Sound racist? Surely does, but I'm not. You play ball, any ball, and you'll find that it can't be explained, but it's true. For whatever the reason, when blacks are on the field or the court, the level of play goes up a few notches.

Defensive linemen, blacks and whites, are by position the first to grab a fistful of Andy's candy. Their battles are mano a mano with the biggest men on the field in that rarefied zone I have earlier termed the Trenches. This is where the real warfare takes place. By the constantly aggressive nature of the job that has to be done, anything that turned the men into the beasts required to patrol that section of the turf has to be employed. It is so frightening to face or even think of these huge men hopped up on speed, conscious and subconscious thought revved to the red line, with total disregard for football or social rules, approaching the level of human demolitionists, killing machines.

You think I'm exaggerating? I'll tell you this now. Offensive linemen, the more rational of the bunch, in the interest of survival often slip a few black beauties down their gullets. Imagine that five-on-five, men as big as houses, chemically induced, or to say it more accurately, chemically controlled. Put yourself in Vinny's place, trying to run a team and execute a game plan against the monsters who outweigh you by eighty to a hundred pounds, quick as pumas, strong as heavy machinery, and totally fucking out of their minds. They have one objective: maul your ass into a grease spot on the carpet. The pills tell them it's entirely possible. Vinny says it's better to not think about it.

The wackos, as we affectionately call them, today without regard to the whereabouts of their uniforms or tape, performed their pregame acquisitions. One at a time in a secretive fashion, Andy dispensed the meds, very skillfully hidden from Father and the militia. We who have seen their rituals many times before are all-knowing. With due respect to our desire for victory, we allow it to happen, a necessary evil, even though we are aware of the fact that at any moment on the field of play the heart muscles of our friends and teammates may just simply explode.

"So, when the fuck are we going to get our gear, coach?" an angry voice from the gallery queried of me.

"I'm working on it," I shouted back, not really knowing any more than he did.

"Get 'em out here, Coach Ivy," yelled John, "or we'll have to go up against Pitt totally nude."

The tension is cut with laughter. "You'd like that, queerbait," Tim Jones, John's second teamer, countered. The team got a big kick out of that. They love any accusation of homosexuality, as ignorant and as latent as it may be. I glanced at Father. He shook his head and smiled. I guess he's heard it all.

Walking around and taking inventory of the situation as my teammates enjoyed just being here, however empty as it is, I listed immediate needs: uniforms, gear, managers to get the uniforms and gear, trainers, tape, braces, a couple of doctors, chalkboards, chalk, headsets, cable, watercoolers, Gatorade; in fact, most everything it takes to run an NCAA Division I football team. The bastards, I thought, those motherfuckers came over here to empty us out with some kind of a half-assed siege. The gall! Well, this a contest of 'chicken' with two '57 Chevys and we shall see who blinks first, if only I knew what to do and if only I can keep my men from pulling a Billy Budd on me. I've lost it. I'm mixing metaphors. Michele would kill me.

It didn't take but a minute later for one of the militiamen to walk from his guardpost at the front door up to me to announce, "Lyndon Fadden is here to see you." Strangely, I found it difficult to erase the smile that sneaked on my face. It's my father coming out in me. I can hear the Bazooka now, 'Bring the son-of-a-bitch on.'

"Michael! Ted!" I shouted. They raised their heads almost simultaneously. "Fagden is here."

Fagden. Our not-so-respectful nickname. Sometimes even I fell into the 'bash the homos' trap.

The big men walked over and arrived at the same time as Dr. Fadden. The Athletic Director looked the part of the major college football administrator: just over six feet, graying hair, ruggedly handsome, camel hair overcoat, five hundred dollar suit, white shirt painstakingly starched, navy and silver rep tie, shoes impeccably polished, socks and underwear probably smelling like cedar. Without a word, we all stepped back into Lawson's office. Arthur joined in, then Vinny, then Father and his immensity made it a crowd. Six against one. That peckerhead Fadden stood there, hands on hips, still thinking he had the upper hand. Staring, glancing, and overall positioning ensued, except for Fadden who did not take his eyes off me. I get the feeling he's not admiring my physique.

"I'll get to the point," The Chief Asshole boomed, loud enough for everyone outside to hear. "Bring the coaches right in right now or I will rescind all scholarships on disciplinary charges." He's bucking for a total breakdown, probably thinking I'm just a young fool and can't hold it together. Maybe he's half-right, but I have faith in my team.

"You can't and won't do that, Dr. Fadden," I countered.

"Consider it done," he threatened.

I looked around. No one budged.

"I'm going to call you on this, Dr. Fadden," I said with a poker reference and a poker face, "Here's what's going to happen. We stay. We coach this game. We need everything to run a game: gear, trainers, doctors, everything. And you're going to provide it all for us. This game will proceed like a normal West Virginia football game, except Lawson and all the other coaches will merely be spectators. Then we talk on Sunday." Michael and Arthur slapped palms. I guess from that I'm on the right track, but you can't tell that from the scowl on Father's face.

"And if we don't?" Fadden asked. Nice comeback, Univac.

"The black guys walk and the white guys won't be far behind, and you're totally embarrassed on national television with Keith Jackson doing the play-by-play." I said with finality.

Dr. Fadden exploded, "You're taking this university down the crapper with your punk antics!"

I moved toward his face, confident I had the upper hand. Father wrapped his big paw around my shoulder, but to no avail. "We're ruining the university?" I said with a manly laugh, "We? Bullshit! I think your bigoted head coach has already done that, Dr. Fadden. Your inability to grasp this situation is startling. You bring the coaching staff back in here and you can forget about recruiting black players for the rest of the century. Contributions and season ticket sales will plummet and the Ridge Runners will disappear from the bowl game radar screen. That's about it, Dr. Fadden," I paused, then the English major in me took over, "You ever wonder what the true meaning of the word 'irony' is? Well, you're lookin' at it. You've gotten yourself in such a mess backing that cross-burner of a coach of yours that we're your only hope!"

Arthur and Father slapped palms. It must be frustrating to be a man earning six figures and lose a battle of wits to a teenager.

Finally, finally, he spoke, "I'll make a deal with you, Mr. Bricker," Fadden's head cocked back with some resignation but definitely a man to never leave empty-handed. He crossed his arms. "I'll get your trainers and doctors and gear and all that. You and your rag-tags can run this game, and this game only, provided you keep that bleeding-heart on the sidelines with you," he said, nodding to Father, who I think is growing more and more ready to cave in his face. "You can do all this, and we'll talk on Sunday, as you wish."

Sounds great, but I know better. "And what's the price?"

"You, Mr. Bricker," the cockster said, "You're the price. You coach today, you play today, and this is the end of the line for you. Maybe you'll stay in school, although I can't guarantee that. That's out of my jurisdiction. But one thing I as the athletic director can count on: this will be your final game, match, meet, anything that has to do with anything with regard to sports here in Montani, boy. When darkness falls, the sun will set on your athletic career at West Virginia."

I'm stunned. This possibility hadn't seriously crossed my mind. I didn't come prepared to give it all up. Of all the opportunities presented to me in my life, I never wanted any of them more than to play football for West Virginia. As an early adolescent, I myself painted my room navy and silver. Pictures of players and banners and streamers hung from the walls. Whenever I became bored in school, I would count the hours and minutes to the next Runners game. Then, for away games I would park myself beside the radio and listen from the first pregame segment to the last interview. Every home game since I was seven years old I was here. I didn't miss, even finding a way upstate after my dad died. I would sit there in the stands with Vinny. I could see The Gunner sailing one to me on the fly headed for the bowl endzone. By God, I was going to be here and play here. My friend and I were. It was the one constant in my life. And even after the U coaches didn't show any interest in my services and all appeared lost for a full ride up here, my fervor had become so well known in my hometown that the editors of my high school senior yearbook still wrote under my portrait, 'Mr. Ridge Runner. Bleeds navy and silver. Most likely to be captain at the U, 1977.' The chance escaped, but the obsession remained. And despite the ignored phone messages and pigeon-holed letters to the coaching staff from one persistent prep, self-described as a 'born hitter,' wanting just one chance at glory at The Ridge, I'm here, ain't I? Against odds, I did turn out to be a Runner, and nobody, nobody wears the uniform with more pride than I, the navy jersey and the silver pants and the silver helmet with the double blue stripes down the middle. Just like my father and I always dreamed I would.

However, and overridingly most importantly right now, the Beach Boys' *Be True To Your School* doesn't even begin to describe how I feel about it all. Especially the team, the tradition, the history. Especially the boys. Especially my teammates.

With moist eyes and a crack in my voice, I gathered all the bravery I have in my soul and said, "Dr. Fadden, I'll do it. You set this game up for us today, let us play and coach, and today's the last day I play for West Virginia."

"No!" Michael shouted, "No, Mason! Don't do it! Don't give in to the son-of-a-bitch!" I thought he was going across the room after Fagden.

"No, Mason!" Vinny yelled, "We'll work it out, honest!" I could see the pain on his face. He and I have the most on the line here.

"He can't make it stick!" Michael said, seething.

"Nope," I said, red-rimmed, "I can tell. This is going to be the only way. And because of that, if you keep the coaches out, I'll play today and stay away. You've got what you want, Dr. Fadden. Now get us our stuff." I used the palms of my hands to dry my face, then looked at the blood-sucking leech in an attempt to transmit all the contempt I had for him and what he represents in one final glare of defiance.

"Are you sure, Mason?" Father asked softly, his right hand on my shoulder. He knows what it means to walk.

"Yes, Father," I said as reassuringly as possible.

Fadden smiled ominously. It's an act. He thought I'd never give in to his demand, but I've spent my life surprising people. It's worth it just to watch that bastard twist in the wind. I felt a very real sense of victory, although the cost of which I know will hit home to me later on today. And other days.

"The truck with the equipment is parked right outside. The trainers, managers, and doctors, and the techs, they'll be here in ten minutes." He craned to look outside the office. "And you can dispense with the baby killers."

"Sorry, Dr. Fadden," I said boldly, "The Mighty Mon stays, if anything as our trump card."

Fadden paused, then said, "Who's the old fart leader of this bunch playing Army?"

"Major Wilmore," I replied.

Fadden yelled, "Major, get in here!"

The Major hup-twoed, front and center, "Sir!" He knows the importance of Fadden.

"You fire one shot," Fadden said, "and I'll have the National Guard on you so fast that silly-looking hat will spin."

The Major took it, "My men are disciplined. You'll have no trouble from us." Wisely, the Major didn't show our cards. We want Fadden and his cronies to think we're loaded.

I'm tiring of Fadden's presence. We'd worked it all out. Now... "We've got a deal, Dr. Fadden. Now let us do our job. Let us beat Pitt."

"Ha!" he shot sarcastically, "Good luck!" On that, my men spread against the walls to show him the way out. He bounded through the room and the door, turned the corner, and disappeared, taking my athletic future with him. 'Ha! Good luck!' I think we have our battlecry.

"Goddamnit, Mason!" pressed Michael, "Why the hell did you do that? You just took yourself out of football! Jesus!" As with most everything, Michael feels responsible. A tinge of survivor's guilt, perhaps. I'm sure he thinks he's the one who should have taken the bullet.

"Listen, guys, a few things here," I started. "One, Fagden read the newspapers this morning, and he wanted my ass. He's not stupid, though. He has to have a ball game. He doesn't want an asterisk on the record, nor the lost revenue. That's why he let me play today. Any disturbance, like taking me out, Deep Throat, we'da walked. But, he made sure he got something."

"So, he gets the game and you," said Father Al.

"Right," I said, "he figures I'm expendable."

"But, you're not, Ivy," Arthur said in an uncharacteristic display of emotion, "You're our leader."

"I accept that, and I'm proud to be your leader," I whispered. I felt whimpers within, "We've talked about it, Michael. I'll do anything for this team." I'm one more sentence away from being Jello in the fetal position.

"I'm with you, man," Michael said, choking back.

Ted sat and buried his head in his hands, a twitching hillside of a man, inconsolable. Vinny walked up to me and embraced me. Our boyhood dreams are quickly fading away.

"Guys," said Father Al, "too much has happened to let this go to waste. Turn this emotion and this newly found faith you have in each other into something positive. There are a lot of different people here. A hundred stories. And there are blacks and there are whites. But, gentlemen, in this room of the leaders of this team, I feel love. I love for a living, dudes, and I know love when it's there. And it's here."

We're quiet. Despite our sincerity, the whole thing is getting kind of cornball. Michael did something about that.

"Love for a living, eh, Father?" he said, "Now there's a scandal." The laughter broke the uneasy strain built up from Fagden's visit. Hell, from the past two weeks.

Father Al laughed, too. "I think you know what I mean," he said grinning.

"You're a cool dude, Father," said Arthur, "We could find you a real good woman." Vinny spat a laugh. I don't think Arthur entirely understands Catholicism.

"Let's say the pope might frown on that," said Father, "So, before you wreck my vow to God and chastity, let's go out there and win this football game."

"I want this game, men," I said, moving up to pudding. "I want it for you. I want it for the fans in the stands. And I want it for me. I want this game." Adrenaline must have rushed in to help me regain composure. I feel stronger, capable of the job ahead. The captains and Arthur and Vinny joined in screams in the coach's office, testament to our found and refound togetherness, a state I'm sure we will have to rediscover all day today. You don't tear down lifetimes of intolerance with one victory over an insolent asshole. The most important thing I'll have to do today is keep the hundred men with the hundred different stories, as Father said, on task. And Fagden the budgetmeister ought to be happy. He's getting me cheap.

"Father," I said, "to paraphrase what they say in your business, let's go tell it to the mountains."

"After you, Coach," he replied, arms outstretched, showing me the way.

I led the five of us out of the office and back into the locker room. Right on time, too. The newness of being in their confines had worn off and the players were restless, close to a critical mass only an unsupervised kindergarten could match. They're looking for new toys. Standing on a chair, I began, "All right, men, here we go, again," I got their attention pretty quickly, so I continued, "Fagden just left and gave us his blessing. The team is officially ours, sanctioned by the administration!"

Cheers of approval rang out. The team broke into the all-too-familiar 'here we go!' chant. That went on for a minute or so until they gave the floor back to me.

"This is our game to win or lose. I think we'll win it." The hundred yelled again, complete with shrill cries and whistles. "Shortly, we'll have everything we'll need to play, including doctors. Of course, Pitt better have their own damn doctors because I feel like there's going to be a lot of hurtin' goin' on their side."

My men liked that one. More cheers interrupted me for several moments. I feel like Jack Kennedy on the stump at a union rally.

"So, just bide your time a little while longer, and hopefully we can at least get the tape over here and possibly the jockstraps so you don't have to sit on the training tables with your scrotums exposed."

More laughter. Now I feel like the white Lenny Bruce.

"Let's have positions meetings again…no, fuck, just relax. We'll have enough time to meet today. Just relax and wait on your gear and we'll take 'er from there."

Various calls of approval sounded out from the group. To be a team that had been jacked around for three days we are collectively in a pretty good mood. Soon, however, the uniforms and the pads will arrive and the familiar aroma of accumulated sweat will waft through the fieldhouse. That will be our sign to get down to the business of college football.

Forty thousand butts in the seats at, at least, ten dollars a pop, with contributions totaling in the hundreds of thousands on a per game basis just to get the choice seats. On top of that are radio and television rights, including the Holy Grail, ABC Sports, concessions, and advertising. Put it all together and you have yourself one mother of a business. I can add the numbers, but consider the sheer magnitude of it all. Compared to my junior high days of bake sales to buy new uniforms, all this can warp your mind if you let it. Fortunately, we have Fagden to take care of those details, and to his credit he does a good job. But he represents everything bad that can happen when you turn a boys' game into a profit center, with mean green looming over why we're really here.

Attention can be positive or negative. It's good, for instance, to have swooning coeds pulling their bras out from under their sweaters and asking you to autograph them. I don't see a problem with that. The bad arises when big business and big influence throw you the big bucks in the name of support, shielding the true intentions of running the show to further their old school sociology of how the team should be. Yes, we need the money...who doesn't? However, when the rich alums subscribe to the old University of Virginia adage, 'Our black boys can beat your niggers,' then the whole system rots from within, and you end up with Lawson and McNabb and one hundred anarchists who are happy as little children right now but don't honestly know without the guidance of a good experienced coach what the hell they're in for.

Saturday, November 8, 1975
10:20 AM

Preparing for the game

I'll say it for the third time: it's too late to turn back now. I'm the
coach for the day. And what a day. And it's going to take every ounce of
effort and faith and luck I can find to keep us believing. I'm committed
to it, but I'm scared shitless. Father just better stay within praying distance because I'm desperately going to need him.

Monty ambled up to me, "Hey, Ivy…Hey, man…I don't know what
to say.…"

"Monty," I said, "you'da done the same thing."

CC approached me, "We're gonna win it for you, Ivy. You're going out
a winner."

"CC, I'm going to win it for you. We're going to show Fagden and his
boys that you don't sell us out. We're going to beat those SOBs and we're
doin' it ourselves."

"Damn straight," said Monty. We put our three hands together
within our circle.

Pittsburgh's dead.

In spite of that display of emotion, I don't even want to think about
life after today, after football. I honestly can't remember ever not playing. My fears of yesterday, of wondering what I'm going to do after the
NFL turns me down; these fears have hit the beach with a resounding
blow. Despite the fact that a big part of my life has but six hours to live,
this isn't about me. We as a team have a lot to prove. We have to show
everyone that we can run and run hard against the racism that perme-
ates our culture and our individual souls while both taking the high
road and coming out on top. We're here. We're better friends than I
thought we would be. Now to complete it, I feel we've gotta win. Pitt's
always been the big rival, but no Pitt game or no college football game

for that matter has held more importance than the one we play in Montani this afternoon.

"Sir," said the nice militiaman who is twice my age but always calls me 'sir,' "The truck is out front at the door waiting to be unloaded." The news was overheard and spread quickly. We all crowded the door as if someone yelled 'Fire!' It was difficult to regain order and, as there are no grunt managers around to do it for us, we had to find some way to get the gear out quickly. So, Monty just lifted the door of the truck, crawled in, and started throwing bags out. Men caught them and searched for their numbers on the bags, a very disorganized way to do this, but who the hell's going to suggest anything different? The unloading continued at a frenetic pace, loud, like dogs fighting over pieces of meat. After only a few minutes of this, everyone had his gear and the bags are being opened and emptied, indicative of how badly my team wants to be normal again.

Now, this is the beginning of the football game day. The general mood has been uplifted as the odd mixture of light-hearted conversation and caveman guttural huffing filled the air. It's not playful. We are getting ready to perform in the man's game of men's games. The time has come to prepare to crack some serious heads. This isn't baseball or a track meet. Sure, the three are alike in that there is competition involved, but that's where it ends. Football goes beyond that. We hurt each other.

As I tried to tell the Taranucci sisters last night, it is very much different playing a game of supervised, controlled violence. Look at the pros. Major League Baseball plays one hundred sixty-two games in a season. The NBA, basketball, gets in eighty-two games. Neither of these includes the playoffs, if you're fortunate enough to make it. But football, NFL football, can barely squeeze in one a week, sixteen in all. If you make it to the Super Bowl, you play three more, and the pros themselves will tell you that's almost too much. As you can see, there is a lot of compensation made for the fact that in many cases it takes the entire week for the players to heal and regenerate. The colleges play fewer games, eleven in the season, and one more if you go to a bowl. But the similarities to the NFL remain. If the body is indeed the temple of the soul, then football is the wrecking ball that swings at it every week. And speaking of the soul, that's where it all comes from, where the courage resides to subject your frame to the incredible abuse it takes every Saturday. I've played a lot of sports and a lot of games. I will always attest to the fact that it takes much more bravery to step onto a football field than any other field or court of play.

We dress, pulling on our protective equipment, enveloping the shoulders, hips, thighs, knees, and the face and head. We get taped, ankles and knees, with braces being applied to us who possess the really bad joints. We get shots of cortisone and novacane, before the game and during the game, to relieve the pain and numb the pulls and rips and tears so we can keep on playin.' This is the sick part about football; the way we disregard any bodily damage in the name of manly fortitude, damage that would be debilitating to anyone in the stands. Through all this we center only on what it takes only what we have to do. This is why the leaders of our country send kids our age into battle. We can get psyched to do it.

The pads also serve to block the world from our brains. They separate us from everything else out there and focus us on the one hundred twenty yard by fifty-four yard rectangle of lined plastic grass where our respective manhoods will be tested in one afternoon fifty or sixty times. Fifty or sixty private battles not only with the man in front of you but also within yourself, where you force your body to do the things almost everyone else in the world wouldn't.

The breakfast. The wait. The arguments. More waiting. Then, finally, the stroll, during which the fans would have laid down palms had they had any (I don't want to think of historically what happened next).

Fadden. Still more waiting. The arrival of the gear. Dressing and taping. The entire process had brought us to twenty minutes after eleven o'clock. So, what do we do now in preparation for a one o'clock game? We wait.

Although there are no real coaches around to tell us what to do, we Runners by rote sat at our lockers in our own quiet astral planes of reflection. Occasionally one would intersect with his neighbors to his sides and across, but calm prevailed. I always thought we readily conformed to the coaches' orders for quiet because we knew within ourselves we had to both conserve energy and get in the right frame of mind. It's a time for right-brained thinking, an incubation of thoughts and beliefs to hatch the intuition it takes to play on this level.

I looked at Vinny. My organizational duties had taken me away from him since we arrived here. I guess I just assumed he's okay. It took a lot of moxie to stand up to his father as he did. It is the best thing that could have happened, for him and for the team. It's interesting how a father-son fight can improve a team's chances against a top-ranked squad, but Vinny looks ready. He worried me on the walk from our house to breakfast. Now, I think it's sunk in that he's his own man and his father knows how he feels. I glanced at him again. He gave me a thumbs up and a grin. I'll have plenty of chances to talk with him during the game as we progress through our unconventional coach-QB relationship, but now I need to check in with the Incredible Hulking Padre.

At the risk of interrupting any meditation he could have been in, I stepped over to Father Al. He saw me.

"What's up, heavy hitter?" Father asked me in a low tone.

I like that. Back to the matter at hand, "Would one call this a beginning, Father?" I asked, somewhat afraid to face the truth about our revolt.

"In a word, yes," he said, "And, it's both good and bad. The good is you're all laying your hearts on the line. The bad is you're all laying your hearts on the line."

I pondered that. "I guess this brings back memories for you," I replied.
"This is different and the same," he said.

"Father, you're packed full with dichotomies today, aren't you?"

"Yes, and allow me to explain," he began, "I know first-hand the dictatorial aspects of this game, benevolent or otherwise. You do what your coaches say, no questions asked. Well, Mason, you not only disobeyed your coaches, you tossed them out in an unprecedented insurrection. Believe me, this has shaken up the team, the entire state, and will eventually affect all college teams. Although all of you are part of it, you're the only one whose name appeared in the newspaper this morning as the guy who started it all."

The way he presented all it to me made my gut tighten up. He went on. "And, as the new leader, your primary job is to keep them facing in the same direction. This thing could get out of hand. I'll do my best, but blood is thicker than water. And you're blood, blood."

"It can't get much worse than this, can it, Father?" I asked, "So, tell me the same part."

"It's the same in that it's the right thing to do," he said, "Like Boston, there was no option. And sometimes that hurts like hell. And that's the reason I'm here."

We sat for a minute and let it all soak in. The heaviness of today could be stifling if I think of all the things that could go wrong. I decided to change the subject.

"You know, Father, we have all types here," I said, "You're well aware of how strange football players can be, even above their drinking, harassing, and overall derangement, much moreso than the average guy." Talk had picked up somewhat among us all and no one could hear us, so I felt safe in discussing my teammates with my priest. "See number sixty-eight over there. That's Andy Baum. He takes extra meat from training table to feed to his tarantulas and pirahhnas. Number fifty-seven near Andy, that's Andy Bruzinski. His house had rodents. He didn't call Orkin. He bought a couple of boas and just turned them loose. No more rats and mice. I've told you about number forty-four, Joe. If Communism kicks in hard, he'll dive in headfirst. He's told me he'll kill anybody for his country. That's special. Number seventy-five, Ted, your man, contracts himself out to events for crowd control. Read: bouncer. I've seen him. The man can bounce. And you know most everything about me," I closed in jest, "I thought about calling the pope to set up a plenary indulgence at the front doors before you got here."

Father Al laughed. "There's no need to do that. First of all, you think your team is odd? Cowboy, you ain't seen odd. We Jets…damn. And second, the plenary indulgence, the idea that one man can call an entrance to anything a cleansing medium? Who says they need to be cleansed anyway? And, speaking of that, and don't tell the bishop this, but I don't necessarily go for all the decorum hoopla of the Catholic Church. I mean, tradition is one thing, but too many of us get caught up in the rituals and forget the real meaning. There are people who won't touch the host with their hands but also won't step across the street to buy a poor man a cup of coffee. Don't get me wrong, Mason. There's a place for everything traditional, but it should be kept in its place."

I never thought I would get into a philosophical discussion with a priest in the fieldhouse before Pitt, but he's old AFL, so there must be something right about it.

"Yeah, Father, I've always wondered about Vatican II. All these things, like eating before mass, things that would have stranded you in purgatory in the fifties are now all of a sudden okay. Makes you think about the possibilities for Vatican III."

"Are you sure you're not going to call the bishop?" Father said, "Because if you're not, I'll tell you sometime how I really feel. You buy the Rolling Rock."

"Tell me now," I replied.

"Huh-uh," Father said, "I need to be half-crocked and you've got a football team to run. You've gotta concentrate on keeping these guys happy. I think you'd better get out on the field."

The fieldhouse clock read just before eleven-thirty. Usually around this time, the three quarterbacks, the two tight ends, and the top five receivers, a group that has included me all season long, went out on the field and threw around. The rest of the team then appeared about twenty minutes later. We all stretched and warmed up for forty minutes, then ajourned back in the fieldhouse for final meetings and instructions. The team always bitched about us receivers and QBs going out there first, always accusing us of grandstanding. With this in mind, I thought we could change some things today.

"Okay! All right! Listen up!" I yelled from my chair pulpit. After I got their attention, I continued, "Okay! Here we go! You know, I was just thinking...."

"Oh, no! Not again!" shouted Tim Seiler from the back. The place roared with laughter. I'm happy to hear that.

"All right! As I said, I was just thinking; the fans in the stands are probably wondering about us. Some of them saw us walking over here, but after this week, well, maybe we should all just go out there and show them we're dressed and ready!"

Sounds of loud affirmations resonated through the locker room. It's wonderful, but this still is one minute at a time.

"Michael, Ted! Lead the way!"

~ ~ ~ ~ ~ ~ ~ ~ ~ ~

Walking down the tunnel, I recalled the history of this stadium my old man passed on to me. Ridge Run is a creek that flows down Lewis Hill to Montani's Pine River, which empties into the Monongahela River and meanders north to Point Park and Three Rivers Stadium in Pittsburgh, there joining with the Allegheny River to form the headwaters of the mighty Ohio River. In 1912, W. T. Williams, a civil engineer and noted futurist and cocaine user, stood near the bottom of Ridge Run hollow (or holler if you're in the Dixie part of the state) and had an idea. If one with wood and concrete were to build rising stands up the sides of the hollow, he thought, one would have just enough space between them to put a football field encircled by a quarter-mile cinder track. And since the U's then-current stadium, Montani Field, a wooden structure seating only ten thousand brave souls, had gone past decrepit, the need for a new home for West Virginia football was definitely there. W. T. proposed his idea to the school's board. The muckity-mucks approved it right away since one of the board members had fallen through the cracked fourth row and broken a leg.

After routing Ridge Run through giant terra cota pipes, Williams, probably on a coke high, placed the field and the track over the pipes one year and built the grandstands the next. By 1914, the engineer had his stadium, and also due to his social behavior and unpopular politics he had his commitment to the state sanitary hospital for 'hallucinations and psychoses.' A week later, the team took the field for the first time in the new stadium named Ridge Field. The team changed its nickname from the Surveyors, a ridiculous sounding moniker that was chosen with respect to George Washington to the equally ridiculous but more geographically correct Ridge Runners, which as I said before is cooler if you use only the second word.

During the Depression decade, the Civilian Conversation Corps, probably again because of politics since Ridge Field has nothing to do with conservation, built free-standing bleacher seats from wood and steel twenty rows high in the space behind the north end zone, up the creek. Finally, employing ex-soldiers returning from the war in the late 40s to build a concrete structure as a replacement for the bleachers, the civil engineering faculty and seniors went to the drawing boards to round the stadium out, making Ridge Field horseshoe-shaped around the gridiron. The Bowl was born. More bleachers were added in the south end zone during the mid 60s and that gives you the current configuration, seating the forty thousand. Ohio State, Michigan, Notre Dame, and Penn State, just to name a few, seat twice as many, but I am convinced that no stadium in the country rocks one end zone as do our students in their half of the horseshoe, The Bowl.

To our pleasure, that's what we ran into as we emerged from the tunnel leading from the fieldhouse under The Bowl to the field. Usually, it takes until twelve thirty to pack everybody in. Today, however, they're at least a full hour early and have the place shaking and rattling. We stood in that north end zone, the same one that enthralled me as a boy, and greeted the students, a hundred of us with arms and fists gyrating in the air, doing our part to start the chain reaction going. We fire them up and they fire us up even more, and on and on until you think the emotions can't get any stronger. But they do; they do for a full five minutes.

I gotta think now the students like what they've read in the papers and heard as scuttlebutt in the streets this morning. We are all typical young adults, trying, pressing, stretching, questioning. Our players have for the most part welcomed the new coaching assignments so far. Think of how the student body feels, who as a whole are more liberal than we are and therefore much more prone to accept change. We are not that far removed from 1968. The students obviously dig this. We've resurrected the protest movements. In doing so, we stuck it to the brass, the big dogs, and have assimilated the fantasies they've held throughout their teen years, chimeras of rebellion against authority, against the government, 'the pigs,' their teachers. Against their parents.

The torch has been passed from the Woodstock Generation to us, the Watergate Kids. We the students and the jocks, banded together as those Kids, raise that torch to the sky, burning bright and hot, but guess what? The Vietnam War is over, Nixon's out, the economic pump has been primed, and protests have left the streets. The hippies, yippies, flower children, and other members of the counterculture have given us all this momentum, but there is nothing to fight against. Until this week. Well, just as before, we're going to raise hell and force ourselves to be heard. But, we're going to do it our way. Instead of a summer of love as in 1967, or, on the other end of the spectrum, instead of using violence as with the bombings by the underground Weathermen, we sneaked in the back door, threw the bums out, incorporated the centuries-old concept of a militia, gave them empty rifles, staged a peaceful march, and invited ten thousand of our fellow Kids to watch us play a football game. Football. We're going to use football, oddly enough one of the institutions our predecessors railed against.

Several years ago, the protesters listened to Bob Dylan while the jocks had their radios tuned to Hank Williams and The Temptations. Clothes, lingo, haircuts, lifestyles; they were miles apart. Today, as Linda Ronstadt sang, we all still march to the beat of a different drum. But by God, one of our black Kids got screwed by the White Establishment. And today, we stand together against the racism that still defines our times in our attempt to effect change. The forum is distinct, but the cause remains the same.

Saturday, November 8, 1975
11:30 AM

The women and friends and family at the game (third person)

Against and within the backdrop of all those students and all that hair and all the yelling and partying and passing of the joints stand two remarkably attractive women, so striking, so well-but-appropriately-for-a-football-Saturday-afternoon dressed. Wool blazers, colorful sweaters, denims, and pricey boots. In silence they take it all in, amused by the energy vibrating throughout that curvature of the stadium. Their actions and reactions to the crowd are consistent with their stations in life. Having a bit more maturity than their neighbors, they're satisfied to do what they would not have done six years ago, decline the marijuana offered to them and just watch.

"There," Joan said, pointing to the players on the field, "that's him. That's Mason. Number eighty-eight."

Pamela Kissinger looked from her seat in row AA to see the player her younger sister referred her to, smaller than the others, but just as cranked up.

"So, that's your new boyfriend," Pamela said with a smile and a dig.

"I don't know what he is," said Joan in a tone of worry, "Up until a couple of days ago, he was my friend and my tutor. Now...."

Pamela had both the added advantage and the curse of being a PhD in psychology also from Northwestern, just finishing her first year in a lucrative downtown Chicago practice with other psychologists and a couple of psychiatrists. It's often good to know what's going on in other people's minds, she has surmised, but sometimes it's not. She'd rather have the day off today and not be in her sister's brain, but the training as well as the years and years of growing up in the same mansion with their sixth generation banker family have landed her there. Oh, well, the doctor is in, she thought. Not wanting to sound like she's treating Joan as a patient, or clients as they are referred to in her posh office, she also doesn't want to miss this opportunity to help her sister out of a jam.

"Now?" asked Pamela.

As a general rule, Joan does not open up to people. She prefers to keep it pleasantly superficial. But this is kin; not just any kin, but her only sister, a person who knows of everything Joan has done because Joan has told her. As Carly Simon, their favorite female artist sang, 'We have no secrets. / We tell each other everything. / About the lovers in our past, / and why they didn't last.'

"Now there are these feelings," Joan replied.

"Feelings? What feelings?" asked Pamela, "Love? Friendship? Horniness?" She decided she was now probing and thought it was better to back it off a couple of turns.

"He started it," Joan said defensively. "He wrote me a letter. In it he told me he loves me."

"Well, that's never happened before," Pamela said sarcastically. Joan gave her a look of disgust.

So far nothing surprised Pamela, having the benefit from previous telephone calls, letters, and a couple of wine-laced visits to know some of the vitals of Mason. She knows he's nineteen, extremely bright, a football player but well read, worked hard, and the students liked him for the same reasons Joan did, because he is a nice guy.

Joan spoke of Mason atypically more than she would a friend, not as a prospective beau, it seemed, but as if she were observing him. It also struck Pamela as interesting that Joan mentioned Mason more than she had any other guy in several years. However, as Joan's talk with Pamela progressed over the past few weeks, the psychologist and sister in her seriously doubted these feelings began just a couple of days ago.

"What does all this mean to you?" asked Pamela, skirting an analysis of Mason for now, "Please forgive me if I sound like your doctor and I won't bill you."

"He's a friend, I think," responded Joan, "That's how I feel, or I think I feel. And just bill Dad."

The sisters laughed, knowing their father would probably pay it.

The Runners left the sideline and end line to the biggest cheers of the day. They spread across their half of the field to loosen up and warm up. The crowd noise then started to die down only slightly, but everybody remained standing. Pamela continued to work.

"Do you find anything unusual about the last statement?" Pamela asked.

"About Dad?" asked Joan.

"We'll eventually get to him, but what you said about Mason being a friend."

Joan still didn't get it. "What about it?"

Pamela gave her one hint, "About Mason being a guy and being a friend."

Clueless, Joan glanced at her sister and shrugged.

"I don't know of any guy friend of yours you talk about as much as you've talked with me about Mason," said Pamela, "I feel like I know him. I've even seen a snapshot of him. Cute, but when have you ever taken the trouble to show me a picture of a guy you weren't going out with?"

Joan looked straight across the field toward the scoreboard in the south end zone. "Are you saying I'm destined to go out with Mason?" Not allowing her sister to respond, she quickly continued, "Go out? I can't do that. There is an explicit stipulation about faculty and students. It can't happen! That can't be tainted with tawdry, cheap…you know. There's a professional trust between us."

Pamela resisted smiling. Her sister is like many of her clients. The more words they emit, the more confused they are. The psychologist sat in silence.

Joan stared at Pamela. From the neck down, they are fantastically the same. But Pamela's eyes are warmer, her hair is lighter and curlier, and her lips are more pronounced. Two knockouts, sitting within whiffs of pot smoke, considering life and romance.

"Usually people use such rules to stop something they can't stop themselves," Pamela started, "But, I know you, Joan. I think you left it open. You didn't close the ultimate door with the rule. You didn't say 'no,' did you?"

"I told him I don't date students," Joan said, "And I have a duty."

"So you didn't say you wouldn't date him. He's a student, but not one of your students. Look, every rejection is code for 'Sell me.' Every rejection is an opportunity to discuss. What does that mean to you?"

Joan sat in silence, blank, not looking as if she's thinking about anything, maybe afraid to think about anything. Afraid to face the rolling of *the thunder. Afraid to face the truth. The truth Pamela knows by being an astute observer. The truth Joan knows by being unable to get the sensuality of the previous night with Mason out of her mind.*

"Mason and I were together last night."

Not surprised in a professional sense, but still astounded by her little sister with the banker's mentality when it concerns matters of love and the flesh, Pamela turned to Joan and said in a deeper voice, "There goes duty. Tell me about it."

"We weren't together together," Joan clarified, softening the admission, "It's scary because that could have happened. I might have let it happen. I think I wanted it to happen."

"Where were you?" asked Pamela, "At your house?"

"We were at Michele's. I went over there because I was sitting lonely at home, thinking of Mason. Kind of sick, right? I had just opened my second beer, and I said to myself, 'I'm drinking alone. I'm pining over a college sophomore, something I hadn't done in almost nine years, and I'm drinking alone!' I had to get out of there, so I called Michele. She invited me over."

Pamela goes down paths such as these daily, but this one was so close to home it had her confused. She knows Joan and knows psych, and figured the best thing to do is to keep her talking.

"I thought you didn't like Michele."

"No, she doesn't like me."

"But she invited to you to her home."

"Well, she must like me better now."

The event surrounding them had quieted and turned into a regular pregame. They lowered the volume. "So, you're at Michele's...," Pamela said, trying to keep her on track.

"I'm there, and she offers me my third beer, but it's that West Virginia brew and it's really like water, I understand, but I'm still a little tipsy.

Michele took that opportunity to tell me Mason's coming over. I hand her my beer and say, 'Give me the hard stuff. Give me a Michelob.'"

Pamela allowed herself a giggle inside and a grin on her lips. Her sister sometimes has a dry wit. But something has been left unexplained.

"What's this between Michele and Mason? Why would he call her and visit her?"

"She's his writing instructor and has this 'special' relationship with her, the bitch."

"Special? Does he love her, too? Is he running through the female faculty?"

"No, it's not like that, they say. And I believe them. I can tell. Mason looks at me differently than he looks at her. They're like frat brothers."

Nothing wrong with that, thought Pamela. But, the 'bitch' comment; envy at its finest.

"Anyway," Joan continued, "Mason arrives and I can tell by the look on his face that he's very surprised to see me. So, we sit, we talk, and then we decide to talk in private."

"Who else is there?"

"Michele's sister MJo and Mason's friend Vinny. He's number twelve down there."

Pamela turns to find a twelve throwing the ball. "So the college quarterback was at this party. That was game night. What were they doing out?"

"Vinny hates his father and Michele offered them, Mason and him, her guest room."

Beginning to think she could be on call here for the entire weekend taking care of everybody, Pamela shook it off to get herself back on task. "Okay, so you and Mason are together, alone."

"Yes," said Joan, "we just talk and talk more. I'm leaning on one end of the bed, he's on the other."

"Bed," replied Pamela.

"Yeah," continued Joan, "It was the only place to sit. Anyway, talk and talk, then I find myself moving over to him and we kiss and kiss."

And there went professional trust, Pamela thought. She paused to reflect on how Mason must have felt then, a kid with a woman like Joan. Wow. "And…," Pamela said, beginning to get caught up in the 'soap' of it all.

"He's such a gentleman, damn him." The two laugh softly. "No, really, he is so sweet. He professed his love, and…."

"Again?"

"Several times," said Joan.

"What did you do?"

"I explained to him that for many reasons there would be too many obstacles to overcome. But, I also told him he could be the one to break my heart."

Damn, thought Pamela, glossing over Joan's 'obstacles.' "Could he really be?"

"I don't know. I really have never met anyone quite like him."

Resisting the overwhelming temptation to make a paperback diagnosis, Pamela dug in to find more questions. After another pause, she asked, "Does that scare you?"

"What?" asked Joan in earnest.

"The fact that Mason is so unique and so close, maybe too close," responded Pamela.

"Yeah, he's close, all right," Joan said, "But, I'd hate to see him go away. Mason has been doing very well as my tutor. He's like an extension of me."

"That's Fruedian."

"Professionally!" exclaimed Joan, maybe a little too loudly. A few students turned. She didn't recognize them and didn't want to risk it again, but she also didn't want to change topics now. 'On their feet' for a semi-private walk meant 'lose their seat,' so Joan decided to stay and continue. All the while, Pamela sat and smiled. She normally led her clients farther through the maze, but this is her sister, a lot has been said, and her opinion

now just may pull out more information. Besides, she knows exactly what's going on here, and she's just about to die!

"Joan," Pamela started, "he's obviously an outstanding young man and you're smitten with him."

"Smitten?" Joan shot back, but softly, "You make it sound like I'm a teen again!"

"Joan, darling," Pamela continued, "Think about it, but not from the aspect of being a teen. Look at college. We're not that far removed, and you're even closer to it than I am because you are with them daily. A couple more years of instruction and a thesis and they're you."

"But those years, Pamela, as I've told Mason, are very critical years."

"That's true, Sis, but for the average college student, especially males, especially frat males or the average football player even. We've already established Mason has moved beyond all that. You two are chronologically apart but romantically converging. Look at you. You're drinking beer again. Remember Jonathan the older guy when you were studying for your masters. He had you on a more sophisticated vodka and water."

Joan looked pensive. Pamela tried to comfort her. "It's only natural, Joan. What I've said, I'm just trying to show you that you are by far not crazy for having these feelings."

"I even set up a joint teaching session yesterday with the two of us," said Joan, "I allowed him in because he as the tutor had been getting along with the students so well. He's so bright, I knew he could do it. I also thought in a sneaky way that I would put him in their element and he'd respond as them and let me off the hook. Besides, there's this coed in there. Jennifer."

"Jennifer," repeated Pamela.

"Jennifer."

From envy to jealousy, smiled Pamela. "What happened?" asked Pamela, already knowing.

"He was like a second professor, the fucker."

Pamela laughed. That pissed off Joan a bit. "Sorry, Sis."

"And the troubles with the team? Guess who ratted to the newspapers about the coach?"

Pamela thought she was beyond surprise. "Why?"

"Someone gave him the evidence and he didn't like the way his black friend was being treated."

"That's very admirable of him," Pamela said, "Did he tell you this?"

"Yes, and it was in this morning's paper that he is the informant."

"He's got scruples," Pamela said. "And balls. That can't be all bad."

"And, I called him at his house this morning," sprung Joan, full of surprises today.

"Joan!" Pamela quietly exclaimed, "You've never called a guy! Have you?"

"No," replied Joan, "He's a first. I was also very suggestive."

"What were you suggesting?" Pamela asked slowly.

"That I want him to meet us tonight and what I wanted to do last night."

"I alter my analysis," said Pamela, "You're beyond smitten."

"What the hell does that mean?"

"You're in love, Joan."

"Oh shit! That can't be!"

"I know you. It could be. It is."

"But, we can't go out," Joan groaned.

"But you can go in," Pamela said.

Realizing her sister might know what she is talking about, Joan whispered, "Oh, God, help me!"

"Think about it, Joan. Maybe He already has."

"What?" Joan asked, shocked at Pamela's assertion.

"What's so bad about it? Live a little. Make this guy's lifetime and help yourself to a hunky slice of the pie in the meantime. Besides, I really think you are in love with Mason. You by your own admission admire him. You said you can't imagine life without him, professionally, you said, but I think there is more to it. You two have talked about everything, and I mean after this morning everything. He admits he loves you. You like that, I *know you do. You've ruminated over him, been jealous of others who vie for his attention, and you've gotten drunk over him. Sounds to me like he's the number one guy in your heart right now. And you know something? There's absolutely nothing wrong with that. Nothing at all."*

"How could I take him home to Mom and Dad? He's so young. They'd crucify me." Joan said.

"When lately have you ever worried about what Mom and Dad think? Stop setting up roadblocks with Mason. Jump in and take it a step at a time, Sis. Explore. If there is something to it, it will all fall into place," said the Head Doctor.

"This is insanity!" Joan anguished.

"I've seen insanity, Joan. Compared to some of the things out there, this is boring. Have some fun! Let it flow. Grasp your man. Love him like I know you want to." Pamela has seen Joan in various states of enchantment, usually enchanting the guys. Now, however, she thinks the table has been turned on her sister. And she thinks it is better than what she the doctor could ever order.

"I could get into a lot of trouble with the school," Joan said, in an attempt to pull herself out of a hole.

"I know. I know. Love never comes without tradeoffs," countered Pamela, "But, I do know you, Joan. You're wise in these matters, and discreet. And it sounds as if he would do anything for you, including sneaking around. Just go for it."

"Oh, I don't...," Joan said, "I'm confused and scared."

"Only natural," said Pamela, "But, don't drop the thought. Think of how nice you say he is. Think of what a gentleman you say he is. You've always had a pretty good handle on that. I believe you. Think of how much he loves you. Then, take one good look at him in those tight football pants down there. What do you think you ought to do?"

The two sisters sat still in contemplation. *After several moments, a student, a male, yelled from behind them, "Hey! I just heard on the radio that the team threw out all the coaches. They're going to run the game themselves!"*

"I'll be damned," exclaimed another student.

"Wonder who got all that started?" giggled a coed to Pamela's right.

Joan quickly looked down and to her left just as Judy Lambert a couple of rows away stood and glanced up and to her right. Their eyes fixed instantly. Despite having seldom few words not pertaining to American Literature, each knew what the other is thinking now.

"Mason, you goddamned fool!" Alice admonished under her breath, hoping her housemate can hear her telepathically, but knowing that if he did he wouldn't listen anyway. Beside Alice in row X sat Judy to her left and Jennifer to her right, who heard the sound of her man's name whisper from her buddy's lips.

"What about Mason?" asked Jennifer.

Alice caught that not-a-clue look on her sorority sister's face and thought seriously about saying she just saw him fall down out on the field somewhere.

No women understand Mason the way Alice and Judy do. From early on, they knew him as a guy who lived on the edge, and unconventional thinker at best, but more realistically as the boy with the big ideas. Mason was Alice's boyfriend for thirteen days as a freshman until she had the gut feel that life with the man as her romantic lover would be one daredevil stunt after another. Judy eventually rates every man with her 'husband material/not husband material' meter and she readily saw Mason pegged it to the latter. But something kept them hanging around, an intrinsic sweetness he displayed, or perhaps his unwavering loyalty for Vinny, a loyalty he readily shared with the girls. He went from interesting to tolerable to a friend in a matter of weeks. They came to view him as a person with the 'stuff' who could back it up, a real stand-up guy.

The four became as good of friends as any eighteen year olds can be. Fortuitous this was for Mason, because the girls were with him as he suffered through the short but tragic illness and death of his mother last spring. Alice and Judy witnessed a vulnerable, very alone side of Mason. They came to the conclusion together, being the good women they are, that he needed them just as much as they needed him. A couple of weeks later they all four signed for the house as the girls shared themselves as Mason's extended family. He knew what they were doing and why. He thanked them endlessly, wondering aloud how he could ever repay them for their kindness. Judy surprised herself by saying simply, "Just be yourself. That's more than enough." Alice wholeheartedly concurred.

Now the two women sit together after one hell of a week, after the Montani newspaper, Joan, the fight with Ron, Vinny's fight with his dad, and what appears to be Mason's leadership of a palace coup.

Alice said to Judy in low tones, "I think Mason's really done it this time."

"No shit," said Judy.

"Alice, honey," said Jennifer, "you keep mentioning Mason. What's up?"

"That fucking bastard," spat Jean. As always, she thought, he's screwing everything up.

Jean held in her mind since she first started paying attention to her mother and to boys what the perfect man would be. As an adolescent she learned early of her propensity through her superior beauty and intellect to command the male gender. She honed these skills in high school, and showed up last year at Montani prepared to find that dream man, with the looks, the brains, the bright future, and the willingness to allow her to rule. To her good fortune, it took but a few weeks. She met him, Vinny Vacca, the new friend of her suitemate Judy. With total disregard to how Judy might feel about this, and while wearing her favorite powder blue tight tee shirt and cut-off denim short-shorts, Jean in a single conversation with Vinny knew she had made the catch. Deeming it both risky and futile to wait for another, she persuaded him with blue-eyed seduction that theirs was the relationship for the ages. Within several days, they were inseparable.

Her only mistake, a common one as far as eighteen year olds and part-
nerships go, was that she didn't take the interview process far enough.
Having already committed herself to Vinny as The One, she did not until
later figure out the prominence Mason held with her man. Jean was surprised to find out how attached the young men were, despite the differences
between the two with respect to reverence to authority and conformity.
This phenomenon really gave her problems when it became obvious that
Vinny without Mason was not an option. She saw the years and decades of
future concessions she would have to make. Mason was the only clinker in
the pursuit of Vinny's perfection, and it was enough to make her consider
scrapping the entire project. That is, until she met Mike Vacca. The two hit
it off instantly as Vinny's father readily saw that he and his son's new girlfriend were in agreement on Vinny's place in the world. Jean decided to
stay. She had Her Program in place with the man on her side, the man who
would be the one to keep her man on track. And it was that program that
allowed her man to share a house with her two friends after her mother
insisted she live with the sorority for at least a year. That, and the fact that
Alice nor Judy didn't have a prayer in matching her body and what she had
learned to do to Vinny with it.

Jean saw football as a line on Vinny's future resume. She figured it was
enough to have simply dressed as a Runner quarterback for Big Eight
accounting firms to take notice, so she didn't concern herself much with
Vinny's advancement on the depth chart. But Jean is an opportunist.
When she saw Vinny's competition go down as walking hospitals, she recognized the potential one start against the number one team in the nation
on national television would have when the offers to become partner are
made in ten years or so. Therefore, she fervently jumped on the new quarterback's bandwagon. She was not even deterred by Vinny's display of
white hot anger this morning and even forgave him for running away last
night, chalking it all up to pregame nerves. She just walked to the game this
morning to await for the seeds to be sown. Now apparently, Mason The
Blight, who else could it be, has led an uprising and therefore threatens to

spoil her man's chance of a lifetime. Vinny will be guilty by association of all his friend's sins. This throws a wrench into the finely tuned works of her Grand Design, and about this she sits in the cool autumn air and does her best slow burn.

This year the Lamberts and the Calires by luck had garnered seats beside Mike, near the seats he had held since 1963. The older Vacca felt good about having his new friends around. It had been a long stretch of loneliness for Mike, an emptiness to which no true man, no true ex-Marine would ever admit. He very much missed the company of his late friend and DI Bazooka Frank, one tough Guadalcanal warrior he looked upon as a personal hero. Having Wayne and Rob with him this season was just what Mike needed to get him through these football afternoons in Montani. Although his two new companions didn't share the same experiences, with Wayne being an old Navy guy stationed at Great Lakes during Korea and Rob in the Army in West Germany far removed from the action, Mike made the best of the enjoyment of having the men with him on these Saturdays.

Today is special, and had also quickly become frustrating. Mike felt the overpowering pride that would of course come from a man who fathered the starting quarterback, giving him the edge he always enjoys having, the edge over the other men. He also would glance down the row at Sal and Dom and imagine Vaccas owning the quarterback position, not only here but possibly the with the Eastern Independents for years to come.

But as always for Mike, he views the world as revolving around him. Just a few minutes ago, he had found out the news of the players' revolt. He knew for a fact who started it all and had guessed correctly who the leader was. Feeling the contradiction of his unwavering respect and admiration for The Bazooka along side his complete disregard and acrimony unable to be quelled for The Bazooka's younger son, Mike was angry beyond words. Mason had indeed rendered his son's day in the sun invalid at the absolute best, ruining the father's chance at greatness, with Vinny's first start to historically become a bad joke.

Wayne and Rob and Geri and Pauline, joined by Patricia, sensed Mike's utter frustration. This time without saying anything to each other they agreed with him. Being the informant to the newspaper was something to be proud of, they collectively thought, but now the kid whom they felt in their own ways a duty to care for had stepped far over the line. They were disappointed in him, and in their varying degrees as responsible adults feared the worst of possible outcomes for the team which represents the college to which they pay all that money.

~ ~ ~ ~ ~ ~ ~ ~ ~ ~

"Who?" pled Jennifer, "Why's Mason a fucking bastard?"

Miss Pierce hasn't a pretentious thought in her mind. In her past she was well cared for by two loving parent partners and allowed to trust, as contrasted to Jean and her autocratic mother and detached father. But, the roomies from the sorority house still get along well even though they have one major difference of opinion. Jennifer believes in Mason. She sees what Jean sees, but she looks at Mason from another angle. Jennifer views her man as having everything she had ever hoped for and is confident that he will fulfill the unlimited potential she thinks he possesses. This sounds somewhat like Jean and Vinny, but she and her friend are going about it different ways. She's going to allow Mason to live as he sees fit. Jennifer thinks the attributes of Mason Jean despises are the ones that will carry him far. Even above all that, beyond his recalcitrance toward and willingness to fight selflessly against anything unfair, Jennifer has found a golden heart in Mason. She has also found that heart to be somewhat scarred by pain. She wants to massage that heart and truly thinks that despite the risk Mason's pain has for her, there is no other man she knows who is more deserving of her affections. That's why she has offered him everything she can to soothe the pain, and proved it to him last night by chasing him across town in nothing but a raincoat and lingerie.

Extremely proud of Mason's contribution to Coach Lawson's demise, Jennifer sees the actions he has taken as a college sophomore are indicative of boundless courage, the trait of his she most admires. She is the woman depicted on the covers of paperback romance novels, clinging to the love of her life, herself idealistic and strong, willing to do anything for the man she so adores, to advance his strengths and help him overcome his demons. Even if that devil is disguised as a very sexy instructor of English.

~ ~ ~ ~ ~ ~ ~ ~ ~ ~ ~

Michele and MJo are seated in Row S off to the left of Joan and Pamela. She also stood to face her colleague when she overheard the radio report of the locker room subversion. Joan saw Michele after glancing at Judy. Michele shrugged. Knowing there was no way she could make it up the several rows to talk, she placed the thumb of her right hand to her ear and the pinkie to her mouth, the sign to 'call me.' Joan nodded and made a mental note to do so

MJo turned to her sister and said, "Can you believe it? We are among the instigators of the topple of university administration! I missed the chance to do it in college. It's damned exciting!"

"When you consider the fact you could refer to me as university administration, it's…fuckin' great!" Michele exclaimed, giggling, "God, I'm so proud of my boy. I've taught him well. He's in a helluva lot of trouble now."

"I love it!" squealed MJo, "I didn't know who I was going to root for today. Last night, that Vinny got me on his side."

"That's not the only thing he got you on."

"I'm true to my marriage, you bitch!" MJo yelled in jest, but for everyone to hear. The crowd around the Taranucci sisters turned in wonder. Michele and MJo didn't care.

"In action. But, thoughts…."

"True, Michele, a different story. Anyway, I want to see the rebels take this one."

"Yeah, wouldn't that be great?" Michele offered dreamily, "I've been Pitt since I can remember, but our boys have stolen my heart."

"Our boys," MJo said, "Ya think Sports Illustrated will want to talk to us if…what the hell am I thinking? Jimmy reads that! Oh, he wouldn't understand!"

Now, the folks in Rows R and T are really being entertained.

"He knows you're faithful," Michele said.

"Yeah, but that's just between him and me. Of course, two more beers, and…."

"Back to the slut days for you, honey."

"Mickey! You're one to talk!"

A guy in the row below Michele turned around to MJo. He'd heard the entire conversation and figured the two foxes are primed. "Uh…I've been listening to you two have your sisterly talk for a while now. I'm Brad. This is Bobby," Brad said, introducing his friend to Michele. "You two wanna come to join us tonight for a party?"

Michele spoke for her sister, "Brad, Bobby, fuck off, okay?"

Saturday November 8, 1975
11:40 AM

On the field for warm-ups

Vinny is putting all his weight on my left leg, stretching the ham out. I studied his face. He is focused and determined and relaxed, just as a quarterback should be, very much unlike The Kid who if the opponent had any chance of winning carried the blurring countenance of worry. However, I'm not fooling myself. I checked out Pitt when they hit the field just a few minutes ago. They're huge, muscular, fast, and worthy of their top billing. I simply feel Vinny can do the job. There is no objective reason to think this. He's vastly inexperienced, not really big, and still young. There is a giant difference between twenty and twenty-two, or so Joan tells me, not counting what she told me this morning. I know my Gunner. I know what goes on in his head. And what's upstairs with the boy today will carry us through. I just know it.

He changed to my right leg. We hadn't said anything during these exercises. Our eyes met. He gave me a wink, one that says, ' and away we go!' Then he smiled. I smiled back, and finally spoke, "We get to work together today, Gunner. Not the way we had planned it, but nevertheless."

"I'll accept any advice you give me," Vinny said as he laid on the field and I began working on his legs. "I'm open."

"Think about this," I said, "Don't shelve your high school passing game. I predict we'll need it by half-time."

"Do you predict this, or plan on it?"

"I come here with no preconceived notions. I'm a virginal neophyte. But, we shall see."

"There's nothing virginal about you, Mason." I considered that as I switched legs. "You're boyishly handsome, but that bullshit stops right there. You'll be able to carry this team."

I'm flattered by my own best friend. What a charmer he is when he's on. If Jean were to check out it would take him, oh, a few minutes to find another extremely suitable companion.

"Thanks, Vinny. I just want to be worthy of the job."

"Worthy or not, you've got it. No one else will want it."

"Don't remind me."

Time for passing drills. Receivers line up on both sides of half the field. The QBs stand in the middle, take snaps from the centers, and throw to the wideouts running routes and working on cuts and timing. This goes on for a little less than a half-hour. Despite my lowly status among my fellow teammates, I got to catch about a baker's dozen of The

Gunner's passes. He is crisp, throwing short and long with accuracy and aplomb. And my confidence, confidence with regard to Michael, Joe, Ted, Arthur, and all the Runners I already possess, grew to cockiness as I watched him. I heard the money had stacked up on Pitt so much Vegas pulled the game from their card. In other words, there is no line. Mathematically speaking, Pitt is an infinite favorite. Standing on the field watching Vinny throwing ropes and rainbows, I feel as if I know something about which the rest of the country has no idea. This must have been how it was for the guy who discovered Norma Jean.

The general mood of the team is uplifting. We spent half the morning not knowing if we would even get out here, so we are excited to be headed in the right direction. And we did not cringe in sharing the field with the preordained national champions. In fact, a lot of jawing and woofing ensued, most of it originating from our guys. We're talking trash, and why not? This is our house. They're coming into our house and expect us to bow down? Not us. Not the 1975 Runners. Penn State was goddamned lucky to escape us and that was with a boy as our quarterback. We've been through more adversity in a couple of days than Pitt has seen all year. We're tough, man. And we've got thousands and thousands of students surrounding us screaming madly. Your championship run goes through Montani, Pitt, and you'd better be ready.

I stole a look at Drew Osberg. Just under six feet, cut high, narrow waist, big legs. He looked fast just talking to one of his coaches. I glanced over at Michael. He's doing the same thing, checking out Drew. Our eyes met. Michael smiled big. Pitt averages forty-nine points a game. Do they possibly think they're going to hang seven touchdowns on Michael? They're nuts if they do.

The lines are really coming off on the count. Because they don't do much of anything during warm-ups, they're difficult to read. I'm difficult to read, too, but I just have this feeling. I can see Pitt players being flat blocked and Pitt QBs on their butts. Of course, I'm one of the world's greatest Runners fans and a charter optimist. We shall see.

What the hell am I going to tell these guys when we get back in the locker room for pre-game? My purpose here is to provide a semblance of order and an impetus. The stories of fiery pre-game speeches are myths, anyway. They don't need anybody, much less a sophomore walk-on, to urge them to play their hearts out. They've shown a lot of heart just walking over here. I don't know what to say. Maybe if I stop worrying about it and just speak from the soul, and not too much, less is more, maybe that will be what we need. I have been able to say the right things lately. Look at Joan. My true feelings came out there, and see what happened? Open-mouthed kisses and All That Jazz. And Thursday, to think it was 'You are so full of shit, Mason Bricker.' I knew the embrace on my porch was meaningful. It was worth the few moments when I didn't know if I was going to live or die.

Saturday November 8, 1975
12:40 PM

The pre-game speech

We left the field to the standing ovation with which we were greeted. The militiamen remained out there guarding the sidelines and our bench to remind the higher-ups concerned they aren't fucking with just anybody. I ran through the tunnel, trying to find a way to keep this crowd in the game. Maybe the secret is to keep us in the game. That's not rocket science. I hope and pray we can pull off this second play of the game. If Vinny finds Dhali, seismologists will register the stadium on the Richter scale.

The men took their places in our last pre-game meetings. I attended with my backs and receivers. Dhali and Clark are bordering on smug. Arthur's pacing the floor, his ritual. He's a sedate man off the field, but the closer it gets to opening kickoff, he's like a thoroughbred in the gate. Frank's sitting in the middle of us, probably channeling his thoughts into the broken leg of some Pitt linebacker. Then, Vinny stepped in like a professor. You could see the respect from the others. They were with him in warm-ups. They caught his passes. We haven't seen anything like that this year. Vinny's eyes, the way he's holding his chin. He oozes surety and conviction. That's being transferred through the air from him to us. The University of West Virginia stole a Blue Chip two years ago. If it weren't for me, he'd be elsewhere. My contribution to my favorite team.

"Dhali," Vinny said, "how does that floater feel?"

"Great, Vinny," replied Dhali, "I think you've got it down to a fine art." Vinny smiled.

"Now," he said, "normal game plan. Establish the run. Loosen them up with the pass. Johnny," Vinny said to the new tight end, a man very nervous, "I'm looking for you. You look for holes underneath and tell me about it." Johnny nodded. His face is really white. "We'll hit the second play, I can feel it." Vinny said, "But, just remember: chip away at these guys. We're good. We'll get our points. Don't worry and by all means, don't get frustrated. I'll take care of you."

I'm chest busting proud of my man Vinny. I can see it. He's got us convinced we are going to win this game.

There wasn't in my estimation much left to say in the meetings. We're becoming repetitive and the players are about to explode…again. The clock read ten 'til one. It's early, but I decided it's time for all to come together and talk about it.

It's also time to drop any concerns I have about PD. This is now a football game. Any ramifications will be dealt with afterwards. It could get really bad. The question remains: who was set up? PD by McNabb or Lawson and me by PD? Put it in the back of your mind….

"Okay, gentlemen," I announced. Funny, addressing my teammates as gentlemen, considering we won't be satisfied until each and every Pitt player is carried off the field on a stretcher. "We're just about ready." I moved to the middle of the long lines of lockers. Gazing around, I see I have everyone's attention. I still can't believe the position I'm in. Responsible for the tempo of this game, everything has led up to this point in time. Still not knowing exactly what to say, I started, "First, and most importantly, allow me to say that being your coach and being part of today is by far the proudest moment of my life. Nothing matches it, or comes even close. And with due regard to that, I'm going to turn it over to the seniors. Seniors, you were my heroes when I was in high school. I then had the feeling you were destined for greatness, and now that I've played with you this season and now that we sit on the throes of the biggest victory in the school's history, I know I couldn't have been more correct. Seniors, you've got the floor."

Michael stood immediately, "We've been through a lot lately. But, here we sit, a team," He hesitated, then, "At times today, I haven't displayed the leadership qualities that you expect from me, but that's all behind me. The Ivy's right. We are destined for greatness. And I promise I'll do my best to help take you there. Thank you for letting me be your captain. I won't let you down. Now, let's beat these fuckers!"

"Oh, yeah! All right! Let's go!" All this resonated through the big room with applause. Not rah-rah, but a display of focus and boldness. Michael sat down. I'm sure it was difficult to do what he did, but it doesn't surprise me. As I said before, Michael is a man I want to be.

Ted, surely inspired by one captain, stood as the other captain. Laced with redneck attitudes but mellowed by the realities of the morning, he started, "I haven't been the model citizen here." I'm surprised that this time of assertions and declarations has turned into true confessions. Anyway. "I've always thought I was the biggest guy on the team and the baddest motherfucker here, and I've been throwing my weight around for two years now. Well, I still feel the same way about myself, but I need you guys. I want this team to rock, and I want to do what I have to make it that way. I've been Runners my whole life. I know what this game means. Let's kick the shit out of Pitt!"

More yelps and applause, maybe just a trifle more subdued because everybody is afraid of Ted and doesn't know what think of him. I can also tell the blacks aren't exactly with the big man, but I think they're going to let up enough to make it all work today.

There's a pause. Monty Cash stood with a simple message, "We're here, man. Just kick ass!" We liked that one. I looked to Arthur. He's still in his own reality. As we fell silent, Father Al cleared his throat and stepped to the middle beside me. Now, he attracted attention. This guy is Super Bowl. Heads raised. Eyes fixed.

Father gazed around. He ended at Ted, and began talking, "I'm going to tell you guys what Weeb Eubanks, my coach with the Jets, told us in the locker room right before the Super Bowl game. You're probably well aware we were seventeen point underdogs and few people gave us a prayer. The Colts had lost two games in two years, and had just annihilated Cleveland at Cleveland. Weeb stood there as we awaited his words of wisdom. He said exactly this, 'When we win, and you carry me off the field, I have a bad hip that's been hurting me lately, so just be careful.' That's all he said."

Smiles flashed all around, as laughter eased into the room, then picked up momentum as we all considered how ludicrous that sounded before the biggest game ever. Father let it go on, then stepped his way back in and brought it home, "So, with that in mind, when we win, there's no way you'll be able to carry me off the field, so just grab a boy like your Ivy and celebrate by throwing him around." Guffaws took over quickly. Some of the bigger black guys just pointed at me and rolled on the floor. Whites and blacks slapped hands as the fun continued for a while. Michael stood up and walked over to me, grabbing my shoulders, laughing, "Man, it would be easier to carry you! Ha!" I looked to Vinny, rocking back in his chair, smiling, shaking his head. I have no choice but to stand here and take it. One could examine the psychology of this event, but that's unnecessary. The effect is the key here. Father pushed the right buttons. I glanced over to him, grinning. He laughed, pretty damned self-righteous for a priest. He got me. In a football player way, where vast bodies are essential, they all got me. I may be the coach and their ordained leader, but I'm still everybody's little brother.

The referee poked his head in the door from the field. "Two minutes, coach," he said to no one in particular.

"We're comin'," I said to him. I turned back to the team, "Well, Father, it's all been said." There are a few residual snickers. I paused. "Let's go!" The rhythmic clapping started. My hair stood on end as I grabbed my helmet and squeezed it my head into it. My respiration quickly picked up pace. Knots tied in my stomach. I did my best to hold down a few sobs as the clapping continued. The players had all stood and are converging around me. "Let's go! Let's go!" shot through the room in abrupt individual sounds. We all then switched to applause, with yells and whistles, displays of our strength.

"Hey, little man!" John Pettibone hollered. "Yeah, you, eighty-eight!" I turned to him. "Let's get out of here. Lead the way!"

"Let's light their fuckin' candles!" I yelled. "Let's go!" I turned to the door and discovered half of the team had moved to the sides to give me a corridor toward the tunnel. For a second, I saw my dad at the door in the olive slacks, tan shirt, the five chevrons on his arms, and the wide-brimmed hat of the Marine Corps drill instructor. 'Get to it, son.' I could hear him say. This is no time to deliberate. I walked with assuredness to and through the door to the tunnel. There's daylight at the end. I continued to walk the fifty or so yards until I was stopped by a very skinny salt-and-peppered-hair man with headphones on his ears and a ski jacket bearing the 'ABC Sports' logo. It's strange. Television and its transmission waves and receivers in homes across America have pervaded our culture in such a way that you're not real until you've been 'on the box.' I have no idea what is going to happen in this game. I may just be as I most always am, the anonymous participant. Who knows? But, I can see one thing for sure: when Keith Jackson announces our arrival on the field, I am going out there first. And I'll get the tape of this and show it to my children and grandchildren. It could be my only chance in my life to be real.

The ABC guy looked into the air of the tunnel, holding me back with his left arm and raising his right arm in the air. I looked over my shoulder to discover my team had followed me out here. With regard to this week, that's a relief. I glanced to a couple of unnamed defensive linemen near me, seeing their eyes were wide and red, emitting soft sounds unintelligible, like a 'Eeeeeaaahhhh,' a sort of a velar sound apparently caused as a result of the black beauties kicking in. I just shook my head and took Vinny's advice, trying not to think about it.

Screams are reverberating through the tunnel. Everything since Thursday had been tainted by the expose. But, with exception to awaiting network television to tell us when we can play our game, the yells, the declarations of loyalty, the fists cracking the pads, the players jumping around, the swearing to God someone's going to fuckin' kill somebody are all very normal, each of us preparing to play the game for keeps.

I can see from my vantage point at the end of the tunnel that the stadium is teeming with inflamed fans. I took a step out to examine The Bowl. It looks as if the students are going to spill out onto the field, a quavering mass of fee-paying humanity. They're incited by our insurgence, tugging on us to get out on the gridiron and get it on. They want to see it us do it. And they, because of a desire all college students hold to simply see wild shit happen, are ours, behind us all the way.

I can't see how our fans can get any more boisterous, but….

The ABC guy dropped his hand and shouted, "Go!" I didn't hesitate one bit, sprinting out on the field, crazed out of my skull, begging, beseeching to break Panthers in half. I stopped at the fifty on our sidelines and the team met me there where we jumped into one pile of pads, muscle, and skin, beating the hell out of each other in preparation for what we are going to do to Pitt. The crowd went ape, vibrating out of control. Our team melee broke up in time to see Pitt take the field. Those fucking bastards are shaking their fists and shooting birds. Boos and catcalls from our fans resounded through the stadium. They may be number one and we may be a team in trouble, but this is a rivalry for the ages and we just hate each other. When Pittsburgh and West Virginia play, you can often throw out the record books and roll the ball on the field and anything will happen. The rest of the nation may think this one will be over by the second quarter, but we have something different in mind.

Vinny's throwing to Dhali and Clark on the sidelines. He hasn't thrown a duck all day. Bullets, missiles, darts. Man. He's grinning. Right now, Vinny's either a complete badass or insane.

Michael and Ted lined up on the fifty to be escorted by one of the game officials to midfield for the coin toss. There, my two captains met Pitt's captains, Hank Gerard, the defensive end Ted will have to face all day, and Miguel Jackson, a talented receiver who, despite rarely touching the ball that mostly belongs to Osberg, will go right after Dhali in the NFL draft. The four of them are civil and sportsmanlike, but the rest of us, on both sides, rushed toward our respective hashmarks, lining up and down the field, throwing foul language and obscene gestures at each other. The crowd is into this game within a game, the fans looking for a rumble or two. No fights resulted, but we made it evident we're going after them. They may be Pittsburgh and they may eventually grab the Golden Ring, but they've crossed the border to the south. Today you don't beat the Runners without earning it.

The coin flipped up in the air. Pitt's Jackson called it. The referee indicated he missed by talking to our captains first. We had won the first battle and cheered accordingly. The ref gave us the choice to kick or receive, or chose ends of the field. Michael, knowing we plan on striking quickly, chose to receive. Pitt elected to defend the south end zone. Jackson and Gerard faced their backs to the south. Michael and Ted backed toward the north. They came out shaking hands, an ironic gesture considering that Michael in the game mode which has now invaded his body would if you're a Pitt man prefer to see you dead than see you at all.

Saturday November 8, 1975
1:05 PM

The Game

   We all left the field of play and convened on the sidelines. A hundred men surrounded me and looked as if they are going to hold onto my every word. I feel like Churchill when Hitler was in the bunker with Eva Braun. I'm ready for this. "Okay, gentlemen, we're here. We're here to do something we know we can do very well. Keep at it. We're at home, and the breaks fall your way at home. Play hard, hit hard, help out your teammates, and *never*, never, I say never give up! Let's get on these bastards! Let's go!"
   The team chanted, "Ho,ho,ho,ho,hey,hey,hey,hey! GO!" We broke and the kickoff receiving team took the field. Arthur and Lucious are back to receive, with the starting five offensive line up just behind the fifty to block. Pitt spread their ten men wide as the kicker, a Berwick, Pa. boy named Eric Archer, teed the ball up. It always takes the referee an inordinate amount of time in these televised games to drop his hand. As he surveyed the situation out there looking for whatever it was he looks for, Vinny and I stood side by side. We simultaneously turned to each other and smiled. The crowd is hot as a firetube boiler. Students screaming, joining in with the middle-aged men in the cheer, 'Here we

go, Runners, here we go!' Those guys are the ones who get you. They put all their energy into that school lament of today and their days. Unable themselves to run and block and tackle, they sit in the stands with pride, knowing we can.

PD didn't set me up....

"Do it, Gunner. Fuck with them," I said, bravado at the max.

"I gotcha covered, Pappy," he replied. "Remember, you get out there, you and I are going downtown." It all seemed very unlikely, but it's nice to think about.

The kick boomed and sailed past the end line, unreturnable. Ten offensive guys headed for the twelve yard line for the huddle. The ball is placed on the West Virginia twenty, eighty yards to go for a TD. Vinny turned to me the coach instinctively for last-second instructions. He had this gleam in his eyes like he was headed up to his room with his hand on Jean's ass. I grinned. It's great. "Off-tackle. No huddle. Throw the floater, even if there's a remote chance of sticking it. Remember: that's Dhali out there," I said.

"Watch this," said Vinny, "Just watch this." He winked and ran on to the field.

Michael stood beside me as we looked upon our team in the huddle. "I understand you have something planned," he said, in the measured tone of a serial killer, part of Michael's gameday personality.

"Watch the second play, Michael," I said, staring at the men in the huddle. They formed an oval with the line closer to the ball, Ted, John, Marty, Reginald, and Monty. The backs, Arthur and Frank, the wide-outs, Dhali and Clark, and the reluctant tight end Johnny Mueller were on the other side, with Vinny for the first time on the right side among the ten men. It is truly exciting just seeing him there.

*   *   *   *   *

The Runners on the field are quiet, awaiting Vinny's instructions. Vinny knelt, scanned the group looking everybody in the eyes, and for his first

time in college gave his orders, "This is where it all begins, and it's going to
be good," Vinny said with a grin, "Two plays. First, flood left, Arthur, 26
slide, 26 slide. Second, no huddle, I repeat, no huddle. Clark split left, tight
left, Dhali split right, 88 streak, 88 streak, Dhali, get a step and look fast.
Watch for my signal. Everybody, after the first play line up fast. Both on set.
Got it?"

"Yeah!"

"Ready?' said Vinny, "Break!"

The Runners broke from the huddle. They are to a man pleasantly sur-
prised to see Vinny so confident right before his first play, recalling how
against Miami and Penn State Bobby Kay always looked as if was going to
toss his tomatoes.

The team spread out to take their positions. The receivers and Johnny
lined up left. Frank took a three-point stance a couple of yards behind
Vinny, while Arthur stood with hands on his knees a couple of yards
behind Frank. Vinny approached the line looking over the Pitt defense.
They are huge up front, no fat, five men snorting.

"Where's your pussy coach, pussies?"

"You get rid of the faggot? He try get some couch time with you?"

"He's in the hotel in bed waiting for you!"

Some were directed at Vinny: "I'm going to bust your ass, queerbait
quarterback!"

"You're going to be sorry you ever took this job, high school superstar!"

Vinny didn't hear them. He saw the linebackers darting and stunting,
showing different looks; blitz, zone. But he ignored all that, noticing the d-
backs are man-to-man. Important for Dhali.

"Three ninety-five! Three ninety-five!" shouted Vinny. In the Runners'
book, any call with a ninety in it means nothing. The plays called in the
huddle stand. "Set!" Monty snapped the ball to the QB, who smartly spun
to his left and around to hand the ball to Arthur led into the line by big
Frank. Cracking and grunts filled the air as Arthur danced at near top
speed through a slit in the line and dodge the first linebacker to arrive at

the scene. The second one got him, but not after he picked up seven yards. The official whistled the play dead.

"Up easy, up easy!" he said, untangling the knotted human limbs. Pitt has lost a little of their verve after Arthur diced them. It took them a couple of moments to notice West Virginia is already lining for the next play.

The Runners moved quickly to their positions and, importantly, got set, holding still in their stances. Vinny glanced at Dhali. He's guarded tight by a Pitt senior, Mark Washington, All-East, extremely confident in his abilities to cover anybody. Vinny looked ahead to find the safety cheating toward Clark on the strong left side. It can't be more perfect, the QB thought. He turned to Clark, flapped his arms, and bent over the center for the snap.

The Bowl crowd knew from the no-huddle something is going on. They turned up the typical first-play noise in anticipation of the unexpected, with anything unexpected being an unusual event considering the tedious nature of the Lawson-coached teams of the recent weeks.

"Set!"

Dhali Sellers hails from eastern Pennsylvania near Philadelphia. Incredible athletes run in his family. His brother Sully was a role player for the New York Knicks during their NBA championship run a few years ago. Dhali always wanted to be like him but, despite his basketball abilities, he concentrated on football. He was a true Blue Chip receiver, pursued by the big schools all over the nation. That is until one day he got mixed up in a racially motivated fight. In a fit of uncontrollable seventeen year old anger, he beat the white guy who had been taunting him for weeks so badly the boy spent days in the hospital in serious condition. Dhali was arrested for assault. By virtue of having a great lawyer and by the fact that he had a spotless record, Dhali was sentenced only to six months probation. But the real punishment was that the big schools rescinded their scholarship offers and all but disappeared from Dhali's life. That's when the Wallflowers stepped in. Lawson immediately upon hearing of Dhali's troubles visited him and offered a chance to come to Montani. It was Dhali's only choice at the time, so he took it.

It had not gone well for Dhali with the Runners. During his tenure, West Virginia started eight different QBs, therefore not allowing Dhali to get any momentum. His numbers are a bit above average, but the pros know a player when they see one. Dhali was just marking his time here with a running team, then take his chances on the next level.

Knowing he is on national TV and knowing the corner has bit the bait, and also knowing he now has a quarterback who can actually pass, he funneled all the frustrations piled on since the day of the fight into this one jaunt down the sidelines. Dhali jumped out of his stance at three-quarters speed, took five strides, did a bossanova move that left Washington holding his jockstrap, and cruised around the right side of the corner. He had his step.

Vinny, while in his three step dropback, looked over to Clark to freeze the safeties. It worked. He then quickly turned right, and without seeing Dhali and without noticing the Pitt d-lineman closing in hard, put up a floater aimed for a point twenty-five yards downfield. Vinny watched the rise of the ball just as he was welcomed to the NCAA by that d-lineman. He didn't see the pass clear the corner's hands and intersect with Dhali. The Man pulled the ball into his chest and ran.

Washington is pretty fast and recovered nicely from getting burned to give chase. But, it's as if Dhali said, 'That's your speed. This is my speed.' The Runner receiver found a fifth gear and accelerated, looking as if he were shot from a cannon. His long legs stretched down the field as the Runner faithful in the stands went from noisy to high-pitched screams, doing their part to carry Dhali to six. He crossed the goal line and slowed down, not stopping until he was in the bleacher seats slapping hands with a bunch of junior high boys, thereby giving them the highlight of their lives.

"Oh, God! Oh, God!" I yelled, clutching Michael as I saw Vinny's strike hit Dhali's hands. "Oh, shit! Damnit! Shit! Look at that! Oh, my

God!" I screamed as Dhali kicked in the four-barrel and left every Panther sitting still. "Goddamn, Michael! Goddamn!"

"It worked! Hahahaha! It worked! Ivy, you're a genius!" Michael shouted as he grabbed me by the head and shook me.

I listened. Well, I really couldn't help but listen. Thirteen years at The Ridge and I've never heard anything like it. It sounds like the tarmac at Laguardia during the height of the shuttle day. It's so loud and the throng of fans is undulating so much, I honest-to-God thought the stadium was going to crumble. This is more reward for our troubles of this week. Deranged fans and first blood.

But wait! I caught myself. I'm coach!

"XP team! XP team! Get out there!" I yelled. I saw Raj kind of dazed. He's got a helluva leg, but sometimes he doesn't understand football. "Raj! Get your ass out there!"

"Already?" he asked with an Indian accent.

"Yeah, man, you gotta kick!" I said. "Let's go!"

The teams changed. The line stayed the same, with some extra second-teamer blockers out there. The receivers came off the field, including The Man. I met him several yards off the sidelines.

"Dhali! Dhali! What a run! Where did you learn to run like that?"

He's always cool, which will come in handy later on I am sure. "Oh, that was nothin,' man." He slapped my shoulders and walked by, then turned back. "Ivy, thanks, man," he said with sparkling eyes. He and I know what that means.

Vinny held and Raj punched the extra point through. Seven zip, West Virginia. I wonder what the viewing public thinks of this?

*   *   *   *   *

Vinny's Pi Gamma Pi friends are celebrating their man's first heroic act. Jean bounced and screamed, forgetting for now the future economic benefits and just enjoying the moment. The housemates knew the boy had it in him a long time ago and congratulated themselves for their foresight with a highfive. A long touchdown pass early! Even Jennifer, despite wanting Mason to be part of the action, is impressed. However, she knows his status on the team. And she knows he is walking out there for the kickoff.

Patricia has her arms clutched around her husband's neck as her son's pass sailed into Dhali's hands. They along with the Calires and the Lamberts jumped and screamed like high school kids as Sellars took it across the goal line, witnessing the Vacca's first-born's first heroic deed as a college quarterback. The past couple of days has been rough ones for the family led by the at-times impudent Mike, but a small victory such as this one tends to take all that away. Mike thought back to his son's Pop Warner days. Patricia took it back even further, back to her swimsuit lying on the floor of the honeymooning couple's hotel and the moment of Vinny's conception she had shared with the most handsome man she ever knew.

MJo and Michele are screaming uncontrollably. "You did it, Mary! You did it!" yelled Michele, "You got him so hot he'll never be quenched!"
MJo laughed and laughed, "I could tell something was working last night, but I guess it just takes a little while for my effect to kick in."
"If the sports public only knew the true story," quipped Michele.
"By the end of the day, I may have plenty to say," MJo said, grinning.
"I bet you will," said Michele with a smirk. Reminded of the previous night, she stood and turned around to catch Joan, also standing with a huge smile. Michele inferred, if Vinny makes her this happy, then, 'I must be right on the money about Maggie and her tutor.' The thought of that made her giggle aloud.

*   *   *   *   *

The XP team jogged to the sidelines, taking great pleasure in their early attack. The Runner bench is cranked, before knowing they could match up with number one, but now believing, I mean believing! Football in a large part is a game of momentum, and we've got it now. Unfortunately, we've got to give the ball up to them. But our defense will keep it alive.

My kickoff team spread across the field. It is a tremendous feeling to be out here with the lead and the fans going absolutely nuts. A few kick coverage men waved their arms up in the air, and the crowd turned it up even more. We responded accordingly.

I am psyched out of my gourd. I screamed Our Kickoff Question to Michael beside me, "Who's gonna get the tackle? Come on, Michael! Who's gonna get him?" I'm doing this maddening jumping thing. Possessing a nice vertical leap, my high school buddies have told me it looks pretty ominous out there when I start doing that. Well, they don't say ominous; they don't know what it means. Anyway, I jump and it fires me up even more.

The ref dropped his hand and Raj ran toward the ball and launched one. I had sprinted about thirty yards down the field when I saw the ball careen through the uprights into the tunnel. Goddamn, what a kick! Although it was a touchback, I completed my run to the wedge and yelled, "Call yourselves lucky, girls! I'm nailing you next time!"

"There won't be a goddamned next time, homo! Ya ain't scorin' no more!" barked the unnamed number forty-eight.

"Hey!" I screamed at him as he walked off, "Clever, peanut brain! Who wrote that one for you?"

Turning to run off the gridiron, whooping and pumping my fist, I saw Vinny for the first time since the second play. It was his first pass, his first completion, and his first touchdown, all rolled into one. He was waiting for me. I jumped into his arms.

"Gunner! Yeah!" I screamed, my voice already hoarse.

"This game's easy! A piece of cake!" replied Vinny. We laughed and laughed, in part because of how absurd his assessment is.

Saturday, November 8, 1975
14:37 remaining in first quarter

The reality of Pitt

Michael and his defense played off the mo'of the score and stopped Pitt's tyrannizing offensive attack in its tracks. Thrice the Panthers went three plays and out, with Drew Osberg running the ball five times for five yards. The loud crowd, despite the action being away from The Bowl, greeted each Runner defensive stuff with approval. I knew the early TD would pump them up, and they are in the stands doing their jobs very well. Now it is up to us to put more points on the board and make Pitt play a catch-up game.

That's a hell of a lot easier said than done. Pitt's defense turned the thumbscrews down on us. Taking advantage of our weakness at tight end, they doubled both Dhali and Clark and loaded up on the run. Consequently, Arthur has no room and is going nowhere. It's strange; there are O'Neill and Osberg, the two premier backs in the East, and the pair is getting no real estate. I hate to say 'I told you so,' but I knew Arthur would be stopped. Our offense is uninventive and unimaginative. The frustrating thing is it's the coach's job to put his players in position to do their best. I tried to do just that with the suggestion for three receivers, but it was Arthur, the man who is now spending a lot of time picking himself off the turf just after he gets the ball who rebuffed the idea. The early election returns don't look good for the favorite sons. I wondered how long it would take Arthur to come around and a worse thought, what the score will be when he does.

It was bound to happen. Pitt's offensive coordinator figured out a way to beat our big D. They came out with altered blocking assignments, concentrating on double-teaming Michael and Joe, getting them out of the way and going one-on-one with the others on their strong side. Surprised at how fast and efficiently they blew us off the ball, I grabbed the phones from David. "Timmy…any suggestions?" I said tersely to the man in the box.

"They're double-teaming Michael and Joe," Timmy said.

"No shit!" I shouted, "Tell me something a sportswriter wouldn't know." It hasn't taken me long to act like a head coach.

"Try loading up on Pitt's strong side. They seem to be going there," Timmy said.

We've been doing that. Great fucking insight. Thinking a six-man line might do it, I turned to David, "Signal Big Load."

"We've been doing that, Ivy."

Oh, Christ….

As we discussed strategy, or lack thereof, Pitt continued to air-tool Osberg through, right or left. The result is yardage, four, five, or six at a crack, consistently moving the ball down the field, melting minutes off the clock despite starting deep in their own territory.

"Timmy…you there?" I shouted.

"Bring the safeties up. Put the corners on an island," he said.

"David, Hit Man Rise," I spat.

"Michael's already doing that," David said.

"David, do we have any fucking idea what's going on out there?"

"You're the coach," he shot back.

Fifteen fuckin' ten on the SAT….

Our attempt to help Michael counter the attack is encountering turbulence. Osberg rammed the ball into our end zone before we knew what we were doing. The score is tied at seven as we near the end of the first quarter.

It's always good for the offense to stay on the field long enough to give the defense a blow. We couldn't do it. Vinny, trying to run The Kid's extremely limited sets and plays, found it difficult to lead our boys anywhere. We spent most of the first and a good deal of the second quarter punting a lot. The only bright spot is Anders, who's booming kicks over the Pitt return men's heads, pinning them back deep and making them run out of poor field position.

"Michael," I said just before my friend hit the field, "Stunt the lines and send Joe in occasionally to rip that Osberg fucker's head off," I offered.

"Good move," Michael said.

Stunting is lining up one way and sending guys the other way, and the Joe blitz is designed to try to stop Osberg in the backfield before he got anywhere. It worked for the first part of the second quarter. Then, as always, as football turns into a match of wits, Pitt's coaches quickly deciphered what we were doing on defense. They read Joe's blitzes and negated him. Mounting another one of those ground-consuming drives, Pitt methodically mowed Drew right through us, injecting him into the end zone for another touchdown.

The score is now Pitt fourteen seven at the midpoint of the second quarter. The fans see what's happening, seeing us getting pushed back and going nowhere. Not a peep came from the stands. Timmy, David, and I are in radio silence.

Fourteen seven doesn't tell the true tale of the game. We are getting manhandled on the field and, much to our dismay, losing the battle of the minds on the sidelines. This is where we needed the experience in coaching it takes to react quickly and decisively. I'm smart enough to figure most anything out and I played a lot of defense in high school, but I remain a college boy trying to do a man's job. Maybe I'll eventually be able to convince Joan I'm up to the task, but I'm not fooling Pitt. Honestly, the way things are going, if something doesn't change Pitt's going to ding our chimes in our own backyard.

Princeton's playing Harvard today. I wonder if they're winning? I bet they have professional adult men coaches who don't take money from Nazis and can successfully execute a declarative sentence.

We are three plays and punt yet again. The defense this time is admirably holding Pitt, without my help, probably to our advantage.

Arthur must have read the stats sheet or something because he came to me like he had his hat in his hands. He looked at me with his big brown eyes and said with disgust, "Ivy, I've got ten yards in seven carries. We gotta change something."

A break. I took a chance on what I thought he's talking about, "Arthur, Vinny's awfully good at running that offense. He's a master. I swear, it'll open things up for you. You might not get a bunch of yards rushing, but you'll get your hands on the ball and we'll get downfield." I let it hang right there.

We stood in silence for a while watching Pitt run a few plays, leaving Michael on his own to figure it out. He's doing a better job than I am. Arthur sighed, finally. "It may be nuts changing everything in the middle of the game…," he said, voice trailing away.

"Arthur, you've got seniority on the offense," I said, "It's your call."

"Let's do it," he said with little hesitation.

Oh, thank God something's going right! It happened as I had hoped, and it's not too late.

Pitt punted to us on the very next play. Since I didn't have time to inform the offense of the major change, even to tell Vinny, I called a time-out. I want to get this going as quickly as possible.

The offense gathered around. I started, "Here we go. Vinny. Three receivers."

He grinned big. "Now you're talking!" he said.

"Johnny, I'm sorry. You're out for now. We'll need you for short yardage, so stand by." I swear he has a look of relief on his cherubic face. "Tom, you're in as the third wideout with Dhali and Clark. All plays from the old way are now officially scrapped. Vinny knows how to do this. I can speak from experience. We'll just draw them in the dirt. Frank, just to let you know, you'll be lining up tight sometimes."

"I know," Frank said, "I gotcha."

"Now, loosen up, be patient, let it flow, and we'll soon see ourselves move that ball. Everybody okay?"

Nods and affirmations went around.

"Okay, men, let's go!"

"GO!"

Vinny put Frank tight the first play just to show Pitt we aren't kidding. Still, it was a little rough at first, with Vinny and his receivers having some difficulty with their timing. That's to be expected, but The Gunner is so accurate and knows how to do this so well I felt as if we'd have that straightened out in no time.

I was right about Arthur. We spread the field out, allowing him to get some room running. Vinny mixed passing and Arthur well, well enough to lead us on a good drive through Pitt's all-star defense. We got inside the twenty, a sure three points at least. Then the wheels fell off. Penalties. Penalties negating gains and forcing us to give back yards we had earned. Stupid things, like holding, clipping, which is blocking a player in the back, very illegal, and personal fouls stemming from frustration. We lost thirty yards due to flags, knocking us out of field goal position and forcing us to send Anders back out there to try to punt them back.

Pitt got a couple of first downs on us, but Michael and the boys held them tight. They punted it back to us and Vinny got us driving again. At midfield, he threw a pass to Tom in an attempt to give him a chance to use his outstanding speed. Just as Tom caught the ball and turned, Jeff Denzel of Pitt unloaded on him. Tom dropped to the turf where he laid unconscious for a couple of minutes. It's a scary time for us. I said a prayer for Tom, which is all a football player can do in this situation. The risk of head injuries is always present. And as I said before, we just don't think about it. Until it happens.

Tom is revived, walking off under his own power with trainers beside him. He wretched only twice as he moved toward the sidelines. Rules state that an injured player has to come out of the game for at least one play, but Dr. McCormick approached me. He let me know that Tom, after the doctor's quick examination of the wideout's pupils, has a big time concussion. He is for his safety out for the day. That puts the hands man Dave in there for good and makes me the first sub. Interesting.

Pitt stopped us and we stopped Pitt, trading punts and putting us back around the forty in our own territory. Vinny threw an out to Dave. He made it near midfield when Jim Bobson, the Pitt corner covering him, hit Dave in the legs from behind for a good, solid tackle. Dave laid there and writhed in pain. Oh, Jesus Christ....

Saturday, November 8, 1975
3:02 remaining in the first half

The Catch

The crowd is hushed as yet another Runner quickly hit the field injured. Michael grabbed the phones to get the word from upstairs.

"It's Dave," said Michael, "He's moving, but the doctor's looking at his leg."

"I know that, goddamnit," I shot at my friend. As a coach, I'm concerned, for Dave's health as well as for the potential loss of his outstanding hands. We need his precision and his consistency to make this three-receiver offense hum. He's a weapon by virtue of his contrasts to Dhali's raw speed and Clark's size. I'd hate to see him go down for the day.

As a player, I'm excited and apprehensive. I'm the next in line to the throne and there are only freshmen behind me, so if the prognosis for Dave is not good, I'm in for the duration. It's what I've anticipated my entire life. Now that the time maybe has come, I'm frankly about to puke.

Dave's been down for a while. To keep my breakfast, I'm preparing, loosening up, hams, arms, calves, and neck. My muscles are cold and my brain is in the coaching mode, so I have some realignment to do to get ready for this possibility that is becoming, as Dave lays there, more and more probable.

He's up, and the trainers are gingerly helping him off the field. Dave hopped on one leg with the other foot held in the air as motionless as possible. It's a knee. He's fried. I'm in. "Michael," I said.

"I know," he replied, "I gotcha covered. Good luck, man. Do it!"

I ran onto the field toward the huddle, passing Dave with a word of encouragement. "Way to go, Dave. You did it for us." I slapped his ass.

"Get 'em, Ivy!" Dave said, with irregular breathing from the pain of having the insides of his knee ripped apart.

I enter the huddle, greeted with applause, not like Johnny Carson, but enough to get me boiling. "Let's go, Coach Ivy!" I heard. "Go, Brick, go!" Vinny looked up to me. I wagged my eyebrows at him. He smiled and nodded. We have an agreement. I think he's going to follow through on it.

The ball is at the Runners' forty-seven. It's second down and three, a good passing situation with that short yardage and extra downs.

I had been watching this for most of the second quarter. Vinny has been throwing in Dhali's direction enough, albeit unsuccessfully. Pitt's All America free safety Denzel has in response been shading toward Sellers. Vinny's obviously seen this, too, and considered it with his next play.

"This is it," Vinny commanded, "Power I backfield, Dhali split right. Ten and out. Clark slot right. Block and hook. Mason left." That was the first time I had heard my name in a college huddle. It gave me goose bumps, "Mason. If you're isolated on the corner, burn post down. Burn post down. On set. Ready?"

"Break!"

I'm assigned to run a deep midfield route at top speed. Vinny is guessing I'll be covered man to man, so it'll be a footrace. I took my position, drawing Mark. He's tough. Fortunately for me, I think I'm faster.

Washington is in my face. I'm the new kid on the block, so he went after me. "What's you doin' here, asshole?"

Vinny barked the signals. Not willing to take anything from anybody, I replied, "It's Mr. Asshole to you." I think that threw him off.

I know this is a go. Vinny's going big to me. I thought about making the catch in the bowl in full view of everybody, but of course Joan specifically. Of course. My love makes me stronger. Makes me feel like the man I want to be. I hope Alan's at this game, too, not with Joan, but…. And I hope I, the man in Joan's one-man universe last night, makes him think and worry. Yeah, Bricker, I mused, second year of college and you're still showing off for the girls and their pansy boyfriends.

"Set!"

I jumped out of my stance and got a chuck from Mark. Then out of my periphery, I saw the cornerback inexplicably stumble and fall into a heap. Washington lay helpless as I turned it on and zipped right past him. What misfortune! However, any elation on my part was very momentary because Denzel did not move toward Dhali. He instead locked onto me, turned, and with a five yard lead ran the post route with me.

~ ~ ~ ~ ~ ~ ~ ~ ~ ~

Backpedaling, Vinny saw Washington fall and also saw Denzel ahead of Mason. It's early enough to call it off and do something smart, like look for

Clark. But Vinny has been frustrated by a series of near misses during Pitt's dominance and wanted to get it all back quickly. Knowing it's his best friend Mason out there, and letting his heart overrule his head, and even after realizing he's throwing to a walk-on covered like a tarp by a future NFL safety, Vinny did what God had built him to do. He cocked and fired the ball in a tight spiraling arc marked for the end zone. His reasoning is faulty, but the pass is very pretty.

It doesn't look good for the Runners. Down fourteen seven late in the second quarter with nothing working against the top-ranked team in the nation and a ball in mid-flight with interception written all over it, it really doesn't look good at all for the home team.

~ ~ ~ ~ ~ ~ ~ ~ ~

Denzil is running straight downfield while I closed in from the left and behind. I knew Jeff had drawn a bead on the ball and is simply going to run under it for the pick-off. Therefore, I positioned myself as the defender.

I feel all forty thousand in the stadium rise to their feet and gasp as Denzel, the ball, and I neared our meeting at the goal line. Exactly when my instincts told me to, I jumped for my only shot at breaking up Jeff's interception, hoping to get to the ball over his head. As it turned out, I couldn't have timed it more perfectly as our hands simultaneously hit the ball. I saw it bounce without wobble into a second parabolic glide with an apex about ten feet over the turf.

~ ~ ~ ~ ~ ~ ~ ~ ~

Denzel's finished, his stride disrupted by Mason's jump. He folded to the turf and therefore missed seeing one of the greatest catches ever executed in a major college football game. Mason, amid his levitation, saw the ball in the corner of his eye from below it, just past his arm's length away. The bump with Denzel had slowly rotated his torso down and his legs up, making him approach a position parallel with the ground. Those in the bowl gasped again, as if right before them they were discovering the mystery of flight.

~ ~ ~ ~ ~ ~ ~ ~ ~ ~

I'm way up in the air. Fully aware I have to come down, I lowered my left foot in search of the turf and, with my eyes firmly fixed on the ball, reflexively extended my right leg for airborne stability. My foot found the ground, slowing my fall enough to allow the ball on its second trip down to drop nearer to me.

Just a couple of feet above her and a full two seconds after having left her, I leaned into Mother Earth and softly received the ball as it fell into my hands.

I laid there in the end zone clutching the leather as if were a leaded crystal vase I had just saved from destruction from its fall from Joan's end table. My world remained silent with concentration, knowing only how incredibly lucky I am to have it.

~ ~ ~ ~ ~ ~ ~ ~ ~ ~

The stadium crowd, especially those in The Bowl, at first all somewhat in disbelief, quickly swelled into an eruption of noise of great proportion. Not only had they seen the potentially tying score against Pitt, but they had also witnessed one hell of a play executed by a smallish sophomore, a player not even worthy of a scholarship, mind you. It was a play that lended beauty to a game defined by wrenching collisions among massive people. They couldn't believe they had seen it. They couldn't believe it had happened. They wanted it to happen again so they could relive the aesthetic pleasure, despite being fully aware that nothing like that play could have been planned on a chalkboard, or choreographed in a dance studio.

Pamela, with her general awareness of those things going on around her, had seen Mason go in. She alerted Joan, who was progressively becoming bored with the game. They watched Mason stride down the field toward them, Joan thinking of how beautifully he runs. She saw Mason go up, lay out, and catch the ball. Despite knowing that isn't how passes are usually caught, it all happened so quickly she didn't quite understand the significance of the play until the overwhelming reaction of the crowd tipped her off that something incredible had just taken place. Then, it happened to her, something she had never experienced at a football game, or anywhere at anytime. As Mason stood facing the crowd with The Bowl continuing to go berserk, Joan felt a squeeze on her heart that pulled a deep breath into her chest and forced her to bring her hands up to her bosom in an attempt to hold it all together. It was 1967 all over again and the nineteen year old inside her that never leaves anyone sent a flash of heat up her neck to her head. The irresistible man whom she last night kissed and kissed is now the subject of the adoration of tens of thousands. As she holds the secret of her evening with him within her, Joan feels she and Mason are one.

"Jesus, what a remarkable catch!" Pamela yelled. "Did you see that?" *Turning to her sister who is fanning herself with her hands, unable to say anything,* Pamela asked, "Are you all right?"

"Of course," *Joan replied, her mind at war with her heart.*

Judy, Alice, Jean, and Jennifer are squealing, looking at each other incredulously. They know what it is. Mason's first play, first catch, first touchdown. And what a way to do it. Leave it to Mason, Judy thought. He can't just make an ordinary touchdown catch. Oh, no. He has to raise the degree of difficulty and perform magic. That's my boy.

He's dreamy, Jennifer thought. She let it all run away with her, and there is nothing left to say.

The jerk's finally done something right, Jean said under her breath.

When I turned him loose last year, Alice thought, what was I thinking? Oh, my God, what the hell am I thinking now?

Michele and MJo were screaming, grabbing each other and hopping.
"Christ almighty!" MJo shouted, "How did he do that?"
"Hey, sweetheart, I don't put anything past the boy," Michele yelled,
"What a guy! What a guy! Complete package, baby! Best student I ever
had."
Bobby turned to Michele with a look of surprise, "You're a teacher?"
"No, Enrico Fermi, I'm the fuckin' homecoming queen," Michele shot,
"What do they do, take your brains away when you join a frat?"
Brad laughed at his brother. Bobby came back, "You know, I really go for
strong women."

"Well, I don't go for idiots," Michele said. Bobby and Brad turned back
sheepishly. MJo cracked up.

~ ~ ~ ~ ~ ~ ~ ~ ~ ~ ~

It occurred to me what happened. Not the series of individual events, but the final analysis: I have my first touchdown as a Runner! Goddamnit, I scored! But I'm not the only one excited about this. I thought The Bowl's going to pour onto me. The crowd's roaring and surging, and we, before my teammates make the fifty yards to celebrate with me, have a few precious seconds alone. I face them and with outstretched arms, ball in the fingertips of my right hand, bowed my head in appreciation for giving me the second biggest thrill of my life, a screaming standing ovation from the best fans in all of sports. Standing there, I soaked it all in. You never know when you're going to be back, so enjoy it.

A wave of my teammates mauled me, like the pictures I had seen of Bill Mazoraski after he hit the two-out seventh-game World Series-winning home run for the Pittsburgh Pirates fifteen years ago. We jumped and slapped and pumped fists.

"Oh, yeah! Ivy!" Dhali screamed, "Ya got ya one!"

Clark got in my face, "It's about time you started pulling your weight around here!" he laughed.

Monty's next, grabbing me by my helmet, "I saw it, man! Make it look easy, baby!"

The Bowl crowd went up further. They carried us with them. We couldn't leave the scene, couldn't adjourn to the sidelines as most all teams do after a touchdown. We stayed there with our fans and milked it for all it's worth. Except for two plays, our first half sucked. But, the only thing that counts is the score, and the board read Pitt fourteen thirteen, with Raj lining up for a sure-thing kick to tie it. Tied at the half, a stunner of a score. The fans know what that means, and they know what it takes to get there against the 1975 Pittsburgh Panthers. And they let us know we are great.

Vinny found me in the middle of the party, holding onto me with a bear hug. It was our first completion, first touchdown. Throughout all the years of all the talk of doing this, all the dreams, just being able to see it and taste it, we got in there, by God. In spite of the incredible odds against us even getting a chance, we did it. As we had done thousands and thousands of times before, Vinny threw it and I caught it. But, this time it was at The Ridge and the Runners needed it and we did it. It is indeed a beautiful moment.

"Perfect pass," Vinny joked, fully aware he had no business throwing the ball my way.

"You put it right in there, buddy," I replied, laughing. "Right in my hands."

"Hey," he yelled, "Six is six, no matter how you cut it."

At that time, the band struck up *The Fight Song*. The dream is complete. As my team ran off the field still in celebration, I walked, slowly, first down the end line, then down the sideline, toward my other crazed teammates awaiting me.

Michael's on his knees screaming. "Oh, goddamn it! Poison Ivy!" he screamed to my smile.

I'm protracting the moment as long as I can. This has been forever coming, and I can tell it will be another forever before I forget it.

Raj converted and we are tied at fourteen, most assuredly confounding the football experts in the United States.

Saturday, November 8, 1975
Halftime and third quarter

The crisis resurfaces

Neither team moved the ball after my catch, so the Runners and the Panthers withdrew to our respective locker rooms with a tie score. We ran by The Bowl crowd amid their rousing approval. The game started tied and halfway into it we're still tied. Our fans love it, almost billowing over top of us. This is the perfect home field advantage. Inertia is certainly on our side as we take a break. We can hear and feel the fans rock through the tunnel roof. Because of this, there are a lot of smiles going into the locker room, a lot of congratulatory slugs, a lot of positive talk and chatter.

I don't want to let on too heavily, but I am not impressed with our play. We caught Pitt not looking twice and took advantage of their mistakes. My catch, The Catch to which it is already being referred much to my simultaneous pride and humility, was lucky. Only I, and possibly Vinny, realize that, but, as always, the scoreboard tells the tale.

Pitt has coaches who spent a full workweek studying film of us looking for tendencies and weaknesses. They're using this halftime to adjust and plan. As it turns out, we're using it to boast and gloat. Apparently, and this is bad, we're satisfied. And that plays us right into Pitt's hands.

"Position meetings! Get them started!" I shouted, "Remember, Pitt's over there thinking and looking hard. Consider that when you talk among yourselves. What worked in the first half may not work in the second." The Runners are still jabbering about the first half, oblivious to the fact that Pitt, as evident by their play, can still bang our gong.

I called on Father Al. "Father, help out the o-line. We've got that new offense and Vinny's going to need time. Tell them how to do it."

"I'll do my best," Father said.

"Tell them how you guys did it for Namath. That certainly worked."

"I'll try to fit it into the conversation," said Father smiling.

"You can do it." I slipped over to the receivers and backs, short of demeanor, like a coach would be. They had just gathered when I got there. Nobody looked around at each other. They looked at me. I guess they want me to say something.

"Look, guys," I said in a low tone to keep the defense from hearing. They're on the other end of the locker room, so it's safe, "We're going to have to outscore them. It really is totally up to us." I said this in regard to the fact that Pitt has figured out a way to ram the ball down our mouths. True, the defense has stopped them more times than they have not, but when Pitt ran over us, they abused us. An offense like that just gets better and better as the game rolls along. They wear our D down, eat up the clock, keep the ball away from us, and render the crowd quiet.

Back to the meeting. I decided that instead of leading off with strategy I would pump up confidence. "Vinny will attest to this; it may take a few series to get the three receiver set going, but it's beautiful when it works. And now, we have an outstanding backfield in Arthur and Frank, greatness in Dhali and Clark, a true leader at quarterback in Vinny, and Mason, who will fuck with everybody in a white shirt and just be disruptive as hell." The men laughed, but I think I got my point across. "Give it time," I reminded them. "Vinny?"

"They'll blitz me, trying to take advantage of my inexperience. That opens holes in a zone and sets up one-on-one mismatches. That's what

I'll be looking for. For instance, Clark, if you see any kind of height mis-match, you'll know I see it, so look for the ball fast. Dhali, any one-on-one with you, you'll get it. Mason, hit the seams in the zones. I'm going to send you over the middle since I know you to be crazy. Frank, you'll draw linebackers, so if they blitz, look fast. And Arthur, they'll be wide open for draws and sweeps. That's how it works. It's flexible, easy to adjust, and makes anything they do a potential mistake. Just be patient with it. Run your routes and report back to me what they're doing. We'll be toolin' soon."

Vinny's damned good. We're going to need a lot of points, and this group of men with this offense will get them. As we continued to meet, my worries of the first half are fading. I now have renewed belief in what I told our fans at our house. We're going to take them down to late in the game and make them scramble to win this one.

"Five minutes, coach," said the official popping his head in the door.

"Okay," I responded. I don't know went on in the other meetings. That's the disadvantage of being a player-head coach and having other players as assistants. I need to talk to Michael to get a feel for what they decided to do. Pitt has the ball first, so we will be tested early. It's not our defense I worry about. It's Pitt and their big running, scoring game. As far as averages go, we're ahead. But statistics can be misleading and mis-used. And I know Michael. He can't be happy with the way things are.

"All right," I shouted. Everyone gathered around quickly. I have their attention, "Thirty minutes remaining," I said, with a twinge in my stom-ach reminding me I have only thirty minutes remaining, "We played as a team in the first half. We faced some tough times, but, hey, the score's tied," I continued, trying to put as positive of a light on this as I could, despite my personal feelings, "Seniors?"

Michael stood, "We're ready. We're ready to show the world we aren't flaky. Let's go back out there and kick some Panther ass!" Manly cheers rang out. It sounds good. Ted stood.

"Y'all. We're close. I've hated Pitt my entire life. This is personal to me. Nobody, nobody, nofuckinbody is getting by the G-man. I challenge everyone else in this room to do what I'm going to do." More manly cheers.

"Seniors?" I asked again.

"Let's do it, man!" yelled Monty.

"It's ours, baby!" screamed Chandler. "Yeah! Yeah!" the Runners shouted.

"Father," I said, offering him the floor. He took it.

"Just one remark," said Father. He commanded us. "The Colts came out ready and proud. All we did was what Ted Gerlach said to do. We concentrated on our individual battles, and played as a team. And, the rest is history."

The loudest Runners screams of the day reverberated through the locker room. Now there's nothing at all left to say.

"Let's go, men!' I shouted. I took off through the doors first and ran through the tunnel and out onto the field. There are enough fans in their seats to give us a great greeting. The beginning of the second half usually drags for the fans as they take their minds off the game for food and socializing. It's also tough on the players, who after having just gotten warmed up and into it were asked to stop. If we had anything to do with it, the players would cut the duration of the halftime in half at least, or possibly do away with it all together. Of course, that would step on the toes of the cheerleaders and the marching band, but what's the reason for the game anyway? They are nice diversions, but trumpets and trombones and girls in short skirts up to their navy panties aren't scoring any points on the board. What's the real reason for the game? For the fan's entertainment, obviously. And that brings me back to halftime. That's why we have it; the fans want it. Jesus, this mental circumlocution I'm putting myself through is not going to help me on the field.

*　　*　　*　　*　　*

The parents sat through the half, mostly thrilled with their 'boys.' Wayne and Rob are in a male way giddy with excitement as they talked of Vinny's two long touchdowns.

"Here we are, Robert," quipped Wayne, "This is worth every dollar of tuition and rent and board paid to date."

"Entertaining," replied Rob, "Vinny's a great one. And, you got to hand it to Mason so far. He's doing a good job as coach, and a receiver. That boy you can't discount him. He's got guts, beyond the general lunatic college student."

"I think he's cute," said Geri, "His enthusiasm is contagious."

"I think he's got a line of bullshit for every occasion," laughed Pauline, "But, that's okay."

"Who else could have talked us into allowing our daughters to move in the same house with two men?" responded Geri, "My apologies, Patricia."

"Think nothing of it," replied Patricia, "I've often wondered what the hell you two were thinking anyway," the women laughed together.

"Ah, the door's locked," said Geri, "What else can we ask for?"

"That," said Pauline, "and the two young men have conducted themselves as gentlemen. That's what Alice tells me. Even Mason." They laughed again.

"What's this thing with him, anyway?" asked Geri.

"Vinny tells his mother everything. The One and Only is the instructor he works for," whispered Patricia.

"Oh…," replied Pauline.

"His idealism is kind of…no, I won't say it," Geri said softly.

"I know," said Pauline.

"Think we've had anything to do with that?" Patricia said, continuing the low tone.

"Probably," said Geri. The women giggled under their breaths.

"Girls," said Wayne, turning around to them sitting in their row, "we've heard every word you said. Let's get back to football, okay?" He's smiling.

"Oh…okay," whined Pauline.

It was a light conversation, except for Mike. He had witnessed Mason with the coach's headset on his ears for the time he didn't play. Being the football fan and the compulsively discerning person he is, he this time agreed with Mason. Mike is concerned for his son and the second half, wondering when Pitt's dominating offense and seasoned coaching staff are just going to take over the game and run it up. For the first time that day, he viewed the event in terms of his son and his son alone. He wanted Vinny to do well for Vinny's sake. Mason's takeover could royally screw it all up, Mike thought. He didn't want that to happen to his eldest son on the day he was taking giant leaps toward becoming a man. The Mike took in a deep breath and tried to relax, something at which he was not very good.

*   *   *   *   *

The Runners encircled me for the second half talk. Again on automatic, I said, "C'mon now. Pitt's a proud bunch, just like the Father said, but we've got more pride than that. It comes down to this, men: we've got to want it. We've got to want it more. Which ever team out here wants it more will win this game…. Now, let's get 'em and get it!"

"Go, go, go, go, GO!" We broke the huddle and hit the field for kickoff.

Lining up, I saw downfield that Drew is shading to the right of us. He's usually in the middle. Odd…Hmmm….

"Who's getting this tackle, Ivy?" Michael shouted.

"I am, Burt," I yelled back, "I've got the son-of-a-bitch!" I'm supposed to bust wedges, not tackle. But, that wouldn't make our ritualistic question fit.

The ref dropped his hand and a couple of seconds later Raj ran to the ball and kicked downfield. The kick is shallower than his others, ending up in Quen Riley's hands, the secondary return man for Pitt. He took off to our right along with my wedge and every other Panther and Runner. Suddenly, Riley handed off to Osberg, who now had the ball going the other way. A reverse!

Pitt has formed a wall of blockers in the middle of the field to spring Drew, who is fast enough to make it work. I quickly saw most of us are surprised by the misdirection. There are only two Runners behind that wall, Dougie Roland and me. It's Dougie's job to protect the outside left. Any outside run is a disaster for coverage teams. The return man must be forced in toward the others so one or some of us can make the tackle. However, this time if Dougie does his job, because the wall of blockers is flattening every other Runner cover man, it'll be just Drew and me. The nationally recognized future NFL star and Heisman Trophy winner-in-waiting and the walk-on American Literature tutor.

I saw Dougie plant his stance to force Osberg in. I could, and should, have played it safe and given myself room to maneuver and react to Drew's cut to the middle off of Dougie. But, consistent with my life, I just said, 'fuck it.' I aimed myself a couple of yards in front of Dougie, right where I thought Osberg would have to cut.

By the luck of the Irish, Drew planted his right foot just there for the quick blast upfield. Right when he turned, I had twenty yards of velocity momentum, the ferocity instilled in me by Bazooka Frank, and the instant acceleration before the point of contact given to me by God. He didn't even see me. I hammered Osberg with the biggest hit of my life. The force was transmitted through my body, rattling every bone, every muscle. I hit the turf, motionless for a couple of moments. I wanted to stay there and recover for the rest of the afternoon, but my instincts told me to get up and look tough. I pulled myself up, glaring through clouds at Osberg on the ground, lying still, holding the ball but minus his headgear.

I could hear the crowd going apeshit, but I could barely see them through the blur. Dougie's the first to me, having been but a few yards from the hit, just out of his mind with celebration. He's grabbing me and shaking me when all I want to do is search the turf to see if I lost any important body parts. Amid his wildness, I looked back over to Drew, who now has three or five people around him, trainers or doctors or rabbis or priests, I don't know because I still can't see straight. Fortunately, Dougie has me in his arms and is moving toward the sidelines because I don't think I can direct myself there under my own will. He then jumped away from me, leaving me in the middle of the turf, still unable to think clearly, afraid I have cavitated part of my brain. I saw a collection of dark shirts I felt safe moving toward. Walking slowly, I looked back again, seeing Drew still on the turf, attended to by a team of surgeons or whomever. It started to come to me what I had just done, but I'm too racked to get it straight in my head.

Vinny is the first to reach me, several yards off the sidelines.

"God-damn, Cheetah! What a shot! You buried the bastard! Jesus H. Christ!" he yelled into my face, "I've never seen a hit like that! What did Joan do to you last night? God! What a pop!" It hurt but Vinny kept yelling, "It was like he cut and there was this navy blur and this cracking noise, then the next instant he's on the ground! Where's his fuckin' helmet, Mason? Jesus! Are you all right?"

"No!" I shouted, "But don't tell anybody. I'll recover."

I got as many congratulations for that hit as I did for the touchdown. The team's all over me, even though I can't make out anybody individually. I know they loved it. That's football. The big hitters come at a premium. With the Runners being so deep at the receivers and at the d-backs, I've always been convinced that my ability to hit is what keeps me in a jersey.

But, the highest compliment, the one I will treasure most came from Father Al.

"Mason, are you okay?" he asked.

"Yeah…no…yeah," I said.

"Mason," Father said in a low tone, "I have never seen a ballcarrier of Osberg's quality go down like that. That was a big time stick, my man. We're talkin' National Football League. Way to hit!"

"Thanks, Father," I said.

"That was horrific," he added.

"Thanks, Father," I said.

Drew must have still been on the turf, because Michael bounced over to me, "What a shot, man, what a hit! Get his dental records! He's not getting up!" he screamed wildly.

"Thank you again, Father," I said.

"Mason, maybe you'd better sit for a while," Father suggested.

"No!' I yelled as everybody jumped back from me, "No way! No way!" I'm not ready for my last play! "No way! I'm here until the end even if they have to put a metal plate in my head! No goddamned way I'm coming out!"

"Okay, Mason," Vinny said in a settling voice, "You're in. Just rest a bit."

Drew pulled himself to his feet to cheers from the Pitt crowd. A trainer recovered his hat, which had bounced a good ten yards from where his head landed. Riley, the second team back, entered the game. Without Osberg, Pitt only got one first down and punted.

Vinny took his troops in on the Runners' thirty-five, tried a couple of passes and a run by Arthur. We didn't go anywhere with it, so we punted. Anders pounded them back deep. Osberg, much to his credit, came back into the game.

From that point, Pitt began one of their patented drives, Osberg right and Osberg left, with the fullback running intermittently to keep us honest. Their line is blowing us off the ball, like getting beaten up in slow motion. I as the coach am bankrupt of ideas, unfairly again leaving it all up to Michael. After a little under seven minutes, Osberg dove over the lines for a touchdown, putting Pitt up by seven. Only by seven, most in the stands probably said, but we on the sidelines are in shock and the defense with their glazed eyes know it is a hell of a lot worse than that.

During Pitt's XP attempt, Michael approached me. He is not pleased.

"Thanks for the help, Coach."

"Hey, we're doing what we can over here," I replied sharply.

"What are you doing over here? Scoping women?" Michael got in my face, hands on hips.

I got closer, "We're lookin' for some way to stop Osberg, fuckhead!"

"Well, fuckhead," Michael yelled, just about jumping into my helmet, "any thoughts on the subject?"

"Yeah," I spat back, our masks touching, "stunt and blitz Joe, except next time make it work!"

"Great idea, Coach! They probably haven't even noticed we've been doing that almost the entire fucking game!" Fellow teammates are doing anything to get away from us. I'm sure the whites love it.

My emotions said think of some snappy answer, but I realized what's going on here and with whom it's happening. I relaxed my stance and pulled back as the more rational side of my mind took over. Michael saw that and his eyes softened. "Look, Michael," I said, in a more normal gameday tone, "In spite of the fact that I can kick your ass all over this field," Michael smiled, "you and I have to stay on the same stanza to make this work."

"Yeah," Michael said, "we asked for this. And we got it."

"You're the true leader here," I said, "I'm just a rabble-rousing fascist." I concluded, recalling Lawson from the last time we talked with him.

"Oh, no. You're not pulling that shit on me," Michael said, smile not leaving, "It's your team. The newspaper says so. Now, you show the way. And I'll help out by stopping Osberg. Deal?"

I sighed. "Deal."

"Good," Michael said, "Now get your mind and whatever else off Dr. Kissinger and coach this goddamned team."

I squinted, "How…."

"Do you think Ellen hasn't noticed?" he said laughing.

"Then why haven't you ever…."

"Ellen tells her big stud a secret, her big stud keeps the secret, okay?" Michael laughed again. He wouldn't stop laughing. Pitt's busting our ass and Michael's guffawing over busting mine. Football's not supposed to be like this.

"I got your white ass," he threw over his shoulder as he walked.

"That's enough," I said, red-faced, "Play ball, big stud." Michael came back to me. We shook hands, again headed in the same direction. Crisis averted.

We took the kickoff with the same result as before. Vinny pass to Dhali for five, Vinny incomplete to Clark, Vinny incomplete to Arthur, then Anders, getting a real workout today, punting. The old offense hadn't a prayer, and I hoped the new offense would start working before tomorrow, possibly?

After the Borgstrom bomb, Pitt started on their own nine, ninety-one yards to go. And go they did. It's a little different this time, however. It's Osberg left, *then* Osberg right, four yards a pop, melting the clock and much of the resolve we have. Ramming and ramming down field, Osberg put himself in the position to again leap over the lines for his fourth score and probably several dozen more Heisman votes. I hate to say anything good about anybody from Pitt, but I pummeled that bastard, and he got back up and back in to score twice. It says a lot for his courage.

Damn, this looked good on paper....

Down twenty-eight fourteen as the gun fired to end the third shortly after Pitt's score, tempers flared on our side. All the old crap came back: the offense, led by Ted, berating the defense, led by Michael, for not doing their jobs and getting the ball for us. He has a point. The stats sheet showed that Pitt had the ball for thirteen minutes thirty-nine seconds to our one minute twenty-one seconds. We had no chance to use our new offense. I'm sure Pitt, after seeing how explosive we can be, decided to play the ball control game. Michael is frustrated, completely unable to accept that they can't stop Pitt, but then again faced with the facts and having them nailed home by Ted.

"Jesus Christ, Burt, stop them!" he shouted, "We can't score if we can't get the ball!" Michael is getting it again, this time from someone with a real agenda.

"Get fucked, Ted! Why don't you fuckers move the damn ball?" Michael replied heatedly.

"Goddamn it, I knew this was a mistake! You black guys don't have the heart!" shouted Ted.

Oh, no. Not that again. Ted's remark hit me hard in the face. We're vulnerable anyway. Knowing the insidious nature of racism and how I'm sure it also remained on the surface, the revolting supremacy that Ted brought back up would probably infect some of the other white guys, leading to our certain demise. In other words, we're in a heap of trouble. Big time.

The brothers stood in attention to that remark. Chandler is the first to speak, "You fuckin' bigot! Let's see you get your ass out there and stop them!"

"That's your job!" Ted yelled back, "And you're not doing it! You and your *brothers* should have gone to one of those colored schools like Grambling or Southern with your kind and left the big time up to us!"

Now we have totally derailed. Ted's under delusions and is pissing off half the team, again. And this time with only fifteen minutes left to play in a game we are in our current state nowhere near having any hope to win. The black guys are congregating, I know preparing again to walk. Ted's startling display of hatred had us splintering fast, with all of us white guys being implicating. Distrust spread like a windblown brushfire. In just a few short moments, we are again dying from within our souls, even worse than it was this morning. I have no choice. The time for words has passed. The physical nature of football is so basal, there's only one thing left to do. I have to give up the seventy-five pounds and seven inches and go after Ted.

Thank God Father Al got there first. With fury, eyeballs to eyeballs, Father got in his face. "This is the wrong place and the wrong time to hear your beliefs, Ted. As much as they sicken me, you'll have plenty of chances to discuss this later, that is, if anyone will want to hear it. But, right now, Gerlach, you're captain and a leader and you're acting like you've got the fire hoses out at Selma and somebody actually cares. No one wants to hear your crap, Gerlach, especially right now. Straighten up, or I as the faculty rep will throw your butt off the team! You decide, do you stay and play, or do you want to have a Ku Klux Klan meeting, somewhere else preferably?"

"You can't do shit here, Al," Ted said to Father, now taking it personally, "Your days are over! You took yourself out of the game to become some fuckin' wimp priest."

Big mistake, Ted. "Oh, yeah?" Father shouted, "Okay, big man! Right here, right now! You wear your pads, and you try to get by me," Father lined up on the sidelines facing the field, "Come on, sissy!" Father yelled, urging, no, shaming Ted to get in front of him, "You make it to that bench behind me, we'll do it your way. I'll even give you three chances. If I stop you three times, you play our way, or you walk. Fair?."

Ted didn't know quite what to do. No one does, including me. Father Al apparently is a few two by fours shy of a house frame. He hasn't blocked anybody since that day at the Orange Bowl. But, seven years later he's here putting it all on the line. Fortunately, he had worn a spare pair of turf shoes, I'm certain divinely guided.

The black guys started closing in up front, liking this action. It's a strange way to spread Al's ministry, but it has Ted confused.

Father has a red face and glowing embers for eyes. He's not bluffing. "Come on, fat boy! Put it to work! Put your beliefs in action. I'm for equality among the races, among all people. I represent the less fortunate, the oppressed. I represent blacks, Jews, Muslims, Buddhists, everybody you despise lives within me. Come on! Three shots. Or," as Father approached Ted frozen in his tracks, "are you the wimp?"

Ted straightened up, "Okay, goddamn it, you got me!" The G-man lined up in front of Father Al.

"You're damned straight I got you," Father spat, "Mason! Blow the whistle!"

Here we are, in the middle of one of the biggest rivalries in all of college sports, in front of forty thousand people, the number one team across the field, on national TV, and a hundred football players circle a piece of the turf for the ultimate Challenge Day, a spiritual shit drill, good vs. evil, a live allegory. Father has no helmet and no shoulder pads, but, as I thought about it more and more, Ted has no chance.

They each got into a three-point stance. I blew. They cracked, and at first they went nowhere, then Ted went quickly on his ass. The black guys whooped it up, and the white guys are not about to jump on Ted's side yet. Father stood above him and even helped him up.

"Two more, pussy!" Father said, uncharacteristically for a priest using the common football derogatory term. They lined up again, this time Ted snorted through his mouthpiece.

Father didn't have a mouthpiece, but it didn't matter because Ted was pancaked again in a matter of a few moments after I blew the whistle. More hoots from the brothers. This time, Father offered no assistance in getting Ted to his feet. He backed up and took his stance for the last time. Father has a gash above his left eye. Blood is pouring down his face, the scent and the feel of which I know brought back even more wrath.

Ted lined up on fire. Gerlach has one more chance and he's going for it if only to save face. I blew the whistle for the final time. Father popped him with the hardest hit I have ever seen from a dead stop. Ted was down in an instant, and the blacks went crazy with their personal victory.

Ted is beaten, in many ways. As Father with the bloodstained collar extended his hand for the sportsmanlike handshake, Ted eschewed it and walked off the field to the dressing room. I thought quickly, sending two of the militiamen with him to back up the two guards protecting our stuff.

As I watch Ted exit the field I hope someday he can win over the hatred he learned from his father and his father's father. I also have the funny feeling that now even without Ted and his skills, we have a chance to win this game.

Saturday, November 8, 1975
Fourth quarter

The comeback

Ted had for the most part held Hank Gerard back. His disappearance leaves a gaping hole in Vinny's protection, because the guy behind Ted at second team left tackle is a freshman, Wayne Lockman. Despite being a big, mean kid, Wayne is still eighteen years old, not the sharpest tool in the shed, and, hailing from Deep Creek, Maryland, a bit naïve. He hasn't played a varsity down of college football in his young life, but why should that concern me, since Vinny and I hadn't either. The problem is Wayne is now being injected in the game in the most pressing fifteen minutes of Runner history. He'll have to learn fast, damned fast.

Luckily, Wayne doesn't carry the philosophical baggage Ted has. His only concerns in life are a) football, b) his girlfriend Dias Ann, who won Miss Daisy Mae of Western Maryland and in the late summer months of the first semester always dressed the part (we all kept our comments to ourselves), c) the television shows *Happy Days* and *Laverne and Shirley*, from which Squiggy is his hero, d) the doo-wop Sha Na Na, and e) his Mustang 283. Everything else doesn't matter. Therefore, being a

Blue Chip who ended up at West Virginia because he didn't make the ACT cut anywhere else and barely made it here, he kept his eligibility by having an army of tutors for every one of his remedial bonehead classes. I saw Wayne's future back in Deep Creek as early as next year as one of the only carburetor repairmen in the world tipping the scales at three hundred while Dias Ann popped out babies and remained stacked for the rest of her life.

The brothers crowded around to congratulate the Father.

"You're one bad mother, Father," said a beaming Monty.

John added, "Way to go, man!"

In fact, the black guys' sentiments can be summed in one colloquial word, "Da-yum!" Like my dad's Marine buddies, my brothers know a badass when they see one.

"Father, what can I say? I think you brought us back to each other," I whispered.

"Think nothing of it," Father said while a trainer placed a butterfly patch on his cut, "I had enough of him."

"No, I mean it, Father. This morning, I asked you to take care of Ted. You sure as hell did. Now, I have another job for you," I said, motioning my head toward Wayne, "There's your next project. Wayne Lockman. He's not too bright, but I think he understands you and he'll pay attention."

We looked at Wayne. He appears to be frighteningly calm, not aware of Pitt or ABC or black or white or Hank Gerard. My inclination is to be optimistic and think he's just mean as hell and simply won't back down to anybody, or possibly any animal.

"He'll be all right," Father Al said, "Just take care of your business, and I'll take care of Wayne."

"Cool, Father," I said, and I forgot all about it. I turned my concerns to the Major. The entire game he and his militiamen have done a fabulous job caring for our sidelines. No one, by that I mean Fadden's or Lawson's infiltrators, had attempted to breech Joe's troops. Maybe few will admit they agree, but I continued to think the employment of the militia is the Idea of the Day. Andy Wilmore allowed us to not worry and play football.

However, we are down two scores against a white hot Pitt team and this would be the perfect time for the administration to come down and take over. And where does the PD mess fit in here? Impotent coaches, an emasculated athletic director, a banker either lying or lied to…or maybe not…perhaps we'd better load those rifles.

I motioned for the Major. "Major," I said, "we're here at the end of the game. I suggest you tighten up and go on red alert or whatever you guys call that."

"I understand, Mason," the Major said, "You'll be just fine. We'll do our job and that means you can do your job."

"Major," I said, extending my hand, "thanks. You've been the key. They've stayed away from us and it's all because of you and your men."

"Just doing our job," replied the Major modestly, "Just doing our job." I smiled and let him get back to work.

I found Vinny. The Gunner is a fourth quarter guy. When everything is on the line, Vinny wants the ball in his hands. In the high school state championship game we played against each other, after his wimp receivers had been beaten physically and emotionally, we still had to contend with Vinny. He took over and gave us a real scare, almost one-manning Madonna to the victory. Now, our cancerous sore has walked and therefore our spirituality is the healthiest I've ever witnessed, but we're still down fourteen and we need a spark.

"Gunner, you know you're going to have to show us the way."

"You bet," said Vinny directly into my eyes.

"The offense is yours, the receivers are primed, you're at The Ridge, the nation is watching, and this is Pitt. Win it for us."

He smiled. "You got it, Pappy."

We shook hands. Vinny tickled the palm of my hand with his index finger much like the sign junior high boys usually give girls for what they think means 'let's have sex.' He smirked, telling me without saying,

'I'll win the damn game for you, okay?' This could be a good omen. But, I probably would have tried to steer the *Titanic* into port. Speaking of that, I think this listing team is miraculously righting itself. And we've got The Gunner. Just another great day to be alive.

Indeed another great day to be alive, but just not as exciting as earlier. Pitt's offense and their two methodical drives for touchdowns has wrung the fervor out of the crowd. It's as if they are beginning to catch on that we are truly getting leveled. You can tell that two more unanswered Panther scores would, with our fans knowing that we haven't beaten these guys since Goldwater ran for president, send them to the exits to get an early start on their Saturday evening parties. The stadium has an atmosphere of the mandatory pre-prom high school assembly on the dangers of drunk driving. However, we as Runner football players know well of the fickle nature of the crowd. They're like my old high school coach used to tell me, 'Son, I'm from Missouri. You gotta show me!' I always thought that was odd since he was from Glen Rogers up some holler, but I got the meaning.

I have all the confidence in the world that Vinny knows what to do. If The Kid had been the man, I mighta walked after *The Star Spangled Banner.* Even if only to satisfy curiousity, I want to stay and find out how The Gunner's going to do this. I bet if Jean isn't beside him topless, he lies in bed and puts himself in these situations and thinks his way out of them. Vinny's the kind of guy who would start a pack-a-day habit just for the challenge of breaking it.

The ten of us huddled after the touchback kickoff with our new man Wayne. I'm sure he has never played in front of this many people before, but he looks to be unfascinated by it all. Maybe he's thinking about what the Fonz is going to do next Tuesday night. I don't know. I just hope he does it because, as he is the man protecting The Gunner's blindside, I'd like to see my friend Vinny make it home tonight in one piece.

Vinny arrived. "Dhall, you are the man. Power I. Dhali wide left. Clark right. Mason slot left. Mason hook. Clark ten and out. Dhali, fifteen and cross. I'm throwing it in front of you. Don't wait. On one. Ready?"

"Break!"

After spending almost the entire third quarter on the pine, we approached the line a bit more timidly than I would have hoped. Pitt, however, has the swagger of national champions. They have us in a hammerlock and just simply wanted to break our necks as soon as they could. However, you can sometimes tie a turnaround to one or two events. And our first one came from, of all people, our big Squiggy.

Pitt's Gerard, the captain who definitely will be playing on Sundays next year, saw the new fresh-faced boy line up in front of him. I was standing but a couple yards from him when he laughed sinisterly, shouting, "Little boy, I'm going to rip your dick off and stomp on it!" I bet he's going to at least try.

Wayne the freshman looked bored. He unceremoniously unsnapped his chinstrap, raised his facemask over his mouth and spat a loogie right in Gerard's face. Wayne's saliva stuck to Hank's nose and cheeks and dripped down onto his jersey. The Pitt d-lineman is frozen in his amazement. Lockman must have been saving all day for that one. Wayne closed by saying, "Get fucked, you miserable pussy!" Wayne then righted his headgear and got into his stance. Thus end my concerns about Wayne. I don't know what Father Al said to him, but it worked.

"Set! Hut!"

Pitt's Bobson stayed with me as I ran my hook. I finished facing Vinny. The second seminal event started with The Gunner. He stood in the pocket as humanity closed on him fast, took one step up and, with the quick release of Namath, shot a rope out of his hand in a hurry. Playing spectator and following the rocket over my head, I turned in time to see Dhali streaking over the middle with Washington giving chase. If the safeties are even the slightest preoccupied, a crossing route, even those poorly thrown, are sure completions. But, if your QB possesses the arm and the accuracy of Vinny, he'll put you in the position to grab the ball in mid-flight at top speed and run for daylight.

That's what Dhali did. In an instant he had the ball and was doing his best Secretariat at Belmont down the home team sidelines. The Runners' fans, who had absolutely nothing to cheer about since I nailed Osberg at the start of the half, leaped to their feet and let out a collective roar. Dhali's headed toward The Bowl as the noise became deafening, cruising at his four three that I'm sure had the dozens of NFL scouts in attendance to see all the horses on the field today in still further wonderment of My Man. Only Denzil, himself fast and coming in at an angle, had a chance with Dhali. The Pitt safety caught up with him at the twenty and finally dragged him down at the ten. Dhali jumped to his feet and stomped around in disgust, being only a tick of the clock away from his second long TD of the day.

He has not a thing to be ashamed of. His marvelous play jump-started the crowd and reminded us we have the stables to beat these assholes.

The next huddle is transformed. We're excited in anticipation of the score, and are awaiting the orders from our headquarters, Vinny.

Vinny started, "This is six. Guaranteed. Clark wide left. Dhali wide right. Mason slot right. Frank tight right. Right side flood right. Clark, fade to the flag left. I'm going to lay it up and duck it a little so you can see it. Get up and get it, Big Man! On two. Ready?"

"Break!"

The duck remark is funny. Vinny is a finely tuned throwing machine. He could probably vary the number of rotations per minute if he had to.

I can from my vantage point see that Pitt doesn't exactly believe they're being threatened. They lined up like it's second and six at midfield against Temple. Dick 'Night Train' Lane, old of the Detroit Lions called this, 'giving them enough rope to hang themselves.' And Vinny is tying the noose right now.

"One ninety six! One ninety-six! Set! Hut! Hut!"

I broke my route because the fan in me wants to see this one. Looking back quickly, I saw Vinny take a two step drop and loft one for the left corner flag. I'll be damned if it didn't have a slight wobble on it! Clark drew Bobson and Denzil, but The Gunner's pass was so perfectly timed and Clark's six-seven went up at just the right moment that he could have caught the ball over the entire University of Pittsburgh student body. Clark got his long fingers around it and brought it in, hit the flag, and the official threw up his arms to signal TD. The crowd pegged the decibel meter again as we drew within a score of the tie. Another end-zone celebration ensued, and Pitt, I know, stood wondering exactly how much they would have to do to put us away; we, the very annoying Runners.

We again took our good ol' time getting from the site of the TD to the sidelines, bringing with us the fans in the stands. By any football standards, the Ridge Runners should be dead and buried by now. But, our faithful doesn't give a damn about strategy or experts or history or ranking in the polls. Pitt has shown they can hold the ball whenever they want to, but we have proven our ability to strike quickly. There are many ways to play this game, and that's why the scoreboard is the only stat that counts. They don't give points for style.

Vinny held and Raj punched the XP through, making it Pitt twenty-eight twenty-one. There are a little over fourteen minutes left in the game, enough time for anything to happen.

As I lined up to take another shot at the Pitt wedge, I considered The Gunner, us the receivers, the new offense, and results. I think we've got it going now. When we get the ball, we'll be able to do it.

Raj sailed the kick so far it bounced into The Bowl on one hop. I thought of the future importance of that while I yelled at my new friend number forty-eight, "Hey, four eight, go fuck yourself!"

"I got your ass next time, pal!" he spat.

"You like my ass, don't you, Trixie?"

Things are falling into place right at the right time. So, not to take any chances, I violated one of my spiritual canons. I prayed for a win.

God didn't give me a sign right away. Pitt's offense took over yet again as Osberg ran as if he's going for a unanimous Heisman verdict. I suggested to Michael to as before bring the safeties up and stack the lines, leaving the corners 'on an island,' meaning they're on their own if Pitt passes. We dared Osberg to run at us. But even with nine on the line, Pitt didn't even try to throw. And they don't have to. The runs lengthened in yardage, taking less time off the clock. In four minutes, Drew swept right untouched for the endzone, and we are back to a two TD deficit.

Runner fans in the stadium and I'm sure across the state are shocked beyond words. The players stood still for the most part with blank stares, like victims of a storm. Michael walked off the field. I patted him on the shoulder as he bolted by me and threw his helmet against the wall. Sitting for a minute with his head in his hands, Michael jerked up and screamed, "No more, goddamnit! That's it!" No one really paid attention to him, the proclaimer of the declarations of a desperate man.

I'm perplexed. I keep turning to the scoreboard, hoping the score, the time, the quarter, something, anything would change the next time I glanced at it. To my dismay, it always remained the same.

I looked around. We Runners are despondent as our beliefs in ourselves start to fade. The kickoff receiving team took the field under the black cloud of hopes unfulfilled, acceding to a disposal of themselves in history in the ranks of the Wallflowers. We missed out on the Big Schools four years ago. We did everything we could against Penn State and castigatingly ended up on the short end on a fluke kick. Now, the only other chance we have to reclaim lost pride is slipping away. It is times like these in all competition when you have to reach down deep and pull out the guts it takes to keep going, to keep yourself in there and fighting. We seem to be reaching and finding nothing.

I wish I could think of something to say to pull us out. I tried and tried, but Jim Morrison haunted my mind, 'This is the end / beautiful friend / this is the end / my only friend, the end / of our elaborate plans, the end / of everything that stands, the end...'

But, somebody forgot to tell Vinny. He stood back behind the bench throwing to Dhali and Clark grinning, like 'I don't give a shit if it's '75 Pitt or the '75 Cincinnati Reds or the Soviet ice hockey team or Satan, I'm going to beat these fuckers.' I've known The Gunboat for about as long as I can remember. I've always thought he was special. But, I've never seen him like this. Ninety-six of us may be ready to throw in the towel, but I quickly pulled myself out, becoming a member of a trio of wideouts ready to follow Our Man. In a matter of moments just looking at Vinny refueled my soul with the zeal it will take to do it. Now I know how the third wave at Midway felt, and you know what happened there.

Vinny sauntered up to Michael, sitting depressed, staring blankly, conceding. The Gunner knelt to get in the captain's face. Michael looked up to see Vinny's right hand jutted before his eyes. The QB held up four fingers.

"This is us, Michael," Vinny said, "This is everything we sweated and heaved for this summer. We prepared ourselves to play in the fourth quarter, when it counts. I've always been a fourth quarter guy, Michael, I own the fourth. Michael, we own the fourth. Look at these four fingers, Michael. We own the fourth."

Michael's eyes quickly blazed. He immediately stood and raised his four fingers back to Vinny. A mischievous grin overtook his face as he nodded his head in the affirmative to Vinny. Michael turned to the bench with his four fingers, "Fourth quarter, dudes. This is it. This is us." Heads turned up. Hands with four fingers extended. First several, then dozens. An entire sidelines of twentysome year olds were refired with a simple hand gesture. Vinny's four fingers and the certitude he put behind them renewed the team's spirit. Sports is strange. The oddest things can get your octane up.

The Gunner winked at me and stepped up beside Michael. He tossed a football to his fingertip and spun it as if it were a Globetrotter basketball. "Men," he proclaimed, "we are ready for prime time."

Cheers and yelps enveloped the sidelines.

Pitt's Archer boomed it out of the endzone. We started on the twenty, consistent with the lousy field position we've had all day. Vinny and I entered the huddle last. The Gunner glanced at me, determined and nodding. Anybody who can live with Mike Vacca has to look at a situation like this as Frisbee in the park.

My boy took control. Vinny called for Clark on the sidelines and hit him for nine yards. He then found Dhali on a hook for thirteen more. After seeing all of us receivers covered, Vinny scrambled about to avoid the Pitt rush long enough to get Arthur open for nine. Three consecutive completions in a minute and we're in Pitt territory. The manic-depressive crowd once again became elated, doing what they could to pull us downfield. On the next play, Vinny sent me to my favorite place, over the middle where my masochistic tendencies take over. Denzil saw me coming and pounded me, but only after I caught the bullet and hung on for thirteen. I jumped right up and jutted the ball in Jeff's mask, saying something like "You're going to have to hit harder than that, you fucking faggot!" We got in each other's faces, discussing various topics.

"Don't be bringin' that weak shit here again. I'll kill you," Jeff offered.

"You and what sorority, princess?"

"You're a motherfucker!"

"So, she was *your* mother?"

No one can outwoof me. My late father taught me to hate Pitt with a passion, and Vinny knows this, running up to me and pulling me away from a sure fight.

"Back off, Ivy," Vinny said. "Drop him next time."

The exchange of words only took the crowd up higher. There is nothing bad about that. So, playing off the spark of my near altercation, Vinny to hit Clark on a deep out for eighteen. The NFL looks for QBs who can put the deep out on a line, and Vinny surely had to impress them with that pass, as well as with the fact that he had just thrown his seventh straight completion.

We are sitting on the Pitt eighteen, surrounded by The Bowl. Nothing can be better. But, this is football and we are the Runners and it is times like these when it just reaches up and bites you on the butt. Vinny is chased out of the pocket on the next play and ran around until he saw our fullback Frank alone on the ten. Making his only mistake of the game, albeit a minor one, Vinny zipped the ball to Frank when a soft liner would have done the job. The pass caught Frank by surprise and bounced off his shoulder pads and in to Mark Washington's hands.

Mark took off with his interception down the Runner sidelines. I caught up to him quickly at the twenty-six and hit him high from behind in an attempt to take the fucker's head off. I inadvertently grabbed his facemask, and knowing I was going to be flagged anyway, and knowing this is my last game for the rest of my life, I decided to attempt some real damage. I twisted it and pulled down hard, jerking his head and the rest of his body smartly to the turf. The Pitt defense didn't agree with my tactics and went after me. Coming to the aid of my body and my honor, the men on our sidelines went after them. Pitt's bench then cleared, with their fiftysome running across the field. Well over a hundred forty men, all of us much larger than the American norm mixed it up. A lot of foul language and promises to kill mothers and have sex with sisters and one another's girlfriends was heard. I found myself in the mass of meat and male hormones standing before Hank Gerard.

"You don't do that to my man, you got it?" Hank boomed, pointing his big finger in my facemask.

I grabbed his mask and replied calmly, "Get your fucking finger out of my face or I'll puke it back into yours."

The finger remained, "I hate you lowlife bastards!"

I bit his finger hard, drawing blood. He screamed in pain.

"Ahhh! You son-of-a-bitch!"

Inspired by Wayne, I spat the blood, his blood onto the front of his white jersey. Hank's red-stained monster fist went way up and back, only to be caught by Monty.

"Play nice, girlfriend!" Monty reminded him. That saved my little ass....

Incredibly, no real fights resulted, but it took a couple of minutes to maintain order. We did jack the crowd up, though. They liked the altercation, despite us losing the ball with the pick-off. I think The Bowl's ready for the endgame.

After we all returned to our respective sidelines, three penalties, only three penalties surprisingly, resulted. The ref called unsportsmanlike conduct on both teams, offsetting penalties with no net yards marked off. Then, the ref called a facemask penalty on me with a warning that if I do anything like that again, I will be ejected from the game. Under my breath, I told him to fuck off. I'm really steamed. He marked off the fifteen yards, placing the ball on the Pitt forty-one with just under nine minutes left in the game. I guess he missed my mid-game snack.

Vinny made sure Frank knew it's not the fullback's fault for the pick-off. "I didn't throw it right, Frank. I take all the blame. Forget about it. I am. The Runners are going to need me and you out there. It's okay." I heard that. It almost made me cry. My man is such the leader.

Vinny and Michael passed each other on the field after the fight. Michael raised the four fingers. A quarter ago, hell, a couple of minutes ago the interception, the first turnover for either side in this extremely competitive and well-played game, would have put us under. However, right now the 'meeting' Pitt had with us flashed our juices. Our defense took the field ready for a rumble. And even though Pitt and Osberg are their stellar selves, we're fired up enough to slow them down to the point where they aren't eating up the yardage in the chunks as they had been doing. The Panthers are finding it more difficult to get through us. They moved slowly, taking four minutes to get only thirty-five yards. Osberg and his buddies were impeded almost single-handedly by Michael. The Runners' captain is a man playing as if this game is the last chance to recover the pride of the seniors and to get paid for the sweat equity he put in this summer. I can see the pump come back to him and getting unleashed on Pitt. Whomever Michael hits has to feel it. I'm just glad he and I are wearing the same color jerseys.

Michael stopped Osberg cold on our twenty-five with a big, I mean huge cleats-up pop to make it fourth-and-eight. We keep laying him out and Osberg keeps taking them. Damn. When's he gonna die?

Pitt's Legendary Coach sent his field goal team out. The attempt will be from forty-two yards, within Eric Archer's range. Four minutes forty-one seconds showed on the clock. If Archer slices this one through, we'll need three scores in less than five minutes against the number one team in the nation. I confessed my sins to God for my less-, much less-than-gentlemanly play, then resubmitted my prayer for victory.

Pitt is set for the kick. Archer's back and ready. The holder knelt. There is no breathing on our sidelines.

Chandler Childress is a three-year starter at cornerback for the Runners. As a high schooler from Penn Hills in Pittsburgh, he set the WPIAL blazing with a great career as a running back. The problem was his size. Only five-eight and one hundred sixty-five pounds, the big schools, despite Chandler proving his ability to compete in one of the best leagues in the country, passed on him. Signing day came and he considered his only choices, Howard, Hofstra, and, in spite of being black, Hampden-Sydney. He said 'screw that,' and drove down the interstate to walk-on here in Montani. His freshman year he was linebacker fodder on the scout team. But through hard work and faith in his outstanding abilities, and also because of a miraculous late growth spurt taking him to five-ten one eighty, Chandler got a first team corner position. It still wasn't easy. His sophomore year he earned the dubious nickname 'Charcoal Chandler Childress' because he was burned for touchdowns a lot. He didn't give up, improving his technique through his junior year, and coming into his senior year as a pre-season All-East pick. Chandler backed that up by not allowing his man a TD all season. He's attracting some NFL looks, but that's not what's important now.

Chandler lined up wide right, ready for the charge. He anticipated the snap perfectly, and zipped by the wingman blocker. With no one else there to get in his way, and with the jump and his acceleration, the diving Chandler arrived beside Wendell as the ball's coming off Archer's foot. He blocked the kick and recovered it in the same leap. The crowd loved that one. A big play such as Chandler's can mainline a spark into a team. Despite still being down fourteen, I feel we now have our best chances of the game. How many times have I said that?

The offense attacked the field, with notable exception to Frank Adams. He's still punishing himself for the botched pass and resulting interception, not ready to play in the best frame of mind. I ran beside him and talked to him.

"C'mon, Frank! Let it go! We're going to need you! You're the toughest guy on the team. If Vinny gets us down close, you're going to be the man. Don't worry about that pass. Vinny threw it too hard. Get tough again, Frank! Pull it out!" Sometimes in the heat of the game things that take hours otherwise happen quickly. I can see the weight being lifted from his shoulders. I think I the English major got him the big fullback ready to play football.

As Vinny approached the huddle, I know Pitt's ready. They know the pick is the luck of the bounce. We have spent the entire last drive either open right away or with Vinny motoring around until one of us became open. The Panthers' d-backs are an extremely talented and proud group. They are also smart and well coached. The DBs have been mixing coverages well in an attempt to anticipate our new passing game. We're making it tough on them, but they're not about to get pushed around like the last time.

Forget about it, Pitt. You've never faced Vinny when he's 'Zoned.' I can tell by just looking at him. He now, right now in the final few minutes, feels as if he is unbeatable. In fairness to The Kid, Bobby Kay actually had the better gun. However, Bobby's a thrower. Vinny's a passer. And a leader. That's why we're moving the ball with The Gunner.

And consider this. Pitt's never this year gone against our three amazing receivers. Yes, three. I've talked about the outstanding talents of Dhali and Clark. I now include me in that group. My best friend's command of the game had rubbed off on me. I honestly feel with my speed and my willingness to go up and out with total disregard to pain, they don't have anyone who can stop me. I know it and, considering my two catches under difficult conditions, they know it. Pitt can't make the mistake of leaving me alone and keying on Dhali and Clark. I'll smoke 'em. Go ahead, like Vinny said yesterday, hurt me. I don't give a fuck.

In spite of not being in the best field position, Vinny continued his march. He hit Dhali for sixteen yards on a deep out Washington had no chance of stopping. Arthur on the next play slipped out of the backfield. In a mismatch with a relatively slow linebacker Vinny spotted Arthur like a pro. Arthur grabbed the pass over the middle for nine. Vinny made the scouts look to Draft Day 1978 by roping one to Clark on an out for fifteen more, landing us on the Pitt end of the field. My buddy then completely frustrated Pitt's d-line by leading them in a chase that culminated in a breakdown of Pitt's coverage, leaving Dhali alone to catch a twenty yarder. I gave Dhali a few of those yards by tattooing the turf with Bobson's body. If I could have gotten to play every play of every game this year and was not allowed to touch the ball and was only allowed to block, I would be a very happy man. I love to hit people.

"Get up, Bobson! You're my meat!"

Jim jumped up. "Come back at me, Bricker! I got something for you!"

"I'll be there, sweetheart! You'll be on your back again!"

Once again, in less than a minute, Vinny has taken us down to scoring territory on the Pitt twenty-one. Once again, we are in the middle of The Bowl, and once again, the fans came alive with hopes of an unprecedented comeback.

Vinny shifted gears at what I thought was the right time and gave the ball to Arthur on a draw play, a run designed to make the defense think pass and open up a hole in the middle. Unfortunately, the Runners looked as if we're going to revert to our old ways. As Arthur saw green turf in front of him, he tripped over Monty's size nineteen shoe and got only one yard, setting up second down and nine. The clock's going to run with less than three forty left, so I directed Arthur to call time out and stop it. We have two remaining, allowing for any time management we'd have to do at crunch time, as if this time isn't crunchy enough.

Vinny sent us out on a zone flood, but in keeping with the frustrations of the year, he got snagged on Monty's foot. Thinking quickly, Vinny dove at Frank with the ball, barely handing it off to the big guy. Frank's power got us two yards on a broken play in which we deserved to lose a few.

It is now third down and seven yards, a passing situation obvious to all God's children. Pitt therefore rushed four and dropped seven back to defend only five of us. We couldn't shake the coverage and get open, even after Vinny ran around, escaping the four time and again, stopping many hearts in The Bowl, I am sure. Several yards off the line of scrimmage occupying Denzel and Bobson, I saw Vinny come my way. He pointed downfield and tucked the ball, indicating to me he is going to run for it. Now, Vinny's not really built to run. We're the same weight, one eighty-five, but, being more muscular and stronger than he, I can take and dish out hits much better. However, Vinny is the ultimate competitor. He'll do anything short of parading naked through the streets of Montani for a win.

The two Pitt d-backs saw The Gunner take off and set themselves for the tackle just short of a first down. I knew three points wouldn't do us much good this late in the game. We needed a first to keep going for seven. I had a four-yard run at Denzel and Bobson, so I shot out at them, spread my frame out sideways and, as I do every kickoff threw it into the two. They apparently went down just enough because as I rolled I saw Vinny helicopter through the air and land behind them. The Gunner and I jumped up and saw he had gotten a yard beyond the sticks as the official marked the ball and indicated the first. The Bowl crowd went nuts, knowing how vital that is. They are also very impressed with Vinny's guts in flinging his QB body into the fray. Responding to the crowd, Vinny and I reacted to our collaboration on the block and run by hugging and slapping each other like we had just taken it all. That's football! That's real football.

"What happened, ladies?" I threw back to the two Pitt d-backs as Vinny and I ran back to the huddle. We are pumping fists and screaming. I glanced at the sidelines to see every Runner jumping, celebrating madly at Vinny's willingness, the skinniest guy on the team, to sell it all out for a very crucial play. We all respect The Gunner's QB skills and his ability to lead, but now he has attained permanent badass status. Because of that, I think every Runner is given the courage to do whatever it will take to win this game.

Vinny's fade lob to Dhali for the score is almost anti-climactic. Raj came in for the XP and we're within a touchdown and two of winning with three minutes and ten seconds left, definitely enough time for our lightning hot QB to do it again.

Lining up with the kickoff team to a huge rush of noise from the fans, I experienced a deep, almost ethereal feeling. This is an urgent moment for the Runners as a team, as an institution, and as a fighting army against bigotry. For me, in keeping with the deal I made with Fagden, it is my final three minutes on a gridiron. All of it quickly came back to me; from learning where the pads went to playing for the pleasure of my father to playing without my father to first donning the navy and silver and looking in the mirror and thinking I had arrived. It occurred to me that this could be my last trip down the field. And as Raj ran to the ball and cranked it through the air, an entire lifestyle of me the boy to the young man was focused into this one run. I decided to make it memorable.

Raj's kick was a boomer, bouncing off The Bowl wall seventy-five yards away. Still running at full tilt, I began scanning the three men of the Pitt wedge looking, as a lion on the savannah would, for my new buddy. There he is, name still unknown, number forty-eight in your program, and number one, as Casey Kasem would say, as the hits keep coming. He's turned away watching Raj's ball. And, just as luck again would have it, that solitary, random son-of-a-bitch turned back toward me. I thought of everything I held against Lawson and McNabb and Fadden and The U President Smith and Ted and the evil men who killed my good friend Michael's father, any and all reasons to concentrate the rage I feel for having the game I love taken away from me, and ripped into the poor bastard like a fuckin' tsunami.

Apparently no one on either sidelines nor the game officials saw it. Everyone wondered why a Pitt man is lying on the field out cold during a touchback. The game had been delayed for a couple of minutes as the Pitt trainers attempted to scrape his sorry ass from the turf. I stood talking to Michael, still dazed by the hit, discussing endgame defensive strategies, feeling like a man who had just pulled off the perfect crime. If indeed that's it for me at The Ridge, I am satisfied.

The excitement every athlete feels late in a close game clinched us and our souls on the sidelines as the twenty-two players squared off at the Pitt twenty. Mentally, Michael is at his best, empowered, taking it as his personal responsibility to stop these bastards and get Vinny the ball back. Despite my friend's overriding purpose, the greatness in Drew Osberg surfaced. On the first play, the Pitt running back reeled off his longest run of the day, taking the ball twenty-six yards to near midfield. The Pitt fans cheered in relief, and again, the Runner crowd is silenced, especially as the action and the game slipped away from them. The clock stopped on the first down, helping us out, saving time for Vinny to work what is slowly turning into the need for a miracle. Michael and the D plugged up the next two plays, and I am forced to use one of our two time-outs to keep our chances alive. On third down, Drew went thirty yards, breaking tackle after tackle, evident of our defense getting tired for being on the field almost all day. I could hear the spikes being hammered into the coffin over my head, and I once again confessed to God, this time for my sins against Jennifer and the lies for cheap sex, and against Joan for hitting the sack with Jennifer after committing my soul to Dr. Kissinger. If that doesn't get that victory prayer on His docket….

The clock showed a minute forty. Our defense lined up and stunted courageously, but I'm quickly realizing why Pitt is number one. They do it when it's in the balance.

I couldn't believe what I saw when the Pitt QB Wendell dropped back for their first pass of the afternoon, a pass called right in the middle of a time when ball control is imperative, a pass so surprising it might work.

~ ~ ~ ~ ~ ~ ~ ~ ~ ~ ~

Drew Osberg sneaked out of the backfield to the Pitt sidelines about ten yards downfield on the fifteen. Pitt planned to isolate him on a linebacker and loft one to him and get closer to a chip shot field goal for a ten point lead, thereby finishing off. Michael, expecting a run right, totally missed him. The Pitt QB put the ball and West Virginia's designs on an upset up in the air.

Joe Osbourne had been frustrated all day with double team blocks, never getting a clear shot at Mr. Heisman. But, the spy in Joe had sniffed this one out early and gave him enough time to draw a bulls-eye on Osberg. The warrior in Joe knew to never give up and knew this was his opportunity to get it all back. The homicidal maniac in Joe quickly achieved full speed and while thinking, 'join that Angolan national, you sad motherfucker,' plowed a very well timed hit into Drew's sternum, a hit so demolishing it cracked it in three places, taking the shock that would have liquefied his cardiorespiratory system and crushed his spine had the protective bone not been there. It's a hit so vehement Drew was rendered unconscious before he found the ground. Needless to say, the pass in Drew's hands popped up in the air.

Keith Shirley is a scholarship senior from Aliquippa, Pa., a career reserve at safety, sometimes lining up in practice on the second team, sometimes on the scout team. He had never consistently played anywhere but kickoffs, although warranting himself valuable with his intelligent coverage and his ability to hit. He comes from a family of eight children, the oldest of a black night-shift steelworker. Because of the large family Keith's only shot at going to college was to get a full ride. In spite of playing behind Drew Osberg in high school, he was impressive enough to attract the Runner's attention. Impressive is a perfect adjective for Keith, because for two reasons this has been the biggest week of his life. One, on Wednesday Keith found out he had parlayed his three eight in chemistry into an early admission at the U medical school for next year. And, two, he's now four strides from the floating ball. Keith took those steps, dove, and with the hands with which he will in the future serve and care for the injured and the ill, cupped under the ball for the interception. First down, Runners.

~ ~ ~ ~ ~ ~ ~ ~ ~ ~ ~

We all, Runners and fans, went absolutely crazy, except for Joe, that is, who stood a few paces back studying his kill. The paramedics gingerly lifted Osberg to the stretcher to be transported to the U Medical Center. Drew led his team with his remarkable talent and style and, after garnering his couple of hundred yards and five touchdowns today, will in all probability get that Heisman. My only hope is they'll have to wheel the fucker into The New York Athletic Club on a gurney to receive it.

Saturday, November 8, 1975
1:33 remaining in the game

The End Game

Mike endured the waves of emotion that have overtaken his heart, watching his son calling and executing, in the mind of the father, a near-perfect game. Vinny has responded to every Pitt threat with a score of his own. Now he has his team primed again. There is a long way to go and a short time to get there, but the father has for now dropped the propensity to be the critic and to second-guess his eldest, becoming Vinny's number one fan. Maybe Vinny was right this morning, he thought. This is a difficult concept for Mike since he never admits he is wrong. So, Mike decided something, of course on his own terms. If Vinny pulls out a victory here, he'll apologize. It's almost scoffing to their relationship, but it's the best he can do.

Patricia watched her son take control as never before. She looked down the row and saw Sal and Dom, admiring them. She thought of the financial success of her family, and even recalled a recent time she had been alone and had gazed with pleasure in the mirror as she donned that swimsuit from the honeymoon, a little tattered and very dated, but still fitting her like a hand in a glove. Patricia considered it all, even the fact that her husband is sometimes arrogant, and knows she is extremely blessed, no matter who wins this ball game. Nevertheless, she crossed her fingers and urged her Vinny down the field.

The other parents were together in their pleasure and zest for having their two favorite Runners on the field for the run at the victory. Geri and Pauline are arm-in-arm, feet stomping.

"*Come on! Come on, boys!*" *yelled Geri.*

"*Do it!*" *said Pauline,* "*Oh, shit, Ger, oh, shit! Where're those bloody Russians when you need one?*"

"*Right here,*" *whispered Geri, handing her buddy a silver flask from her pleated slacks,* "*without the blood.*" *They shared a couple of swigs in preparation for the final march. Patricia saw them and grabbed the flask for a big belt of her own.*

Their husbands are so engrossed in the game examining Pitt's defensive alignments they don't see their wives drinking. "*What's Pitt going to do?*" *Rob asked.*

"*Probably lose,*" *Wayne said. The two slapped palms like teen boys.*

I ran onto the field, excited as hell. A minute thirty-three left, down by seven, but eighty-five yards to go. We're in a helluva hole, but we've got the ball and we've got Vinny.

To be in a situation like this is the reason you play. You wait your entire life to be tested in a big game with it all on the line, just to see if you have the mettle.

Arriving in the huddle, I checked out my teammates. The linemen are smiling and slapping each other on the ass. Arthur is intent. Frank is clapping. Dhali and Clark, knowing we have to pass to go so far in such a short amount of time, grinned. We look as if we have already done it, just what I want to see.

Vinny walked in and knelt. Ten hands with four fingers each went up. Vinny responded and grinned.

He started with the utmost self-assurance. "We're celebrating tonight, boys. West Virginia beats Pitt. Here's how it's going to happen. Dhali and Clark right. Clark slot. Flood right. Mason left," he said, then after shooting his brown eyes into my blues, "Twilley." The other players glanced around at each other, but I know what he means. "On one. Ready?"

"Break!" huffed us Runners.

In Super Bowl VII in January, 1973, the undefeated Miami Dolphins were facing the Washington Redskins. The experts, citing Miami's creampuff schedule, doubted their ability to beat the venerable George Allen and his battle-tough squad. But with the score tied late in the first half and the ball around the 'Skins thirty, Dolphin QB Bob Griese sent Howard Twilley, a possession receiver out of the pass-happy University of Tulsa, on a special route designed to put him near the goal line. Twilley did that, running downfield and turning three steps slanting inside, bringing with him 'Skin corner Pat Fischer. Twilley then shot smartly on a slant out, leaving Fischer standing just as Griese laid it out. It was a beautifully timed pass and Howard pulled it in, dragging the barely recovering Pat Fischer into the end zone for the score. The network showed the instant replay several times from several angles. Impressive, I thought. The phone rang.

"Did you see that?" exclaimed Vinny from his home in Weirton to my home in Mullens. "Wasn't that great?"

"Wild, man," I the hipster said, "Bitchin'!"

The next week I drove up north to see Vinny. During our standard several hours on Madonna Field we must have run the route we called Twilley three dozen times. In fact, every time after Super Bowl VII we played pass and catch, we worked and worked Twilley until we could do it in the dark. Now….

Twenty-two men, eleven each, line up, by this time in the game having total disdain for one another, silent with exception to the seething breaths hissing through their teeth.

"Two ninety-two! Two ninety-two!" bellowed Vinny, "Set! Hut!"

The lines collided with raging fervor. I exploded as Bobsen ran with me, giving me the outside. I took it downfield fifteen, sold the inside, and cut out on the slant.

~ ~ ~ ~ ~ ~ ~ ~ ~ ~

Vinny dropped back five steps looking to the middle of the field. He pumped on Mason's first cut, then fired a rainbow toward a spot on the sidelines thirty-five yards downfield knowing after hundreds of reps his friend would be there.

~ ~ ~ ~ ~ ~ ~ ~ ~ ~

I looked back after my second cut and saw the ball in mid-flight. The pass is so well thrown I'm the only person on the field who can get to it. Turning it on, I reached for the ball, hauled it in, tiptoed, and fell out of bounds. On the ground, I glanced up to see the ref signal catch on about the West Virginia forty-five. First down, clock stopped at a minute twenty-four, and we're way out of the hole.

Thank you, Howard Twilley.

We huddled with renewed inducement. Monty said, "So that's a Twilley. I've always wondered what a goddamned Twilley was. Now I know."

~ ~ ~ ~ ~ ~ ~ ~ ~ ~

Vinny called for another flood right, this time with Mason and Clark in the inside slot. The three receivers are triplets, looking as if they're going to race. The Gunner took the snap, almost immediately saw all of his wide-outs are covered, stepped up into the pocket, and got flushed out to the left. He ran along the line of scrimmage, waiting, waiting, then seeing Dhali break free. Vinny on the fly drilled the ball into Dhali's gut. Both the QB

*and the receiver were hit hard but not before the Runners had a first down
in enemy territory on the forty-three. The clock stopped at a minute six.*

*The fans are honestly surprised to see their team move so far so fast. It
looked rather bleak in the beginning, but now noise returned to the stadium as the Runners injected life into the crowd that Drew Osberg and his
two big runs had earlier deflated. They are excited in anticipation of what
this final sixty-six seconds would bring.*

~ ~ ~ ~ ~ ~ ~ ~ ~ ~

Vinny split me out left and put Clark in my slot, leaving Dhali on the
right. Frank lined up slot right. He indicated in the huddle he wanted
Dhali, Frank, and me to run outs while sending Clark in over the middle. We all did just that. It didn't work. All four of us were well covered
by Pitt's zone defense, almost impenetrable with all the All-Somethings
forming it. Again Vinny had to scramble to buy time. The confusion
peeled valuable seconds off the clock and also drove the fans in the
stands completely bonkers. The pitch of the screams got higher as the
Pitt front four chased Vinny around like a cat in a garage. While I
worked to get open, The Gunner found Arthur hiding over on the left
sidelines. He hit him with the pass and Arthur got eight before the Pitt
linebackers caught up with him. Wisely, he got out of bounds on the
Pitt thirty-five to stop the clock at forty-four seconds. No first down,
but we still looked good.

~ ~ ~ ~ ~ ~ ~ ~ ~ ~

*Vinny again called for Clark over the middle. He's the best candidate for
that route. Clark is an ex-Runner basketball player who on a whim
decided to use his one year of eligibility remaining with the football team.
He doesn't possess blazing speed, but he's fast enough and is a huge target
with soft hands, able and willing to stretch it out and catch any ball near
him. Pitt changed coverages this time and oddly left a six-one linebacker*

on Clark, a gross mismatch. Vinny picked up on that quickly and fired one to Nestor high over the 'backers hands and into Clark's. The receiver was hit after a ten yard gain, a first down at the Pittsburgh twenty-five and a stopped clock at thirty-four seconds.

~ ~ ~ ~ ~ ~ ~ ~ ~ ~

You'd be hard-pressed to tell my man is a sophomore in his first varsity start. Vinny has moved us the entire fourth quarter like Namath or Johnny Unitas, this time sixty yards in about a minute. As a result of The Gunner's brilliant play, three things are happening. First, we Runners have gone from confident to cocksure, now thinking it's a matter of just a few seconds before our field general put us in the end zone to tie this mama. Second, we are moving closer and closer to The Bowl, where the students yelling with insanity are forcing themselves back into the game. And third, the Pitt defenders are shocked at our ability to push them back. With all they have at stake and with their inability to respond in kind to us, they are glass-eyed and sucking compost gas. Beautiful.

The huddle formed at the thirty-two. Vinny is gazing downfield, thinking, searching. Twilley has my confidence pumping hard. And the party's almost over for me. I got a feeling. I decided to give my buddy an idea.

"Vinny!" I shouted right beside him through the crowd noise.

"What?"

I closed in to his earhole, "What would Machiavelli say right now?"

Vinny is well aware that I am a closet academic freak, so he went along. Plus he has a soft spot in his heart for Italian philosophers.

"What?"

I grabbed his jersey, "He'd say, 'Give me the fuckin' football!'" I left on that to enter the huddle.

Vinny joined us. "Okay. Clark left. Mason slot left. Dhali right. I formation. The two big guys run deep outs. Mason Machiavelli, flag. Look fast. On set. Ready?"

"Break!" I know my Runners are wondering: first Twilley, now this Mack dude. What's this game coming to?

~ ~ ~ ~ ~ ~ ~ ~ ~ ~ ~

The teams lined up. Pitt didn't become number one by fading away. They dug in and dared the Runners to get another yard. They're rocking, jumping, snorting. During all this, Vinny spotted something. It's basically invisible to others, but after staring at the same guys all day you pick up on traits. He noticed a difference; two linebackers in the middle are trying their bests to disguise it, but they're leaning ever so slightly in toward the line. They're bringing a blitz, Vinny thought. He then knew he wouldn't have time enough to develop that flag to Mason, and it's too late and too loud to change the play with everybody. So, he did the only thing he could do. He looked at Mason.

~ ~ ~ ~ ~ ~ ~ ~ ~ ~ ~

I from my slot saw the linebackers, both of them, cheating a bit. I glared at Vinny as he glanced at me. Knowing then the play is off, I thought, now what? Then I thought again. The reels rolled through my mind again: all the games up here with Vinny and me in the stands, hoping, dreaming; the conversations, endless, about everything; the girls, from discovery to Jean and Joan; pass and catch, wind, rain, snow, broiling sunshine; attacking adolescence head-on and winning most of it; our embrace after our only face-to-face meeting on the gridiron; now college and the sensation of it all; and spending a season together on the scout team. My stare remained and he glanced a second time. Years and years and years with the same man. Our minds connected.

Vinny took the snap as the very athletic and aggressive Pitt line-backers went. I lost The Gunner in the fracas as I broke my assigned route and eased into the space the 'backers evacuated. Suddenly, there's the ball, splitting the two men and their flailing arms. A lovely bullet, hitting me right in the hands. I knew Vinny would do this! I clutched the ball a few yards in front of the line and high-tailed it.

There is nothing in front of me but twenty yards of artificial grass. I'm there! Even in my focus, I can hear The Bowl explode. That caused my adrenaline glands to burst and, with Pitt's Denzil and Washington closing in on me in front of the goal line, led me to give it all up as I attempt to hurdle them. One of them clipped my ankle and I flipped, landing on my head then flopping onto my back. Disoriented, I still managed to leap to my feet to find out where I ended up. Four yard line! Christ! That goddamned close! First down. Clock stopped. Twenty-seven ticks.

The Bowl crowd is beside themselves, totally unhinged. We're knocking on the door with seconds remaining and they can hardly stand it, much less believe it.

~ ~ ~ ~ ~ ~ ~ ~ ~ ~

Joan had picked up some football knowledge over the past few weeks, reading and thinking about the game in a more-than-subconscious response to her Battle with the Feelings for Mason. She recently learned what possession and a drive meant. Now it is all unfolding before her, with Mason figuring prominently in this attack. She wants desperately to see the Runners score, mostly if not all because she wanted good things and only good things for Mason. The age-old questions of age and position still cause confusion to bind the back of her mind, but she put that aside for now and did what she could in row AA to keep him going.

Pamela has done some work with the Chicago Bears this season, so she knows what's going on here. It's an entertaining game for her, especially this last drive where she has seen the two friends-for-life take over and eat up most of the yardage to get the Runners this close. As a psychologist, she's fascinated by the dynamics between Mason and Vinny, finding it mind-provoking that when it had to be done and done decisively and quickly, the

QB went right to the man he knows best, trusted most, the man with whom he has the most history.

"Mason's done an outstanding job," Pamela shouted to Joan above the roar of the crowd.

Joan has a worried look on her face, "Now every coed on campus will want him, and what's an old woman like me going to do to deal with that?"

"Remember that you're number one in his heart, meet him at the jazz club tonight, and tell him unequivocally how you feel," Pamela said more softly, on the verge of a major breakthrough with her longtime client.

"Oh, fuck you!" exclaimed Joan. Pamela smiled, smiling for Mason, knowing then her sister is his.

Two rows below, the four ladies are delirious. Judy, Alice, Jennifer, and Jean are wrapped up together, hands folded in front of their faces, apparently holding a makeshift prayer meeting. Jean is astounded by Vinny, never having seen this side of him. She always viewed him as your average bright, handsome man. Yet, today he has led the Runners, the state's only decent 'game in town' near the upset. West Virginia football is the source of pride and prestige for the residents of this small anonymous section on a map, from Chester to War, from Hurricane to Shenandoah Junction. Vinny has taken his team from certain defeat to where they are now, standing on the doorstep of the Upset of the Decade. It takes a special guy to face that challenge and come through, she joyfully thought. Maybe he'll be partner before age thirty.

Jennifer is most impressed. Her man got the ball. She imagined in ten years sitting in their family room, kids in bed asleep, popping open a bottle of chilled chardonnay, then making wild love on the floor, on the sofa, on the stairs, on the butcher's block, and in the backyard under the cloak of night. Jennifer's always been rather enamored by just the general nature of Mason, but today his athletic prowess has seized her. She's decided tonight is the night she, with her parents downstairs, is going to lead Mason to his room and drive him to delirium.

Judy and Alice aren't thinking in terms of marriage, sex, or accounting. Their friends, their housemates, the best man friends any woman could want are having the games of their lives, fulfilling the dreams they have often told the girls about. The two sat in The Bowl incredibly happy, tears flowing, jumping, screaming, wanting Vinny and Mason to finish this off so they can earn their places in the Runners' hall of fame. Judy and Alice, together exclaiming things like,'ohshitohshitohshitohshit!' just know they will do it.

Michele and MJo are under the influence of Bobby's and Brad's pot, the two women slightly buzzed, the two guys stoned. The sisters are insane with joy, watching their projects get the Runners into upset position.

"That goddamned Joan, that stupid bitch," Michele said, "I'm gonna give her until New Year's Day, then the Brick is mine."

"Go for it now, Professor!" the red-eyed Brad said in response, "I won't tell anybody."

"Nah. I don't know," Michele replied, "Why screw up a good thing?"

"Screw, Mickey, being an important concept here," MJo observed.

Michele laughed a laugh of an intelligent high woman, "Jo, you're evil. We'll see. Joan, you fool!" She turned around to Dr. Kissinger, quickly getting her attention. As the two instructors looked at each other in the midst of one huge party, Michele alternately pointed to Joan and pointed to the field, repeating the gesture a few times, trying to communicate, 'What the hell are you waiting for?' Michele then stretched out her arms beside her as if to say, 'Why not?' The point is made. Joan can only bite her lower lip and stare at Mickey as if trying to break through her indecision. Pamela nodded to Michele in approval.

The crowd loved the hit and the interception. They haven't sat since the first play. Each one of Vinny's five consecutive completions turned up the juice more and more until they found their team right with them, within spitting distance of The Bowl, just a few steps from immortality. If they have to, they'll just scream until they will their beloved Runners in there.

The Runners kept the same eleven: Wayne, John, Monty, Reginald, and Monty up front; Mason, Clark, and Dhali out wide; Arthur and Frank in the backfield, with Vinny at the wheel. Pitt brought in a couple extra d-linemen to bolster against the power run. But, Vinny has a plan. In the entire fourth quarter, Pitt hasn't touched him. The Runners' line has protected him, keeping the very strong, very fast Panthers at bay. Due to Pitt's excellent coverage, Vinny had to at times run out of the pocket to make things happen, but he has for the most part stayed on his feet, much to the frustration of the Pitt line. He decided to reward his six big guys with the highest of compliments. He's going to run his Runners directly down the throats of the number one team in the nation when both teams need it the most because he knows Wayne, John, Monty, Reginald, and Monty can shove Pitt back, way back.

~ ~ ~ ~ ~ ~ ~ ~ ~ ~

We huddled a few yards behind the ball. Vinny entered and smiled, looking into all our eyes, "Okay. You know, you guys have played so well today you're making everybody out there think I know what I'm doing," Vinny said. We laughed. First and goal on the four with seconds remaining and down a TD and our QB's a comedian. "So, here you go, line. It's all yours. Mason wide left. Dhali wide right. Clark tight right. Pro set backfield. Frank; 35 power. 35 power. On three. Listen! Late count. On three. Ready?"

"Break!" grunted the Runners.

The big guys sauntered to the line with the looks on their faces that they aren't going to take any crap from the Panthers. The wideouts and backs took their positions definitively. Vinny walked up to the center to a hard rush of human noise from The Bowl. He waived his arms over his head to quiet the crowd, and they responded like fourth graders to a twenty-five year veteran teacher.

This is a day of firsts and bests and mosts. I'm standing in the loudest Bowl ever. This is the best I've ever played, considering the level of the competition; two catches in the biggest of drives, man! This fourth quarter is the best the Runners have ever played as long as I've ever seen them. We've had plenty of chances to check out, and we've stayed in there. Now, here we are with a great opportunity, the second in three weeks to put ourselves among the elite. It'll affect recruiting, contributions, and future television. But to hell with all that. We just want it because we are a team.

~ ~ ~ ~ ~ ~ ~ ~ ~ ~

Frank Adams is the bruiser in the Runners' backfield. He comes from good stock for fullbacks. His grandfather Franklin was the big man in Penn State's single wing in the twenties. His father Bernard played the power guy for the Nittany Lions in the post-war years. And his older brother Brent was the tractor for Penn State's undefeated teams of the late sixties. So, when it came time for Frank to leave high school and move on, it was certain he would follow his family's legacy.

However, a lack of need for fullbacks in Happy Valley in the early seventies led Penn State to seek other players in other positions. Despite all the Adams' history, Frank was passed over for a ride with the Nitts. And if that weren't difficult enough to take, one of the assistants provided the final blow by telling Bernard that scouting and film determined that his younger son lacked the heart and desire it took to play for the school to which the Adams have given so much.

Treated by his family as if he had gone AWOL in battle, Frank in shame took the only other decent offer extended to him, the Statue of Liberty of college football, taking your tired, your poor, your huddled masses: The University of West Virginia. Frank arrived in Montani not in the best mental condition. He was rude and had a terrible attitude. True, his family's response wasn't helping matters much, but during Frank's first few weeks he was a drag on the team.

In radical introspection, he decided he couldn't continue living like that. He did a total turn around, throwing himself into the team, always hustling, the first in line for everything. During off-season, you had to bribe him with women to get him out of the weight room, and then only after another half-hour round of one more set, one more lift. Frank was a daily communicant at St. Mary's for the growth of his soul. And, odd for any football player of the seventies, he maintained a client relationship with a school psychologist to unlock his mind, completely hidden from his family who had they found that out would have considered legally disowning him.

Through it all, over the years, Frank became that big school fullback to which his family thought they had a birthright, better than any Penn State or Pitt had to offer. Better than his brother was. Thing is, now Frank is on the Runners' side of the ball. Vinny has called his number, he's on national television, and he knows this is his chance of a lifetime.

~ ~ ~ ~ ~ ~ ~ ~ ~ ~

Pitt dug in like a retaining wall. We are collectively aligned like a battering ram. Twenty-two major college athletes with world-class egos. Something has to give. Somebody is going to make a play here.

I lined up in my wide left position, my job to occupy the corner and keep the safety honest. I'm not going to be in the brawl. At one eighty-five, I wouldn't do much good, so they think. Maybe I'll get a chance to nail Denzel, the son-of-a-bitch.

~ ~ ~ ~ ~ ~ ~ ~ ~ ~

The crowd swelled again, then died down when Vinny raised his arms. As he called the signals, the Runners are perfectly still, as they have to be. The Panthers are bolting around, stunting, faking, trying to incite movement and earn a Runner penalty. The offense showed restraint and discipline and awaited Vinny's signal to kill.

The Bowl held its collective breath in anticipation. Will it be?"Set! Hut! Hut! Hut!"

Vinny took the snap, spun right, and laid the ball in Frank's belly as he ran left toward the line. Pitt put up a good fight and there wasn't much room to run. But, as Frank hit the line, a sliver of daylight appeared. He sliced through that, then squared his shoulders. A linebacker hit Frank low and a safety jumped on his back. It's not enough. Frank churned his legs and lowered his torso, carrying the two Panthers with him toward paydirt. A third guy met Frank at the one, but all he got was Frank's helmet in his gut. The four men ended up collapsed two yards deep into the endzone. In a classic fullback power run, Frank got his team the score they needed to put them down by one. Pitt thirty-five thirty-four. Twenty-three seconds remaining.

~ ~ ~ ~ ~ ~ ~ ~ ~ ~

Touchdown, baby! Frank showed his family a thing or two, the pricks! I ran over to greet him.

"Frank! Frank!" I shouted through the biggest Bowl commotion of the day as he disentangled himself from the three Panthers who didn't have one goddamned chance of stopping him. "Frank! Oh, yeah! Way to punch it in, Cement Head!"

Frank is beyond speech. He tossed the ball to the ref and accepted more congrats as we jumped around before the next play.

The next play! Oh hell! That's my call! I ran toward the sidelines, not really knowing where to go, meeting Michael halfway on the field. Arthur joined us, as did Vinny. The choices are these: go for an almost certain one point kick for a tie, thereby playing Not To Lose, or line up to run a play for two points, a more difficult endeavor, going for The Win.

The Bowl crowd is still celebrating wildly, having never lost faith in us, but never, never three-and-a-half hours ago dreaming of anything like this. Michael, Arthur, and Vinny are silent as they looked to me, the appointed head coach; I, English student, hopeless romantic, lover of an older woman…supreme competitor.

The captains and the quarterback await my verdict. Purposefully neglecting to evaluate and analyze the events and probabilities that lead to a decision of this gravity, it took me an instant to figure it all out.

"We're going to win it! Go for two!" I exclaimed, holding up two fingers in the hook-em-horns sign.

"All right!" screamed Vinny.

"Here we go, baby!" yelled Arthur.

I kept the fingers in the air as I ran back to the line, indicating to the other eight to stay out there for the next play. The crowd saw that and got it, torquing the noise up even further. Their Rebel Runners are doing the impossible. And I'm here to witness it, surely each fan thought. In my estimation, there's now not a one of them out there, not a D-Day vet, a Korea survivor, a Pork Chop Hill grunt, a Rosie the Riveter, a USO girl, a bandage roller, a sixties campus burner, a women's lib bra-burner, or a seventies joint burner, or just your ordinary, average citizen; not a one of them don't identify with our football team right now. We are America. We are symbolic of what every fan stands for. We are doing what everyone wishes they could do.

Taking a quick glance around the stadium, I see all in attendance out of his or her seats and on their feet. You can barely hear yourself think.

Vinny knelt in the huddle. He sported a grin. The Kid would be in a strait jacket at this point. But then again, he never, never, no way, would have gotten us here.

"Let's put it in, then let's party. Mason wide left. Clark and Dhali left slot. Stay behind the line. No offsides. Frank tight right. Flood right zone. No primary receiver. I'll roll right and try to find someone open. Let's go, baby! Let's take this game! On one. Ready?"

"Break!"

The two teams lined up, against one another all afternoon, but now boiling it down to one play. This is beyond national championships and bowl games and the pride of upsets. This is one play, West Virginia and Pittsburgh, separated by an hour's worth of interstate, mortal enemies since the turn of the century. This is even beyond football. We'da been satisfied if the refs would have simply turned us loose and let us beat the fuck out of each other.

I am the widest, so I'm to go in the end zone and run along the end line. Dhali has the middle of the end zone, while Clark is to run along the goal line. Frank and Arthur are to dash right then find an opening to Vinny's left. Pretty good set up Vinny called. It gives us a good chance.

Vinny barked the signals. "Set! Hut!" He took the ball from Monty and dropped back as he rolled right. We are all five, including Arthur and Frank, covered with a tent. Vinny kept rolling, hoping something would break. Through my concentration, I could hear the high pitch of the fans. I worked and worked the d-backs as The Gunner seemingly moved in slow motion. Finally, suddenly, I found a seam between Denzil and Bobsen. As I'm stationed on the end line, Vinny saw me. But with Denzel nearby, he'd have to throw it high.

I saw my man rock back on his right foot and launch a lasso just as a Pitt lineman crushed him. The pass is sailing, but within my reach. I jumped as never before with Joan in the back of my mind, running faster, jumping higher, my five-eleven skying for the ball. I got it with both my hands, my fingertips squeezing it in, a textbook catch. I came down on both feet after trying to pull them in toward the field to stay inbounds. This pushed me off balance and I fell with the ball firmly in my hands. Hitting the turf and rolling, I looked up amid screams to see the official running to the spot at which I landed. He hesitated for what seemed to be an eternity, then signaled first the waving crossed arms of an incomplete pass, then the sweeping motion indicating I came down past the end line.

My first instinct is to argue. I stood face-to-face with the official, "I was in! I saw my feet! They were in!" I yelled, not really knowing this but considering my duty to proclaim so.

"No, son, both your feet were barely on the line. Out," he said with the finality of a murder verdict. The score remained Pitt thirty-five thirty-four.

Groans and boos filled the stadium. I'm right in the middle of them, right where I had pointed out to my dad thirteen years earlier. I'm disappointed and exasperated.

Feeling as if I have blown the whole game, I handed the ball to the official. I walked away dazed, knowing I have let everybody down.

~ ~ ~ ~ ~ ~ ~ ~ ~ ~

Michele stood clapping her hands hard, "C'mon, boys! You're not going to lose this game! You've come way too far now!" She turned to MJo, "They're not going to lose this game, Jo."

"No way, baby! Go! Go! Go!" MJo shouted. In an attempt at the power of positive thinking, MJo said to her sister, "We gonna hit the field when they win?"

"Hell, yes!" Michele yelled, "Brad and Bobby here will protect us."

Bobby turned to Michele and passed out at her feet. "Well, maybe not," said MJo, "But, let's rush it anyway."

"A couple of old ladies! Yeah!" Michele exclaimed.

Joan had seen the play and the official and the result. She used to attend football games at Northwestern just to see who could out-sorority one another. Never paying attention to what or who or why, even if he was 'boyfriend of the month,' she and her sisters had one highlight of the after-noon. With Northwestern being such a doormat in the Big Ten albeit a most outstanding academic institution, the student body would late in the fourth quarter of a rout start the cheer, 'That's all right / that's okay / we're gonna be your boss someday!'

That was then. This is now. And she is now heartsick for Mason, feeling his disappointment, knowing his passions have brought him to this sum-mit, and a bad break has taken it all away from him. Joan felt an empti-ness and assuaged it by promising herself to stop being so obsessed with their differences and do something for him to make him feel special. After all of Mason's efforts to show his worthiness of her love, through being invaluable as her tutor, his respect for her as a woman and a professional, the propriety and maturity he displayed in his romance for her, especially with the letter and with the way he treated her like a lady at Michele's despite making his intentions very clear; after it all Joan allowed herself to find the humor in the fact that she finally yielded to her love for Mason during his football game. After taking Pamela's advice and after giving it all a chance to sink in, she decided to tell him what he wanted to hear, what she now believes in her mind and her soul to be true.

Pamela turned to Joan, saying, "They've got one more chance. It's remote. But it's a chance."

"What is it?" Joan asked.

"An onsides kick."

"I don't know what the hell that is, Pam, but I hope it works. My man is hurting."

Pamela held Joan in support of her sister and the price of her admission.

~ ~ ~ ~ ~ ~ ~ ~ ~ ~

Strangely, I quickly stopped feeling sorry for myself and got back into my role as the head man and chief cheerleader. I ran to our sidelines as the crowd was its quietest of the day. The fans were jolted out of the game and we had but one more opportunity to pull them back in.

The kickoff coverage team is huddled up at the fifty on our sidelines. The team has to my relief given me the rule of this entire game. I hope these next couple of plays will go as smoothly.

Entering the huddle, I see they're all anxiously awaiting my directives. Here goes. "We will do an onsides kick and we therefore need the 'hands team' out there. To review, Raj, tee it up on the right hash. Line up seven on the left and three on the right. On Raj's signal, the right side will run over to the left. Get set for a second. Raj, dribble a bouncer to hit ten yards down near the left sidelines. You all know who the 'hands team' is."

Keith, Dhali, Clark, Arthur, Dougie Roland, Joe, Michael, Chandler, Monty, and I comprise the 'hands team.' We are the guys who can catch and handle the ball the best. The reason why we need guys with good hands is because of the nature of the onsides kick. Football rules state that once the kickoff travels ten yards, in this case from the Runners' forty to the fifty, it's anybody's ball. So, instead of launching a kick downfield, Raj will chip one on the ground to land ten yards down near the sidelines, putting us in the position after we have run the ten yards to catch it or recover it. If we do, it's first down West Virginia and we'll have another chance to score. If we don't, that's the ball game and Pitt wins.

"All right! Get nasty and get the ball!" I shouted, "One, two, three, go!" "GO!"

The hands team lined up as directed. But, it's not that simple. Everybody in the world knows we're going to do an onsides kick, including Pitt, which has their own hands team out there, stacked near the midfield stripe, five between the fifty and the Pitt forty-five and the rest directly behind them. Because of the oblong shape of the football and the strange bounces it takes, and because there are twenty one guys with sure hands headed for the ball at the same place, and because the ball has to kicked, you just don't know what's going to happen.

Saturday, November 8, 1975
0:22 remaining in the game

Dream...dream...dream

There is more luck in football than any of us participants would admit, but the onsides kick, Jeez, it's the bingo of sports.

Raj raised his hand and the three hands men from the right dashed over with us on the left. After we were all set Raj approached the ball on the tee. As he practices daily except this time with the complete bedlam of the crowd in the background, he with his left kicking foot did a little pooch pop on the side of the ball. All of us Runners headed left for the fifty as the ball dribbled along the turf, on target to intersect with about ten of us, Runners and Panthers, in just a second.

I had lined up second man from the sidelines. Now inside the fifty and legal to bring the ball in, I saw it hit parallel to me five yards to the side. The ball did its second roll on the fifty jumped up on its third. Keith and Denzil from Pitt just beside me went up for it, colliding in mid-air. The ball careened off their pads.

Maybe it was that sweet older lady out the road whose porch I painted as a teenager for no charge. Or possibly it was the day I talked one of my high school classmates out of running away from home. Or maybe it is nothing. Maybe it goes back to my response after the landing gear engaged on the plane coming home from Penn State. Maybe I would rather be lucky than good. Regardless, the ball is heading for my knees. I crouched down, brought it into my arms, and hit the turf, rolling up to protect it.

Bingo!

Rolling back over to look up, I saw ten Runners jumping excitedly, pumping their right arms with the First Down West Virginia sign. The ref made the sign, too, and the crowd exploded. Just lost it. We are forty-nine yards away from the endzone, and there are only twenty-one seconds left on the clock, but it is cause for celebration. We're going to take the number one team in the nation down to the last play. Our destiny is in our hands. The fans in the stands like a good story, and they let us know it.

Because of the aforementioned field position and the short clock, this is not going to be easy. But it's a helluva lot better chance than anybody was giving us a day, Christ, even an hour ago. So, away we go!

Vinny and I met at midfield several yards away from the huddle. As quarterback and head coach, it is up to us to map out the final seconds of the game. Eighty-nine years of Runners' football and the biggest decisions to date rest with two sophomores who share joint ownership of several ounces of stash, a big bong and a few water pipes. I love this country.

We stared at each other for a couple of seconds as the forty thousand around us are setting new standards for the word berserk. I can tell we have reached the same conclusion, but Vinny said, "You say it."

Vinny told me something a few weeks ago that is foremost in our minds right now. Raj's longest kick in a game was from fifty-four yards last year for the win against the University of Virginia, a school which by the way each year offers degrees to the dicks of our society. He said Raj has in practice hit consistently with a snap and hold sixty yard field goals, a boss distance in comparison to other college kickers. At this point, adding ten for the endzone and seven for the snap, we're now sitting at sixty-six yards. We need to get just a little closer.

I said it, "One run. Arthur. Bleed the clock. Raj kick."

Vinny grinned, "Fifteen fuckin' ten on the SAT and you've finally said something smart." I laughed.

The starting offense huddled up at the West Virginia forty-five. Vinny and I joined them. The Gunner spoke. He has the plan. "Here's the deal. Twenty-one seconds. One time-out, which we've gotta save for the last play, probably a field goal. This play is: Mason left. Clark slot right. Dhali wide right. Frank, tight right. Arthur, off-tackle right. Get toward the middle of the field, get as many yards as you can, protect the ball. On three. Ready?"

"Go!" and we headed for the line.

As I stood in my position with the blasts of sound coming from the stands, I snuck a glance over the Pitt bench to the seats of my childhood in Row I. A big smile is pasted on my face. As the boy of then fantasized, I'm here.

Goddamn, go Arthur, go. He probably won't get a touchdown, but this is the biggest clutch run of the senior's career.

"Set! Hut." Pitt has no idea what the hell we're going to do. Are we going to go for broke and fling it down the field? Throw it underneath? Run it? Just what? I can sense the confusion among them

"Hut." It was supposed to be a lot easier than this for them. But they're on the field, seconds left, trying to save everything that is anything to a football team. I keep smiling.

"Hut!" Vinny took the ball, spun left, and gave it Arthur, who danced up the field, sidestepping, breaking grasps, holding the ball with two hands, spinning, then finally being tackled for a nine yard gain; nine of the toughest, most essential yards in Runner history. The official whistles blew. It's not a first down or out of bounds, so the clock kept running.

"Mason!" yelled Vinny, "Take over!"

I found Arthur, the captain. "Arthur, at three seconds, call the time out."

"Got'cha." Arthur ran over to the official. I heard him, "Sir, at three seconds, I'm going to call a time out."

"Okay, son."

"Take a breather, guys," I said to my teammates on the field, "At three seconds, we're going to win this son-of-a-bitch."

Thirteen, twelve....

"Raj?" asked Monty.

"Yep," I replied.

"Sweet, man! Sweet!" he said. He knows.

We stood in the huddle, with the exception of Arthur who's positioned right beside the referee. Pitt also has a time-out remaining, but they didn't burn it. They think our upcoming kick is in desperation. It is. I'll never admit it, but it is. This time, however, we've got our own wind gust. We've got Raj.

Eight, seven....

I'm not ten yards from the Panther head coach, watching him. He looked at me, too. This is probably the closest in proximity head coaches have ever been in the heat of the battle. I wonder if he knows I'm the head man? I wonder if it matters at all. Then I shot him the bird.

Six, five....

Half of the fans didn't know what we are doing. The other half know and disagree. Considering the distance, fifty-seven yards, most everyone thought it's too far for a kick. They want to see us put it up and get closer, at least. I gambled. Knowing what Vinny had told me about Raj and his kicking prowess, and knowing Pitt would drop back in an eight man zone, thereby making any passing very difficult, and knowing that any play could result in a lost fumble or an interception, taking all chances away from us, I decided to go for one play, a field goal, and run the clock down so after that field goal, Pitt won't have another crack at it.

Four, three....

"Time out!" Arthur yelled, making the T with his hands. The ref stopped the clock and signaled time out, West Virginia.

The crowd is on their collective feet, but cheers and yells have been replaced by conversation and buzzing. Sometimes that's what's wrong with a sporting event. The end of the game becomes a chess match and destroys crowd momentum. Now we all stand still at three seconds, with the only activity being Monty practicing long snaps on the sidelines as Vinny held for Raj's warm-up kicks into a stationary net. Everybody else in the stadium just had to wait.

I decided I should check in with Raj, thinking that maybe if I talk with him about anything but football, he'll stay loose. That's a good head coach thing to do.

Walking to Raj and Vinny, I found RR pounding the football into the net with incredible force, thinking on the next one the ball just might blow.

"Hello, Mason Bricker," Raj said, accent a hybrid of American and Indian.

"Whatdya say, Raj?" I asked.

Vinny held and he kicked the shit out of another one. Thinking he had to answer the question literally, Raj said, "I say I'm loose, but I'd better kick a few more."

I know Raj has an American home, but I didn't know where. That's a shame. I should know my teammates better than that. I hadn't had much contact with him until I was named coach for the day. Raj and Anders spend the practice alone together, kicking back and forth until it's time to hit the showers.

"Where did you go to high school, Raj?"

"South Charleston," he replied, pounding another one.

"Hey, so there are four West Virginians on this team. Great!" Well, three....

"I was only there for a year," Raj said, "My father was transferred from Indonesia to South Charleston."

"What does your father do, if you don't mind me asking."

"He's a chemical engineer with Union Carbide. They've a big research facility in South Charleston."

"I didn't know that," I said, "Research, huh? What's he working on?"

"His company will soon have a proprietary process for the low energy manufacturing of low density polyethylene." Raj wound up and hit another one.

Duh…"What's that, Raj?"

"Baggies, Glad trash bags, things like that." Things essential.

A game official walked over to me. "Pitt just called their final time-out," he said. Trying to ice my man Raj, I thought. Well! I continued the conversation with him, "Pretty good stuff. Is your family here today?"

"This is the first game they've all together watched me play. My parents and my high school sister." Raj is a handsome guy. For some reason, probably because of Joan and Edie Loden, I wonder what Raj's sister looks like.

"First game. They've come to a big one."

"My father never wanted me to play football. He wanted me to be a tennis player in the Ivy League. Tennis is for, how you say here in your country, wimps."

I laughed, "You're right. How did you ever talk him into it?"

Raj jerked another one into the net, "I was a pretty good soccer player in Indonesia. Over here, I kicked some for South Charleston High. I loved it! The U wanted me to try out. My father was very much against it. I pleaded. So, he said, 'You take me to the high school field. Line up the ball from fifty yards.' He'd studied the game to know that was a long distance. He said, 'If you hit all five tries I will give you, you may kick for West Virginia.'"

"How did that go?" asked Vinny, still kneeling.

"I was very nervous. But I kicked all five right down the fucking middle," said Raj, proudly smiling.

"Damn good thing, Raj," I said, "because I believe you're the only one on the East Coast who can ace this one." I pointed out to the crossbar to our left in the north endzone.

He smiled again. Vinny lined up a hold and Raj blasted one into the net. The game official came by again. "Thirty seconds."

"Okay, Raj," I said, "Time to shine."

"Don't you worry, Mason Bricker," Raj said, hand on my shoulder, "I will make you a hero." And with that and his flat field goal tee, he's off.

Vinny stopped by me on his way out, "The motherfucker's going to do it." He shrugged and ran out onto the gridiron. I don't know why I was worried about Raj. He's got the soul of Gandhi and the big leg of Pele.

Raj set the tee down fifty-seven yards from the goal posts and backed away three paces, then stepped over to the right two more. He's the definition of concentration as Vinny placed himself on one knee to the left of the tee. The line is set. Monty's over the ball ready for the snap. The eleven Pitt players are trying to find the most advantageous position to get free for the block. The crowd noise picked up quickly and hard, although not to the extent it was when we were scoring touchdowns. You could tell they didn't quite believe. Well, had they had the opportunity to talk to Raj, they might feel better. I think Raj felt more pressure kicking for his old man than he's experiencing right now.

It's interesting. West Virginia is a state filled with Baptists, Methodists, and Presbyterians, with Jesus Christ as the only Lord and Savior. They're watching their team go for its biggest victory ever, and it rests on the foot of a Hindu.

Raj kicked five past the forty in Miami, virtually winning the game for us. Every extra point this season has been perfect. He hasn't missed a field goal since 1973. Monty's never botched a snap, and Vinny has spun and placed every ball probably in the same exact spot. It all looked good, maybe too good.

Not a butt is in a seat. Cheers swelled. Michael stood beside me to my left, bravely witnessing this event. Not true for almost all of our players on the sidelines. It looked funny, nearly eighty men with their faces to the turf, hiding from the sight of the attempt, or in four- or five-man prayer circles, heads bowed. Father Al appeared on my right, patting my shoulder. Joe stood there, too. We three players still had our helmets on, the ultimate shields. We held hands.

Vinny pointed at Raj with his right hand, his left hand touching the tee. Raj nodded to Vinny in acknowledgment. Then The Gunner placed his right hand on the tee and pointed to Monty with his left. Then both hands were up to receive the snap.

Sunday I got the box. Monday I became Deep Throat. Thursday the newspaper told the story, releasing the expose. This morning the world discovered I got it all started. A couple of hours later we pulled our own Columbia-University-president's-office takeover. In a half-hour I was the head coach. It's now late afternoon and the Runners are in a position in which by all rights we should not be. We're fifty-seven yards of air space away from an upset of monumental proportions, something every one of us players on the field and of any sport across the nation have dreamed about since we were boys.

But this is much more than football. We told The U administration and the rich boosters to take their exclusionary philosophies and fuck off. And as I had begged this morning, we did indeed come together as a team. Now at the throes of a victory symbolic to those fighting freedom for all, we will keep the flame burning.

I'm thrilled beyond words to be the leader. How I got us here I'll never know. Or even if I had much to do with it. One thing's for sure: if Raj doesn't make this, I'll look like a real idiot.

Monty snapped the ball. I'm unaware of the struggle at the line, fixing my eyes on Vinny. The Gunner almost casually caught the snap, spun the laces away from Raj's foot, placed the tip of the ball on the tee, and held it straight up with his left hand, his right arm swinging out of the way. Raj burst out of his stance, took two quick, long strides toward the ball, and with his head bent over the tee just as the kickers in the clinics say, exploded his foot into the football. It jumped off the turf, high and long. I sucked in a breath and watched it go, not sail, but as if flung from a catapult. I know it's long enough. Hell, there's plenty of distance left over for ten more yards. But is it true? Oh, shit.

The ball passed the goalposts. I saw out of the corner of my eye Raj and Vinny going nuts, but what the hell do they know? The important guys are the two refs stationed under each upright. They each took three strides in toward the field and simultaneously raised both arms to signal 'Good!' I looked back to the line. No flags! I looked to the board. The clock read zeroes and: West Virginia thirty-seven, Pitt thirty-five. Oh, my God! Oh, my God!

Michael grabbed me with such force he knocked me to the ground. I squirmed on the turf. "Oh, God! Oh, God! We won this sucker! We won it! I can't believe it!" Then, I didn't know what else to say. I just looked up from the carpet in time to see Father run on to the field with Michael. The Bowl emptied. Thousands of students are running and jumping around, total pandemonium. It's one of those crowd things where your life is in more danger than you realize, but you don't give a damn. The Runners sidelines is vacated, every player mixing it up with just about every student. It is totally bitchin' wild! But, my reaction's strange. My behavior is eerily calm. Here I am, always considering myself to be one of the more emotional Runners and all I want to do is sit back and watch. I'm very content with this. Strange.

The celebration on the field is not letting up. In fact, it may be gathering momentum. I looked up in The Bowl, the Empty Bowl, with the exception of a hundred or so observing souls just as me. I decided to go up there and check this big party out. I walked the length of the field, found the steps just behind the north end zone, ascended them, and continued up to one of the aisles. As I'm doing this, I realize I still have my helmet on. Figuring it's now safe to remove it, I took my hat off my head and kept walking up. I remembered my game days up here last year, in civvies, with Jean, Judy, and Alice, practicing through the week but assigned to the stadium stands on Saturdays. Though I knew as little as everybody else about what the future held, I always carried even a flicker of hope I would be down there. Now, merely a year later, watching the fans go absolutely nuts, I finally show emotion. I laugh uncontrollably, sitting down, doubled over.

After a minute or so, I finally caught my breath and regained control. Glancing directly to my right, I am pleasantly surprised to see Joan two sections over. She's with another woman I assumed is her sister. Shaking my head in an effort to align the oddities of my life, I negotiated my way through the bleacher seats on that one row which will take me to my girl. Occasionally I stopped to watch the festivities. There are no Pitt players on the field, and I think it's safe to say there are no West Virginia players in the locker room. A bunch of navy jerseys are peppered among the student partyers, a quivering horde of humans. I find myself in Joan's section. She still has not discovered me. I walk more and got closer to her, stop, and not wanting to startle her too much, said in a low voice, "Pretty damned good game, wasn't it?"

She turned slowly, then with saucers for eyes yelled, "Mason! What the hell…What…Mason! You're supposed to be down there!" Sometimes Joan is awfully rigid and she therefore believes people should be where they belong. The other woman looked around Joan to me. It seemed to be okay for her I'm up here. I introduced myself.

"Hi," I said, extending my hand, despite realizing I smell like I had been playing football all afternoon, "I'm Mason Bricker. I assume you're Pamela Kissinger."

"Why, yes," Pamela said pleasantly, clasping my hand, "It's great to meet you! I knew I would eventually get to you, but this is a surprise!"

You can tell they're sisters. I'll leave it at that. Pamela is wearing a black leather blazer over a red sweater and black denims and black boots, very attractive. Joan is beautiful in a tweed blazer and a turquoise sweater, faded-but-well-cared-for straight leg denims in black over-the-calf boots. And she wonders what I'm doing up here?

The party on the field continued hardily. The crowd is nowhere near dispersing. Joan's still awestruck, you know, one of those times when you're not prepared to say anything, so you don't say anything. Pamela picked up on this and spoke.

"Mason, you were magnificent," she said with admiration.

"Oh, thank you," I replied, "You flatter me."

"It's true, Mason," Pamela continued, "That catch you made down here early. That was a work of art."

Joan didn't want to concede to her sister, so she joined in, "Oh, Mason, that was wonderful. Even I the sports imbecile know that."

I laughed. "Thank you. Thanks. Sometimes you get lucky, and other times you get really lucky."

"Mason, you are too modest," Joan said, placing her hand in my arm and looking at me with that Joan Look, the one after which I usually do anything she says.

"Okay, I'm too modest," I said. Pamela giggled. I guess she's in on what's going on with me. "But we had a lot of players just rise to the occasion. Vinny, Vinny, did you notice him?"

Pamela said, "Oh, he was outstanding."

"That was his first start, Pamela."

"That's incredible!" she said. Pamela is trying to interact with me. I hope she likes me. That's important, seeing as how I'm hopelessly, irretrievably in love with her sister.

It's funny. Just very recently I was virulently out for blood, real blood, Pitt's blood. Now, at Mach speed in a full one eighty on the emotional circle, my heart is melting.

"A lot of other things took place, guys playing and overachieving and not giving up, especially in light of the circumstances of the past two days. I don't want to bore you with the details," I said, trying my damnedest to maintain while standing before Joan.

"Mason," Joan said as we're still arm-in-arm, "we heard your team threw the coaches out and your team ran the game. Is that true?"

"Well," I responded, knowing now everything is going to come out, "yes."

"Did you have something to do with that?" Joan asked, probably already knowing the answer. This won't go along with her quest for order in the world. And now she's pulling that 'I'm older and wiser' stuff on me. Damn....

The only thing to do is answer truthfully, "Yes, I...I was the instigator."

"How did that take place?" asked Pamela. The party is still going on.

"Well, to give you the short version...I'm uncomfortable talking about it...," I said.

"Go ahead, Mason," Joan said, "Pamela's a psychologist. Don't you think she's seen and heard it all?" Joan laughed.

"It's pretty pathological, Pamela" I said, fading away again.

"What's wrong?" Joan asked in a whisper.

I paused and I could feel my chest tighten. Here I am, dressed in a complete football uniform, fresh after a major victory in which I led the team and played very well, with every reason to be proud, but I'm afraid. I'm afraid....

"Joan, I'm really concerned you're not going to like what happened today, that you're going to think I'm out of control, and with regard to...what you think about me is so very important to me, to say the absolute least," There, I said it.

"Oh, Mason," said Joan, "Mason, I haven't begun to tell you what I think of you. Whatever you tell me now, I know it was just what you had to do. You've had a very difficult week, and you've taken on many things most everybody would just walk away from. Darling, it'll be all right. Trust me."

Our eyes met. Joan has never looked at me like that. She gave me strength, that is, after I first felt faint.

"Mason, really, I'm her sister," Pamela said with a smile, "It's okay."

I started again. I told them of the breakfast and Lawson, and the call for the players' only meeting. Then I moved on to the near-fight and the decision to go it alone. I talked about the militia and the distrust and the walk and the police and the National Guard. I left out the news about PD because because it could be negate everything in such a manner that I don't want to think about it right now. Then....

"We got to the locker room and we had no gear, nothing. The administration had moved it out."

"Damn," said Pamela, "Hardball."

"Then, the athletic director comes over. First, he tries to take all of our scholarships away. We told him to get screwed. Then he dropped the bomb...he told me if we expected to play today, it would have to be my last game here ever."

"Mason!" exclaimed Joan, "No! He can't do that!"

"He did it. And I had seconds to make the choice. It was a really nasty power play to get me back for the newspaper. I couldn't abandon my teammates. And he knew that. And he couldn't kick me off the team for what I'd done because of the potential for a backlash today. So, he got his game, he kept his players, and he got rid of me. A really politically astute son-of-a-bitch he is."

We paused a while. "I'm sorry, Mason," said Pamela with her mouth and her eyes. "I'm so sorry."

I continued. "It would have been too noisy to release me just because of the expose, but insubordination is a different story. He needed this game today, and he basically set me up to complete the revolt. So, here I am. When the kick went through the goal posts, I wasn't a part of the team anymore. They're down there. I'm here with you."

"Oh, Mason," Joan said, "I'm sorry."

"Thanks, Joan," I said, "You two may not agree with this, but my fate was sealed when the banker placed the box of evidence on my doorstep.

I couldn't ignore it. I had to act on it. And I knew it was going to be trouble. The events are unfortunate, but it had to be done."

"No, Mason, I do agree with that," said Pamela, "Sometimes that's just the way it goes. And you seem to be doing an admirable job accepting it."

"Thank you," I replied, "Accepting it for now. I'm sure tough times are ahead."

"But, Mason," Joan said, her head tilting on my shoulder, "you don't get to play any more. And you're so good."

"Thanks," I said, becoming upbeat. Compliments from Joan will do that to me. "But, you know something, and Pamela, you the psychologist may think I'm in denial by saying this, but what a way to go out! We beat number one. Vinny and I connected on a long ball, a dream of ours from since we ever thought it was possible. The final drive, I caught two balls. And I got to hit the Heisman Trophy winner so hard his helmet flew off," Pamela laughed. "No, seriously, it really can't get much better than that."

"There are lawyers, Mason," Joan said, trying her best to be helpful, "maybe you can get reinstated."

"Maybe," I said, "but if it's over right now, it was a helluva ride."

The conversation stopped as we saw two State Troopers approach us carrying my athletic bag.

"Are you Mason Bricker?" one of the troopers asked.

"Yes, sir," I replied.

"Mr. Bricker, I am under the orders from the governor to escort you from the stadium. I have your clothes, and this." He handed me the black plastic sign from my locker, reading in white '88' on the top line, and 'Bricker' on the bottom line. Holding that sign struck the finality of it all.

"So, you by bringing me my clothes here, you're telling me I can't dress here?" I said, stating the obvious.

"Yes, sir. You are banned from the locker room and the stadium," said the other trooper.

"This is goddamned ridiculous," said Joan, possibly the most she had ever resisted authority in her life. "I've never seen such totalitarian tactics used in this country!" She is livid.

"Mr. Bricker, you have to leave now," said the first trooper.

"Well," responded Joan, "we have no reason to stay here, either." And we left. The troopers flanked me with Joan and Pamela behind me. We walked toward then through the exit at the top of the stands near The Bowl. A sidewalk led out to the campus, intersecting with the street on which we as a team had paraded just several hours earlier. The troopers left us there. Yet, in a turn of their tone, each trooper offered his hand to me. They then in unison saluted me. With a lump in my throat, I returned the salutes. I have never been saluted so much in my life.

I'm still in my full uniform, carrying my bag in one hand and my helmet in the other, getting some whoops and applause from students walking down the street looking for the nearest beer. Dusk is ready to fall and it's getting close to dinner. I haven't had a meal since breakfast and after a game of football I'm famished. Joan and Pamela and I stood in a circle of three, trying to figure out what to do next, not really wanting to part.

"Mason, you know I just live ten minutes up the hill," Joan said, "I've got some beer, we'll order Chinese, and you can get cleaned up and join us for dinner."

I have an unusual life. Very few things in my years on earth have gone by the book. Consequently, I possess the corresponding attitudes and feelings associated with living like this. A normal athlete who caught four passes for a hundred twentysome yards and a touchdown, a couple of them key grabs very late in the game, would be screeching in the locker room, still wearing his jockstrap, flipping teammates on the ass with towels, celebrating the biggest of victories with those with whom he achieved it, then interviewing with *Sports Illustrated*. Not I. I'm going to shower in the home of a woman for whom I have always at least had an undying infatuation, and then suck moo goo guy pan out of quart containers and wash it down with Miller Lite in the company of that woman and her equally beautiful sister. College tradition dictates the former way should be the way. I'm sorry. I'll go with Joan.

"Joan, thank you! I just live a mile and so from here. I could go there and not trouble you," I said, trying to be nice. I'll give her one chance to rescind, then I'm up the hill.

"But, I want to have dinner with you, Mason Bricker," said Joan, "And you need a shower." She grabbed my upper arm and squeezed, smiling at me then giving me for my benefit a derivative of The Laugh, The Giggle. At that time, I would have cleaned up with a water hose in front of the High Ridge if she asked.

We walked to her house; my love, her sister, and I, the displaced wide receiver. "What happens to the team from here?" asked Pamela.

"I have no idea. I wish them only good things. But, they have to deal with the football establishment. That could get ugly fast."

"Mason, you said 'they,'" said Joan. "Don't quit."

"It's too late. I can't worry about it right now. I can't even think about it right now. But as I said before, I got mine. I got it good!"

"I just want you to be happy," Joan said, resting her head on my shoulder. Happy, I wanted to say. I think I know what would make me extremely happy.

"Tonight is going to be wild as hell," Pamela said, "This will be something like we never saw in Evanston. Northwestern never beat anybody this big I can remember."

"Maybe we should go out and observe it later on this evening," I said, joyously signing myself up as their escort for the remainder of the day.

"Maybe we should go out and get right in the middle of it this evening," Joan proclaimed.

I dared to say it. "Joan, you and I, in public?"

"I don't see why not," she replied. My eyes caught Pamela's. She wagged her eyebrows. Okay, now they're fuckin' with me....

"I've never been with the hero of the football game," Joan said.

"I'm sure that's not true," I said smiling.

"Sure it is," Pamela added, "There were no football heroes at Northwestern." Joan giggled.

"Yes, there was one. Mike Adamle," I said, my obscure knowledge of minutiae surfacing.

"Oh, he wasn't hot until after we were in grad school," Pamela said. I was a big fan of his when I was in junior high. Shut up, Mason.

"Then, Joan, you're with your first football hero only by default," I said.

"Whatever. That's all a million miles away now," Joan said, again putting the squeeze on my tricep. I know she likes that.

There before we knew it, we walked up the front walk. Joan unlocked the door and we entered. I hadn't been here since the week before school started. It looked the same, immaculately clean hardwood floors, decorated walls, the right furniture, and well-appointed lamps and prints. The house is probably smaller than she's used to, but she's just starting out and it's all hers. With a little help, but all hers.

Pamela walked into the kitchen to the left. "Beers for all," she said, clinking three bottles out of the fridge. "Doctor's orders." She passed them around. We cracked them open. Standing in the dining room with the two ladies, I said as I waived around the house, "May the locker rooms of the future look like this," Joan giggled, "And," motioning to Joan and Pamela, I said, "may the locker room attendants look like you." We swigged.

"Thank you, Mason," said Pamela, smiling big.

"Well, Mason, as your attendant, follow me. I'll get your towel and show you your private shower," Joan said, seductively glancing over her shoulder. I followed. Who wouldn't?

We ended up in Joan's bedroom. "This is my bedroom," Joan said, smiling, eyes half closed, peeling the label off her beer bottle. There is a big bay window adorned with curtains, open now, looking onto the wooded area behind her house. The walls are a tasteful, soft yellow with the ceiling and baseboards and trim along the windows painted an eggshell white. Hardwood floors are covered by a couple of those cable rugs, for lack of a better description, and the feet of the queen-size bed are resting on a large rug. The bedposts are brass, old brass, like they're a family heirloom or as if she had found them at an estate sale. The bureaus and large vanity are eggshell. The vanity is well-lit, with female stuff, cologne, perfume, powder, about in an orderly fashion. She stood there before me as I looked around. I turned back to Joan and her eyes are still sleepy and she's still smiling and the label still hasn't come off the bottle.

"Joan, this is very nice," I said, in a low tone and sincerely. Pamela must have just put on some music because I heard Fleetwood Mac in the background. 'Monday morning you sure look fine. / I've got traveling on my mind.'

"Thank you, Mason," she said, eyes not deviating from me.

I'm still carrying my bag and my helmet. "You can put your things down here, Mason," Joan said. She walked into her bath and opened the linen closet to fetch a towel and a washcloth. "Here," she said, handing them to me, "I'll order, and by the time you're clean and dressed, we'll eat."

Being in Joan's bedroom in full gear and home uniform seems like some surreal dream I would have right before I wake up, one of those you think about all day in an attempt to figure out why you had it.

"I bet I look pretty damned stupid right now, don't I?"

"No. I mean, it's unusual. It's never happened to me," Joan said, "But, in a way, it's sexy."

Oh…sexy…great thought…"Thanks. I'll be normal here shortly," I said.

"No, Mason, I don't think you'll ever be normal. You're an extraordinary man. You're bright. You're sweet. And, as I saw today, you're an outstanding athlete. And, courageous. And you and I have a lot to talk about. But, first, you get clean."

The breath was sucked out of my lungs. What ever could she mean? "Joan," I said, venturing into the unknown, searching for absolute in the middle of the dance, "our talk. Tell me, is it good? Just tell me that."

"Mason, it's wonderful. It's wonderful." Joan kissed my mouth, vaulting me into the next day. She laughed, "How am I ever going to get my arms around you with all this stuff on? Get clean, my darling, and meet me in the rec room. You have enough beer?"

"I'm good."

"I bet you are." And with that, she turned and walked.

Saturday, November 8, 1975
5:30 PM

Joan talks to me

God, Joan could never shower at my place. This is spotless! I'm afraid I'm not rinsing enough, like I'll leave too much soap scum here and she'll think I'm the animal I sometimes am. I can't believe I'm standing naked where Joan stands naked everyday. I'd better not think about this too much, you know, get, uh, too premature. One thing I can think about: tell me on this past Thursday I would have been here. No way! No way I would have guessed this. This whole day has been the total liberation of the unconscious. God, my torso is one big pain. Man, rigor mortis is setting in. I need beer, jazz, and sweet love. What is she going to say to me? Today, it could be anything. I hope her parents aren't in town. I've had enough of that. What if they are, and they're in the living room, and I walk out there in a towel dragging my helmet and my shoulder pads? I don't think I'm their ideal mate for her. I don't think I'm their ideal parking valet for her. Oh, shit, that hurts. I know where I got it. I got it when I got Drew. He was like hitting a concrete pylon, but I dropped him like a ton of bricks. I'll remember that one for a long time. I'll remember it all night tonight, like everytime I move. I can barely wash my hair. What am I going to do without football? I've been sticking people all season long, hell, for years. What's going to replace that? Maybe rugby. I'll still have to lift weights. And run. I'm going to miss Vinny. Right when he latches onto the Saturn V, I'm gone. I'll just have to be his biggest fan. I could transfer and play elsewhere. But, Joan's about to talk with me, and she says it's good. No, wonderful, she says. I'm hanging around for this. Man, Pitt, we beat Pitt! No one in his or her right mind thought we would beat Pitt. Well, I did, but you know, the right mind thing. Vinny's pretty level headed, and he believed. Jesus, he's great! He's NFL. Who's going to coach? Wonder what happened in the locker room? I haven't seen TV or heard radio or talked to a reporter. It's like I disappeared. No one knows where I am. No one! No one would know to look here. Hey, Vinny, I'm in Joan's shower, alone. See if that works. What a guy! He said if I got out there, we were going big. We did it. 555-2468. What the hell is that? I'm hungry. I hope they ordered a gallon of Szechwan chicken for me. I'll have to tone down the eating of massive quantities today. I don't want to look like a nineteen year old. It's over. A lot of things I'll miss. Vinny, Michael, Joe, even. Shit, we're going to a bowl game! Damnit! I think I'm going to need a psychologist to get through this. I think I'm going to need a psychologist whatever Joan says. Either way, I'm going to a shrink. It looks good, but what if it's bad? What will I do? Jennifer? No, I'm afraid not. Way too serious. I'm too abnormal for Jennifer. I'm sorry, Jen. When will I ever talk to her? When I get home. When will I ever get home? I'll let

Joan decide that. If Joan says no…You know what I'll miss the most about game day? The walk from the High Ridge to the stadium. Oh, my, oh, my, Edie Loden. 555-2468. Oh. Okay, never fear. If Joan says no, call Edie Loden. She is so intriguingly beautiful. Not to take anything away from Joan. Not at all. Joan is gorgeous, everywhere. She's like a Playmate with brains. Edie is exotic with brains. She's that babe in black Vinny says I need. I can't believe I'm in Joan's shower thinking of another woman! Where are my morals?

~ ~ ~ ~ ~ ~ ~ ~ ~ ~ ~

The ladies drank the first beers quickly. Pamela is calm, as always. It helps to have delved into the human mind. As a psychologist, she knows to trust her gut. She has vivid memories of her sister ever since boys and men starting paying attention to them. Easily able to review the history of all the men who pursued Joan, and after spending time talking about Mason, then meeting him, Pamela has decided it will be difficult for her sister to find any other man who would or could love Joan the way Mason does. The differences and the difficulties are certainly there, she thought. But how often in a woman's life will she meet that man? When again would it all fall into place so well, so, so perfectly; the looks, the brains, the talent, the kindness, and most importantly the unlimited adoration he has for her? Pamela laughed as she thought how happy for and how envious she is of her sis.

Joan, on the other hand, is jittery. The alcohol is about ten minutes from taking effect, and she is running over and over in her brain what she is going to say. Having never told a college sophomore she loves him, even when she herself was a college sophomore, the nerves are unsettling. And just how long does it take to shower?

"*Do it, Joan,*" *Pamela said, "There are no words to describe how much I approve of him. I've only actually known him for a quarter-hour, but I've spent an entire lifetime making decisions quickly. I'm seldom if ever wrong." She pulled the Lite bottle to her smug lips.*

Joan didn't hear a word Pamela said. "I'm trying to keep myself from running in there, ripping the door open, and screaming it!" she exclaimed, taking one long suck on her beer.

"It won't be long now. I'll just leave you two alone, and you let your feelings run the course," suggested Pamela.

There is just a bit of twilight in the air. The food is slow in coming, most assuredly because of everybody in town eating and partying after the unprecedented victory. Even from Joan's hillside abode, car horns and hoots from students can be heard. Montani is destined to be one giant wasteland of wasted people.

Joan had put on Aerosmith's Toys in the Attic. *Pamela commented, "Joan. Aerosmith? You've really fallen hard for that guy in your shower, haven't you?"*

"We've already established that," Joan said, now enjoying the easing effect of the alcohol on her brain.

~ ~ ~ ~ ~ ~ ~ ~ ~ ~

I took one last glance in the mirror. Charcoal slacks, narrow waist, blue shirt, still starched, Brightonions rep tie, loose, wool navy blazer, Bass cordovans, black hose, slightly damp hair, kind of messed up. I like this look. Let's see what happens. I open Joan's bedroom door, checking one more time that I have kept the place neat, and walk down the hallway, past her living room. I found them in her entertainment room, complete with bookcases, sounds turned on, and a television turned off. Joe Perry is finishing off *Sweet Emotion*. I smell food. I swear to God eating right now will be better than sex. Maybe I should reserve judgment on that.

"Ladies," I said.

"I bet you feel better," Pamela said.

"I'm stiff and I have an aching head, but I can live with that," I said. "Pitt went down."

Joan silently smiled at me. My heart raced.

"Mason," said Pamela, "Look. Food."

"That's the second best sentence I could hear right now," I said, truthfully.

~ ~ ~ ~ ~ ~ ~ ~ ~ ~

I sat on one sofa beside Pamela as Joan sat on the other. We dug in and drained beer like we hadn't eaten for days. After a few minutes of that, Joan finally laughed. "God, we're pigs!"

"Just as long as we're all pigs together," I said.

"Yeah," said Pamela, "Table manners are relative."

Despite our admission, the eatfest continued. "Now I know what it feels like to be at dinner at a fraternity house," Joan said laughing again.

"Like you didn't know before," Pamela said, winking at me.

"Tell me all about this, Dr. Kissinger," I jokingly said.

"It was so long ago it doesn't even count any more," Joan replied. We all grinned. The age issue has been tested and passed.

After a while, there's nothing remaining but a pile of cartons, scattered chopsticks, and fortune cookies. Pamela cracked hers open first. She read, "'Honesty is the best policy.' Lucky numbers 4, 8, 11, 15. What a joke! 'Honesty is the best policy.' Of course! Well, not always…Jesus! Give me a real fortune! Tell me what's going to happen in my life! Call these bastards." An interesting side of a Kissinger….

"Really, Sis!" Joan said, "Okay, here's mine, 'Tonight is your night. Lucky numbers 6, 13,16, 22.' Tonight, eh?" Joan stared at me, overpoweringly. My body stayed seated, but my soul fell to its knees. Hours went by.

"Uh…Mason…you there," I heard Pamela say.

I snapped out of it. "Okay…Okay…that was fantasy, this is reality. I know the difference." The women laughed big.

"Read yours, Mason," Joan asked me.

I opened the cookie. It read, 'Kindness will be rewarded soon.' I said, "You will be victorious in a violent game, then party hardy with two gorgeous women from Chicago. Lucky numbers 3, 12, 88"

"Oh, bullshit, Mason," Joan exclaimed, reaching, "Let me see that! I read mine. You read yours!" I stuffed the slip in my blazer pocket.

She shocked me by leaping from her sofa and pouncing on me, forcing her hand into my coat. "Give it to me!" Joan spat playfully.

"No!" I replied, "You'll have to get it yourself." If she only knew how much my body hurt…but if pain is present, like the tree falling in the forest….

"You think I can't, big man? I'm a mean little hussy." We wrestled, giggling wildly.

"Uh…I'll be in my room reading," I heard Pamela say, "Excuse me." She got up and walked out.

"Nice having dinner with you," I said, actually straining against this tough girl.

Still clenched, but out of breath, our faces ended up inches apart. Her eyes grew soft as she gazed at me. At *me*, damn it. She's gazing at me. Joan lifted herself from me and returned to her seat on the sofa. She patted the space beside her, I guess indicating I am to be there. In no time flat, I am.

Joan turned to her right. I turned to my left. I didn't have a beer. She did, so she got up and got me one. When she came back, she sat in the same place, in the same position, looking at me the same way. I have no idea what's going to happen here. Joan in no way is tipping her hand. Fearing the worst, I keep thinking, 'Edie Loden.'

Joan inhaled, then spoke with confidence directly into my eyes, "Mason, I have been fighting and fighting and fighting." She paused. "After I left you last night, I fought. After I called you this morning, I fought still more. At the game, I fought harder than you." Another pause. I smiled, and she's still in my eyes. "I'm tired of fighting. There's no more fight left in me. I throw caution to the wind. I give up. I surrender." Joan went silent, eyes never deviating. She breathed again. I am experiencing the total lack of molecular motion.

"I…I am so much in love with you," Joan said, finally. Finally! "It's not supposed to work this way. This is not the way things are meant to be. But, your sweetness, your mind, your body, your lips, your eyes, I've had it. By God, I'm in love with you. And there's not a thing I can do about it. There's not a thing I want to do about it. I love you, Mason. Do you understand? Everything I have said, I've ever said, anything that had anything to do with any excuse about why we couldn't be together, they were all the blind assertions of a woman desperately afraid of the truth. The embrace on your porch? You were right. I loved you then, Mason Bricker. I love you now, and I hope you still love me."

I became dumbfounded. I heard it all, everything she said. But I sat there; waiting to wake up and find myself in my bed, clock buzzing at six-thirty, facing yet another day with another dream and Joan and unrequited love. I reached for her hand, something tactile, like real three-D. She did have a hand, and I did feel it, and I'm screwing around here too long and leaving her hanging and not giving her an answer and risking that she might change her mind….

"Oh, Joan," I sighed, "It's been so long, so long that I have loved you. Do I still love you? Yes. Yes! I love you, Joan. I love you more than anybody could ever know, could ever guess. And to hear you…and to find out you…." Now I'm afraid….

"Go ahead and say it, Mason. To hear that I love you. To find out that I love you. Go ahead and say it. Say it, because it's all true. It could never be more true."

We sat there, hand-in-hand, gazing, smiling, basking in the heat of the moment. Suddenly, we jumped in each other's arms and kissed a hard, passionate kiss, long, holding tight, just like you would think, just like two people who had been together daily for weeks and weeks and weeks, knowing something, but for various reasons afraid to admit it, fearful to come to terms with it. Last night, we flirted with the possibilities. This morning, we participated in some harmless titillation. Those were all tests, toe-dips, important in their own way, but not nearly as now...the beginning of the journey.

We parted, staring at each other, breathless, each of us amazed at the passions unleashed, prepared to ride those passions, the waves, the crests.

"Mason, my darling, my darling, this is the craziest thing I have ever done. I have my entire life been so normal, so boring."

"Joan, don't beat yourself up over that. You could be normal. You could have been anything. You are the most beautiful, fantastic woman I have ever known. You could call your shots. Normal worked. It's okay."

"But it wouldn't have worked this time. If I would have stayed normal, I would have never fallen in love with you. And I would have then missed out on you and everything wonderful about you. I risk it. You do that to me."

"Joan...," and then I just started crying.

"Oh, Mason, oh.... It's okay. It's okay." She held me to her shoulder.

"I know," I said through the deluge, "You've got to know this about me. I'm just so fuckin' emotional. I'm all right." Jesus, what a week!

"I know. That's what's so sweet about you. Usually, the guys only cry after I break up with them. You're so unique. You're the first to do this."

I laughed, laughed big, an odd combination with the tears. "Damnit. Damnit, Joan." I gathered myself and rallied back, still laughing. I bet she's told more than her share of guys to take a hike. Why is that so funny?

"Mason, the way I could and can tell how special I am to you has always been and still is really something, but through it all you really have remained such a gentleman. Through it all you really have treated me like a lady, with respect, not like a piece of meat, but like a friend."

"I'm sorry, Joan, but I have to tell you I probably had more than the average number of sex dreams about you."

Joan Laughed. I thought the blood was going to rush from my head. "Mason, when we're in bed together, which will be the minute after my sister leaves," she giggled with her hand over her lips. Cute. "you can tell me more, and I'll tell you about mine. Deal?"

Hers? Ohhh…"We have to make up for a lot of lost time," I said, arching my eyebrows.

Joan Laughed again, then fell silent, still smiling.

"There's something we have to discuss," she started, one knee touching mine, our hands squeezed, "Let me tell you how all this is going to happen. I have thought this through. You know I could get into big trouble with the university for dating a student. I know you hate that word. Now so do I. But, anyway, here goes: we cool it during the week. And on Friday, after school, since your weekends will be free, you come over here, and I'm going to lock the doors, and you won't be able to get out until Sunday evening. Except for lunch, maybe. But, it's going to be bed and bathrobes for the entire weekend. Can you stand it?" She snuggled into my chest.

The prospects of that are absolutely incredible. "Of course. I'm man enough"

"I can tell," Joan said, caressing my chest. "But, there's more. Don't be mad at this, but we have to have diversions."

I'm confused. "Meaning?"

"Camouflaged dates."

At first, I couldn't believe what I had just heard. Then I became inwardly incensed. This doesn't work. She just told me she loves me and we're still dating? I'm not usually a jealous man, but this…hell, yes, I'm a jealous man! I don't think I can take another man having her atten-tions during…Edie Loden.

"Well, Joan, I don't like it, not very much at all, but it's probably a good idea. I mean, it's not ideal, not at all, but if it means you and me and baths and romps and making love for an entire weekend, I guess we'll just do it that way." Considering everything, Ivy Punk, *what the fuck are you thinking!?*

"Mason," Joan said, leaning into my face, "Mason, you've got to real-ize, you'll be my man. My only man. Why would I want any other man? This other guy, whomever he may be, he won't be my man," she said, placing her hand On Me, "I can only have one man," I am speechless, "And you're that man." She finished her explanation, but didn't move her hand.

"Well, I think you've gotten your point across," I said with a little raspiness, unable to be any more aroused. We heard a tapping coming down the hallway. Joan quickly released and sat on my lap to hide Me. I drew a long breath as Pamela walked into the room.

"Never mind me, kids," Pamela said, "I'm just getting my magazine." She glanced at me and grinned, then stepped back out.

"Pamela's all for this, by the way," Joan said, holding my arm tightly, "She helped me through it, even before she met you. Hell, she's been hearing about you since early September."

"Uh, Joan," I said, "you could have just had me then and…."

"And," she said.

"And…I don't know…never mind. This has worked out perfectly," I replied, living for the moment, bringing her to me for a kiss. We simply sat there, quietly acquiescing.

"Mason?" Joan asked.

"Yes, my sweet?" I've never called any woman 'my sweet' before…espe-cially only hours after trying to break a guy's neck.…

"Mason, who's going to be your weekday woman?" Impressive. I can tell she's a little worried.

"I don't know," I responded, "but I know who it's not going to be."

"Who's that?" She knows. She just wants to hear me say it.

"It won't be Jennifer," I said, "As of this morning, after the phone rang," Joan smiled, "she's out of my romantic life. She's in her own world. That wouldn't work with our plans. It's going to piss my friends off, but Joan and Jen can't coexist, not like this. And, besides, I love you. And, that's the whole reason for the weekday chick. It's so I can love you."

She nuzzled into my chest. Well, that drives me wild. "Don't get anybody from the classes," Joan ordered nicely.

"Oh, that would be smart," I said facetiously.

"The thought of sharing you with anybody, in any way, boils my blood," Joan whispered.

Then, why…forget it…"You're not sharing me, Joan," I replied, repeating her intentions, "After you get through with me, there will be nothing left to go around."

Another Laugh. Boy, I'll never get used to that. "Still, I may have to rethink that." She's confusing me. But, when has that not happened?

"Who's your guy?"

"Maybe Alan."

"Wait a second," I felt a flash, "The guy you were mad over just two weeks ago?" I said more calmly, contorting my face.

"Don't you see, sweetmeat? I was just trying to make you envious," she Laughed.

"Well, darling, it worked," I said, half grinning.

"God, I was crazy for you then."

"You're kidding?"

"No."

The consternation, the doubt, the pain of that week. I'll never forget it. The hell with it. I won. "You tried your best, babe, but you couldn't chase me away."

"I know. As you say, it's a good thing."

I steered back to the Rule of Weekday Dating, "Thinking about your rethinking, Joan; anytime you want to ditch that rule, I'm all for it."

"It feels okay now, but the first time that slut, whomever she is, comes to your office to see you, the rule will probably be gone. If you had to pick one right now, who would it be?"

"I don't know. Kate Jackson. Jaclyn Smith." Joan cracked me hard in the ribs. God, I didn't know I'm hurt there! Oww!

"Mason Bricker!"

"To answer your question, Joan, I don't know."

"Now, I've already told you Alan."

"Fuckin' wimp."

Joan smiled. She moved a leg over to straddle me, a preview, I guess, of coming attractions, "There has to be one. You have to know of one." Joan laid a great kiss on my mouth. She's going to draw it out of me. I just feel it. I'm going to tell Joan about Edie.

"Joan, how can I possibly think of other women when you've positioned yourself on me so?" Her breasts are in my face. If I had a dollar for every time I wanted her to do that....

"Just tell me." Another kiss, this time tonguing my uvula. This is getting kind of sick. I'm starting to like it.

"Okay."

"Who is she?" she asked, now her face in my face.

"You don't know her."

"Yet."

"She's never been to the office."

"Oh, Mason, I'm not going to be angry. I'm so strict with my life that in some convoluted way, this has to be done. You can tell me," Joan whispered.

"She's in my Physics class. I saw her today during our parade. She thanked me profusely for the newspaper deal. Then she gave me her telephone number and told me to call her. There, dammit, I told you. I don't feel right about it. I love you. I want only you. I don't want to love this girl. I don't like your rule, but if it means I get to be with you, then I'll call Edie and see her."

"Edie. What does she look like?" Joan mouthed my neck. I do have an interesting life.

"Not like you." In principle, I lied.

"So, I'm not threatened in any way?" Joan asked, biting my lip.

"Am I threatened by Alan?"

"I frustrate Alan. He can't understand why I won't go to bed with him. Does Edie want to have sex with you?"

Probably…"I don't know, but the point's moot. I only want you. I'll say it again: I understand the need for the rule. But, I'll be counting the hours from Sunday evening to Friday evening, every week."

"Maybe we can make it Monday morning," Joan said, grinding herself against me.

"Joan…Joan…."

"I can't wait any longer," she said, pulling my face into her breasts, "Let me go tell Pamela to give me a little bit of time. Meet me in my bedroom. I love you." Joan kissed me wet, and turned to go to Pamela's room.

If this day gets any better, I'll die.

Saturday, November 8, 1975
7:00 PM

The first day of the rest of my life

Our first trek into the ultimate of passion was intense and extremely pleasurable, and had the duration of lightning for both of us. Maybe it was because Pamela was just three rooms away and we had to keep acoustics in mind. Maybe it was weeks and weeks of what Michele described as 'Just do each other already!' Well, Michele…Maybe it was the tease of the buildup of the past twenty-four hours. Maybe that's just Joan and me. Maybe for a while every venture into lovemaking for the two of us will be like a ride past the stratosphere in the X-1, short, exhilarating, with a great view of the stars. You're not going to hear me argue about it.

I thought my imagination had a pretty good handle on how Joan looked under her clothing. Well, I'm off the mark. She's legendary. And she commented on how much she liked the looks of me. Then she said she's understating it to the max. It's nice to know we fit.

With regard to Pamela, we didn't have much time to lounge around this evening. Just as I suggested we get dressed and pay a visit to her sister, Joan had another idea.

"Call Edie."

"What?" I asked, face screwed into amazement.

"Call Edie. Now's as good a time as any," Joan said, with the look of a vanquisher.

"Joan, I love you and I go along with you on most anything, well…really everything, but I have to draw the line on telephoning another woman while naked in bed with you."

"I say it's okay. Call her. Make her your Weekday Woman."

This is a side of Joan that I had no idea existed. It's an ornery part of her, not malevolent, I think, and always done with a smile and a glint in her eyes. She says she's been boring and conservative her entire life. Where did this come from? And for that matter, where did I come from?

But, I'm always up for a good weird thing. "Okay."

"Good!" she exclaimed, reaching for the phone and handing it to me. "You need the book?"

"No." Uh-oh. I answered that one too quickly.

"What!" Joan's eyes became fiery.

"Not to worry. I have a good memory for numbers. She just gave it to me this morning. It's all association. 555-2468. Two-four-six-eight, who do we appreciate? You, Joan. That's who we appreciate." I think I talked her down.

"Okay. You're off the hook. This time." She's not smiling.

I leaned a pillow on the bedpost, sat against it, and punched in the number. My love sat beside me and placed her hand on my belly. It's kinda rippled. I know she likes that. In two rings, a female answered.

"Hello?"

"Hello. Hi. May I please speak with Edie Loden?"

"Loden," Joan whispered, "Edie Loden. What a bitch."

I shot Joan a look. Another female voice appeared.

"Hello?"

"Hello, Edie? Good evening. This is Mason Bricker."

"Mason!" Edie said my name so loudly Joan heard her. That didn't go over well. Joan gave me a hard punch in the abs. "Mason! What a surprise!"

"Now, Edie," I said, trying to be myself despite being hit in the gut and having this entire conversation under duress, "you asked me to call."

"But I didn't think you'd call so soon." I didn't either, sweetheart.

"So, here I am," I said, with Joan remaining in good behavior.

"Mason, that was a wonderful game today. You played extremely well. That catch for that touchdown; my God, Mason, that could do a girl in."

"Thank you, Edie." Joan waved her hands, the signal for, 'get on with it.' It's very difficult looking at Joan's heavenly body while talking to Edie, and Dr. Kissinger made sure she stayed in the line of sight.

"And I heard all about it on the radio tonight. No coaches. What a revolutionary you are."

"Reactionary could be another word." Joan cleared her throat and wagged her tongue at me. I'm beginning to think, did she miss out on part of her teen years and is acting it out on me? Back to Edie. "I've got a lot to tell you on that subject."

"We should get together and talk about it, soon." Great. She made it so easy for me.

"That sounds wonderful," I said, "I must admit, Edie, that's the reason I called." On that, Joan crawled on top of me and laid there, the side of her head on my solar plexus. Why is she putting herself through this?

"I figured it is, since I told you just this morning I love you," Edie said, laughing, making light of herself.

"Well, Edie, I'll give you a chance to take that back, if you wish," I said. Joan bolted up, turning, hitting a bruised rib. Luckily, I have a high pain threshold. She scrambled around in her nightstand drawer, fanny jutting in the air. Stop it!

"Maybe, for now, Mason," Edie said, still giggling.

I recovered. "Whatever you feel comfortable with," I said. At that time, Joan shoved a note in my face. It read, 'Monday, seven, Bill's.'

"How about Monday evening, say around seven, at Bill's?"

"How did you know my favorite place? That sounds great. A little sludge coffee, a little conversation. You can give me the inside perspective on the team."

"Gladly," I replied, "I'll see you then. For now, I don't want to hold you too long. I'm sure you have some important partying to do."

"Yeah, I'm going to All That Jazz," Edie said as my stomach dropped through the floor.

"Great," I said, "I might see you there."

"You like jazz, Mason?"

"I'm a jazz novice. A friend and her sister have invited me there. I'm going because I like them." Joan then stood on her knees and slowly caressed her navel. I am in awe. She grinned big.

"Just to tell you, I'm meeting my boyfriend there," said Edie.

"Oh," I must have sounded concerned because she backpedaled.

"He goes to school at Westminster," she explained, "He's here some weekends. Actually, he's not a great boyfriend, but we see each other."

"Oh, that's cool," I said, wondering what the hell truly was going on here.

"Mason," Edie said reassuringly, "don't worry. Let me be totally up front with you. I've seen enough of you in the very few times you've been to class to know I'd like to have you during the week, as it may. If you choose to accept the position?"

What is it with these women and their fuckin' schemes? Works for me. "Actually, Edie," I said, "I also have weekend activities. So, that seems okay." Joan thrusted her arms in the air for victory. That is a sight.

"I won't ask you who she is," Edie said.

"Good."

"See, Mason," Edie said with a smile in her voice, "we are made to work. My weekday guy. I couldn't have chosen anyone better than you to get me through the drudgery of the week. Besides, I'm going to need help with Physics. How do you ace the tests and never come to class?"

"Physics comprises of three laws which are applied to everything on earth. I'll show you," I said. Joan wrote me another note, 'End it!' I assume she meant the conversation. "Oh, I'm sorry, I'm holding you up talking about Isaac Newton."

"Yeah, unfortunately, I'd better go," she said, "Mason, I'd rather be with you than Nick tonight. I don't know what I'm going to do when I see you there." You happy, Joan? You've created a monster.

"Hey, we're classmates. That'll be okay."

"Until Monday night?" Edie said softly.

"Until then, Edie," I said.

"Until then, Mason."

"See ya."

"Bye, for now." I hung on until I heard the click, then softly placed the phone in its cradle. I crawled from the bed and stood, exposing my entire bare body to the woman of my heart.

"Oh, Mason," she said in a sultry fashion.

"Okay, Joan, your evil plan is in place," I said, barely smiling.

"Oh, Mason, don't…."

"Look, listen to me. We'll do this. Edie's going to Jazz tonight. She'll be with her boyfriend, her weekend boyfriend."

"See, Mason, this…," she said cheerily until I interrupted her.

"Wait, Joan, I have something to say. You're not going to like her. You're *really* not going to like her. Recall the most beautiful Jewish American…I can't believe I thought that! I'm not going to say that…anyway, the most beautiful…you've ever seen. Edie's better. But, that's okay, because I don't like Alan. I haven't liked the son-of-a-bitch since we were first introduced. I'd rather drop the fucker than look at him. I can't stand the fact that he'll be anywhere near your arms."

"Mason," Joan cooed, standing and cozying up to me, "no one's getting anywhere near my arms but you. Why, darling, as you said, we'll be spending the week recovering from our weekends. No one will have a prayer with me. And speaking of prayer, I've prayed that you would somehow be delivered to me. And I've been answered. You are so sweet to be so concerned, but I'm your woman. Always remember that." She hung her arms around me and kissed me for a couple of days.

Joan can get me to do anything. Is she unfazed by Edie? Of course. She's like the devil. That's one of the reasons I love her.

"Okay, Joan," I said, as a statement of fact, "I love you and I'd run naked in the snow for you."

"Don't do that," she said, hands firmly placed on my hips, "or you'll have way too many weekday women."

Saturday evening, November 8, 1975
8:15 PM

Vinny and I celebrate

Joan and I are in her BMW silently traversing the town to my house.
The plan is to drop me off, have me glad-hand the public for a while,
explain to Jennifer why I can't be with her tonight, blame it on my new
girlfriend, get out before I create any more trouble, and meet Joan and
Pamela at Jazz, where Joan is going to see Edie for the first time and get
what she deserves for coming up with such an ill-conceived operation.
A big evening to finish off an unusual day.

We left Pamela at Joan's to nap in preparation for a night on the
town. I had my gear, so smelly we had to put it in a Glad bag, thanks to
Union Carbide and Dr. Retnitraj. The bag is minus my double eight jersey which I left for Joan. She is truly touched, vowing to sleep in it every
night, thereby solidifying the fact that we are going steady and making
the reality of my Susan St. James fantasy I've had since the first episode
of *McMillan and Wife.*

Montani is party central. It's as if all the dorms and the apartment
houses have unloaded into the streets, where the constant clamor from
the stadium has found a home. Traffic is jammed packed, thereby taking us a quarter hour to make it the two miles to my house. This is college as I had always thought it should be. We sat amid all the cars and
people witnessing the spectacle. Joan finally spoke.

"What are you going to tell Jennifer?"

"Nothing tonight. I'm just in, say hello to everybody, and out.
Anything else will get too messy."

"How deep did it get with you two?"

"The Mariana Trench with her. But, I told her I can't make commitments."

"Why?"

"Why? You, Joan. I always held out hope, sometimes for hope's sake."

Joan took her hand off the wheel to massage the back of my neck. "It'll be fun to review with you the past few months, you know, about you and me. It'll give me something to do in between screwing you out of your mind."

I considered that. I considered how very fortunate I am. I considered how I did not want this to end, even before it got started in earnest.

"Sweetheart," I said, "you'd better be prepared to have the passions I have held so long for you flooding you, with you, for you. They're endless, bottomless, infinite, powerful."

Joan drew in a deep breath. "Mason…Mason, you're nothing like anything ever before. God, I've got to stop thinking about it before I rear-end somebody! Tomorrow, sweetthing. Tomorrow."

"Tomorrow, it is."

We are content, minds contemplating as one, silently. Joan has been the soothing touch to take away the sting of being out of football. I had no time to think about it, with the gorgeous woman at my side since just minutes after Raj split the uprights. I now find myself very much lacking concern for the postgame, not out of any animosity I hold from the circumstances, but just because my heart is overly filled otherwise. I am finally with, certainly with the woman for whom my feelings accelerated quickly from amazement to admiration to infatuation to a crush to the hots to passion, all the way up to and beyond friendship and respect, now perching on boundless love. I reached to her and squeezed her knee. Joan smiled a huge smile and shook her head.

"I've got you. I finally got you," she announced to me and the windshield.

My eyes closed as I thought about how wonderful it is to have Joan want me. "You surely do," I said, turning to her and softly kissing her cheek. She is lovely. Then I turned back to find we are a half-block from my house.

Joan drove a bit more to come up beside a figure walking on the sidewalk. It's Vinny. Very much excited to see him, having not talked with him since just before he took the field to hold for Raj and therefore not even having the chance to celebrate with him, I said to Joan, "Here. Stop, please. Here's Vinny."

"Oh!" she said, mirroring my pleasure, probably considering the new relationship she'll have with My Gunner. She rolled her window down and said, "Hey, studboy!" I rocked back in laughter.

Vinny turned nonchalantly, then went bug-eyed when he saw who it is.

"Great game, Vinny. Here's your friend." Joan turned to me, "Go in, shake hands, go out, come see me before I ask around for Edie and beat the shit out of her." After getting over the initial shock of Joan new image she's projecting to me, I have grown to just adore the way she acts.

"See you there, baby," I said, reaching for my bag, "I love you."

"I love you, too," she said. I opened the door, "And, Mason…uh…even better than imagined." Joan twitched her nose at me.

My heart burst. "We'll talk about the fulfilling of imaginations later," I barely got it out.

"See ya." And she drove away.

"Where the hell have you been?" asked Vinny from across the street.

Jolted out of my state of ga-ga, I said, "I tried to contact you through our minds. Didn't you get my message?"

"No, goddamnit. What happened?"

"I was escorted from the stadium," I said.

"By Joan?"

"No, by the State Storm Troopers sent by the governor."

"You're kidding?" Vinny replied. Even in the dark of the streetlight, I could tell he still had the fourth quarter glow. My man.

"Sad but true," I said, "The field party was in full swing and I was out of there on my ass."

"Damnit, that sucks. That really sucks…but, listen to this. It might make you feel better. Man, you wouldn't believe what happened. But, first, what's up with Joan?"

"We've come to an agreement. We're lovers."

"Wait a minute. You get a touchdown, you coach a huge victory, and you get the prettiest girl? What is this? A made-for-TV movie? *Greg Brady: The College Years?*"

"I've had a good day. I had a good day? You had a good day!"

"Pretty remarkable. I want to thank you. If it weren't for you and your insanity, I wouldn't have had this chance."

I'm proud. "Think nothing of it, Gunner."

"No, I mean it. It was big. You kept us together so we could do our magic."

"Your magic, Magic Man. What a fourth you had! We decided it was going to take just that, and you did it. You did it."

"Hey, what did I tell you about our man Raj?"

"Goddamn, what a Howitzer!"

Vinny started to change the subject. I can tell he wants to tell me something important, "Now lemme tell you what happened. We finally made it to the locker room. It was crawling with the press. It was bizarre! They were all over my locker. I couldn't think straight. Then, Michael must have looked over to your locker and saw your stuff missing and your nameplate gone. He fuckin' went spastic! He single-handedly chased almost every reporter out, going off on a tirade about them being part of the big problem, of them sucking up to the administration and setting up the, as he put it, 'racism doctrine of college sports.' Huh, Cheetah? How about that? He lashed out to them as they were fuckin' scared to death, with Michael holding you up as an example of someone who stands up for what he believes and in the end, as he pointed to your empty locker, gets screwed. He told them what Fagden did to you, then he went off on them again as too gutless to do anything about it. He was very hot. I know he's true to you, but I think the thirty-five points had something to do with it."

I am shocked. Michael. My hero. Ohhh…"Shit, Vinny. Damn." My voice is weak.

Vinny grabbed my shoulder. "It gets better. Michael set the whole team afire. We all, black and white, piled our headgear in your locker and told the brave reporters who risked their lives and stayed there that we aren't playing until we institute changes in the system. We will get lawyers, Michael said, we will keep our scholarships, but we won't play until the administration, including the U president and the governor, meet with us and meet our demands."

"What are the demands?"

"We don't know yet. Michael, Arthur, Joe, Monty, and I are going to get together tomorrow and figure it out. One of them is to get you back."

I hesitated, because what I am about to say is not going to go along with the program. "Vinny. Forget me. There are more important issues here, like big money influence and how blacks are treated. I made a deal with that asshole Fagden. Unlike him, I live by my deals. Work on others. I'll even help, you know, like a consultant or something. But, go for the big stuff. And besides…" I thought about PD, "you can't repeat what I'm about to tell you."

"What?" Vinny asked.

"My contact, the banker."

"What?"

"He was arraigned for embezzlement yesterday."

Vinny's jaw dropped. I think he got it. "Oh, Jesus…when did you find out?"

"It was the story right beside mine in the paper this morning."

"Why didn't you say something?"

"Ohh…man, the implications of that are large and totally unknown. Michael and his guys were already moving. It was rolling too hard. I just kept my mouth closed and concentrated on Pitt."

"This means…oh, Christ."

"You bet. Somebody might have been set up. The banker, by McNabb. Or, if the banker's a lying bastard, me, and consequently Lawson."

"Oh, fuck…," sighed Vinny, "Oh, shit!" He started laughing. "Why am I laughing? This whole day could have been bogus. We could have thrown out an innocent man. A stupid man for starting The Kid, but not a bigot."

"Man, we don't know anything…I might try to talk to PD tonight."

"PD? PD Doughtery. My dad knows him."

"Oh, fuck, Vinny…This isn't getting any better…." Why me, God? Except for wanting a lot of sex, I've been a good guy….

"Look "Vinny started, "We have the paperwork. Bank photostats, affidavits. Christ, even a picture. That's real…just like you told Gerlach; it would be hard to just come up with that stuff. We've got to assume PD is telling the truth."

"And if he is," I said, "my ass is eventually grass."

"Ohh…," moaned Vinny.

"If they, the ubiquitous they, got PD, they're coming after me. Or, I submitted false evidence against a public employee."

"Man," Vinny said, "Joan looks great, but I'd hate to be you."

"I've got to call my lawyer."

We paused to gather our thoughts. The darkness surrounded us, metaphorical with regard to the unknown. Yet, like the kids we really are, Vinny continued, "Still, Mason, you gotta be with us, Mason," said Vinny, almost pleading, "We just got started, you and me. This is what we waited our whole lives for, man."

"And we got ours, today," I said, putting my tenuous future aside, "We got ours when everybody, I mean everybody, thought we couldn't. We got ours in the biggest of big games. We needed that last drive. It was crucial, and you and I, Vinny, moved it down the field against the number two defense in the nation. But, you, Gunner, you have a bright future here, buddy. Right now, you're the man. We're going bowling, pal, and if we beat Syracuse here next week, it could be New Years' Day. The national stage for you again, Vinny. There's a lot at stake. Your negotiations will be highly important. Don't fuck them up over one guy, over me. Especially in light of the current situation with PD."

Vinny stood in thought, then, "Man, we were something else, weren't we?"

"When it counted most, we delivered. You and me, Vinny. Just like we always knew it would be."

"I'll never forget your face when you hit the huddle for the first time. We knew what to do."

"The pass sucked," I joked.

"I was trying to make you look good," Vinny said with a smile.

"Well, you made up for it with Twilley. And the telepathic blitz check. Beautiful, Vinny."

"Worth all that work, wasn't it?"

I paused for emphasis, then reiterated, "Vinny, you guys in your meeting tomorrow, save the team. Save the Runners. Make it better. Look, the circumstances got me. I'm going to move on. You do the same."

Vinny got emotional, "Shit, Cheetah, I don't want you to go." When Vinny gets emotional, his speech lowers in volume and becomes more deliberate. But, he showed some capitulation to the events of the day, the cards we Runners have been dealt, "Hey, you're still going to live out the street from me and save me from the, as you say, trappings of the pursuit of the American dream, aren't you?"

"Vinny, I wouldn't miss messin' with Jean's head for the rest of her life for anything in the world."

My man laughed heartily. "I'm sure she'll appreciate it."

"I love you, man."

"I love you, too, man."

We embraced, two friends, at diverging crossroads, but with dreams fulfilled. And, as men caught in the trap of the honest expression of feelings, we steered the conversation toward something more man-friendly.

"Now, tell me again, what's going on with Joan?"

"We're a pair, Vinny."

"What's in the bag?"

"My gear."

"Have you been here already?"

"Nope. Got cleaned up at Joan's"

"You showered in Joan's shower? Damn."

"Hey, we're in love. What can I say?"

"What about her job, is one thing you can say."

I told Vinny about Joan's diabolical plan and the weekends and Alan and Edie. He's astounded.

"I thought she might be a sane influence, but it turns out she's as fuckin' nuts as you are…But, you get Edie during the week. Son-of-a-bitch. What a deal. Two gorgeous women. I guess you're not as crazy as I thought you were. But, tell me, and I think I already know, what about Jennifer?"

"Ohhh…I'm going to make a lot of people mad."

"Uh-oh. It's not going to be a pretty sight."

"I don't want to think about it right now."

"Are you coming in before you go to All That Jazz?"

"No."

"They're all expecting you," Vinny said like a parent.

"It's Jennifer, man. I can't face her yet."

Vinny became pensive. He gazed into the clouded night sky, then looked to me. "Look, I'm your best buddy. Whatever you do, I'll back it up. I told Michele and MJo last night I was starting to become a little concerned about Jen and her grand design for you, anyway. That may work with me, but you're different. You artsy-fartsy types gotta be handled in a special way. It's pretty apparent that Joan, just by going for your line of bullshit, that she's as unconventional as you are."

"Go ahead and say weird," I said, half-joking.

"And Edie, what's her deal?"

"She's an art major a senior...."

"I rest my case. See, Mason, I'm smart enough to know that if we were all alike, we'd get nowhere. So, we, you and I, keep each other from being obliterated off the face of the earth. I mean, if you didn't have me, you'd be dead right now with no trace of your body to be found."

"Yeah, you're probably right, Vinny."

"And maybe, just maybe, if you're out of football, that will give us more differences and more experiences and make us even better."

"That's a good way to look at it," I said with a smile, "I do hope you guys can get this thing settled tomorrow."

"We may take you up on your consultant offer. You were damned good today. Jesus, Mason, we were near boiling all day, and you kept it simmering and aimed at Pitt. Man, especially after what you knew about PD. What a guy! Good show!"

"The big priest didn't hurt. Was he with you after the game?"

"No. It was like you. He just vaporized. I don't know where he is."

"I guess we won," I said, "so his job is done."

"Anyway, we'll call if we need you."

"Well, I'll be at Joan's"

"I don't even want to ask."

"All I know is the doors will be locked and the curtains will be pulled and sometimes the phone may be off the hook. But, just keep dialing. Other than that, it's all a mystery to me. If I'm not back by Wednesday evening, send food, preferably Chinese."

Vinny laughed, "When are you going to find time for Edie?"

"That's Monday night, at Bill's"

"I take it back. I want your life."

"Let me live it for a while. You might change your mind."

"You two are crazy. You know that sissy Alan. Does she know Edie?"

"She'll see her at Jazz tonight."

"Oh, hell, I'd love to be there for that!"

"Come with me. Joan's sister Pamela is in town. She was very impressed with your game today. You never know."

"Mason, remember? I'm the ordinary one, the orthodox man, as you've called me many times. I've got Jean upstairs and the lifetime sentence. A sentence I'm willing to accept."

"You know more than I do about that."

"Believe me, there are reasons."

"I can see that much from my vantage point."

"Are you lusting after my girlfriend, future wife, and mother of my children?"

"Occasionally."

"That's probably good. It says you're not Joan-deaf."

"Joan-deaf! Witty for a male model."

"I keep hearing that. But, look at you! You must be doing something right," Vinny replied. Another pause. "I guess I'd better get upstairs,"

"I'll be here tomorrow morning until about ten."

"Pamela leaving at nine fifty-nine?"

"On the nose."

"What do I tell Jennifer, if she asks?"

"Tell her I'm too bummed to be there, or if she doesn't buy that, tell her I'm in Iran looking for alternative energy sources."

"That'll work."

"Vinny, buddy, I am proud to have been your target today. Thank you for everything you've done." I extended my hand. He clasped it, then pulled me in to hug him.

"Mason, we couldn't have written a better script." Vinny said.

"And the voyage continues." I said.

"And it does."

Vinny turned and walked up the steps to the porch. He faced me again, gave me the thumbs-up, the same thumbs-up he gave me all day today, then turned again to open the door. The house erupted. I smiled, satisfied.

Saturday, November 8, 1975
8:45 PM

The war hero

Holding my bag full of my football stuff, I turned away from my house, a most difficult thing to do since I too could have been a subject of their adulation. My inability to face Jennifer right now, my total lack of guts, a position in which I honestly seldom if ever find myself, is a source of dismay. I rationalized that my lack of true feelings for her would be a future disaster, causing more pain then than the truth will now. Trouble is, I'm not telling her the truth now. Just this morning, we made love. Well, she made love. I just had sex with an irresistible and available long-legged college girl. Worse, I promised her more. She's up there right now wondering where I am. And there is no instrument fine enough to measure my interest. I have really botched this one and I don't want to think about it because I won in the pursuit of my dream woman. That woman is now my love life. Well, she along with the absolutely stunning Edie Loden, but I'll have to find a way to keep that in perspective, like continue to lobby with Joan to drop her ludicrous idea. I'm only hoping she'll come to her senses, but from what I've witnessed this afternoon and this evening, Vinny's right. She has as much sense as I do.

I walked to the Tazmanian Devil, looking it over from the outside and chuckling. What if Joan's parents saw this car? Then I thought that maybe I am Joan's mute protest against the society in which she was raised. I pondered that. Then I remembered Joan naked. She can use me to piss her parents off any time she wishes.

Throwing the bag in the back seat, I reached in my pocket for my keys. I sat at the wheel, inserted the keys into the ignition lock, wondered for an instant if Fagden had wired a bomb to the electrical system of the car, decided that probability is remote, turned the key, and nothing happened but a clicking sound. I paused, turned the key again, and the grating of stripped gears came from under the hood. The starter's shot. "Fuck!" I exclaimed under my breath. The car's dead for now. No starter, no hope to start the car. If I were on a hill, I could drift start it, but then how embarrassing would that be at the flat lot of Jazz in front of Joan, Pamela, and Edie. And I can't go up to the house and ask anybody for a ride. Almost immediately, I decided my only choice is to use the Universal College Transit System. I will hitchhike.

I'm still in blazer, tie, and overcoat, so I'm an attractive rider. But, that doesn't make much sense. How many mutilating murderers have access to good clothes? And automobiles? Nevertheless, Joan awaits, so I walked to the curb of Wagner and Donnelly and stuck out my thumb.

It took a couple of moments for even one car to come by. And go by. Another minute. Another car, come and gone. This took place several times until a black Lincoln Continental, even longer than Vinny's Caprice, stopped just ahead of me. I walked to the door. The gentleman driving reached across the seat to unlatch the door for me. I opened it and stepped into the auto's front passenger side and sat.

"Thank you, sir," I said, thinking that most hitchhikers aren't lucid nor mannerly.

"You're welcome," the driver said, his voice deep and educated, his body short and round, his head fat and bald. "Where are you off to, son?"

"Over to the Pinehurst area, on States Drive."

"Where are you going to there?"

"A jazz club, All That Jazz," I replied. I glanced his way, then did a double take. I recognized him, but couldn't place where. We rode in quiet for a few minutes.

"Looks like I can take you right there, Mr. Bricker."

Okay, that scares me. He's either a fan, a predator, or a predator fan. Captive in his car, I have no choice but to confront this right away.

"So, you know me," I said.

"I surely do," the man said, "I was at the game today. You played well."

"Thank you," I said, sincerely.

"I didn't at all agree with your team's, what you might call, overall philosophy today, but you won. You won on your own, no coaches. I'm sure you're proud of yourselves."

Great. I've hitched a ride with one of the dissenters. "Actually, sir, we'd rather none of this would have happened. But, you do what you have to do."

"So, you think you had to do it," the man said in a low voice.

I looked at him to respond, "Sir, considering everything, yes, we had to." Then, my heart fell into my suddenly cramping stomach. I know who this dude is. I've seen his picture. It's Myron McNabb. This ride is now officially irony. What do I do? Do I acknowledge who he is? Or, do I just hope to make it anywhere near the jazz club? Or, do I open the door and roll out right now?

Ahh, I'll just stay and fuck with his mind.

"Yes, sir, Mr. McNabb," I said, "We had a lot to prove. More than just football. And we did it."

"Do you honestly think you changed any thoughts or beliefs among your fans with your childish expression of resistance?" McNabb asked as he continued to drive, at least in the general direction of Jazz.

"I think we either changed them or gave them cause to think," I said proudly. "Most importantly, we did what was right."

"You did what you thought was right," he said, "But, was it really? You're so young, you don't know. You don't know what a fine country this was."

"It is a fine country, right now, Mr. McNabb," I said.

"It was much better. It was much purer. People used to know their places. Now we're all mixed. It's dangerous, Mr. Bricker. You don't know the danger you face by your…togetherness."

I am in the midst of a true, card-carrying racist. This man has caused me a lot of grief. I'm out of football because of this asshole. And I'm in the mood to argue, "What dangers? What's so dangerous about it?"

"They'll take over your employment possibilities. They'll take over your neighborhood. They'll overrun your Roman Catholicism. You see the Mexicans and the Puerto Ricans doing that already, Mr. Bricker. And they'll steal your women. You have a girlfriend, Mr. Bricker?"

"Yeah, she's Jewish," I said, feeling a little badly about using Edie to mess with McNabb. She might approve, though.

"You've fallen for the trap worse than I thought, Mr. Bricker. Hitler was right. They're unclean. Watch your Juden woman closely. They don't do things the way we do."

"You're pissing me off, Mr. McNabb."

"And the only reason I picked you up tonight is because I wanted to meet you. My nemesis. The doer of good. Fighting my evil. You'll see evil, Mr. Bricker, when the coloreds and the Jews and the ethnics take over. You won't have a chance."

This guy's a real piece of work. "I'm sorry, Mr. McNabb. I don't agree with your assessment of the future of the world. I think we are stronger and more compassionate with our diversity. I'm white, and I'm a male, and I'm from one of the most backwoods states in the nation, but I embrace my black friends, and my Italian-American friend, and, much to your alarm, my Jewish friend. We're all in this together, and we're better for it."

We are nearing Jazz. I'm on. I almost wished we had more time, but getting this hyperbigot out of my sight will be a relief.

"You'll find out, Mr. Bricker," McNabb said.

I felt an overwhelming urge to get to the bottom of this, all this. "Let me ask you, Mr. McNabb," I said, "Why did you do it? Why did you pay Lawson off to play Kay? Why football? Why us?"

"Mr. Bricker," he answered almost immediately, "I'm a very wealthy man. I have it to spare. And there are people out there, desperate people, who want a slice of my pie. I'll admit it to you, but I'll swear I never said it, but your Lawson is one of those folks. And I saw a way to make a statement. I don't like the way the blacks are taking over American sports. It reached a critical point with the Kansas City Chiefs winning the Super Bowl with all those coloreds. It's gone downhill since then. Do you know half your team is black?"

"Yeah. It's great. They're great guys," I said in defiance.

"I couldn't see a black playing quarterback for my home state's football team. Quarterback. The position of skill and intelligence. They can take over with their running and jumping ability, but quarterback belongs to us. And I made sure that happened." McNabb finished, cool, collected, depraved.

"Mr. McNabb, you fell for the trap," I said with fire, "You had to pay Lawson off because Lendel was so damn good. He was the best man for the job. He was benched because of your money, and only because of your money. Is this what it takes? Whites can't win on their own merits anymore, so you pull your wallet out? And we're the superrace?"

"It worked with your friend from First National," McNabb said.

Just as I thought. Lawson and PD. Another brought down by this bastard. I'm seething. But in a way I am also relieved. PD had been telling me the truth. But, for it he got hung. I thought about that again and went back to being mad. I decided to face it head-on, "So you set up

PD Doughtery. He had you dead to rights, Mr. McNabb. Hiding behind your bankroll again, aren't you? So, now what are you going to do to me?" I asked the question fearlessly, despite worrying about it a good part of the day. He is going to nail me. Joan. Oh, shit, now we're dragging her into this. Ohh....

"Mr. Bricker," McNabb started, "you are naïve. You with Mr. Burton, Mr. Ward, Mr. Doughtery, and your Hebrew woman. You'll see. Mr. Doughtery has already proved himself to be less than a credit to his race by stupidly getting too close to one of his accounts and thereby leaving himself open."

"So, he almost did it and you just gave it a little push. You are a jerk." I feel pain for PD, for a career he had worked so long to build. For his reputation. For his credibility. For his family. He got me involved to save his people and himself. Now he's had it. I feel terribly for him. I'm going to do whatever I can to pull him out of it. The first thing is to call Rex and tell him about McNabb and this.

McNabb ignored my comment, "You'll find out. But, if people like you run the country, when you find out it will be too late." McNabb paused and changed the way he looked at me. He talked again, "You know, with Lyndon Fadden kicking you out of football, and with your status as a student frankly in question, I could use a bright, talented young man like you in my coal organization. You would be a very good understudy."

I am shocked almost to the point of laughter, "Mr. McNabb, no," is my simple response.

"Are you sure?" he asked.

I don't know what I did or said to make him think I would want to be associated with him, so I reaffirmed, "No."

"If you were to accept my offer, you wouldn't be the first Bricker in my organization," he said with a smile as we pulled into the parking lot at All That Jazz.

"I'm not doing it, Mr. McNabb," I said again.

After bringing his car to a halt and putting it in park, McNabb reached into his back seat for a briefcase. He swung it up front and rested it on the steering wheel. Opening it, he leafed through some papers and produced a manila envelope which he handed to me. I took it, peered at him, and opened it. There is a single photograph in there, an eight-by-ten black-and-white glossy of a group of men, all in street clothes. A banner of a *swastika* hung behind the men. My heart broke. I saw my punishment for going against swelling tide of discrimination. The second man from the right is my father.

McNabb must have seen the expression on my face fall. "Frank Bricker," he began, "Congressional Medal of Honor. USMC track man. Husband. Father of four. Railroader. Union secretary-treasurer. Welcome to his secret life, Mr. Bricker."

I don't recall being so devastated in my entire life. Everything, my belief structure, my hero ideals, foundations built on decades of what I thought were true, on what I trusted, trusted implicitly; everything began to crack and crumble before me. I took one more look at the picture. It made me want to wretch. I couldn't even hold it any more. Placing it back into its envelope, I handed it to McNabb, resigned to the fact that my father for reasons unknown to me, reasons known only by him and carried to his grave, was part of a group of men whom everything they espoused I was fighting-mad against. My father was a Neonazi.

"Your father was a drunk, Mr. Bricker," McNabb said, cowardly kicking me while I am down, "A sot. He could barely hold his job. He often had to mark-off because he was either hung over or just couldn't take it. Your father was one of those desperate souls. He needed money, and I had the money, and I, Mr. Bricker, saw him coming. His job was a special one. A charismatic individual he was, so he recruited for me. Brought in a lot of good men, a lot of men, the frantic and the furious, a lot of men who saw what I saw, who saw a nation, a nation whom many of them fought for falling apart under the guise of diversity. There are many like us, Mr. Bricker. We have cause, purpose. We are going to save a race, and at the same time save a country. Now, after seeing that you are a legacy, you might reconsider joining me."

The dissonance is clanging in my brain. I just finished playing our dream game, ours, my father's and mine. He taught me how to play, and taught me other things important to me. I thought he was a brave man. I thought he encouraged me to take a stand for my beliefs. The irony of this ride continued with blinding lights and cacophony as I recalled the past week and thought of how I drew upon the memory of my father to keep me going when all seemed impossible and lost. I knew he drank too much, but he seemed to handle his weakness so well. I never knew he hurt for money so badly, so implausibly badly that he would go against everything he carried a rifle for in pursuit of it. Ron said he saw McNabb in the basement once. I thought it was just a cheap shot. I'll be damned if it's not true.

"Think about it, Mr. Bricker," McNabb continued, "I put the clothes on your back. You've already joined me. Just make it official, right now."

"No," I answered firmly.

"Well, then, Mr. Bricker," McNabb said, "you leave me no choice. You want to stay with your niggers and your dago and your kike whore? I have the power to get this picture published in *The Montani Mail*. And I have the power to get you expelled. What do you think they'll think of you then, Mr. Bricker?"

I am angry beyond concept. The foul names he has for my friends, the unveiling of my father and his identity, the audacity he has in even considering me as a recruit, I found it difficult to keep it all under control. It would be incredibly foolish to beat the mortal shit out of a multimillionaire. As despoiled as my emotional state is, I have to do what my father was unable to do. I have to pick up the pieces.

"Print it, McNabb," I said, knowing there really is nothing else he can do to me. "Go ahead. And get me kicked out school while you're at it.

You've got all the money in the world, but you don't know my friends. They're aware of something you're not. I'm not my father. I'm *Mason Bricker.* Surely, I've discovered an evil side of the man I most admire. And, to understate it, it's goddamned disappointing. But, it's not me. And whatever you think I might become because of some choices my father made at some time, I'm not going to do the same things. Never."

"We'll see after the photo hits the papers," McNabb said.

"Print it, you fucking son-of-a-bitch," I said.

"I'll be around," he said, a persistent bastard, "And, Admissions will be contacting you."

"If you think you're going to back me down, you're wasting your time. I'd rather die than join you," I said, "So long, Mr. McNabb." Not waiting for his goodbyes, I opened the door and stepped out of his car.

Walking away in some direction I am unaware of, I am hurting. McNabb drove off. I know I have the resolve to be my own man, but now I feel so desolate, so empty. I'm trying to move on, but the road before me looks so long and winding and daunting. Finding a curbside in the parking lot beside a Volkswagen Karmen Ghia, I sat on the butt of my overcoat and sobbed.

Saturday, November 8, 1975
9:15 PM

Dealing with the sins of my father

I have achieved that point of draining emotions where I am nearly in a stupor. Sitting between two cars now, since a Datsun B210 had parked beside the Karmen Ghia, possibly unaware I was there or thinking I was just another drunk, it didn't matter to me at that time. Feelings are hitting, I mean hitting me from all sides. I am angry, damned mad at my father for doing this, for being such a fucking wimp and not being responsible. Here's a man who was a war hero. He saved the lives of ten men with his bravery. He acted when it was most essential that he do so. Yet, when it came time to simply care for a family the right way, when it was safe and there were no bullets flying, he choked.

I'm embarrassed, too. I told McNabb to print it, but I do dread my friends, and anybody else, seeing the picture in the paper. I made such a big goddamned fuss over Lawson, and now look at the mess I'm in. This is going to make a lot of people who didn't agree with my tactics and actions very happy. And talk about loss of credibility...no, I don't want to talk about that. It's better for the team that they figure it all out for themselves, and I fall on my sword. What's Joan going to say when she finds out my father was a Nazi? Oh, God, Edie? Oh, what a fuckin' mess.

But, you know what I also feel? I feel sorry for my father. I'm in a mess? He really screwed it up, screwed it up so terribly that he was trapped and couldn't find any other way out except McNabb. It must have been hell for him. Think of the rationalizations he had to make to just look in the mirror. Or just to look at me, who saw him as some sort of a Roman god. It was almost as if his life ended when he signed on with McNabb. And, that brings up the possibilities of the locomotive accident. Maybe it wasn't an accident. I was just semi-joking about going to see a psychologist. Now, it's the best thing to do. I'm going to need some help in figuring this out. I know I'm not going to get anywhere by myself. I might as well just suck it up and go to a professional. First, losing football. Then, choosing a peculiar but loving relationship with an older woman. Now, this. I'd better do something about it before I turn into my father. Going to a shrink will take the pressure off me. No, it'll probably uncover some really ugly things, but, hell, from this curb I don't see any other way.

"Mason?"

I had my head down and my left hand in my hair when I heard a sweet voice say my name. Looking up to find Edie standing at the rear of the Datsun, all I can think of is she is the worst possible person I can run into right now. I know I just have to stand up and act coherent because I'm sure I look like a pothead sitting between two automobiles. Worse still, I have to explain what's going on. I've lied enough today with Jennifer, and I've learned from the picture of my father that it is better to face the music.

"Oh, Edie," I said, sounding badly, I know.

"Mason, are you okay?" she said. I think she is genuinely concerned.

Edie is resplendent in a denim jacket over a black leotard and tight black corduroy slacks and jazz dance shoes. I could lay in bed all night long and just look at her face. She's awesome. She wears no makeup, a natural beauty, even in the most unnatural of streetlights. You'd better say something, Cheetah.

"Uh, Edie, no, I'm not okay."

"What's wrong, Mason?" she asked, "Is there something I can help you with?"

After I hesitated because of the weight bearing down on me, I said, "Actually, I hope so. I have something to tell you."

"What is it, dear?" She reached to touch my arm.

"Edie, you're the first person I have told this to, because I just learned about it. It has rocked my world, and after I tell you, I hope you don't hate me."

"Oh, Mason…," Edie said, not knowing what to say.

"I hitched a ride over here, and, wouldn't you know it, the guy who picked me up was McNabb."

"Oh, my!" Edie's face looked pained.

"We had philosophical arguments on the way over here, as you may be able to imagine. I outwitted the son-of-a-bitch, but those kinds of guys are ill, so they don't know any better. The killer is…" I sighed. Edie squeezed my arm tighter. "he showed me a picture of my late father as part of his organization, a picture of him with other men standing in front of a *swastika*."

Edie's hand jumped in front of her mouth in horror.

"Edie," I said, choking back as hard as possible, "I never knew this. I just found out. The bastard McNabb is going to publish the picture in the newspaper."

"Just to get you back, huh?" she said.

"I guess. Oh, shit, Edie, I'm sorry…I'm sorry for what my father did to you…." It is thirty years after the Nazi's attempt at the genocide of Jews, but I have a very real feeling my father is responsible. I am close to collapse.

"Mason!" she said, "Mason! Oh, you dear, sweet thing!" Edie held me in her arms, "Oh, Mason, you're dad didn't do that. He's just part of those hanging on. And, Mason, it's not you. It's your dad. He's the one in the photo. I'm sure this hurts you so badly, but you, Mason, you did wonderful things. Courageous things! Oh, I don't hate you. In fact, I'm kind of impressed you can face me with this." I stood against her, shaking. Edie kept holding me. "Mason, I'm not kidding! What you did this week, well, you used to be just another good-looking guy. But now, you're that and much more. Oh, I'm going to go see that whatever I date. I promised him, but I'll be in there, looking at you, wanting to be with you. I can't wait to see you Monday night. It looks like we've got some things to discuss. Some good things."

I raised my face directly in front of hers. Our lips immediately met, and I forgot where I am and why I'm there. Edie and I parted, gazing, smiling.

"I'd better get in there," she said.

"I…uh…yeah…well."

She laughed.

"I…I…as soon as I cure my speech impediment…," Edie laughed. She really is beautiful. I could kick myself for the 'princess' insinuation I made with Joan. *Joan*!! Oh, hell, "I've got to get in there, too," I said.

"Yeah, we'd better not walk in together. People can always tell."

"Yeah, I don't want to make yours, or mine, mad."

"Well, my knight in shining armor, until later?"

"Until later."

Miss Loden's acceptance of me has done a lot to put my father in perspective for now. Edie kissed her fingertips and touched my lips with them. That's a lovely gesture. She grinned and walked.

And here I am, back to Women Problems. Call the shrink first thing Monday.

Saturday November 8, 1975
9:40 PM

Dealing with the sins of our fathers

A solitary figure in the parking lot, I stand among the increasing amount of cars filtering in. Joan expected me to go to the party, so I'm not alarmingly late. That gives me time to get a hold of myself. A memorable day this has been. Football is such an emotionally taxing sport. I'm sure part of my problem right now is that I did not allow myself to celebrate, the natural extension of a big victory in the closest of games. It would have completed the circuit. I followed my instincts at the time, but I am becoming aware that maybe it was a mistake. Of course, being thrown out of the stadium put a damper on my party, but it's as if I went from being a kid to Joan's young adult life and her inviting shower and all the head rushes associated with her. I did this at light speed and I will pay.

Joan's *interesting* right now. It makes me wonder just how mercurial she is. Can she keep a relationship going, and can she keep one going with me? How long will she be able to accept the secrecy? I guess I'll have to buy her a lot of stuff and jet us off to places. We could be rather anonymous in New York City. That would be fun. I wonder if Stan the Money Man will understand the sale of Batavia Bank stock to court the daughter of its CEO. Too bad the pursuit of love and dynamite sex isn't tax deductible. This, of course, could all be moot if the picture of my Nazi father frightens her off. Once again, for the second time in just a few hours, I test Joan with Edie as the backstop. Whatever, this is much better than being the husband of Jennifer Pierce Bricker. It was a nasty job, but I feel I did the right thing, even though the Catwoman is still waiting for me to walk through the door. But I've always believed that what comes around goes around. I'll get my head handed to me some-time as penance, but I've accepted the way I live. Kind of reminds me of my father from long range, except I'll try to be a helluva lot more hon-est with myself.

The shrink idea still sounds good to me. I wonder how Joan will go with that? You'd think with regard to Pamela she'd be okay with it, but people are funny about those mental things. I'll go during the week on the sly, setting up the appointments during class. Assuming, of course, I'm still a student. If not, I'll just become a professional investor, maybe a money manager. Maybe Stan will let me extend for him here in West Virginia. Goddamn, I am going to put the food on this shrink's table for a long time. She'll be able to make a career out of me. She? That would be a disaster in waiting. Can you imagine me spilling my feelings from the innermost recesses of my mind to a woman who would have total control over me? A woman? Nope. A compelling story, but not good, not with my more recent history. I need a man shrink. He'd understand men and fathers, men and hitting people, men and love. I'm already looking forward to it, which is testament to just how crazy I am.

As I walk toward the door of The Jazz, the gamesman in me antici-pated Edie/Joan with a smile. It's strange; I love Joan, but I want to see her squirm over this stupid fuckin' idea of hers. I'll just be cool about it. The opportunity to point my little friend out will come in its own time.

Sit back, buddy, and let it unfold. Jesus, there are two things I have to pop on Joan tonight. Keep Pamela around. She's rather grounded, a total contrast to her sister whom has turned out to be unlocked. No complaints, however. This should be fun, if she accepts the sins of my father.

Entering, I paid my cover with a five and stepped into the big room. I discovered All That Jazz to be pleasingly simple, in comparison to the superficially opulent discos which are popping up all over the place offering bump and grind dancing and women doing some serious booty shaking. The walls are wood paneling, real wood, a darkened knotty pine. Art hangs all around, ranging from Monet to abstract to the incomprehensible. Plants are suspended from macramé cordage, which is nothing more than decorative rope. There is a small stage at the farthest point from the front door with drums and mikes and stools and no musicians. Must be a break. Tables are randomly placed throughout the room, with candles in colored jars as centerpieces. That reminds me…ah, there…there's the fire exit. I'll have to get Joan and Pamela and Edie out of here. That'll be tricky.

The place is about three-quarters full with the dominant color of clothing being black. Possessing no knowledge of jazz as a music genre and with my gray overcoat and dress slacks and tie draping me, making me look like a young businessman who has just stumbled in, I'm out of it. I notice the people in black examining me, as if I am a tax CPA or the FBI. Oh, fuck 'em.

I see Joan and Pamela. Pamela is wearing a black turtleneck and faded denims, common clothes for an uncommon woman. Joan is my dream, literally. She's wearing that black mohair cardigan and black tight slacks from my fantasy of the night before. Kreskin the Tutor. Edie and her guy are sitting at the table right next to Joan and Pamela. At this point, there is nothing to do but laugh.

The sisters waved. I moved their way, passing directly in front of Edie, behind her man. I winked. She quickly glanced and grinned. The man must have caught this, because he turned. I had already walked by, so he missed me. I sat down beside Joan and across from Pamela.

"Hi, Mason," Joan said, looking at me very seductively. If this is what jazz does to her, I'm running out to buy every Dizzy Gillespie or whoever LP I can find tomorrow.

"Hello, Mason," said Pamela. She is smoking. There is also a loaded ashtray in front of Joan. I caught a whiff of burning tobacco on her breath. That's kind of a turn-on. Of course, since August everything about her has been. They've been drinking beer. Cool.

"That didn't take too long," Joan said, placing her hand halfway up my right thigh.

"No, I just talked to Vinny for a while and didn't go in," I said, "The house was shaking. They may have never let me out."

"I'm glad you made it," Joan said, grinning. She owns my soul.

"How's your friend Vinny?" asked Pamela. Well....

"Doin' pretty well. Understandable coming off such a great game," I replied, "It was good to see him. Vinny and I are heading into uncharted territory, with him playing ball and me just being a regular student."

"I still think you can fight that, Mason," said Joan. She must have liked that aspect of me.

"Well, ladies, after I tell you this, you may see why it will just be better for me to walk."

"What is it?" Pamela asked as Joan squinted a question on her pretty face.

"It's bad."

"Oh, no, Mason," Joan said, very concerned.

I explained to them softly, with regard to Edie being just next door, about the dead car and the hitchhike out here. I told them about McNabb picking me up and about how appallingly racist he is, even moreso in person. I told them about PD. Then, I got to the part where he tried to recruit me. And....

"The son-of-a-bitch pulled out a large photo of men standing in front of a banner with a *swastika*. One of the men was my late father. McNabb said he's going to get the picture published in *The Montani Mail* and get me thrown out of school if I don't join him. No way in hell will I ever do that." I stopped talking for the response.

The ladies looked at me in astonishment. I glanced at each of them for clues. I got none. So, I continued, "Joan, one of the first things I thought about was us, was about how you'd feel about me when you saw this picture in the paper."

"Oh, Mason, no. Don't worry about me. This is your father, not you. You've proven yourself in a way no one could ever. I know of your allegiances to fairness. Don't worry, sweetheart. I love you. You, Mason. And I know who you are. And you're not some...I can't even say it...you're just not that way."

Goddamnit, I want to cry but I've had enough of that this week.

"Mason, it's okay," Pamela said, reaching across the table and clasping my hand, "Your reaction to that terrible picture you saw is completely natural. But, Joan's right. It's not you. Believe me. I know." She smiled a smile of assurance, then continued, "Your friend PD; well you know maybe we don't know the whole story there. That could border on extortion, I think."

"Yeah," said Joan, "You've got to talk to him, Mason. You've got to tell him about your conversation with McNabb."

"I've got to call him soon," I added, "I feel kind of responsible."

"I certainly understand your feelings. They're consistent with the good man you are," said Joan as she squeezed my arm, "Just don't worry about that." Wow...good man...Joan, you've locked up my heart and thrown away the key.

"Yeah, I have enough to worry about," I replied, in recovery, "The fat bastard is coming after me." Joan placed her cheek against my shoulder.

These two women are doing a damn good job of relieving my pain. And believe me, I hurt. "The father I had no idea existed came back to haunt me and went right for where it counts," I continued, "I want to be a good man. I want to save the Bricker name."

Joan and Pamela looked intently at each other for the longest time. I sat there waiting for something, whatever. Joan reached for the pack of Mores to her right, got out two, handed one to Pamela, picked up the disposable lighter and lit them both. The Kissingers took simultaneous draws and exhales. They looked to each other again. This is curious.

"Tell him," Pamela said, eyes askance.

"Think I should?" Joan asked.

"Yep. Now's the time. It'll help things," said Pamela.

I waited. Joan took another puff. The waitress delivered more beers to the sisters. I ordered a Miller Lite.

"Mason, Pamela and I know all about fathers," began Joan, "Ours is the perfect jackass."

I really don't know what to say to that, but I'm certainly hip.

She went on, "He screws everything. Brothers, business associates, secretaries, wives of business associates. He's an arrogant man out of control. He has his own rules. And he doesn't care what anybody thinks of him, except his daughters, whom he thinks he has fooled. Ha! And, here's the real kicker, he's so filthy rich he can get by with anything. He's Mr. Charisma. He'll shake your right hand and stab you with his left, and he's so damned adept at it, no one cares. We live in fear that some brave soul is going to get so pissed off at him he's going to kill him.

"My mother, Jesus, it's almost worse. She just turns her back and puts up with it. We used to think she was afraid of him, but now we know she's just greedy and being twenty years younger, she's waiting for someone to blow him away or for him just to be stricken dead."

"I'm...Gee...I'm sorry, girls," I said, in light of everything keeping it simple.

"Last October, when the stock price was so low," Joan said, "you remember. Pamela, just to keep you up to date, Mason owns stock in Batavia."

Wide-eyed and agape, Pamela asked, "How did that happen?"

"It's a long story," I said, "My money guy was looking for value, and he found your family's bank."

"Mason's been talking to Sally for a long time," said Joan, hammering away at still more irony in my fantastically ironic life.

"Most serendipitous," Pamela said, shaking her head, smiling, "It's meant to be."

Despite her earlier lack of interest in my small ownership of her family's bank, I can tell by Joan's look of approval she liked the thought of Batavia and me. "Anyway," she continued, "our father accumulated through less-than-ethical tactics large amounts of the stock, looking at the same value you were seeing, but not satisfied until he had wrested total control from his family members. Now he's king."

"What I'm happy for," Pamela said, "is that our mother is, at forty-eight, young enough to be the next in line for the fortune and hold on to it for a long time, thereby preventing me…."

" And me…," said Joan.

"Yes, both of us, from having to make a decision on what to do with this tainted money. True, he's put us through school, sent us to Europe, set us up in practices and homes, but to be frank with you, he presents one giant motherfucker of a conundrum for us. What do you do?"

"You see, Mason," Joan said, "he's our father, and there's always hope out there that he'll change, way out there most of the time. But he has passed it on. Our older brother Jack has turned out to be just like him, right down to fucking anything that walks. Sally acts as if she doesn't know a thing."

We sat in silence, letting it all soak in; one father a foolhardy Nazi, the other a capitalist pig gone mad. I restarted the conversation with a bent of a nineteen-year-old, "Dads are just ass-rippers."

"I couldn't have said it better myself," said Pamela.

"Pamela and I figured this out when we were in high school," said Joan, "Since then, we've managed to stick together, and that's how we've survived, right, Sis?"

"Right," responded Pamela, "It's all about making it through the day. You string those along and you've got a life."

"So, Mason," Joan said, "not meaning to belittle your painful discovery, I just want to let you know that you're not alone." She grabbed my thigh again and kissed my cheek. I am most appreciative of their efforts to pull me through this. I have also lost track of Edie. I wonder what she thinks of Joan and her rack? I stole a glance over to her table. She looked to me at the same time. Joan didn't see me, but she caught Edie.

"It is now time to forget fathers for the night," Joan announced, "But, Mason, there is another question burning in my soul."

Knowing what that might be, I asked, "And what might that be?"

"Excuse me," said Pamela, standing and heading for the ladies' room, probably trying to get out of the line of fire.

I looked directly into her eyes. Whispering, most likely because she already knows, Joan asked, "Where's Edie?"

Imprudently, I paused. And paused.

"Well?" Joan pressed.

I moved my face right next to hers, and said, "With the guy, directly to my left. Short, black hair."

Joan glanced obliquely three times, then hesitated, and gave her a fourth. I know, I just know this is not going to be good. That face…Holy Mary, Edie looks like the young Elizabeth Taylor. I can tell because I love her that Joan is burning mad right now.

All hands are off me. There is no touching, not the sides of legs or arms or shoulders. There are cigarette smoking, lots of staring straight ahead, and lots and lots of eerie silence. It is probably my jock arrogance taking over that makes me feel I have the upper hand here. I mean, Alan, Mr. Country Club, suntan in the bowels of autumn. Joan has not a leg to stand on. But, as I recalled from studying the philosophy of investing, reward is relative and risk is absolute. And I can see Joan absolutely despised my choice for my Weekday Woman.

Joan dashed out one cigarette and lit another. She swigged her beer. It's as if I'm not here. It's as if we are married.

I didn't know when to say something. With the Joan of old, I'd know: stay true to the story, hang on in spite of it all. With the new Joan, anything can set her off, impelling her to jump over me and onto Edie's table and claw her. Part of me is actually laughing, deeply inside, of course. There's a good possibility that considering her uniqueness, Joan has never had such close personal proximity to a woman who is competition and who in some ways, well, in many ways, actually closer than I want to admit, matches her beauty. But there's Edie, smiling, beaming, the candlelight reflecting from her face just perfectly. In a way it's not fair causing Joan such concern. I have to wonder, if I got my wish and she called off Alan, would I be willing to give up Edie? It's difficult to say. I guess I'm thinking like a nineteen year old, but maybe I could risk Alan for Edie. So, here's the big question: would I during the weekdays make love with Edie? Even after the promises to Joan? I don't know the answer to that question.... Oh, hell yes I know the answer to that question. I'm just afraid of it. I am a college sophomore. The reality is...oh, I hate myself for thinking this sacrificing everything I've dreamed since I met Margaret Joan...I'd just think of Alan, knock on Edie's door, and be her true-to-the-flesh Weekday Man.

That would be incredibly foolish. I have to get out of this as soon as possible.

"Consider this, Joan," I said, eyes straight ahead, "You drop Alan. Edie takes a walk, too. We're committed to each other, exclusively, like I think we truly want it. I only want you. I don't want Edie, or any other woman for that matter. We'll just be very careful and I won't do anything stupid like unbutton your blouse in your office or camp out under your desk and run my face up your thighs when you sit down...." I noticed I got a little smile from her on that one, but she refused to even glance at me, "Joan, I respect and admire you and your career. You know, professionally, I want to be like you someday. It's sort of funny to hold up the woman you make love with as a role model, but it's true," Joan's smile grew wider, "You have a classroom presence of which I have never witnessed. You're good. I will never do anything to harm that. Nothing at all. But, I also don't want anybody to come between us, not even in a titular nature. I want it all. I want you to be a college professor, or anything you want to be. I'm behind you one hundred and ten percent. And I want to be your lover. And I want to be your friend. I simply want you. And I want you to want me. And I'll do anything for you. Anything. I do have to be honest with you and tell you that I hope that anything doesn't involve Alan and Edie."

Wouldn't you know it, right at the moment Joan broke her starefest and turned to me, Edie looked at me, too. I saw it. They caught each other. Edie glanced away quickly. Joan held her position.

"Okay, smart-ass," Joan said, smiling, "You got me. You picked the loveliest coed on campus and you nailed me. I never admit defeat, but I do love you, and as it turns out I end up doing a lot of things with you I've never done. So, here it is. Alan's history. Poor guy. He'll have to drown his sorrows with booze and a whore. Edie's gone. For her own sake she'll have to find a way to dump that clown she's with, but she's gorgeous, Mason, goddamn you, and she'll land on her feet. I'm getting a restraining order on Jennifer, and you might as well tell me now: are there any other women in your life?"

"No," I said into her eyes, "There's no room."

"You're sweet," Joan said. She meant it, "More rules. You can't tell anybody about us. Well, Vinny knows, but I can tell, he'll keep a secret."

"Funny you should say that," I said, "He will, for me, even with Jean. Vinny and I have a pact. Nothing is repeated."

"It's wonderful you have him," Joan said, "I'm happy you have him. He's like Pamela. He may even be prettier than Pamela."

I laughed near convulsions. The Brunette Barbie is dead. Long live the Wild Child.

"We're just buddies, according to the new rules," Joan continued, "We will comport ourselves as buddies at the college. That of course means I will get you home every night and make you happy you are going to neglect every other woman in the world."

"That's good, sweetness, because I don't think you'll want to have roaming eyes, either."

"I only have eyes for you," Joan said.

Cool.

The clown has been fondling Edie's hand for minutes now. They stood, he dropped some bills on the table, and they left. Edie passed a glance and a smile at me over her shoulder. Joan saw it. Why are they were leaving so early? Why do I care?

"She doesn't know how closely she came to shedding blood," Joan said. I have a feeling that's not an idle threat. She then placed her hand back on my thigh and scooted in closer. "Mason, dear, you have been most difficult to accept. Guys used to be easier for me. Is it because I'm getting older?"

That's the first time I had ever heard Joan mention age in terms of a rue. I feel sorry for her. I'm sure she was queen of Northwestern, not officially, like homecoming. I don't really know that, but I bet she in a romantic sense had a reign and an orb and a scepter. It's my job to make her feel like the superwoman she is. Darn. I guess someone's gotta do it.

"Joan, don't in anyway blame yourself, for anything. Our situation is an unusual one. It took a lot to get here, and we'll always have to work at it. But, I would have it no other way. Not at all. I want you just as you are. I don't want you to be any other way. In my eyes, you're just perfect, and I'm damned lucky to be with you."

"Mason...," she whispered.

"You want to talk difficulties?" I offered, "I'm kind of an oddball guy. I always have been. So, if this has been tougher than usual, I'm sure I had a lot to do with it."

"Oh, Mason," she said, kissing me on the cheek, "I fell in love with the oddball. I don't want you to be any other way either. So, there is only one thing left to do."

"What's that?" I asked.

"Let's go into the parking lot, get in the back seat of my car, and make out," Joan said, seduction on high beams.

"Follow me," I said.

"Wait," Joan said, "Where's Pamela?"

I scanned the room and couldn't find her.

"There she is," Joan said, "Over there talking to that guy."

I looked diagonally across and saw her, "Damn. What a handsome guy," I said. That's an older-dude comment. It's true: we football players are constantly surveying each other's bodies, but none of us would dare say anything. I must be growing up!

"We Kissinger chicks have extremely high standards," Joan said, "C'mon. The car awaits."

~ ~ ~ ~ ~ ~ ~ ~ ~ ~

Ten minutes and a few very steamed up automobile windows later, Joan and I decided that a) she has a house, b) we could do this and much more at said house, c) we should find Pamela and tell her we've heard enough jazz, even though I haven't caught my first note, d) encourage Pamela to leave, e) call Vinny and ask him to pack some clothes and essentials in a bag for me, f) swing by my house and have Vinny meet us with my bag on the sly, g) go to Joan's, where I along with Pamela will be an honored guest, h) humor Pamela until she's gets the drift, and i) find out just how quiet and unleashed Joan and I can be at the same time. It's a great plan.

We reentered Jazz. Joan is assigned to convince Pamela it's time for all good girls to be home. I'm to call Vinny.

I found a phone and deposited the dime. Dialing 555-8486, the last four numbers of which spelled, 'Vgun,' I hoped, prayed he would be the one to answer.

"Vinny." I heard a party in the background.

"Gunner, it's Mason."

"Lemme go upstairs," he said quickly. Vinny put me on hold. A few seconds later, Vinny picked up. "Okay, Cheetah, I gotcha. I had to come up here because I was standing right beside Judy, Jean, and Jennifer. They're drunk."

"Good for you, buddy," I said.

"You're a hot topic of conversation here. *Sports Illustrated*, the Montani newspaper, the Charleston newspaper, and the Pittsburgh newspaper are all looking for you. Alice has called the police. They're all grilling me, but I know nothing. Also, the SI reporter is hitting on Jennifer, and I think it might happen."

"Let them use my room."

"You're a sick man. Why did you call?"

"I have to ask you a favor."

"Shoot."

"Could you please pack for me a pair of Levis, a denim shirt, a pullover sweater, socks, razor, cream, runt, and a toothbrush?"

"Huh-huh! I thought you two were going to wait until her sister left?"

"Well, you know, the best laid plans."

"Laid, huh? I'll do it, but how do I get it to you?"

"Sneak out our fire escape and meet us on Upper Ridgeway." Upper Ridgeway is the street behind our house, shielded by pines, and a good place for Joan, Pamela, and me to hide and await Vinny.

"I think it'll work. I'll do it."

"Thanks, pal. So, you've got SI at the house. Is it cover boy for you?"

"Who knows? But, we have talked a lot, and Michael's been here, as well as Dhali and Arthur. And with the Jennifer factor, this could be a good article for the Runners. But, they're looking for you. Don't screw up and get caught at 7-11 buying rubbers."

I laughed. "We're going straight from our house to Joan's house."

"What about Monday when Alice, Judy, Jean, and Jennifer go to their nine o'clock with Joan and you're in your office and life's back to normal except for you and Joan, as you two won't be able to go three hours without doing each other? You think the girls won't see through that? Have you thought about that?"

"Uh…no."

"I didn't expect you to. Have fun tonight and tomorrow, because reality awaits, and it could be a real bite."

"What it will be is a wall-to-wall carpet of denial. Joan and I are more than capable of that."

"I'm sure you are. I'll help anyway I can. I have been. I finally think you and Joan are good for each other. I bet she looks good in a swimsuit. I know you do."

"Okay, sweetie, I'll see you in a few minutes. Oh, I almost forgot to tell you. I hitchhiked and McNabb gave me a ride to Jazz."

"That's damned weird. Shit. Oh, shit, here comes someone. I'll get your stuff. Man, we've got to talk about this."

"Okay."

"Oh, fuck! I'd better go. You okay?"

"Yeah. One more thing. McNabb said he did set up PD."

"Thank God! That's a relief! Why did I say that? Fuck! Gotta go."

"Yeah. I'll see you soon."

"You bet, lover."

"See ya." I can tell Vinny about the picture tomorrow. After talking to Edie, Joan, and Pamela, it isn't such a crisis. For now, of course. I'm sure the shrink will make it one until he makes it better.

Saturday November 8, 1975
10:30 PM

Pamela's suggestion

About the time I hung up, Pamela walked by toward the door with Joan in tow. Joan looked at me, pointed to her sister, and held two fingers to her mouth, making the face of a toker. She shook her head and grinned. I quickly got the point, being a marijuana connoisseur. Pamela, the psychologist to the rich and famous of the Second City, is high. This should be fun.

There is an unrecognizable song coming from the sax, upright, and drums on stage. Too bad I'm going to miss out on jazz. It could have been good. It could have made me a more well rounded person. Later.

I approached Joan. "I just talked to Vinny. He's going to meet us behind my house with an overnight bag." I smiled a toothy grin.

"Great!" said Joan, herself smiling, "Great news. We'll just care for Pamela for a while, then I get my dream. I get to wake up in your arms. I've had to go to work a couple of times over the past weeks with that nighttime dream on my mind." Her face was so close I could feel her breath.

Air rushed into my lungs. My eyes are becoming watery. Whatever you were doing during that time, Mason, just keep it up. "Gee, Joan, I, uh, wish you would have said something. I mean, I could have broken away from my studies and been there for you."

"You don't study, silly!" she said with the Laugh. I had an out-of-body experience.

"Uh, lovers," slurred Pamela, "pay attention to me. In fact, Mason, come here. I want to talk to you."

Pamela is a woman of poise and confidence. Now she's a smoked-up woman of poise and confidence. I excused myself from Joan and stepped over to her sister. I looked back to see Joan rolling her eyes.

I started, "Pamela, where did you get the pot?"

"That guy. I think he wanted me to go to bed with him, but I had just met him. I have standards. I have to know a man two or three days before that happens." Then she cackled a resinous laugh, "Oh, Mason, Mason, I'm just kidding. You don't think I'm like that, do you?"

"Of course not, Pamela," I said reassuringly.

"Well, I'm not," she said, head weaving slightly. I turned back to Joan. She sat on a bench, arms crossed, smiling at me, but not having fun.

"Look, Mason, what I want to talk to you about is this," she said, slowly, "Are you going to make my sister an honest woman or what?"

Stunned, getting half of what I thought she meant, I stared at her with a question on my face, saying nothing.

Joan stood and walked our way. "We're going, Pamela," she said, not irritated, but just wanting to move on.

I want desperately to finish this conversation with her. Where is she going with it?

"I really need some ice cream," said Pamela, "Chocolate mint. Yeah." Her eyes became dreamy. She has the supremo munchies. How much did she smoke? I just love seeing this side of people. My first book will discuss this. Title: *Ordinary People and Other Folks: Ripped.* I've done some research….

We exited the Jazz and headed for Joan's navy BMW. Pamela crawled in the back seat, I sat on the passenger side, with Joan driving. There is a Kroger about a half-mile down the street. "We'll get you that ice cream,

Sis," said Joan. She reached across the seat and squeezed my quadriceps, several times. Oh, yeah....

"I'm not finished with you, Mason," said Pamela. "We'll talk in the dairy section."

Saying nothing in response to Pamela, Joan pulled into the supermarket lot and parked. We got out of the car. Walking into the store, a manager stopped us and said, "Sorry, we're out of beer. I think the whole county's out." I'm proud. My team created a run on alcohol. All right!

"We're...not here...for beer," said Pamela, drawing it out like poetry, to her pleasure.

"Oh, I'm just telling you," the manager said, "It's amazing. We were empty by eight." I raised my fist indicating, 'Righteous!' and entered.

"I need some groceries," said Joan to me softly, "I'll take care of that, and you take care of Pamela. She has a weakness for Cracker Jacks." Joan grinned. I guess she's been through this before. Joan then kissed my lips and covered her mouth, "Oh, my! Public display of affection!" she exclaimed.

I held my index finger and thumb an inch apart in front of her face. "We're this close to a public display of body heat," I said. A Laugh ensued. That's it, Mason. That's the secret. Keep her Laughing. Joan crinkled her nose at me, a nonverbal communication tactic women learn early, like adolescence. She turned and walked. My eyes crossed. Pamela appeared at my side.

"Okay, Pamela, let's get your food," I said. We headed for the frozen food section.

"Wait, we haven't finished talking," she said, "So, answer the question."

"Uh...please clarify," I said.

"Mason, come on...you're bright...," Pamela said as we walked by the cereal, "You know, an honest woman...connubial arrangements...the big leap...'til death do us part...tuxedoes and gowns...ice sculptures...a priest…one of the sacraments…honeymoon in Maui…Dr. Kissinger-Bricker…a kiss for luck, and you're on your way…we've only just begun…me for a sister-in-law and all that stuff."

Damn…damn! I stared straight ahead, buying time in consideration of my answer. This could be an even more important statement than Joan's 'Mason, I'm untying my robe now.' "Pamela," I began, "just between me and you for now, that's the direction in which I'd like to move. Your sister's a dreamboat. I love her so much. But if I were to tell her my thoughts, wouldn't that just frighten the hell out of her?"

"Mason," Pamela announced, "we're not getting any younger. I'll tell you a secret. I want a husband, a partner. So does my sister. This summer, Joan and I talked. She said, 'Pamela, I get the feeling the next guy will be the one. I don't why.' She said she just felt that way. Guess what, Mason? You're up!" Pamela's head rocked back in laughter. She's weird right now. Pamela sounds like a psychologist one second, then suddenly she's a Tri Sig weaving with a hash pipe. "You were so confusing to her," she said as the head doctor returned, "because you're the only nice guy she's ever known who wasn't totally incapacitated by her. Enchanted, maybe. But not plowed under. Well, that and the fact that you're eight years younger than her, but she's worked past that. It happened today. She worked past it. Mason, you've held your ground, and that's impressed her."

"Jesus, Pamela," I said, as we reached the freezer, "I always felt like I was barely under control around her."

"Barely, maybe, but you were under control. She's always in control."

"I've seen that," I returned.

"But, now you're in control. I can tell from my conversations with her, my sister's presenting herself to you. She's ready for you. I mean, ready," Pamela said, "Oh, my God, there's my ice cream." She opened the door and grabbed a half-gallon, "This should be enough. Now, let's get some Cracker Jacks to sprinkle on top."

"Pamela, how do you keep your girlish figure?" I asked.

"Genetics," she replied, "I'm destined to look like this. Isn't it something?" She winked at me.

'Pamela, I'm not commenting on the body of my future sister-in-law. It's just not right."

"Then you'll marry my sister?"

I'm in college. I live with college students. I attend classes with other college students. Today, I have kissed two college girls, an extremely unusual event in my life, but one that is part of my college experience. I also played college football today. I even through an unusual series of events coached the college football team. All my friends are associated with the college. I work at a college, under a college instructor. I have two-and-a-half years of college remaining, and then I go to post-collegiate studies. Everything Mason is so collegiate, so anchored to that time of one's life during which one makes the transition from fantasyland to the real world. Today, however, that same college instructor and I have professed our love for each other. And her sister, maintaining altitude but still brilliant, is asking me to ask her sister the college instructor for her hand in marriage. That's the real world there over the horizon, pal, closing in fast. Also, I'm wondering, what's going to happen at midnight tonight? Will all this reach a state of nihility, with I awakening under a table at a bar, or is this really taking place?

But, has contemplation ever stopped me from doing anything I wanted to do?

"Yes, Pamela, however, I'm going to need some help. I can't do this alone. Joan's got to mention it first. I have stuck my neck out and risked with her all the dignity I've ever had. If she brings the topic up in any way, I'll take it from there. In spite of your observations, I just don't want to scare her to the point to where she questions being with me. Life without Joan is not a chance I want to take"

"Young man, it's in place," Pamela said, with her arm in mine, "Now, where the fuck are the Cracker Jacks?"

We found them in aisle four with the potato chips. Pamela grabbed a half-dozen boxes, handed a couple of them to me, and led me to the checkout line.

"Mason, don't be scared," Pamela said.

"Pammy, honey, I am. Has she said anything about this? About me being this?"

"Maybe, in a way. Not directly, but she's never acted this way about any man. This afternoon she referred to you as 'her man.' That's pretty good. And she's had the choice of the lot, Mason. My sister Joan has always found a way to be detached with men. But, you, darling, have her full attention. Mason, I read people for a living. I should be a poker player in Vegas, but it wouldn't be fair. I know what she's thinking. And I know you. And I approve of you. I embrace you. But, when I do embrace you, you'd better not press your body too hard against my boobs." She spat a laugh at herself, letting me know the Tri Sig is back.

"Oh, God," she wailed, "Whew! Now, here's the plan."

"Great, Natasha," I said in a Russian accent, "Now we can get rid of Moose and Squirrel."

Pamela completely lost it, knees buckling, ice cream dropping, screaming "Moose and Squirrel! Ohhh!" just as we rounded the corner to the checkout line. She and her PhD were slumped on the floor of the grocery store, convulsing in laughter. I stood above her as an observer, knowing this is the best reaction I've had to my Flying Squirrel joke and also wondering if Pam had gotten into some Thai sticks or something wicked.

We turned the corner to find Joan holding a basket of various and sundry items, just stepping up to the line. I looked at the younger Dr. Kissinger and saw for the first time my future wife. I am thrilled, apprehensive, and obligated. I turned back to the older Dr. Kissinger in hope that we don't before it's all over have to bail her out of jail.

"Well, you two have been having fun," Joan said. She really is a bit suspicious. Maybe there's been some competition in the past. Look at them…I'm almost sure of it. Well, Joan, allow me to allay your fears….

I walked up to my love and threw the fuel on the charm, that sincere kind I have I know to be irresistible. "Darling, you are the only woman with whom I will ever have fun. From now and into and through the twenty-first century." I looked at her. She looked at me. I had rendered her speechless. Our eyes couldn't part. Joan dropped her basket to her side. Groceries rolled everywhere, but neither of us cared.

We'll pick up the groceries and Pamela in a minute….

Saturday November 8, 1975
11:20 PM

The eleven o'clock news

Pamela sat on one of Joan's entertainment room sofa cross-legged with the container of chocolate mint between her legs and four empty boxes of Cracker Jacks scattered about. She held a serving spoon in her hand and interestingly didn't eat voraciously and without a word like most stonies do, but slowly savored each dip into the box and every lick of the spoon, describing the experience to us.

"This is good. You guys sure you don't want some?" Pamela asked.

"No, Pamela," Joan replied, "We wouldn't want to take anything away from you."

"Actually, Pamela," I said, "This is close enough for me."

"Man, you can't believe what this does for me," she said. "The richness of the dark chocolate, the freshness of the mint, the coolness on my palate, the crack of the Cracker Jacks," She laughed loudly, and stuck another spoonful between her lips. I had to stop watching her. It is very sensuous.

Joan is sitting on my lap. I leaned back against the corner of the love seat, the same seat where she just hours before gave me The Word. Time has slowed, like the reverse of Einstein's relativity. Despite this, I feel as if I have known her for years. That makes sense; it seemed like years since August, the summer day Joan sprung into my life. I then existed, the most essential of being, in her house in awe, knowing I wanted her so badly and knowing equally well so did everybody else in that room and the campus and for that matter any man who had ever come in contact with her. I thought there was no chance. What I didn't know at the time was the profundity she would have on my life, and then once I had figured that out, I didn't know how unbelievably hopeless I would feel, right up to the first sit on this seat. What a moon shot this has been. Joan in my heart has been one small step for me, but being in her soul is one giant leap for my kind. Chicago's society girl and the boy from the coalfields, all wrapped up in one another, watching the late news, waiting for the sports report. Only in America!

We had met Vinny behind my house to get my bag. He was most gracious and I was definitely appreciative. So was Joan. So was Pamela, who got out of the car and threw her hemped-up self into The Gunner's arms, gushing over his game. Vinny took it all like a man. I told him he should have joined us, but I'm sure an inebriated Jean is eventually more fun. Considering it all, he made the better choice. As I can attest, once you go Kissinger, you don't go back.

"This ladies and gentlemen," Pamela announced, "is better than a good screw."

"Not any more," Joan said right before she planted her lips on my mouth, launching me into the next county. Pamela is intently digging the spoon into the ice cream, oblivious to her sister and, as the psychologist has crowned me, her future brother in-law. My philosophy of living in the moment and I simply dug it all.

Sated, finally, Pamela sat with us as the sports just came on the box.

"And, Pat, speaking of surprises," said the perky news anchor from KDKA with her segue into the world of sports from a man proposing marriage to a woman by stringing Christmas lights on her porch spelling, 'Marry me,' "Pitt was handed their first defeat of their remarkable season this afternoon."

"That's right, Andi," said Pat, "The West Virginia Ridge Runners, or in this case, the runaway Ridge Runners, without their coaches, sent the Panthers packing today. Everyone by now is well aware of the troubles in Montani. Well, the Runners made a statement today and did it all themselves, coming from a two touchdown fourth quarter deficit and beating Pitt thirty-seven thirty-five on a last second desperation field goal. The loss, with Penn State and Alabama still undefeated, all but derails the Panthers' chances for a national championship, and puts the Runners back in contention for a major bowl. We'll show you highlights of the game."

"This guy's pretty boring," said Pamela. She's right. Ron could do a much better job than this, I'm sure.

"Shhh!' hissed Joan, "Watch!"

"The Runners came out firing, with Vinny Vacca, barely alive on the depth charts as late as Monday, throwing a beautiful pass to Philly's Dhali Sellers for the opening TD."

It is truly exciting to see Vinny on the tube stroking one down the field, validating his talent. Yeah!

"Then, Pitt took control, ball control, that is, as their Heisman candidate Drew Osberg led the Panthers in two long touchdown drives. Here's the first score midway in the first...and here's the second in the second."

"Droll, man," said Pamela, "This weekend crap is crap." Still high.

"However, late in the half...."

"All right, Pamela, right here, shut the fuck up," said Joan. Boy, I like that....

"Okay, Sis. I need some more food."

"Mason Bricker, reserve receiver and by many accounts the leader in running the coaches off, made the catch of his life. Watch this."

I indeed watched it. Denzil and I went up, the ball bounced up, Denzil went down, and I never took my eyes off the ball and, diving, pulled it into my hands. Damn, I'm impressed.

"I told you it was special," Joan said, kissing my cheek.

"That mid-air collision and miracle catch tied the game fourteen all at the half. But, the Panthers were not to be outdone. Two long drives, both resulting in touchdowns by Osberg, put Pitt up twenty-eight fourteen going into the fourth." The anchor showed film of some Osberg action. "Then, Vacca took over, leading the Runners for one score." They showed Vinny's lob to Clark. "The Panthers responded with Osberg's fifth TD." There was Drew's last one.... "Vacca drove again late to put the Runners within seven." More Vinny scrambling and passing. He makes great highlight films. "Then, the killer. Pitt has the ball and all they have to do is run out the clock. Osberg receives a pass, but is leveled by the Runners' Joe Osbourne." Leveled, hell, he was demolished! That was a scary hit, even scarier in person. "West Virginia's Keith Shirley picks off the pass and the Runners have new life. Vacca takes them down the field quickly." The tape showed Twilley. Oh, wow! "And State College product Frank Adams rams it in. Alas, the try for two failed." 'Alas'...bozo...but, I got to see the catch. I was in, goddamnit. "And the Runners had one final chance. Their onsides kick was successful."

"Successful," mocked Pamela, "What a maroon" as I saw the ball fall into my hands. "And West Virginia had just enough time for a field goal attempt, which kicker Roger Retina nailed from fifty-seven yards, setting off the celebration in Montani. A great game if you're West Virginia, but Pitt has everybody back next year and should be in the running for the title. Elsewhere in the college ranks...." You can tell that was a Pittsburgh TV report. They made the whole event sound as exciting as a Boy Scout spaghetti dinner.

Pamela has control of the channel changer and clunked the TV off at that point. "I can't take that guy any more." She sat up and walked out, taking her ice cream with her.

"What did you think after seeing the game, Mason?" Joan asked, beaming.

"Aside from the fact that Roger's real name is Raj Retnitraj, it's pretty cool," I said, "Actually, I can't think of anything to say. It's…uh…overwhelming." I feel emotional and don't want to cry, for the seventy-second goddamned time in two weeks. Eating the feelings, I just breathed slowly, sat there, and held on to Joan. I think she's aware of what I'm going through.

"Oh, Mason. My Mason," Joan whispered to me as Pamela fiddled with the stereo, putting on *The Eagles: Greatest Hits*. I listened to the beginning of *Take It Easy*, remembering the time just, oh, a few hours ago when I had seven women on my mind. Four who want to own me: Joan, Jennifer, Edie, and maybe Alice again. Two that want to stone me: Jean and Judy. And one, Michele, who says she's a friend of mine. Take it easy.

'I was standin' on a corner in Winslow, Arizona, / and what a fine sight to see. / It's a girl, my Lord, / in a flatbed Ford, / slowin' down to take a look at me.' I have Joan in my arms and now I finally understand what Jackson Browne is talking about.

"Come on, baby," I said to Joan at the appropriate time in the song, "Don't say maybe."

"No maybes here," Joan said, "It'll either be yes, or hell, yes."

"With that in mind, you've always got to wonder: where's Pamela?" I asked. We heard stirring in the house, then looked at each other, grinning. Prying ourselves from one another, difficult for me since my body is stiff and Joan feels so damned good, we walked into the kitchen to find the sister rummaging through the cupboards, refrigerator door open, foraging for food like a raccoon would.

"Stoners," said Joan to me softly, "You can't live with them. You can't live without them."

"I heard that," Pamela said, "Don't you have anything to eat around here? Any peanut butter?"

"Top right shelf," said Joan, placing her hand on my butt.

"Any vanilla wafers?"

"You're in luck," Joan said, "Beside the peanut butter." Joan looked to me and added, "How do you think I got through the past couple of weeks?" I'm flattered. I drove the woman to junk food. While she was sending me to the smoker. How will I give up weed....

'You can't hide your lyin' eyes' Don Henley and Glenn Frey continued as my woman and I repaired back to the rec room, assuming the same position, I on the leather sofa, Joan on me. Now, this is how I thought college was going to be when I would daydream about it in high school algebra. Pamela is right behind us with the cookies, the peanut butter, and a tablespoon. She, without full control of her motor functions, plopped down on her sofa and continued eating, not breaking stride from the ice cream.

'She woke up and poured herself a strong one...'

"She's so engrossed in her food she won't notice," purred Joan, "Just tongue me."

I did. I kissed her big.

"That's good, Mason, but I didn't mean there." Joan lost it in her laughter. I froze. "I got you. Your face is priceless!" More Laughter.

"You'll pay for that," I said calmly.

"Oh, I hope," Joan whispered.

"I know you guys are talking about sex over there," Pamela mumbled with a full vanilla wafer sandwich in her mouth. "I know. I'm an expert of the human mind. I deal with perpetually horny people like you two all day long."

"Well, tell me, Pamela," Joan said slyly, "When you talk with these people, does it ever make you horny?"

"Occasionally," she said, "about once a day, really."

"What do you do about it?" Joan asked, then looking at me with an impish face.

"I don't want to hear this," I said.

"Oh, hell, Mason," said Pamela, stuffing in another cookie, "Don't be so uptight."

"Pamela?" asked Joan again. I don't know whom she was trying to make squirm more, her sister or me. It couldn't have been Pamela, though. She seemed to be handling it a lot better than I am.

"I have a man, a friend, with whom I have an agreement," said Pamela, "So, he's either there or I just take matters into my own hands." There it is. That's the part I didn't want to hear. "Are you okay with that, Mason?" Pamela closed.

"A-okay, Pamela," I said, "We all have to do it once in a while." I surprised myself with my casual appraisal of the subject.

"Those days are over for us, big boy," Joan said softly. I'm sure I am one big stupid looking grin right now.

"You guys are too much for me," Pamela said, "I'm taking my cookies into my room, reading, and eating myself into the sublimation of my sexual desires you two are stirring within me. Goodnight. If you hear me moaning uncontrollably, bring me more peanut butter." We laughed, except Pamela. I think she's serious. She stood, walked to Joan and kissed her cheek. Then, without warning, she stuck a spoonful of that peanut butter in her mouth and bent down to place her open lips on my mouth. Despite her beauty, it feels like exactly what it is, like kissing your sister when she has a mouth full of food. Both women laughed uncontrollably. I smiled and let them have their fun.

"Goodnight, sweet man," Pamela mumbled, and off she went.

"She is so wild," Joan said, still laughing, rolling over on my lap. "I've got stories. For later. Right now, I have desires."

"That's so crazy, because I do, too," I said with fake amazement.

"I know."

"Yeah, it's always so obvious with guys," I said, Joan remaining in my lap.

"I've got a game we can play."

"I'm good at games."

"Let's," Joan said, drawing it out for emphasis, "stay out here until we can't stand it any longer. We'll just talk and things like that, you know, like we've been doing the whole semester."

"Well, honey," I said, "It's been since August. You know I'm good at that." She Laughed. How long we gotta stay here?

"Tell me, how did the game feel today?"

"It was unbelievable," I said, attempting to explain the feelings I had in way she could relate to. Does she really want to hear this? I guess. "During a game like that, the emotions swing wildly. We surprised them and scored early and first, but they just solidly kicked our butts for the rest of the half."

"How do you mean?" Joan asked, doing that chest rub thing again. This is not going to be an easy game.

"They ran at will, controlled us when we had the ball, and nothing we were doing worked. Something like that really tests you, and you have to keep yourself up, because nobody's going to do it for you. Then, Vinny found me with that long touchdown, and all of a sudden, we're walking into the locker room at the half and the score's tied."

"What do you guys do then?" she said, resting her head on my shoulder and nibbling my neck. Oh, God. "C'mon. Keep talking." What I am saying and what I am thinking are exclusive, but I'll do it. It's Joan. Of course I'll do it. Anything.

"We discuss things and make adjustments and try to keep that momentum going. There's not much time, so we concentrate mostly on keeping ourselves going. Especially after what we had been through this week."

"Then what happened?" Joan said into my ear after she ran her mouth up the side of my face. I hesitated. "Mason, you've got to talk or you're not playing this game right."

"Well," I said as my voice cracked, "we went back out there and they manhandled us. Our third quarter was the worst. We were down fourteen. And all the racial animosity came back. Father Al then beat the shit out of..." I'm breathless as Joan sat up and unbuttoned the mohair, seductively exposing a very sheer black brassiere.

"And," she said. I moved to her face to kiss her. She placed her two fingers to my mouth, impeding my progress. "And...."

Okay. I talked fast. "And we were in big trouble so I told Vinny you've got to win it for us Vinny's the kind of guy who responds to those tough times he wanted the ball and he pulled us out of out funk with spectacular play we really fought as a team thanks to Vinny so we won. Can I kiss you now?"

"Yes, you may." I did.

"That was great. You with your leadership did a wonderful job. It's like a JFK turn on."

"Wow! Thank you!"

"Oh, I was thirteen or fourteen when he was in office. Oh, my God, what a heartthrob! I remember it was a terrible, disheartening day when he was killed."

This is one of those times Judy and Alice were bitching about. Still, I offered my observations. "I could feel it, too. I could feel the despair." Joan bought it and moved on.

"You know, Mason, this is good. This is good for us," she said, I guess referring to our years apart, "We can provide our perspectives and both learn from them."

"I agree, Joan. I've always thought that."

"Well, you convinced me," and she stood up and took her cords off, sitting down back on my lap, yes, in her underwear. Black. Jennifer flashed into my mind, but I quickly got rid of that image and concentrated on whom was before me. Oh, the past three weeks from no women, to two women, to three women, now one woman, a setting more amenable to my emotional structure, especially when that one woman is Dr. Kissinger.

"You look good," I said, my eyes everywhere but in her eyes.

"I'm happy you think so. I want to look good to you, for you, with you," Maybe it's time for the Magic Carpet Ride. "But, I have more things I want to know," she said. She's going to kill me. "You never hit on any of my students. Why's that?"

I'm ready for this one. "Uh…as with everything, it's never just one thing. Primarily, however, I wanted to hit on you," Joan giggled, and jiggled, in her underwear, "so I…um…was saving myself."

Joan grinned, "Nice, safe answer. Okay, let's pretend I, for some reason, am out of the picture. Now, why don't you hit on my students?"

I responded almost immediately, "It's difficult to imagine you out of the picture, but it would have sooo…predictable. It would have been so sophomoric, with emphasis on the 'moric.' Everybody would have been expecting it, and I didn't feel like playing the game."

"But, you played the game with me," she said.

"No, I didn't," I said. "There was no wile, no unctuous presumption involved with my love for you. I was direct as possible, and in retrospect, if I did anything wrong, I waited too long. You should have been sitting in my lap in your underwear in September."

"I had a dream about that in September," Joan said, chin up and mouth slightly open. "Now, back to my coeds…you had your pick, Mason. You've got the goods. And, we're going back in there on Monday, and in their eyes, nothing's changed. Except except with regard to us, the women will know. That knowledge, and because of the game and because you've been so damned unavailable all semester long will make it much more urgent for them. Now, what are you going to do about that?"

I took Joan into my arms and stood with her, lifting her from my lap into the air. Boy, it really hurt, but as I've said before, when has pain ever stopped me from doing anything?

"What are you doing?" she said, "I'm not finished."

"Joan, you're an intelligent girl," I said, "You can do two things at once. Besides, to answer your last question, I do need to talk with you, but I also have some visual aids I have to employ." I carried her toward her bedroom.

"I can walk to my bedroom, you know," Joan said with a fake serious face.

"I know, but this is more to my liking," I said, stepping with her through the threshold. I used her feet to softly shut the door. We retired for the night.

Sunday, November 9, 1975
10:10 AM

Every new beginning is some other new beginning's end.

The Sunday edition of *The Montani Mail* is strewn about the table in Joan's breakfast nook. I first spent several minutes flipping through all the pages in search of the picture of my dad. I didn't find it. Reminded of PD, I know it's inevitable. Well, that gives me something to look forward to.

I'm holding the sports section, of course, the headline of which proclaimed, 'UNBELIEVABLE!' There are several stories of the game; the account of the game itself, a story about Vinny and his rise to glory, a story about the retribution of the seniors, a story about the players' revolt, and, most inquisitively, a story entitled, 'Where Is Mason Bricker?'

As I always do, before I read the stories of our games I find the statistics section. This year that search has rendered, with our offense being so dull and Vinny and I not being involved at all, little to my liking. Today is different. The breakdown of the scores glared like a Jimi Hendrix black light poster. The fourth item read, 'W. Va. Bricker 53 yd. from Vacca (Retnitraj kick).' How long have I waited to see that! It's verified now: I scored for the Runners. Sweet! I continued through the other scores, with Osberg's five TDs dominating. And speaking of dominating, my perusal through the stats showed something I found stupendous, but not surprising. Under the Passing summary: 'Vacca 27-42-473-4-1,' meaning twenty-seven completions on forty-two attempts for four hundred seventy-three yards, four touchdowns and one interception. In black-and-white, Vinny showed that he both got his due and that he is undeniably the Runner QB of the future. I have a head-spin of pride for my man. I wish I were there with him reading this.

I dropped down to the Receiving section. The line 'Sellars 8-221-2,' eight catches for two hundred twenty-one yards and two TDs, is proof of how remarkable Dhali is and showed the pros watching at The Ridge and in TV land that he's a catch himself. But, goddamn, there it is. 'Bricker 4-117-1,' four receptions, one hundred seventeen yards and one TD. Mr. Walk-On, 1975. I've been reading stats such as these since I can remember first opening a newspaper and finding out what they meant, and now here I am. Jesus! Even under the Rushing section, 'Osberg, 34-277-5,' thirty-four carries, two hundred seventy-seven yards, and five TDs, as commanding as that is, it does not take away from the fact that 'you look at the scoreboard and see who's behind.' What a performance all around, but fuck Pitt for now, what a performance by the Runners! Some will call us lucky, but the truly lucky ones were the forty thousand at The Ridge and the whatever number of folks comprising our Nielsen rating watching on the box.

Already knowing how the game progressed and turned out, I read Vinny's article next. His journey to Montani is outlined, and his travails on the scout team are addressed. But, and most correctly, with the press this time getting it right, the article stressed Vinny coming through in the fourth, accurately assessing that he is the man who got it running and kept it going.

"By staying in the pocket when he had to even though Pitt's line was bearing down hard, and by scrambling around waiting, looking for the open man," the newspaper article read, "Vacca made the Runners hum in the critical final period and was definitely the game's most outstanding player. He led his team to victory by seeing things others had no chance of finding and by making things work in ways few other college quarterbacks ever could. He was a true coach on the field on this victorious day when West Virginia needed both the coach and the victory." Quotes from Dhali and Clark are used, affirming the sophomore QB and my soulmate as "one of the best they had ever seen or played with," and "a born leader." That just about got me.

I read his fourth quarter numbers: seventeen completions on eighteen attempts for two hundred sixty-eight yards and two TDs with only one interception. Vinny went nuclear, and it came at a time when there was no other choice, when, as I've said and said again, it had to be done. What a guy!

Sitting across from Joan, up early to see Pamela off when the Pittsburgh airport shuttle drove by to pick her up, I'm showered (not alone), shaved (for only the third time this week, but no one knows that), and dressed in a forest green cotton pullover sweater, a light denim shirt, Levis, and boots. Well, I'm happy…I'm in the breakfast company of a gorgeous woman and I have the sports page and it's talking all about a game I won yesterday.

I read the revolt article. Just as Vinny said: it read as if it was written by a sportswriter who was about to get his head taken off by Michael. That means it read in our favor, the way it should be reading. This writer makes the athletic administration look like the Nixon White House, almost verbatim from what Vinny told me Michael flew off the handle about: the "administration of lies," 'supporting the racism dogma of sports (the guy plagiarized Michael), and how I tried to do the right thing and ended up "being screwed by Fadden." I realize that in these years after Watergate, every newspaper hack is looking for a way to convey this message. As far as The University of West Virginia goes, this time it's true. And now it's out there for the people to read and believe. We got those bastards!

Onto the 'where am I' article. It addressed my lead role in the uprising, my contribution to the game, both as the coach and a player, "unprecedented in the history of the game," it read (how insightful) my expulsion from both the stadium and the team, and my ultimate disappearance directly after the game. Journalism thrives on the unknown, and no one has any idea where I am, except Vinny, and he's not saying anything.

Joan got her wish. I awoke, looked to my left, and there she was, lying on her side, staring at me, smiling, seemingly satiated. I wondered why. My hair usually looks like I combed it with a brush ax when I wake up, and I bet my breath was bad. But it's her dream and she called the shots. She liked it, so I go along. My eyes weren't open but a second when I immediately thought of my previous night's talk with Pamela, the 'kiss for luck' conversation. 'Don't be afraid, Mason,' she offered. However, with Pamela now physically removed from the scene, my resolve personified gone, and even while sitting near the awesome woman who could be my wife of the future, I still don't know what to think.

We had ten minutes before we had to get up and help get Pamela ready, and we made the best use of it. With the Alan/Edie Project scrapped, it looks as if a lot of my time will be put to its best use. Golly, I could get use to that. Pamela wants me to sign on for life. If the decision had to be made while I am in the middle of making love with Joan, there would be absolutely no question. I would have been a married man the very first instant. She is that powerful.

Joan is relaxed in an oxford blouse, tight black cords (again, what is it with that?) and houseslippers. Of course, she's a burlap sack girl, so she's always lookin' good. The front page is on the table in front of her, with its half page picture of the crowd storming the field right after the game. She has the Local section in hand, opened to a middle page. I need coffee, so I stood and stepped over to the pot beside us. I filled my cup and took it over to Joan to offer her some. She kindly accepted. As I poured I see Joan is reading the wedding and engagements announcements. It is something like when cues and clues appear over a period of time, and despite them getting progressively more and more obvious, you ignore them over and over until they pin you by the throat, forcing you to pay due attention. I think that's what's happening.

"Mason."

"Yes, sugar?"

"How much money do you have?"

"Well I've got a twenty on me. Do you want some donuts?"

"No, Mason how much *money* do you have?"

Now I'm sure that's what's happening. Oh, boy, Pamela, we are in play, aren't we? Man, I've never been asked this question with everything on the line like it is now. Come to think of it, I've never been asked this question period. My boyish charm was always sufficient in the past. Hell, for the past several months there hasn't even been a fuckin' past. Damn, this married stuff is serious. Just answer the lady, okay?

I silently pulled in a breath. "Uh…I had two of the three banks bought out Friday, an unusual event I learned of when Stan called that evening and have until now forgotten all about, thank you for reminding me. It was a precursor to how my weekend was going to turn out. So that puts me at, after taxes, around a hundred eighty-five thousand. I have no debt, fees paid through spring, a thousand dollars left on a rent agreement, no real estate, a four-dollar-an-hour job, and a car that works occasionally." Carly Simon keeps reappearing. No secrets. Or, I'm so vain....

Joan glanced up from the paper at me, then dropped her eyes back to the brides. "That's pretty good, Mason. It'll get better. Pamela tells me Daddy's arranged for a buy-out for Batavia."

"Uh...That's insider information. I didn't hear that," I said.

"Okay," Joan said, still looking at the paper, not at all concerned with securities law violations, "It's funny. The bank's been in our family for so long, but I'm sure Daddy will end up on top. That's his favorite position, I understand."

I snickered. "What about you, Joan, sweetheart?" referring to her jingle, with an educated guess any position is her favorite. Oh, hell, here goes. Get ready to get blown out of the financial water, Mason.

"I'm a trust baby," she admitted, "I'm paid three thousand dollars a month from the trust, which has a lot of money in it. I don't really know how much. I don't care. I get it free and clear at age thirty if my parents approve of me. I earn twenty-five thousand a year as an instructor, of which I am much more proud. I have about thirty thousand equity in this house, a sixty thousand dollar mortgage, some bank stock, no other real estate, and a BMW."

"You're doing pretty well. Just don't piss your parents off," I said thoughtlessly as I scanned the rest of the sports, trying to imagine bowl matchups. It'll give me a chance for Pamela and her assertions and now Joan and her balance sheet inquiries to sink in. Let's see, Alabama and Penn State in the Sugar Bowl for the national title, if Penn State beats Pitt minus Osberg up the road here, which they should. Damn, we were so damned close. Ohio State and UCLA in the Rose. Texas and therefore Pitt in the Cotton. That leaves undefeated Oklahoma out because they are so totally fucking out of their minds and on probation, and sending number nine Nebraska in their place to the Orange. If the pollsters look favorably on our performance against two of the top three teams at the time, beating number one, and considering other Top Ten teams such as Michigan, Notre Dame (which as a Catholic I should die for but I'd rather see suffer infinitely), and the rising Arizona State were upset and upset badly this weekend, losing respectively to Northwestern, Navy, and Utah, and also considering the fact that a few second ten teams were beaten, and if we beat Syracuse, we could, finally concluding this run-on sentence, find ourselves against the Cornhuskers, a nickname as stupid as the Ridge Runners, in Miami. Vinny and NBC and Dick Enberg and Merlin Olson. Wow!

On the other hand, bowls at times have nothing to do with the college football to which I gave all. They are political and run by sponsors. So the question remains: what sponsors would want to get with our revolution? 'When you talk about destruction / don't you know that you can count me out.' The Beatles. Huh…the fear of Watergate as well as the early Boomers, fans of the late socially conscious Beatles, coming of age…Corporate America just might line up behinds us. That would be cutting-edge. Destruction. We did destroy a few things. Like Pitt.

"To hell with my parents," Joan said, after a pause, not looking up and shaking me out of college football and back into my new reality. "I don't care what they think. I just want the opportunity to teach, the opportunity to publish, and, most of all, true love. Everything else is extraneous."

I could feel Pamela's presence. "Good. We have the same goals," I said.

Her beautiful brown eyes peered again over the paper, "That is good, Mason. That's very good." She went back to Montani's society pages, which certainly pale dramatically to those in the Chicago area she is used to reading. I'd lay out a thousand to find out what the hell is she thinking right now.

Save your money! When is it going to be more crystal clear? Pamela reappeared as I quickly ran over in my mind how to ask the next question. I decided: a) don't be overly clever, b) don't string Christmas lights outside, c) be simple, d) be direct, e) be confident, f) be sincere, and g) believe in Pamela.

I began as she continued to read the same pages, over and over. What the hell's she doing, memorizing the attendant's dresses? Then, I stalled. What am I doing? I'm just a kid! Friday might have been my last day of school here at West Virginia. If that's true, then no college degree, no more tutor, nothing. Christ, my car won't even start! I mean, I look good, but what self-respecting man would want to be a gigolo? Joan won't want me as a freeloading husband. I'd have to, as my only choice, have Stan set me up as an investment advisor here in Montani. That means for a long time I would be my only client and I'd have to make fifty percent on my money just to match Joan's salary after taxes, and on top of that another twenty percent for growth. What do I think I am, a stock market wizard? Even if, I'd have to hustle for clients. "Hello, Mr. Prospective Client. I know I just screwed up Runners football for the foreseeable future and I am a smooth-faced man-child not yet twenty years old, but would you consider allowing me to help you manage your investments?" We'd starve! I'd have to start a newsletter or something, like Martin Zweig. Who the hell would read it? When has my future ever sucked any more than now?

I find myself staring out the kitchen window from my seat at the table in quiet desperation. Feeling something on the side of my face, I glanced over to see Joan gazing at me as only she can, with what I interpreted as loving dedication. The thick clouds in my mind instantly cleared. Before I knew it, I said with pride, "Joan, I would like to be your husband. Will you please marry me?"

Without hesitation nor movement of her head, Joan replied, "Is that a proposal of marriage, Mason?"

What? She's good at this. "Yes, Joan, it is indeed."

More silence. I don't know what that means. She has been keeping me guessing for eightysomething days. By now, there's got to be a hole in my stomach somewhere.

"All my friends from college, they're all married now," Joan finally said, looking back down to the brides.

"Sounds like a Carly Simon song," I said, a smart-ass. And, why does that woman with the big mouth and headlights keep figuring into my life, anyway?

She smiled a bit, "They all married bankers, stockbrokers…."

I thought about the fortuity of being Stan's West Virginia man and mentioning to her my most recent career path. No, that's way too much. Deciding to sell myself, my true self, with a wink of the eye I said, "Well, you just had an ex-college football coach ask for your hand. It's unique. Be the first on your block." She's never lived on a block…Mason, get a grip.

More smiles. She started, "It all happened two, three years ago. Late spring and early summer, almost every weekend there was something to do with a wedding. A party, a shower, then a wedding itself. What a time that was."

"It sounds pretty crazy," is all my nineteen-year-old mind can think to say.

She finally laid the paper down and looked at me, "Every ceremony was an event. The competition was at times unbearable. It was as if there was a matrimony Olympics."

"You know, men can find the best women at a wedding," I said, probably not too wisely. I hope she didn't hear me.

"I was almost married," Joan confessed.

"Oh," I responded, then zipped my lip, wanting to hear about this.

"He was a finance officer at First Chicago. James Bryant. It all seemed so right at first. Handsome. The right schools. The right career. The right family. Then, I saw him for the moron he was. He was so caught up in it, just like the way you described George Babbitt. He is Babbitt.

Funny you and I led that discussion Friday." Joan gave another smile.
Keep on smilin', baby....

"Anyway, my parents and his parents thought it was a match made in
heaven. I had other feelings. So did Pamela. He was from a long line of
legacies with no brains and no talent."

"You're a good judge of quality men. Obviously," I said to her grin with
my palms facing me, "How did you get mixed up with a guy like that?"

"Years and years of the indoctrination of high society," Joan replied,
"It's frightening just how close I came to being another one. I'm proud
of my breakaway. I couldn't have done it without Pamela, though. She's
still around there, but she's out of it, too. I got a map out and marked on
it my good offers. With a string I found geographically the school with
the most miles between it and Chicago. The University of West
Virginia."

"Good job. Good move on your part," I said, reassuringly, trying to
cover the jealousy I strangely harbor even after Joan's explanation. She
was preordained as my woman and this Jimmy dude almost fucked it
up for me.

Still, consider the map and the string and Joan's escape from her
early years, Mason. Then consider the weekend you told Princeton
something they seldom hear, *No, thank you. Looks like West Virginia.*
Consider also the pull toward your early years. Preordained.

"Surely was a good decision. Mrs. James Bryant. Makes me want to
throw up. My mom and dad really haven't been too happy with me
since then."

"You're your own woman. That's one of the many reasons why I love
you," I said, still sitting on my side of the table, in an attempt to bring
this discussion back to me.

Joan smiled again, "You're pure, Mason. You're the only man to ever
look at me the way you do, like you really admire me, the person, the

academic, the woman, everything I am, Mason; with no motives, just because you do."

I carried the new momentum through, "You're right. One couldn't describe my feelings for you any better. Admire. That's a good word. Adore is closer. Veneration is up there, but probably too formal, sounding like it comes from The Bible." This is no time for some feeble attempt at humor, my man. Get serious. "Respect, Joan. Love says it all, however. I love you. I love you, Joan. I don't really remember what love was before you, and I can't imagine what love would be like without you," I concluded in praise, directly into her eyes.

She gazed at me in silence for the longest time. I think that's a good sign.

"How do you feel about children?" Joan asked.

"I'm all for 'em," I said, masking my elation, "I want to raise them, care for them, love them as much as I love their mother. You'll have to actually give birth to them, but I'll be there from beginning and beyond. How do you feel about kids?"

Joan grinned more, "I want to be a mommy."

God, that is sweet. "C'mon, then," I continued, being the Mason Bricker I am, damning the doubts, reaching across the table to take her hand, "You've got you an ex-college jock with a perfect eight hundred on his SAT verbals, a good lookin' man, I've heard, good breeding stock…who's crazy in love with you. We'll make smart, fast, pretty babies."

"You'd be a great father," she said. My heart melted. But, I had to make sure.

"Is there anything concerning you? Like my father?"

"No, Mason," Joan answered into my eyes, "I'm my own woman. You are your own man. We can break the chains of those who came before us."

We?

Damn, that sounds great. However, I had to get it out in the open. "McNabb could get nasty with me. That could hurt you with your administration. Would anything like that give you problems?"

"I know what happened, Mason. Nothing he could go after you with would bother me. Besides, I think Dr. Cost is a free-thinker and is also on your side, our side."

That's true, but how does she know that? I'm not asking the question for her. However…"Does Dr. Cost think freely enough to accept us…you and me…married?"

"Could be worth a shot."

I like that, but, the biggie, "Could money, or the relative lack thereof bother you, perhaps?"

"Money is of little concern to me. I've seen the damage it can do. From what I have heard, we will get by fine."

We?

Silence. Joan looked at me and glanced all around. This went on for several moments. She always takes me down to the final play. To keep my determination, I found it necessary to refer back to the sports section.

"I do have two conditions," she stated.

I jumped. Anything! "Yes?" I asked, gut tied up like it was yesterday morning.

"One: we elope. I don't want to play those ridiculous wedding games with my family and their friends. We'll elope and then have parties and let everyone else deal with it from there."

Shocking! "Very romantic!" I remained composed. Joan looked like she was negotiating a business deal, with exception of the sexy smirk on her face.

"Two: we elope tonight for a civil ceremony tomorrow. I'm not giving one more coed even the slightest chance with you. Edie, Jennifer, they're my wake-up calls. I want them on the outside looking in. When we return to school, you'll be mine. And you'll be my husband. And how could the school really think that is inappropriate?"

She may be stretching that one, but who am I to argue? Besides, I have been as a result of her dumbfounded more times than with any other person or any other anything in my life. That's a good sign for the future, our future. I have no choice but to just one-word it. "Glorious!"

"Ya think?" she asked, smiling even wider.

"Most definitely!" I replied.

We sat and stared across the table into each other's eyes, I guess it never occurring to us that we should get up and leap into one another, dance throughout her house, and scream it to the world. Instead, one hand held the other; then both hands, then I stood and lifted her litheness and lightness into my meaty torso, carried her out of the kitchen into her living room, and simply remained there, holding her, gazing at the marvel of her face, with no chance of the huge smile leaving mine. She covered her lips with her free hand and declared, "Oh, shit, I'm getting married!"

"You're getting married? I'm getting married!" I exclaimed.

Joan squirmed while I held her, "Damnit! Damnit! Damnit! I'm getting married! I didn't think I'd ever get married!"

"You didn't think you'd ever get married? I never thought I'd get married!"

"Well, think it now, bucko, because we're both getting married," Joan shouted, "And we're getting married to each other!"

"Baby, I'm never going to get married without you!" I said, "So, you're stuck now!"

"Oh, no!" Joan said, face beaming as never before, "You're the one who's stuck! You're never getting out of my sight, boy! I saw how my girls were looking, no, leering at you on Friday. I'm serious. No way am I going to send you back out on that campus without my mark on you!"

That's all right with me. I'll be her little possessive playtoy. But…"Me? Me? Gaze into the mirror, sweetheart. Every walk around campus with you is a new adventure in the real-time lust of the American male! I'm afraid you've had it, darling. My mark is on you."

"Had it?" Joan said, teeth actually bared, "I'm going to get it when-ever I want it. You're going to be my husband, and you're going to have to give it to me whenever I say!"

I feigned pensiveness. "Okay," I said with nonchalance.

"Like right now, big man!" Her eyes are afire.

I carried my fiancee into her bedroom to celebrate. The bed's not yet made. My hope is that we spend an entire marriage never getting around to making the bed.

~ ~ ~ ~ ~ ~ ~ ~ ~ ~

We laid side-by-side on the bare sheets, comforter and blanket on the floor at our feet, not a word, a picture of complete satisfaction, holding hands and looking up. This would be an ideal time to have a mirror on the ceiling.

"Where are we going to get married?" Joan asked.

"I don't know. I've been thinking about that," I replied.

"You have not," Joan said, "You've been thinking about ravishing my body."

"I've been thinking about that since I was first at your house."

"And you have since treated me like a lady."

"Easy."

"Well, I've been thinking about ravishing your body since, oh, the first time I saw my students lusting for you."

"You keep saying that. Even the guys?"

"Some of them."

Interesting. "Again, Joan, I wish you would have written me a note or shot off a flare or, even better, just sat on my desk."

"You're enigmatic, Mason," Joan said, rolling over toward me, in full view to me, always an experience marked by excitement and light-head-edness, "It took a while for the truth to foment."

"And all the while, it turned out we are foment for each other."

A Laugh. "You're a killer, Mason! It'll be just wonderful to live with you."

"So, you're going to let me move in?" I asked in jest.

"No, I'm going to demand you move in."

"Okay "I kissed her lips softly.

"We've got so much to do today," Joan said, giggling like a schoolgirl.

I glanced at her clock. It read ten fifty, just flipping over to ten fifty-one. "Okay, here's the checklist," I said.

"Yeah, you do that. I'm too giddy right now. I'm getting married tomorrow, you know."

I rolled to her, held her face in my right hand and wet-kissed her. "Ohh," she moaned. I'd give her half my stock for that moan. Wait, I am going to do that.

"Mason, list. I can't think."

"Okay," I said, shaking myself into action, thinking myself how she has gone like quantum light from not dating students to marrying one. Drop it, Mason. "We've got to call people. You've got to find somebody to teach or cancel your classes, or replace them with wedding showers."

"Okay," Joan said, laughing, "Michele. She'll do something with them."

"Great," I responded, "Okay, chiquita, that means Michele has to know."

"Oh, my! Oh, God! We're going to spread the word!"

"Damn right! We've got to call Pamela, since she was very instrumental in this."

Joan sat up. "I wondered what you two were talking about last night."

"Believe me, she only confirmed an idea I had since, say, late September?"

"And you should be back at school?" Joan said smiling.

"That's right, Maggie J. But, instead, I'm really happy I saw your face."

"Oh, Mason!" Joan said, "You charming, poetic man, you. How will I ever repay you for what you do to me?" My appreciations to Rod Stewart.

Outwardly, I grinned. Inwardly, I detonated in a flash of passion. With regard to all the planning we have to do and to avoid taking her under me, again, for wild lovemaking, again, I found it best to joke, "Oh, Joan, you repaid me just a second ago when you sat up." Another Laugh. Oh, Christ….

"Mason, I love you, so, so much," she said, moving over and on top of me. "Can you still think while I'm up here?" she grinned onerously.

"It'll be challenging, but…." The only thing I could think of was, 'the glass turf shoe fits.' "Okay! Back at it! Michele."

"What's she going to say?"

"You'll be surprised. Pamela. Vinny. Vinny!"

"What'll he say?"

"Again, you'll be surprised."

"Tell me!"

"Michele and Vinny will love it. I'll leave their exact words up to them when we stand before them and announce our intentions. Michele has been hinting at the possibilities of us for some time now. Vinny? Well, Vinny has seen me do some unusual things in my life. This will be just another one. He takes them in stride. Besides, he said just last night we were good together. He said we'd both look good in swimsuits."

Joan Laughed. Damn…"Let's call Michele right now."

"Let's."

"Dial the phone. I'm *sure* you know her number."

"Now what's that all about?" I asked, all knowing.

"You two used to burn me up. You were too close for my comfort," admitted Joan.

"Joan, baby, just as I said earlier, she was and is one of your biggest proponents."

"I never knew that. I just saw you two laughing a lot."

"Whatever, Joan, but now it's all ancient history. You've got me. I'll dial her." I did just that. One ring.

"Talk to me!" Michele said.

"Michele! Mason!"

"Where in the hell have you been? I called your house last night. No one knew where in the hell you were! I even called Joan. No answer. What's up with you?"

"Mickey, I'm at Joan's right now."

"And, I'm sure you didn't just arrive to take her to mass."

"I confess. We also have other confessions, to get to the point. But, I'll let her tell you." I handed the phone to a willing Joan.

"Mickey."

"Joan, what the fuck are you doing with my student?"

"To put it succinctly, Michele, I'm going to marry him tomorrow."

"Why does that not surprise me?"

"It's true, Michele. We've reached an agreement."

"I'm relieved to know the deal was struck. You two. I knew it! I knew this was going to happen! I was going to give you until New Year's, then I was going to have my own Bicentennial beefcake. You eked out, honey."

"Too late, Mick."

"I'm so happy for you both. Honestly. God bless you both."

"I think He did," Joan reached for my hand.

"I don't mean to rush you, but MJo and I are just out to The Dining Room because she has to get back to her married grind. Oh, I'm sorry…."

"No, you're not," Joan said as she laughed. "I'll get to it. I have a favor to ask you."

"I'll take care of your classes tomorrow. I'll make them write something. The topic, 'What Do You Really Think of Mason and Joan Getting Married?' I'm sure the men will have a different viewpoint than the women."

"Make it ten percent of their grade."

"Nice touch. Don't worry. I'll take care of you. You just take care of my friend, friend."

"No problem."

"Where you going?"

"We don't know yet."

"What's your name going to be?"

"I don't know yet."

"When you coming back?"

"That I do know. We'll be back for Tuesday morning. Listen, I don't want to hold you. Thank you for your help with my classes, and Michele...."

"Yes?"

"Thank you for everything. I really think I've hit the jackpot here." Joan said, wrapping her legs around mine.

"I've got to have a party for you two. You think the English administration is going to have a problem with this?"

"I don't know yet. But, how can they stop the spouse of a member of the faculty from taking classes?"

"I just love your 'I don't know yets.' You've come a long way, banker's daughter.

"Now that I have faced the truth, it's all a lot easier to handle."

"You're all right, Dr. Brick."

"That has a nice ring to it. Thanks again."

"Next time I see you, you'll be an old married woman."

"It'll have its benefits."

"I'm counting on it."

"Bye, Michele."

"See you Tuesday."

Joan hung up the telephone. "God, she's nice. How did we not ever get along? I think it's you, Mason. You've brought Mickey and me together." Her legs squeezed mine again. I'll give her a day to stop that.

Joan then jumped from me. "Let's get dressed and get started! We'll talk along the way!" In no time, she's clothed. It's almost as erotic watching her put her clothes on.

"Move it, Mason! Monty going to be my husband, so I'm Monty boss." She giggled wildly.

~ ~ ~ ~ ~ ~ ~ ~ ~ ~

On the way to my house, Joan drove while I continued to make the list, "I gotta pack," I said, "You gotta pack. Hell's bells, we've gotta decide where to go! We need plane tickets! We need rings! I guess you get them there, where ever there is."

"I love surprises! What a surprise this will be! We don't even know where we are going!" exclaimed Joan, "As if this entire weekend is not a surprise enough."

"Believe me," I said, "It'll get better." I kissed her cheek. "But, let me ask you a question, if you please."

"I please," said Joan, "I got what I pleased. I'm sorry. I'm nuts! I'm crazy! I'm a happy idiot! Go ahead."

An idiot Joan is much better than a rational any-other-woman. "Forgive me for bringing this up, and I hope it's at the right time, but what do you want to do about your name?"

"Funny you should ask. Michele mentioned the same thing. I haven't thought about it. Well, I wrote 'Joan Bricker' like a schoolgirl in the margins of some lesson notes I was taking once, but other than that…I actually did that, Mason," Joan grinned. "Is that the silliest thing you ever heard? I'm a fawning junior high girl around you."

I'm breathless. The despair of blind faith came back to me and all the while she was writing my name…our name…fawning…I like her better when she's paying attention to me.

"Mason," Joan said, nudging my leg.

I came to. "God I'm…I'm…."

"I know," she said, smiling.

Inhaling deeply, I said, "May I give you my thoughts, then?"

"Go ahead, sweet thing." Joan said. I love that.

"You are welcome, more than welcome to my name. I would be honored, very much so. But, as I said before, I don't want to change a thing about you. Anything. I'll take you any way I can get you. You worked hard with your name. You've got three degrees and a profession with your name. I don't mean to throw the entire thing in your lap, so those are just my feelings."

"I don't know what to do," Joan said, "In Chicago, it was easy. The men there would have never considered the wife keeping her name. Mason, Monty so…so…seventies."

"Thank you…since you can't decide, I would if I were you keep Kissinger. That doesn't bother me in the least. I'm really proud of you. I want you to be Joan Kissinger. She's the woman I fell in love with, by the way."

"That's sweet, Mason. You got it…I'll keep my name. Realize, however, now I really am the boss," Joan joked.

"As all wives are," I said astutely. And wisely. "You can be the boss. Just let me slip your panties off occasionally, okay?"

"Oh, Mason what a thought…Ohh…" I think I handled that well. Joan continued, "Now that we have that settled, back to the lists. You'll still have to do it for me. I'm in nirvana right now and can't think clearly."

My God, I've put Joan Kissinger in a state of bliss. Righteous, dude. "Where to go?" I said.

"Not West Virginia," Joan posed, "You need three days."

"How do you know that?"

"Do you think this idea just occurred to Joan Bricker? Come on, Mason." She smiled big. I momentarily lost brain function. "Vegas? Deliciously tacky. Illinois? Same day matrimony, while you wait!"

"Deliciously ironic," I said, returning.

"Could be…," Joan said, running it through her mind. "But, I say Vegas. We may even be married tonight."

"Excellent!" I said. "Vegas it is. We'll pack and get the tickets at the airport."

"How spontaneous of me!" Joan said proudly, "Of course, the idea of marrying you is far from that."

"Again, I wish you'da said something," I reiterated, "But, considering everything, the timing couldn't be more perfect."

"Yeah, we waited until we both were like, in heat."

"'A kiss for luck and we're on our way,'" I said, repeating my conversation with Pamela.

"Sweet, Mason. Karen Carpenter was singing that song right in the middle of all those weddings, and right in the middle of me telling James Bryant to go to hell. That brings back good memories. All those brides thought I was crazy. We'll see what they think now when I take you home."

The prospect of being Joan Kissinger's filet mignon on the platter aroused me. My house is in sight. Gee, I hope nobody's home. Well, my car isn't home. Montani has an ordinance to solve its constant parking problem: after forty-eight hours in one space on the street, Monty tow bait.

"Looks like I need a new car," I said.

"You're...whatever you call...it is scary anyway. Sell some of that stock and buy you a new one," Joan said, giving me her First Wifely Directive. Funny, it made me ill when Jennifer did it, but Joan...It's okay! It's just another way to start anew." Joan pulled into my old space. We hopped out of the car. It's eleven thirty. Who's here? Who knows? My fiancee and I couldn't care less.

We climbed the stairs to my porch. I tested the knob. The door's locked. As I fumbled through my pocket for keys, I could see Joan out of the corner of my eye standing there with arms outstretched, pulling me through space to her.

"Mason, this is where we were just two weeks ago," she said wistfully, "This is where we held each other for the first time. I'll never forget it." I moved to her arms. "You felt so, so strong. I wanted to stay there. I thought you were gone, but then I held you and everything was all right."

"Joan, I remember it well. It was the point of no return for me. I was a lost ball in high weeds."

She laughed, "I should have kissed you."

"You're right. You should have."

We then made up for our negligence of that Saturday night. How many times...I mean, Mary, Mother of Christ, is this going to happen everytime I kiss Joan? Is my heart going to do a freefall ad infinitum? I can only hope so....

The door cracked open. Joan and I didn't budge.

"There you are!" I heard Judy's voice say. "Hi, Dr. Kissinger." We are caught in the act.

I looked to Judy and smiled, then glanced back at Joan to assess her reaction to this latest development. To my pleasure, Joan is her New Joan normal self.

"Good morning, Judy," Joan said, "And, due to these circumstances, you can always call me Joan."

"Hi, Judy," I said, canary in mouth.

"Would you two like to come in?" Judy asked.

"Uh...yeah," I said. "Joan?" I gentlemanly presented to her the way.

The house is very un-collegiatelike clean, amazing considering how the victory party must have gone last night.

"Oh, a most beautiful place, Judy!" Joan said sincerely.

"Thank you!" Judy said. Lambert's a combustive soul. Is she looking for the right moment to strangle Joan, or what? As I thought about that, Alice appeared from upstairs.

"Mason! Dr. Kissinger! What a surprise!"

"Hi, Alice," Joan said. This is going better than I thought. For Joan, I mean. She's must be really serious about taking me for as a mate for life.

Judy and Alice? Still to early to tell…especially when Alice excused her-self quickly and rushed upstairs to my side of the house.

"We have coffee," Judy said, "Please join us."

Joan and I accepted and followed Judy into the kitchen. Coffee's poured all around and we sat at the table and prepared to chat.

"Mason, I never knew you lived so well," Joan said, smiling, "It has to be the female influence." She grinned at Judy, fully aware of the head wind she is running against here.

Judy giggled, "Yeah, if it weren't for us women, the boys would still have pizza on the coffee table from October." Joan laughed a polished, appropriate laugh.

"Now, wait a minute," I said, "Pizza is at its best after curing in the liv-ing room for a couple of weeks." Before anyone could respond to that which I always think is funny, Alice bounded back downstairs and joined us in the kitchen. She poured coffee and took one huge gulp. Her eyes are more startled than normal, and I don't think it's just because of Joan and me.

"Mason, I never had a chance to tell you, great game yesterday!" said Judy, really being too nice. "I wish we could have celebrated last night." Interpretation: 'Why did you stand up Jennifer and spend the night with this slut?'

"Yeah, Mason, that was a close one indeed," Alice said, "The best game I've seen here. We partied here all night last night." Same message.

Joan looked at me and grinned. I grinned back. Interpretation: 'I told you girls you were full of shit when you said I had no chance with Joan.' So, why waste any more precious time?

"Well, I just came here to pick up a few things. Joan and I are going out of town for a couple of days." I said.

"Oh," Alice said with a surprised look, "Where are you going? Any place special?"

"We don't know yet," Joan said, fully aware of where we are going, showing her aptitude for girl games. I looked to the ceiling and quelled a laugh.

"Oh," said Judy. The two roomies glanced at each other, a trifle confused.

"If you ladies will excuse me, I'll step upstairs and…."

"I'll go with you "said Joan.

"NO!" yelled Alice, "I mean, no, Jean's in Vinny's room showering."

"Jean showers all the time when I'm upstairs, Alice," I said, "She's very modest, Joan. No worries."

"Do I look worried?" said Joan. She did not, and it is a major turn-on. But, what isn't?

"I'll be back down in a bit," I said. Joan and I stood.

"Mason," Judy said in resignation, "you can't go up there because there are guests in your room. We leased it out because…well, we didn't know where you were and it was late and they were drunk…God, Joan, you're going to think we're just awful."

"No!" Joan said in a friendly, reassuring fashion, "Yesterday was a big day. There was a guest in my room, too. Think nothing of it." Wow! Joan! Lay it on the line. I guess it's my turn. My woman has given me the will to lead my friends to the truth. I want to rub their faces in it. This is going to be wild!

"Ladies," I started, "There's something I we have to tell you. We do know where we're going today. We're going to Las Vegas, and we're not there to gamble."

"Well, in a sense…," Joan said grinning, putting a loving squeeze on my forearm. Alice and Judy became frozen with inquiring looks. They're smart girls. They know.

"Alice, Judy. Joan and I are eloping. We're getting married tonight." I grabbed Joan's hand. We stood before my friends bearing all, hoping for approval, but settling for tolerance. Plus, I want to rub their faces in it.

They are silent, trance-like. We are the definition of assuredness. You can hear the spigot drip.

"Well, girls, at least wish us luck," I said.

More silence. Then, "You two!" proclaimed Alice. "This is crazy! I mean when? Oh, hell…What a surprise! Mason…Joan, you must be some woman because I always thought Mason would be the last to marry." I started to interrupt Alice's chatter before she said something in her shock she might regret. Judy possibly felt the same way because she took over.

"Kids "she said, "Congratulations! I'm happy for you…I just don't know what else to say."

"I understand," Joan said, stepping in to help out, "This, Mason and I, I know we're odd. It's difficult to explain. But, that's romance. We worked side-by-side for this semester, and we therefore had a lot of time to talk and become friends. Then, ol' Mason here takes it a step higher," she said, punching my arm, "and I after so much playing hard-to-get…."

"Two weeks," I interrupted. A Laugh

"A couple of months," Joan said, correcting me as a wife would, and will, "Time just compressed," Joan said. I examined Alice and Judy. They are being agreeable, probably without agreeing. "Anyway, here we are," Joan closed simply.

"Ladies, I you mean a lot to me. So, I wanted to tell you, and ask for your blessing," I said. I may be over the face-rubbing, but a blessing…a little too much.

"Mason…Doctor—Joan…," said Judy, "It's just so fast. I can't tell you what to do, but you guys are wasting no time at all. Are you sure about this?"

"Judy, Alice, romance is timeless. It can take decades, or lunch. But, when it happens, it happens. And there's no sense sitting around waiting for the calendar to flip. Joan and I are in love. So…."

I can see Judy's bullshit alarm go off. "I hesitate to ask this," Alice said slowly, "but, when did this happen?"

"Some time ago, for me," Joan said, making me tingle, "But, I was so damned obstinate, I allowed it to linger to the point of not being able to go through one night without dreaming of your friend," Joan then clutched my hand. My diaphragm stopped working. "You know, dreams are our way of dealing with unresolved issues, and I was not allowing my issue with my fiancee here to be resolved."

The perpetually direct Judy hit it on the head, "It's understandable, Joan. There are your ages…and the fact you're faculty." A left jab….

"What do you think kept me away?" asked Joan, "If not for those things, I would have jumped in his arms before the first day of fall. I mean, just look at him!" Joan gave me a gaze that usually precedes sweet love. This is the best time I've ever had in my kitchen. But, 'just look at him?' That doesn't work on Judy and Alice. They don't look at me that way. I changed tacks.

"Don't worry, girls," I said, ready to drive it home, "I'll honor my rent agreement. In fact, I'll pay it all today."

Not good. "Mason, this isn't about that!" Alice said, flaring, "This is…oh, fuck. Just run off and get married! Good luck to you." Alice left and went back upstairs to my room. "Jennifer! Ken!" I heard her yell, "MOVE IT!' Joan shot me a surprised look followed by a grin. "Vinny! Your buddy's here! Get down here, and you'd better hurry!"

Ken? Jennifer's Ken doll? This is too much! I checked Joan to see her response to Alice's tirade. My lady is composed. She smiled.

"Good luck," Judy said perfunctorily. Then, in kindness, sometimes aberrant to her nature when caught off-guard, she said, "I'm sorry, for both Alice and me. Just give us a chance to get used to it. I know it makes perfectly good sense to you. Joan, we all in this house had a conversation about Mason and his feelings for you recently, and I know from that he certainly loves you, so you'll be just fine. Even better. Just take care of him, or I'll beat the shit out of you. Just kidding…no, I'm not."

Joan extended her arms to Judy, embraced her, and said, "Judy, he's in good hands. I'm happy my Mason has such great friends who are so concerned for him. Don't worry. You won't have to make good on your threat," Joan concluded, smiling, calming Judy. A strange exchange....

"Excuse me," Judy said. She then walked through the door.

"That went well," Joan said, kissing me on the lips.

"It's all you can expect for right now," I said. I reached across the table to pour coffee as we sat at the table awaiting to receive more well-wishers.

"I can't wait to see your room," Joan said.

"Yeah, it's where I thought about you a lot. In fact, I thought about you so much there I'm sure there are a few of your apparitions remaining."

"I wonder if Barbie and Ken saw any last night?" Joan asked in jest. I fought to keep from choking on coffee. I honestly hate to do that to Jennifer, but such are the mishaps of love. I don't mean to be so casual over it, but what can I do now? And, she certainly knows how to take care of herself. Besides, she finally had sex in my room. The silver medal. She'll get me, though. Mr. and Dr. Bricker get to see her on Wednesday. Ho, boy! You're back to one step at a time, Ivy Boy.

Vinny appeared, bounding into the room. "Congratulations!" he said in all sincerity as he gave us both big hugs, still acting like a man who had just gone seventeen for eighteen in the fourth against the number one team in the nation, "I mean it, unlike our roomies. But, let it grow on 'em. Anyway, I knew this was going to happen. Joan, you can thank me for this. I told Mason to go for it. I even kept progress on him. He's right on schedule."

Joan laughed, "You mean, Mason, you had to have third party inter-vention to get you going on us," she said, bantering, "I'm insulted. Wasn't I, my mere presence, enough?" Joan grabbed my arm and pulled herself closely. Another nose crinkle. How many men have fallen for that?

"Sometimes you need help, even for that which slaps you in the face," I said.

"Damnit, Cheetah," Vinny said, "I thought it was going to take you forever to get hitched. You still going to take care of me, aren't you?"

"Cheetah?" asked Joan.

"Yeah, it's an old reference to his footspeed," said Vinny.

"Oh, I like the animal thing," Joan cooed, hands around my torso. I shot Vinny a smile.

The Gunner readily picked up on that, "Well, I see you guys are going to have a good time. Just answer the phone occasionally when I call."

"On occasion," Joan said.

We heard footsteps tapping in staccato down our stairway. By the fading sound, I could tell they didn't turn for the kitchen.

"I think your room's ready," said Vinny.

"That was the SI reporter?" I asked.

"Yep. It's curious that he didn't come in here for a quick interview," Vinny said, "But, maybe not."

"It's always good to get a writer for *Sports Illustrated* laid whenever he's in town," Joan said. Vinny and I paused, pleasantly flabbergasted at Joan. Then we both howled. Joan joined us.

"Oh, God," I said, recovering, "Where's Jean?"

"She left with Jennifer. She sends her love," Vinny said.

"I'm sure," I replied.

"I think there's an early sorority prayer breakfast or something. Or maybe they have to meet the Pierces. I don't know. I have a meeting myself."

"Yes, Vinny," Joan said, "Mason's told me about what you and your teammates are going to do. Good luck. It's been tough, but don't give an inch."

"Thanks, Joan," Vinny said, "Mason, are you sure you don't want us to put you on the bargaining table?"

"In light of everything," I said, responding confidently, "I'm out. I had my day in the sun. It was wonderful. You guys go for the important stuff. With regard to it all," as I thought about my father and PD and

McNabb and his retribution, "I bow out. Save it for the guys who count, Vinny: the young boys." I recalled Vinny and Mason, 1967, the year before the nation exploded, a couple of sixth-graders in Row I on the fifty, sometimes in the middle of non-stop chatter, other times eyes glued to the turf and imagining 'what's it going to be like for us?'

I looked to Joan. Again, 1967, walking around the Evanston campus, just about as pretty as a nineteen-year-old girl can be, leaving a wake of college men on their knees, her entire life ahead of her. One of the sixth graders, ahead of her. How did we happen, I ask. She gazed at me admiringly. Sometimes, Mason, you ask too many goddamn questions. Holding Joan's shoulder in my right arm and Vinny's in my left, I tied the three of us together, "I'm going to miss being on the field with you, Gunner."

"I'm going to miss you, too," Vinny said after a breath, "But, you'll still remain unconventional and keep me sane as I progress through the dreary life of the superhero Attorney Man, won't you?"

"I'll be there for you, Vinny," I said. I have never discussed this with Joan, but with her awareness of Vinny and me and her experience with her years of rampant preoccupation with materialistic ideals, I can tell with one glance she understood completely.

"I'd better go. I have to be at Michael's in five minutes."

"Tell them I said hello, and tell them I said to give them hell." Vinny and I embraced again. He took Joan into his arms. "Weddings make me cry," he said to her, grinning, "You bringing him back Tuesday?"

"Yes," Joan said, "We'll have you over next week. I'll make Mason cook."

"Jesus! Henpecked already!" Vinny exclaimed. "See you guys. Have a safe trip." He turned and walked out of the kitchen and I heard him go through the front door. Then, I heard more footsteps. He reappeared. "Hey, Mason, you read the paper this morning?"

"Oh, yeah!" I said.

"We did it, man. You and I did it. There's nothing like a plan coming together."

"No doubt," I said. We clasped hands. He tickled my palm again, just like the fourth quarter. I laughed. He patted me on the back, sporting a huge grin. Backing out of the door, Vinny issued yet another thumbs-up and is gone.

"We cleared this place out, didn't we?" I said, turning to Joan.

"That only means one thing: carry me upstairs and make love with me."

My focus shifted instantly. What an opportunity! In my room! Didn't The Beach Boys sing that? Who gives a damn....

"You're so demanding," I said, "But, if you insist."

~ ~ ~ ~ ~ ~ ~ ~ ~ ~ ~

We're dressed. I sat in my lounge chair as Joan stood, taking advantage of her first chance to examine my room. "The wall color. The polished floor. The matching rugs. Mason, you're a man. You had to have a decorator."

"Okay. I confess."

"Framed posters?"

"I knew you'd eventually be here, so I didn't think tape would be suave enough."

"Ken Kesey. What college student would even know whom Ken Kesey is? I'm impressed. Your mind first attracted me to you. Your mind and your butt."

"Thank you. You don't do too badly yourself."

"Thank you." She continued to scan the walls. "The Lizard King."

"He can do anything."

"And he did. We Northwestern girls were in love with him. A bunch of us went to a Doors concert in Chicago. They're all married now. Wait until they hear about me. Who's that?" Joan asked, pointing to the Oakland Raider in black.

"Jack Tatum. I like the way he plays, which is one of the reasons I'm glad I'm out."

"I never got it. You're not an animal."

"Not in public. But, when I play football, I flick a switch and I hit people to hurt them. To inflict pain and injury. As I've said before, there's no single reason why I chose to leave the game, but one of them is I can't reconcile playing the way I played and being your lover, and your husband. I can't explain why that makes sense to me. It's just a feeling I have. And, I feel like I'm doing the right thing."

Joan studied my face, impelling me to become paranatural with regard to the recent events, "Maybe, just maybe, Joan, I was born into football just for yesterday. The box. The newspaper. The takeover. Maybe all those years and all those dreams took place to prepare me for what somebody had to do this week. Not that I was the only guy who could have done it...."

"I know, sweetie," Joan picked up, sitting on my lap, "But you were the man who did it. Maybe you were the one chosen to start it all, and you can be happy with your success. From what you have said, the change is now rolling on its own. Blacks and whites are working together, Mason, because of your sacrifice." She held my hand and rested her head on my shoulder.

"I don't know if I'd particularly call it a sacrifice. I ended up with you. It looks like I won first prize," Joan smiled big, "If my teammates become a team after it all, then it puts the lifetime of dedication on a much higher order. It makes the blood and the sweat even more meaningful than it already is. Worldly. I hope I'm right about that. Much more than just a game." I paused to reflect, then asked my love, "Does that sound pompous?"

"Most definitely not," Joan answered, "I understand completely, Mason. I truly do. I am so proud of you." Her head remained on my shoulder as she lightened it up, putting it all into our new perspective, "Just do what you can to keep that body, especially this summer when I take you to my old club pool where the girls still hang out and, not unlike the men they married, I can show you off as my trophy spouse." Joan pivoted onto my lap and draped herself around my shoulders. She kissed me. It feels as if she's the only woman who ever kissed me. I know now she is serious about this. If she wants to put me on display, well….

"That's the second time you've mentioned that," I said, "You really want these women to…."

"Cream."

Oh, hell! Joan Laughed. She knew she got me. "So, I'm your man," I said, in recovery, "but only if your adorn my arm occasionally for the benefit of the public."

"It's a deal." Her attentions quickly turned to my desk where I had framed and propped the black-and-white photo of us, Joan and me. Little did the couple know, little did anybody know, other arrangements would be made at a later date, TBA.

"Mason, that's us! That's the picture from the newspaper." Joan said, standing up to pick up the picture.

"On the money, Joan," I replied.

"Where did you get this?" she asked with a pleasant smile.

"I had to beg, but I got it."

"Darling, that's so sweet! You had a picture of us. On your desk! I never knew."

"Joan," I started, "had you known, that might have frightened you. As it turned out, there are many things you didn't know. Things I didn't have enough guts to tell you."

"You came through when you had to, sweetie. You had the guts. I didn't. I didn't know what to do. For instance, the day I introduced you to ol' what's-his-name, I had you two together there in the hallway for the direct comparison," Joan put the picture back and straddled me again, "I knew who I wanted. And I went to lunch with the other guy. How damned…will you ever forgive me?"

I remembered. It's time. "Wait here. Don't lose that thought. Excuse me." Joan stood again as I stepped over to my bookcase and scooted it back, exposing the small wall safe. Twice right, to forty, once left, to twenty-four, then back right directly to thirty-one. I turned the handle down and the door popped open. The only contents were the box and the receipt. I reached in and retrieved the box. Standing back up to Joan, I said, "You went to lunch with ol' what's-his-name, and I took a walk downtown and ended up with this. I bought it for you, and I now give it to you." Joan accepted the box from me, glanced at it, looked up to me with a face of wonderment, and finally fulfilling yet another dream, opened it. Her mouth went wide and tears filled her eyes. She emitted an, "Ohhhh," removed the ring from the box. My woman simply held it and stared at it. I then took it from her with no resistance, held her left hand in mine, and with my right hand slipped the ring, beauteous stone and all, on the proper finger. It fit perfectly. Joan pulled herself from the ring and looked up to me, crying.

"Now, will you marry me?" I asked with a smile.

"Oh, Mason, yes! The answer's yes, just like before, but this time, this time, after the most, the positively most romantic thing anyone has ever done for me." The tears kept coming. I'm fine, for once, remaining collected, but Joan is a lovely mess, and she doesn't give a damn. "You mean you bought this ring for me after you met Alan? After I had ignored you? After I chased you to your porch, then spent the next week just going on and on about that…right in front of you? Oh, Mason, I don't deserve you. The letter. The respect. The patience. The absolute love you had, you have for me." She couldn't stop crying. "And now, this? This ring you bought for me right when I was in the middle of trying to deny the feelings I had for you? You bought this ring when I was giving you no clues whatsoever about how much I loved you? When I was denying it all myself? Oh, Mason, what a man of faith you are! Oh, what a man you are!" Joan leapt into my arms and held tighter than she has ever held. The tears had turned to sobs and she can't let go of me. And I don't want her to. Despite having my heart squeezed lovingly and my skin burning, I talked to her through it all.

"Joan, I just knew. I couldn't explain it. It would have sounded too…daft…for anyone else to understand. I just held on. I knew I would have the opportunity to give you this ring sometime. I didn't know how. Vinny didn't even know about it, the ring. Frankly, I'm surprised it came so early, but you don't hear me fussin' about it." She is still crying. I kept talking. "The past is interesting, something we can sit on the plane this afternoon and laugh about. I know I've done some funny things since September." At this point I want to make her laugh, "Here's one you'll enjoy. I just had to go into your office every five minutes or so. Hell, I wanted to move into your desk beside you. So I played a strange game. I couldn't walk through your door until the minute hand swept past the two or the seven. That kept me from being even more obsessed than I already was."

"Mason, you were a touch transparent," Joan said laughing through tears, "The real question is: why didn't I just…." She started crying hard again.

I pulled her even closer, "But, Joan, it doesn't matter any more. In fact, most everything is now incidental, because I have my woman. And you have your man. And we can now do all those things I've dreamed about. They're going to be fun."

Joan is having a difficult time becoming composed. "You must have thought I was a real grade-A bitch. I mean, Mason, I went out of my way to show you I wasn't interested. 'I don't date students,' I said, when all I wanted to do was throw myself in your arms. I got your letter that Sunday and that Alan was coming over in a half-hour. I was crying like now, I couldn't stop. It was such a beautiful letter. God, you're talented. I just laid on my bed and bawled. But, what did I do? I avoided most conversation with you for days then said 'I'm sorry, Mason, we can't date,'" She gazed at me with incessant tears streaming from her eyes, "How goddamned stupid could I get? Date? This man loves me, like no other man has ever or is even capable of, and I'm talking about dating." Joan swallowed hard and continued, "You said we transcend dating. Men don't even get that. I did, but I was afraid, I guess. It didn't stop me from thinking, though. That week I would sneak a look at you, every chance I got. All I wanted to do was simply invite you over for dinner and talk about my hopes and our opportunities. I got so close at times, but I can't tell you what pulled me away."

"It was risky, darling," I said, trying to help her out, "Don't worry. I understand."

Joan went on with more surprises, "My comment to you after you told us about leaving the U with Vinny I was the supercilious professor on the outside. Within, I was screaming, 'Don't leave me!' I fell apart. It was all so bad for you. I felt so badly for you. But, the thought of you going without knowing how…I…oh…." She buried her face in my chest.

"It's okay," I said, squeezing her tightly, helping her hold on, "It didn't happen. I don't think it could have, really. Besides, I'll never leave you. I can't be without you." My throat went dry.

"God, you were incredible in my class," Joan confessed, "Afterwards, I was so depressed I went to my office, sat down at my desk, and I couldn't move. I watched Jennifer that morning. She's so pretty. And I gave you to her. But, I wanted you. I thought it was all over."

"Then, at Michele's, I had another chance. I wanted to say, 'I'll ride the rocket with you.' But, the next thing I knew, I was in my bed, alone, in tears. Damn, Mason, how can you stand to be with me?" Joan asked, raising her head to me.

"How can I stand not to be with you?" I held her face and kissed her lips, hoping to let her know just that. Placing my hands on her shoulders and looking directly at her, I said, "Joan, it was a lot easier for me. You, Joan…you're our hero." Joan's look of anguish lessened. I paused. "Look, lover, I'm going to pack, so we can go get married."

"And I'll just sit here and lose it," she choked out, plopping herself on the edge of my bed, folding her face into her hands.

I sat beside her to comfort her. "And I'll drive you home, and you pack, and let's hop on the next plane to Vegas, the capital of the profuse, and become husband and wife. That's the way I heard it should be."

Joan raised her mascara-streaked face to me. "Yes, Mason. That's the way I *always* heard it should be."

"Do you want to marry me?" I sang.

Joan brought Carly home, "We'll marry."

We stared for a three count, "Damn, we're terrible," Joan said giggling, "Remind me to never allow us to sing in public."

"Then we won't do *Anticipation*, okay?" I joked. Joan laughed.

"Although, Mason "she added, "these are the good ol' days."

On that, we bowed to each other. Our foreheads touched lightly. My eyes are closed. Total silence enveloped us. One minute. Then another. We didn't move.

I have always been afraid of stillness, as if motion ceased all the pain in my life would creep up on me. Yet after my most chaotic week ever, the clocks have stopped. The world is held in suspension. An entire galaxy spins around me, but the only thing that matters to me is the woman I met on the big hill.

Joan has brought me peace.

CPSIA information can be obtained
at www.ICGtesting.com
Printed in the USA
LVHW091235010322
712320LV00009BA/12